# The Headless Horseman

## A Strange Tale of Texas

by
Captain Mayne Reid

# Contents

# Prologue

The stag of Texas, reclining in midnight lair, is startled from his slumbers by the hoofstroke of a horse.

He does not forsake his covert, nor yet rise to his feet. His domain is shared by the wild steeds of the savannah, given to nocturnal straying. He only uprears his head; and, with antlers o'ertopping the tall grass, listens for a repetition of the sound.

Again is the hoofstroke heard, but with altered intonation. There is a ring of metal—the clinking of steel against stone.

The sound, significant to the ear of the stag, causes a quick change in his air and attitude. Springing clear of his couch, and bounding a score of yards across the prairie, he pauses to look back upon the disturber of his dreams.

In the clear moonlight of a southern sky, he recognises the most ruthless of his enemies—man. One is approaching upon horseback.

Yielding to instinctive dread, he is about to resume his flight: when something in the appearance of the horseman—some unnatural seeming—holds him transfixed to the spot.

With haunches in quivering contact with the sward, and frontlet faced to the rear, he continues to gaze—his large brown eyes straining upon the intruder in a mingled expression of fear and bewilderment.

What has challenged the stag to such protracted scrutiny?

The horse is perfect in all its parts—a splendid steed, saddled, bridled, and otherwise completely caparisoned. In it there appears nothing amiss—nothing to produce either wonder or alarm. But the man—the rider? Ah! About him there *is* something to cause both—something weird—something *wanting*!

By heavens! it is the head!

Even the unreasoning animal can perceive this; and, after gazing a moment with wildered eyes—wondering what abnormal monster thus mocks its cervine intelligence—terror-stricken it continues its retreat; nor again pauses, till it has plunged through the waters of the

Leona, and placed the current of the stream between itself and the ghastly intruder.

Heedless of the affrighted deer—either of its presence, or precipitate flight—the Headless Horseman rides on.

He, too, is going in the direction of the river. Unlike the stag, he does not seem pressed for time; but advances in a slow, tranquil pace: so silent as to seem ceremonious.

Apparently absorbed in solemn thought, he gives free rein to his steed: permitting the animal, at intervals, to snatch a mouthful of the herbage growing by the way. Nor does he, by voice or gesture, urge it impatiently onward, when the howl-bark of the prairie-wolf causes it to fling its head on high, and stand snorting in its tracks.

He appears to be under the influence of some all-absorbing emotion, from which no common incident can awake him. There is no speech—not a whisper—to betray its nature. The startled stag, his own horse, the wolf, and the midnight moon, are the sole witnesses of his silent abstraction.

His shoulders shrouded under a *serapé*, one edge of which, flirted up by the wind, displays a portion of his figure: his limbs encased in "water-guards" of jaguar-skin: thus sufficiently sheltered against the dews of the night, or the showers of a tropical sky, he rides on—silent as the stars shining above, unconcerned as the cicada that chirrups in the grass beneath, or the prairie breeze playing with the drapery of his dress.

Something at length appears to rouse from his reverie, and stimulate him to greater speed—his steed, at the same time. The latter, tossing up its head, gives utterance to a joyous neigh; and, with outstretched neck, and spread nostrils, advances in a gait gradually increasing to a canter. The proximity of the river explains the altered pace.

The horse halts not again, till the crystal current is surging against his flanks, and the legs of his rider are submerged knee-deep under the surface.

The animal eagerly assuages its thirst; crosses to the opposite side; and, with vigorous stride, ascends the sloping bank.

Upon the crest occurs a pause: as if the rider tarried till his steed should shake the water from its flanks. There is a rattling of saddle-flaps, and stirrup-leathers, resembling thunder, amidst a cloud of vapour, white as the spray of a cataract.

Out of this self-constituted *nimbus*, the Headless Horseman emerges; and moves onward, as before.

Apparently pricked by the spur, and guided by the rein, of his rider, the horse no longer strays from the track; but steps briskly forward, as if upon a path already trodden.

A treeless savannah stretches before—selvedged by the sky. Outlined against the azure is seen the imperfect centaurean shape gradually dissolving in the distance, till it becomes lost to view, under the mystic gloaming of the moonlight!

# 1. The Burnt Prairie

On the great plain of Texas, about a hundred miles southward from the old Spanish town of San Antonio de Bejar, the noonday sun is shedding his beams from a sky of cerulean brightness. Under the golden light appears a group of objects, but little in unison with the landscape around them: since they betoken the presence of human beings, in a spot where there is no sign of human habitation.

The objects in question are easily identified—even at a great distance. They are waggons; each covered with its ribbed and rounded tilt of snow-white "Osnaburgh."

There are ten of them—scarce enough to constitute a "caravan" of traders, nor yet a "government train." They are more likely the individual property of an emigrant; who has landed upon the coast, and is wending his way to one of the late-formed settlements on the Leona.

Slowly crawling across the savannah, it could scarce be told that they are in motion; but for their relative-position, in long serried line, indicating the order of march.

The dark bodies between each two declare that the teams are attached; and that they are making progress is proved, by the retreating antelope, scared from its noonday *siesta*, and the long-shanked curlew, rising with a screech from the sward—both bird and beast wondering at the string of strange *behemoths*, thus invading their wilderness domain.

Elsewhere upon the prairie, no movement may be detected—either of bird or quadruped. It is the time of day when all tropical life becomes torpid, or seeks repose in the shade; man alone, stimulated by the love of gain, or the promptings of ambition, disregarding the laws of nature, and defying the fervour of the sun.

So seems it with the owner of the tilted train; who, despite the relaxing influence of the fierce mid-day heat, keeps moving on.

That he is an emigrant—and not one of the ordinary class—is evidenced in a variety of ways. The ten large waggons of Pittsburgh build, each hauled by eight able-bodied mules; their miscellaneous contents: plenteous provisions, articles of costly furniture, even of *luxe*, live stock in the shape of coloured women and children; the groups of black and yellow bondsmen, walking alongside, or straggling foot-sore in the rear; the light travelling carriage in the lead, drawn by a span of sleek-coated Kentucky mules, and driven by a black Jehu, sweltering in a suit of livery; all bespeak, not a poor Northern-States settler in search of a new home, but a rich Southerner who has already purchased one, and is on his way to take possession of it.

And this is the exact story of the train. It is the property of a planter who has landed at Indianola, on the Gulf of Matagorda; and is now travelling overland—*en route* for his destination.

In the *cortège* that accompanies it, riding habitually at its head, is the planter himself—Woodley Poindexter—a tall thin man of fifty, with a slightly sallowish complexion, and aspect proudly severe. He is simply though not inexpensively clad: in a loosely fitting frock of alpaca cloth, a waistcoat of black satin, and trousers of nankin. A shirt of finest linen shows its plaits through the opening of his vest—its collar embraced by a piece of black ribbon; while the shoe, resting in his stirrup, is of finest tanned leather. His features are shaded by a broad-brimmed Leghorn hat.

Two horsemen are riding alongside—one on his right, the other on the left—a stripling scarce twenty, and a young man six or seven years older. The former is his son—a youth, whose open cheerful countenance contrasts, not only with the severe aspect of his father, but with the somewhat sinister features on the other side, and which belong to his cousin.

The youth is dressed in a French blouse of sky-coloured "cottonade," with trousers of the same material; a most appropriate costume for a southern climate, and which, with the Panama hat upon his head, is equally becoming.

The cousin, an ex-officer of volunteers, affects a military undress of dark blue cloth, with a forage cap to correspond.

There is another horseman riding near, who, only on account of having a white skin—not white for all that—is entitled to description. His coarser features, and cheaper habiliments; the keel-coloured "cowhide" clutched in his right hand, and flirted with such evident skill, proclaim him the overseer—and whipper up—of the swarthy pedestrians composing the *entourage* of the train.

5

The travelling carriage, which is a "carriole"—a sort of cross between a Jersey waggon and a barouche—has two occupants. One is a young lady of the whitest skin; the other a girl of the blackest. The former is the daughter of Woodley Poindexter—his only daughter. She of the sable complexion is the young lady's handmaid.

The emigrating party is from the "coast" of the Mississippi—from Louisiana. The planter is not himself a native of this State—in other words a *Creole*; but the type is exhibited in the countenance of his son—still more in that fair face, seen occasionally through the curtains of the carriole, and whose delicate features declare descent from one of those endorsed damsels—*filles à la casette*—who, more than a hundred years ago, came across the Atlantic provided with proofs of their virtue—in the *casket*!

A grand sugar planter of the South is Woodley Poindexter; one of the highest and haughtiest of his class; one of the most profuse in aristocratic hospitalities: hence the necessity of forsaking his Mississippian home, and transferring himself and his "penates,"—with only a remnant of his "niggers,"—to the wilds of south-western Texas.

The sun is upon the meridian line, and almost in the zenith. The travellers tread upon their own shadows. Enervated by the excessive heat, the white horsemen sit silently in their saddles. Even the dusky pedestrians, less sensible to its influence, have ceased their garrulous "gumbo;" and, in straggling groups, shamble listlessly along in the rear of the waggons.

The silence—solemn as that of a funereal procession—is interrupted only at intervals by the pistol-like crack of a whip, or the loud "wo-ha," delivered in deep baritone from the thick lips of some sable teamster.

Slowly the train moves on, as if groping its way. There is no regular road. The route is indicated by the wheel-marks of some vehicles that have passed before—barely conspicuous, by having crushed the culms of the shot grass.

Notwithstanding the slow progress, the teams are doing their best. The planter believes himself within less than twenty miles of the end of his journey. He hopes to reach it before night: hence the march continued through the mid-day heat.

Unexpectedly the drivers are directed to pull up, by a sign from the overseer; who has been riding a hundred yards in the advance, and who is seen to make a sudden stop—as if some obstruction had presented itself.

6

He comes trotting back towards the train. His gestures tell of something amiss. What is it?

There has been much talk about Indians—of a probability of their being encountered in this quarter.

Can it be the red-skinned marauders? Scarcely: the gestures of the overseer do not betray actual alarm.

"What is it, Mr Sansom?" asked the planter, as the man rode up.

"The grass air burnt. The prairy's been afire."

"*Been* on fire! Is it on fire *now*?" hurriedly inquired the owner of the waggons, with an apprehensive glance towards the travelling car- riage. "Where? I see no smoke!"

"No, sir—no," stammered the overseer, becoming conscious that he had caused unnecessary alarm; "I didn't say it air afire now: only thet it hez been, an the hul ground air as black as the ten o' spades."

"Ta—tat! what of that? I suppose we can travel over a black prai- rie, as safely as a green one?

"What nonsense of you, Josh Sansom, to raise such a row about nothing—frightening people out of their senses! Ho! there, you nig- gers! Lay the leather to your teams, and let the train proceed. Whip up!—whip up!"

"But, Captain Calhoun," protested the overseer, in response to the gentleman who had reproached him in such chaste terms; "how air we to find the way?"

"Find the way! What are you raving about? We haven't lost it— have we?"

"I'm afeerd we hev, though. The wheel-tracks ain't no longer to be seen. They're burnt out, along wi' the grass."

"What matters that? I reckon we can cross a piece of scorched prairie, without wheel-marks to guide us? We'll find them again on the other side."

"Ye-es," naïvely responded the overseer, who, although a "down- easter," had been far enough west to have learnt something of frontier life; "if theer air any other side. I kedn't see it out o' the seddle—ne'er a sign o' it."

"Whip up, niggers! whip up!" shouted Calhoun, without heeding the remark; and spurring onwards, as a sign that the order was to be obeyed.

The teams are again set in motion; and, after advancing to the edge of the burnt tract, without instructions from any one, are once more brought to a stand.

The white men on horseback draw together for a consultation. There is need: as all are satisfied by a single glance directed to the ground before them.

Far as the eye can reach the country is of one uniform colour—black as Erebus. There is nothing green—not a blade of grass—not a reed nor weed!

It is after the summer solstice. The ripened culms of the *gramineae*, and the stalks of the prairie flowers, have alike crumbled into dust under the devastating breath of fire.

In front—on the right and left—to the utmost verge of vision extends the scene of desolation. Over it the cerulean sky is changed to a darker blue; the sun, though clear of clouds, seems to scowl rather than shine—as if reciprocating the frown of the earth.

The overseer has made a correct report—there is no trail visible. The action of the fire, as it raged among the ripe grass, has eliminated the impression of the wheels hitherto indicating the route. "What are we to do?"

The planter himself put this inquiry, in a tone that told of a vacillating spirit.

"Do, uncle Woodley! What else but keep straight on? The river must be on the other side? If we don't hit the crossing, to a half mile or so, we can go up, or down the bank—as the case may require."

"But, Cassius: if we should lose our way?"

"We can't. There's but a patch of this, I suppose? If we do go a little astray, we must come out somewhere—on one side, or the other."

"Well, nephew, you know best: I shall be guided by you."

"No fear, uncle. I've made my way out of a worse fix than this. Drive on, niggers! Keep straight after *me*."

The ex-officer of volunteers, casting a conceited glance towards the travelling carriage—through the curtains of which appears a fair face, slightly shadowed with anxiety—gives the spur to his horse; and with confident air trots onward.

A chorus of whipcracks is succeeded by the trampling of four-score mules, mingled with the clanking of wheels against their hubs. The waggon-train is once more in motion.

The mules step out with greater rapidity. The sable surface, strange to their eyes, excites them to brisker action—causing them to raise the hoof, as soon as it touches the turf. The younger animals show fear—snorting, as they advance.

In time their apprehensions become allayed; and, taking the cue from their older associates, they move on steadily as before.

A mile or more is made, apparently in a direct line from the point of starting. Then there is a halt. The self-appointed guide has ordered it. He has reined up his horse; and is sitting in the saddle with less show of confidence. He appears to be puzzled about the direction.

The landscape—if such it may be called—has assumed a change; though not for the better. It is still sable as ever, to the verge of the horizon. But the surface is no longer a plain: it *rolls*. There are ridges—gentle undulations—with valleys between. They are not entirely treeless—though nothing that may be termed a tree is in sight. There have been such, before the fire—*algarobias, mezquites*, and others of the acacia family—standing solitary, or in copses. Their light pinnate foliage has disappeared like flax before the flame. Their existence is only evidenced by charred trunks, and blackened boughs.

"You've lost the way, nephew?" said the planter, riding rapidly up.

"No uncle—not yet. I've only stopped to have a look. It must lie in this direction—down that valley. Let them drive on. We're going all right—I'll answer for it."

Once more in motion—adown the slope—then along the valley—then up the acclivity of another ridge—and then there is a second stoppage upon its crest.

"You've lost the way, Cash?" said the planter, coming up and repeating his former observation.

"Damned if I don't believe I have, uncle!" responded the nephew, in a tone of not very respectful mistrust. "Anyhow; who the devil could find his way out of an ashpit like this? No, no!" he continued, reluctant to betray his embarrassment as the carriole came up. "I see now. We're all right yet. The river must be in this direction. Come on!"

On goes the guide, evidently irresolute. On follow the sable teamsters, who, despite their stolidity, do not fail to note some signs of vacillation. They can tell that they are no longer advancing in a direct line; but circuitously among the copses, and across the glades that stretch between.

All are gratified by a shout from the conductor, announcing recovered confidence. In response there is a universal explosion of whipcord, with joyous exclamations.

Once more they are stretching their teams along a travelled road—where a half-score of wheeled vehicles must have passed before them. And not long before: the wheel-tracks are of recent impress—the hoof-prints of the animals fresh as if made within the hour. A train of waggons, not unlike their own, must have passed over the burnt prairie!

Like themselves, it could only be going towards the Leona: perhaps some government convoy on its way to Fort Inge? In that case they have only to keep in the same track. The Fort is on the line of their march—but a short distance beyond the point where their journey is to terminate.

Nothing could be more opportune. The guide, hitherto perplexed—though without acknowledging it—is at once relieved of all anxiety; and with a fresh exhibition of conceit, orders the route to be resumed.

For a mile or more the waggon-tracks are followed—not in a direct line, but bending about among the skeleton copses. The countenance of Cassius Calhoun, for a while wearing a confident look, gradually becomes clouded. It assumes the profoundest expression of despondency, on discovering that the four-and-forty wheel-tracks he is following, have been made by ten Pittsburgh waggons, and a carriole—the same that are now following him, and in whose company he has been travelling *all the way from the Gulf of Matagorda*!

# 2. The Trail of the Lazo

Beyond doubt, the waggons of Woodley Poindexter were going over ground already traced by the tiring of their wheels.

"Our own tracks!" muttered Calhoun on making the discovery, adding a fierce oath as he reined up.

"Our own tracks! What mean you, Cassius? You don't say we've been travelling—"

"On our own tracks. I do, uncle; that very thing. We must have made a complete circumbendibus of it. See! here's the hind hoof of my own horse, with half a shoe off; and there's the foot of the niggers. Besides, I can tell the ground. That's the very hill we went down as we left our last stopping place. Hang the crooked luck! We've made a couple of miles for nothing."

Embarrassment is no longer the only expression upon the face of the speaker. It has deepened to chagrin, with an admixture of shame. It is through him that the train is without a regular guide. One, engaged at Indianola, had piloted them to their last camping place. There, in consequence of some dispute, due to the surly temper of the ex-captain of volunteers, the man had demanded his dismissal, and gone back.

For this—as also for an ill-timed display of confidence in his power to conduct the march—is the planter's nephew now suffering under a sense of shame. He feels it keenly as the carriole comes up, and bright eyes become witnesses of his discomfiture.

Poindexter does not repeat his inquiry. That the road is lost is a fact evident to all. Even the barefooted or "broganned" pedestrians have recognised their long-heeled footprints, and become aware that they are for the second time treading upon the same ground.

There is a general halt, succeeded by an animated conversation among the white men. The situation is serious: the planter himself believes it to be so. He cannot that day reach the end of his journey—a thing upon which he had set his mind.

That is the very least misfortune that can befall them. There are others possible, and probable. There are perils upon the burnt plain. They may be compelled to spend the night upon it, with no water for their animals. Perhaps a second day and night—or longer—who can tell how long?

How are they to find their way? The sun is beginning to descend; though still too high in heaven to indicate his line of declination. By waiting a while they may discover the quarters of the compass.

But to what purpose? The knowledge of east, west, north, and south can avail nothing now: they have lost their *line of march*.

Calhoun has become cautious. He no longer volunteers to point out the path. He hesitates to repeat his pioneering experiments—after such manifest and shameful failure.

A ten minutes' discussion terminates in nothing. No one can suggest a feasible plan of proceeding. No one knows how to escape from the embrace of that dark desert, which appears to cloud not only the sun and sky, but the countenances of all who enter within its limits.

A flock of black vultures is seen flying afar off. They come nearer, and nearer. Some alight upon the ground—others hover above the heads of the strayed travellers. Is there a boding in the behaviour of the birds?

Another ten minutes is spent in the midst of moral and physical gloom. Then, as if by a benignant mandate from heaven, does cheerfulness re-assume its sway. The cause? A horseman riding in the direction of the train!

An unexpected sight: who could have looked for human being in such a place? All eyes simultaneously sparkle with joy; as if, in the approach of the horseman, they beheld the advent of a saviour!

"He's coming this way, is he not?" inquired the planter, scarce confident in his failing sight.

"Yes, father; straight as he can ride," replied Henry, lifting the hat from his head, and waving it on high: the action accompanied by a shout intended to attract the horseman.

The signal was superfluous. The stranger had already sighted the halted waggons; and, riding towards them at a gallop, was soon within speaking distance.

He did not draw bridle, until he had passed the train; and arrived upon the spot occupied by the planter and his party.

"A Mexican!" whispered Henry, drawing his deduction from the habiliments of the horseman.

"So much the better," replied Poindexter, in the same tone of voice; "he'll be all the more likely to know the road."

"Not a bit of Mexican about him," muttered Calhoun, "excepting the rig. I'll soon see. *Buenos dias, cavallero! Esta V. Mexicano?*" (Good day, sir! are you a Mexican?)

"No, indeed," replied the stranger, with a protesting smile. "Anything but that. I can speak to you in Spanish, if you prefer it; but I dare say you will understand me better in English: which, I presume, is your native tongue?"

Calhoun, suspecting that he had spoken indifferent Spanish, or indifferently pronounced it, refrains from making rejoinder.

"*American*, sir," replied Poindexter, his national pride feeling slightly piqued. Then, as if fearing to offend the man from whom he intended asking a favour, he added: "Yes, sir; we are all Americans—from the *Southern States*."

"That I can perceive by your following." An expression of contempt—scarce perceptible—showed itself upon the countenance of the speaker, as his eye rested upon the groups of black bondsmen. "I can perceive, too," he added, "that you are strangers to prairie travelling. You have lost your way?"

"We have, sir; and have very little prospect of recovering it, unless we may count upon your kindness to direct us."

"Not much kindness in that. By the merest chance I came upon your trail, as I was crossing the prairie. I saw you were going astray; and have ridden this way to set you right."

"It is very good of you. We shall be most thankful, sir. My name is Poindexter—Woodley Poindexter, of Louisiana. I have purchased a property on the Leona river, near Fort Inge. We were in hopes of reaching it before nightfall. Can we do so?"

"There is nothing to hinder you: if you follow the instructions I shall give."

On saying this, the stranger rode a few paces apart; and appeared to scrutinise the country—as if to determine the direction which the travellers should take.

Poised conspicuously upon the crest of the ridge, horse and man presented a picture worthy of skilful delineation.

A steed, such as might have been ridden by an Arab sheik—blood-bay in colour—broad in counter—with limbs clean as culms of cane, and hips of elliptical outline, continued into a magnificent tail sweeping rearward like a rainbow: on his back a rider—a young man of not more than five-and-twenty—of noble form and features; habited

13

in the picturesque costume of a Mexican *ranchero*—spencer jacket of velveteen—*calzoneros* laced along the seams—*calzoncillos* of snow-white lawn—*botas* of buff leather, heavily spurred at the heels—around the waist a scarf of scarlet crape; and on his head a hat of black glaze, banded with gold bullion. Picture to yourself a horseman thus habited; seated in a deep tree-saddle, of Moorish shape and Mexican manufacture, with housings of leather stamped in antique patterns, such as were worn by the caparisoned steeds of the Conquistadores; picture to yourself such a *cavallero*, and you will have before your mind's eye a counterpart of him, upon whom the planter and his people were gazing.

Through the curtains of the travelling carriage he was regarded with glances that spoke of a singular sentiment. For the first time in her life, Louise Poindexter looked upon that—hitherto known only to her imagination—a man of heroic mould. Proud might he have been, could he have guessed the interest which his presence was exciting in the breast of the young Creole.

He could not, and did not. He was not even aware of her existence. He had only glanced at the dust-bedaubed vehicle in passing—as one might look upon the rude incrustation of an oyster, without suspecting that a precious pearl may lie gleaming inside.

"By my faith!" he declared, facing round to the owner of the waggons, "I can discover no landmarks for you to steer by. For all that, I can find the way myself. You will have to cross the Leona five miles below the Fort; and, as I have to go by the crossing myself, *you* can follow the tracks of my horse. Good day, gentlemen!"

Thus abruptly bidding adieu, he pressed the spur against the side of his steed; and started off at a gallop.

An unexpected—almost uncourteous departure! So thought the planter and his people.

They had no time to make observations upon it, before the stranger was seen returning towards them!

In ten seconds he was again in their presence—all listening to learn what had brought him back.

"I fear the tracks of my horse may prove of little service to you. The *mustangs* have been this way, since the fire. They have made hoof-marks by the thousand. Mine are shod; but, as you are not accustomed to trailing, you may not be able to distinguish them—the more so, that in these dry ashes all horse-tracks are so nearly alike."

"What are we to do?" despairingly asked the planter.

"I am sorry, Mr Poindexter, I cannot stay to conduct you, I am riding express, with a despatch for the Fort. If you *should* lose my trail, keep the sun on your right shoulders: so that your shadows may fall to the left, at an angle of about fifteen degrees to your line of march. Go straight forward for about five miles. You will then come in sight of the top of a tall tree—a *cypress*. You will know it by its leaves being *in the red*. Head direct for this tree. It stands on the bank of the river; and close by is the crossing."

The young horseman, once more drawing up his reins, was about to ride off; when something caused him to linger. It was a pair of dark lustrous eyes—observed by him for the first time—glancing through the curtains of the travelling carriage.

Their owner was in shadow; but there was light enough to show that they were set in a countenance of surpassing loveliness. He perceived, moreover, that they were turned upon himself—fixed, as he fancied, in an expression that betokened interest—almost tenderness!

He returned it with an involuntary glance of admiration, which he made but an awkward attempt to conceal. Lest it might be mistaken for rudeness, he suddenly faced round; and once more addressed himself to the planter—who had just finished thanking him for his civility.

"I am but ill deserving thanks," was his rejoinder, "thus to leave you with a chance of losing your way. But, as I've told you, my time is measured."

The despatch-bearer consulted his watch—as though not a little reluctant to travel alone.

"You are very kind, sir," said Poindexter; "but with the directions you have given us, I think we shall be able to manage. The sun will surely show us—"

"No: now I look at the sky, it will not. There are clouds looming up on the north. In an hour, the sun may be obscured—at all events, before you can get within sight of the cypress. It will not do. Stay!" he continued, after a reflective pause, "I have a better plan still: *follow the trail of my lazo!*"

While speaking, he had lifted the coiled rope from his saddlebow, and flung the loose end to the earth—the other being secured to a ring in the pommel. Then raising his hat in graceful salutation—more than half directed towards the travelling carriage—he gave the spur to his steed; and once more bounded off over the prairie.

The lazo, lengthening out, tightened over the hips of his horse; and, dragging a dozen yards behind, left a line upon the cinereous surface—as if some slender serpent had been making its passage across the plain.

"An exceedingly curious fellow!" remarked the planter, as they stood gazing after the horseman, fast becoming hidden behind a cloud of sable dust. "I ought to have asked him his name?"

"An exceedingly conceited fellow, I should say," muttered Calhoun; who had not failed to notice the glance sent by the stranger in the direction of the carriole, nor that which had challenged it. "As to his name, I don't think it matters much. It mightn't be his own he would give you. Texas is full of such swells, who take new names when they get here—by way of improvement, if for no better reason."

"Come, cousin Cash," protested young Poindexter; "you are unjust to the stranger. He appears to be educated—in fact, a gentleman—worthy of bearing the best of names, I should say."

"A gentleman! Deuced unlikely: rigged out in that fanfaron fashion. I never saw a man yet, that took to a Mexican dress, who wasn't a *Jack*. He's one, I'll be bound."

During this brief conversation, the fair occupant of the carriole was seen to bend forward; and direct a look of evident interest, after the form of the horseman fast receding from her view.

To this, perhaps, might have been traced the acrimony observable in the speech of Calhoun.

"What is it, Loo?" he inquired, riding close up to the carriage, and speaking in a voice not loud enough to be heard by the others. "You appear impatient to go forward? Perhaps you'd like to ride off along with that swaggering fellow? It isn't too late: I'll lend you my horse."

The young girl threw herself back upon the seat—evidently displeased, both by the speech and the tone in which it was delivered. But her displeasure, instead of expressing itself in a frown, or in the shape of an indignant rejoinder, was concealed under a guise far more galling to him who had caused it. A clear ringing laugh was the only reply vouchsafed to him.

"So, so! I thought there must be something—by the way you behaved yourself in his presence. You looked as if you would have relished a *tête-à-tête* with this showy despatch-bearer. Taken with his stylish dress, I suppose? Fine feathers make fine birds. His are borrowed. I may strip them off some day, along with a little of the skin that's under them."

"For shame, Cassius! your words are a scandal!"

"'Tis you should think of scandal, Loo! To let your thoughts turn on a common scamp—a masquerading fellow like that! No doubt the letter carrier, employed by the officers at the Fort!"

"A letter carrier, you think? Oh, how I should like to get love letters by such a postman!"

"You had better hasten on, and tell him so. My horse is at your service."

"Ha! ha! ha! What a simpleton you show yourself! Suppose, for jesting's sake, I *did* have a fancy to overtake this prairie postman! It couldn't be done upon that dull steed of yours: not a bit of it! At the rate he is going, he and his blood-bay will be out of sight before you could change saddles for me. Oh, no! he's not to be overtaken by me, however much I might like it; and perhaps I *might like it*!"

"Don't let your father hear you talk in that way."

"Don't let him hear *you* talk in that way," retorted the young lady, for the first time speaking in a serious strain. "Though you *are* my cousin, and papa may think you the pink of perfection, I don't—not I! I never told you I did—did I?" A frown, evidently called forth by some unsatisfactory reflection, was the only reply to this tantalising interrogative.

"You *are* my cousin," she continued, in a tone that contrasted strangely with the levity she had already exhibited, "but you are nothing more—nothing more—Captain Cassius Calhoun! You have no claim to be my counsellor. There is but one from whom I am in duty bound to take advice, or bear reproach. I therefore beg of you, Master Cash, that you will not again presume to repeat such sentiments—as those you have just favoured me with. I shall remain mistress of my own thoughts—and actions, too—till I have found a master who can control them. It is not you!"

Having delivered this speech, with eyes flashing—half angrily, half contemptuously—upon her cousin, the young Creole once more threw herself back upon the cushions of the carriole.

The closing curtains admonished the ex-officer, that further conversation was not desired.

Quailing under the lash of indignant innocence, he was only too happy to hear the loud "gee-on" of the teamsters, as the waggons commenced moving over the sombre surface—not more sombre than his own thoughts.

# 3. The Prairie Finger-Post

The travellers felt no further uneasiness about the route. The snake-like trail was continuous; and so plain that a child might have followed it.

It did not run in a right line, but meandering among the thickets; at times turning out of the way, in places where the ground was clear of timber. This had evidently been done with an intent to avoid obstruction to the waggons: since at each of these windings the travellers could perceive that there were breaks, or other inequalities, in the surface.

"How very thoughtful of the young fellow!" remarked Poindexter. "I really feel regret at not having asked for his name. If he belong to the Fort, we shall see him again."

"No doubt of it," assented his son. "I hope we shall."

His daughter, reclining in shadow, overheard the conjectural speech, as well as the rejoinder. She said nothing; but her glance towards Henry seemed to declare that her heart fondly echoed the hope.

Cheered by the prospect of soon terminating a toilsome journey—as also by the pleasant anticipation of beholding, before sunset, his new purchase—the planter was in one of his happiest moods. His aristocratic bosom was moved by an unusual amount of condescension, to all around him. He chatted familiarly with his overseer; stopped to crack a joke with "Uncle" Scipio, hobbling along on blistered heels; and encouraged "Aunt" Chloe in the transport of her piccaninny.

"Marvellous!" might the observer exclaim—misled by such exceptional interludes, so pathetically described by the scribblers in Lucifer's pay—"what a fine patriarchal institution is slavery, after all! After all we have said and done to abolish it! A waste of sympathy—sheer philanthropic folly to attempt the destruction of this ancient edifice—worthy corner-stone to a 'chivalric' nation! Oh, ye abolition fanatics! why do ye clamour against it? Know ye not that some must suffer—must work and starve—that others may enjoy the luxury of idleness? That some must be slaves, that others may be free?"

Such arguments—at which a world might weep—have been of late but too often urged. Woe to the man who speaks, and the nation that gives ear to them!

The planter's high spirits were shared by his party, Calhoun alone excepted. They were reflected in the faces of his black bondsmen, who regarded him as the source, and dispenser, of their happiness, or misery—omnipotent—next to God. They loved him less than God, and feared him more; though he was by no means a bad master—that is, *by comparison.* He did not absolutely take delight in torturing them. He liked to see them well fed and clad—their epidermis shining with the exudation of its own oil. These signs bespoke the importance of their proprietor—himself. He was satisfied to let them off with an occasional "cow-hiding"—salutary, he would assure you; and in all his "stock" there was not one black skin marked with the mutilations of vengeance—a proud boast for a Mississippian slave-owner, and more than most could truthfully lay claim to.

In the presence of such an exemplary owner, no wonder that the cheerfulness was universal—or that the slaves should partake of their master's joy, and give way to their garrulity.

It was not destined that this joyfulness should continue to the end of their journey. It was after a time interrupted—not suddenly, nor by any fault on the part of those indulging in it, but by causes and circumstances over which they had not the slightest control.

As the stranger had predicted: the sun ceased to be visible, before the cypress came in sight.

There was nothing in this to cause apprehension. The line of the lazo was conspicuous as ever; and they needed no guidance from the sun: only that his cloud-eclipse produced a corresponding effect upon their spirits.

"One might suppose it close upon nightfall," observed the planter, drawing out his gold repeater, and glancing at its dial; "and yet it's only three o'clock! Lucky the young fellow has left us such a sure guide. But for him, we might have floundered among these ashes till sundown; perhaps have been compelled to sleep upon them."

"A black bed it would be," jokingly rejoined Henry, with the design of rendering the conversation more cheerful. "Ugh! I should have such ugly dreams, were I to sleep upon it."

"And I, too," added his sister, protruding her pretty face through the curtains, and taking a survey of the surrounding scene: "I'm sure I should dream of Tartarus, and Pluto, and Proserpine, and—"

"Hya! hya! hya!" grinned the black Jehu, on the box—enrolled in the plantation books as *Pluto Poindexter*—"De young missa dream 'bout *me* in de mids' ob dis brack praira! Golly! dat am a good joke—berry! Hya! hya! hya!"

"Don't be too sure, all of ye," said the surly nephew, at this moment coming up, and taking part in the conversation—"don't be too sure that you won't have to make your beds upon it yet. I hope it may be no worse."

"What mean you, Cash?" inquired the uncle.

"I mean, uncle, that that fellow's been misleading us. I won't say it for certain; but it looks ugly. We've come more than five miles—six, I should say—and where's the tree? I've examined the horizon, with a pair of as good eyes as most have got, I reckon; and there isn't such a thing in sight."

"But why should the stranger have deceived us?"

"Ah—why? That's just it. There may be more reasons than one."

"Give us one, then!" challenged a silvery voice from the carriole. "We're all ears to hear it!"

"You're all ears to take in everything that's told you by a stranger," sneeringly replied Calhoun. "I suppose if I gave my reason, you'd be so charitable as to call it a false alarm!"

"That depends on its character, Master Cassius. I think you might venture to try us. We scarcely expect a false alarm from a soldier, as well as traveller, of your experience."

Calhoun felt the taunt; and would probably have withheld the communication he had intended to make, but for Poindexter himself.

"Come, Cassius, explain yourself!" demanded the planter, in a tone of respectful authority. "You have said enough to excite something more than curiosity. For what reason should the young fellow be leading us astray?"

"Well, uncle," answered the ex-officer, retreating a little from his original accusation, "I haven't said for certain that he *is*; only that it looks like it."

"In what way?"

"Well, one don't know what may happen. Travelling parties as strong, and stronger than we, have been attacked on these plains, and plundered of every thing—murdered."

"Mercy!" exclaimed Louise, in a tone of terror, more affected than real.

"By Indians," replied Poindexter.

"Ah—Indians, indeed! Sometimes it may be; and sometimes, too, they may be whites who play at that game—not all Mexican whites, neither. It only needs a bit of brown paint; a horsehair wig, with half a dozen feathers stuck into it; that, and plenty of hullabalooing. If we were to be robbed by a party of *white* Indians, it wouldn't be the first time the thing's been done. We as good as half deserve it—for our greenness, in trusting too much to a stranger."

"Good heavens, nephew! this is a serious accusation. Do you mean to say that the despatch-rider—if he be one—is leading us into—into an ambuscade?"

"No, uncle; I don't say that. I only say that such things have been done; and it's possible he *may*."

"But not *probable*," emphatically interposed the voice from the carriole, in a tone tauntingly quizzical.

"No!" exclaimed the stripling Henry, who, although riding a few paces ahead, had overheard the conversation. "Your suspicions are unjust, cousin Cassius. I pronounce them a calumny. What's more, I can prove them so. Look there!"

The youth had reined up his horse, and was pointing to an object placed conspicuously by the side of the path; which, before speaking, he had closely scrutinised. It was a tall plant of the *columnar cactus*, whose green succulent stem had escaped scathing by the fire.

It was not to the plant itself that Henry Poindexter directed the attention of his companions; but to a small white disc, of the form of a parallelogram, impaled upon one of its spines. No one accustomed to the usages of civilised life could mistake the "card." It was one.

"Hear what's written upon it!" continued the young man, riding nearer, and reading aloud the directions pencilled upon the bit of pasteboard.

"The cypress in sight!"

"Where?" inquired Poindexter.

"There's a hand," rejoined Henry, "with a finger pointing—no doubt in the direction of the tree."

All eyes were instantly turned towards the quarter of the compass, indicated by the cipher on the card.

Had the sun been shining, the cypress might have been seen at the first glance. As it was, the sky—late of cerulean hue—was now of a

21

leaden grey; and no straining of the eyes could detect anything along the horizon resembling the top of a tree.

"There's nothing of the kind," asserted Calhoun, with restored confidence, at the same time returning to his unworthy accusation. "It's only a dodge—another link in the chain of tricks the scamp is playing us."

"You mistake, cousin Cassius," replied that same voice that had so often contradicted him. "Look through this lorgnette! If you haven't lost the sight of those superior eyes of yours, you'll see something *very like a tree*—a tall tree—and a cypress, too, if ever there was one in the swamps of Louisiana."

Calhoun disdained to take the opera glass from the hands of his cousin. He knew it would convict him: for he could not suppose she was telling an untruth.

Poindexter availed himself of its aid; and, adjusting the focus to his failing sight, was enabled to distinguish the red-leafed cypress, topping up over the edge of the prairie.

"It's true," he said: "the tree is there. The young fellow is honest: you've been wronging him, Cash. I didn't think it likely he should have taken such a queer plan to make fools of us. He there! Mr Sansom! Direct your teamsters to drive on!"

Calhoun, not caring to continue the conversation, nor yet remain longer in company, spitefully spurred his horse, and trotted off over the prairie.

"Let me look at that card, Henry?" said Louise, speaking to her brother in a restrained voice. "I'm curious to see the cipher that has been of such service to us. Bring it away, brother: it can be of no further use where it is—now that we have sighted the tree."

Henry, without the slightest suspicion of his sister's motive for making the request, yielded obedience to it.

Releasing the piece of pasteboard from its impalement, he "chucked" it into her lap.

"*Maurice Gerald!*" muttered the young Creole, after deciphering the name upon the card. "Maurice Gerald!" she repeated, in apostrophic thought, as she deposited the piece of pasteboard in her bosom. "Whoever you are—whence you have come—whither you are going—what you may be—*Henceforth there is a fate between us!* I feel it—I know it—sure as there's a sky above! Oh! how that sky lowers! Am I to take it as a type of this still untraced destiny?"

# 4. The Black Norther

For some seconds, after surrendering herself to the Sybilline thoughts thus expressed, the young lady sate in silence—her white hands clasped across her temples, as if her whole soul was absorbed in an attempt, either to explain the past, or penetrate the future.

Her reverie—whatever might be its cause—was not of long duration. She was awakened from it, on hearing exclamations without—mingled with words that declared some object of apprehension.

She recognised her brother's voice, speaking in tones that betokened alarm.

"Look, father! don't you see them?"

"Where, Henry—where?"

"Yonder—behind the waggons. You see them now?"

"I do—though I can't say what they are. They look like—like—" Poindexter was puzzled for a simile—"I really don't know what."

"Waterspouts?" suggested the ex-captain, who, at sight of the strange objects, had condescended to rejoin the party around the carriole. "Surely it can't be that? It's too far from the sea. I never heard of their occurring on the prairies."

"They are in motion, whatever they be," said Henry. "See! they keep closing, and then going apart. But for that, one might mistake them for huge obelisks of black marble!"

"Giants, or ghouls!" jokingly suggested Calhoun; "ogres from some other world, who've taken a fancy to have a promenade on this abominable prairie!"

The ex-officer was only humorous with an effort. As well as the others, he was under the influence of an uneasy feeling.

And no wonder. Against the northern horizon had suddenly become upreared a number of ink-coloured columns—half a score of them—unlike anything ever seen before. They were not of regular columnar form, nor fixed in any way; but constantly changing size, shape, and place—now steadfast for a time—now gliding over the charred surface like giants upon skates—anon, bending and balancing towards one another in the most fantastic figurings!

It required no great effort of imagination, to fancy the Titans of old, resuscitated on the prairies of Texas, leading a measure after some wild carousal in the company of Bacchus!

In the proximity of phenomena never observed before—unearthly in their aspect—unknown to every individual of the party—it was but natural these should be inspired with alarm.

And such was the fact. A sense of danger pervaded every bosom. All were impressed with a belief: that they were in the presence of some *peril of the prairies*.

A general halt had been made on first observing the strange objects: the negroes on foot, as well as the teamsters, giving utterance to shouts of terror. The animals—mules as well as horses, had come instinctively to a stand—the latter neighing and trembling—the former filling the air with their shrill screams.

These were not the only sounds. From the sable towers could be heard a hoarse swishing noise, that resembled the sough of a waterfall—at intervals breaking into reverberations like the roll of musketry, or the detonations of distant thunder!

These noises were gradually growing louder and more distinct. The danger, whatever it might be, was drawing nearer!

Consternation became depicted on the countenances of the travellers, Calhoun's forming no exception. The ex-officer no longer pretended levity. The eyes of all were turned towards the lowering sky, and the band of black columns that appeared coming on to crush them!

At this crisis a shout, reaching their ears from the opposite side, was a source of relief—despite the unmistakable accent of alarm in which it was uttered.

Turning, they beheld a horseman in full gallop—riding direct towards them.

The horse was black as coal: the rider of like hue, even to the skin of his face. For all that he was recognised: as the stranger, upon the trail of whose lazo they had been travelling.

The perceptions of woman are quicker than those of man: the young lady within the carriole was the first to identify him. "Onward!" he cried, as soon as within speaking distance. "On—on! as fast as you can drive!"

"What is it?" demanded the planter, in bewildered alarm. "Is there a danger?"

"There is. I did not anticipate it, as I passed you. It was only after reaching the river, I saw the sure signs of it."

"Of what, sir?"

"The *norther*."

"You mean the storm of that name?"

"I do."

"I never heard of its being dangerous," interposed Calhoun, "except to vessels at sea. It's precious cold, I know; but—"

"You'll find it worse than cold, sir," interrupted the young horseman, "if you're not quick in getting out of its way. Mr Poindexter," he continued, turning to the planter, and speaking with impatient emphasis, "I tell you, that you and your party are in peril. A norther is not always to be dreaded; but this one—look yonder! You see those black pillars?"

"We've been wondering—didn't know what to make of them."

"They're nothing—only the precursors of the storm. Look beyond! Don't you see a coal-black cloud spreading over the sky? That's what you have to dread. I don't wish to cause you unnecessary alarm: but I tell you, there's death in yonder shadow! It's in motion, and coming this way. You have no chance to escape it, except by speed. If you do not make haste, it will be too late. In ten minutes' time you may be enveloped, and then—quick, sir, I entreat you! Order your drivers to hurry forward as fast as they can! The sky—heaven itself—commands you!"

The planter did not think of refusing compliance, with an appeal urged in such energetic terms. The order was given for the teams to be set in motion, and driven at top speed.

Terror, that inspired the animals equally with their drivers, rendered superfluous the use of the whip.

The travelling carriage, with the mounted men, moved in front, as before. The stranger alone threw himself in the rear—as if to act as a guard against the threatening danger.

At intervals he was observed to rein up his horse, and look back: each time by his glances betraying increased apprehension.

Perceiving it, the planter approached, and accosted him with the inquiry:

"Is there still a danger?"

"I am sorry to answer you in the affirmative," said he: "I had hopes that the wind might be the other way."

"Wind, sir? There is none—that I can perceive."

25

"Not here. Yonder it is blowing a hurricane, and this way too—direct. By heavens! it is nearing us rapidly! I doubt if we shall be able to clear the burnt track."

"What is to be done?" exclaimed the planter, terrified by the announcement.

"Are your mules doing their best?"

"They are: they could not be driven faster."

"I fear we shall *be too late, then*!"

As the speaker gave utterance to this gloomy conjecture, he reined round once more; and sate regarding the cloud columns—as if calculating the rate at which they were advancing.

The lines, contracting around his lips, told of something more than dissatisfaction.

"Yes: too late!" he exclaimed, suddenly terminating his scrutiny. "They are moving faster than we—far faster. There is no hope of our escaping them!"

"Good God, sir! is the danger so great? Can we do nothing to avoid it?"

The stranger did not make immediate reply. For some seconds he remained silent, as if reflecting—his glance no longer turned towards the sky, but wandering among the waggons.

"Is there no chance of escape?" urged the planter, with the impatience of a man in presence of a great peril.

"There is!" joyfully responded the horseman, as if some hopeful thought had at length suggested itself. "There *is a chance*. I did not think of it before. We cannot shun the storm—the danger we may. Quick, Mr Poindexter! Order your men to muffle the mules—the horses too—otherwise the animals will be blinded, and go mad. Blankets—cloaks—anything will do. When that's done, let all seek shelter within the waggons. Let the tilts be closed at the ends. I shall myself look to the travelling carriage."

Having delivered this chapter of instructions—which Poindexter, assisted by the overseer, hastened to direct the execution of—the young horseman galloped towards the front.

"Madame!" said he, reining up alongside the carriole, and speaking with as much suavity as the circumstances would admit of, "you must close the curtains all round. Your coachman will have to get inside; and you, gentlemen!" he continued, addressing himself to Henry and Calhoun—"and you, sir;" to Poindexter, who had just come up. "There will be room for all. Inside, I beseech you! Lose no time. In a few seconds the storm will be upon us!"

"And you, sir?" inquired the planter, with a show of interest in the man who was making such exertions to secure them against some yet unascertained danger. "What of yourself?"

"Don't waste a moment upon me. I know what's coming. It isn't the first time I have encountered it. In—in, I entreat you! You haven't a second to spare. Listen to that shriek! Quick, or the dust-cloud will be around us!"

The planter and his son sprang together to the ground; and retreated into the travelling carriage.

Calhoun, refusing to dismount, remained stiffly seated in his saddle. Why should *he* skulk from a visionary danger, that did not deter a man in Mexican garb?

The latter turned away; as he did so, directing the overseer to get inside the nearest waggon—a direction which was obeyed with alacrity—and, for the first time, the stranger was left free to take care of himself.

Quickly unfolding his *serapé*—hitherto strapped across the cantle of his saddle—he flung it over the head of his horse. Then, drawing the edges back, he fastened it, bag-fashion, around the animal's neck. With equal alertness he undid his scarf of China crape; and stretched it around his sombrero—fixing it in such a way, that one edge was held under the bullion band, while the other dropped down over the brim— thus forming a silken visor for his face.

Before finally closing it, he turned once more towards the carriole; and, to his surprise, saw Calhoun still in the saddle. Humanity triumphed over a feeling of incipient aversion.

"Once again, sir, I adjure you to get inside! If you do not you'll have cause to repent it. Within ten minutes' time, you may be a dead man!"

The positive emphasis with which the caution was delivered produced its effect. In the presence of mortal foeman, Cassius Calhoun was no coward. But there was an enemy approaching that was not mortal—not in any way understood. It was already making itself manifest, in tones that resembled thunder—in shadows that mocked the darkness of midnight. Who would not have felt fear at the approach of a destroyer so declaring itself?

The ex-officer was unable to resist the united warnings of earth and heaven; and, slipping out of his saddle with a show of reluctance—intended to save appearances—he clambered into the carriage, and ensconced himself behind the closely-drawn curtains.

To describe what followed is beyond the power of the pen. No eye beheld the spectacle: for none dared look upon it. Even had this been possible, nothing could have been seen. In five minutes after the muffling of the mules, the train was enveloped in worse than Cimmerian darkness.

The opening scene can alone be depicted: for that only was observed by the travellers. One of the sable columns, moving in the advance, broke as it came in collision with the waggon-tilts. Down came a shower of black dust, as if the sky had commenced raining gunpowder! It was a foretaste of what was to follow.

There was a short interval of open atmosphere—hot as the inside of an oven. Then succeeded puffs, and whirling gusts, of wind—cold as if projected from caves of ice, and accompanied by a noise as though all the trumpets of Aeolus were announcing the advent of the Storm-King!

In another instant the *norther* was around them; and the waggon train, halted on a subtropical plain, was enveloped in an atmosphere, akin to that which congeals the icebergs of the Arctic Ocean!

Nothing more was seen—nothing heard, save the whistling of the wind, or its hoarse roaring, as it thundered against the tilts of the waggons. The mules having instinctively turned stern towards it, stood silent in their traces; and the voices of the travellers, in solemn converse inside, could not be distinguished amid the howling of the hurricane.

Every aperture had been closed: for it was soon discovered, that to show a face from under the sheltering canvas was to court suffocation. The air was surcharged with ashes, lifted aloft from the burnt plain, and reduced, by the whirling of the wind, to an impalpable but poisonous powder.

For over an hour did the atmosphere carry this cinereous cloud; during which period lasted the imprisonment of the travellers.

At length a voice, speaking close by the curtains of the carriole, announced their release.

"You can come forth!" said the stranger, the crape scarf thrown back above the brim of his hat. "You will still have the storm to contend against. It will last to the end of your journey; and, perhaps, for three days longer. But you have nothing further to fear. The ashes are all swept off. They've gone before you; and you're not likely to overtake them this side the Rio Grande."

"Sir!" said the planter, hastily descending the steps of the carriage, "we have to thank you for—for—"

"Our lives, father!" cried Henry, supplying the proper words. "I hope, sir, you will favour us with your name?"

"*Maurice Gerald*!" returned the stranger; "though, at the Fort, you will find me better known as *Maurice the mustanger.*"

"A mustanger!" scornfully muttered Calhoun, but only loud enough to be heard by Louise.

"Only a mustanger!" reflected the aristocratic Poindexter, the fervour of his gratitude becoming sensibly chilled.

"For guide, you will no longer need either myself, or my lazo," said the hunter of wild horses. "The cypress is in sight: keep straight towards it. After crossing, you will see the flag over the Fort. You may yet reach your journey's end before night. I have no time to tarry; and must say adieu."

Satan himself, astride a Tartarean steed, could not have looked more like the devil than did Maurice the Mustanger, as he separated for the second time from the planter and his party. But neither his ashy envelope, nor the announcement of his humble calling, did aught to damage him in the estimation of one, whose thoughts were already predisposed in his favour—Louise Poindexter.

On hearing him declare his name—by presumption already known to her—she but more tenderly cherished the bit of cardboard, chafing against her snow-white bosom; at the same time muttering in soft pensive soliloquy, heard only by herself:—

"Maurice the mustanger! despite your sooty covering—despite your modest pretence—you have touched the heart of a Creole maiden. *Mon Dieu—mon Dieu! He is too like Lucifer for me to despise him!*"

# 5. The Home of the Horse-Hunter

Where the *Rio de Nueces* (River of Nuts) collects its waters from a hundred tributary streams—lining the map like the limbs of a grand genealogical tree—you may look upon a land of surpassing fairness. Its surface is "rolling prairie," interspersed with clumps of post-oak and pecân, here and there along the banks of the watercourses uniting into continuous groves.

In some places these timbered tracts assume the aspect of the true *chapparal*—a thicket, rather than a forest—its principal growth being various kinds of acacia, associated with copaiva and creosote trees, with wild aloes, with eccentric shapes of cereus, cactus, and arborescent yucca.

These spinous forms of vegetation, though repulsive to the eye of the agriculturist—as proving the utter sterility of the soil—present an attractive aspect to the botanist, or the lover of Nature; especially when the cereus unfolds its huge wax-like blossoms, or the *Fouquiera splendens* overtops the surrounding shrubbery with its spike of resplendent flowers, like a red flag hanging unfolded along its staff.

The whole region, however, is not of this character. There are stretches of greater fertility; where a black calcareous earth gives nourishment to trees of taller growth, and more luxuriant foliage. The "wild China"—a true *sapindal*—the pecân, the elm, the hackberry, and the oak of several species—with here and there a cypress or Cottonwood—form the components of many a sylvan scene, which, from the blending of their leaves of various shades of green, and the ever changing contour of their clumps, deserves to be denominated fair.

The streams of this region are of crystal purity—their waters tinted only by the reflection of sapphire skies. Its sun, moon, and stars are scarcely ever concealed behind a cloud. The demon of disease has not found his way into this salubrious spot: no epidemic can dwell within its borders.

Despite these advantages, civilised man has not yet made it his home. Its paths are trodden only by the red-skinned rovers of the prairie—Lipano or Comanche—and these only when mounted, and upon the *maraud* towards the settlements of the Lower Nueces, or Leona.

It may be on this account—though it would almost seem as if they were actuated by a love of the beautiful and picturesque—that the true children of Nature, the wild animals, have selected this spot as their favourite habitat and home. In no part of Texas does the stag bound up so often before you; and nowhere is the timid antelope so frequently seen. The rabbit, and his gigantic cousin, the mule-rabbit, are scarcely ever out of sight; while the polecat, the opossum, and the curious peccary, are encountered at frequent intervals.

Birds, too, of beautiful forms and colours, enliven the landscape. The quail whirrs up from the path; the king vulture wheels in the ambient air; the wild turkey, of gigantic stature, suns his resplendent gorget by the side of the pecân copse, and the singular tailor-bird—known among the rude Rangers as the "bird of paradise"—flouts his long scissors-like tail among the feathery fronds of the acacia.

Beautiful butterflies spread their wide wings in flapping flight; or, perched upon some gay corolla, look as if they formed part of the flower. Huge bees (*Meliponae*), clad in velvet liveries, buzz amid the blossoming bushes, disputing possession with hawkmoths and humming-birds not much larger than themselves.

They are not all innocent, the denizens of this lovely land. Here the rattlesnake attains to larger dimensions than in any other part of North America, and shares the covert with the more dangerous *moccasin*. Here, too, the tarantula inflicts its venomous sting; the scorpion poisons with its bite; and the centipede, by simply crawling over the skin, causes a fever that may prove fatal!

Along the wooded banks of the streams may be encountered the spotted ocelot, the puma, and their more powerful congener, the jaguar; the last of these *felidae* being here upon the northern limit of its geographical range.

Along the edges of the chapparal skulks the gaunt Texan wolf—solitarily and in silence; while a kindred and more cowardly species, the *coyoté*, may be observed, far out upon the open plain, hunting in packs.

Sharing the same range with these, the most truculent of quadrupeds, may be seen the noblest and most beautiful of animals—perhaps nobler and more beautiful than man—certainly the most distinguished of man's companions—the horse!

Here—independent of man's caprice, his jaw unchecked by bit or curb, his back unscathed by pack or saddle—he roams unrestrained; giving way to all the wildness of his nature.

But even in this, his favourite haunt, he is not always left alone. Man presumes to be his pursuer and tamer: for here was he sought, captured, and conquered, by *Maurice the Mustanger*.

On the banks of the *Alamo*—one of the most sparkling streamlets that pay tribute to the Nueces—stood a dwelling, unpretentious as any to be found within the limits of Texas, and certainly as picturesque.

Its walls were composed of split trunk of the arborescent yucca, set stockade-fashion in the ground; while its roof was a thatch furnished by the long bayonet-shaped loaves of the same gigantic lily.

The interstices between the uprights, instead of being "chinked" with clay—as is common in the cabins of Western Texas—were covered by a sheeting of horse-skins; attached, not by iron tacks, but with the sharp spines that terminate the leaves of the *pita* plant.

On the bluffs, that on both sides overlooked the rivulet—and which were but the termination of the escarpment of the higher plain—grew in abundance the material out of which the hut had been constructed: tree yuccas and *magueys*, amidst other rugged types of sterile vegetation; whereas the fertile valley below was covered with a growth of heavy timber—consisting chiefly of red-mulberry, post-oak, and pecân, that formed a forest of several leagues in length. The timbered tract was, in fact, conterminous with the bottom lands; the tops of the trees scarce rising to a level with the escarpment of the cliff.

It was not continuous. Along the edge of the streamlet were breaks—forming little meads, or savannahs, covered with that most nutritious of grasses, known among Mexicans as *grama*.

In the concavity of one of these, of semicircular shape—which served as a natural lawn—stood the primitive dwelling above described; the streamlet representing the chord; while the curve was traced by the trunks of the trees, that resembled a series of columns supporting the roof of some sylvan coliseum.

The structure was in shadow, a little retired among the trees; as if the site had been chosen with a view to concealment. It could have been seen but by one passing along the bank of the stream; and then only with the observer directly in front of it. Its rude style of architecture, and russet hue, contributed still further to its *inconspicuousness*.

The house was a mere cabin—not larger than a marquee tent—with only a single aperture, the door—if we except the flue of a slender clay chimney, erected at one end against the upright posts. The doorway had a door, a light framework of wood, with a horse-skin stretched over it, and hung upon hinges cut from the same hide.

In the rear was an open shed, thatched with yucca leaves, and supported by half a dozen posts. Around this was a small enclosure, obtained by tying cross poles to the trunks of the adjacent trees.

A still more extensive enclosure, containing within its circumference more than an acre of the timbered tract, and fenced in a similar manner, extended rearward from the cabin, terminating against the bluff. Its turf tracked and torn by numerous hoof-prints—in some places trampled into a hard surface—told of its use: a "corral" for wild horses—*mustangs*.

This was made still more manifest by the presence of a dozen or more of these animals within the enclosure; whose glaring eyeballs, and excited actions, gave evidence of their recent capture, and how ill they brooked the imprisonment of that shadowy paddock.

The interior of the hut was not without some show of neatness and comfort. The sheeting of mustang-skins that covered the walls, with the hairy side turned inward, presented no mean appearance. The smooth shining coats of all colours—black, bay, snow-white, sorrel, and skewbald—offered to the eye a surface pleasantly variegated; and there had evidently been some taste displayed in their arrangement.

The furniture was of the scantiest kind. It consisted of a counter-feit camp bedstead, formed by stretching a horse-hide over a framework of trestles; a couple of stools—diminutive specimens on the same model; and a rude table, shaped out of hewn slabs of the yucca-tree. Something like a second sleeping place appeared in a remote corner—a "shakedown," or "spread," of the universal mustang-skin.

What was least to be expected in such a place, was a shelf containing about a score of books, with pens, ink, and *papéterie*; also a newspaper lying upon the slab table.

Further proofs of civilisation, if not refinement, presented themselves in the shape of a large leathern portmanteau, a double-barrelled gun, with "Westley Richards" upon the breech; a drinking cup of chased silver, a huntsman's horn, and a dog-call.

Upon the floor were a few culinary utensils, mostly of tin; while in one corner stood a demijohn, covered with wicker, and evidently containing something stronger than the water of the Alamo.

Other "chattels" in the cabin were perhaps more in keeping with the place. There was a high-peaked Mexican saddle; a bridle, with headstall of plaited horsehair, and reins to correspond; two or three spare *serapés*, and some odds and ends of raw-hide rope.

Such was the structure of the mustanger's dwelling—such its surroundings—such its interior and contents, with the exception of its living occupants—two in number.

On one of the stools standing in the centre of the floor was seated a man, who could not be the mustanger himself. In no way did he present the semblance of a proprietor. On the contrary, the air of the servitor—the mien of habitual obedience—was impressed upon him beyond the chance of misconstruction.

Rude as was the cabin that sheltered him, no one entering under its roof would have mistaken him for its master.

Not that he appeared ill clad or fed, or in any way stinted in his requirements. He was a round plump specimen, with a shock of carrot-coloured hair and a bright ruddy skin, habited in a suit of stout stuff—half corduroy, half cotton-velvet. The corduroy was in the shape of a pair of knee-breeches, with gaiters to correspond; the velveteen, once bottle green, now faded to a brownish hue, exhibited itself in a sort of shooting coat, with ample pockets in the breast and skirts.

A "wide-awake" hat, cocked over a pair of eyes equally deserving the appellation, completed the costume of the individual in question—if we except a shirt of coarse calico, a red cotton kerchief loosely knotted around his neck, and a pair of Irish *brogues* upon his feet.

It needed neither the brogues, nor the corduroy breeches, to proclaim his nationality. His lips, nose, eyes, air, and attitude, were all unmistakably Milesian.

Had there been any ambiguity about this, it would have been dispelled as he opened his mouth for the emission of speech; and this he at intervals did, in an accent that could only have been acquired in the shire of Galway. As he was the sole human occupant of the cabin, it might be supposed that he spoke only in soliloquy. Not so, however. Couched upon a piece of horse-skin, in front of the fire, with snout half buried among the ashes, was a canine companion, whose appearance bespoke a countryman—a huge Irish staghound, that looked as if he too understood the speech of Connemara.

Whether he did so or not, it was addressed to him, as if he was expected to comprehend every word.

"Och, Tara, me jewel!" exclaimed he in the corduroys, fraternally interrogating the hound; "hadn't yez weesh now to be back in Ballyballagh? Wadn't yez loike to be wance more in the coortyard av the owld castle, friskin' over the clane stones, an bein' tripe-fed till there wasn't a rib to be seen in your sides—so different from what they are now—when I kyan count ivery wan av them? Sowl! it's meself that ud loike to be there, anyhow! But there's no knowin' when the young masther 'll go back, an take us along wid him. Niver mind, Tara! He's goin' to the Sittlements soon, ye owld dog; an he's promised to take us thare; that's some consolashun. Be japers! it's over three months since I've been to the Fort, meself. Maybe I'll find some owld acquaintance among them Irish sodgers that's come lately; an be me sowl, av I do, won't there be a dhrap betwane us—won't there, Tara?"

The staghound, raising his head at hearing the mention of his name, gave a slight sniff, as if saying "Yes" in answer to the droll interrogatory.

"I'd like a dhrap now," continued the speaker, casting a covetous glance towards the wickered jar; "mightily I wud that same; but the dimmyjan is too near bein' empty, an the young masther might miss it. Besides, it wudn't be raal honest av me to take it widout lave—wud it, Tara?"

The dog again raised his head above the ashes, and sneezed as before.

"Why, that was *yis*, the last time ye spoke! Div yez mane is for the same now? Till me, Tara!"

Once more the hound gave utterance to the sound—that appeared to be caused either by a slight touch of influenza, or the ashes having entered his nostrils.

"'Yis' again? In trath that's just fwhat the dumb crayther manes! Don't timpt me, ye owld thief! No—no; I won't touch the whisky. I'll only draw the cork out av the dimmyjan, an take a smell at it. Shure the masther won't know anything about that; an if he did, he wudn't mind it! Smellin' kyant do the pothyeen any harm."

During the concluding portion of this utterance, the speaker had forsaken his seat, and approached the corner where stood the jar.

Notwithstanding the professed innocence of his intent, there was a stealthiness about his movements, that seemed to argue either a want of confidence in his own integrity, or in his power to resist temptation.

He stood for a short while listening—his eyes turned towards the open doorway; and then, taking up the demijohn, he drew out the stopper, and held the neck to his nose.

For some seconds he remained in this attitude: giving out no other sign than an occasional "sniff," similar to that uttered by the hound, and which he had been fain to interpret as an affirmative answer to his interrogatory. It expressed the enjoyment he was deriving from the *bouquet* of the potent spirit.

But this only satisfied him for a very short time; and gradually the bottom of the jar was seen going upwards, while the reverse end descended in like ratio in the direction of his protruding lips.

"Be japers!" he exclaimed, once more glancing stealthily towards the door, "flesh and blood cudn't stand the smell av that bewtiful whisky, widout tastin' it. Trath! I'll chance it—jist the smallest thrifle to wet the tap av my tongue. Maybe it'll burn the skin av it; but no matther—here goes!"

Without further ado the neck of the demijohn was brought in contact with his lips; but instead of the "smallest thrifle" to wet the top of his tongue, the "gluck—gluck" of the escaping fluid told that he was administering a copious saturation to the whole lining of his larynx, and something more.

After half a dozen "smacks" of the mouth, with other exclamations denoting supreme satisfaction, he hastily restored the stopper; returned the demijohn to its place; and glided back to his seat upon the stool.

"Tara, ye owld thief!" said he, addressing himself once more to his canine companion, "it was you that timpted me! No matther, man: the masther 'll niver miss it; besides, he's goin' soon to the Fort, an can lay in a fresh supply."

For a time the pilferer remained silent; either reflecting on the act he had committed, or enjoying the effects which the "potheen" had produced upon his spirits.

His silence was of short duration; and was terminated by a soliloquy.

"I wondher," muttered he, "fwhat makes Masther Maurice so anxious to get back to the Sittlements. He says he'll go wheniver he catches that spotty mustang he has seen lately. Sowl! isn't he bad aft-her that baste! I suppose it must be somethin' beyant the common—the more be token, as he has chased the crayther three times widout bein' able to throw his rope over it—an mounted on the blood-bay, too. He sez he won't give it up, till he gets howlt of it. Trath! I hope it'll be grupped soon, or wez may stay here till the marnin' av dooms-day. Hush! fwhat's that?"

Tara springing up from his couch of skin, and rushing out with a low growl, had caused the exclamation.

"Phelim!" hailed a voice from the outside. "Phelim!"

"It's the masther," muttered Phelim, as he jumped from his stool, and followed the dog through the doorway.

# 6. The Spotted Mustang

Phelim was not mistaken as to the voice that had hailed him. It was that of his master, Maurice Gerald.

On getting outside, he saw the mustanger at a short distance from the door, and advancing towards it.

As the servant should have expected, his master was mounted upon his horse—no longer of a reddish colour, but appearing almost black. The animal's coat was darkened with sweat; its counter and flanks speckled with foam.

The blood-bay was not alone. At the end of the lazo—drawn taut from the saddle tree—was a companion, or, to speak more accurately, a captive. With a leathern thong looped around its under jaw, and firmly embracing the bars of its mouth, kept in place by another passing over its neck immediately behind the ears, was the captive secured.

It was a mustang of peculiar appearance, as regarded its markings; which were of a kind rarely seen—even among the largest "gangs" that roam over the prairie pastures, where colours of the most eccentric patterns are not uncommon.

That of the animal in question was a ground of dark chocolate in places approaching to black—with white spots distributed over it, as regularly as the contrary colours upon the skin of the jaguar.

As if to give effect to this pleasing arrangement of hues, the creature was of perfect shape—broad chested, full in the flank, and clean limbed—with a hoof showing half a score of concentric rings, and a head that might have been taken as a type of equine beauty. It was of large size for a mustang, though much smaller than the ordinary English horse; even smaller than the blood-bay—himself a mustang—that had assisted in its capture.

The beautiful captive was a mare—one of a *manada* that frequented the plains near the source of the Alamo; and where, for the third time, the mustanger had unsuccessfully chased it.

In his case the proverb had proved untrue. In the third time he had not found the "charm"; though it favoured him in the fourth. By the fascination of a long rope, with a running noose at its end, he had secured the creature that, for some reason known only to himself, he so ardently wished to possess.

Phelim had never seen his master return from a horse-hunting excursion in such a state of excitement; even when coming back—as he often did—with half a dozen mustangs led loosely at the end of his lazo.

But never before at the end of that implement had Phelim beheld such a beauty as the spotted mare. She was a thing to excite the admiration of one less a connoisseur in horse-flesh than the *ci-devant* stable-boy of Castle Ballagh.

"Hooch—hoop—hoora!" cried he, as he set eyes upon the captive, at the same time tossing his hat high into the air. "Thanks to the Howly Vargin, an Saint Pathrick to boot, Masther Maurice, yez have cotched the spotty at last! It's a mare, be japers! Och! the purthy crayther! I don't wondher yez hiv been so bad about gettin' howlt av her. Sowl! if yez had her in Ballinasloe Fair, yez might ask your own price, and get it too, widout givin' sixpence av luckpenny. Oh! the purty crayther! Where will yez hiv her phut, masther? Into the corral, wid the others?"

"No, she might get kicked among them. We shall tie her in the shed. Castro must pass his night outside among the trees. If he's got any gallantry in him he won't mind that. Did you ever see anything so beautiful as she is, Phelim—I mean in the way of horseflesh?"

"Niver, Masther Maurice; niver, in all me life! An' I've seen some nice bits av blood about Ballyballagh. Oh, the purty crayther! she looks as if a body cud ate her; and yit, in trath, she looks like she wud ate you. Yez haven't given her the schoolin' lesson, have yez?"

"No, Phelim: I don't want to break her just yet—not till I have time, and can do it properly. It would never do to spoil such perfection as that. I shall tame her, after we've taken her to the Settlements."

"Yez be goin' there, masther Maurice? When?"

"To-morrow. We shall start by daybreak, so as to make only one day between here and the Fort."

"Sowl! I'm glad to hear it. Not on me own account, but yours, Masther Maurice. Maybe yez don't know that the whisky's on the idge of bein' out? From the rattle av the jar, I don't think there's more than three naggins left. Them sutlers at the Fort aren't honest. They chate ye in the mizyure; besides watherin' the whisky, so that it won't bear a dhrap more out av the strame hare. Trath! a gallon av Innishowen wud last ayqual to three av this Amerikin *rotgut*, as the Yankees themselves christen it."

"Never mind about the whisky, Phelim—I suppose there's enough to last us for this night, and fill our flasks for the journey of to-morrow. Look alive, old Ballyballagh! Let us stable the spotted mare; and then I shall have time to talk about a fresh supply of 'potheen,' which I know you like better than anything else—except yourself!"

"And you, Masther Maurice!" retorted the Galwegian, with a comical twinkle of the eye, that caused his master to leap laughingly out of the saddle.

The spotted mare was soon stabled in the shed, Castro being temporarily attached to a tree; where Phelim proceeded to groom him after the most approved prairie fashion.

The mustanger threw himself on his horse-skin couch, wearied with the work of the day. The capture of the "yegua pinta" had cost him a long and arduous chase—such as he had never ridden before in pursuit of a mustang.

There was a motive that had urged him on, unknown to Phelim—unknown to Castro who carried him—unknown to living creature, save himself.

Notwithstanding that he had spent several days in the saddle—the last three in constant pursuit of the spotted mare—despite the weariness thus occasioned, he was unable to obtain repose. At intervals he rose to his feet, and paced the floor of his hut, as if stirred by some exciting emotion.

For several nights he had slept uneasily—at intervals tossing upon his *catré*—till not only his henchman Phelim, but his hound Tara, wondered what could be the meaning of his *unrest*.

The former might have attributed it to his desire to possess the spotted mare; had he not known that his master's feverish feeling antedated his knowledge of the existence of this peculiar quadruped.

It was several days after his last return from the Fort that the "yegua pinta" had first presented herself to the eye of the mustanger. That therefore could not be the cause of his altered demeanour.

His success in having secured the animal, instead of tranquillising his spirit, seemed to have produced the contrary effect. At least, so thought Phelim: who—with the freedom of that relationship known as "foster-brother"—had at length determined on questioning his master as to the cause of his inquietude. As the latter lay shifting from side to side, he was saluted with the interrogatory—

"Masther Maurice, fwhat, in the name of the Howly Vargin, is the matther wid ye?"

"Nothing, Phelim—nothing, *mabohil*! What makes you think there is?"

"*Alannah*! How kyan I help thinkin' it! Yez kyant get a wink av sleep; niver since ye returned the last time from the Sittlement. Och! yez hiv seen somethin' there that kapes ye awake? Shure now, it isn't wan av them Mixikin girls—*mowchachas*, as they call them? No, I won't believe it. You wudn't be wan av the owld Geralds to care for such trash as them."

"Nonsense, my good fellow! There's nothing the matter with me. It's all your own imagination."

"Trath, masther, yez arr mistaken. If there's anything asthray wid me imaginashun, fhwat is it that's gone wrong wid your own? That is, whin yez arr aslape—which aren't often av late."

"When I'm asleep! What do you mean, Phelim?"

"What div I mane? Fwhy, that wheniver yez close your eyes an think yez are sleepin', ye begin palaverin', as if a preast was confessin' ye!"

"Ah! Is that so? What have you heard me say?"

"Not much, masther, that I cud make sinse out av. Yez be always tryin' to pronounce a big name that appares to have no indin', though it begins wid a *point*!"

"A name! What name?"

"Sowl! I kyan't till ye exakly. It's too long for me to remimber, seein' that my edicashun was intirely neglicted. But there's another name that yez phut before it; an that I kyan tell ye. It's a wuman's name, though it's not common in the owld counthry. It's Looaze that ye say, Masther Maurice; an then comes *the point*."

"Ah!" interrupted the young Irishman, evidently not caring to converse longer on the subject. "Some name I may have heard—somewhere, accidentally. One does have such strange ideas in dreams!"

"Trath! yez spake the truth there; for in your drames, masther, ye talk about a purty girl lookin' out av a carriage wid curtains to it, an tellin' her to close them agaynst some danger that yez are going to save her from."

"I wonder what puts such nonsense into my head?"

"I wondher meself," rejoined Phelim, fixing his eyes upon his young master with a stealthy but scrutinising look. "Shure," he continued, "if I may make bowld to axe the quistyun—shure, Masther

Maurice, yez haven't been makin' a Judy Fitzsummon's mother av yerself, an fallin' in love wid wan of these Yankee weemen out hare? Och an-an-ee! that wud be a misforthune; an thwat wud she say—the purty colleen wid the goodlen hair an blue eyes, that lives not twinty miles from Ballyballagh?"

"Poh, poh! Phelim! you're taking leave of your senses, I fear."

"Trath, masther, I aren't; but I know somethin' I wud like to take lave av."

"What is that? Not me, I hope?"

"You, *alannah*? Niver! It's Tixas I mane. I'd like to take lave of that; an you goin' along wid me back to the owld sad. Arrah, now, fhwat's the use av yer stayin' here, wastin' the best part av yer days in doin' nothin'? Shure yez don't make more than a bare livin' by the horse-catchin'; an if yez did, what mathers it? Yer owld aunt at Castle Ballagh can't howld out much longer; an when she's did, the bewtiful demane 'll be yours, spite av the dhirty way she's thratin' ye. Shure the property's got a tail to it; an not a mother's son av them can kape ye out av it!"

"Ha! ha! ha!" laughed the young Irishman: "you're quite a law-yer, Phelim. What a first-rate attorney you'd have made! But come! You forget that I haven't tasted food since morning. What have you got in the larder?"

"Trath! there's no great stock, masther. Yez haven't laid in any-thin' for the three days yez hiv been afther spotty. There's only the cowld venison an the corn-bread. If yez like I'll phut the venison in the pat, an make a hash av it."

"Yes, do so. I can wait."

"Won't yez wait betther afther tastin' a dhrap av the crayther?"

"True—let me have it."

"Will yez take it nate, or with a little wather? Trath! it won't carry much av that same."

"A glass of grog—draw the water fresh from the stream."

Phelim took hold of the silver drinking-cup, and was about step-ping outside, when a growl from Tara, accompanied by a start, and followed by a rush across the floor, caused the servitor to approach the door with a certain degree of caution.

The barking of the dog soon subsided into a series of joyful whimperings, which told that he had been gratified by the sight of some old acquaintance.

"It's owld Zeb Stump," said Phelim, first peeping out, and then stepping boldly forth—with the double design of greeting the new-comer, and executing the order he had received from his master.

The individual, who had thus freely presented himself in front of the mustanger's cabin, was as unlike either of its occupants, as one from the other.

He stood fall six feet high, in a pair of tall boots, fabricated out of tanned alligator skin; into the ample tops of which were thrust the bot-toms of his pantaloons—the latter being of woollen homespun, that had been dyed with "dog-wood ooze," but was now of a simple dirt colour. A deerskin under shirt, without any other, covered his breast and shoulders; over which was a "blanket coat," that had once been green, long since gone to a greenish yellow, with most of the wool worn off.

There was no other garment to be seen: a slouch felt hat, of grey-ish colour, badly battered, completing the simple, and somewhat scant, collection of his wardrobe.

He was equipped in the style of a backwoods hunter, of the true Daniel Boone breed: bullet-pouch, and large crescent-shaped powder-horn, both suspended by shoulder-straps, hanging under the right arm; a waist-belt of thick leather keeping his coat closed and sustaining a skin sheath, from which protruded the rough stag-horn handle of a long-bladed knife.

He did not affect either mocassins, leggings, nor the caped and fringed tunic shirt of dressed deerskin worn by most Texan hunters. There was no embroidery upon his coarse clothing, no carving upon his accoutrements or weapons, nothing in his *tout ensemble* intended as ornamental. Everything was plain almost to rudeness: as if dictated by a spirit that despised "fanfaron."

Even the rifle, his reliable weapon—the chief tool of his trade—looked like a rounded bar of iron, with a piece of brown unpolished wood at the end, forming its stock; stock and barrel, when the butt rested on the ground, reaching up to the level of his shoulder.

The individual thus clothed and equipped was apparently about fifty years of age, with a complexion inclining to dark, and features that, at first sight, exhibited a grave aspect.

On close scrutiny, however, could be detected an underlying stra-tum of quiet humour; and in the twinkle of a small greyish eye there was evidence that its owner could keenly relish a joke, or, at times, perpetrate one.

The Irishman had pronounced his name: it was Zebulon Stump, or "Old Zeb Stump," as he was better known to the very limited circle of his acquaintances.

"Kaintuck, by birth an raisin'," —as he would have described himself, if asked the country of his nativity—he had passed the early part of his life among the primeval forests of the Lower Mississippi—his sole calling that of a hunter; and now, at a later period, he was performing the same *métier* in the wilds of south-western Texas.

The behaviour of the staghound, as it bounded before him, exhibiting a series of canine welcomes, told of a friendly acquaintance between Zeb Stump and Maurice the mustanger.

"Evenin'!" laconically saluted Zeb, as his tail figure shadowed the cabin door.

"Good evening', Mr Stump!" rejoined the owner of the hut, rising to receive him. "Step inside, and take a seat!"

The hunter accepted the invitation; and, making a single stride across the floor, after some awkward manoeuvring, succeeded in planting himself on the stool lately occupied by Phelim. The lowness of the seat brought his knees upon a level with his chin, the tall rifle rising like a pikestaff several feet above his head.

"Durn stools, anyhow!" muttered he, evidently dissatisfied with the posture; "an' churs, too, for thet matter. I likes to plant my starn upon a log: thur ye've got somethin' under ye as ain't like to guv way."

"Try that," said his host, pointing to the leathern portmanteau in the corner: "you'll find it a firmer seat."

Old Zeb, adopting the suggestion, unfolded the zigzag of his colossal carcase, and transferred it to the trunk.

"On foot, Mr Stump, as usual?"

"No: I got my old critter out thur, tied to a saplin'. I wa'n't a huntin'."

"You never hunt on horseback, I believe?"

"I shed be a greenhorn if I dud. Anybody as goes huntin' a hossback must be a durnation fool!"

"But it's the universal fashion in Texas!"

"Univarsal or no, it air a fool's fashion—a durned lazy fool's fashion! I kill more meat in one day afut, then I ked in a hul week wi' a hoss atween my legs. I don't misdoubt that a hoss air the best thing for you—bein' as yur game's entire different. But when ye go arter baar, or deer, or turkey eyther, ye won't see much o' them, trampin' about through the timmer a hossback, an scarrin' everythin' es hes got ears 'ithin the circuit o' a mile. As for hosses, I shodn't be bothered wi' ne'er a one no how, ef twa'n't for packin' the meat: thet's why I keep my ole maar."

"She's outside, you say? Let Phelim take her round to the shed. You'll stay all night?"

"I kim for that purpiss. But ye needn't trouble about the maar: she air hitched safe enuf. I'll let her out on the laryitt, afore I take to grass."

"You'll have something to eat? Phelim was just getting supper ready. I'm sorry I can't offer you anything very dainty—some hash of venison."

"Nothin' better 'n good deermeat, 'ceptin it be baar; but I like both done over the coals. Maybe I can help ye to some'at thet'll make a roast. Mister Pheelum, ef ye don't mind steppin' to whar my critter air hitched, ye'll find a gobbler hangin' over the horn o' the seddle. I shot the bird as I war comin' up the crik."

"Oh, that is rare good fortune! Our larder has got very low—quite out, in truth. I've been so occupied, for the last three days, in chasing a very curious mustang, that I never thought of taking my gun with me. Phelim and I, and Tara, too, had got to the edge of starvation."

"Whet sort o' a mustang?" inquired the hunter, in a tone that betrayed interest, and without appearing to notice the final remark.

"A mare; with white spots on a dark chocolate ground—a splendid creature!"

"Durn it, young fellur! thet air's the very bizness thet's brung me over to ye."

"Indeed!"

"I've seed that mustang—maar, ye say it air, though I kedn't tell, as she'd niver let me 'ithin hef a mile o' her. I've seed her several times out on the purayra, an I jest wanted ye to go arter her. I'll tell ye why. I've been to the Leeona settlements since I seed you last, and since I seed her too. Wal, theer hev kum thur a man as I knowed on the Mississippi. He air a rich planter, as used to keep up the tallest kind o' doin's, 'specially in the feestin' way. Many's the jeint o' deermeat, and many's the turkey-gobbler this hyur coon hes surplied for his table. His name air Peintdexter."

"Poindexter?"

"Thet air the name—one o' the best known on the Mississippi from Orleens to Saint Looey. He war rich then; an, I reck'n, ain't poor now—seein' as he's brought about a hunderd niggers along wi' him. Beside, thur's a nephew o' hisn, by name Calhoun. He's got the dollars, an nothin' to do wi' 'em but lend 'em to his uncle—the which, for a sartin reezun, I think he *will*. Now, young fellur, I'll tell ye why I wanted to see *you*. Thet 'ere planter hev got a darter, as air dead bent upon hossflesh. She used to ride the skittishest kind o' cattle in Loozeyanner, whar they lived. She heern me tellin' the old 'un 'bout the spotted mustang; and nothin' would content her thur and then, till he promised he'd offer a big price for catchin' the critter. He sayed he'd give a kupple o' hunderd dollars for the anymal, ef 'twur anythin like what I sayed it wur. In coorse, I knowed thet 'ud send all the mustangers in the settlement straight custrut arter it; so, sayin' nuthin' to nobody, I kim over hyur, fast as my ole maar 'ud fetch me. You grup thet 'ere spotty, an Zeb Stump 'll go yur bail ye'll grab them two hunderd dollars."

"Will you step this way, Mr Stump?" said the young Irishman, rising from his stool, and proceeding in the direction of the door.

The hunter followed, not without showing some surprise at the abrupt invitation.

Maurice conducted his visitor round to the rear of the cabin; and, pointing into the shed, inquired—

"Does that look anything like the mustang you've been speaking of?"

"Dog-gone my cats, ef 'taint the eyedenticul same! Grupped already! Two hunderd dollars, easy as slidin' down a barked saplin'! Young fellur, yur in luck: two hunderd, slick sure!—and durn me, ef the anymal ain't worth every cent o' the money! Geehosofat! what a putty beest it air! Won't Miss Peintdexter be pleezed! It'll turn that young critter 'most crazy!"

46

# 7. Nocturnal Annoyances

The unexpected discovery, that his purpose had been already anticipated by the capture of the spotted mustang, raised the spirits of the old hunter to a high pitch of excitement.

They were further elevated by a portion of the contents of the demijohn, which held out beyond Phelim's expectations: giving all hands an appetising "nip" before attacking the roast turkey, with another go each to wash it down, and several more to accompany the post-cenal pipe.

While this was being indulged in, a conversation was carried on; the themes being those that all prairie men delight to talk about: Indian and hunter lore.

As Zeb Stump was a sort of living encyclopaedia of the latter, he was allowed to do most of the talking; and he did it in such a fashion as to draw many a wondering ejaculation, from the tongue of the astonished Galwegian.

Long before midnight, however, the conversation was brought to a close. Perhaps the empty demijohn was, as much as anything else, the monitor that urged their retiring to rest; though there was another and more creditable reason. On the morrow, the mustanger intended to start for the Settlements; and it was necessary that all should be astir at an early hour, to make preparation for the journey. The wild horses, as yet but slightly tamed, had to be strung together, to secure against their escaping by the way; and many other matters required attending to previous to departure.

The hunter had already tethered out his "ole maar"—as he designated the sorry specimen of horseflesh he was occasionally accustomed to bestride—and had brought back with him an old yellowish blanket, which was all he ever used for a bed.

"You may take my bedstead," said his courteous host; "I can lay myself on a skin along the floor."

"No," responded the guest; "none o' yer shelves for Zeb Stump to sleep on. I prefer the solid groun'. I kin sleep sounder on it; an bus-sides, thur's no fear o' fallin' over."

"If you prefer it, then, take the floor. Here's the best place. I'll spread a hide for you."

"Young fellur, don't you do anythin' o' the sort; ye'll only be wastin' yur time. This child don't sleep on no floors. His bed air the green grass o' the purayra."

"What! you're not going to sleep outside?" inquired the mustan-ger in some surprise—seeing that his guest, with the old blanket over his arm, was making for the door.

"I ain't agoin' to do anythin' else."

"Why, the night is freezing cold—almost as chilly as a norther!"

"Durn that! It air better to stan' a leetle chillishness, than a feelin' o' suffercation—which last I wud sartintly hev to go through ef I slep inside o' a house."

"Surely you are jesting, Mr Stump?"

"Young fellur!" emphatically rejoined the hunter, without making direct reply to the question. "It air now nigh all o' six yeer since Zeb Stump hev stretched his ole karkiss under a roof. I oncest used to hev a sort o' a house in the hollow o' a sycamore-tree. That wur on the Mas-sissippi, when my ole ooman wur alive, an I kep up the 'stablishment to 'commerdate her. Arter she went under, I moved into Loozeyanny; an then arterward kim out hyur. Since then the blue sky o' Texas hev been my only kiver, eyther wakin' or sleepin'."

"If you prefer to lie outside—"

"I prefar it," laconically rejoined the hunter, at the same time stalking over the threshold, and gliding out upon the little lawn that lay between the cabin and the creek.

His old blanket was not the only thing he carried along with him. Beside it, hanging over his arm, could be seen some six or seven yards of a horsehair rope. It was a piece of a *cabriesto*—usually employed for tethering horses—though it was not for this purpose it was now to be used.

Having carefully scrutinised the grass within a circumference of several feet in diameter—which a shining moon enabled him to do—he laid the rope with like care around the spot examined, shaping it into a sort of irregular ellipse.

Stepping inside this, and wrapping the old blanket around him, he quietly let himself down into a recumbent position. In an instant after he appeared to be asleep.

And he was asleep, as his strong breathing testified: for Zeb Stump, with a hale constitution and a quiet conscience, had only to summon sleep, and it came.

He was not permitted long to indulge his repose without interruption. A pair of wondering eyes had watched his every movement—the eyes of Phelim O'Neal.

"Mother av Mozis!" muttered the Galwegian; "fwhat can be the manin' av the owld chap's surroundin' himself wid the rope?"

The Irishman's curiosity for a while struggled with his courtesy, but at length overcame it; and just as the slumberer delivered his third snore, he stole towards him, shook him out of his sleep, and propounded a question based upon the one he had already put to himself.

"Durn ye for a Irish donkey!" exclaimed Stump, in evident displeasure at being disturbed; "ye made me think it war mornin'! What do I put the rope roun' me for? What else wud it be for, but to keep off the varmints!"

"What varmints, Misther Stump? Snakes, div yez mane?"

"Snakes in coorse. Durn ye, go to your bed!"

Notwithstanding the sharp rebuke, Phelim returned to the cabin apparently in high glee. If there was anything in Texas, "barrin' an above the Indyins themselves," as he used to say, "that kept him from slapin', it was them vinamous sarpints. He hadn't had a good night's rest, iver since he'd been in the counthry for thinkin' av the ugly vipers, or dhramin' about thim. What a pity Saint Pathrick hadn't paid Tixas a visit before goin' to grace!"

Phelim in his remote residence, isolated as he had been from all intercourse, had never before witnessed the trick of the *cabriesto*.

He was not slow to avail himself of the knowledge thus acquired. Returning to the cabin, and creeping stealthily inside—as if not wishing to wake his master, already asleep—he was seen to take a *cabriesto* from its peg; and then going forth again, he carried the long rope around the stockade walls—paying it out as he proceeded.

Having completed the circumvallation, he re-entered the hut; as he stepped over the threshold, muttering to himself—

"Sowl! Phalim O'Nale, you'll slape sound for this night, spite ov all the snakes in Tixas!"

For some minutes after Phelim's soliloquy, a profound stillness reigned around the hut of the mustanger. There was like silence inside; for the countryman of Saint Patrick, no longer apprehensive on the score of reptile intruders, had fallen asleep, almost on the moment of his sinking down upon his spread horse-skin.

For a while it seemed as if everybody was in the enjoyment of perfect repose, Tara and the captive steeds included. The only sound heard was that made by Zeb Stump's "maar," close by cropping the sweet *grama* grass.

Presently, however, it might have been perceived that the old hunter was himself stirring. Instead of lying still in the recumbent attitude to which he had consigned himself, he could be seen shifting from side to side, as if some feverish thought was keeping him awake.

After repeating this movement some half-score of times, he at length raised himself into a sitting posture, and looked discontentedly around.

"Dod-rot his ignorance and imperence—the Irish cuss!" were the words that came hissing through his teeth. "He's spoilt my night's rest, durn him! 'Twould sarve him 'bout right to drag him out, an giv him a duckin' in the crik. Dog-goned ef I don't feel 'clined torst doin' it; only I don't like to displeeze the other Irish, who air a somebody. Possible I don't git a wink o' sleep till mornin'.".

Having delivered himself of this peevish soliloquy, the hunter once more drew the blanket around his body, and returned to the horizontal position.

Not to sleep, however; as was testified by the tossing and fidgeting that followed—terminated by his again raising himself into a sitting posture.

A soliloquy, very similar to his former one, once more proceeded from his lips; this time the threat of ducking Phelim in the creek being expressed with a more emphatic accent of determination.

He appeared to be wavering, as to whether he should carry the design into execution, when an object coming under his eye gave a new turn to his thoughts.

On the ground, not twenty feet from where he sate, a long thin body was seen gliding over the grass. Its serpent shape, and smooth lubricated skin—reflecting the silvery light of the moon—rendered the reptile easy of identification.

"Snake!" mutteringly exclaimed he, as his eye rested upon the reptilian form. "Wonder what sort it air, slickerin' aboout hyur at this time o' the night? It air too large for a *rattle*; though thur air some in these parts most as big as it. But it air too clur i' the colour, an thin about the belly, for ole rattle-tail! No; 'tain't one o' them. Hah—now I ree-cog-nise the varmint! It air a *chicken*, out on the sarch arter eggs, I reck'n! Durn the thing! it air comin' torst me, straight as it kin crawl!"

The tone in which the speaker delivered himself told that he was in no fear of the reptile—even after discovering that it was making approach. He knew that the snake would not cross the *cabriesto*; but on touching it would turn away: as if the horsehair rope was a line of living fire. Secure within his magic circle, he could have looked tranquilly at the intruder, though it had been the most poisonous of prairie serpents.

But it was not. On the contrary, it was one of the most innocuous—harmless as the "chicken," from which the species takes its trivial title—at the same time that it is one of the largest in the list of North-American *reptilia*.

The expression on Zeb's face, as he sat regarding it, was simply one of curiosity, and not very keen. To a hunter in the constant habit of couching himself upon the grass, there was nothing in the sight either strange or terrifying; not even when the creature came close up to the *cabriesto*, and, with head slightly elevated, rubbed its snout against the rope!

After that there was less reason to be afraid; for the snake, on doing so, instantly turned round and commenced retreating over the sward.

For a second or two the hunter watched it moving away, without making any movement himself. He seemed undecided as to whether he should follow and destroy it, or leave it to go as it had come—unscathed. Had it been a rattlesnake, "copperhead," or "mocassin," he would have acted up to the curse delivered in the garden of Eden, and planted the heel of his heavy alligator-skin boot upon its head. But a harmless chicken-snake did not come within the limits of Zeb Stump's antipathy: as was evidenced by some words muttered by him as it slowly receded from the spot.

"Poor crawlin' critter; let it go! It ain't no enemy o' mine; though it do suck a turkey's egg now an then, an in coorse scarcities the breed o' the birds. Thet air only its nater, an no reezun why I shed be angry wi' it. But thur's a durned good reezun why I shed be wi' thet Irish—the dog-goned, stinkin' fool, to ha' woke me es he dud! I feel dod-rotted like sarvin' him out, ef I ked only think o' some way as wudn't diskermode the young fellur. Stay! By Geehosofat, I've got the idee—the very thing—sure es my name air Zeb Stump!"

On giving utterance to the last words, the hunter—whose countenance had suddenly assumed an expression of quizzical cheerfulness—sprang to his feet; and, with bent body, hastened in pursuit of the retreating reptile.

A few strides brought him alongside of it; when he pounced upon it with all his ten digits extended.

In another moment its long glittering body was uplifted from the ground, and writhing in his grasp.

"Now, Mister Pheelum," exclaimed he, as if apostrophising the serpent, "ef I don't gi'e yur Irish soul a scare thet 'll keep ye awake till mornin', I don't know buzzart from turkey. Hyur goes to purvide ye wi' a bedfellur!"

On saying this, he advanced towards the hut; and, silently skulking under its shadow, released the serpent from his gripe—letting it fall within the circle of the *cabriesto*, with which Phelim had so craftily surrounded his sleeping-place.

Then returning to his grassy couch, and once more pulling the old blanket over his shoulders, he muttered—

"The varmint won't come out acrost the rope—thet air sartin; an it ain't agoin' to leave a yurd o' the groun' 'ithout explorin' for a place to git clur—thet's eequally sartin. Ef it don't crawl over thet Irish greenhorn 'ithin the hef o' an hour, then ole Zeb Stump air a greenhorn hisself. Hi! what's thet? Dog-goned of 'taint on him arready!"

If the hunter had any further reflections to give tongue to, they could not have been heard: for at that moment there arose a confusion of noises that must have startled every living creature on the Alamo, and for miles up and down the stream.

It was a human voice that had given the cue—or rather, a human howl, such as could proceed only from the throat of a Galwegian. Phelim O'Neal was the originator of the infernal *fracas*.

His voice, however, was soon drowned by a chorus of barkings, snortings, and neighings, that continued without interruption for a period of several minutes.

"What is it?" demanded his master, as he leaped from the *catré*, and groped his way towards his terrified servitor. "What the devil has got into you, Phelim? Have you seen a ghost?"

"Oh, masther!—by Jaysus! worse than that: I've been murdhered by a snake. It's bit me all over the body. Blessed Saint Pathrick! I'm a poor lost sinner! I'll be shure to die!"

"Bitten you, you say—where?" asked Maurice, hastily striking a light, and proceeding to examine the skin of his henchman, assisted by the old hunter—who had by this time arrived within the cabin.

"I see no sign of bite," continued the mustanger, after having turned Phelim round and round, and closely scrutinised his epidermis.

"Ne'er a scratch," laconically interpolated Stump.

"Sowl! then, if I'm not bit, so much the better; but it crawled all over me. I can feel it now, as cowld as charity, on me skin."

"Was there a snake at all?" demanded Maurice, inclined to doubt the statement of his follower. "You've been dreaming of one, Phelim—nothing more."

"Not a bit of a dhrame, masther: it was a raal sarpint. Be me sowl, I'm shure of it!"

"I reck'n thur's been snake," drily remarked the hunter. "Let's see if we kin track it up. Kewrious it air, too. Thur's a hair rope all roun' the house. Wonder how the varmint could ha' crossed thet? Thur— thur it is!"

The hunter, as he spoke, pointed to a corner of the cabin, where the serpent was seen spirally coiled.

"Only a chicken!" he continued: "no more harm in it than in a suckin' dove. It kedn't ha' bit ye, Mister Pheelum; but we'll put it past bitin', anyhow."

Saying this, the hunter seized the snake in his hands; and, raising it aloft, brought it down upon the floor of the cabin with a "thwank" that almost deprived it of the power of motion.

"Thru now, Mister Pheelum!" he exclaimed, giving it the finishing touch with the heel of his heavy boot, "ye may go back to yur bed agin, an sleep 'ithout fear o' bein' disturbed till the mornin'— leastwise, by snakes."

Kicking the defunct reptile before him, Zeb Stump strode out of the hut, gleefully chuckling to himself, as, for the third time, he extended his colossal carcase along the sward.

# 8. The Crawl of the Alacran

The killing of the snake appeared to be the cue for a general return to quiescence. The howlings of the hound ceased with those of the henchman. The mustangs once more stood silent under the shadowy trees.

Inside the cabin the only noise heard was an occasional shuffling, when Phelim, no longer feeling confidence in the protection of his *cabriesto*, turned restlessly on his horseskin.

Outside also there was but one sound, to disturb the stillness though its intonation was in striking contrast with that heard within. It might have been likened to a cross between the grunt of an alligator and the croaking of a bull-frog; but proceeding, as it did, from the nostrils of Zeb Stump, it could only be the snore of the slumbering hunter. Its sonorous fulness proved him to be soundly asleep.

He was—had been, almost from the moment of re-establishing himself within the circle of his *cabriesto*. The *revanche* obtained over his late disturber had acted as a settler to his nerves; and once more was he enjoying the relaxation of perfect repose.

For nearly an hour did this contrasting duet continue, varied only by an occasional *recitative* in the hoot of the great horned owl, or a *cantata penserosa* in the lugubrious wail of the prairie wolf.

At the end of this interval, however, the chorus recommenced, breaking out abruptly as before, and as before led by the vociferous voice of the Connemara man.

"Meliah murdher!" cried he, his first exclamation not only startling the host of the hut, but the guest so soundly sleeping outside. "Howly Mother! Vargin av unpurticted innocence! Save me—save me!"

"Save you from what?" demanded his master, once more springing from his couch and hastening to strike a light. "What is it, you confounded fellow?"

"Another snake, yer hanner! Och! be me sowl! a far wickeder sarpent than the wan Misther Stump killed. It's bit me all over the breast. I feel the place burnin' where it crawled across me, just as if the horse-shoer at Ballyballagh had scorched me wid a rid-hot iron!"

"Durn ye for a stinkin' skunk!" shouted Zeb Stump, with his blanket about his shoulder, quite filling the doorway. "Ye've twicest spiled my night's sleep, ye Irish fool! 'Scuse me, Mister Gerald! Thur air fools in all countries, I reck'n, 'Merican as well as Irish—but this hyur follerer o' yourn air the durndest o' the kind iver I kim acrost. Dog-goned if I see how we air to get any sleep the night, 'less we drownd *him* in the crik fust!"

"Och! Misther Stump dear, don't talk that way. I sware to yez both there's another snake. I'm shure it's in the kyabin yit. It's only a minute since I feeled it creepin' over me."

"You must ha' been dreemin?" rejoined the hunter, in a more complacent tone, and speaking half interrogatively. "I tell ye no snake in Texas will cross a hosshair rope. The tother 'un must ha' been in-side the house afore ye laid the laryitt roun' it. 'Taint likely there keel ha' been two on 'em. We kin soon settle that by sarchin'."

"Oh, murdher! Luk hare!" cried the Galwegian, pulling off his shirt and laying bare his breast. "Thare's the riptoile's track, right ac-rass over me ribs! Didn't I tell yez there was another snake? O blissed Mother, what will become av me? It feels like a strake av fire!"

"Snake!" exclaimed Stump, stepping up to the affrighted Irish-man, and holding the candle close to his skin. "Snake i'deed! By the 'tarnal airthquake, it air no snake! It air wuss than that!"

"Worse than a snake?" shouted Phelim in dismay. "Worse, yez say, Misther Stump? Div yez mane that it's dangerous?"

"Wal, it mout be, an it moutn't. Thet ere 'll depend on whether I kin find somethin' 'bout hyur, an find it soon. Ef I don't, then, Mister Pheelum, I won't answer—"

"Oh, Misther Stump, don't say thare's danger!"

"What is it?" demanded Maurice, as his eyes rested upon a red-dish line running diagonally across the breast of his follower, and which looked as if traced by the point of a hot spindle. "What is it, anyhow?" he repeated with increasing anxiety, as he observed the se-rious look with which the hunter regarded the strange marking. "I never saw the like before. Is it something to be alarmed about?"

"All o' thet, Mister Gerald," replied Stump, motioning Maurice outside the hut, and speaking to him in a whisper, so as not to be over-heard by Phelim.

"But what is it?" eagerly asked the mustanger. "*It air the crawl o' the pisen centipede.*"

"The poison centipede! Has it bitten him?"

"No, I hardly think it hez. But it don't need thet. The *crawl* o' it-self air enuf to kill him!"

"Merciful Heaven! you don't mean that?"

"I do, Mister Gerald. I've seed more 'an one good fellur go under wi' that same sort o' a stripe acrost his skin. If thur ain't somethin' done, an thet soon, he'll fust get into a ragin' fever, an then he'll go out o' his senses, jest as if the bite o' a mad dog had gin him the hydrophoby. It air no use frightenin' him howsomdever, till I sees what I kin do. Thur's a yarb, or rayther it air a plant, as grows in these parts. Ef I kin find it handy, there'll be no defeequilty in curin' o' him. But as the cussed lack wud hev it, the moon hez sneaked out o' sight; an I kin only get the yarb by gropin'. I know there air plenty o' it up on the bluff; an ef you'll go back inside, an keep the fellur quiet, I'll see what kin be done. I won't be gone but a minute."

The whispered colloquy, and the fact of the speakers having gone outside to carry it on, instead of tranquillising the fears of Phelim, had by this time augmented them to an extreme degree: and just as the old hunter, bent upon his herborising errand, disappeared in the darkness, he came rushing forth from the hut, howling more piteously than ever.

It was some time before his master could get him tranquillised, and then only by assuring him—on a faith not very firm—that there was not the slightest danger.

A few seconds after this had been accomplished, Zeb Stump reappeared in the doorway, with a countenance that produced a pleasant change in the feelings of those inside. His confident air and attitude proclaimed, as plainly as words could have done, that he had discovered that of which he had gone in search—the "yarb." In his right hand he held a number of oval shaped objects of dark green colour—all of them bristling with sharp spines, set over the surface in equidistant clusters. Maurice recognised the leaves of a plant well known to him—the *oregano* cactus.

"Don't be skeeart, Mister Pheelum!" said the old hunter, in a consolatory tone, as he stepped across the threshold. "Thur's nothin' to fear now. I hev got the bolsum as 'll draw the burnin' out o' yur blood, quicker 'an flame ud scorch a feather. Stop yur yellin', man! Ye've rousted every bird an beast, an creepin' thing too, I reckon, out o' thar slumbers, for more an twenty mile up an down the crik. Ef you go on at that grist much longer, ye'll bring the Kumanchees out o' thur mountains, an that 'ud be wuss mayhap than the crawl o' this hunderd-legged critter. Mister Gerald, you git riddy a bandige, whiles I pur-pares the powltiss."

Drawing his knife from its sheath, the hunter first lopped off the spines; and then, removing the outside skin, he split the thick succulent leaves of the cactus into slices of about an eighth of an inch in thickness. These he spread contiguously upon a strip of clean cotton stuff already prepared by the mustanger; and then, with the ability of a hunter, laid the "powltiss," as he termed it, along the inflamed line, which he declared to have been made by the claws of the centipede, but which in reality was caused by the injection of venom from its poison-charged mandibles, a thousand times inserted into the flesh of the sleeper!

The application of the *oregano* was almost instantaneous in its effect. The acrid juice of the plant, producing a counter poison, killed that which had been secreted by the animal; and the patient, relieved from further apprehension, and soothed by the sweet confidence of security—stronger from reaction—soon fell off into a profound and restorative slumber.

After searching for the centipede and failing to find it—for this hideous reptile, known in Mexico as the *alacran*, unlike the rattle-snake, has no fear of crossing a *cabriesto*—the improvised physician strode silently out of the cabin; and, once more committing himself to his grassy couch, slept undisturbed till the morning.

At the earliest hour of daybreak all three were astir—Phelim having recovered both from his fright and his fever. Having made their matutinal meal upon the *débris* of the roast turkey, they hastened to take their departure from the hut. The quondam stable-boy of Ballyballagh, assisted by the Texan hunter, prepared the wild steeds for transport across the plains—by stringing them securely together—while Maurice looked after his own horse and the spotted mare. More especially did he expend his time upon the beautiful captive—carefully combing out her mane and tail, and removing from her glossy coat the stains that told of the severe chase she had cost him before her proud neck yielded to the constraint of his lazo.

"Durn it, man!" exclaimed Zeb, as, with some surprise, he stood watching the movements of the mustanger, "ye needn't ha' been hef so purtickler! Wudley Pointdexter ain't the man as 'll go back from a barg'in. Ye'll git the two hunderd dollars, sure as my name air Zeblun

Stump; an dog-gone my cats, ef the maar ain't worth every red cent o' the money!"

Maurice heard the remarks without making reply; but the half suppressed smile playing around his lips told that the Kentuckian had altogether misconstrued the motive for his assiduous grooming.

In less than an hour after, the mustanger was on the march, mounted on his blood-bay, and leading the spotted mare at the end of his lazo; while the captive *cavallada*, under the guidance of the Gal-wegian groom, went trooping at a brisk pace over the plain.

Zeb Stump, astride his "ole maar," could only keep up by a con-stant hammering with his heels; and Tara, picking his steps through the spinous *mezquite* grass, trotted listlessly in the rear.

The hut, with its skin-door closed against animal intruders, was left to take care of itself; its silent solitude, for a time, to be disturbed only by the hooting of the horned owl, the scream of the cougar, or the howl-bark of the hungering coyoté.

# 9. The Frontier Fort

The "star-spangled banner" suspended above Fort Inge, as it flouts forth from its tall staff, flings its fitful shadow over a scene of strange and original interest.

It is a picture of pure frontier life—which perhaps only the pencil of the younger Vernet could truthfully portray—half military, half civilian—half savage, half civilised—mottled with figures of men whose complexions, costumes, and callings, proclaim them appertaining to the extremes of both, and every possible gradation between.

Even the *mise-en-scène*—the Fort itself—is of this *miscegenous* character. That star-spangled banner waves not over bastions and battlements; it flings no shadow over casemate or covered way, fosse, scarpment, or glacis—scarce anything that appertains to a fortress. A rude stockade, constructed out of trunks of *algarobia*, enclosing shed-stabling for two hundred horses; outside this a half-score of buildings of the plainest architectural style—some of them mere huts of "wattle and daub"—*jacalés*—the biggest a barrack; behind it the hospital, the stores of the commissary, and quartermaster; on one side the guard-house; and on the other, more pretentiously placed, the messroom and officers' quarters; all plain in their appearance—plastered and white-washed with the lime plentifully found on the Leona—all neat and clean, as becomes a cantonment of troops wearing the uniform of a great civilised nation. Such is Fort Inge.

At a short distance off another group of houses meets the eye—nearly, if not quite, as imposing as the cluster above described bearing the name of "The Fort." They are just outside the shadow of the flag, though under its protection—for to it are they indebted for their origin and existence. They are the germ of the village that universally springs up in the proximity of an American military post—in all probability, and at no very remote period, to become a town—perhaps a great city.

At present their occupants are a sutler, whose store contains "knick-knacks" not classed among commissariat rations; an hotel-keeper whose bar-room, with white sanded floor and shelves sparkling with prismatic glass, tempts the idler to step in; a brace of gamblers whose rival tables of *faro* and *monté* extract from the pockets of the soldiers most part of their pay; a score of dark-eyed señoritas of questionable reputation; a like number of hunters, teamsters, *mustangers*, and nondescripts—such as constitute in all countries the hangers-on of a military cantonment, or the followers of a camp.

The houses in the occupancy of this motley corporation have been "sited" with some design. Perhaps they are the property of a single speculator. They stand around a "square," where, instead of lamp-posts or statues, may be seen the decaying trunk of a cypress, or the bushy form of a hackberry rising out of a *tapis* of trodden grass.

The Leona—at this point a mere rivulet—glides past in the rear both of fort and village. To the front extends a level plain, green as verdure can make it—in the distance darkened by a bordering of woods, in which post-oaks and pecâns, live oaks and elms, struggle for existence with spinous plants of cactus and anona; with scores of creepers, climbers, and parasites almost unknown to the botanist. To the south and east along the banks of the stream, you see scattered houses: the homesteads of plantations; some of them rude and of recent construction, with a few of more pretentious style, and evidently of older origin. One of these last particularly attracts the attention: a structure of superior size—with flat roof, surmounted by a crenelled parapet—whose white walls show conspicuously against the green background of forest with which it is half encircled. It is the hacienda of *Casa del Corvo.*

Turning your eye northward, you behold a curious isolated eminence—a gigantic cone of rocks—rising several hundred feet above the level of the plain; and beyond, in dim distance, a waving horizontal line indicating the outlines of the Guadalupe mountains—the outstanding spurs of that elevated and almost untrodden plateau, the *Llano Estacado.*

Look aloft! You behold a sky, half sapphire, half turquoise; by day, showing no other spot than the orb of its golden god; by night, studded with stars that appear clipped from clear steel, and a moon whose well-defined disc outshines the effulgence of silver.

Look below—at that hour when moon and stars have disappeared, and the land-wind arrives from Matagorda Bay, laden with the fragrance of flowers; when it strikes the starry flag, unfolding it to the eye of the morn—then look below, and behold the picture that should have been painted by the pencil of Vernet—too varied and vivid, too plentiful in shapes, costumes, and colouring, to be sketched by the pen.

In the tableau you distinguish soldiers in uniform—the light blue of the United States infantry, the darker cloth of the dragoons, and the almost invisible green of the mounted riflemen.

You will see but few in full uniform—only the officer of the day, the captain of the guard, and the guard itself.

Their comrades off duty lounge about the barracks, or within the stockade enclosure, in red flannel shirts, slouch hats, and boots innocent of blacking.

They mingle with men whose costumes make no pretence to a military character: tall hunters in tunics of dressed deerskin, with leggings to correspond—herdsmen and mustangers, habited *à la Mexicaine*—Mexicans themselves, in wide *calzoneros*, *serapés* on their shoulders, *botas* on their legs, huge spurs upon their heels, and glazed *sombreros* set jauntily on their crowns. They palaver with Indians on a friendly visit to the Fort, for trade or treaty; whose tents stand at some distance, and from whose shoulders hang blankets of red, and green, and blue—giving them a picturesque, even classical, appearance, in spite of the hideous paint with which they have bedaubed their skins, and the dirt that renders sticky their long black hair, lengthened by tresses taken from the tails of their horses.

Picture to the eye of your imagination this jumble of mixed nationalities—in their varied costumes of race, condition, and calling; jot in here and there a black-skinned scion of Ethiopia, the body servant of some officer, or the emissary of a planter from the adjacent settlements; imagine them standing in gossiping groups, or stalking over the level plain, amidst some half-dozen halted waggons; a couple of six-pounders upon their carriages, with caissons close by; a square tent or two, with its surmounting fly—occupied by some eccentric officer who prefers sleeping under canvas; a stack of bayoneted rifles belonging to the soldiers on guard,—imagine all these component parts, and you will have before your mind's eye a truthful picture of a military fort upon the frontier of Texas, and the extreme selvedge of civilisation.

---

About a week after the arrival of the Louisiana planter at his new home, three officers were seen standing upon the parade ground in front of Fort Inge, with their eyes turned towards the hacienda of Casa del Corvo.

They were all young men: the oldest not over thirty years of age. His shoulder-straps with the double bar proclaimed him a captain; the second, with a single cross bar, was a first lieutenant; while the youngest of the two, with an empty chevron, was either a second lieutenant or "brevet."

They were off duty; engaged in conversation—their theme, the "new people" in Casa del Corvo—by which was meant the Louisiana planter and his family.

"A sort of housewarming it's to be," said the infantry captain, alluding to an invitation that had reached the Fort, extending to all the commissioned officers of the garrison. "Dinner first, and dancing afterwards—a regular field day, where I suppose we shall see paraded the aristocracy and beauty of the settlement."

"Aristocracy?" laughingly rejoined the lieutenant of dragoons. "Not much of that here, I fancy; and of beauty still less."

"You mistake, Hancock. There are both upon the banks of the Leona. Some good States families have strayed out this way. We'll meet them at Poindexter's party, no doubt. On the question of aristocracy, the host himself, if you'll pardon a poor joke, is himself a host. He has enough of it to inoculate all the company that may be present; and as for beauty, I'll back his daughter against anything this side the Sabine. The commissary's niece will be no longer belle about here."

"Oh, indeed!" drawled the lieutenant of rifles, in a tone that told of his being chafed by this representation. "Miss Poindexter must be deuced good-looking, then."

"She's all that, I tell you, if she be anything like what she was when I last saw her, which was at a Bayou Lafourche ball. There were half a dozen young Creoles there, who came nigh crossing swords about her."

"A coquette, I suppose?" insinuated the rifleman.

"Nothing of the kind, Crossman. Quite the contrary, I assure you. She's a girl of spirit, though—likely enough to snub any fellow who might try to be too familiar. She's not without some of the father's pride. It's a family trait of the Poindexters."

"Just the girl I should cotton to," jocosely remarked the young dragoon. "And if she's as good-looking as you say, Captain Sloman, I shall certainly go in for her. Unlike Crossman here, I'm clear of all entanglements of the heart. Thank the Lord for it!"

"Well, Mr Hancock," rejoined the infantry officer, a gentleman of sober inclinings, "I'm not given to betting; but I'd lay a big wager you won't say that, after you have seen Louise Poindexter—that is, if you speak your mind."

"Pshaw, Sloman! don't you be alarmed about me. I've been too often under the fire of bright eyes to have any fear of them."

"None so bright as hers."

"Deuce take it! you make a fellow fall in love with this lady without having set eyes upon her. She must be something extraordinary—incomparable."

"She was both, when I last saw her."

"How long ago was that?"

"The Lafourche ball? Let me see—about eighteen months. Just after we got back from Mexico. She was then 'coming out' as society styles it:—

"A new star in the firmament, to light and glory born!"

"Eighteen months is a long time," sagely remarked Crossman—"a long time for an unmarried maiden—especially among Creoles, where they often get spliced at twelve, instead of 'sweet sixteen.' Her beauty may have lost some of its bloom?"

"I believe not a bit. I should have called to see; only I knew they were in the middle of their 'plenishing,' and mightn't desire to be visited. But the major has been to Casa del Corvo, and brought back such a report about Miss Poindexter's beauty as almost got him into a scrape with the lady commanding the post."

"Upon my soul, Captain Sloman!" asseverated the lieutenant of dragoons, "you've excited my curiosity to such a degree, I feel already half in love with Louise Poindexter!"

"Before you get altogether into it," rejoined the officer of infantry, in a serious tone, "let me recommend a little caution. There's a *bête noir* in the background."

"A brother, I suppose? That is the individual usually so regarded."

"There is a brother, but it's not he. A free noble young fellow he is—the only Poindexter I ever knew not eaten up with pride, he's quite the reverse."

"The aristocratic father, then? Surely he wouldn't object to a quartering with the Hancocks?"

"I'm not so sure of that; seeing that the Hancocks are Yankees, and he's a *chivalric Southerner*! But it's not old Poindexter I mean."

"Who, then, is the black beast, or what is it—if not a human?"

"It is human, after a fashion. A male cousin—a queer card he is—by name Cassius Calhoun."

"I think I've heard the name."

"So have I," said the lieutenant of rifles.

"So has almost everybody who had anything to do with the Mexican war—that is, who took part in Scott's campaign. He figured there extensively, and not very creditably either. He was captain in a volunteer regiment of Mississippians—for he hails from that State; but he was oftener met with at the *monté-table* than in the quarters of his regiment. He had one or two affairs, that gave him the reputation of a bully. But that notoriety was not of Mexican-war origin. He had earned it before going there; and was well known among the desperadoes of New Orleans as a *dangerous man*."

"What of all that?" asked the young dragoon, in a tone slightly savouring of defiance. "Who cares whether Mr Cassius Calhoun be a dangerous man, or a harmless one? Not I. He's only the girl's cousin, you say?"

"Something more, perhaps. I have reason to think he's her lover."

"Accepted, do you suppose?"

"That I can't tell. I only know, or suspect, that he's the favourite of the father. I have heard reasons why; given only in whispers, it is true, but too probable to be scouted. The old story—influence springing from mortgage money. Poindexter's not so rich as he has been—else we'd never have seen him out here."

"If the lady be as attractive as you say, I suppose we'll have Captain Cassius out here also, before long?"

"Before long! Is that all you know about it? He *is* here; came along with the family, and is now residing with them. Some say he's a partner in the planting speculation. I saw him this very morning—down in the hotel bar-room—'liquoring up,' and swaggering in his old way."

"A swarthy-complexioned man, of about thirty, with dark hair and moustaches; wearing a blue cloth frock, half military cut, and a Colt's revolver strapped over his thigh?"

"Ay, and a bowie knife, if you had looked for it, under the breast of his coat. That's the man."

"He's rather a formidable-looking fellow," remarked the young rifleman. "If a bully, his looks don't belie him."

"Damn his looks!" half angrily exclaimed the dragoon. "We don't hold commissions in Uncle Sam's army to be scared by looks, nor bullies either. If he comes any of his bullying over me, he'll find I'm as quick with a trigger as he."

At that moment the bugle brayed out the call for morning parade—a ceremony observed at the little frontier fort as regularly as if a whole *corps-d'armée* had been present—and the three officers separating, betook themselves to their quarters to prepare their several companies for the inspection of the major in command of the cantonment.

# 10. Casa Del Corvo

The estate, or "hacienda," known as Casa del Corvo, extended along the wooded bottom of the Leona River for more than a league, and twice that distance southwards across the contiguous prairie.

The house itself—usually, though not correctly, styled the *hacienda*—stood within long cannon range of Fort Inge; from which its white walls were partially visible; the remaining portion being shadowed by tall forest trees that skirted the banks of the stream.

Its site was peculiar, and no doubt chosen with a view to defence: for its foundations had been laid at a time when Indian assailants might be expected; as indeed they might be, and often are, at the present hour.

There was a curve of the river closing upon itself, like the shoe of a racehorse, or the arc of a circle, three parts complete; the chord of which, or a parallelogram traced upon it, might be taken as the groundplan of the dwelling. Hence the name—Casa del Corvo—"the House of the Curve" (curved river).

The façade, or entrance side, fronted towards the prairie—the latter forming a noble lawn that extended to the edge of the horizon—in comparison with which an imperial park would have shrunk into the dimensions of a paddock.

The architecture of Casa del Corvo, like that of other large country mansions in Mexico, was of a style that might be termed Morisco-Mexican: being a single story in height, with a flat roof—*azotea*—spouted and parapeted all round; having a courtyard inside the walls, termed *patio*, open to the sky, with a flagged floor, a fountain, and a stone stairway leading up to the roof; a grand entrance gateway—the *saguan*—with a massive wooden door, thickly studded with bolt-heads; and two or three windows on each side, defended by a *grille* of strong iron bars, called *reja*. These are the chief characteristics of a

Mexican hacienda; and Casa del Corvo differed but little from the type almost universal throughout the vast territories of Spanish America.

Such was the homestead that adorned the newly acquired estate of the Louisiana planter—that had become his property by purchase.

As yet no change had taken place in the exterior of the dwelling; nor much in its interior, if we except the *personnel* of its occupants. A physiognomy, half Anglo-Saxon, half Franco-American, presented itself in courtyard and corridor, where formerly were seen only faces of pure Spanish type; and instead of the rich sonorous language of Andalusia, was now heard the harsher guttural of a semi-Teutonic tongue—occasionally diversified by the sweeter accentuation of Creolian French.

Outside the walls of the mansion—in the village-like cluster of yucca-thatched huts which formerly gave housing to the *peons* and other dependants of the hacienda—the transformation was more striking. Where the tall thin *vaquero*, in broad-brimmed hat of black glaze, and chequered *serapé*, strode proudly over the sward—his spurs tinkling at every step—was now met the authoritative "overseer," in blue jersey, or blanket coat—his whip cracking at every corner; where the red children of Azteca and Anahuac, scantily clad in tanned sheepskin, could be seen, with sad solemn aspect, lounging listlessly by their *jacalés*, or trotting silently along, were now heard the black sons and daughters of Ethiopia, from morn till night chattering their gay "gumbo," or with song and dance seemingly contradicting the idea: that slavery is a heritage of unhappiness!

Was it a change for the better upon the estate of Casa del Corvo?

There was a time when the people of England would have answered—no; with a unanimity and emphasis calculated to drown all disbelief in their sincerity.

Alas, for human weakness and hypocrisy! Our long cherished sympathy with the slave proves to have been only a tissue of sheer dissembling. Led by an oligarchy—not the true aristocracy of our country: for these are too noble to have yielded to such, deep designings—but an oligarchy composed of conspiring plebs, who have smuggled themselves into the first places of power in all the four estates—guided by these prurient conspirators against the people's rights—England has proved untrue to her creed so loudly proclaimed—truculent to the trust reposed in her by the universal acclaim, of the nations.

On a theme altogether different dwelt the thoughts of Louise Poindexter, as she flung herself into a chair in front of her dressing-glass, and directed her maid Florinda to prepare her for the reception of guests—expected soon to arrive at the hacienda.

It was the day fixed for the "house-warming," and about an hour before the time appointed for dinner to be on the table. This might have explained a certain restlessness observable in the air of the young Creole—especially observed by Florinda; but it did not. The maid had her own thoughts about the cause of her mistress's disquietude—as was proved by the conversation that ensued between them.

Scarce could it be called a conversation. It was more as if the young lady were thinking aloud, with her attendant acting as an echo. During all her life, the Creole had been accustomed to look upon her sable handmaid as a thing from whom it was not worth while conceal-ing her thoughts, any more than she would from the chairs, the table, the sofa, or any other article of furniture in the apartment. There was but the difference of Florinda being a little more animated and com-panionable, and the advantage of her being able to give a vocal response to the observations addressed to her.

For the first ten minutes after entering the chamber, Florinda had sustained the brunt of the dialogue on indifferent topics—her mistress only interfering with an occasional ejaculation.

"Oh, Miss Looey!" pursued the negress, as her fingers fondly played among the lustrous tresses of her young mistress's hair, "how bewful you hair am! Like de long 'Panish moss dat hang from de cy-prus-tree; only dat it am ob a diff'rent colour, an shine like the sugar-house 'lasses."

As already stated, Louise Poindexter was a Creole. After that, it is scarce necessary to say that her hair was of a dark colour; and—as the sable maid in rude speech had expressed it—luxuriant as Spanish moss. It was not black; but of a rich glowing brown—such as may be observed in the tinting of a tortoise-shell, or the coat of a winter-trapped sable.

"Ah!" continued Florinda, spreading out an immense "hank" of the hair, that glistened like a chestnut against her dark palm, "if I had dat lubbly hair on ma head, in'tead ob dis cuss'd cully wool, I fotch em all to ma feet—ebbry one oh dem."

"What do you mean, girl?" inquired the young lady, as if just aroused from some dreamy reverie. "What's that you've been saying? Fetch them to your feet? Fetch whom?"

"Na, now; you know what dis chile mean?"

68

"'Pon honour, I do not."

"Make em lub me. Dat's what I should hab say."

"But whom?"

"All de white gen'l'm. De young planter, de officer ob de Fort—all ob dem. Wif you hair, Miss Looey, I could dem all make conquess."

"Ha—ha—ha!" laughed the young lady, amused at the idea of Florinda figuring under that magnificent chevelure. "You think, with my hair upon your head, you would be invincible among the men?"

"No, missa—not you hair alone—but wif you sweet face—you skin, white as de alumbaster—you tall figga—you grand look. Oh, Miss Looey, you am so 'plendidly bewful! I hear de white gen'l'm say so. I no need hear em say it. I see dat for masef."

"You're learning to flatter, Florinda."

"No, 'deed, missa—ne'er a word ob flattery—ne'er a word, I swa it. By de 'postles, I swa it."

To one who looked upon her mistress, the earnest asseveration of the maid was not necessary to prove the sincerity of her speech, however hyperbolical it might appear. To say that Louise Poindexter was beautiful, would only be to repeat the universal verdict of the society that surrounded her. A single glance was sufficient to satisfy any one upon this point—strangers as well as acquaintances. It was a kind of beauty that needed no *discovering*—and yet it is difficult to describe it. The pen cannot portray swell a face. Even the pencil could convey but a faint idea of it: for no painter, however skilled, could represent upon cold canvas the glowing ethereal light that emanated from her eyes, and appeared to radiate over her countenance. Her features were purely classic: resembling those types of female beauty chosen by Phidias or Praxiteles. And yet in all the Grecian Pantheon there is no face to which it could have been likened: for it was not the countenance of a goddess; but, something more attractive to the eye of man, the face of a woman.

A suspicion of sensuality, apparent in the voluptuous curving of the lower lip—still more pronounced in the prominent rounding beneath the cheeks—while depriving the countenance of its pure spiritualism, did not perhaps detract from its beauty. There are men, who, in this departure from the divine type, would have perceived a superior charm: since in Louise Poindexter they would have seen not a divinity to be worshipped, but a woman to be loved.

Her only reply vouchsafed to Florinda's earnest asseveration was a laugh—careless, though not incredulous. The young Creole did not

69

need to be reminded of her beauty. She was not unconscious of it: as could be told by her taking more than one long look into the mirror before which her toilet was being made. The flattery of the negress scarce called up an emotion; certainly not more than she might have felt at the fawning of a pet spaniel; and she soon after surrendered herself to the reverie from which the speech had aroused her.

Florinda was not silenced by observing her mistress's air of abstraction. The girl had evidently something on her mind—some mystery, of which she desired the *éclaircissement*—and was determined to have it.

"Ah!" she continued, as if talking to herself; "if Florinda had half de charm ob young missa, she for nobody care—she for nobody heave do deep sigh!"

"Sigh!" repeated her mistress, suddenly startled by the speech. "What do you mean by that?"

"Pa' dieu, Miss Looey, Florinda no so blind you tink; nor so deaf neider. She you see long time sit in de same place; you nebber 'peak no word—you only heave de sigh—de long deep sigh. You nebba do dat in de ole plantashun in Loozyanny."

"Florinda! I fear you are taking leave of your senses, or have left them behind you in Louisiana? Perhaps there's something in the climate here that affects you. Is that so, girl?"

"Pa' dieu, Miss Looey, dat question ob youself ask. You no be angry case I 'peak so plain. Florinda you slave—she you lub like brack sisser. She no happy hear you sigh. Dat why she hab take de freedom. You no be angry wif me?"

"Certainly not. Why should I be angry with you, child? I'm not. I didn't say I was; only you are quite mistaken in your ideas. What you've seen, or heard, could be only a fancy of your own. As for sighing, heigho! I have something else to think of just now. I have to entertain about a hundred guests—nearly all strangers, too; among them the young planters and officers whom you would entangle if you had my hair. Ha! ha! ha! *I* don't desire to enmesh them—not one of them! So twist it up as you like—without the semblance of a snare in it."

"Oh! Miss Looey, you so 'peak?" inquired the negress with an air of evident interest. "You say none ob dem gen'l'm you care for? Dere am two, tree, berry, berry, berry han'som'. One planter dar be, and two ob de officer—all young gen'l'm. You know de tree I mean. All ob dem hab been 'tentive to you. You sure, missa, tain't one ob dem dat you make sigh?"

"Sigh again! Ha! ha! ha! But come, Florinda, we're losing time. Recollect I've got to be in the drawing-room to receive a hundred guests. I must have at least half an hour to compose myself into an attitude befitting such an extensive reception."

"No fear, Miss Looey—no fear. I you toilette make in time— plenty ob time. No much trouble you dress. Pa' dieu, in any dress you look 'plendid. You be de belle if you dress like one ob de fiel' hand ob de plantashun."

"What a flatterer you are grown, Florinda! I shall begin to suspect that you are after some favour. Do you wish me to intercede, and make up your quarrel with Pluto?"

"No, missa. I be friend nebber more wid Pluto. He show hisseff such great coward when come dat storm on de brack prairee. Ah, Miss Looey! what we boaf do if dat young white gen'l'm on de red hoss no come ridin' dat way?"

"If he had not, cher Florinde, it is highly probable neither of us should now have been here."

"Oh, missa! wasn't he real fancy man, dat 'ere? You see him bewful face. You see him thick hair, jess de colour ob you own—only curled leetle bit like mine. Talk ob de young planter, or dem officer at de Fort! De brack folk say he no good for nuffin, like dem—he only poor white trash. Who care fo' dat? He am de sort ob man could dis chile make sigh. Ah! de berry, berry sort!"

Up to this point the young Creole had preserved a certain tran- quillity of countenance. She tried to continue it; but the effort failed her. Whether by accident or design, Florinda had touched the most sensitive chord in the spirit of her mistress.

She would have been loth to confess it, even to her slave; and it was a relief to her, when loud voices heard in the courtyard gave a colourable excuse for terminating her toilette, along with the delicate dialogue upon which she might have been constrained to enter.

# 11. An Unexpected Arrival

"Say, ye durnationed nigger! whar's yur master?"

"Mass Poindex'er, sar? De ole massr, or de young 'un?"

"Young 'un be durned! I mean Mister Peintdexter. Who else shed I? Whar air he?"

"Ho—ho! sar! dey am boaf at home—dat is, dey am boaf away from de house—de ole massr an de young Massr Henry. Dey am down de ribber, wha de folk am makin' de new fence. Ho! ho! you find 'em dar."

"Down the river! How fur d'ye reck'n?"

"Ho! ho! sar. Dis nigger reck'n it be 'bout tree or four mile—dat at de berry leas'."

"Three or four mile? Ye must be a durnationed fool, nigger. Mister Peintdexter's plantation don't go thet fur; an I reck'n he ain't the man to be makin' a fence on some'dy else's clarin'. Lookee hyur! What time air he expected hum? Ye've got a straighter idee o' thet, I hope?"

"Dey boaf 'pected home berry soon, de young massr and de ole massr, and Mass Ca'houn too. Ho! ho! dar's agwine to be big dooin's 'bout dis yar shanty—yer see dat fo' yeseff by de smell ob de kitchen. Ho! ho! All sorts o' gran' feassin'—do roas' an de bile, an de barbecue; de pot-pies, an de chicken fixins. Ho! ho! ain't thar agwine to go it hyar jess like de ole times on de coass ob de Massippy! Hoora fo' ole Mass Poindex'er! He de right sort. Ho! ho! 'tranger! why you no holla too: you no friend ob de massr?"

"Durn you, nigger, don't ye remember me? Now I look into yur ugly mug, I recollex you."

"Gorramighty! 'tain't Mass 'Tump—'t use to fotch de ven'son an de turkey gobbla to de ole plantashun? By de jumbo, it am, tho'. Law, Mass 'Tump, dis nigga 'members you like it wa de day afore yesserday. Ise heern you called de odder day; but I war away from 'bout de place. I'm de coachman now—dribes de carriage dat carries de lady ob de 'tablishment—de bewful Missy Loo. Lor, massr, she berry fine gal. Dey do say she beat Florinday into fits. Nebba mind, Mass 'Tump, you better wait till ole massr come home. He am *a bound to be hya*, in de shortess poss'ble time."

"Wal, if thet's so, I'll wait upon him," rejoined the hunter, leisurely lifting his leg over the saddle—in which up to this time he had retained his seat. "Now, ole fellur," he added, passing the bridle into the hands of the negro, "you gi'e the maar half a dozen yeers o' corn out o' the crib. I've rid the critter better 'n a score o' miles like a streak o' lightnin'—all to do yur master a sarvice."

"Oh, Mr Zebulon Stump, is it you?" exclaimed a silvery voice, followed by the appearance of Louise Poindexter upon the verandah.

"I thought it was," continued the young lady, coming up to the railings, "though I didn't expect to see you so soon. You said you were going upon a long journey. Well—I am pleased that you are here; and so will papa and Henry be. Pluto! go instantly to Chloe, the cook, and see what she can give you for Mr Stump's dinner. You have not dined, I know. You are dusty—you've been travelling? Here, Morinda! Haste you to the sideboard, and pour out some drink. Mr Stump will be thirsty, I'm sure, this hot day. What would you prefer—port, sherry, claret? Ah, now, if I recollect, you used to be partial to Monongahela whisky. I think there is some. Morinda, see if there be! Step into the verandah, dear Mr Stump, and take a seat. You were inquiring for papa? I expect him home every minute. I shall try to entertain you till he come."

Had the young lady paused sooner in her speech, she would not have received an immediate reply. Even as it was, some seconds elapsed before Zeb made rejoinder. He stood gazing upon her, as if struck speechless by the sheer intensity of his admiration.

"Lord o' marcy, Miss Lewaze!" he at length gasped forth, "I thort when I used to see you on the Mississippi, ye war the puttiest critter on the airth; but now, I think ye the puttiest thing eyther on airth or in hewing. Geehosofat!"

The old hunter's praise was scarce exaggerated. Fresh from the toilette, the gloss of her luxuriant hair untarnished by the notion of the atmosphere; her cheeks glowing with a carmine tint, produced by the application of cold water; her fine figure, gracefully draped in a robe of India muslin—white and semi-translucent—certainly did Louise Poindexter appear as pretty as anything upon earth—if not in heaven.

"Geehosofat!" again exclaimed the hunter, following up his complimentary speech, "I hev in my time seed what I thort war some putty critters o' the sheemale kind—my ole 'ooman herself warn't so bad-lookin' when I fast kim acrost her in Kaintuck—thet she warn't. But I will say this, Miss Lewaze: ef the puttiest bits o' all o' them war clipped out an then jeined thegither agin, they wudn't make up the thousanth part o' a angel sech as you."

"Oh—oh—oh! Mr Stump—Mr Stump! I'm astonished to hear *you* talk in this manner. Texas has quite turned you into a courtier. If you go on so, I fear you will lose your character for plain speaking! After that I am sure you will stand in need of a very big drink. Haste, Morinda! I think you said you would prefer whisky?"

"Ef I didn't say it, I thunk it; an that air about the same. Yur right, miss, I prefar the corn afore any o' them thur furrin lickers; an I sticks to it whuriver I kin git it. Texas hain't made no alterashun in me in the matter o' lickerin'."

"Mass 'Tump, you it hab mix wif water?" inquired Florinda, coming forward with a tumbler about one-half full of "Monongahela."

"No, gurl. Durn yur water! I hev hed enuf o' thet since I started this mornin'. I hain't hed a taste o' licker the hul day—ne'er as much as the smell o' it."

"Dear Mr Stump! surely you can't drink it that way? Why, it will burn your throat! Have a little sugar, or honey, along with it?"

"Speil it, miss. It air sweet enuf 'ithout that sort o' docterin'; 'specially arter you hev looked inter the glass. Yu'll see ef I can't drink it. Hyur goes to try!"

The old hunter raised the tumbler to his chin; and after giving three gulps, and the fraction of a fourth, returned it empty into the hands of Florinda. A loud smacking of the lips almost drowned the simultaneous exclamations of astonishment uttered by the young lady and her maid.

"Burn my throat, ye say? Ne'er a bit. It hez jest eiled thet ere jugewlar, an put it in order for a bit o' a palaver I wants to hev wi' yur father—'bout thet ere spotty mow-stang."

"Oh, true! I had forgotten. No, I hadn't either; but I did not suppose you had time to have news of it. Have you heard anything of the pretty creature?"

"Putty critter ye may well pernounce it. It ur all o' thet. Besides, it ur a maar."

"A ma-a-r! What is that, Mr Stump? I don't understand."

"A maar I sayed. Shurly ye know what a maar is?"

"Ma-a-r—ma-a-r! Why, no, not exactly. Is it a Mexican word? *Mar* in Spanish signifies the sea."

"In coorse it air a Mexikin maar—all mowstangs air. They air all on 'em o' a breed as wur oncest brought over from some European country by the fust o' them as settled in these hyur parts—leesewise I hev heern so."

"Still, Mr Stump, I do not comprehend you. What makes this mustang a ma-a-r?"

"What makes her a *maar*? 'Case she ain't a *hoss*; thet's what make it, Miss Peintdexter."

"Oh—now—I—I think I comprehend. But did you say you have heard of the animal—I mean since you left us?"

"Heern o' her, seed her, an feeled her."

"Indeed!"

"She air grupped."

"Ah, caught! what capital news! I shall be so delighted to see the beautiful thing; and ride it too. I haven't had a horse worth a piece of orange-peel since I've been in Texas. Papa has promised to purchase this one for me at any price. But who is the lucky individual who accomplished the capture?"

"Ye mean who grupped the maar?"

"Yes—yes—who?"

"Why, in coorse it wur a mowstanger."

"A mustanger?"

"Ye-es—an such a one as thur ain't another on all these purayras—eyther to ride a hoss, or throw a laryitt over one. Yo may talk about yur Mexikins! I never seed neery Mexikin ked manage hoss-doin's like that young fellur; an thur ain't a drop o' thur pisen blood in his veins. He ur es white es I am myself."

"His name?"

"Wal, es to the name o' his family, that I niver heern. His Christyun name air Maurice. He's knowed up thur 'bout the Fort as Maurice the mowstanger."

The old hunter was not sufficiently observant to take note of the tone of eager interest in which the question had been asked, nor the sudden deepening of colour upon the cheeks of the questioner as she heard the answer.

Neither had escaped the observation of Florinda.

"La, Miss Looey!" exclaimed the latter, "shoo dat de name ob de

"Geehosofat, yes!" resumed the hunter, relieving the young lady from the necessity of making reply. "Now I think o't, he told me o' thet suckumstance this very mornin', afore we started. He air the same. Thet's the very fellur es hev trapped spotty; an he air toatin' the critter along at this eyedentical minnit, in kump'ny wi' about a dozen others o' the same cavyurd. He oughter be hyur afore sundown. I pushed my ole maar ahead, so 's to tell yur father the spotty war comin', and let him git the fust chance o' buyin'. I know'd as how thet ere bit o' hos-doin's don't get druv fur into the Settlements efore someb'dy snaps her up. I thort o' *you*, Miss Lewaze, and how ye tuk on so when I tolt ye 'bout the critter. Wal, make yur mind eezy; ye shell hev the fast chance. Ole Zeb Stump 'll be yur bail for thet."

"Oh, Mr Stump, it is so kind of you! I am very, very grateful. You will now excuse me for a moment. Father will soon be back. We have a dinner-party to-day; and I have to prepare for receiving a great many people. Florinda, see that Mr Stump's luncheon is set out for him. Go, girl—go at once about it!"

"And, Mr Stump," continued the young lady, drawing nearer to the hunter, and speaking in a more subdued tone of voice, "if the young—young gentleman should arrive while the other people are here—perhaps he don't know them—will you see that he is not neglected? There is wine yonder, in the verandah, and other things. You know what I mean, dear Mr Stump?"

"Durned if I do, Miss Lewaze; that air, not adzackly. I kin unnerstan' all thet ere 'bout the licker' an other fixins. But who air the young gen'leman yur speakin' o'? Thet's the thing as bamboozles me."

"Surely you know who I mean! The young gentleman—the young man—who, you say, is bringing in the horses."

"Oh! ah! Maurice the mowstanger! That's it, is it? Wal, I reck'n yur not a hundred mile astray in calling *him* a gen'leman; tho' it ain't offen es a mowstanger gits thet entitlement, or desarves it eyther. *He air one*, every inch o' him—a gen'leman by barth, breed, an raisin'—tho' he air a hoss-hunter, an Irish at thet."

The eyes of Louise Poindexter sparkled with delight as she listened to opinions so perfectly in unison with her own.

"I must tell ye, howsomdiver," continued the hunter, as some doubt had come across his mind, "it won't do to show that 'ere young fellur any sort o' second-hand hospertality. As they used to say on the Massissippi, he air 'as proud as a Peintdexter.' Excuse me, Miss Lewaze, for lettin' the word slip. I did think o't thet I war talkin' to a Peintdexter—not the proudest, but the puttiest o' the name."

"Oh, Mr Stump! you can say what you please to me. You know that I could not be offended with you, you dear old giant!"

"He'd be meaner than a dwurf es ked eyther say or do anythin' to offend you, miss."

"Thanks! thanks! I know your honest heart—I know your devotion. Perhaps some time—some time, Mr Stump,"—she spoke hesitatingly, but apparently without any definite meaning—"I might stand in need of your friendship."

"Ye won't need it long afore ye git it, then; thet ole Zeb Stump kin promise ye, Miss Peintdexter. He'd be stinkiner than a skunk, an a bigger coward than a coyoat, es wouldn't stan' by sech as you, while there wur a bottle-full o' breath left in the inside o' his body."

"A thousand thanks—again and again! But what were you going to say? You spoke of second-hand hospitality?"

"I dud."

"You meant—?"

"I meaned thet it 'ud be no use o' my inviting Maurice the mow-stanger eyther to eat or drink unner this hyur roof. Unless yur father do that, the young fellur 'll go 'ithout tastin'. You unnerstan, Miss Le-waze, he ain't one o' thet sort o' poor whites as kin be sent roun' to the kitchen."

The young Creole stood for a second or two, without making re-joinder. She appeared to be occupied with some abstruse calculation, that engrossed the whole of her thoughts.

"Never mind about it," she at length said, in a tone that told the calculation completed. "Never mind, Mr Stump. You need not invite him. Only let *me* know when he arrives—unless we be at dinner, and then, of course, he would not expect any one to appear. But if he *should* come at that time, *you* detain him—won't you?"

"Boun' to do it, ef you bid me."

"You will, then; and let me know he is here. *I* shall ask him to eat."

"Ef ye do, miss, I reck'n ye'll speil his appetite. The sight o' you, to say nothin' o' listenin' to your melodyus voice, ud cure a starvin' wolf o' bein' hungry. When I kim in hyur I war peckish enuf to swaller a raw buzzart. Neow I don't care a durn about eatin'. I ked go 'ithout chawin' meat for month."

of the patio; where her maid was seer emerging from the "cocina," carrying a light tray—followed by Pluto with one of broader dimensions, more heavily weighted.

"You great giant!" was the reply, given in a tone of sham reproach; "I won't believe you have lost your appetite, until you have eaten Jack. Yonder come Pluto and Morinda. They bring something that will prove more cheerful company than I; so I shall leave you to enjoy it. Good bye, Zeb—good bye, or, as the natives say here, *hasta luego!*"

Gaily were these words spoken—lightly did Louise Poindexter trip back across the covered corridor. Only after entering her chamber, and finding herself *chez soi-même*, did she give way to a reflection of a more serious character, that found expression in words low murmured, but full of mystic meaning:—

"It is my destiny: I feel—I know that it is! I dare not meet, and yet I cannot shun it—I may not—I would not—I *will not!*"

78

# 12. Taming a Wild Mare

The pleasantest *apartment* in a Mexican house is that which has the roof for its floor, and the sky for its ceiling—the *azotea*. In fine weather—ever fine in that sunny clime—it is preferred to the drawing-room; especially after dinner, when the sun begins to cast rose-coloured rays upon the snow-clad summits of Orizava, Popocatepec, Toluca, and the "Twin Sister;" when the rich wines of Xeres and Madeira have warmed the imaginations of Andalusia's sons and daughters—descendants of the Conquistadores—who mount up to their house-tops to look upon a land of world-wide renown, rendered famous by the heroic achievements of their ancestors.

Then does the Mexican "cavallero," clad in embroidered habiliments, exhibit his splendid exterior to the eyes of some señorita—at the same time puffing the smoke of his paper cigarito against her cheeks. Then does the dark-eyed donçella favourably listen to soft whisperings; or perhaps only pretends to listen, while, with heart distraught, and eye wandering away, she sends stealthy glances over the plain towards some distant hacienda—the home of him she truly loves.

So enjoyable a fashion, as that of spending the twilight hours upon the housetop, could not fail to be followed by any one who chanced to be the occupant of a Mexican dwelling; and the family of the Louisiana planter had adopted it, as a matter of course.

On that same evening, after the dining-hall had been deserted, the roof, instead of the drawing-room, was chosen as the place of re-assemblage; and as the sun descended towards the horizon, his slanting rays fell upon a throng as gay, as cheerful, and perhaps as resplendent, as ever trod the azotea of Casa del Corvo. Moving about over its tessellated tiles, standing in scattered groups, or lined along the parapet owner used to distribute hospitality to the *hidalgos* of the land—the *bluest* blood in Coahuila and Texas.

The company now collected to welcome the advent of Woodley Poindexter on his Texan estate, could also boast of this last distinction. They were the *élite* of the Settlements—not only of the Leona, but of others more distant. There were guests from Gonzales, from Castroville, and even from San Antonio—old friends of the planter, who, like him, had sought a home in South-Western Texas, and who had ridden—some of them over a hundred miles—to be present at this, his first grand "reception."

The planter had spared neither pains nor expense to give it *éclat*. What with the sprinkling of uniforms and epaulettes, supplied by the Fort—what with the brass band borrowed from the same convenient repository—what with the choice wines found in the cellars of Casa del Corvo, and which had formed part of the purchase—there could be little lacking to make Poindexter's party the most brilliant ever given upon the banks of the Leona.

And to insure this effect, his lovely daughter Louise, late belle of Louisiana—the fame of whose beauty had been before her, even in Texas—acted as mistress of the ceremonies—moving about among the admiring guests with the smile of a queen, and the grace of a goddess.

On that occasion was she the cynosure of a hundred pairs of eyes, the happiness of a score of hearts, and perhaps the torture of as many more: for not all were blessed who beheld her beauty.

Was she herself happy?

The interrogatory may appear singular—almost absurd. Surrounded by friends—admirers—one, at least, who adored her—a dozen whose incipient love could but end in adoration—young planters, lawyers, embryo statesmen, and some with reputation already achieved—sons of Mars in armour, or with armour late laid aside—how could she be otherwise than proudly, supremely happy?

A stranger might have asked the question; one superficially acquainted with Creole character—more especially the character of the lady in question.

But mingling in that splendid throng was a man who was no stranger to either; and who, perhaps, more than any one present, watched her every movement; and endeavoured more than any other to interpret its meaning. Cassius Calhoun was the individual thus occupied.

She went not hither, nor thither, without his following her—not close, like a shadow; but by stealth, flitting from place to place; upstairs, and downstairs; standing in corners, with an air of apparent abstraction; but all the while with eyes turned askant upon his cousin's face, like a plain-clothes policeman employed on detective duty.

Strangely enough he did not seem to pay much regard to her speeches, made in reply to the compliments showered upon her by several would-be winners of a smile—not even when these were conspicuous and respectable, as in the case of young Hancock of the dragoons. To all such he listened without visible emotion, as one listens to a conversation in no way affecting the affairs either of self or friends.

It was only after ascending to the azotea, on observing his cousin near the parapet, with her eye turned interrogatively towards the plain, that his detective zeal became conspicuous—so much so as to attract the notice of others. More than once was it noticed by those standing near: for more than once was repeated the act which gave cause to it.

At intervals, not very wide apart, the young mistress of Casa del Corvo might have been seen to approach the parapet, and look across the plain, with a glance that seemed to interrogate the horizon of the sky.

Why she did so no one could tell. No one presumed to conjecture, except Cassius Calhoun. He had thoughts upon the subject—thoughts that were torturing him.

When a group of moving forms appeared upon the prairie, emerging from the garish light of the setting sun—when the spectators upon the azotea pronounced it a drove of horses in charge of some mounted men—the ex-officer of volunteers had a suspicion as to who was conducting that *cavallada*.

Another appeared to feel an equal interest in its advent, though perhaps from a different motive. Long before the horse-drove had attracted the observation of Poindexter's guests, his daughter had noted its approach—from the time that a cloud of dust soared up against the horizon, so slight and filmy as to have escaped detection by any eye not bent expressly on discovering it.

From that moment the young Creole, under cover of a conversation carried on amid a circle of fair companions, had been slyly scanning the dust-cloud as it drew nearer; forming conjectures as to what was causing it, upon knowledge already, and as she supposed, exclusively her own.

"Wild horses!" announced the major commandant of Fort Inge,

I see now—it's Maurice the mustanger, who occasionally helps our men to a remount. He appears to be coming this way—direct to your place, Mr Poindexter."

"If it be the young fellow you have named, that's not unlikely," replied the owner of Casa del Corvo. "I bargained with him to catch me a score or two; and maybe this is the first instalment he's bringing me."

"Yes, I think it is," he added, after a look through the telescope.

"I am sure of it," said the planter's son. "I can tell the horseman yonder to be Maurice Gerald."

The planter's daughter could have done the same; though she made no display of her knowledge. She did not appear to be much interested in the matter—indeed, rather indifferent. She had become aware of being watched by that evil eye, constantly burning upon her.

The *cavallada* came up, Maurice sitting handsomely on his horse, with the spotted mare at the end of his lazo.

"What a beautiful creature!" exclaimed several voices, as the captured mustang was led up in front of the house, quivering with excitement at a scene so new to it.

"It's worth a journey to the ground to look at such an animal!" suggested the major's wife, a lady of enthusiastic inclinings. "I propose we all go down! What say you, Miss Poindexter?"

"Oh, certainly," answered the mistress of the mansion, amidst a chorus of other voices crying out—

"Let us go down! Let us go down!"

Led by the majoress, the ladies filed down the stone stairway—the gentlemen after; and in a score of seconds the horse-hunter, still seated in his saddle, became, with his captive, the centre of the distinguished circle.

Henry Poindexter had hurried down before the rest, and already, in the frankest manner, bidden the stranger welcome.

Between the latter and Louise only a slight salutation could be exchanged. Familiarity with a horse-dealer—even supposing him to have had the honour of an introduction—would scarce have been tolerated by the "society."

Of the ladies, the major's wife alone addressed him in a familiar way; but that was in a tone that told of superior position, coupled with condescension. He was more gratified by a glance—quick and silent—when his eye changed intelligence with that of the young Creole.

Hers was not the only one that rested approvingly upon him. In truth, the mustanger looked splendid, despite his travel-stained habiliments. His journey of over twenty miles had done little to fatigue him. The prairie breeze had freshened the colour upon his cheeks; and his full round throat, naked to the breast-bone, and slightly bronzed with the sun, contributed to the manliness of his mien. Even the dust clinging to his curled hair could not altogether conceal its natural gloss, nor the luxuriance of its growth; while a figure tersely knit told of strength and endurance beyond the ordinary endowment of man. There were stolen glances, endeavouring to catch his, sent by more than one of the fair circle. The pretty niece of the commissary smiled admiringly upon him. Some said the commissary's wife; but this could be only a slander, to be traced, perhaps, to the doctor's better half—the Lady Teazle of the cantonment.

"Surely," said Poindexter, after making an examination of the captured mustang, "this must be the animal of which old Zeb Stump has been telling me?"

"It ur thet eyedenticul same," answered the individual so described, making his way towards Maurice with the design of assisting him. "Ye-es, Mister Peintdexter; the eyedenticul critter—a maar, es ye kin all see for yurselves—"

"Yes, yes," hurriedly interposed the planter, not desiring any further elucidation.

"The young fellur hed grupped her afore I got thur; so I wur jess in the nick o' time 'bout it. She mout a been tuck elswhar, an then Miss Lewaze thur mout a missed hevin' her."

"It is true indeed, Mr Stump! It was very thoughtful of you. I know not how I shall ever be able to reciprocate your kindness?"

"Reciperkate! Wal, I spose thet air means to do suthin in return. Ye kin do thet, miss, 'ithout much difeequilty. I han't dud nothin' for you, ceptin' make a bit o' a journey acrost the purayra. To see yur bewtyful self mounted on thet maar, wi' yur ploomed het upon yur head, an yur long-tailed pettykote streakin' it ahint you, 'ud pay old Zeb Stump to go clur to the Rockies, and back agin."

"Oh, Mr Stump! you are an incorrigible flatterer! Look around you! you will see many here more deserving of your compliments than I."

"Wal, wal!" rejoined Zeb, casting a look of careless scrutiny towards the ladies, "I ain't a goin' to deny thet thur air gobs o' putty critters hyur—dog-goned putty critters; but es they used to say in ole Loozyanney, thur air but one Lewaze Peintdexter."

"I shall owe you two hundred dollars for this," said the planter, addressing himself to Maurice, and pointing to the spotted mare. "I think that was the sum stipulated for by Mr Stump."

"I was not a party to the stipulation," replied the mustanger, with a significant but well-intentioned smile. "I cannot take your money. *She* is not for sale."

"Oh, indeed!" said the planter, drawing back with an air of proud disappointment; while his brother planters, as well as the officers of the Fort, looked astonished at the refusal of such a munificent price. Two hundred dollars for an untamed mustang, when the usual rate of price was from ten to twenty! The mustanger must be mad?

He gave them no time to descant upon his sanity.

"Mr Poindexter," he continued, speaking in the same good-humoured strain, "you have given me such a generous price for my other captives—and before they were taken too—that I can afford to make a present—what we over in Ireland call a 'luckpenny.' It is our custom there also, when a horse-trade takes place at the house, to give the *douceur*, not to the purchaser himself, but to one of the fair members of his family. May I have your permission to introduce this Hibernian fashion into the settlements of Texas?"

"Certainly, by all means!" responded several voices, two or three of them unmistakably with an Irish accentuation.

"Oh, certainly, Mr Gerald!" replied the planter, his conservatism giving way to the popular will—"as you please about that."

"Thanks, gentlemen—thanks!" said the mustanger, with a patronising look towards men who believed themselves to be his masters. "This mustang is my luckpenny; and if Miss Poindexter will condescend to accept of it, I shall feel more than repaid for the three days' chase which the creature has cost me. Had she been the most cruel of coquettes, she could scarce have been more difficult to subdue."

"I accept your gift, sir; and with gratitude," responded the young Creole—for the first time prominently proclaiming herself, and stepping freely forth as she spoke. "But I have a fancy," she continued, pointing to the mustang—at the same time that her eye rested inquiringly on the countenance of the mustanger—"a fancy that your captive is not yet *tamed*? She but trembles in fear of the unknown future. She may yet kick against the traces, if she find the harness not to her liking; and then what am I to do—poor I?"

"True, Maurice!" said the major, widely mistaken as to the meaning of the mysterious speech, and addressing the only man on the ground who could possibly have comprehended it; "Miss Poindexter

84

speaks very sensibly. That mustang has not been tamed yet—any one may see it. Come, my good fellow! give her the lesson.

"Ladies and gentlemen!" continued the major, turning towards the company, "this is something worth your seeing—those of you who have not witnessed the spectacle before. Come, Maurice; mount, and show us a specimen of prairie horsemanship. She looks as though she would put your skill to the test."

"You are right, major: she does!" replied the mustanger, with a quick glance, directed not towards the captive quadruped, but to the young Creole; who, with all her assumed courage, retired tremblingly behind the circle of spectators.

"No matter, my man," pursued the major, in a tone intended for encouragement. "In spite of that devil sparkling in her eye, I'll lay ten to one you'll take the conceit out of her. Try!"

Without losing credit, the mustanger could not have declined acceding to the major's request. It was a challenge to skill—to equestrian prowess—a thing not lightly esteemed upon the prairies of Texas.

He proclaimed his acceptance of it by leaping lightly out of his saddle, resigning his own steed to Zeb Stump, and exclusively giving his attention to the captive.

The only preliminary called for was the clearing of the ground. This was effected in an instant—the greater part of the company—with all the ladies—returning to the azotea.

With only a piece of raw-hide rope looped around the under jaw, and carried headstall fashion behind the ears—with only one rein in hand—Maurice sprang to the back of the wild mare.

It was the first time she had ever been mounted by man—the first insult of the kind offered to her.

A shrill spiteful scream spoke plainly her appreciation of and determination to resent it. It proclaimed defiance of the attempt to degrade her to the condition of a slave!

With equine instinct, she reared upon her hind legs, for some seconds balancing her body in an erect position. Her rider, anticipating the trick, had thrown his arms around her neck; and, close clasping her throat, appeared part of herself. But for this she might have poised over upon her back, and crushed him beneath her.

The uprearing of the hind quarters was the next "trick" of the mustang—sure of being tried, and most difficult for the rider to meet without being thrown. From sheer conceit in his skill, he had declined these he could not have claimed accomplishment of the boasted feat of the prairies—*to tame the naked steed.*

He performed it without them. As the mare raised her hind quarters aloft, he turned quickly upon her back, threw his arms around the barrel of her body, and resting his toes upon the angular points of her fore shoulders, successfully resisted her efforts to unhorse him.

Twice or three times was the endeavour repeated by the mustang, and as often foiled by the skill of the mustanger; and then, as if conscious that such efforts were idle, the enraged animal plunged no longer; but, springing away from the spot, entered upon a gallop that appeared to have no goal this side the ending of the earth.

It must have come to an end somewhere; though not within sight of the spectators, who kept their places, waiting for the horse-tamer's return.

Conjectures that he might be killed, or, at the least, badly "crippled," were freely ventured during his absence; and there was one who wished it so. But there was also one upon whom such an event would have produced a painful impression—almost as painful as if her own life depended upon his safe return. Why Louise Poindexter, daughter of the proud Louisiana sugar-planter—a belle—a beauty of more than provincial repute—who could, by simply saying yes, have had for a husband the richest and noblest in the land—why she should have fixed her fancy, or even permitted her thoughts to stray, upon a poor horse-hunter of Texas, was a mystery that even her own intellect—by no means a weak one—was unable to fathom.

Perhaps she had not yet gone so far as to fix her fancy upon him. She did not think so herself. Had she thought so, and reflected upon it, perhaps she would have recoiled from the contemplation of certain consequences, that could not have failed to present themselves to her mind.

She was but conscious of having conceived some strange interest in a strange individual—one who had presented himself in a fashion that favoured fanciful reflections—one who differed essentially from the common-place types introduced to her in the world of social distinctions.

She was conscious, too, that this interest—originating in a word, a glance, a gesture—listened to, or observed, amid the ashes of a burnt prairie—instead of subsiding, had ever since been upon the increase!

It was not diminished when Maurice the mustanger came riding back across the plain, with the wild mare between his legs—no more wild—no longer desiring to destroy him—but with lowered crest and mien submissive, acknowledging to all the world that she had found her master!

Without acknowledging it to the world, or even to herself, the young Creole was inspired with a similar reflection.

"Miss Poindexter!" said the mustanger, gliding to the ground, and without making any acknowledgment to the plaudits that were showered upon him—"may I ask you to step up to her, throw this lazo over her neck, and lead her to the stable? By so doing, she will regard you as her tamer; and ever after submit to your will, if you but exhibit the sign that first deprived her of her liberty."

A prude would have paltered with the proposal—a coquette would have declined it—a timid girl have shrunk back.

Not so Louise Poindexter—a descendant of one of the *filles-à-la-casette*. Without a moment's hesitation—without the slightest show of prudery or fear—she stepped forth from the aristocratic circle; as instructed, took hold of the horsehair rope; whisked it across the neck of the tamed mustang; and led the captive off towards the *caballeriza* of Casa del Corvo.

As she did so, the mustanger's words were ringing in her ears, and echoing through her heart with a strange foreboding weird signification.

*"She will regard you as her tamer; and ever after submit to your will, if you but exhibit the sign that first deprived her of her liberty."*

# 13. A Prairie Pic-Nic

The first rays from a rosy aurora, saluting the flag of Fort Inge, fell with a more subdued light upon an assemblage of objects occupying the parade-ground below—in front of the "officers' quarters."

A small sumpter-waggon stood in the centre of the group; having attached to it a double span of tight little Mexican mules, whose quick impatient "stomping," tails spitefully whisked, and ears at intervals turning awry, told that they had been for some time in harness, and were impatient to move off—warning the bystanders, as well, against a too close approximation to their heels.

Literally speaking, there were no bystanders—if we except a man of colossal size, in blanket coat, and slouch felt hat; who, despite the obscure light straggling around his shoulders, could be identified as Zeb Stump, the hunter.

He was not standing either, but seated astride his "ole maar," that showed less anxiety to be off than either the Mexican mules or her own master.

The other forms around the vehicle were all in motion—quick, hurried, occasionally confused—hither and thither, from the waggon to the door of the quarters, and back again from the house to the vehicle.

There were half a score of them, or thereabouts; varied in costume as in the colour of their skins. Most were soldiers, in fatigue dress, though of different arms of the service. Two would be taken to be mess-cooks; and two or three more, officers' servants, who had been detailed from the ranks.

A more legitimate specimen of this profession appeared in the person of a well-dressed darkie, who moved about the ground in a very authoritative manner; deriving his importance, from his office of *valet de tout* to the major in command of the cantonment. A sergeant, as shown by his three-barred chevron, was in charge of the mixed party, directing their movements; the object of which was to load the waggon with eatables and drinkables—in short, the paraphernalia of a pic-nic.

That it was intended to be upon a grand scale, was testified by the amplitude and variety of the *impedimenta*. There were hampers and baskets of all shapes and sizes, including the well known parallel-opipedon, enclosing its twelve necks of shining silver-lead; while the tin canisters, painted Spanish brown, along with the universal sardine-case, proclaimed the presence of many luxuries not indigenous to Texas.

However delicate and extensive the stock of provisions, there was one in the party of purveyors who did not appear to think it complete. The dissatisfied Lucullus was Zeb Stump.

"Lookee hyur, surgint," said he, addressing himself confidentially to the individual in charge, "I hain't seed neery smell o' corn put inter the veehicle as yit; an', I reck'n, thet out on the purayra, thur'll be some folks ud prefar a leetle corn to any o' thet theer furrin French stuff. Sham-pain, ye call it, I b'lieve."

"Prefer corn to champagne! The horses you mean?"

"Hosses be durned. I ain't talkin' 'bout hoss corn. I mean M'nongaheela."

"Oh—ah—I comprehend. You're right about that, Mr Stump. The whisky mustn't be forgotten, Pomp. I think I saw a jar inside, that's intended to go?"

"Yaw—yaw, sagint," responded the dark-skinned domestic; "dar am dat same wesicle. Hya it is!" he added, lugging a large jar into the light, and swinging it up into the waggon.

Old Zeb appearing to think the packing now complete, showed signs of impatience to be off.

"Ain't ye riddy, surgint?" he inquired, shifting restlessly in his stirrups.

"Not quite, Mr Stump. The cook tells me the chickens want another turn upon the spit, before we can take 'em along."

"Durn the chickens, an the cook too! What air any dung-hill fowl to compare wi' a wild turkey o' the purayra; an how am I to shoot one, arter the sun hev clomb ten mile up the sky? The major sayed I war to git him a gobbler, whativer shed happen. 'Tain't so durnation eezy to kill turkey gobbler arter sun-up, wi' a clamjamferry like this comin' clost upon a fellur's heels? Ye mustn't surpose, surgint, that thet ere bird air as big a fool as the sodger o' a fort. Of all the cunnin' critters helf way roun' one o' 'em, ye must be up along wi' the sun; and pree-hap a leetle urlier."

"True, Mr Stump. I know the major wants a wild turkey. He told me so; and expects you to procure one on the way."

"No doubt he do; an preehap expex me likeways to purvid him wi' a baffler's tongue, an hump—seein' as thur ain't sech a anymal on the purayras o' South Texas—nor hain't a been for good twenty yurs past—noterthstandin' what Eur-óp-ean writers o' books hev said to the contrary, an 'specially French 'uns, as I've heern. Thur ain't no burner 'bout hyur. Thur's baar, an deer, an goats, an plenty o' gobblers; but to hev one o' these critters for yur dinner, ye must git it urly enuf for yur breakfist. Unless I hev my own time, I won't promise to guide yur party, an git gobbler both. So, surgint, ef ye expex yur grand kumpny to chaw turkey-meat this day, ye'll do well to be makin' tracks for the purayra."

Stirred by the hunter's representation, the sergeant did all that was possible to hasten the departure of himself and his parti-coloured company; and, shortly after, the provision train, with Zeb Stump as its guide, was wending its way across the extensive plain that lies be-tween the Leona and the "River of Nuts."

The parade-ground had been cleared of the waggon and its escort scarce twenty minutes, when a party of somewhat different appearance commenced assembling upon the same spot.

There were ladies on horseback; attended, not by grooms, as at the "meet" in an English hunting-field, but by the gentlemen who were to accompany them—their friends and acquaintances—fathers, broth-ers, lovers, and husbands. Most, if not all, who had figured at Poindexter's dinner party, were soon upon the ground.

The planter himself was present; as also his son Henry, his nephew Cassius Calhoun, and his daughter Louise—the young lady mounted upon the spotted mustang, that had figured so conspicuously on the occasion of the entertainment at Casa del Corvo.

The affair was a reciprocal treat—a simple return of hospitality; the major and his officers being the hosts, the planter and his friends the invited guests. The entertainment about to be provided, if less pre-tentious in luxurious appointments, was equally appropriate to the time and place. The guests of the cantonment were to be gratified by wit-nessing a spectacle—grand as rare—a chase of wild steeds!

The arena of the sport could only be upon the wild-horse prai-ries—some twenty miles to the southward of Fort Inge. Hence the necessity for an early start, and being preceded by a vehicle laden with an ample *commissariat*.

Just as the sunbeams began to dance upon the crystal waters of the Leona, the excursionists were ready to take their departure from the parade-ground—with an escort of two-score dragoons that had been ordered to ride in the rear. Like the party that preceded them, they too were provided with a guide—not an old backwoodsman in battered felt hat, and faded blanket coat, astride a scraggy roadster; but a horseman completely costumed and equipped, mounted upon a splendid steed, in every way worthy to be the chaperone of such a distinguished expedition.

"Come, Maurice!" cried the major, on seeing that all had assembled, "we're ready to be conducted to the game. Ladies and gentlemen! this young fellow is thoroughly acquainted with the haunts and habits of the wild horses. If there's a man in Texas, who can show us how to hunt them, 'tis Maurice the mustanger."

"Faith, you flatter me, major!" rejoined the young Irishman, turning with a courteous air towards the company; "I have not said so much as that. I can only promise to show you where you may *find* them."

"Modest fellow!" soliloquised one, who trembled, as she gave thought to what she more than half suspected to be an untruth.

"Lead on, then!" commanded the major; and, at the word, the gay cavalcade, with the mustanger in the lead, commenced moving across the parade-ground—while the star-spangled banner, unfurled by the morning breeze, fluttered upon its staff as if waving them an elegant adieu!

A twenty-mile ride upon prairie turf is a mere bagatelle—before breakfast, an airing. In Texas it is so regarded by man, woman, and horse.

It was accomplished in less than three hours—without further inconvenience than that which arose from performing the last few miles of it with appetites uncomfortably keen.

Fortunately the provision waggon, passed upon the road, came close upon their heels; and, long before the sun had attained the meridian line, the excursionists were in full pic-nic under the shade of a gigantic pecân tree, that stood near the banks of the Nueces.

No incident had occurred on the way—worth recording. The mustanger, as guide, had ridden habitually in the advance; the company, leaping clear over a prairie stream, or dry arroyo, which others were fain to ford, or cross by the crooked path.

There may have been a suspicion of bravado in this behaviour—a desire to exhibit. Cassius Calhoun told the company there was. Perhaps the ex-captain spoke the truth—for once.

If so, there was also some excuse. Have you ever been in a hunting-field, at home, with riding habits trailing the sward, and plumed hats proudly nodding around you? You have: and then what? Be cautious how you condemn the Texan mustanger. Reflect, that he, too, was under the artillery of bright eyes—a score pair of them—some as bright as ever looked love out of a lady's saddle. Think, that Louise Poindexter's were among the number—think of that, and you will scarce feel surprised at the ambition to "shine."

There were others equally demonstrative of personal accomplishments—of prowess that might prove manhood. The young dragoon, Hancock, frequently essayed to show that he was not new to the saddle; and the lieutenant of mounted rifles, at intervals, strayed from the side of the commissary's niece for the performance of some equestrian feat, without looking exclusively to her, his reputed sweetheart, as he listened to the whisperings of applause.

Ah, daughter of Poindexter! Whether in the *salons* of civilised Louisiana, or the prairies of savage Texas, peace could not reign in thy presence! Go where thou wilt, romantic thoughts must spring up— wild passions be engendered around thee!

# 14. The Manada

Had their guide held the prairies in complete control—its denizens subject to his secret will—responsible to time and place—he could not have conducted the excursionists to a spot more likely to furnish the sport that had summoned them forth.

Just as the sparkling Johannisberger—obtained from the German wine-stores of San Antonio—had imparted a brighter blue to the sky, and a more vivid green to the grass, the cry "Musteños!" was heard above the hum of conversation, interrupting the half-spoken sentiment, with the peal of merry laughter. It came from a Mexican *vaquero*, who had been stationed as a vidette on an eminence near at hand.

Maurice—at the moment partaking of the hospitality of his employers, freely extended to him—suddenly quaffed off the cup; and springing to his saddle, cried out—

"*Cavallada?*"

"No," answered the Mexican; "*manada.*"

"What do the fellows mean by their gibberish?" inquired Captain Calhoun.

"*Musteños* is only the Mexican for mustangs," replied the major; "and by 'manada' he means they are wild mares—a drove of them. At this season they herd together, and keep apart from the horses; unless when—"

"When what?" impatiently asked the ex-officer of volunteers, interrupting the explanation.

"When they are attacked by asses," innocently answered the major.

A general peal of laughter rendered doubtful the *naïveté* of the major's response—imparting to it the suspicion of a personality not intended.

succumb to an unlucky accident of speech. On the contrary, he perceived the chance of a triumphant reply; and took advantage of it.

"Indeed!" he drawled out, without appearing to address himself to any one in particular. "I was not aware that mustangs were so dangerous in these parts."

As Calhoun said this, he was not looking at Louise Poindexter or he might have detected in her eye a glance to gratify him.

The young Creole, despite an apparent coolness towards him, could not withhold admiration at anything that showed cleverness. His case might not be so hopeless?

The young dragoon, Hancock, did not think it so; nor yet the lieutenant of rifles. Both observed the approving look, and both became imbued with the belief that Cassius Calhoun had—or might have—in his keeping, the happiness of his cousin.

The conjecture gave a secret chagrin to both, but especially to the dragoon.

There was but short time for him to reflect upon it; the manada was drawing near.

"To the saddle!" was the thought upon every mind, and the cry upon every tongue.

The bit was rudely inserted between teeth still industriously grinding the yellow corn; the bridle drawn over shoulders yet smoking after the quick skurry of twenty miles through the close atmosphere of a tropical morn; and, before a hundred could have been deliberately counted, every one, ladies and gentlemen alike, was in the stirrup, ready to ply whip and spur.

By this time the wild mares appeared coming over the crest of the ridge upon which the vidette had been stationed. He, himself a horse-catcher by trade, was already mounted, and in their midst—endeavouring to fling his lazo over one of the herd. They were going at mad gallop, as if fleeing from a pursuer—some dreaded creature that was causing them to "whigher" and snort! With their eyes strained to the rear, they saw neither the sumpter waggon, nor the equestrians clustering around it, but were continuing onward to the spot; which chanced to lie directly in the line of their flight.

"They are chased!" remarked Maurice, observing the excited action of the animals.

"What is it, Crespino?" he cried out to the Mexican, who, from his position, must have seen any pursuer that might be after them.

There was a momentary pause, as the party awaited the response. In the crowd were countenances that betrayed uneasiness, some even alarm. It might be Indians who were in pursuit of the mustangs!

"*Un asino cimmaron!*" was the phrase that came from the mouth of the Mexican, though by no means terminating the suspense of the picknickers. "*Un macho!*" he added.

"Oh! That's it! I thought it was!" muttered Maurice. "The rascal must be stopped, or he'll spoil our sport. So long as he's after them, they'll not make halt this side the sky line. Is the macho coming on?"

"Close at hand, Don Mauricio. Making straight for myself."

"Fling your rope over him, if you can. If not, cripple him with a shot—anything to put an end to his capers."

The character of the pursuer was still a mystery to most, if not all, upon the ground: for only the mustanger knew the exact signification of the phrases—"un asino cimmaron," "un macho."

"Explain, Maurice!" commanded the major. "Look yonder!" replied the young Irishman, pointing to the top of the hill.

The two words were sufficient. All eyes became directed towards the crest of the ridge, where an animal, usually regarded as the type of slowness and stupidity, was seen advancing with the swiftness of a bird upon the wing.

But very different is the "asino cimmaron" from the ass of civilisation—the donkey be-cudgelled into stolidity.

The one now in sight was a male, almost as large as any of the mustangs it was chasing; and if not fleet as the fleetest, still able to keep up with them by the sheer pertinacity of its pursuit!

The tableau of nature, thus presented on the green surface of the prairie, was as promptly produced as it could have been upon the stage of a theatre, or the arena of a hippodrome.

Scarce a score of words had passed among the spectators, before the wild mares were close up to them; and then, as if for the first time, perceiving the mounted party, they seemed to forget their dreaded pursuer, and shied off in a slanting direction.

"Ladies and gentlemen!" shouted the guide to a score of people, endeavouring to restrain their steeds; "keep your places, if you can. I know where the herd has its haunt. They are heading towards it now; and we shall find them again, with a better chance of a chase. If you pursue them at this moment, they'll scatter into yonder chapparal; and ten to one if we ever more get sight of them.

The Mexican, detaching a short gun—"escopeta"—from his saddle-flap, and hastily bringing its butt to his shoulder, fired at the wild ass.

The animal brayed on hearing the report; but only as if in defiance. He was evidently untouched. Crespino's bullet had not been truly aimed.

"I must stop him!" exclaimed Maurice, "or the mares will run on till the end of daylight."

As the mustanger spoke, he struck the spur sharply into the flanks of his horse. Like an arrow projected from its bow, Castro shot off in pursuit of the jackass, now galloping regardlessly past.

Half a dozen springs of the blood bay, guided in a diagonal direction, brought his rider within casting distance; and like a flash of lightning, the loop of the lazo was seen descending over the long ears.

On launching it, the mustanger halted, and made a half-wheel— the horse going round as upon a pivot; and with like mechanical obedience to the will of his rider, bracing himself for the expected pluck.

There was a short interval of intense expectation, as the wild ass, careering onward, took up the slack of the rope. Then the animal was seen to rise erect on its hind legs, and fall heavily backward upon the sward—where it lay motionless, and apparently as dead, as if shot through the heart!

It was only stunned, however, by the shock, and the quick tightening of the loop causing temporary strangulation; which the Mexican mustanger prolonged to eternity, by drawing his sharp-edged *macheté* across its throat.

---

The incident caused a postponement of the chase. All awaited the action of the guide; who, after "throwing" the macho, had dismounted to recover his lazo.

He had succeeded in releasing the rope from the neck of the prostrate animal, when he was seen to coil it up with a quickness that betokened some new cause of excitement—at the same time that he ran to regain his saddle.

Only a few of the others—most being fully occupied with their own excited steeds—observed this show of haste on the part of the mustanger. Those who did, saw it with surprise. He had counselled patience in the pursuit. They could perceive no cause for the eccentric change of tactics, unless it was that Louise Poindexter, mounted on the spotted mustang, had suddenly separated from the company, and was galloping off after the wild mares, as if resolved on being foremost of the field!

But the hunter of wild horses had not construed her conduct in this sense. That uncourteous start could scarce be an intention—except on the part of the spotted mustang? Maurice had recognised the manada, as the same from which he had himself captured it: and, no doubt, with the design of rejoining its old associates, it was running away with its rider!

So believed the guide; and the belief became instantly universal.

Stirred by gallantry, half the field spurred off in pursuit. Calhoun, Hancock, and Crossman leading, with half a score of young planters, lawyers, and legislators close following—each as he rode off reflecting to himself, what a bit of luck it would be to bring up the runaway.

But few, if any, of the gentlemen felt actual alarm. All knew that Louise Poindexter was a splendid equestrian; a spacious plain lay before her, smooth as a race-track; the mustang might gallop till it tired itself down; it could not throw her; there could be little chance of her receiving any serious injury?

There was one who did not entertain this confident view. It was he who had been the first to show anxiety—the mustanger himself.

He was the last to leave the ground. Delayed in the rearrangement of his lazo—a moment more in remounting—he was a hundred paces behind every competitor, as his horse sprang forward upon the pursuit.

Calhoun was a like distance in the lead, pressing on with all the desperate energy of his nature, and all the speed he could extract from the heels of his horse. The dragoon and rifleman were a little in his rear; and then came the "ruck."

Maurice soon passed through the thick of the field, overlapped the leaders one by one; and forging still further ahead, showed Cassius Calhoun the heels of his horse.

A muttered curse was sent hissing through the teeth of the ex-officer of volunteers, as the blood bay, bounding past, concealed from his sight the receding form of the spotted mustang.

The sun, looking down from the zenith, gave light to a singular tableau. A herd of wild mares going at reckless speed across the prairie; one of their own kind, with a lady upon its back, following about four hundred yards behind; at a like distance after the lady, a steed of red bay colour, bestridden by a cavalier picturesquely attired, and apparently intent upon overtaking her; still further to the rear a string of group of ladies and gentlemen—also mounted, but motionless, on the plain, or only stirring around the same spot with excited gesticulations!

In twenty minutes the tableau was changed. The same personages were upon the stage—the grand *tapis vert* of the prairie—but the grouping was different, or, at all events, the groups were more widely apart. The manada had gained distance upon the spotted mustang; the mustang upon the blood bay; and the blood bay—ah! his competitors were no longer in sight, or could only have been seen by the far-piercing eye of the *caracara*, soaring high in the sapphire heavens.

The wild mares—the mustang and its rider—the red horse, and his—had the savanna to themselves!

# 15. The Runaway Overtaken

For another mile the chase continued, without much change. The mares still swept on in full flight, though no longer screaming or in fear. The mustang still uttered an occasional neigh, which its old associates seemed not to notice; while its rider held her seat in the saddle unshaken, and without any apparent alarm.

The blood bay appeared more excited, though not so much as his master; who was beginning to show signs either of despondency or chagrin.

"Come, Castro!" he exclaimed, with a certain spitefulness of tone. "What the deuce is the matter with your heels—to-day of all others? Remember, you overtook her before—though not so easily, I admit. But now she's weighted. Look yonder, you dull brute! Weighted with that which is worth more than gold—worth every drop of your blood, and mine too. The yegua pinta seems to have improved her paces. Is it from training; or does a horse run faster when ridden?

"What if I lose sight of her? In truth, it begins to look queer! It would be an awkward situation for the young lady. Worse than that— there's danger in it—real danger. If I should lose sight of her, she'd be in trouble to a certainty!"

Thus muttering, Maurice rode on: his eyes now fixed upon the form still flitting away before him; at intervals interrogating, with uneasy glances, the space that separated him from it.

Up to this time he had not thought of hailing the rider of the runaway.

His shouts might have been heard; but no words of warning, or instruction. He had refrained: partly on this account; partly because he was in momentary expectation of overtaking her; and partly because he knew that acts, not words, were wanted to bring the mustang to a

All along he had been flattering himself that he would soon be near enough to fling his lazo over the creature's neck, and control it at discretion. He was gradually becoming relieved of this hallucination.

The chase now entered among copses that thickly studded the plain, fast closing into a continuous chapparal. This was a new source of uneasiness to the pursuer. The runaway might take to the thicket, or become lost to his view amid the windings of the wood.

The wild mares were already invisible—at intervals. They would soon be out of sight altogether. There seemed no chance of their old associate overtaking them.

"What mattered that? A lady lost on a prairie, or in a chapparal—alone, or in the midst of a manada—either contingency pointed to certain danger."

A still more startling peril suggested itself to the mind of the mustanger—so startling as to find expression in excited speech.

"By heavens!" he ejaculated, his brow becoming more clouded than it had been from his first entering upon the chase. "*If the stallions should chance this way*! 'Tis their favourite stamping ground among these mottos. They were here but a week ago; and this—yes—'tis the month of their madness!"

The spur of the mustanger again drew blood, till its rowels were red; and Castro, galloping at his utmost speed, glanced back upbraidingly over his shoulder.

At this crisis the manada disappeared from, the sight both of the blood-bay and his master; and most probably at the same time from that of the spotted mustang and its rider. There was nothing mysterious in it. The mares had entered between the closing of two copses, where the shrubbery hid them from view.

The effect produced upon the runaway appeared to proceed from some magical influence. As if their disappearance was a signal for discontinuing the chase, it suddenly slackened pace; and the instant after came to a standstill!

Maurice, continuing his gallop, came up with it in the middle of a meadow-like glade—standing motionless as marble—its rider, reins in hand, sitting silent in the saddle, in an attitude of easy elegance, as if waiting for him to ride up!

"Miss Poindexter!" he gasped out, as he spurred his steed within speaking distance: "I am glad that you have recovered command of that wild creature. I was beginning to be alarmed about—"

"About what, sir?" was the question that startled the mustanger.

"Your safety—of course," he replied, somewhat stammeringly. "Oh, thank you, Mr Gerald; but I was not aware of having been in any danger. Was I really so?"

"Any danger!" echoed the Irishman, with increased astonishment. "On the back of a runaway mustang—in the middle of a pathless prairie!"

"And what of that? The thing couldn't throw me. I'm too clever in the saddle, sir."

"I know it, madame; but that accomplishment would have availed you very little had you lost yourself, a thing you were like enough to have done among these chapparal copses, where the oldest Texan can scarce find his way."

"Oh—*lost myself*! That was the danger to be dreaded?"

"There are others, besides. Suppose you had fallen in with—"

"Indians!" interrupted the lady, without waiting for the mustanger to finish his hypothetical speech. "And if I had, what would it have mattered? Are not the Comanches *en paz* at present? Surely they wouldn't have molested me, gallant fellows as they are? So the major told us, as we came along. 'Pon my word, sir, I should seek, rather than shun, such an encounter. I wish to see the noble savage on his native prairie, and on horseback; not, as I've hitherto beheld him, reeling around the settlements in a state of debasement from too freely partaking of our fire-water."

"I admire your courage, miss; but if I had the honour of being one of your friends, I should take the liberty of counselling a little caution. The 'noble savage' you speak of, is not always sober upon the prairies; and perhaps not so very gallant as you've been led to believe. If you had met him—"

"If I had met him, and he had attempted to misbehave himself, I would have given him the go-by, and ridden, straight back to my friends. On such a swift creature as this, he must have been well mounted to have overtaken me. You found some difficulty—did you not?"

The eyes of the young Irishman, already showing astonishment, became expanded to increased dimensions—surprise and incredulity being equally blended in their glance.

"But," said he, after a speechless pause, "you don't mean to say that you could have controlled— that the mustang was not running away with you? Am I to understand—"

that is, at the first—but I—I found, that is—at the last—I found I could easily pull her up. In fact I did so: you saw it?"

"And could you have done it sooner?"

A strange thought had suggested the interrogatory; and with more than ordinary interest the questioner awaited the reply.

"Perhaps—perhaps—I might; no doubt, if I had dragged a little harder upon the rein. But you see, sir, I like a good gallop—especially upon a prairie, where there's no fear of running over pigs, poultry, or people."

Maurice looked amaze. In all his experience—even in his own native land, famed for feminine *braverie*—above all in the way of bold riding—he had met no match for the clever equestrian before him.

His astonishment, mixed with admiration, hindered him from making a ready rejoinder.

"To speak truth," continued the young lady, with an air of charming simplicity, "I was not sorry at being run off with. One sometimes gets tired of too much talk—of the kind called complimentary. I wanted fresh air, and to be alone. So you *see*, Mr Gerald, it was rather a bit of good fortune: since it saved explanations and adieus."

"You wanted to be alone?" responded the mustanger, with a disappointed look. "I am sorry I should have made the mistake to have intruded upon you. I assure you, Miss Poindexter, I followed, because I believed you to be in danger."

"Most gallant of you, sir; and now that I know there *was* danger, I am truly grateful. I presume I have guessed aright: you meant the Indians?"

"No; not Indians exactly—at least, it was not of them I was thinking."

"Some other danger? What is it, sir? You will tell me, so that I may be more cautious for the future?"

Maurice did not make immediate answer. A sound striking upon his ear had caused him to turn away—as if inattentive to the interrogatory.

The Creole, perceiving there was some cause for his abstraction, likewise assumed a listening attitude. She heard a shrill scream, succeeded by another and another, close followed by a loud hammering of hoofs—the conjunction of sounds causing the still atmosphere to vibrate around her.

It was no mystery to the hunter of horses. The words that came quick from his lips—though not designed—were a direct answer to the question she had put.

"*The wild stallions*!" he exclaimed, in a tone that betokened alarm. "I knew they must be among those mottes; and they are!"

"Is that the danger of which you have been speaking?"

"It is."

"What fear of them? They are only mustangs!"

"True, and at other times there is no cause to fear them. But just now, at this season of the year, they become as savage as tigers, and equally as vindictive. Ah! the wild steed in his rage is an enemy more to be dreaded than wolf, panther, or bear."

"What are we to do?" inquired the young lady, now, for the first time, giving proof that she felt fear—by riding close up to the man who had once before rescued her from a situation of peril, and gazing anxiously in his face, as she awaited the answer.

"If they should charge upon us," answered Maurice, "there are but two ways of escape. One, by ascending a tree, and abandoning our horses to their fury."

"The other?" asked the Creole, with a *sang froid* that showed a presence of mind likely to stand the test of the most exciting crisis. "Anything but abandon our animals! 'Twould be but a shabby way of making our escape!"

"We shall not have an opportunity of trying it, I perceive it is impracticable. There's not a tree within sight large enough to afford us security. If attacked, we have no alternative but to trust to the fleetness of our horses. Unfortunately," continued he, with a glance of inspection towards the spotted mare, and then at his own horse, "they've had too much work this morning. Both are badly blown. That will be our greatest source of danger. The wild steeds are sure to be fresh."

"Do you intend us to start now?"

"Not yet. The longer we can breathe our animals the better. The stallions may not come this way; or if so, may not molest us. It will depend on their mood at the moment. If battling among themselves, we may look out for their attack. Then they have lost their reason—if I may so speak—and will recklessly rush upon one of their own kind—even with a man upon his back. Ha! 'tis as I expected: they are in conflict. I can tell by their cries! And driving this way, too!"

"But, Mr Gerald; why should we not ride off at once, in the opposite direction?"

"'Twould be of no use. There's no cover to conceal us, on that side—nothing but open plain. They'll be out upon it before we could are now upon the direct path to it, if I can judge by what I hear; and, if we start too soon, we may ride into their teeth. We must wait, and try to steal away behind them. If we succeed in getting past, and can keep our distance for a two-mile gallop, I know a spot, where we shall be as safe as if inside the corrals of Casa del Corvo. You are sure you can control the mustang?"

"Quite sure," was the prompt reply: all idea of deception being abandoned in presence of the threatening peril.

# 16. Chased by Wild Stallions

The two sat expectant in their saddles—she, apparently, with more confidence than he: for she confided in him. Still but imperfectly comprehending it, she knew there must be some great danger. When such a man showed sign of fear, it could not be otherwise. She had a secret happiness in thinking: that a portion of this fear was for her own safety.

"I think we may venture now;" said her companion, after a short period spent in listening; "they appear to have passed the opening by which we must make our retreat. Look well to your riding, I entreat you! Keep a firm seat in the saddle, and a sure hold of the rein. Gallop by my side, where the ground will admit of it; but in no case let more than the length of my horse's tail be between us. I must perforce go ahead to guide the way. Ha! they are coming direct for the glade. They're already close to its edge. Our time is up!"

The profound stillness that but a short while before pervaded the prairie, no longer reigned over it. In its stead had arisen a fracas that resembled the outpouring of some overcrowded asylum; for in the shrill neighing of the steeds might have been fancied the screams of maniacs—only ten times more vociferous. They were mingled with a thunder-like hammering of hoofs—a swishing and crashing of branches—savage snorts, accompanied by the sharp snapping of teeth—the dull "thud" of heels coming in contact with ribs and rounded hips—squealing that betokened spite or pain—all forming a combination of sounds that jarred harshly upon the ear, and caused the earth to quake, as if oscillating upon its orbit!

It told of a terrible conflict carried on by the wild stallions; who, still unseen, were fighting indiscriminately among themselves, as they held their way among the mottes.

Not much longer unseen. As Maurice gave the speckled crowd showed itself in an opening betwee moment more it filled the gangway-like gap, and commenced disgorging into the glade, with the impetus of an avalanche!

It was composed of living forms—the most beautiful known in nature: for in this man must give way to the horse. Not the unsexed horse of civilisation, with hunched shoulders, bandied limbs, and bowed frontlet—scarce one in a thousand of true equine shape—and this, still further, mutilated by the shears of the coper and gentleman jockey—but the wild steed of the savannas, foaled upon the green grass, his form left free to develop as the flowers that shed their fragrance around him.

Eye never beheld a more splendid sight than a *cavallada* of wild stallions, prancing upon a prairie; especially at that season when, stirred by strong passions, they seek to destroy one another. The spectacle is more than splendid—it is fearful—too fearful to be enjoyed by man, much less by timid woman. Still more when the spectator views it from an exposed position, liable to become the object of their attack.

In such situation were the riders of the blood bay and spotted mustang. The former knew it by past experience—the latter could not fail to perceive it by the evidence before her.

"This way!" cried Maurice, lancing his horse's flanks with the spur, and bending so as to oblique to the rear of the cavallada.

"By heaven—they've discovered us! On—on! Miss Poindexter! Remember you are riding for your life!"

The stimulus of speech was not needed. The behaviour of the stallions was of itself sufficient to show, that speed alone could save the spotted mustang and its rider.

On coming out into the open ground, and getting sight of the ridden horses, they had suddenly desisted from their internecine strife; and, as if acting under the orders of some skilled leader, come to a halt. In line, too, like cavalry checked up in the middle of a charge!

For a time their mutual hostility seemed to be laid aside—as if they felt called upon to attack a common enemy, or resist some common danger!

The pause may have proceeded from surprise; but, whether or no, it was favourable to the fugitives. During the twenty seconds it continued, the latter had made good use of their time, and accomplished the circuit required to put them on the path of safety.

Only on the path, however. Their escape was still problematical: for the steeds, perceiving their intention, wheeled suddenly into the line of pursuit, and went galloping after, with snorts and screams that betrayed a spiteful determination to overtake them.

From that moment it became a straight unchanging chase across country—a trial of speed between the horses without riders, and the horses that were ridden.

At intervals did Maurice carry his chin to his shoulder; and though still preserving the distance gained at the start, his look was not the less one of apprehension.

Alone he would have laughed to scorn his pursuers. He knew that the blood-bay—himself a prairie steed—could surpass any competitor of his race. But the mare was delaying him. She was galloping slower than he had ever seen her—as if unwilling, or not coveting escape—like a horse with his head turned away from home!

"What can it mean?" muttered the mustanger, as he checked his pace, to accommodate it to that of his companion. "If there should be any baulk at the crossing, we're lost! A score of seconds will make the difference."

"We keep our distance, don't we?" inquired his fellow-fugitive, noticing his troubled look.

"So far, yes. Unfortunately there's an obstruction ahead. It remains to be seen how we shall get over it. I know you are a clever rider, and can take a long leap. But your mount? I'm not so sure of the mare. You know her better than I. Do you think she can carry you over—"

"Over what, sir?"

"You'll see in a second. We should be near the place now."

The conversation thus carried on was between two individuals riding side by side, and going at a gallop of nearly a mile to the minute!

As the guide had predicted, they soon came within sight of the obstruction; which proved to be an arroyo—a yawning fissure in the plain full fifteen feet in width, as many in depth, and trending on each side to the verge of vision.

To turn aside, either to the right or left, would be to give the pursuers the advantage of the diagonal; which the fugitives could no longer afford.

The chasm must be crossed, or the stallions would overtake them.

It could only be crossed by a leap—fifteen feet at the least. Maurice knew that his own horse could go over it—he had done it before. But the mare?

"Do you think she can do it?" he eagerly asked, as, in slackened pace, they approached the edge of the barranca.

"I am sure she can," was the confident reply.

"But are you sure you can sit her over it?"

"Ha! ha! ha!" scornfully laughed the Creole. "What a question for an Irishman to ask! I'm sure, sir, one of your own countrywomen would be offended at your speech. Even I, a native of swampy Louisiana, don't regard it as at all gallant. Sit her over it! Sit her anywhere she can carry me."

"But, Miss Poindexter," stammered the guide, still doubting the powers of the spotted mustang, "suppose she cannot? If you have any doubts, had you not better abandon her? I know that my horse can bear us both to the other side, and with safety. If the mustang be left behind, in all likelihood we shall escape further pursuit. The wild steeds—"

"Leave Luna behind! Leave her to be trampled to death, or torn to pieces—as you say she would! No—no, Mr Gerald. I prize the spotted mare too much for that. She goes with me: over the chasm, if we can. If not, we both break our necks at the bottom. Come, my pretty pet! This is he who chased, captured, and conquered you. Show him you're not yet so *subdued*, but that you can escape, when close pressed, from the toils of either friend or enemy. Show him one of those leaps, of which you've done a dozen within the week. Now for a flight in the air!"

Without even waiting for the stimulus of example, the courageous Creole rode recklessly at the arroyo; and cleared it by one of those leaps of which she had "done a dozen within the week."

There were three thoughts in the mind of the mustanger—rather might they be called emotions—as he sate watching that leap. The first was simple astonishment; the second, intense admiration. The third was not so easily defined. It had its origin in the words—"*I prize the spotted mare too much for that.*"

"Why?" reflected he, as he drove his spur-rowels into the flanks of the blood bay; and the reflection lasted as long as Castro was suspended in mid-air over the yawning abysm.

Cleverly as the chasm was crossed, it did not ensure the safety of the fugitives. It would be no obstruction to the steeds. Maurice knew it, and looked back with undiminished apprehension.

Rather was it increased. The delay, short as it was, had given the pursuers an advantage. They were nearer than ever! They would not be likely to make a moment's pause, but clear the crevasse at a single bound of their sure-footed gallop.

And then—what then?

The mustanger put the question to himself. He grew paler, as the reply puzzled him.

On alighting from the leap, he had not paused for a second, but gone galloping on—as before, close followed by his fugitive companion. His pace, however, was less impetuous. He seemed to ride with irresolution, or as if some half-formed resolve was restraining him.

When about a score lengths from the edge of the arroyo, he reined up and wheeled round—as if he had suddenly formed the determination to ride back!

"Miss Poindexter!" he called out to the young lady, at that moment just up with him. "You must ride on alone."

"But why, sir?" asked she, as she jerked the muzzle of the mustang close up to its counter, bringing it almost instantaneously to a stand.

"If we keep together we shall be overtaken. I must do something to stay those savage brutes. Here there is a chance—nowhere else. For heaven's sake don't question me! Ten seconds of lost time, and 'twill be too late. Look ahead yonder. You perceive the sheen of water. 'Tis a prairie pond. Ride straight towards it. You will find yourself between two high fences. They come together at the pond. You'll see a gap, with bars. If I'm not up in time, gallop through, dismount, and put the bars up behind you."

"And you, sir? You are going to undergo some great danger?"

"Have no fear for me! Alone, I shall run but little risk. 'Tis the mustang.—For mercy's sake, gallop forward! Keep the water under your eyes. Let it guide you like a beacon fire. Remember to close the gap behind you. Away—away!"

For a second or two the young lady appeared irresolute—as if reluctant to part company with the man who was making such efforts to ensure her safety—perhaps at the peril of his own.

By good fortune she was not one of those timid maidens who turn frantic at a crisis, and drag to the bottom the swimmer who would save them. She had faith in the capability of her counsellor—believed that he knew what he was about—and, once more spurring the mare into a gallop, she rode off in a direct line for the prairie pond.

At the same instant, Maurice had given the rein to his horse, and was riding in the opposite direction—back to the place where they had leaped the arroyo!

On parting from his companion, he had drawn from his saddle holster the finest weapon ever wielded upon the prairies—either for attack or defence, against Indian, buffalo, or bear. It was the six-chambered revolver of Colonel Colt—not the spurious *improvement* of Deane, Adams, and a host of retrograde imitators—but the genuine article from the "land of wooden nutmegs," with the Hartford brand upon its breech.

"They must get over the narrow place where we crossed," muttered he, as he faced towards the stallions, still advancing on the other side of the arroyo.

"If I can but fling one of them in his tracks, it may hinder the others from attempting the leap; or delay them—long enough for the mustang to make its escape. The big sorrel is leading. He will make the spring first. The pistol's good for a hundred paces. He's within range now!"

Simultaneous with the last words came the crack of the six-shooter. The largest of the stallions—a sorrel in colour—rolled headlong upon the sward; his carcass falling transversely across the line that led to the leap.

Half-a-dozen others, close following, were instantly brought to a stand; and then the whole cavallada!

The mustanger stayed not to note their movements. Taking advantage of the confusion caused by the fall of their leader, he reserved the fire of the other five chambers; and, wheeling to the west, spurred on after the spotted mustang, now far on its way towards the glistening pond.

Whether dismayed by the fall of their chief—or whether it was that his dead body had hindered them from approaching the only place where the chasm could have been cleared at a leap—the stallions abandoned the pursuit; and Maurice had the prairie to himself as he swept on after his fellow fugitive.

He overtook her beyond the convergence of the fences on the shore of the pond. She had obeyed him in everything—except as to the closing of the gap. He found it open—the bars lying scattered over the ground. He found her still seated in the saddle, relieved from all apprehension for his safety, and only trembling with a gratitude that longed to find expression in speech.

The peril was passed.

# 17. The Mustang Trap

No longer in dread of any danger, the young Creole looked interrogatively around her.

There was a small lake—in Texan phraseology a "pond"—with countless horse-tracks visible along its shores, proving that the place was frequented by wild horses—their excessive number showing it to be a favourite watering place. There was a high rail fence—constructed so as to enclose the pond, and a portion of the contiguous prairie, with two diverging wings, carried far across the plain, forming a funnel-shaped approach to a gap; which, when its bars were up, completed an enclosure that no horse could either enter or escape from.

"What is it for?" inquired the lady, indicating the construction of split rails.

"A mustang trap," said Maurice.

"A mustang trap?"

"A contrivance for catching wild horses. They stray between the *wings*; which, as you perceive, are carried far out upon the plain. The water attracts them; or they are driven towards it by a band of mustangers who follow, and force them on through the gap. Once within the *corral*, there is no trouble in taking them. They are then lazoed at leisure."

"Poor things! Is it yours? You are a mustanger? You told us so?"

"I am; but I do not hunt the wild horse in this way. I prefer being alone, and rarely consort with men of my calling. Therefore I could not make use of this contrivance, which requires at least a score of drivers. My weapon, if I may dignify it by the name, is this—the lazo."

"You use it with great skill? I've heard that you do; besides having myself witnessed the proof."

"It is complimentary of you to say so. But you are mistaken. There are men on these prairies 'to the manner born'—Mexicans—who regard, what you are pleased to call skill, as sheer clumsiness."

"Are you sure, Mr Gerald, that your modesty is not prompting *you* to overrate your rivals? I have been told the very opposite."

"By whom?"

"Your friend, Mr Zebulon Stump."

"Ha—ha! Old Zeb is but indifferent authority on the subject of the lazo."

"I wish I could throw the lazo," said the young Creole. "They tell me 'tis not a lady-like accomplishment. What matters—so long as it is innocent, and gives one a gratification?"

"Not lady-like! Surely 'tis as much so as archery, or skating? I know a lady who is very expert at it."

"An American lady?"

"No; she's Mexican, and lives on the Rio Grande; but sometimes comes across to the Leona—where she has relatives."

"A young lady?"

"Yes. About your own age, I should think, Miss Poindexter."

"Size?"

"Not so tall as you."

"But much prettier, of course? The Mexican ladies, I've heard, in the matter of good looks, far surpass us plain *Americanos*."

"I think Creoles are not included in that category," was the reply, worthy of one whose lips had been in contact with the famed boulder of Blarney.

"I wonder if I could ever learn to fling it?" pursued the young Creole, pretending not to have been affected by the complimentary remark. "Am I too old? I've been told that the Mexicans commence almost in childhood; that that is why they attain to such wonderful skill?"

"Not at all," replied Maurice, encouragingly. "'Tis possible, with a year or two's practice, to become a proficient lazoer. I, myself, have only been three years at; and—"

He paused, perceiving he was about to commit himself to a little boasting.

"And you are now the most skilled in all Texas?" said his companion, supplying the presumed finale of his speech.

"No, no!" laughingly rejoined he. "That is but a mistaken belief on the part of Zeb Stump, who judges my skill by comparison, making use of his own as a standard."

"Is it modesty?" reflected the Creole. "Or is this man mocking me? If I thought so, I should go mad!"

"Perhaps you are anxious to get back to your party?" said Maurice, observing her abstracted air. "Your father may be alarmed by your long absence? Your brother—your cousin—"

"Ah, true!" she hurriedly rejoined, in a tone that betrayed either pique, or compunction. "I was not thinking of that. Thanks, sir, for reminding me of my duty. Let us go back!"

Again in the saddle, she gathered up her reins, and plied her tiny spur—both acts being performed with an air of languid reluctance, as if she would have preferred lingering a little longer in the "mustang trap."

Once more upon the prairie, Maurice conducted his protégée by the most direct route towards the spot where they had parted from the picnic party.

Their backward way led them across a peculiar tract of country—what in Texas is called a "weed prairie," an appellation bestowed by the early pioneers, who were not very choice in their titles.

The Louisianian saw around her a vast garden of gay flowers, laid out in one grand parterre, whose borders were the blue circle of the horizon—a garden designed, planted, nurtured, by the hand of Nature.

The most plebeian spirit cannot pass through such a scene without receiving an impression calculated to refine it. I've known the illiterate trapper—habitually blind to the beautiful—pause in the midst of his "weed prairie," with the flowers rising breast high around him, gaze for a while upon their gaudy corollas waving beyond the verge of his vision; then continue his silent stride with a gentler feeling towards his fellow-man, and a firmer faith in the grandeur of his God.

"*Pardieu!* 'tis very beautiful!" exclaimed the enthusiastic Creole, reining up as if by an involuntary instinct.

"You admire these wild scenes, Miss Poindexter?"

"Admire them? Something more, sir! I see around me all that is bright and beautiful in nature: verdant turf, trees, flowers, all that we take such pains to plant or cultivate; and such, too, as we never succeed in equalling. There seems nothing wanting to make this picture complete—'tis a park perfect in everything!"

"Except the mansion?"

"That would spoil it for me. Give me the landscape where there is not a house in sight—slate, chimney, or tile—to interfere with the out-

The word: "love" uppermost in her thoughts—was upon the tip of her tongue.

She dexterously restrained herself from pronouncing it—changing it to one of very different signification—"die."

It was cruel of the young Irishman not to tell her that she was speaking his own sentiments—repeating them to the very echo. To this was the prairie indebted for his presence. But for a kindred inclination—amounting almost to a passion—he might never have been known as *Maurice the mustanger*.

The romantic sentiment is not satisfied with a "sham." It will soon consume itself, unless supported by the consciousness of reality. The mustanger would have been humiliated by the thought, that he chased the wild horse as a mere pastime—a pretext to keep him upon the prairies. At first, he might have condescended to make such an acknowledgment—but he had of late become thoroughly imbued with the pride of the professional hunter.

His reply might have appeared chillingly prosaic.

"I fear, miss, you would soon tire of such a rude life—no roof to shelter you—no society—no—"

"And you, sir; how is it *you* have not grown tired of it? If I have been correctly informed—your friend, Mr Stump, is my authority—you've been leading this life for several years. Is it so?"

"Quite true: I have no other calling."

"Indeed! I wish I could say the same. I envy you your lot. I'm sure I could enjoy existence amid these beautiful scene for ever and ever!"

"Alone? Without companions? Without even a roof to shelter you?"

"I did not say that. But, you've not told me. How do you live? Have *you* a house?"

"It does not deserve such a high-sounding appellation," laughingly replied the mustanger. "Shed would more correctly serve for the description of my *jacalé*, which may be classed among the lowliest in the land."

"Where is it? Anywhere near where we've been to-day?"

"It is not very far from where we are now. A mile, perhaps. You see those tree-tops to the west? They shade my hovel from the sun, and shelter it from the storm."

"Indeed! How I should like to have a look at it! A real rude hut, you say?"

"In that I have but spoken the truth."

"Standing solitary?"

"I know of no other within ten miles of it."

"Among trees, and picturesque?"

"That depends upon the eye that beholds it."

"I should like to see it, and judge. Only a mile you say?"

"A mile there—the same to return—would be two."

"That's nothing. It would not take us a score of minutes."

"Should we not be trespassing on the patience of your people?"

"On your hospitality, perhaps? Excuse me, Mr Gerald!" continued the young lady, a slight shadow suddenly overcasting her countenance. "I did not think of it! Perhaps you do not live *alone*? Some other shares your—jacalé—as you call it?"

"Oh, yes, I have a companion—one who has been with me ever since I—"

The shadow became sensibly darker.

Before the mustanger could finish his speech, his listener had pictured to herself a certain image, that might answer to the description of his companion: a girl of her own age—perhaps more inclining to *embonpoint*—with a skin of chestnut brown; eyes of almond shade, set piquantly oblique to the lines of the nose; teeth of more than pearly purity; a tinge of crimson upon the cheeks; hair like Castro's tail; beads and bangles around neck, arms, and ankles; a short kirtle elaborately embroidered; mocassins covering small feet; and fringed leggings, laced upon limbs of large development. Such were the style and equipments of the supposed companion, who had suddenly become outlined in the imagination of Louise Poindexter.

"Your fellow tenant of the jacalé might not like being intruded upon by visitors—more especially a stranger?"

"On the contrary, he's but too glad to see visitors at any time—whether strangers or acquaintances. My foster-brother is the last man to shun society; of which, poor fellow! he sees precious little on the Alamo."

"Your foster-brother?"

"Yes. Phelim O'Neal by name—like myself a native of the Emerald Isle, and shire of Galway; only perhaps speaking a little better brogue than mine."

"Oh! the Irish brogue. I should so like to hear it spoken by a native of Galway. I am told that theirs is the richest. Is it so, Mr Gerald?"

"Being a Galwegian myself, my judgment might not be reliable;

hour, he will, no doubt, give you an opportunity of judging for yourself."

"I should be delighted. 'Tis something so new. Let papa and the rest of them wait. There are plenty of ladies without me; or the gentlemen may amuse themselves by tracing up our tracks. 'Twill be as good a horse hunt as they are likely to have. Now, sir, I'm ready to accept your hospitality."

"There's not much to offer you, I fear. Phelim has been several days by himself, and as he's but an indifferent hunter, his larder is likely to be low. 'Tis fortunate you had finished luncheon before the *stampede*."

It was not Phelim's larder that was leading Louise Poindexter out of her way, nor yet the desire to listen to his Connemara pronunciation. It was not curiosity to look at the jacalé of the mustanger; but a feeling of a far more irresistible kind, to which she was yielding, as if she believed it to be her fate!

---

She paid a visit to the lone hut, on the Alamo; she entered under its roof; she scanned with seeming interest its singular *penates*; and noted, with pleased surprise, the books, writing materials, and other chattels that betokened the refinement of its owner; she listened with apparent delight to the *palthogue* of the Connemara man, who called her a "coleen bawn;" she partook of Phelim's hospitality— condescendingly tasting of everything offered, except that which was most urgently pressed upon her, "a dhrap of the crayther, drawn fresh from the dimmyjan;" and finally made her departure from the spot, apparently in the highest spirits.

Alas! her delight was short-lived: lasting only so long as it was sustained by the excitement of the novel adventure. As she recrossed the flower prairie, she found time for making a variety of reflections; and there was one that chilled her to the very core of her heart.

Was it the thought that she had been acting wrongly in keeping her father, her brother, and friends in suspense about her safety? Or had she become conscious of playing a part open to the suspicion of being unfeminine?

Not either. The cloud that darkened her brow in the midst of that blossoming brightness, was caused by a different, and far more distressing, reflection. During all that day, in the journey from the fort, after overtaking her in the chase, in the pursuit while protecting her, lingering by her side on the shore of the lake, returning across the prairie, under his own humble roof—in short everywhere—her companion had only been polite—*had only behaved as a gentleman*!

# 18. Jealousy upon the Trail

Of the two-score rescuers, who had started in pursuit of the runaway, but few followed far. Having lost sight of the wild mares, the mustang, and the mustanger, they began to lose sight of one another; and before long became dispersed upon the prairie—going single, in couples, or in groups of three and four together. Most of them, unused to tracking up a trail, soon strayed from that taken by the manada; branching off upon others, made, perhaps, by the same drove upon some previous stampede.

The dragoon escort, in charge of a young officer—a fresh fledgling from West Point—ran astray upon one of these ramifications, carrying the hindmost of the field along with it.

It was a rolling prairie through which the pursuit was conducted, here and there intersected by straggling belts of brushwood. These, with the inequalities of the surface, soon hid the various pursuing parties from one another; and in twenty minutes after the start, a bird looking from the heavens above, might have beheld half a hundred horsemen, distributed into half a score of groups—apparently having started from a common centre—spurring at full speed towards every quarter of the compass!

But one was going in the right direction—a solitary individual, mounted upon a large strong-limbed chestnut horse; that, without any claim to elegance of shape, was proving the possession both of speed and bottom. The blue frock-coat of half military cut, and forage cap of corresponding colour, were distinctive articles of dress habitually worn by the ex-captain of volunteer cavalry—Cassius Calhoun. He it was who directed the chestnut on the true trail; while with whip and spur he was stimulating the animal to extraordinary efforts. He was himself stimulated by a thought—sharp as his own spurs—that caused him to concentrate all his energies upon the abject in hand.

Like a hungry hound he was laying his head along the trail, in hopes of an issue that might reward him for his exertions.

What that issue was he had but vaguely conceived; but on occasional glance towards his holsters—from which protruded the butts of a brace of pistols—told of some sinister design that was shaping itself in his soul.

But for a circumstance that assisted him, he might, like the others, have gone astray. He had the advantage of them, however, in being guided by two shoe-tracks he had seen before. One, the larger, he recollected with a painful distinctness. He had seen it stamped upon a charred surface, amid the ashes of a burnt prairie. Yielding to an undefined instinct, he had made a note of it in his memory, and now remembered it.

Thus directed, the *ci-devant* captain arrived among the copses, and rode into the glade where the spotted mustang had been pulled up in such a mysterious manner. Hitherto his analysis had been easy enough. At this point it became conjecture. Among the hoof-prints of the wild mares, the shoe-tracks were still seen, but no longer going at a gallop. The two animals thus distinguished must have been halted, and standing in juxtaposition.

Whither next? Along the trail of the manada, there was no imprint of iron; nor elsewhere! The surface on all sides was hard, and strewn with pebbles. A horse going in rude gallop, might have indented it; but not one passing over it at a tranquil pace.

And thus had the spotted mustang and blood bay parted from that spot. They had gone at a walk for some score yards, before starting on their final gallop towards the mustang trap.

The impatient pursuer was puzzled. He rode round and round, and along the trail of the wild mares, and back again, without discovering the direction that had been taken by either of the ridden horses.

He was beginning to feel something more than surprise, when the sight of a solitary horseman advancing along the trail interrupted his uncomfortable conjectures.

It was no stranger who was drawing near. The colossal figure, clad in coarse habiliments, bearded to the buttons of his blanket coat, and bestriding the most contemptible looking steed that could have been found within a hundred miles of the spot, was an old acquaintance. Cassius Calhoun knew Zebulon Stump, and Zeb Stump knew Cash Calhoun, long before either had set foot upon the prairies of

"You hain't seed nuthin' o' the young lady, hev ye, Mister Cal-houn?" inquired the hunter, as he rode up, with an unusual impressiveness of manner. "No, ye hain't," he continued, as if deduc-ing his inference from the blank looks of the other. "Dog-gone my cats! I wonder what the hell hev becomed o' her! Kewrious, too; sech a rider as she air, ter let the durned goat o' a thing run away wi' her. Wal! thur's not much danger to be reeprehended. The mowstanger air putty sartin to throw his rope aroun' the critter, an that 'll put an eend to its capers. Why hev ye stopped hyur?"

"I'm puzzled about the direction they've taken. Their tracks show they've been halted here; but I can see the shod hoofs no farther."

"Whoo! whoo! yur right, Mister Cashus! They hev been halted hyur; an been clost thegither too. They hain't gone no further on the trail o' the wild maars. Sartin they hain't. What then?"

The speaker scanned the surface of the plain with an interrogative glance; as if there, and not from Cassius Calhoun, expecting an answer to his question.

"I cannot see their tracks anywhere," replied the ex-captain.

"No, kan't ye? I kin though. Lookee hyur! Don't ye see them thur bruises on the grass?"

"No."

"Durn it! thur plain es the nose on a Jew's face. Thur's a big shoe, an a little un clost aside o' it. Thet's the way they've rud off, which show that they hain't follered the wild maars no further than hyur. We'd better keep on arter them?"

"By all means!"

Without further parley, Zeb started along the new trail; which, though still undiscernible to the eye of the other, was to him as con-spicuous as he had figuratively declared it.

In a little while it became visible to his companion—on their arri-val at the place where the fugitives had once more urged their horses into a gallop to escape from the cavallada, and where the shod tracks deeply indented the turf.

Shortly after their trail was again lost—or would have been to a scrutiny less keen than that of Zeb Stump—among the hundreds of other hoof-marks seen now upon the sward.

"Hilloo!" exclaimed the old hunter, in some surprise at the new sign. "What's been a doin' hyur? This air some 'at kewrious."

"Only the tracks of the wild mares!" suggested Calhoun. "They appear to have made a circuit, and come round again?"

"If they hev it's been arter the others rud past them. The chase must a changed sides, I reck'n."

"What do you mean, Mr Stump?"

"That i'stead o' them gallupin' arter the maars, the maars hev been gallupin' arter them."

"How can you tell that?"

"Don't ye see that the shod tracks air kivered by them o' the maars? Maars—no! By the 'turnal airthquake!—them's not maar-tracks. They air a inch bigger. Thur's been *studs* this way—a hul cavayurd o' them. Geehosofat! I hope they hain't—"

"Haven't what?"

"Gone arter Spotty. If they hev, then thur will be danger to Miss Peintdexter. Come on!"

Without waiting for a rejoinder, the hunter started off at a shambling trot, followed by Calhoun, who kept calling to him for an explanation of his ambiguous words.

Zeb did not deign to offer any—excusing himself by a backward sweep of the hand, which seemed to say, "Do not bother me now: I am busy."

For a time he appeared absorbed in taking up the trail of the shod horses—not so easily done, as it was in places entirely obliterated by the thick trampling of the stallions. He succeeded in making it out by piecemeal—still going on at a trot.

It was not till he had arrived within a hundred yards of the arroyo that the serious shadow disappeared from his face; and, checking the pace of his mare, he vouchsafed the explanation once more demanded from him.

"Oh! that was the danger," said Calhoun, on hearing the explanation. "How do you know they have escaped it?"

"Look thur!"

"A dead horse! Freshly killed, he appears? What does that prove?"

"That the mowstanger hes killed him."

"It frightened the others off, you think, and they followed no further?"

"They follered no further; but it wa'n't adzackly thet as scared 'em off. Thur's the thing as kep them from follerin'. Ole Hickory, what a jump!"

The speaker pointed to the arroyo, on the edge of which both rid-

"Leaped it clur as the crack o' a rifle. Don't ye see thur toe-marks, both on this side an the t'other? An' Miss Peintdexter fust, too! By the jumpin' Geehosofat, what a gurl she air sure enuf! They must both a jumped afore the stellyun war shot; else they kedn't a got at it. Thur's no other place whar a hoss ked go over. Geeroozalem! wa'n't it cunnin' o' the mowstanger to throw the stud in his tracks, jest in the very gap?"

"You think that he and my cousin crossed here together?"

"Not adzackly thegither," explained Zeb, without suspecting the motive of the interrogatory. "As I've sayed, Spotty went fust. You see the critter's tracks yonner on t'other side?"

"I do."

"Wal—don't ye see they air kivered wi' them o' the mowstanger's hoss?"

"True—true."

"As for the stellyuns, they hain't got over—ne'er a one o' the hul cavayurd. I kin see how it hez been. The young fellur pulled up on t'other side, an sent a bullet back inter this brute's karkidge. 'Twar jest like closin' the gap ahint him; an the pursooers, seein' it shet, guv up the chase, an scampered off in a different direckshun. Thur's the way they hev gone—up the side o' the gully!"

"They may have crossed at some other place, and continued the pursuit?"

"If they dud, they'd hev ten mile to go, afore they ked git back hyur—five up, an five back agin. Not a bit o' that, Mister Calhoun. To needn't be uneezy 'bout Miss Lewaze bein' pursooed by *them* any further. Arter the jump, she's rud off along wi' the mowstanger—both on 'em as quiet as a kupple o' lambs. Thur wa'n't no danger then; an by this time, they oughter be dog-goned well on torst rejoinin' the people as stayed by the purvision waggon."

"Come on!" cried Calhoun, exhibiting as much impatience as when he believed his cousin to be in serious peril. "Come on, Mr Stump! Let us get back as speedily as possible!"

"Not so fast, if you pleeze," rejoined Zeb, permitting himself to slide leisurely out of his saddle, and then drawing his knife from his sheath. "I'll only want ye to wait for a matter o' ten minutes, or there-about."

"Wait! For what?" peevishly inquired Calhoun.

"Till I kin strip the hide off o' this hyur sorrel. It appear to be a skin o' the fust qualerty; an oughter fetch a five-dollar bill in the settlements. Five-dollar bills ain't picked up every day on these hyur pu-rayras."

"Damn the skin!" angrily ejaculated the impatient Southerner. "Come on, an leave it!"

"Ain't a goin' to do anythin' o' the sort," coolly responded the hunter, as he drew the sharp edge of his blade along the belly of the prostrate steed. "You kin go on if ye like, Mister Calhoun; but Zeb Stump don't start till he packs the hide of this hyur stellyun on the krupper o' his old maar. Thet he don't."

"Come, Zeb; what's the use of talking about my going back by myself? You know I can't find my way?"

"That air like enough. I didn't say ye ked."

"Look here, you obstinate old case! Time's precious to me just at this minute. It 'll take you a full half-hour to skin the horse."

"Not twenty minutes."

"Well, say twenty minutes. Now, twenty minutes are of more importance to me than a five-dollar bill. You say that's the value of the skin? Leave it behind; and I agree to make good the amount."

"Wal—that air durned gin'rous, I admit—dog-goned gin'rous. But I mussent except yur offer. It 'ud be a mean trick o' me—mean enuf for a yeller-bellied Mexikin—to take yur money for sech a sarvice as thet: the more so es I ain't no stranger to ye, an myself a goin' the same road. On the t'other hand, I kan't afford to lose the five dollars' worth o' hoss-hide which ud be rotten as punk—to say nuthin' o' it's bein' tored into skreeds by the buzzarts and coyoats—afore I mout find a chance to kum this way agin."

"'Tis very provoking! What am I to do?"

"You *air* in a hurry? Wal—I'm sorry to discommerdate ye. But—stay! Thur's no reezun for yur waitin' on me. Thur's nuthin' to hinder ye from findin' yur way to the waggon. Ye see that tree stannin' up agin the sky-line—the tall poplar yonner?"

"I do."

"Wal; do you remember ever to hev seed it afore? It air a queery lookin' plant, appearin' more like a church steeple than a tree."

"Yes—yes!" said Calhoun. "Now you've pointed it out, I do remember it. We rode close past it while in pursuit of the wild mares?"

"You dud that very thing. An' now, as ye know it, what air to hinder you from ridin' past it agin; and follering the trail o' the maars back'ard? That ud bring ye to yur startin'-peint; where, ef I ain't out o' m          e'll find yur cousin, Miss Peintdexter, an the hul o' yur pa          themselves wi' that 'ere French stuff, they call sham-pain. I hope they'll stick to it, and spare the Monongaheela—of which licker I shed like to hev a triflin' suck arter I git back myself."

Calhoun had not waited for the wind-up of this characteristic speech. On the instant after recognising the tree, he had struck the spurs into the sides of his chestnut, and gone off at a gallop, leaving old Zeb at liberty to secure the coveted skin.

"Geeroozalem!" ejaculated the hunter, glancing up, and noticing the quick unceremonious departure. "It don't take much o' a head-piece to tell why he air in sech a durned hurry. I ain't myself much guv torst guessin'; but if I ain't doggonedly mistaken it air a clur case o' jellacy on the trail!"

Zeb Stump was not astray in his conjecture. It *was* jealousy that urged Cassius Calhoun to take that hasty departure—black jealousy, that had first assumed shape in a kindred spot—in the midst of a charred prairie; that had been every day growing stronger from cir-cumstances observed, and others imagined; that was now intensified so as to have become his prevailing passion.

The presentation and taming of the spotted mustang; the accep-tance of that gift, characteristic of the giver, and gratifying to the receiver, who had made no effort to conceal her gratification; these, and other circumstances, acting upon the already excited fancy of Cas-sius Calhoun, had conducted him to the belief: that in Maurice the mustanger he would find his most powerful rival.

The inferior social position of the horse-hunter should have hin-dered him from having such belief, or even a suspicion.

Perhaps it might have done so, had he been less intimately ac-quainted with the character of Louise Poindexter. But, knowing her as he did—associating with her from the hour of childhood—thoroughly understanding her independence of spirit—the *braverie* of her disposi-tion, bordering upon very recklessness—he could place no reliance on the mere idea of gentility. With most women this may be depended upon as a barrier, if not to *mésalliance*, at least to absolute impru-dence; but in the impure mind of Cassius Calhoun, while contemplating the probable conduct of his cousin, there was not even this feeble support to lean upon!

Chafing at the occurrences of the day—to him crookedly inauspi-cious—he hurried back towards the spot where the pic-nic had been held. The steeple-like tree guided him back to the trail of the manada; and beyond that there was no danger of straying. He had only to return along the path already trodden by him.

He rode at a rapid pace—faster than was relished by his now tired steed—stimulated by bitter thoughts, which for more than an hour were his sole companions—their bitterness more keenly felt in the tranquil solitude that surrounded him.

He was but little consoled by a sight that promised other companionship: that of two persons on horseback, riding in advance, and going in the same direction as himself, upon the same path. Though he saw but their backs—and at a long distance ahead—there was no mistaking the identity of either. They were the two individuals that had brought that bitterness upon his spirit.

Like himself they were returning upon the trail of the wild mares; which, when first seen, they had just struck, arriving upon it from a lateral path. Side by side—their saddles almost chafing against each other—to all appearance absorbed in a conversation of intense interest to both, they saw not the solitary horseman approaching them in a diagonal direction.

Apparently less anxious than he to rejoin the party of picknickers, they were advancing at a slow pace—the lady a little inclining to the rear.

Their proximity to one another—their attitudes in the saddle—their obvious inattention to outward objects—the snail-like pace at which they were proceeding—these, along with one or two other slighter circumstances observed by Calhoun, combined to make an impression on his mind—or rather to strengthen one already made—that almost drove him mad.

To gallop rapidly up, and rudely terminate the *tête-à-tête*, was but the natural instinct of the *chivalric* Southerner. In obedience to it he spitefully plied the spur; and once more forced his jaded chestnut into an unwilling canter.

In a few seconds, however, he slackened pace—as if changing his determination. The sound of his horse's hoofs had not yet warned the others of his proximity—though he was now less than two hundred yards behind them! He could hear the silvery tones of his cousin's voice bearing the better part of the conversation. How interesting it must be to both to have hindered them from perceiving his approach!

If he could but overhear what they were saying?

It seemed a most unpropitious place for playing eavesdropper; and yet there might be a chance?

The seeming interest of the dialogue to the individuals engaged in it gave promise of such opportunity. The turf of the savannah was soft

125

as velvet. The hoof gliding slowly over it gave forth not the slightest sound.

Calhoun was still too impatient to confine himself to a walk; but his chestnut was accustomed to that gait, peculiar to the horse of the South-Western States—the "pace"; and into this was he pressed.

With hoofs horizontally striking the sward—elevated scarce an inch above the ground—he advanced swiftly and noiselessly; so quick withal, that in a few seconds he was close upon the heels of the spotted mustang, and the red steed of the mustanger!

He was then checked to a pace corresponding to theirs; while his rider, leaning forward, listened with an eagerness that evinced some terrible determination. His attitude proclaimed him in the vein for vituperation of the rudest kind—ready with ribald tongue; or, if need be, with knife and pistol!

His behaviour depended on a contingency—on what might be overheard.

As chance, or fate, willed it, there was nothing. If the *two* equestrians were insensible to external sounds, their steeds were not so absorbed. In a walk the chestnut stepped heavily—the more so from being fatigued. His footfall proclaimed his proximity to the sharp ears, both of the blood-bay and spotted mustang; that simultaneously flung up their heads, neighing as they did so.

Calhoun was discovered.

"Ha! cousin Cash!" cried the lady, betraying more of pique than surprise; "you there? Where's father, and Harry, and the rest of the people?"

"Why do you ask that, Loo? I reckon you know as well as I."

"What! haven't you come out to meet us? And they too—ah! your chestnut is all in a sweat! He looks as if you had been riding a long race—like ourselves?"

"Of coarse he has. I followed you from the first—in hopes of being of some service to you."

"Indeed! I did not know that you were after us. Thank you, cousin! I've just been saying thanks to this gallant gentleman, who also came after, and has been good enough to rescue both Luna and myself from a very unpleasant dilemma—a dreadful danger I should rather call it. Do you know that we've been chased by a drove of wild steeds, and had actually to ride for our lives?"

"I am aware of it."

"You saw the chase then?"

"No. I only knew it by the tracks."

"The tracks! And were you able to tell by that?"

"Yes—thanks to the interpretation of Zeb Stump."

"Oh! he was with you? But did you follow them to—to—how far did you follow them?"

"To a crevasse in the prairie. You leaped over it, Zeb said. Did you?"

"Luna did."

"With you on her back?"

"I *wasn't anywhere else*! What a question, cousin Cash! Where would you expect me to have been? Clinging to her tail? Ha! ha! ha!"

"Did *you* leap it?" inquired the laugher, suddenly changing tone. "Did you follow us any farther?"

"No, Loo. From the crevasse I came direct here, thinking you had got back before me. That's how I've chanced to come up with you."

The answer appeared to give satisfaction.

"Ah! I'm glad you've overtaken us. We've been riding slowly. Luna is so tired. Poor thing! I don't know how I shall ever get her back to the Leona."

Since the moment of being joined by Calhoun, the mustanger had not spoken a word. However pleasant may have been his previous intercourse with the young Creole, he had relinquished it, without any apparent reluctance; and was now riding silently in the advance, as if by tacit understanding he had returned to the performance of the part for which he had been originally engaged.

For all that, the eye of the ex-captain was bent blightingly upon him—at times in a demoniac glare—when he saw—or fancied—that another eye was turned admiringly in the same direction.

A long journey performed by that trio of travellers might have led to a tragical termination. Such finale was prevented by the appearance of the picknickers; who soon after surrounding the returned runaway, put to flight every other thought by the chorus of their congratulations.

# 19. Whisky and Water

In the embryo city springing up under the protection of Fort Inge, the "hotel" was the most conspicuous building. This is but the normal condition of every Texan town—whether new or founded forty years ago; and none are older, except the sparse cities of Hispano-Mexican origin—where the *presidio* and convent took precedence, now surpassed by, and in some instances transformed into, the "tavern."

The Fort Inge establishment, though the largest building in the place, was, nevertheless, neither very grand nor imposing. Its exterior had but little pretence to architectural style. It was a structure of hewn logs, having for ground-plan the letter T according to the grotesque alphabet—the shank being used for eating and sleeping rooms, while the head was a single apartment entirely devoted to drinking—smoking and *expectorating* included. This last was the bar-room, or "saloon."

The sign outside, swinging from the trunk of a post-oak, that had been *pollarded* some ten feet above the ground, exhibited on both sides the likeness of a well known military celebrity—the hero of that quarter of the globe—General Zachariah Taylor. It did not need looking at the lettering beneath to ascertain the name of the hotel. Under the patronage of such a portrait it could only be called "Rough and Ready."

There was a touch of the apropos about this designation. Outside things appeared rough enough; while inside, especially if you entered by the "saloon," there was a readiness to meet you half way, with a mint julep, a sherry cobbler, a gin sling, or any other *mixed* drink known to trans-Mississippian tipplers—provided always that you were ready with the *picayunes* to pay for them.

The saloon in question would not call for description, had you ever travelled in the Southern, or South-Western, States of America. If so, no Lethean draught could ever efface from your memory the "bar-room" of the hotel or *tavern* in which you have had the unhappiness to sojourn. The counter extending longitudinally by the side; the shelved wall behind, with its rows of decanters and bottles, containing liquors, of not only all the colours of the prism, but every possible combination of them; the elegant young fellow, standing or sidling between counter and shelves, ycleped "clerk"—don't call him a "barkeeper," or you may get a decanter in your teeth—this elegant young gentleman, in blouse of blue *cottonade*, or white linen coat, or maybe in his shirt sleeves—the latter of finest linen and lace—ruffled, in the year of our Lord eighteen hundred and fifty—this elegant young gentleman, who, in mixing you a sherry cobbler, can look you straight in the face, talk to you the politics of the day, while the ice, and the wine, and the water, are passing from glass to glass, like an iris sparkling behind his shoulders, or an aureole surrounding his perfumed head! Traveller through the Southern States of America you; cannot fail to remember him?

If so, my words will recall him, along with his surroundings—the saloon in which he is the presiding administrator, with its shelves and coloured decanters; its counter; its floor sprinkled with white sand, at times littered with cigar stumps, and the brown asterisks produced by *expectoration*—its odour of mint, absinthe, and lemon-peel, in which luxuriate the common black fly, the blue-bottle, and the sharp-tongued mosquito. All these must be sharply outlined on the retina of your memory.

The hotel, or tavern, "Rough and Ready," though differing but little from other Texan houses of entertainment, had some points in particular. Its proprietor, instead of being a speculative Yankee, was a German—in this part of the world, as elsewhere, found to be the best purveyors of food. He kept his own bar; so that on entering the saloon, instead of the elegant young gentleman with ruffled shirt and odorous chevelure, your "liquor" was mixed for you by a staid Teuton, who looked as sober as if he never tasted—notwithstanding the temptation of wholesale price—the delicious drinks served out to his customers. Oberdoffer was the name he had imported with him from his fatherland; transformed by his Texan customers into "Old Duffer."

There was one other peculiarity about the bar-room of the "Rough and Ready," though it scarce deserved to be so designated; since it was not uncommon elsewhere. As already stated, the building was shaped like a capital T; the saloon representing the head of the letter. The counter extended along one side, that contiguous to the shank; while at each end was a door that opened outward into the public square of the incipient city.

This arrangement had been designed to promote the circulation of the air—a matter of primary importance in an atmosphere where the thermometer for half the year stands at 90 degrees in the shade.

The hotels of Texas or the South-Western States—I may say every part of the American Union—serve the double purpose of exchange and club-house. Indeed, it is owing to the cheap accommodation thus afforded—often of the most convenient kind—that the latter can scarce be said to exist.

Even in the larger cities of the Atlantic states the "club" is by no means a necessity. The moderate charges of the hotels, along with their excellent *cuisine* and elegant accommodations, circumscribe the prosperity of this institution; which in America is, and ever must be, an unhealthy exotic.

The remark is still more true of the Southern and South-western cities; where the "saloon" and "bar-room" are the chief places of resort and rendezvous.

The company, too, is there of a more miscellaneous character. The proud planter does not disdain—for he does not dare—to drink in the same room with the "poor white trash;" often as proud as himself.

There is no *peasant* in that part of the world—least of all in the state called Texas; and in the saloon of "Rough and Ready" might often be seen assembled representatives of every class and calling to be met with among the settlements.

Perhaps not upon any occasion since "Old Duffer" had hung out the sign of his tavern, was he favoured with a larger company, or served more customers across his counter, than upon that night, after the return of the horse-hunting party to Fort Inge.

With the exception of the ladies, almost every one who had taken part in the expedition seemed to think that a half-hour spent at the "Rough and Ready" was necessary as a "nightcap" before retiring to rest; and as the Dutch clock, quaintly ticking among the coloured decanters, indicated the hour of eleven, one after another—officers of the Fort—planters living near along the river—Sutlers—commissariat contractors—"sportsmen"—and others who might be called nondescripts—came dropping in; each as he entered marching straight up to the counter, calling for his favourite drink, and then falling back to converse with some group already occupying the floor.

One of these groups was conspicuous. It consisted of some eight or ten individuals, half of them in uniform. Among the latter were the three officers already introduced; the captain of infantry, and the two lieutenants—Hancock of the dragoons, and Crossman of the mounted rifles.

Along with these was an officer older than any of them, also higher in authority, as could be told by the embroidery on his shoulder-strap, that proclaimed him of the rank of major. As he was the only "field officer" at Fort Inge, it is unnecessary to say he was the commandant of the cantonment.

These gentlemen were conversing as freely as if all were subalterns of equal rank—the subject of the discourse being the incidents of the day.

"Now tell us, major!" said Hancock: "you must know. Where did the girl gallop to?"

"How should I know?" answered the officer appealed to. "Ask her cousin, Mr Cassius Calhoun."

"We have asked him, but without getting any satisfaction. It's clear he knows no more than we. He only met them on the return—and not very far from the place where we had our bivouac. They were gone a precious long time; and judging by the sweat of their horses they must have had a hard ride of it. They might have been to the Rio Grande, for that matter, and beyond it."

"Did you notice Calhoun as he came back?" inquired the captain of infantry. "There was a scowl upon his face that betokened some very unpleasant emotion within his mind, I should say."

"He did look rather unhappy," replied the major; "but surely, Captain Sloman, you don't attribute it to—?"

"Jealousy. I do, and nothing else."

"What! of Maurice the mustanger? Poh—poh! impossible—at least, very improbable."

"And why, major?"

"My dear Sloman, Louise Poindexter is a lady, and Maurice Gerald—"

"May be a gentleman for aught that is known to the contrary."

"Pshaw!" scornfully exclaimed Crossman; "a trader in horses! The major is right—the thing's improbable—impossible."

"Ah, gentlemen!" pursued the officer of infantry, with a significant shake of the head. "You don't know Miss Poindexter, so well as I. An eccentric young lady—to say the least of her. You may have already observed that for yourselves."

"Come, come, Sloman!" said the major, in a bantering way; "you are inclined to be talking scandal, I fear. That would be a scandal. Perhaps you are yourself interested in Miss Poindexter, notwithstanding your pretensions to be considered a Joseph? Now, I could understand your being jealous if it were handsome Hancock here, or Crossman—supposing him to be disengaged. But as for a common mustanger—poh—poh!"

"He's an Irishman, major, this mustanger; and if he be what I have some reason to suspect—"

"Whatever he be," interrupted the major, casting a side glance towards the door, "he's there to answer for himself; and as he's a sufficiently plain-spoken fellow, you may learn from him all about the matter that seems to be of so much interest to you."

"I don't think you will," muttered Sloman, as Hancock and two or three others turned towards the new-comer, with the design of carrying out the major's suggestion.

Silently advancing across the sanded floor, the mustanger had taken his stand at an unoccupied space in front of the counter.

"A glass of whisky and water, if you please?" was the modest request with which to saluted the landlord.

"Visky und vachter!" echoed the latter, without any show of eagerness to wait upon his new guest. "Ya, woe, visky und vachter! It ish two picayunsh the glass."

"I was not inquiring the price," replied the mustanger, "I asked to be served with a glass of whisky and water. Have you got any?"

"Yesh—yesh," responded the German, rendered obsequious by the sharp rejoinder. "Plenty—plenty of visky und vachter. Here it ish."

While his simple potation was being served out to him, Maurice received nods of recognition from the officers, returning them with a free, but modest air. Most of them knew him personally, on account of his business relations with the Fort.

They were on the eve of interrogating him—as the major had suggested—when the entrance of still another individual caused them to suspend their design.

The new-comer was Cassius Calhoun. In his presence it would scarce have been delicacy to investigate the subject any further.

Advancing with his customary swagger towards the mixed group of military men and civilians, Calhoun saluted them as one who had spent the day in their company, and had been absent only for a short interval. If not absolutely intoxicated, it could be seen that the ex-officer of volunteers was under the influence of drink. The unsteady sparkle of his eyes, the unnatural pallor upon his forehead—still further clouded by two or three tossed tresses that fell over it—with the somewhat grotesque set of his forage cap—told that he had been taking one beyond the limits of wisdom.

"Come, gentlemen!" cried he, addressing himself to the major's party, at the same time stepping up to the counter; "let's hit the waggon a crack, or old Dunder-und-blitzen behind the bar will say we're wasting his lights. Drinks all round. What say you?"

"Agreed—agreed!" replied several voices.

"You, major?"

"With pleasure, Captain Calhoun."

According to universal custom, the intended imbibers fell into line along the counter, each calling out the name of the drink most to his liking at the moment.

Of these were ordered almost as many kinds as there were individuals in the party; Calhoun himself shouting out—"Brown sherry for me;" and immediately adding—"with a dash of bitters."

"Prandy und pitters, you calls for, Mishter Calhoun?" said the landlord, as he leant obsequiously across the counter towards the reputed partner of an extensive estate.

"Certainly, you stupid Dutchman! I said brown sherry, didn't I?"

"All rights, mein herr; all rights! Prandy und pitters—prandy und pitters," repeated the German Boniface, as he hastened to place the decanter before his ill-mannered guest.

With the large accession of the major's party, to several others already in the act of imbibing, the whole front of the long counter became occupied—with scarce an inch to spare.

Apparently by accident—though it may have been design on the part of Calhoun—he was the outermost man on the extreme right of those who had responded to his invitation.

This brought him in juxtaposition with Maurice Gerald, who alone—as regarded boon companionship—was quietly drinking his whisky and water, and smoking a cigar he had just lighted.

The two were back to back—neither having taken any notice of the other.

"A toast!" cried Calhoun, taking his glass from the counter.

"Let us have it!" responded several voices.

"America for the Americans, and confusion to all foreign interlopers—especially the damned Irish!"

On delivering the obnoxious sentiment, he staggered back a pace; which brought his body in contact with that of the mustanger—at the moment standing with the glass raised to his lips.

133

The collision caused the spilling of a portion of the whisky and water; which fell over the mustanger's breast.

Was it an accident? No one believed it was—even for a moment. Accompanied by such a sentiment the act could only have been an affront intended and premeditated.

All present expected to see the insulted man spring instantly upon his insulter. They were disappointed, as well as surprised, at the manner in which the mustanger seemed to take it. There were some who even fancied he was about to submit to it.

"If he does," whispered Hancock in Sloman's ear, "he ought to be kicked out of the room."

"Don't you be alarmed about that," responded the infantry officer, in the same *sotto voce*. "You'll find it different. I'm not given to betting, as you know; but I'd lay a month's pay upon it the mustanger don't back out; and another, that Mr Cassius Calhoun will find him an ugly customer to deal with, although just now he seems more concerned about his fine shirt, than the insult put upon him. Odd devil he is!"

While this whispering was being carried on, the man to whom it related was still standing by the bar—to use a hackneyed phrase, "the observed of all observers."

Having deposited his glass upon the counter, he had drawn a silk handkerchief from his pocket, and was wiping from his embroidered shirt bosom the defilement of the spilt whisky.

There was an imperturbable coolness about the action, scarce compatible with the idea of cowardice; and those who had doubted him perceived that they had made a mistake, and that there was something to come. In silence they awaited the development.

They had not long to wait. The whole affair—speculations and whisperings included—did not occupy twenty seconds of time; and then did the action proceed, or the speech which was likely to usher it in.

"*I* am an Irishman," said the mustanger, as he returned his handkerchief to the place from which he had taken it.

Simple as the rejoinder may have appeared, and long delayed as it had been, there was no one present who mistook its meaning. If the hunter of wild horses had tweaked the nose of Cassius Calhoun, it would not have added emphasis to that acceptance of his challenge. Its simplicity but proclaimed the serious determination of the acceptor.

"You?" scornfully retorted Calhoun, turning round, and standing with his arms *akimbo*. "You?" he continued, with his eye measuring the mustanger from head to foot, "you an Irishman? Great God, sir, I should never have thought so! I should have taken you for a Mexican, judging by your rig, and the elaborate stitching of your shirt."

"I can't perceive how my rig should concern you, Mr Cassius Calhoun; and as you've done my shirt no service by spilling half my liquor upon it, I shall take the liberty of unstarching yours in a similar fashion."

So saying, the mustanger took up his glass; and, before the ex-captain of volunteers could duck his head, or get out of the way, the remains of the mixed Monongahela were "swilled" into his face, sending him off into a fit of alternate sneezing and coughing that appeared to afford satisfaction to more than a majority of the bystanders.

The murmur of approbation was soon suppressed. The circumstances were not such as to call for speech; and the exclamations that accompanied the act were succeeded by a hush of silence. All saw that the quarrel could not be otherwise than a serious one. The affair must end in a fight. No power on earth could prevent it from coming to that conclusion.

# 20. An Unsafe Position

On receiving the alcoholic douche, Calhoun had clutched his six-shooter, and drawn it from its holster. He only waited to get the whisky out of his eyes before advancing upon his adversary.

The mustanger, anticipating this action, had armed himself with a similar weapon, and stood ready to return the fire of his antagonist—shot for shot.

The more timid of the spectators had already commenced making their escape out of doors tumbling over one another, in their haste to get out of harm's way.

A few stayed in the saloon from sheer irresolution; a few others, of cooler courage, from choice; or, perhaps, actuated by a more astute instinct, which told them that in attempting to escape they might get a bullet in the back.

There was an interval—some six seconds—of silence, during which a pin might have been heard falling upon the floor. It was but the interlude that often occurs between resolution and action; when the mind has completed its task, and the body has yet to begin.

It might have been more brief with other actors on the scene. Two ordinary men would have blazed away at once, and without reflection. But the two now confronting each other were not of the common kind. Both had seen *street fighting* before—had taken part in it—and knew the disadvantage of an idle shot. Each was determined to take sure aim on the other. It was this that prolonged the interval of inaction.

To those outside, who dared not even look through the doors, the suspense was almost painful. The cracking of the pistols, which they expected every moment to hear, would have been a relief. It was almost a disappointment when, instead, they heard the voice of the major—who was among the few who had stayed inside—raised in a loud authoritative tone.

"Hold!" commanded he, in the accent of one accustomed to be obeyed, at the same time whisking his sabre out of its scabbard, and interposing its long blade between the disputants.

"Hold your fire—I command you both. Drop your muzzles; or by the Almighty I'll take the arm off the first of you that touches trigger! Hold, I say!"

"Why?" shouted Calhoun, purple with angry passion. "Why, Major Ringwood? After an insult like that, and from a low fellow—"

"You were the first to offer it, Captain Calhoun."

"Damn me if I care! I shall be the last to let it pass unpunished. Stand out of the way, major. The quarrel is not yours—you have no right to interfere!"

"Indeed! Ha! ha! Sloman! Hancock! Crossman! hear that? I have no right to interfere! Hark ye, Mr Cassius Calhoun, ex-captain of volunteers! Know you where you are, sir? Don't fancy yourself in the state of Mississippi—among your slave-whipping chivalry. This, sir, is a military post—under military law—my humble self its present administrator. I therefore command you to return your six-shooter to the holster from which you have taken it. This instant too, or you shall go to the guard-house, like the humblest soldier in the cantonment!"

"Indeed!" sneeringly replied the Mississippian. "What a fine country you intend Texas to become! I suppose a man mustn't fight, however much aggrieved, without first obtaining a licence from Major Ringwood? Is that to be the law of the land?"

"Not a bit of it," retorted the major. "I'm not the man—never was—to stand in the way of the honest adjustment of a quarrel. You shall be quite at liberty—you and your antagonist—to kill one another, if it so please you. But not just now. You must perceive, Mr Calhoun, that your sport endangers the lives of other people, who have not the slightest interest in it. I've no idea of being bored by a bullet not intended for me. Wait till the rest of us can withdraw to a safe distance; and you may crack away to your heart's content. Now, sir, will that be agreeable to you?"

Had the major been a man of ordinary character his commands might have been disregarded. But to his official weight, as chief officer of the post, was added a certain reverence due to seniority in age—along with respect for one who was himself known to wield a weapon with dangerous skill, and who allowed no trilling with his authority.

His sabre had not been unsheathed by way of empty gesticulation. The disputants knew it; and by simultaneous consent lowered the muzzles of their pistols—still holding them in hand.

Calhoun stood, with sullen brow, gritting his teeth, like a beast of prey momentarily withheld from making attack upon its victim; while the mustanger appeared to take things as coolly as if neither angry, nor an Irishman.

"I suppose you are determined upon fighting?" said the major, knowing that, there was not much chance of adjusting the quarrel.

"I have no particular wish for it," modestly responded Maurice. "If Mr Calhoun will apologise for what he has said, and also what he has done—"

"He ought to do it: he began the quarrel!" suggested several of the bystanders.

"Never!" scornfully responded the ex-captain. "Cash Calhoun ain't accustomed to that sort of thing. Apologise indeed! And to a masquerading monkey like that!"

"Enough!" cried the young Irishman, for the first time showing serious anger; "I gave him a chance for his life. He refuses to accept it: and now, by the Mother of God, we don't both leave this room alive! Major! I insist that you and your friends withdraw. I can stand his insolence no longer!"

"Ha—ha—ha!" responded the Southerner, with a yell of derisive laughter; "a chance for my life! Clear out, all of ye—clear out; and let me at him!"

"Stay!" cried the major, hesitating to turn his back upon the duellist. "It's not quite safe. You may fancy to begin your game of touch-trigger a second too soon. We must get out of doors before you do. Besides, gentlemen!" he continued, addressing himself to those around him, "there should be some system about this. If they are to fight, let it be fair for both sides. Let them be armed alike; and go at it on the square!"

"By all means!" chorused the half-score of spectators, turning their eyes towards the disputants, to see if they accepted the proposal.

"Neither of you can object?" continued the major, interrogatively.

"I sha'n't object to anything that's fair," assented the Irishman—"devil a bit!"

"I shall fight with the weapon I hold in my hand," doggedly declared Calhoun.

"Agreed! the very weapon for me!" was the rejoinder of his adversary.

"I see you both carry Colt's six-shooter Number 2," said the major, scanning the pistols held in hand. "So far all right! you're armed exactly alike."

138

"Have they any other weapons?" inquired young Hancock, suspecting that under the cover of his coat the ex-captain had a knife.

"I have none," answered the mustanger, with a frankness that left no doubt as to his speaking the truth.

All eyes were turned upon Calhoun, who appeared to hesitate about making a reply. He saw he must declare himself.

"Of course," he said, "I have my toothpick as well. You don't want me to give up that? A man ought to be allowed to use whatever weapon he has got."

"But, Captain Calhoun," pursued Hancock, "your adversary has no knife. If you are not afraid to meet him on equal terms you should surrender yours."

"Certainly he should!" cried several of the bystanders. "He must! he must!"

"Come, Mr Calhoun!" said the major, in a soothing tone. "Six shots ought to satisfy any reasonable man; without having recourse to the steel. Before you finish firing, one or the other of you—"

"Damn the knife!" interrupted Calhoun, unbuttoning his coat. Then drawing forth the proscribed weapon, and flinging it to the farthest corner of the saloon, he added, in a tone of bravado, intended to encowardice his adversary. "I sha'n't want it for such a spangled jaybird as that. I'll fetch him out of his boots at the first shot."

"Time enough to talk when you've done something to justify it. Cry boo to a goose; but don't fancy your big words are going to frighten me, Mr Calhoun! Quick, gentlemen! I'm impatient to put an end to his boasting and blasphemy!"

"Hound!" frantically hissed out the chivalric Southerner. "Low dog of an Irish dam! I'll send you howling to your kennel! I'll—"

"Shame, Captain Calhoun!" interrupted the major, seconded by other voices. "This talk is idle, as it is unpolite in the presence of respectable company. Have patience a minute longer; and you may then say what you like. Now, gentlemen!" he continued, addressing himself to the surrounding, "there is only one more preliminary to be arranged. They must engage not to begin firing till we have got out of their way?"

A difficulty here presented itself. How was the engagement to be given? A simple promise would scarce be sufficient in a crisis like that? The combatants—one of them at least—would not be over scrupulous as to the time of pulling trigger.

"There must be a signal," pursued the major. "Neither should fire till that be given. Can any one suggest what it is to be?"

"I think. I can," said the quiet Captain Sloman, advancing as he spoke. "Let the gentlemen go outside, along with us. There is—as you perceive—a door at each end of the room. I see no difference between them. Let them enter again—one at each door, with the understanding that neither is to fire before setting foot across the threshold."

"Capital! the very thing!" replied several voices. "And what for a signal?" demanded the major. "A shot?"

"No. Ring the tavern bell!"

"Nothing could be better—nothing fairer," conclusively declared the major, making for one of the doors, that led outward into the square.

"Mein Gott, major!" screamed the German Boniface, rushing out from behind his bar; where, up to this time, he had been standing transfixed with fear. "Mein Gott—surely the shentlemens pe not going to shoot their pisthols inside the shaloon: Ach! they'll preak all my pottles, and my shplendid looking-glashes, an my crystal clock, that hash cost me von—two hundred dollars. They'll shpill my pesht liquors—ach! Major, it'll ruin me—mein Gott—it will!"

"Never fear, Oberdoffer!" rejoined the major, pausing to reply. "No doubt you'll be paid for the damage. At all events, you had better betake yourself to some place of safety. If you stay in your saloon you'll stand a good chance of getting a bullet through your body, and that would be worse than the preaking of your pottles."

Without further parley the major parted from the unfortunate landlord, and hurried across the threshold into the street, whither the combatants, who had gone out by separate doors, had already preceded him.

"Old Duffer," left standing in the middle of his sanded floor, did not remain long in that perilous position. In six seconds after the major's coat-tail had disappeared through the outer door, an inner one closed upon his own skirts; and the bar-room, with its camphine lamps, its sparkling decanters, and its costly mirrors, was left in untenanted silence—no other sound being heard save the ticking of its crystal clock.

# 21. A Duel within Doors

Once outside, the major took no further part in the affair. As the commanding officer of the post, it would have been out of place for him to have given encouragement to a fight—even by his interfering to see that it should be a fair one. This, however, was attended to by the younger officers; who at once set about arranging the conditions of the duel.

There was not much time consumed. The terms had been expressed already; and it only remained to appoint some one of the party to superintend the ringing of the bell, which was to be the signal for the combat to commence.

This was an easy matter, since it made no difference who might be entrusted with the duty. A child might have sounded the summons for the terrible conflict that was to follow.

A stranger, chancing at that moment to ride into the rude square of which the hotel "Rough and Ready" formed nearly a side, would have been sorely puzzled to comprehend what was coming to pass. The night was rather dark, though there was still light enough to make known the presence of a conglomeration of human beings, assembled in the proximity of the hotel. Most were in military garb: since, in addition to the officers who had lately figured inside the saloon, others, along with such soldiers as were permitted to pass the sentries, had hastened down from the Fort on receiving intelligence that something unusual was going on within the "square." Women, too, but scantily robed—soldiers' wives, washerwomen, and "señoritas" of more questionable calling—had found their way into the street, and were endeavouring to extract from those who had forestalled them an explanation of the *fracas*.

The conversation was carried on in low tones. It was known that the commandant of the post was present, as well as others in authority;

and this checked any propensity there might have been for noisy demonstration.

The crowd, thus promiscuously collected, was not in close proximity with the hotel; but standing well out in the open ground, about a dozen yards from the building. Towards it, however, the eyes of all were directed, with that steady stare which tells of the attention being fixed on some engrossing spectacle. They were watching the movements of two men, whose positions were apart—one at each end of the heavy blockhouse, known to be the bar-room of the hotel; and where, as already stated, there was a door.

Though separated by the interposition of two thick log walls, and mutually invisible, these men were manoeuvring as if actuated by a common impulse. They stood contiguous to the entrance doors, at opposite ends of the bar-room, through both of which glared the light of the camphine lamps—falling in broad divergent bands upon the rough gravel outside. Neither was in front of the contiguous entrance; but a little to one side, just clear of the light. Neither was in an upright attitude, but crouching—not as if from fear, but like a runner about to make a start, and straining upon the spring.

Both were looking inwards—into the saloon, where no sound could be heard save the ticking of a clock. Their attitudes told of their readiness to enter it, and that they were only restrained by waiting for some preconcerted signal.

That their purpose was a serious one could be deduced from several circumstances. Both were in their shirt sleeves, hatless, and stripped of every rag that might form an impediment to action; while on their faces was the stamp of stern determination—alike legible in the attitudes they had assumed.

But there was no fine reflection needed to discover their design. The stranger, chancing to come into the square, could have seen at a glance that it was deadly. The pistols in their hands, cocked and tightly clutched; the nervous energy of their attitudes; the silence of the crowd of spectators; and the concentrated interest with which the two men were regarded, proclaimed more emphatically than words, that there was danger in what they were doing—in short, that they were engaged in some sort of a strife, with death for its probable consummation!

So it was at that moment when the crisis had come. The duellists stood, each with eye intent upon the door, by which he was to make entrance—perhaps into eternity! They only waited for a signal to cross the threshold; and engage in a combat that must terminate the existence of one or the other—perhaps both.

Were they listening for that fatal formulary:—One—two—fire?

No. Another signal had been agreed upon; and it was given.

A stentorian voice was heard calling out the simple monosyllable—

"Ring!"

Three or four dark figures could be seen standing by the shorn trunk on which swung the tavern bell. The command instantly set them in motion; and, along with the oscillation of their arms—dimly seen through the darkness—could be heard the sonorous tones of a bell. That bell, whose sounds had been hitherto heard only as symbols of joy—calling men together to partake of that which perpetuates life—was now listened to as a summons of death!

The "ringing in" was of short duration. The bell had made less than a score of vibrations, when the men engaged at the rope saw that their services were no longer required. The disappearance of the duellists, who had rushed inside the saloon, the quick, sharp cracking of pistols; the shivering of broken glass, admonished the ringers that theirs was but a superfluous noise; and, dropping the rope, they stood like the rest of the crowd, listening to the conflict inside.

No eyes—save those of the combatants themselves—were witnesses to that strange duel.

At the first dong of the bell both combatants had re-entered the room. Neither made an attempt to skulk outside. To have done so would have been a ruin to reputation. A hundred eyes were upon them; and the spectators understood the conditions of the duel—that neither was to fire before crossing the threshold.

Once inside, the conflict commenced, the first shots filling the room with smoke. Both kept their feet, though both were wounded—their blood spurting out over the sanded floor.

The second shots were also fired simultaneously, but at random, the smoke hindering the aim.

Then came a single shot, quickly followed by another, and succeeded by an interval of quiet.

Previous to this the combatants had been heard rushing about through the room. This noise was no longer being made.

Instead there was profound silence. Had they killed one another? Were both dead? No! Once more the double detonation announced that both still lived. The suspension had been caused as they stood peering through the smoke in the endeavour to distinguish one another. Neither spoke or stirred in fear of betraying his position.

Again there was a period of tranquillity similar to the former, but more prolonged.

It ended by another exchange of shots, almost instantly succeeded by the falling of two heavy bodies upon the floor.

There was the sound of sprawling—the overturning of chairs—then a single shot—the eleventh—and this was the last that was fired!

The spectators outside saw only a cloud of sulphurous smoke oozing out of both doors, and dimming the light of the camphine lamps. This, with an occasional flash of brighter effulgence, close followed by a crack, was all that occurred to give satisfaction to the eye.

But the ear—that was gratified by a greater variety. There were heard shots—after the bell had become silent, other sounds: the sharp shivering of broken glass, the duller crash of falling furniture, rudely overturned in earnest struggle—the trampling of feet upon the boarded floor—at intervals the clear ringing crack of the revolvers; but neither of the voices of the men whose insensate passions were the cause of all this commotion! The crowd in the street heard the confused noises, and noted the intervals of silence, without being exactly able to interpret them. The reports of the pistols were all they had to proclaim the progress of the duel. Eleven had been counted; and in breathless silence they were listening for the twelfth.

Instead of a pistol report their ears were gratified by the sound of a voice, recognised as that of the mustanger.

"My pistol is at your head! I have one shot left—an apology, or you die!"

By this the crowd had become convinced that the fight was approaching its termination. Some of the more fearless, looking in, beheld a strange scene. They saw two men lying prostrate on the plank floor; both with bloodstained habiliments, both evidently disabled; the white sand around them reddened with their gore, tracked with tortuous trails, where they had crawled closer to get a last shot at each other—one of them, in scarlet scarf and slashed velvet trousers, slightly surmounting the other, and holding a pistol to his head that threatened to deprive him of life.

Such was the tableau that presented itself to the spectators, as the sulphurous smoke, drifted out by the current between the two doors, gave them a chance of distinguishing objects within the saloon.

At the same instant was heard a different voice from the one which had already spoken. It was Calhoun's—no longer in roistering bravado, but in low whining accents, almost a whisper. "Enough, damn it! Drop your shooting-iron—I apologise."

# 22. An Unknown Donor

In Texas a duel is not even a nine days' wonder. It oftener ceases to be talked about by the end of the third day; and, at the expiration of a week, is no longer thought of, except by the principals themselves, or their immediate friends and relatives.

This is so, even when the parties are well known, and of respectable standing in society. When the duellists are of humble position—or, as is often the case, strangers in the place—a single day may suffice to doom their achievement to oblivion; to dwell only in the memory of the combatant who has survived it—oftener one than both—and perhaps some ill-starred spectator, who has been bored by a bullet, or received the slash of a knife, not designed for him.

More than once have I been witness to a "street fight"—improvised upon the pavement—where some innocuous citizen, sauntering carelessly along, has become the victim—even unto death—of this irregular method of seeking "satisfaction."

I have never heard of any punishment awarded, or damages demanded, in such cases. They are regarded as belonging to the "chapter of accidents!"

Though Cassius Calhoun and Maurice Gerald were both comparatively strangers in the settlement—the latter being only seen on occasional visits to the Fort—the affair between them caused something more than the usual interest; and was talked about for the full period of the nine days, the character of the former as a noted bully, and that of the latter as a man of singular habitudes, gave to their duello a certain sort of distinction; and the merits and demerits of the two men were freely discussed for days after the affair had taken place nowhere with more earnestness than upon the spot where they had shed each other's blood—in the bar-room of the hotel.

The conqueror had gained credit and friends. There were few who favoured his adversary; and not a few who were gratified at the result for, short as had been the time since Calhoun's arrival, there was more than one saloon lounger who had felt the smart of his insolence. For this it was presumed the young Irishman had administered a cure; and there was almost universal satisfaction at the result.

How the ex-captain carried his discomfiture no one could tell. He was no longer to be seen swaggering in the saloon of the "Rough and Ready;" though the cause of his absence was well understood. It was not chagrin, but his couch; to which he was confined by wounds, that, if not skilfully treated, might consign him to his coffin.

Maurice was in like manner compelled to stay within doors. The injuries he had received, though not so severe as those of his antagonist, were nevertheless of such a character as to make it necessary for him to keep to his chamber—a small, and scantily furnished bedroom in "Old Duffer's" hotel; where, notwithstanding the *éclat* derived from his conquest, he was somewhat scurvily treated.

In the hour of his triumph, he had fainted from loss of blood. He could not be taken elsewhere; though, in the shabby apartment to which he had been consigned, he might have thought of the luxurious care that surrounded the couch of his wounded antagonist. Fortunately Phelim was by his side, or he might have been still worse attended to.

"Be Saint Pathrick! it's a shame," half soliloquised this faithful follower. "A burnin' shame to squeeze a gintleman into a hole like this, not bigger than a pig-stoy! A gintleman like you, Masther Maurice. An' thin such aytin' and drinkin'. Och! a well fid Oirish pig wud turn up its nose at such traytment. An' fwhat div yez think I've heerd Owld Duffer talkin' about below?"

"I hav'n't the slightest idea, my dear Phelim; nor do I care straw to know what you've heard Mr Oberdoffer saying below; but if you don't want him to hear what you are saying above, you'll moderate your voice a little. Remember, *ma bohil*, that the partitions in this place are only lath and plaster."

"Divil take the partitions; and divil burn them, av he loikes. Av yez don't care fur fwhat's sed, I don't care far fwhat's heeurd—not the snappin' av me fingers. The Dutchman can't trate us any worse than he's been doin' already. For all that, Masther Maurice, I thought it bist to lit you know."

"Let me know then. What is it he has been saying?"

"Will, thin; I heerd him tellin' wan av his croneys that besoides the mate an the dhrink, an the washin', an lodgin', he intinded to make you pay for the bottles, and glasses, an other things, that was broke on the night av the shindy."

"Me pay?"

"Yis, yerself, Masther Maurice; an not a pinny charged to the Yankee. Now I call that downright rascally mane; an nobody but a dhirty Dutchman wud iver hiv thought av it. Av there be anythin' to pay, the man that's bate should be made to showldor the damage, an that wasn't a discindant av the owld Geralds av Ballyballagh. Hoo—hooch! wudn't I loike to shake a shaylaylah about Duffer's head for the matther of two minutes? Wudn't I?"

"What reason did he give for saying that I should pay? Did you hear him state any?"

"I did, masther—the dhirtiest av all raisuns. He sid that you were the bird in the hand; an he wud kape ye till yez sittled the score."

"He'll find himself slightly mistaken about that; and would perhaps do better by presenting his bill to the bird in the bush. I shall be willing to pay for half the damage done; but no more. You may tell him so, if he speak to you about it. And, in troth, Phelim, I don't know how I am to do even that. There must have been a good many breakages. I remember a great deal of jingling while we were at it. If I don't mistake there was a smashed mirror, or clock dial, or something of the kind."

"A big lookin'-glass, masther; an a crystal somethin', that was set over the clock. They say two hunderd dollars. I don't belave they were worth wan half av the money."

"Even so, it is a serious matter to me—just at this crisis. I fear, Phelim, you will have to make a journey to the Alamo, and fetch away some of the household gods we have hidden there. To get clear of this scrape I shall have to sacrifice my spurs, my silver cup, and perhaps my gun!"

"Don't say that, masther! How are we to live, if the gun goes?"

"As we best can, *ma bohil*. On horseflesh, I suppose: and the lazo will supply that."

"Be Japers! it wudn't be much worse than the mate Owld Duffer sits afore us. It gives me the bellyache ivery time I ate it."

The conversation was here interrupted by the opening of the chamber door; which was done without knocking. A slatternly servant—whose sex it would have been difficult to determine from outward indices—appeared in the doorway, with a basket of palm sinnet held extended at the termination of a long sinewy arm.

"Fwhat is it, Gertrude?" asked Phelim, who, from some previous information, appeared to be acquainted with the feminine character of the intruder.

147

"A shentlemans prot this."

"A gentleman! Who, Gertrude?"

"Not know, mein herr; he wash a stranger shentlemans."

"Brought by a gentleman. Who can he be? See what it in, Phelim."

Phelim undid the fastenings of the lid, and exposed the interior of the basket. It was one of considerable bulk: since inside were discovered several bottles, apparently containing wines and cordials, packed among a paraphernalia of sweetmeats, and other delicacies—both of the confectionery and the kitchen. There was no note accompanying the present—not even a direction—but the trim and elegant style in which it was done up, proved that it had proceeded from the hands of a lady.

Maurice turned over the various articles, examining each, as Phelim supposed, to take note of its value. Little was he thinking of this, while searching for the "invoice."

There proved to be none—not a scrap of paper—not so much as a *card*!

The generosity of the supply—well-timed as it was—bespoke the donor to be some person in affluent circumstances. Who could it be?

As Maurice reflected, a fair image came uppermost in his mind; which he could not help connecting with that of his unknown benefactor. Could it be Louise Poindexter?

In spite of certain improbabilities, he was fain to believe it might; and, so long as the belief lasted, his heart was quivering with a sweet beatitude.

As he continued to reflect, the improbabilities appeared too strong for this pleasant supposition; his faith became overturned; and there remained only a vague unsubstantial hope.

"A gintleman lift it," spoke the Connemara man, in semi-soliloquy. "A gintleman, she sez; a kind gintleman, I say! Who div yez think he was, masther?"

"I haven't the slightest idea; unless it may have been some of the officers of the Port; though I could hardly expect one of them to think of me in this fashion."

"Nayther yez need. It wasn't wan av them. No officer, or gintleman ayther, phut them things in the basket."

"Why do you think that?"

"Pwhy div I think it! Och, masther! is it yerself to ask the quistyun? Isn't there the smell av swate fingers about it? Jist look at the nate way them papers is tied up. That purty kreel was niver packed

148

by the hand av a man. It was done by a wuman; and I'll warrant a raal lady at that."

"Nonsense, Phelim! I know no lady who should take so much interest in me."

"Aw, murdher! What a thumpin' big fib! I know won that shud. It wud be black ungratytude av she didn't—afther what yez did for her. Didn't yez save her life into the bargain?"

"Of whom are you speaking?"

"Now, don't be desateful, masther. Yez know that I mane the purty crayther that come to the hut ridin' Spotty that you presinted her, widout resavin' a dollar for the mare. If it wasn't her that sint ye this hamper, thin Phaylim Onale is the biggest numskull that was iver born about Ballyballagh. Be the Vargin, masther, speakin' of the owld place phuts me in mind of its paple. Pwhat wud the blue-eyed colleen say, if she knew yez were in such danger heeur?"

"Danger! it's all over. The doctor has said so; and that I may go out of doors in a week from this time. Don't distress yourself about that."

"Troth, masther, yez be only talkin'. That isn't the danger I was drhamin' av. Yez know will enough what I mane. Maybe yez have resaved a wound from bright eyes, worse than that from lid bullets. Or, maybe, somebody ilse has; an that's why ye've had the things sint ye."

"You're all wrong, Phelim. The thing must have come from the Fort; but whether it did, or not, there's no reason why we should stand upon ceremony with its contents. So, here goes to make trial of them!"

Notwithstanding the apparent relish with which the invalid partook of the products—both of collar and *cuisine*—while eating and drinking, his thoughts were occupied with a still more agreeable theme; with a string of dreamy conjectures, as to whom he was indebted for the princely present.

Could it be the young Creole—the cousin of his direst enemy as well as his reputed sweetheart?

The thing appeared improbable.

If not she, who else could it be?

The mustanger would have given a horse—a whole drove—to have been assured that Louise Poindexter was the provider of that luxurious refection.

Two days elapsed, and the donor still remained unknown.

Then the invalid was once more agreeably surprised, by a second present—very similar to the first—another basket, containing other bottles, and crammed with fresh "confections."

The Bavarian wench was again questioned; but with no better result. A "shentlemans" had "prot" it—the same "stranger shentlemans" as before. She could only add that "the shentlemans" was very "*Schwartz*," wore a glazed hat, and came to the tavern mounted upon a mule.

Maurice did not appear to be gratified with this description of the unknown donor; though no one—not even Phelim—was made the confidant of his thoughts.

In two days afterwards they were toned down to their former sobriety—on the receipt of a third basket, "prot by the Schwartz gentleman" in the glazed hat, who came mounted upon a mule.

The change could not be explained by the belongings in the basket—almost the counterpart of what had been sent before. It might be accounted for by the contents of a *billet doux*, that accompanied the gift—attached by a ribbon to the wickerwork of palm-sinnet.

"'Tis only Isidora!" muttered the mustanger, as he glanced at the superscription upon the note.

Then opening it with an air of indifference, he read:—

"*Querido Señor!*

"*Soy quedando por una semana en la casa del tio Silvio. De questra desfortuna he oido—tambien que V. esta mal ciudado en la fonda. He mandado algunas cositas. Sea graciosa usarlos, coma una chiquitita memoria del servicio grande de que vuestra deudor estoy. En la silla soy escribando, con las espuelas preparadas sacar sangre de las ijadas del mio cavallo. En un momento mas, partira por el Rio Grande.*

"*Bienhichor—de mi vida Salvador—y de que a una mujer esa mas querida, la honra—adios—adios!*

"*Isidora Covarubio De Los Llanos.*

"*Al Señor Don Mauricio Gerald.*"

Literally translated, and in the idiom of the Spanish language, the note ran thus:—

"Dear Sir,—I have been staying for a week at the house of Uncle Silvio. Of your mischance I have heard—also, that you are indifferently cared for at the hotel. I have sent you some little things. Be good enough to make use of them, as a slight souvenir of the great service for which I am your debtor. I write in the saddle, with my spurs ready to draw blood from the flanks of my horse. In another moment I am off for the Rio Grande!

"Benefactor—preserver of my life—of what to a woman is dearer—my honour—adieu! adieu!

"Isidora Covarubio De Los Llanos."

"Thanks—thanks, sweet Isidora!" muttered the mustanger, as he refolded the note, and threw it carelessly upon the coverlet of his couch. "Ever grateful—considerate—kind! But for Louise Poindexter, I might have loved you!"

# 23. Vows of Vengeance

Calhoun, chafing in his chamber, was not the object of such assiduous solicitude. Notwithstanding the luxurious appointments that surrounded him, he could not comfort himself with the reflection: that he was cared for by living creature. Truly selfish in his own heart, he had no faith in friendships; and while confined to his couch—not without some fears that it might be his death-bed—he experienced the misery of a man believing that no human being cared a straw whether he should live or die.

Any sympathy shown to him, was upon the score of relationship. It could scarce have been otherwise. His conduct towards his cousins had not been such as to secure their esteem; while his uncle, the proud Woodley Poindexter, felt towards him something akin to aversion, mingled with a subdued fear.

It is true that this feeling was only of recent origin; and rose out of certain relations that existed between uncle and nephew. As already hinted, they stood to one another in the relationship of debtor and creditor—or mortgagor and mortgagee—the nephew being the latter. To such an extent had this indebtedness been carried, that Cassius Calhoun was in effect the real owner of Casa del Corvo; and could at any moment have proclaimed himself its master.

Conscious of his power, he had of late been using it to effect a particular purpose: that is, the securing for his wife, the woman he had long fiercely loved—his cousin Louise. He had come to know that he stood but little chance of obtaining her consent: for she had taken but slight pains to conceal her indifference to his suit. Trusting to the peculiar influence established over her father, he had determined on taking no slight denial.

These circumstances considered, it was not strange that the ex-officer of volunteers, when stretched upon a sick bed, received less sympathy from his relatives than might otherwise have been extended to him.

While dreading, death—which for a length of time he actually did—he had become a little more amiable to those around him. The agreeable mood, however, was of short continuance; and, once assured of recovery, all the natural savageness of his disposition was restored, along with the additional bitterness arising from his recent discomfiture.

It had been the pride of his life to exhibit himself as a successful bully—the master of every crowd that might gather around him. He could no longer claim this credit in Texas; and the thought harrowed his heart to its very core.

To figure as a defeated man before all the women of the settlement—above all in the eyes of her he adored, defeated by one whom he suspected of being his rival in her affections—a more nameless adventurer—was too much to be endured with equanimity. Even an ordinary man would have been pained by the infliction. Calhoun writhed under it.

He had no idea of enduring it, as an ordinary man would have done. If he could not escape from the disgrace, he was determined to revenge himself upon its author; and as soon as he had recovered from the apprehensions entertained about the safety of his life, he commenced reflecting upon this very subject.

Maurice, the mustanger, must die! If not by his (Calhoun's) own hand, then by the hand of another, if such an one was to be found in the settlement. There could not be much difficulty in procuring a confederate. There are *bravoes* upon the broad prairies of Texas, as well as within the walls of Italian cities. Alas! there is no spot upon earth where gold cannot command the steel of the assassin.

Calhoun possessed gold—more than sufficient for such a purpose; and to such purpose did he determine upon devoting at least a portion of it.

In the solitude of his sick chamber he set about maturing his plans; which comprehended the assassination of the mustanger. He did not purpose doing the deed himself. His late defeat had rendered him fearful of chancing a second encounter with the same adversary—even under the advantageous circumstances of a surprise. He had become too much encowardised to play the assassin. He wanted an accomplice—an arm to strike for him. Where was he to find it?

Unluckily he knew, or fancied he knew, the very man. There was a Mexican at the time making abode in the village—like Maurice himself—a mustanger; but one of those with whom the young Irishman had shown a disinclination to associate.

As a general rule, the men of this peculiar calling are amongst the greatest reprobates, who have their home in the land of the "Lone Star." By birth and breed they are mostly Mexicans, or mongrel Indians; though, not unfrequently, a Frenchman, or American, finds it a congenial calling. They are usually the outcasts of civilised society—oftener its outlaws—who, in the excitement of the chase, and its concomitant dangers, find, perhaps, some sort of *salvo* for a conscience that has been severely tried.

While dwelling within the settlements, these men are not unfrequently the pests of the society that surrounds them—ever engaged in broil and debauch; and when abroad in the exercise of their calling, they are not always to be encountered with safety. More than once is it recorded in the history of Texas how a company of mustangers has, for the nonce, converted itself into a band of *cuadrilla* of *salteadores*; or, disguised as Indians, levied black mail upon the train of the prairie traveller.

One of this kidney was the individual who had become recalled to the memory of Cassius Calhoun. The latter remembered having met the man in the bar-room of the hotel; upon several occasions, but more especially on the night of the duel. He remembered that he had been one of those who had carried him home on the stretcher; and from some extravagant expressions he had made use of, when speaking of his antagonist, Calhoun had drawn the deduction, that the Mexican was no friend to Maurice the mustanger.

Since then he had learnt that he was Maurice's deadliest enemy—himself excepted.

With these data to proceed upon the ex-captain had called the Mexican to his counsels, and the two were often closeted together in the chamber of the invalid.

There was nothing in all this to excite suspicion—even had Calhoun cared for that. His visitor was a dealer in horses and horned cattle. Some transaction in horseflesh might be going on between them. So any one would have supposed. And so for a time thought the Mexican himself: for in their first interview, but little other business was transacted between them. The astute Mississippian knew better than to declare his ultimate designs to a stranger; who, after completing an advantageous horse-trade, was well supplied with whatever he chose to drink, and cunningly cross-questioned as to the relations in which he stood towards Maurice the mustanger.

In that first interview, the ex-officer volunteers learnt enough, to know that he might depend upon his man for any service he might require—even to the committal of murder.

The Mexican made no secret of his heartfelt hostility to the young mustanger. He did not declare the exact cause of it; but Calhoun could guess, by certain innuendos introduced during the conversation, that it was the same as that by which he was himself actuated—the same to which may be traced almost every quarrel that has occurred among men, from Troy to Texas—a woman!

The Helen in this case appeared to be some dark-eyed *donçella* dwelling upon the Rio Grande, where Maurice had been in the habit of making an occasional visit, in whose eyes he had found favour, to the disadvantage of her own *conpaisano*.

The Mexican did not give the name; and Calhoun, as he listened to his explanations, only hoped in his heart that the damsel who had slighted him might have won the heart of his rival.

During his days of convalescence, several interviews had taken place between the ex-captain and the intended accomplice in his purposes of vengeance—enough, one might suppose, to have rendered them complete.

Whether they were so, or not, and what the nature of their hellish designs, were things known only to the brace of kindred confederates. The outside world but knew that Captain Cassius Calhoun and Miguel Diaz—known by the nickname "El Coyote," appeared to have taken a fancy for keeping each other's company; while the more respectable portion of it wondered at such an ill-starred association.

# 24. On the Azotea

There are no sluggards on a Texan plantation. The daybreak begins the day; and the bell, conch, or cow-horn, that summons the dark-skinned proletarians to their toil, is alike the signal for their master to forsake his more luxurious couch.

Such was the custom of Casa del Corvo under its original owners: and the fashion was followed by the family of the American planter—not from any idea of precedent, but simply in obedience to the suggestions of Nature. In a climate of almost perpetual spring, the sweet matutinal moments are not to be wasted in sleep. The *siesta* belongs to the hours of noon; when all nature appears to shrink under the smiles of the solar luminary—as if surfeited with their superabundance.

On his reappearance at morn the sun is greeted with renewed joy. Then do the tropical birds spread their resplendent plumage—the flowers their dew-besprinkled petals—to receive his fervent kisses. All nature again seems glad, to acknowledge him as its god.

Resplendent as any bird that flutters among the foliage of southwestern Texas—fair as any flower that blooms within it—gladdest was she who appeared upon the housetop of Casa del Corvo.

Aurora herself, rising from her roseate couch, looked not fresher than the young Creole, as she stood contemplating the curtains of that very couch, from which a Texan sun was slowly uplifting his globe of burning gold.

She was standing upon the edge of the azotea that fronted towards the east; her white hand resting upon the copestone of the parapet still wet with the dews of the night, under her eyes was the garden, enclosed within a curve of the river; beyond the bluff formed by the opposite bank; and further still, the wide-spreading plateau of the prairie.

Was she looking at a landscape, that could scarce fail to challenge admiration? No.

Equally was she unconscious of the ascending sun; though, like some fair pagan, did she appear to be in prayer at its apprising!

Listened she to the voices of the birds, from garden and grove swelling harmoniously around her?

On the contrary, her ear was not bent to catch any sound, nor her eye intent upon any object. Her glance was wandering, as if her thoughts went not with it, but were dwelling upon some theme, neither present nor near.

In contrast with the cheerful brightness of the sky, there was a shadow upon her brow; despite the joyous warbling of the birds, there was the sign of sadness on her cheek.

She was alone. There was no one to take note of this melancholy mood, nor inquire into its cause.

The cause was declared in a few low murmured words, that fell, as if involuntarily, from her lips.

"He may be dangerously wounded—perhaps even to death?"

Who was the object of this solicitude so hypothetically expressed?

The invalid that lay below, almost under her feet, in a chamber of the hacienda—her cousin Cassius Calhoun?

It could scarce be he. The doctor had the day before pronounced him out of danger, and on the way to quick recovery. Any one listening to her soliloquy—after a time continued in the same sad tone—would have been convinced it was not he.

"I may not send to inquire. I dare not even ask after him. I fear to trust any of our people. He may be in some poor place—perhaps uncourteously treated—perhaps neglected? Would that I could convey to him a message—something more—without any one being the wiser! I wonder what has become of Zeb Stump?"

As if some instinct whispered her, that there was a possibility of Zeb making his appearance, she turned her eyes towards the plain on the opposite side of the river—where a road led up and down. It was the common highway between Fort Inge and the plantations on the lower Leona. It traversed the prairie at some distance from the river bank; approaching it only at one point, where the channel curved in to the base of the bluffs. A reach of the road, of half a mile in length, was visible in the direction of the Fort; as also a cross-path that led to a ford; thence running on to the hacienda. In the opposite direction—down the stream—the view was open for a like length, until the chapparal on both sides closing in, terminated the savanna.

157

The young lady scanned the road leading towards Fort Inge. Zeb Stump should come that way. He was not in sight; nor was any one else.

She could not feel disappointment. She had no reason to expect him. She had but raised her eyes in obedience to an instinct.

Something more than instinct caused her, after a time, to turn round, and scrutinise the plain in the opposite quarter.

If expecting some one to appear that way, she was not disappointed. A horse was just stepping out from among the trees, where the road debouched from the chapparal. He was ridden by one, who, at first sight, appeared to be a man, clad in a sort of Arab costume; but who, on closer scrutiny, and despite the style of equitation—*à la Duchesse de Berri*—was unquestionably of the other sex—a lady. There was not much of her face to be seen; but through the shadowy opening of the *rebozo*—rather carelessly *tapado*—could be traced an oval facial outline, somewhat brownly "complected," But with a carmine tinting upon the cheeks, and above this a pair of eyes whose sparkle appeared to challenge comparison with the brightest object either on the earth, or in the sky.

Neither did the loosely falling folds of the lady's scarf, nor her somewhat *outré* attitude in the saddle, hinder the observer from coming to the conclusion, that her figure was quite as attractive as her face.

The man following upon the mule, six lengths of his animal in the rear, by his costume—as well as the respectful distance observed—was evidently only an attendant.

"Who can that woman be?" was the muttered interrogatory of Louise Poindexter, as with quick action she raised the lorgnette to her eyes, and directed it upon the oddly apparelled figure. "Who *can* she be?" was repeated in a tone of greater deliberation, as the glass came down, and the naked eye was entrusted to complete the scrutiny. "A Mexican, of course; the man on the mule her servant. Some grand señora, I suppose? I thought they had all gone to the other side of the Rio Grande. A basket carried by the attendant. I wonder what it contains; and what errand she can have to the Port—it may be the village. 'Tis the third time I've seen her passing within this week? She must be from some of the plantations below!"

What an outlandish style of riding! *Par Dieu*! I'm told it's not uncommon among the daughters of Anahuac. What if I were to take to it myself? No doubt it's much the easiest way; though if such a spectacle were seen in the States it would be styled unfeminine. How our Puritan mammas would scream out against it! I think I hear them. Ha, ha, ha!

The mirth thus begotten was but of momentary duration. There came a change over the countenance of the Creole, quick as a drifting cloud darkens the disc of the sun. It was not a return to that melancholy so late shadowing it; though something equally serious—as might be told by the sudden blanching of her cheeks.

The cause could only be looked for in the movements of the scarfed equestrian on the other side of the river. An antelope had sprung up, out of some low shrubbery growing by the roadside. The creature appeared to have made its first bound from under the counter of the horse—a splendid animal, that, in a moment after, was going at full gallop in pursuit of the affrighted "pronghorn;" while his rider, with her rebozo suddenly flung from her face, its fringed ends streaming behind her back, was seen describing, with her right arm, a series of circular sweeps in the air!

"What is the woman going to do?" was the muttered interrogatory of the spectator upon the house-top. "Ha! As I live, 'tis a lazo!"

The señora was not long in giving proof of skill in the use of the national implement:—by flinging its noose around the antelope's neck, and throwing the creature in its tracks!

The attendant rode up to the place where it lay struggling; dismounted from his mule; and, stooping over the prostrate pronghorn, appeared to administer the *coup de grace*. Then, flinging the carcass over the croup of his saddle, he climbed back upon his mule, and spurred after his mistress—who had already recovered her lazo, readjusted her scarf, and was riding onward, as if nothing had occurred worth waiting for!

It was at that moment—when the noose was seen circling in the air—that the shadow had reappeared upon the countenance or the Creole. It was not surprise that caused it, but an emotion of a different character—a thought far more unpleasant.

Nor did it pass speedily away. It was still there—though a white hand holding the lorgnette to her eye might have hindered it from being seen—still there, as long as the mounted figures were visible upon the open road; and even after they had passed out of sight behind the screening of the acacias.

"I wonder—oh, I wonder if it be she! My own age, he said—not quite so tall. The description suits—so far as one may judge at this distance. Has her home on the Rio Grande. Comes occasionally to the Leona, to visit some relatives. Who are they? Why did I not ask him the name? *I wonder—oh, I wonder if it be she!*"

## 25. A Gift Ungiven

For some minutes after the lady of the lazo and her attendant had passed out of sight, Louise Poindexter pursued the train of reflection—started by the somewhat singular episode of which she had been spectator. Her attitude, and air, of continued dejection told that her thoughts had not been directed into a more cheerful channel.

Rather the reverse. Once or twice before had her mind given way to imaginings, connected with that accomplished *equestrienne*; and more than once had she speculated upon her purpose in riding up the road. The incident just witnessed had suddenly changed her conjectures into suspicions of an exceedingly unpleasant nature.

It was a relief to her, when a horseman appeared coming out of the chapparal, at the point where the others had ridden in; a still greater relief, when he was seen to swerve into the cross path that conducted to the hacienda, and was recognised, through the lorgnette, as Zeb Stump the hunter.

The face of the Creole became bright again—almost to gaiety. There was something ominous of good in the opportune appearance of the honest backwoodsman.

"The man I was wanting to see!" she exclaimed in joyous accents. "*He* can bear me a message; and perhaps tell who *she* is. He must have met her on the road. That will enable me to introduce the subject, without Zeb having any suspicion of my object. Even with him I must be circumspect—after what has happened. Ah, me! Not much should I care, if I were sure of *his* caring for me. How provoking his indifference! And to me—Louise Poindexter! *Par dieu!* Let it proceed much further, and I shall try to escape from the toils if—if—I should crush my poor heart in the attempt!"

It need scarce be said that the individual, whose esteem was so coveted, was not Zeb Stump.

Her next speech, however, was addressed to Zeb, as he reined up in front of the hacienda.

"Dear Mr Stump!" hailed a voice, to which the old hunter delighted to listen. "I'm so glad to see you. Dismount, and come up here! I know you're a famous climber, and won't mind a flight of stone stairs. There's a view from this housetop that will reward you for your trouble."

"Thur's suthin' on the house-top theear," rejoined the hunter, "the view o' which 'ud reward Zeb Stump for climbin' to the top o' a steamboat chimbly; 'an thet's yurself, Miss Lewaze. I'll kum up, soon as I ha' stabled the ole maar, which shall be dud in the shakin' o' a goat's tail. Gee-up, ole gal!" he continued, addressing himself to the mare, after he had dismounted, "Hold up yur head, an may be Plute hyur 'll gie ye a wheen o' corn shucks for yur breakfist."

"Ho—ho! Mass 'Tump," interposed the sable coachman, making his appearance in the *patio*. "Dat same do dis nigga—gub um de shucks wi' de yaller corn inside ob dem. Ho—ho! You gwup 'tairs to de young missa; an Plute he no 'gleck yar ole mar."

"Yur a dod-rotted good sample o' a nigger, Plute; an the nix occashun I shows about hyur, I'll fetch you a 'possum—wi' the meat on it as tender as a two-year old chicken. Thet's what I'm boun' ter do."

After delivering himself of this promise, Zeb commenced ascending the stone stairway; not by single steps, but by two, and sometimes three, at a stride.

He was soon upon the housetop; where he was once more welcomed by the young mistress of the mansion.

Her excited manner, and the eagerness with which she conducted him to a remote part of the azotea, told the astute hunter, that he had been summoned thither for some other purpose than enjoying the prospect.

"Tell me, Mr Stump!" said she, as she clutched the sleeve of the blanket coat in her delicate fingers, and looked inquiringly into Zeb's grey eye—"You must know all. How is he? Are his wounds of a dangerous nature?"

"If you refar to Mister Cal-hoon—"

"No—no—no. I know all about him. It's not of Mr Calhoun I'm speaking."

"Wall, Miss Lewasse; thur air only one other as I know of in these parts thet hev got wownds; an thet air's Maurice the mowstanger. Mout it be thet ere individooal yur inquirin' abeout?"

"It is—it is! You know I cannot be indifferent to his welfare, notwithstanding the misfortune of his having quarrelled with my cousin. You are aware that he rescued me—twice I may say—from imminent peril. Tell me—is he in great danger?"

Such earnestness could no longer be trifled with. Zeb without further parley, made reply:—

"Ne'er a morsel o' danger. Thur's a bullet-hole jest above the ankle-jeint. It don't signerfy more'n the scratch o' a kitting. Thur's another hev goed through the flesh o' the young fellur's left arm. It don't signerfy neyther—only thet it drawed a good sup o' the red out o' him. Howsomdever, he's all right now; an expecks to be out o' doors in a kupple o' days, or tharabout. He sez that an hour in the seddle, an a skoot acrosst the purayra, 'ud do him more good than all the docters in Texas. I reckon it wud; but the docter—it's the surgint o' the Fort as attends on him—he won't let him git to grass yit a bit."

"Where is he?"

"He air stayin' at the hotel—whar the skrimmage tuk place."

"Perhaps he is not well waited upon? It's a rough place, I've heard. He may not have any delicacies—such as an invalid stands in need of? Stay here, Mr Stump, till I come up to you again. I have something I wish to send to him. I know I can trust you to deliver it. Won't you? I'm sure you will. I shall be with you in six seconds."

Without waiting to note the effect of her speech, the young lady tripped lightly along the passage, and as lightly descended the stone stairway.

Presently she reappeared—bringing with her a good-sized hamper; which was evidently filled with eatables, with something to send them down.

"Now dear old Zeb, you will take this to Mr Gerald? It's only some little things that Florinda has put up; some cordials and jellies and the like, such as sick people at times have a craving for. They are not likely to be kept in the hotel. Don't tell *him* where they come from—*neither him, nor any one else*. You won't? I know you won't, you dear good giant."

"He may depend on Zeb Stump for thet, Miss Lewaze. Nobody air a goin' to be a bit the wiser about who sent these hyur delekissies; though, for the matter o' cakes an kickshaws, an all that sort o' thing, the mowstanger hain't had much reezun to complain. He hev been serplied wi' enuf o' them to hev filled the bellies o' a hul school o' shugar-babbies."

"Ha! Supplied already! By whom?"

"Wal, thet theer this chile can't inform ye, Miss Lewaze; not be-knowin' it hisself. I on'y hyurd they wur fetched to the tavern in bas-kets, by some sort o' a sarving-man as air a Mexikin. I've seed the man myself. Fact, I've jest this minnit met him, ridin' arter a wuman sot stridy legs in her seddle, as most o' these Mexikin weemen ride. I reck'n he be her sarvingt, as he war keepin' a good ways ahint, and toatin' a basket jest like one o' them Maurice hed got arready. Like enuf it air another lot o' Rickshaws they wur takin' to the tavern."

There was no need to trouble Zeb Stump with further cross-questioning. A whole history was supplied by that single speech. The case was painfully clear. In the regard of Maurice Gerald, Louise Poindexter had a rival—perhaps something more. The lady of the lazo was either his *fiancée*, or his mistress!

It was not by accident—though to Zeb Stump it may have seemed so—that the hamper, steadied for a time, upon the coping of the balus-trade, and still retained in the hand of the young Creole, escaped from her clutch, and fell with a crash upon the stones below. The bottles were broken, and their contents spilled into the stream that surged along the basement of the wall.

The action of the arm that produced this effect, apparently spring-ing from a spasmodic and involuntary effort, was nevertheless due to design; and Louise Poindexter, as she leant over the parapet, and con-templated the ruin she had caused, felt as if her heart was shattered like the glass that lay glistening below!

"How unfortunate!" said she, making a feint to conceal her cha-grin. "The dainties are destroyed, I declare! What will Florinda say? After all, if Mr Gerald be so well attended to, as you say he is, he'll not stand in need of them. I'm glad to hear he hasn't been neglected—one who has done me a service. But, Mr Stump, you needn't say any-thing of this, or that I inquired after him. You know his late antagonist is our near relative; and it might cause scandal in the settlement. Dear Zeb, you promise me?"

"Swa-ar it ef ye like. Neery word, Miss Lewaze, neery word; ye kin depend on ole Zeb."

"I know it. Come! The sun is growing hot up here. Let as go down, and see whether we can find you such a thing as a glass of your favourite Monongahela. Come!"

With an assumed air of cheerfulness, the young Creole glided across the azotea; and, trilling the "New Orleans Waltz," once more commenced descending the *escalera*.

In eager acceptance of the invitation, the old hunter followed close upon her skirts; and although, by habit, stoically indifferent to feminine charms—and with his thoughts at that moment chiefly bent upon the promised Monongahela—he could not help admiring those ivory shoulders brought so conspicuously under his eyes.

But for a short while was he permitted to indulge in the luxurious spectacle. On reaching the bottom of the stair his fair hostess bade him a somewhat abrupt adieu. After the revelations he had so unwittingly made, his conversation seemed no longer agreeable; and she, late desirous of interrogating, was now contented to leave him alone with the Monongahela, as she hastened to hide her chagrin in the solitude of her chamber.

For the first time in her life Louise Poindexter felt the pangs of jealousy. It was her first real love: for she was in love with Maurice Gerald.

A solicitude like that shown for him by the Mexican señora, could scarce spring from simple friendship? Some closer tie must have been established between them? So ran the reflections of the now suffering Creole.

From what Maurice had said—from what she had herself seen—the lady of the lazo was just such a woman as should win the affections of such a man. Hers were accomplishments he might naturally be expected to admire.

Her figure had appeared perfect under the magnifying effect of the lens. The face had not been so fairly viewed, and was still undetermined. Was it in correspondence with the form? Was it such as to secure the love of a man so much master of his passions, as the mustanger appeared to be?

The mistress of Casa del Corvo could not rest, till she had satisfied herself on this score. As soon as Zeb Stump had taken his departure, she ordered the spotted mare to be saddled; and, riding out alone, she sought the crossing of the river; and thence proceeded to the highway on the opposite side.

Advancing in the direction of the Fort, as she expected, she soon encountered the Mexican señora on her return; no *señora* according to the exact signification of the term, but a *señorita*—a young lady, not older than herself.

At the place of their meeting, the road ran under the shadow of the trees. There was no sun to require the coifing of the rebozo upon the crown of the Mexican equestrian. The scarf had fallen upon her shoulders, laying bare a head of hair, in luxuriance rivalling the tail of a wild steed, in colour the plumage of a crow. It formed the framing of a face, that, despite a certain darkness of complexion, was charmingly attractive.

Good breeding permitted only a glance at it in passing; which was returned by a like courtesy on the part of the stranger. But as the two rode on, back to back, going in opposite directions, neither could restrain herself from turning round in the saddle, and snatching a second glance at the other.

Their reflections were not very dissimilar: if Louise Poindexter had already learnt something of the individual thus encountered, the latter was not altogether ignorant of *her* existence.

We shall not attempt to portray the thoughts of the señorita consequent on that encounter. Suffice it to say, that those of the Creole were even more sombre than when she sallied forth on that errand of inspection; and that the young mistress of Casa del Corvo rode back to the mansion, all the way seated in her saddle in an attitude that betokened the deepest dejection.

"Beautiful!" said she, after passing her supposed rival upon the road. "Yes; too beautiful to be his friend!"

Louise was speaking to her own conscience; or she might have been more chary of her praise.

"I cannot have any doubt," continued she, "of the relationship that exists between them—He loves her!—he loves her! It accounts for his cold indifference to me? I've been mad to risk my heart's happiness in such an ill-starred entanglement!

"And now to disentangle it! Now to banish him from my thoughts! Ah! 'tis easily said! Can I?"

"I shall see him no more. That, at least, is possible. After what has occurred, he will not come to our house. We can only meet by accident; and that accident I must be careful to avoid. Oh, Maurice Gerald! tamer of wild steeds! you have subdued a spirit that may suffer long—perhaps never recover from the lesson!"

# 26. Still on the Azotea

To banish from the thoughts one who has been passionately loved is a simple impossibility. Time may do much to subdue the pain of an unreciprocated passion, and absence more. But neither time, nor absence, can hinder the continued recurrence of that longing for the lost loved one—or quiet the heart aching with that void that has never been satisfactorily filled.

Louise Poindexter had imbibed a passion that could not be easily stifled. Though of brief existence, it had been of rapid growth—vigorously overriding all obstacles to its indulgence. It was already strong enough to overcome such ordinary scruples as parental consent, or the inequality of rank; and, had it been reciprocated, neither would have stood in the way, so far as she herself was concerned. For the former, she was of age; and felt—as most of her countrywomen do—capable of taking care of herself. For the latter, who ever really loved that cared a straw for class, or caste? Love has no such meanness in its composition. At all events, there was none such in the passion of Louise Poindexter.

It could scarce be called the first illusion of her life. It was, however, the first, where disappointment was likely to prove dangerous to the tranquillity of her spirit.

She was not unaware of this. She anticipated unhappiness for a while—hoping that time would enable her to subdue the expected pain.

At first, she fancied she would find a friend in her own strong will; and another in the natural buoyancy of her spirit. But as the days passed, she found reason to distrust both: for in spite of both, she could not erase from her thoughts the image of the man who had so completely captivated her imagination.

There were times when she hated him, or tried to do so—when she could have killed him, or seen him killed, without making an effort to save him! They were but moments; each succeeded by an interval of more righteous reflection, when she felt that the fault was hers alone, as hers only the misfortune.

*No* matter for this. It mattered not if he had been her enemy—the enemy of all mankind. If Lucifer himself—to whom in her wild fancy she had once likened him—she would have loved him all the same!

And it would have proved nothing abnormal in her disposition—nothing to separate her from the rest of womankind, all the world over. In the mind of man, or woman either, there is no connection between the *moral* and the *passional*. They are as different from each other as fire from water. They may chance to run in the same channel; but they may go diametrically opposite. In other words, we may love the very being we hate—ay, the one we despise!

Louise Poindexter could neither hate, nor despise, Maurice Gerald. She could only endeavour to feel indifference.

It was a vain effort, and ended in failure. She could not restrain herself from ascending to the azotea, and scrutinising the road where she had first beheld the cause of her jealousy. Each day, and almost every hour of the day, was the ascent repeated.

Still more. Notwithstanding her resolve, to avoid the accident of an encounter with the man who had made her miserable, she was oft in the saddle and abroad, scouring the country around—riding through the streets of the village—with no other object than to meet him.

During the three days that followed that unpleasant discovery, once again had she seen—from the housetop as before—the lady of the lazo *en route* up the road, as before accompanied by her attendant with the pannier across his arm—that Pandora's box that had bred such mischief in her mind—while she herself stood trembling with jealousy—envious of the other's errand.

She knew more now, though not much. Only had she learnt the name and social standing of her rival. The Doña Isidora Covarubio de los Llanos—daughter of a wealthy haciendado, who lived upon the Rio Grande, and niece to another whose estate lay upon the Leona, a mile beyond the boundaries of her father's new purchase. An eccentric young lady, as some thought, who could throw a lazo, tame a wild steed, or anything else excepting her own caprices.

Such was the character of the Mexican señorita, as known to the American settlers on the Leona.

A knowledge of it did not remove the jealous suspicions of the Creole. On the contrary, it tended to confirm them. Such practices were her own predilections. She had been created with an instinct to admire them. She supposed that others must do the same. The young Irishman was not likely to be an exception.

There was an interval of several days—during which the lady of the lazo was not seen again.

"He has recovered from his wounds?" reflected the Creole. "He no longer needs such unremitting attention."

She was upon the azotea at the moment of making this reflection—lorgnette in hand, as she had often been before.

It was in the morning, shortly after sunrise: the hour when the Mexican had been wont to make her appearance. Louise had been looking towards the quarter whence the señorita might have been expected to come.

On turning her eyes in the opposite direction, she beheld—that which caused her something more than surprise. She saw Maurice Gerald, mounted on horseback, and riding down the road!

Though seated somewhat stiffly in the saddle, and going at a slow pace, it was certainly he. The glass declared his identity; at the same time disclosing the fact, that his left arm was suspended in a sling.

On recognising him, she shrank behind the parapet—as she did so, giving utterance to a suppressed cry.

Why that anguished utterance? Was it the sight of the disabled arm, or the pallid face: for the glass had enabled her to distinguish both?

Neither one nor the other. Neither could be a cause of surprise. Besides, it was an exclamation far differently intoned to those of either pity or astonishment. It was an expression of sorrow, that had for its origin some heartfelt chagrin.

The invalid was convalescent. He no longer needed to be visited by his nurse. He was on the way to visit *her*!

Cowering behind the parapet—screened by the flower-spike of the *yucca*—Louise Poindexter watched the passing horseman. The lorgnette enabled her to note every movement made by him—almost to the play of his features.

She felt some slight gratification on observing that he turned his face at intervals and fixed his regard upon Casa del Corvo. It was increased, when on reaching a copse, that stood by the side of the road, and nearly opposite the house, he reined up behind the trees, and for a long time remained in the same spot, as if reconnoitring the mansion.

She almost conceived a hope, that he might be thinking of its mistress!

It was but a gleam of joy, departing like the sunlight under the certain shadow of an eclipse. It was succeeded by a sadness that might be appropriately compared to such shadow: for to her the world at that moment seemed filled with gloom.

Maurice Gerald had ridden on. He had entered the chapparal; and become lost to view with the road upon which he was riding.

Whither was he bound? Whither, but to visit Doña Isidora Covarubio de los Llanos?

It mattered not that he returned within less than an hour. They might have met in the woods—within eyeshot of that jealous spectator—but for the screening of the trees. An hour was sufficient interview—for lovers, who could every day claim unrestricted indulgence.

It mattered not, that in passing upwards he again cast regards towards Casa del Corvo; again halted behind the copse, and passed some time in apparent scrutiny of the mansion.

It was but mockery—or exultation. He might well feel triumphant; but why should he be cruel, with kisses upon his lips—the kisses he had received from the Doña Isidora Covarubio de los Llanos?

## 27. I Love You!—I Love You!

Louise Poindexter upon the azotea again—again to be subjected to a fresh chagrin! That broad stone stairway trending up to the house-top, seemed to lead only to spectacles that gave her pain. She had mentally vowed no more to ascend it—at least for a long time. Something stronger than her strong will combatted—and successfully—the keeping of that vow. It was broken ere the sun of another day had dried the dew from the grass of the prairie.

As on the day before, she stood by the parapet scanning the road on the opposite side of the river; as before, she saw the horseman with the slung arm ride past; as before, she crouched to screen herself from observation.

He was going downwards, as on the day preceding. In like manner did he cast long glances towards the hacienda, and made halt behind the clump of trees that grew opposite.

Her heart fluttered between hope and fear. There was an instant when she felt half inclined to show herself. Fear prevailed; and in the next instant he was gone.

Whither?

The self-asked interrogatory was but the same as of yesterday. It met with a similar response.

Whither, if not to meet Doña Isidora Covarubio de los Llanos?

Could there be a doubt of it?

If so, it was soon to be determined. In less than twenty minutes after, a parded steed was seen upon the same road—and in the same direction—with a lady upon its back.

The jealous heart of the Creole could hold out no longer. No truth could cause greater torture than she was already suffering through suspicion. She had resolved on assuring herself, though the knowledge should prove fatal to the last faint remnant of her hopes.

She entered the chapparal where the mustanger had ridden in scarce twenty minutes before. She rode on beneath the flitting shadows of the acacias. She rode in silence upon the soft turf—keeping close to the side of the path, so that the hoof might not strike against stones. The long pinnate fronds, drooping down to the level of her eyes, mingled with the plumes in her hat. She sate her saddle crouchingly, as if to avoid being observed—all the while with earnest glance scanning the open space before her.

She reached the crest of a hill which commanded a view beyond. There was a house in sight surrounded by tall trees. It might have been termed a mansion. It was the residence of Don Silvio Martinez, the uncle of Doña Isidora. So much had she learnt already.

There were other houses to be seen upon the plain below; but on this one, and the road leading to it, the eyes of the Creole became fixed in a glance of uneasy interrogation.

For a time she continued her scrutiny without satisfaction. No one appeared either at the house, or near it. The private road leading to the residence of the haciendado, and the public highway, were alike without living forms. Some horses were straying over the pastures; but not one with a rider upon his back.

Could the lady have ridden out to meet him, or Maurice gone in?

Were they at that moment in the woods, or within the walls of the house? If the former, was Don Silvio aware of it? If the latter, was he at home—an approving party to the assignation?

With such questions was the Creole afflicting herself, when the neigh of a horse broke abruptly on her ear, followed by the chinking of a shod hoof against the stones of the causeway. She looked below: for she had halted upon the crest, a steep acclivity. The mustanger was ascending it—riding directly towards her. She might have seen him sooner, had she not been occupied with the more distant view.

He was alone, as he had ridden past Casa del Corvo. There was nothing to show that he had recently been in company—much less in the company of an *inamorata*.

It was too late for Louise to shun him. The spotted mustang had replied to the salutation of an old acquaintance. Its rider was constrained to keep her ground, till the mustanger came up.

"Good day, Miss Poindexter?" said he—for upon the prairies it is *not* etiquette for the lady to speak first. "Alone?"

"Alone, sir. And why not?"

"'Tis a solitary ride among the chapparals. But true: I think I've heard you say you prefer that sort of thing?"

"You appear to like it yourself, Mr Gerald. To you, however, it is not so solitary, I presume?"

"In faith I do like it; and just for that very reason. I have the misfortune to live at a tavern, or 'hotel,' as mine host is pleased to call it; and one gets so tired of the noises—especially an invalid, as I have the bad luck to be—that a ride along this quiet road is something akin to luxury. The cool shade of these acacias—which the Mexicans have vulgarised by the name of *mezquites*—with the breeze that keeps constantly circulating through their fan-like foliage, would invigorate the feeblest of frames. Don't you think so, Miss Poindexter?"

"You should know best, sir," was the reply vouchsafed, after some seconds of embarrassment. "You, who have so often tried it."

"Often! I have been only twice down this road since I have been able to sit in my saddle. But, Miss Poindexter, may I ask how you knew that I have been this way at all?"

"Oh!" rejoined Louise, her colour going and coming as she spoke, "how could I help knowing it? I am in the habit of spending much time on the housetop. The view, the breeze, the music of the birds, ascending from the garden below, makes it a delightful spot—especially in the cool of the morning. Our roof commands a view of this road. Being up there, how could I avoid seeing you as you passed—that is, so long as you were not under *the shade of the acacias*?"

"You saw me, then?" said Maurice, with an embarrassed air, which was not caused by the innuendo conveyed in her last words—which he could not have comprehended—but by a remembrance of how he had himself behaved while riding along the reach of open road.

"How could I help it?" was the ready reply. "The distance is scarce six hundred yards. Even a lady, mounted upon a steed much smaller than yours, was sufficiently conspicuous to be identified. When I saw her display her wonderful skill, by strangling a poor little antelope with her lazo, I knew it could be no other than she whose accomplishments you were so good as to give me an account of."

"Isidora?"

"Isidora!"

"Ah; true! She has been here for some time."

"And has been very kind to Mr Maurice Gerald?"

"Indeed, it is true. She has been very kind; though I have had no chance of thanking her. With all her friendship for poor me, she is a great hater of us foreign invaders; and would not condescend to step over the threshold of Mr Oberdoffer's hotel."

"Indeed! I suppose she preferred meeting you under the *shade of the acacias*!"

"I have not met her at all; at least, not for many months; and may not for months to come—now that she has gone back to her home on the Rio Grande."

"Are you speaking the truth, sir? You have not seen her since— she is gone away from the house of her uncle?"

"She has," replied Maurice, exhibiting surprise. "Of course, I have not seen her. I only knew she was here by her sending me some delicacies while I was ill. In truth, I stood in need of them. The hotel *cuisine* is none of the nicest; nor was I the most welcome of Mr Ober-doffer's guests. The Doña Isidora has been but too grateful for the slight service I once did her."

"A service! May I ask what it was, Mr Gerald?"

"Oh, certainly. It was merely a chance. I had the opportunity of being useful to the young lady, in once rescuing her from some rude Indians—Wild Oat and his Seminoles—into whose hands she had fallen, while making a journey from the Rio Grande to visit her uncle on the Leona—Don Silvio Martinez, whose house you can see from here. The brutes had got drunk; and were threatening—not exactly her life—though that was in some danger, but—well, the poor girl was in trouble with them, and might have had some difficulty in getting away, had I not chanced to ride up."

"A slight service, you call it? You are modest in your estimate, Mr Gerald. A man who should do that much for *me*!"

"What would you do for *him*?" asked the mustanger, placing a significant emphasis on the final word.

"I should *love* him," was the prompt reply.

"Then," said Maurice, spurring his horse close up to the side of the spotted mustang, and whispering into the ear of its rider, with an earnestness strangely contrasting to his late reticence, "I would give half my life to see you in the hands of Wild Cat and his drunken comrades—the other half to deliver you from the danger."

"Do you mean this, Maurice Gerald? Do not trifle with me: I am not a child. Speak the truth! Do you mean it?"

"I do! As heaven is above me, I do!"

The sweetest kiss I ever had in my life, was when a woman—a fair creature, in the hunting field—leant over in her saddle and kissed me as I sate in mine.

The fondest embrace ever received by Maurice Gerald, was that given by Louise Poindexter; when, standing up in her stirrup, and laying her hand upon his shoulder, she cried in an agony of earnest passion—

*"Do with me as thou wilt: I love you, I love you!"*

# 28. A Pleasure Forbidden

Ever since Texas became the scene of an Anglo-Saxon immigration—I might go a century farther back and say, from the time of its colonisation by the descendants of the Conquistadores—the subject of primary importance has been the disposition of its aborigines.

Whether these, the lawful lords of the soil, chanced to be in a state of open war—or whether, by some treaty with the settlers they were consenting to a temporary peace—made but slight difference, so far as they were talked about. In either case they were a topic of daily discourse. In the former it related to the dangers to be hourly apprehended from them; in the latter, to the probable duration of such treaty as might for the moment be binding them to hold their tomahawks entombed.

In Mexican times these questions formed the staple of conversation, at *desayuno, almuerzo, comida, y cena*; in American times, up to this present hour, they have been the themes of discussion at the breakfast, dinner, and supper tables. In the planter's piazza, as in the hunter's camp, bear, deer, cougar, and peccary, are not named with half the frequency, or half the fear-inspiring emphasis, allotted to the word "Indian." It is this that scares the Texan child instead of the stereotyped nursery ghost, keeping it awake upon its moss-stuffed mattress—disturbing almost as much the repose of its parent.

Despite the surrounding of strong walls—more resembling those of a fortress than a gentleman's dwelling—the inmates of Casa del Corvo were not excepted from this feeling of apprehension, universal along the frontier. As yet they knew little of the Indians, and that little only from report; but, day by day, they were becoming better acquainted with the character of this natural "terror" that interfered with the slumbers of their fellow settlers.

That it was no mere "bogie" they had begun to believe; but if any of them remained incredulous, a note received from the major commanding the Fort—about two weeks after the horse-hunting expedition—was calculated to cure them of their incredulity. It came in the early morning, carried by a mounted rifleman. It was put into the hands of the planter just as he was about sitting down to the breakfast-table, around which were assembled the three individuals who composed his household—his daughter Louise, his son Henry, and his nephew Cassius Calhoun.

"Startling news!" he exclaimed, after hastily reading, the note. "Not very pleasant if true; and I suppose there can be no doubt of that, since the major appears convinced."

"Unpleasant news, papa?" asked his daughter, a spot of red springing to her cheek as she put the question.

The spoken interrogatory was continued by others, not uttered aloud.

"What can the major have written to him? I met him yesterday while riding in the chapparal. He saw me in company with—Can it be that? *Mon Dieu*! if father should hear it—"

"'The Comanches on the war trail'—so writes the major."

"Oh, that's all!" said Louise, involuntarily giving voice to the phrase, as if the news had nothing so very fearful in it. "You frightened us, sir. I thought it was something worse."

"Worse! What trifling, child, to talk so! There is nothing worse, in Texas, than Comanches on the war trail—nothing half so dangerous."

Louise might have thought there was—a danger at least as difficult to be avoided. Perhaps she was reflecting upon a pursuit of wild steeds—or thinking of the *trail of a lazo*.

She made no reply. Calhoun continued the conversation.

"Is the major sure of the Indians being up? What does he say, uncle?"

"That there have been rumours of it for some days past, though not reliable. Now it is certain. Last night Wild Cat, the Seminole chief, came to the Fort with a party of his tribe; bringing the news that the painted pole has been erected in the camps of the Comanches all over Texas, and that the war dance has been going on for more than a month. That several parties are already out upon the maraud, and may be looked for among the settlements at any moment."

"And Wild Cat himself—what of him?" asked Louise, an unpleasant reminiscence suggesting the inquiry. "Is that renegade Indian to be trusted, who appears to be as much an enemy to the whites as to the people of his own race?"

"Quite true, my daughter. You have described the chief of the Seminoles almost in the same terms as I find him spoken of, in a post-script to the major's letter. He counsels us to beware of the two-faced old rascal, who will be sure to take sides with the Comanches, when-ever it may suit his convenience to do so."

"Well," continued the planter, laying aside the note, and betaking himself to his coffee and waffles, "I trust we sha'n't see any redskins here—either Seminoles or Comanches. In making their marauds, let us hope they will not like the look of the crenelled parapets of Casa del Corvo, but give the hacienda a wide berth."

Before any one could respond, a sable face appearing at the door of the dining-room—which was the apartment in which breakfast was being eaten—caused a complete change in the character of the conver-sation.

The countenance belonged to Pluto, the coachman.

"What do you want, Pluto?" inquired his owner.

"Ho, ho! Massr Woodley, dis chile want nuffin 't all. Only look in t' tell Missa Looey dat soon's she done eat her brekfass de spotty am unner de saddle, all ready for chuck de bit into him mouf. Ho! ho! dat critter do dance 'bout on de pave stone as ef it wa' mad to 'treak it back to de smoove tuff ob de praira."

"Going out for a ride, Louise?" asked the planter with a shadow upon his brow, which he made but little effort to conceal.

"Yes, papa; I was thinking of it."

"You must not."

"Indeed!"

"I mean, that you must not ride out *alone*. It is not proper."

"Why do you think so, papa? I have often ridden out alone."

"Yes; perhaps too often."

This last remark brought the slightest tinge of colour to the cheeks of the young Creole; though she seemed uncertain what con-struction she was to put upon it.

Notwithstanding its ambiguity, she did not press for an explana-tion. On the contrary, she preferred shunning it; as was shown by her reply.

"If you think so, papa, I shall not go out again. Though to be cooped up here, in this dismal dwelling, while you gentlemen are all abroad upon business—is that the life you intend me to lead in Texas?"

"Nothing of the sort, my daughter. I have no objection to your riding out as much as you please; but Henry must be with you, or your cousin Cassius. I only lay an embargo on your going alone. I have my reasons."

"Reasons! What are they?"

The question came involuntarily to her lips. It had scarce passed them, ere she regretted having asked it. By her uneasy air it was evident she had apprehensions as to the answer.

The reply appeared partially to relieve her.

"What other reasons do you want," said the planter, evidently endeavouring to escape from the suspicion of duplicity by the Statement of a convenient fact—"what better, than the contents of this letter from the major? Remember, my child, you are not in Louisiana, where a lady may travel anywhere without fear of either insult or outrage; but in Texas, where she may dread both—where even her life may be in danger. Here there are Indians."

"My excursions don't extend so far from the house, that I need have any fear of Indians. I never go more than five miles at the most."

"Five miles!" exclaimed the ex-officer of volunteers, with a sardonic smile; "you would be as safe at fifty, cousin Loo. You are just as likely to encounter the redskins within a hundred yards of the door, as at the distance of a hundred miles. When they are on the war trail they may be looked for anywhere, and at any time. In my opinion, uncle Woodley is rights you are very foolish to ride out alone."

"Oh! *you* say so?" sharply retorted the young Creole, turning disdainfully towards her cousin. "And pray, sir, may I ask of what service your company would be to me in the event of my encountering the Comanches, which I don't believe there's the slightest danger of my doing? A pretty figure we'd cut—the pair of us—in the midst of a war-party of painted savages! Ha! ha! The danger would be yours, not mine: since I should certainly ride away, and leave you to your own devices. Danger, indeed, within five miles of the house! If there's a horseman in Texas—savages not excepted—who can catch up with my little Luna in a five mile stretch, he must ride a swift steed; which is more than you do, Mr Cash!"

"Silence, daughter!" commanded Poindexter. "Don't let me hear you talk in that absurd strain. Take no notice of it, nephew. Even if there were no danger from Indians, there are other outlaws in these parts quite as much to be shunned as they. Enough that I forbid you to ride abroad, as you have of late been accustomed to do."

"Be it as you will, papa," rejoined Louise, rising from the breakfast-table, and with an air of resignation preparing to leave the room. "Of course I shall obey you—at the risk of losing my health for want of exercise. Go, Pluto!" she added, addressing herself to the darkey, who still stood grinning in the doorway, "turn Luna loose into the corral—the pastures—anywhere. Let her stray back to her native prairies, if the creature be so inclined; she's no longer needed here."

With this speech, the young lady swept out of the *sala*, leaving the three gentlemen, who still retained their seats by the table, to reflect upon the satire intended to be conveyed by her words.

They were not the last to which she gave utterance in that same series. As she glided along the corridor leading to her own chamber, others, low murmured, mechanically escaped from her lips. They were in the shape of interrogatories—a string of them self-asked, and only to be answered by conjecture.

"What can papa have heard? Is it but his suspicions? Can any one have told him? Does he knew that we have met?"

# 29. El Coyote at Home

Calhoun took his departure from the breakfast-table, almost as abruptly as his cousin; but, on leaving the *sala* instead of returning to his own chamber, he sallied forth from the house.

Still suffering from wounds but half healed, he was nevertheless sufficiently convalescent to go abroad—into the garden, to the stables, the corrals—anywhere around the house.

On the present occasion, his excursion was intended to conduct him to a more distant point. As if under the stimulus of what had turned up in the conversation—or perhaps by the contents of the letter that had been read—his feebleness seemed for the time to have forsaken him; and, vigorously plying his crutch, he proceeded up the river in the direction of Fort Inge.

In a barren tract of land, that lay about half way between the hacienda and the Fort—and that did not appear to belong to any one—he arrived at the terminus of his limping expedition. There was a grove of *mezquit*, with, some larger trees shading it; and in the midst of this, a rude hovel of "wattle and dab," known in South-Western Texas as a *jacalé*.

It was the domicile of Miguel Diaz, the Mexican mustanger—a lair appropriate to the semi-savage who had earned for himself the distinctive appellation of *El Coyote* ("Prairie Wolf.")

It was not always that the wolf could be found in his den—for his *jacalé* deserved no better description. It was but his occasional sleeping-place; during those intervals of inactivity when, by the disposal of a drove of captured mustangs, he could afford to stay for a time within the limits of the settlement, indulging in such gross pleasures as its proximity afforded.

Calhoun was fortunate in finding him at home; though not quite so fortunate as to find him in a state of sobriety. He was not exactly intoxicated—having, after a prolonged spell of sleep, partially recovered from this, the habitual condition of his existence.

"*H'la ñor!*" he exclaimed in his provincial patois, slurring the salutation, as his visitor darkened the door of the *jacalé*. "*P'r Dios*! Who'd have expected to see you? *Sientese*! Be seated. Take a chair. There's one. A chair! Ha! ha! ha!"

The laugh was called up at contemplation of that which he had facetiously termed a chair. It was the skull of a mustang, intended to serve as such; and which, with another similar piece, a rude table of cleft yucca-tree, and a couch of cane reeds, upon which the owner of the *jacalé* was reclining, constituted the sole furniture of Miguel Diaz's dwelling.

Calhoun, fatigued with his halting promenade, accepted the invitation of his host, and sate down upon the horse-skull.

He did not permit much time to pass, before entering upon the object of his errand.

"Señor Diaz!" said he, "I have come for—"

"Señor Americano!" exclaimed the half-drunken horse-hunter, cutting short the explanation, "why waste words upon that? *Carrambo*! I know well enough for what you've come. You want me to *wipe out* that devilish *Irlandes*!"

"Well!"

"Well; I promised you I would do it, for five hundred *pesos*—at the proper time and opportunity. I will. Miguel Diaz never played false to his promise. But the time's not come, *ñor capitan*; nor yet the opportunity, *Carajo*! To kill a man outright requires skill. It can't be done—even on the prairies—without danger of detection; and if detected, ha! what chance for me? You forget, *ñor capitan*, that I'm a Mexican. If I were of your people, I might slay Don Mauricio; and get clear on the score of its being a quarrel. *Maldita*! With us Mexicans it is different. If we stick our macheté into a man so as to let out his life's blood, it is called murder; and you Americanos, with your stupid juries of twelve *honest* men, would pronounce it so: ay, and hang a poor fellow for it. *Chingaro*! I can't risk that. I hate the Irlandes as much as you; but I'm not going to chop off my nose to spite my own face. I must wait for the time, and the chance—*carrai*, the time and the chance."

"Both are come!" exclaimed the tempter, bending earnestly towards the bravo. "You said you could easily do it, if there was any Indian trouble going on?"

"Of course I said so. If there was that—"

181

"You have not heard the news, then?"

"What news?"

"That the Comanches are starting on the war trail."

"*Carajo!*" exclaimed El Coyote, springing up from his couch of reeds, and exhibiting all the activity of his namesake, when roused by the scent of prey. "*Santissima Virgen!* Do you speak the truth, *ñor capitan?*"

"Neither more nor less. The news has just reached the Fort. I have it on the best authority—the officer in command."

"In that case," answered the Mexican reflecting!—"in that case, Don Mauricio may die. The Comanches can kill him. Ha! ha! ha!"

"You are sure of it?"

"I should be surer, if his scalp were worth a thousand dollars, instead of five hundred."

"It *is* worth that sum."

"What sum?"

"A thousand dollars."

"You promise it?"

"I do."

"Then the Comanches *shall* scalp him, *ñor capitan.* You may return to Casa del Corvo, and go to sleep with confidence that whenever the opportunity arrives, your enemy will lose his hair. You understand?"

"I do."

"Get ready your thousand *pesos.*"

"They wait your acceptance."

"*Carajo!* I shall earn them in a trice. Adios! Adios!"

"*Santissima Virgen!*" exclaimed the profane ruffian, as his visitor limped out of sight. "What a magnificent fluke of fortune! A perfect *chiripé.* A thousand dollars for killing the man I intended to kill on my own account, without charging anybody a single *claco* for the deed!

"The Comanches upon the war trail! *Chingaro!* can it be true? If so, I must look up my old disguise—gone to neglect through these three long years of accursed peace. *Viva la guerra de los Indios!* Success to the pantomime of the prairies!"

# 30. A Sagittary Correspondence

Louise Poindexter, passionately addicted to the sports termed "manly," could scarce have overlooked archery.

She had not. The bow, and its adjunct the arrow, were in her hands as toys which she could control to her will.

She had been instructed in their *manège* by the Houma Indians; a remnant of whom—the last descendants of a once powerful tribe—may still be encountered upon the "coast" of the Mississippi, in the proximity of Point Coupé and the *bayou* Atchafalaya.

For a long time her bow had lain unbent—unpacked, indeed, ever since it had formed part of the paraphernalia brought overland in the waggon train. Since her arrival at Casa del Corvo she had found no occasion to use the weapon of Diana; and her beautiful bow of Osage-orange wood, and quiver of plumed arrows, had lain neglected in the lumber-room.

There came a time when they were taken forth, and honoured with some attention. It was shortly after that scene at the breakfast table; when she had received the paternal command to discontinue her equestrian excursions.

To this she had yielded implicit obedience, even beyond what was intended: since not only had she given up riding out alone, but declined to do so in company.

The spotted mustang stood listless in its stall, or pranced frantically around the corral; wondering why its spine was no longer crossed, or its ribs compressed, by that strange caparison, that more than aught else reminded it of its captivity.

It was not neglected, however. Though no more mounted by its fair mistress, it was the object of her daily—almost hourly—solicitude. The best corn in the *granaderias* of Casa del Corvo was selected, the most nutritions grass that grows upon the lavanna—the *gramma*—

furnished for its manger; while for drink it had the cool crystal water from the current of the Leona.

Pluto took delight in grooming it; and, under his currycomb and brushes, its coat had attained a gloss which rivalled that upon Pluto's own sable skin.

While not engaged attending upon her pet, Miss Poindexter divided the residue of her time between indoor duties and archery. The latter she appeared to have selected as the substitute for that pastime of which she was so passionately fond, and in which she was now denied indulgence.

The scene of her sagittary performances was the garden, with its adjacent shrubbery—an extensive enclosure, three sides of which were fenced in by the river itself, curving round it like the shoe of a race-horse, the fourth being a straight line traced by the rearward wall of the hacienda.

Within this circumference a garden, with ornamental grounds, had been laid out, in times long gone by—as might have been told by many ancient exotics seen standing over it. Even the statues spoke of a past age—not only in their decay, but in the personages they were intended to represent. Equally did they betray the chisel of the Spanish sculptor. Among them you might see commemorated the figure and features of the great Condé; of the Campeador; of Ferdinand and his energetic queen; of the discoverer of the American world; of its two chief *conquistadores*—Cortez and Pizarro; and of her, alike famous for her beauty and devotion, the Mexican Malinché.

It was not amidst these sculptured stones that Louise Poindexter practised her feats of archery; though more than once might she have been seen standing before the statue of Malinché, and scanning the voluptuous outline of the Indian maiden's form; not with any severe thought of scorn, that this dark-skinned daughter of Eve had succumbed to such a conqueror as Cortez.

The young creole felt, in her secret heart, that she had no right to throw a stone at that statue. To one less famed than Cortez—though in her estimation equally deserving of fame—she had surrendered what the great conquistador had won from Marina—her heart of hearts.

In her excursions with the bow, which were of diurnal occurrence, she strayed not among the statues. Her game was not there to be found; but under the shadow of tall trees that, keeping the curve of the river, formed a semicircular grove between it and the garden. Most of these trees were of indigenous growth—wild Chinas, mulberries, and pecâns—that in the laying out of the grounds had been permitted to remain where Nature, perhaps some centuries ago, had scattered their seed.

It was under the leafy canopy of these fair forest trees the young Creole delighted to sit—or stray along the edge of the pellucid river, that rolled dreamily by.

Here she was free to be alone; which of late appeared to be her preference. Her father, in his sternest mood, could not have denied her so slight a privilege. If there was danger upon the outside prairie, there could be none within the garden—enclosed, as it was, by a river broad and deep, and a wall that could not have been scaled without the aid of a thirty-round ladder. So far from objecting to this solitary strolling, the planter appeared something more than satisfied that his daughter had taken to these tranquil habits; and the suspicions which he had conceived—not altogether without a cause—were becoming gradually dismissed from his mind.

After all he might have been misinformed? The tongue of scandal takes delight in torturing; and he may have been chosen as one of its victims? Or, perhaps, it was but a casual thing—the encounter of which he had been told, between his daughter and Maurice the mustanger? They may have met by accident in the chapparal? She could not well pass, without speaking to, the man who had twice rescued her from a dread danger. There might have been nothing in it, beyond the simple acknowledgment of her gratitude?

It looked well that she had, with such willingness, consented to relinquish her rides. It was but little in keeping with her usual custom, when crossed. Obedience to that particular command could not have been irksome; and argued innocence uncontaminated, virtue still intact.

So reasoned the fond father; who, beyond conjecture, was not permitted to scrutinise too closely the character of his child. In other lands, or in a different class of society, he might possibly have asked direct questions, and required direct answers to them. This is not the method upon the Mississippi; where a son of ten years old—a daughter of less than fifteen—would rebel against such scrutiny, and call it inquisition.

Still less might Woodley Poindexter strain the statutes of parental authority—the father of a Creole belle—for years used to that proud homage whose incense often stills, or altogether destroys, the simpler affections of the heart.

Though her father, and by law her controller, he knew to what a short length his power might extend, if exerted in opposition to her will. He was, therefore, satisfied with her late act of obedience—rejoiced to find that instead of continuing her reckless rides upon the prairie, she now contented herself within the range of the garden—with bow and arrow slaying the small birds that were so unlucky as to come under her aim.

Father of fifty years old, why reason in this foolish fashion? Have you forgotten your own youth—the thoughts that then inspired you—the deceits you practised under such inspiration—the counterfeits you assumed—the "stories" you told to cloak what, after all, may have been the noblest impulse of your nature?

The father of the fair Louise appeared to have become oblivious to recollections of this kind: for his early life was not without facts to have furnished them. They must have been forgotten, else he would have taken occasion to follow his daughter into the garden, and observe her—himself unobserved—while disporting herself in the shrubbery that bordered the river bank.

By doing so, he would have discovered that her disposition was not so cruel as may have been supposed. Instead of transfixing the innocent birds that fluttered in such foolish confidence around her, her greatest feat in archery appeared to be the impaling of a piece of paper upon the point of her arrow, and sending the shaft thus charged across the river, to fall harmlessly into a thicket on the opposite side.

He would have witnessed an exhibition still more singular. He would have seen the arrow thus spent—after a short interval, as if dissatisfied with the place into which it had been shot, and desirous of returning to the fair hand whence it had taken its departure—come back into the garden with the same, or a similar piece of paper, transfixed upon its shaft!

The thing might have appeared mysterious—even supernatural—to an observer unacquainted with the spirit and mechanism of that abnormal phenomenon. There was no observer of it save the two individuals who alternately bent the bow, shooting with a single arrow; and by them it was understood.

"Love laughs at locksmiths." The old adage is scarce suited to Texas, where lock-making is an unknown trade.

"Where there's a will, there's a way," expresses pretty much the same sentiment, appropriate to all time and every place. Never was it more correctly illustrated than in that exchange of bow-shots across the channel of the Leona.

Louise Poindexter had the will; Maurice Gerald had suggested the way.

# 31. A Stream Cleverly Crossed

The sagittary correspondence could not last for long. They are but lukewarm lovers who can content themselves with a dialogue carried on at bowshot distance. Hearts brimful of passion must beat and burn together—in close proximity—each feeling the pulsation of the other. "If there be an Elysium on earth, it is this!"

Maurice Gerald was not the man—nor Louise Poindexter the woman—to shun such a consummation.

It came to pass: not under the tell-tale light of the sun, but in the lone hour of midnight, when but the stars could have been witnesses of their social dereliction.

Twice had they stood together in that garden grove—twice had they exchanged love vows—under the steel-grey light of the stars; and a third interview had been arranged between them.

Little suspected the proud planter—perhaps prouder of his daughter than anything else he possessed—that she was daily engaged in an act of rebellion—the wildest against which parental authority may pronounce itself.

His own daughter—his only daughter—of the best blood of Southern aristocracy; beautiful, accomplished, everything to secure him a splendid alliance—holding nightly assignation with a horse-hunter!

Could he have but dreamt it when slumbering upon his soft couch, the dream would have startled him from his sleep like the call of the eternal trumpet!

He had no suspicion—not the slightest. The thing was too improbable—too monstrous, to have given cause for one. Its very monstrosity would have disarmed him, had the thought been suggested.

He had been pleased at his daughter's compliance with his late injunctions; though he would have preferred her obeying them to the letter, and riding out in company with her brother or cousin—which she still declined to do. This, however, he did not insist upon. He could well concede so much to her caprice: since her staying at home could be no disadvantage to the cause that had prompted him to the stern counsel.

Her ready obedience had almost influenced him to regret the prohibition. Walking in confidence by day, and sleeping in security by night, he fancied, it might be recalled.

---

It was one of those nights known only to a southern sky, when the full round moon rolls clear across a canopy of sapphire; when the mountains have no mist, and look as though you could lay your hand upon them; when the wind is hushed, and the broad leaves of the tropical trees droop motionless from their boughs; themselves silent as if listening to the concert of singular sounds carried on in their midst, and in which mingle the voices of living creatures belonging to every department of animated nature—beast, bird, reptile, and insect.

Such a night was it, as you would select for a stroll in company with the being—the one and only being—who, by the mysterious dictation of Nature, has entwined herself around your heart—a night upon which you feel a wayward longing to have white arms entwined around your neck, and bright eyes before your face, with that voluptuous gleaming that can only be felt to perfection under the mystic light of the moon.

It was long after the infantry drum had beaten tattoo, and the cavalry bugle sounded the signal for the garrison of Fort Inge to go to bed—in fact it was much nearer the hour of midnight—when a horseman rode away from the door of Oberdoffer's hotel; and, taking the down-river road, was soon lost to the sight of the latest loiterer who might have been strolling through the streets of the village.

It is already known, that this road passed the hacienda of Casa del Corvo, at some distance from the house, and on the opposite side of the river. It is also known that at the same place it traversed a stretch of open prairie, with only a piece of copsewood midway between two extensive tracts of chapparal.

This clump of isolated timber, known in prairie parlance as a "motte" or "island" of timber, stood by the side of the road, along which the horseman had continued, after taking his departure from the village.

On reaching the copse he dismounted; led his horse in among the underwood; "hitched" him, by looping his bridle rein around the topmost twigs of an elastic bough; then detaching a long rope of twisted horsehair from the "horn" of his saddle, and inserting his arm into its coil, he glided out to the edge of the "island," on that side that lay towards the hacienda.

Before forsaking the shadow of the copse, he cast a glance towards the sky, and at the moon sailing supremely over it. It was a glance of inquiry, ending in a look of chagrin, with some muttered phrases that rendered it more emphatic.

"No use waiting for that beauty to go to bed? She's made up her mind, she won't go home till morning—ha! ha!"

The droll conceit, which has so oft amused the nocturnal inebriate of great cities, appeared to produce a like affect upon the night patroller of the prairie; and for a moment the shadow, late darkening his brow, disappeared. It returned anon; as he stood gazing across the open space that separated him from the river bottom—beyond which lay the hacienda of Casa del Corvo, clearly outlined upon the opposite bluff, "If there *should* be any one stirring about the place? It's not likely at this hour; unless it be the owner of a bad conscience who can't sleep. Troth! there's one such within those walls. If he be abroad there's a good chance of his seeing me on the open ground; not that I should care a straw, if it were only myself to be compromised. By Saint Patrick, I see no alternative but risk it! It's no use waiting upon the moon, deuce take her! She don't go down for hours; and there's not the sign of a cloud. It won't do to keep *her* waiting. No; I must chance it in the clear light. Here goes?"

Saying this, with a swift but stealthy step, the dismounted horseman glided across the treeless tract, and soon readied the escarpment of the cliff, that formed the second height of land rising above the channel of the Leona.

He did not stay ten seconds in this conspicuous situation; but by a path that zigzagged down the bluff—and with which he appeared familiar—he descended to the river "bottom."

In an instant after he stood upon the bank; at the convexity of the river's bend, and directly opposite the spot where a skiff was moored, under the sombre shadow of a gigantic cotton-tree.

For a short while he stood gazing across the stream, with a glance that told of scrutiny. He was scanning the shrubbery on the other side; in the endeavour to make out, whether any one was concealed beneath its shadow.

Becoming satisfied that no one was there, he raised the loop-end of his lazo—for it was this he carried over his arm—and giving it half a dozen whirls in the air, cast it across the stream.

The noose settled over the cutwater of the skiff; and closing around the stem, enabled him to tow the tiny craft to the side on which he stood.

Stepping in, he took hold of a pair of oars that lay along the planking at the bottom; and, placing them between the thole-pins, pulled the boat back to its moorings.

Leaping out, he secured it as it had been before, against the drift of the current; and then, taking stand under the shadow of the cotton-tree, he appeared to await either a signal, or the appearance of some one, expected by appointment.

His manoeuvres up to this moment, had they been observed, might have rendered him amenable to the suspicion that he was a housebreaker, about to "crack the crib" of Casa del Corvo.

The phrases that fell from his lips, however, could they have been heard, would have absolved him of any such vile or vulgar intention. It is true he had designs upon the hacienda; but these did not contemplate either its cash, plate, or jewellery—if we except the most precious jewel it contained—the mistress of the mansion herself.

It is scarce necessary to say, that the man who had hidden his horse in the "motte," and so cleverly effected the crossing of the stream, was Maurice the mustanger.

# 32. Light and Shade

He had not long to chafe under the trysting-tree, if such it were. At the very moment when he was stepping into the skiff, a casement window that looked to the rear of the hacienda commenced turning upon its hinges, and was then for a time held slightly ajar; as if some one inside was intending to issue forth, and only hesitated in order to be assured that the "coast was clear."

A small white hand—decorated with jewels that glistened under the light of the moon—grasping the sash told that the individual who had opened the window was of the gentler sex; the tapering fingers, with their costly garniture, proclaimed her a lady; while the majestic figure—soon after exhibited outside, on the top of the stairway that led down to the garden—could be no other than that of Louise Poindexter.

It was she.

For a second or two the lady stood listening. She heard, or fancied she heard, the dip of an oar. She might be mistaken; for the stridulation of the cicadas filled the atmosphere with confused sound. No matter. The hour of assignation had arrived; and she was not the one to stand upon punctilios as to time—especially after spending two hours of solitary expectation in her chamber, that had appeared like as many. With noiseless tread descending the stone stairway, she glided sylph-like among the statues and shrubs; until, arriving under the shadow of the cotton-wood, she flung herself into arms eagerly outstretched to receive her.

Who can describe the sweetness of such embrace—strange to say, sweeter from being stolen? Who can paint the delicious emotions experienced at such a moment—too sacred to be touched by the pen?

It is only after long throes of pleasure had passed, and the lovers had begun to converse in the more sober language of life, that it becomes proper, or even possible to report them.

Thus did they speak to each other, the lady taking the initiative:—

"To-morrow night you will meet me again—to-morrow night, dearest Maurice?"

"To-morrow, and to-morrow, and to-morrow,—if I were free to say the word."

"And why not? Why are you not free to say it?"

"To-morrow, by break of day, I am off for the Alamo."

"Indeed! Is it imperative you should go?"

The interrogatory was put in a tone that betrayed displeasure. A vision of a sinister kind always came before the mind of Louise Poindexter at mention of the lone hut on the Alamo.

And why? It had afforded her hospitality. One would suppose that her visit to it could scarce fail to be one of the pleasantest recollections of her life. And yet it was not!

"I have excellent reasons for going," was the reply she received.

"Excellent reasons! Do you expect to meet any one there?"

"My follower Phelim—no one else. I hope the poor fellow is still above the grass. I sent him out about ten days ago—before there was any tidings of these Indian troubles."

"Only Phelim you expect to meet? Is it true, Gerald? Dearest! do not deceive me! Only him?"

"Why do you ask the question, Louise?"

"I cannot tell you why. I should die of shame to speak my secret thoughts."

"Do not fear to speak them! I could keep no secret from you—in truth I could not. So tell me what it is, love!"

"Do you wish me, Maurice?"

"I do—of course I do. I feel sure that whatever it may be, I shall be able to explain it. I know that my relations with you are of a questionable character; or might be so deemed, if the world knew of them. It is for that very reason I am going back to the Alamo."

"And to stay there?"

"Only for a single day, or two at most. Only to gather up my household gods, and bid a last adieu to my prairie life."

"Indeed!"

"You appear surprised."

"No! only mystified. I cannot comprehend you. Perhaps I never shall!"

"'Tis very simple—the resolve I have taken. I know you will forgive me, when I make it known to you."

"Forgive you, Maurice! For what do you ask forgiveness?"

"For keeping it a secret from you, that—that I am not what I seem."

"God forbid you should be otherwise than what you seem to me—noble, grand, beautiful, rare among men! Oh, Maurice! you know not how I esteem—how I love you!"

"Not more than I esteem and love you. It is that very esteem that now counsels me to a separation."

"A separation?"

"Yes, love; but it is to be hoped only for a short time."

"How long?"

"While a steamer can cross the Atlantic, and return."

"An age! And why this?"

"I am called to my native country—Ireland, so much despised, as you already know. 'Tis only within the last twenty hours I received the summons. I obey it the more eagerly, that it tells me I shall be able soon to return, and prove to your proud father that the poor horse-hunter who won his daughter's heart—have I won it, Louise?"

"Idle questioner! Won it? You know you have more than won it—conquered it to a subjection from which it can never escape. Mock me not, Maurice, nor my stricken heart—henceforth, and for ever-more, your slave!"

During the rapturous embrace that followed this passionate speech, by which a high-born and beautiful maiden confessed to have surrendered herself—heart, soul, and body—to the man who had made conquest of her affections, there was silence perfect and profound.

The grasshopper amid the green herbage, the cicada on the tree-leaf, the mock-bird on the top of the tall cotton-wood, and the nightjar soaring still higher in the moonlit air, apparently actuated by a simultaneous instinct, ceased to give utterance to their peculiar cries: as though one and all, by their silence, designed to do honour to the sacred ceremony transpiring in their presence!

But that temporary cessation of sounds was due to a different cause. A footstep grating upon the gravelled walk of the garden—and yet touching it so lightly, that only an acute ear could have perceived the contact—was the real cause why the nocturnal voices had suddenly become stilled.

The lovers, absorbed in the sweet interchange of a mutual affection, heard it not. They saw not that dark shadow, in the shape of man or devil, flitting among the flowers; now standing by a statue; now under cover of the shrubbery, until at length it became stationary behind the trunk of a tree, scarce ten paces from the spot where they were kissing each other!

Little did they suspect, in that moment of celestial happiness when all nature was hushed around them, that the silence was exposing their passionate speeches, and the treacherous moon, at the same time, betraying their excited actions.

That shadowy listener, crouching guilty-like behind the tree, was a witness to both. Within easy earshot, he could hear every word—even the sighs and soft low murmurings of their love; while under the silvery light of the moon, with scarce a sprig coming between, he could detect their slightest gestures.

It is scarce necessary to give the name of the dastardly eavesdropper. That of Cassius Calhoun will have suggested itself.

It was he.

# 33. A Torturing Discovery

How came the cousin of Louise Poindexter to be astir at that late hour of the night, or, as it was now, the earliest of the morning? Had he been forewarned of this interview of the lovers; or was it merely some instinctive suspicion that had caused him to forsake his sleeping-chamber, and make a tour of inspection within the precincts of the garden?

In other words, was he an eavesdropper by accident, or a spy acting upon information previously communicated to him?

The former was the fact. Chance alone, or chance aided by a clear night, had given him the clue to a discovery that now filled his soul with the fires of hell.

Standing upon the housetop at the hour of midnight—what had taken him up there cannot be guessed—breathing vile tobacco-smoke into an atmosphere before perfumed with the scent of the night-blooming *cereus*; the ex-captain of cavalry did not appear distressed by any particular anxiety. He had recovered from the injuries received in his encounter with the mustanger; and although that bit of evil fortune did not fail to excite within him the blackest chagrin, whenever it came up before his mind, its bitterness had been, to some extent, counteracted by hopes of revenge—towards a plan for which he had already made some progress.

Equally with her father, he had been gratified that Louise was contented of late to stay within doors: for it was himself who had secretly suggested the prohibition to her going abroad. Equally had he remained ignorant as to the motive of that garden archery, and in a similar manner had misconceived it. In fact, he had begun to flatter himself, that, after all, her indifference to himself might be only a feint on the part of his cousin, or an illusion upon his. She had been less cynical for some days; and this had produced upon him the pleasant impression, that he might have been mistaken in his jealous fears.

He had as yet discovered no positive proof that she entertained a partiality for the young Irishman; and as the days passed without any renewed cause for disquiet, he began to believe that in reality there was none.

Under the soothing influence of this restored confidence, had he mounted up to the azotea; and, although it was the hour of midnight, the careless *insouciance* with which he applied the light to his cigar, and afterwards stood smoking it, showed that he could not have come there for any very important purpose. It may have been to exchange the sultry atmosphere of his sleeping-room for the fresher air outside; or he may have been tempted forth by the magnificent moon—though he was not much given to such romantic contemplation.

Whatever it was, he had lighted his cigar, and was apparently enjoying it, with his arms crossed upon the coping of the parapet, and his face turned towards the river.

It did not disturb his tranquillity to see a horseman ride out from the chapparal on the opposite side, and proceed onward across the open plain.

He knew of the road that was there. Some traveller, he supposed, who preferred taking advantage of the cool hours of the night—a night, too, that would have tempted the weariest wayfarer to continue his journey. It might be a planter who lived below, returning home from the village, after lounging an hour too long in the tavern saloon.

In daytime, the individual might have been identified; by the moonlight, it could only be made out that there was a man on horseback.

The eyes of the ex-officer accompanied him as he trotted along the road; but simply with mechanical movement, as one musingly contemplates some common waif drifting down the current of a river.

It was only after the horseman had arrived opposite the island of timber, and was seen to pull up, and then ride into it, that the spectator upon the housetop became stirred to take an interest in his movements.

"What the devil can that mean?" muttered Calhoun to himself, as he hastily plucked the cigar stump from between his teeth. "Damn the man, he's dismounted!" continued he, as the stranger re-appeared, on foot, by the inner edge of the copse.

"And coming this way—towards the bend of the river—straight as he can streak it!

"Down the bluff—into the bottom—and with a stride that shows him well acquainted with the way. Surely to God he don't intend making his way across into the garden? He'd have to swim for that; and anything he could get there would scarce pay him for his pains. What the old Scratch can be his intention? A thief?"

This was Calhoun's first idea—rejected almost as soon as conceived. It is true that in Spanish-American countries even the beggar goes on horseback. Much more might the thief?

For all this, it was scarce probable, that a man would make a midnight expedition to steal fruit, or vegetables, in such cavalier style.

What else could he be after?

The odd manoeuvre of leaving his horse under cover of the copse, and coming forward on foot, and apparently with caution, as far as could be seen in the uncertain light, was of itself evidence that the man's errand could scarce be honest and that he was approaching the premises of Casa del Corvo with some evil design.

What could it be?

Since leaving the upper plain he had been no longer visible to Calhoun upon the housetop. The underwood skirting the stream on the opposite side, and into which he had entered, was concealing him.

"What can the man be after?"

After putting this interrogatory to himself, and for about the tenth time—each with increasing emphasis—the composure of the ex-captain was still further disturbed by a sound that reached his ear, exceedingly like a plunge in the river. It was slight, but clearly the concussion of some hard substance brought in contact with water.

"The stroke of an oar," muttered he, on hearing it. "Is, by the holy Jehovah! He's got hold of the skiff, and's crossing over to the garden. What on earth can he be after?"

The questioner did not intend staying on the housetop to determine. His thought was to slip silently downstairs—rouse the male members of the family, along with some of the servants; and attempt to capture the intruder by a clever ambuscade.

He had raised his arm from the copestone, and was in the act of stepping back from the parapet, when his ear was saluted by another sound, that caused him again to lean forward and look into the garden below.

This new noise bore no resemblance to the stroke of an oar; nor did it proceed from the direction of the river. It was the creaking of a door as it turned upon its hinge, or, what is much the same, a casement window; while it came from below—almost directly underneath the spot where the listener stood.

On craning over to ascertain the cause, he saw, what blanched his cheeks to the whiteness of the moonlight that shone upon them—what sent the blood curdling through every corner of his heart.

The casement that had been opened was that which belonged to the bed-chamber of his cousin Louise. He knew it. The lady herself was standing outside upon the steps that led to the level of the garden, her face turned downward, as if she was meditating a descent.

Loosely attired in white, as though in the negligé of a *robe de chambre*, with only a small kerchief coifed over her crown, she resembled some fair nymph of the night, some daughter of the moon, whom Luna delighted to surround with a silvery effulgence!

Calhoun reasoned rapidly. He could not do otherwise than connect her appearance outside the casement with the advent of the man who was making his way across the river.

And who could this man be? Who but Maurice the mustanger?

A clandestine meeting! And by appointment!

There could be no doubt of it; and if there had, it would have been dissolved, at seeing the white-robed figure glide noiselessly down the stone steps, and along the gravelled walks, till it at length disappeared among the trees that shadowed the mooring-place of the skiff.

Like one paralysed with a powerful stroke, the ex-captain continued for some time upon the azotea—speechless and without motion. It was only after the white drapery had disappeared, and he heard the low murmur of voices rising from among the trees, that he was stimulated to resolve upon some course of proceeding.

He thought no longer of awaking the inmates of the house—at least not then. Better first to be himself the sole witness of his cousin's disgrace; and then—and then—

In short, he was not in a state of mind to form any definite plan; and, acting solely under the blind stimulus of a fell instinct, he hurried down the *escalera*, and made his way through the house, and out into the garden.

He felt feeble as he pressed forward. His legs had tottered under him while descending the stone steps. They did the same as he glided along the gravelled walk. They continued to tremble as he crouched behind the tree trunk that hindered him from being seen—while playing spectator of a scene that afflicted him to the utmost depths of his soul.

He heard their vows; their mutual confessions of love; the determination of the mustanger to be gone by the break of the morrow's day; as also his promise to return, and the revelation to which that promise led.

With bitter chagrin, he heard how this determination was combated by Louise, and the reasons why she at length appeared to consent to it.

He was witness to that final and rapturous embrace, that caused him to strike his foot nervously against the pebbles, and make that noise that had scared the cicadas into silence.

Why at that moment did he not spring forward—put a termination to the intolerable *tête-à-tête*—and with a blow of his bowie-knife lay his rival low—at his own feet and that of his mistress? Why had he not done this at the beginning—for to him there needed no further evidence, than the interview itself, to prove that his cousin had been dishonoured?

There was a time when he would not have been so patient. What, then, was the *punctilio* that restrained him? Was it the presence of that piece of perfect mechanism, that, with a sheen of steel, glistened upon the person of his rival, and which under the bright moonbeams, could be distinguished as a "Colt's six-shooter?"

Perhaps it may have been. At all events, despite the terrible temptation to which his soul was submitted, something not only hindered him from taking an immediate vengeance, but in the mid-moments of that maddening spectacle—the final embrace—prompted him to turn away from the spot, and with an earnestness, even keener than he had yet exhibited, hurry back in the direction of the house: leaving the lovers, still unconscious of having been observed, to bring their sweet interview to an ending—sure to be procrastinated.

## 34. A Chivalrous Dictation

Where went Cassius Calhoun?

Certainly not to his own sleeping-room. There was no sleep for a spirit suffering like his.

He went not there; but to the chamber of his cousin. Not hers—now untenanted, with its couch unoccupied, its coverlet undisturbed—but to that of her brother, young Henry Poindexter.

He went direct as crooked corridors would permit him—in haste, without waiting to avail himself of the assistance of a candle.

It was not needed. The moonbeams penetrating through the open bars of the *reja*, filled the chamber with light—sufficient for his purpose. They disclosed the outlines of the apartment, with its simple furniture—a washstand, a dressing-table, a couple of chairs, and a bed with "mosquito curtains."

Under those last was the youth reclining; in that sweet silent slumber experienced only by the innocent. His finely formed head rested calmly upon the pillow, over which lay scattered a profusion of shining curls.

As Calhoun lifted the muslin "bar," the moonbeams fell upon his face, displaying its outlines of the manliest aristocratic type.

What a contrast between those two sets of features, brought into such close proximity! Both physically handsome; but morally, as Hyperion to the Satyr.

"Awake, Harry! awake!" was the abrupt salutation extended to the sleeper, accompanied by a violent shaking of his shoulder.

"Oh! ah! you, cousin Cash? What is it? not the Indiana, I hope?"

"Worse than that—worse! worse! Quick! Rouse yourself, and see! Quick, or it will be too late! Quick, and be the witness of your own disgrace—the dishonour of your house. Quick, or the name of Poindexter will be the laughing-stock of Texas!"

After such summons there could be no inclination for sleep—at least on the part of a Poindexter; and at a single bound, the youngest representative of the family cleared the mosquito curtains, and stood upon his feet in the middle of the floor—in an attitude of speechless astonishment.

"Don't wait to dress," cried his excited counsellor, "stay, you may put on your pants. Damn the clothes! There's no time for standing upon trifles. Quick! Quick!"

The simple costume the young planter was accustomed to wear, consisting of trousers and Creole blouse of Attakapas *cottonade*, were adjusted to his person in less than twenty seconds of time; and in twenty more, obedient to the command of his cousin—without understanding why he had been so unceremoniously summoned forth—he was hurrying along the gravelled walks of the garden.

"What is it, Cash?" he inquired, as soon as the latter showed signs of coming to a stop. "What does it all mean?"

"See for yourself! Stand close to me! Look through yonder opening in the trees that leads down to the place where your skiff is kept. Do you see anything there?"

"Something white. It looks like a woman's dress. It is that. It's a woman!"

"It *is* a woman. Who do you suppose she is?"

"I can't tell. Who do you say she is?"

"There's another figure—a dark one—by her side."

"It appears to be a man? It is a man!"

"And who do you suppose *he* is?"

"How should I know, cousin Cash? Do you?"

"I do. That man is Maurice the mustanger!"

"And the woman?"

"*Is Louise—your sister—in his arms!*"

As if a shot had struck him through the heart, the brother bounded upward, and then onward, along the path.

"Stay!" said Calhoun, catching hold of, and restraining him. "You forget that you are unarmed! The fellow, I know, has weapons upon him. Take this, and this," continued he, passing his own knife and pistol into the hands of his cousin. "I should have used them myself, long ere this; but I thought it better that you—her brother—should be the avenger of your sister's wrongs. On, my boy! See that you don't hurt *her*; but take care not to lose the chance at him. Don't give him a word of warning. As soon as they are separated, send a bullet into his belly; and if all six should fail, go at him with the knife. I'll stay near, and

201

take care of you, if you should get into danger. Now! Steal upon him, and give the scoundrel hell!"

It needed not this blasphemous injunction to inspire Henry Poindexter to hasty action. The brother of a sister—a beautiful sister—erring, undone!

In six seconds he was by her side, confronting her supposed seducer.

"Low villain!" he cried, "unclasp your loathsome arm from the waist of my sister. Louise! stand aside, and give me a chance of killing him! Aside, sister! Aside, I say!"

Had the command been obeyed, it is probable that Maurice Gerald would at that moment have ceased to exist—unless he had found heart to kill Henry Poindexter; which, experienced as he was in the use of his six-shooter, and prompt in its manipulation, he might have done.

Instead of drawing the pistol from its holster, or taking any steps for defence, he appeared only desirous of disengaging himself from the fair arms still clinging around him, and for whose owner he alone felt alarm.

For Henry to fire at the supposed betrayer, was to risk taking his sister's life; and, restrained by the fear of this, he paused before pulling trigger.

That pause produced a crisis favourable to the safety of all three. The Creole girl, with a quick perception of the circumstances, suddenly released her lover from the protecting embrace; and, almost in the same instant, threw her arms around those of her brother. She knew there was nothing to be apprehended from the pistol of Maurice. Henry alone had to be held doing mischief.

"Go, go!" she shouted to the former, while struggling to restrain the infuriated youth. "My brother is deceived by appearances. Leave me to explain. Away, Maurice! away!"

"Henry Poindexter," said the young Irishman, as he turned to obey the friendly command, "I am not the sort of villain you have been pleased to pronounce me. Give me but time, and I shall prove, that your sister has formed a truer estimate of my character than either her father, brother, or cousin. I claim but six months. If at the end of that time I do not show myself worthy of her confidence—her love—then shall I make you welcome to shoot me at sight, as you would the cowardly coyoté, that chanced to cross your track. Till then, I bid you adieu."

Henry's struggle to escape from his sister's arms—perhaps stronger than his own—grew less energetic as he listened to these

202

words. They became feebler and feebler—at length ceasing—when a plunge in the river announced that the midnight intruder into the enclosed grounds of Casa del Corvo was on his way back to the wild prairies he had chosen for his home.

It was the first time he had recrossed the river in that primitive fashion. On the two previous occasions he had passed over in the skiff; which had been drawn back to its moorings by a delicate hand, the tow-rope consisting of that tiny lazo that had formed part of the caparison presented along with the spotted mustang.

"Brother! you are wronging him! indeed you are wronging him!" were the words of expostulation that followed close upon his departure. "Oh, Henry—dearest Hal, if you but knew how noble he is! So far from desiring to do me an injury, 'tis only this moment he has been disclosing a plan to—to—prevent—scandal—I mean to make me happy. Believe me, brother, he is a gentleman; and if he were not—if only the common man you take him for—I could not help what I have done—I could not, for *I love him*!"

"Louise! tell me the truth! Speak to me, not as to your brother, but as to your own self. From what I have this night seen, more than from your own words, I know that you love this man. Has he taken advantage of your—your—unfortunate passion?"

"No—no—no. As I live he has not. He is too noble for that—even had I—Henry! he is innocent! If there be cause for regret, I alone am to blame. Why—oh! brother! why did you insult him?"

"Have I done so?"

"You have, Henry—rudely, grossly."

"I shall go after, and apologise. If you speak truly, sister, I owe him that much. I shall go this instant. I liked him from the first—you know I did? I could not believe him capable of a cowardly act. I can't now. Sister! come back into the house with me. And now, dearest Loo! you had better go to bed. As for me, I shall be off *instanter* to the hotel, where I may still hope to overtake him. I cannot rest till I have made reparation for my rudeness."

So spoke the forgiving brother; and gently leading his sister by the hand, with thoughts of compassion, but not the slightest trace of anger, he hastily returned to the hacienda—intending to go after the young Irishman, and apologise for the use of words that, under the circumstances, might have been deemed excusable.

As the two disappeared within the doorway, a third figure, hitherto crouching among the shrubbery, was seen to rise erect, and follow them up the stone steps. This last was their cousin, Cassius Calhoun.

He, too, had thoughts of *going after* the mustanger.

# 35. An Uncourteous Host

"The chicken-hearted fool! Fool myself, to have trusted to such a hope! I might have known she'd cajole the young calf, and let the scoundrel escape. I could have shot him from behind the tree—dead as a drowned rat! And without risking anything—even disgrace! Not a particle of risk. Uncle Woodley would have thanked me—the whole settlement would have said I had done right. My cousin, a young lady, betrayed by a common scamp—a horse, trader—who would have said a word against it? Such a chance! Why have I missed it? Death and the devil—it may not trump up again!"

Such were the reflections of the ex-captain of cavalry, while at some paces distance following his two cousins on their return to the hacienda.

"I wonder," muttered he, on re-entering the *patio*, "whether the blubbering baby be in earnest? Going after to apologise to the man who has made a fool of his sister! Ha—ha! It would be a good joke were it not too serious to be laughed at. He *is* in earnest, else why that row in the stable? 'Tis he bringing but his horse! It is, by the Almighty!"

The door of the stable, as is customary in Mexican haciendas opened upon the paved *patio*.

It was standing ajar; but just as Calhoun turned his eye upon it, a man coming from the inside pushed it wide open; and then stepped over the threshold, with a saddled horse following close after him.

The man had a Panama hat upon his head, and a cloak thrown loosely around his shoulders. This did not hinder Calhoun from recognising his cousin Henry, as also the dark brown horse that belonged to him.

"Fool! So—you've let him off?" spitefully muttered the ex-captain, as the other came within whispering distance. "Give me back my bowie and pistol. They're not toys suited to such delicate fingers as yours! Bah! Why did you not use them as I told you? You've made a mess of it!"

"I have," tranquilly responded the young planter. "I know it. I've insulted—and grossly too—a noble fellow."

"Insulted a noble fellow! Ha—ha—ha! You're mad—by heavens, you're mad!"

"I should have been had I followed your counsel, cousin Cash. Fortunately I did not go so far. I have done enough to deserve being called worse than fool; though perhaps, under the circumstances, I may obtain forgiveness for my fault. At all events, I intend to try for it, and without losing time."

"Where are you going?"

"After Maurice the mustanger—to apologise to him for my misconduct."

"Misconduct! Ha—ha—ha! Surely you are joking?"

"No. I'm in earnest. If you come along with me, you shall see!"

"Then I say again you are mad! Not only mad, but a damned natural-born idiot! you are, by Jesus Christ and General Jackson!"

"You're not very polite, cousin Cash; though, after the language I've been lately using myself, I might excuse you. Perhaps you will, one day imitate me, and make amends for your rudeness."

Without adding another word, the young gentleman—one of the somewhat rare types of Southern chivalry—sprang to his saddle; gave the word, to his horse; and rode hurriedly through the *saguan*.

Calhoun stood upon the stones, till the footfall of the horse became but faintly distinguishable in the distance.

Then, as if acting under some sudden impulse, he hurried along the verandah to his own room; entered it; reappeared in a rough overcoat; crossed back to the stable; went in; came out again with his own horse saddled and bridled; led the animal along the pavement, as gently as if he was stealing him; and once outside upon the turf, sprang upon his back, and rode rapidly away.

For a mile or more he followed the same road, that had been taken by Henry Poindexter. It could not have been with any idea of overtaking the latter: since, long before, the hoofstrokes of Henry's horse had ceased to be heard; and proceeding at a slower pace, Calhoun did not ride as if he cared about catching up with his cousin.

He had taken the up-river road. When about midway between Casa del Corvo and the Fort, he reined up; and, after scrutinising the chapparal around him, struck off by a bridle-path leading back toward the bank of the river. As he turned into it he might have been heard muttering to himself—

"A chance still left; a good one, though not so cheap as the other. It will cost me a thousand dollars. What of that, so long as I get rid of this Irish curse, who has poisoned every hour of my existence! If true to his promise, he takes the route to his home by an early hour in the morning. What time, I wonder. These men of the prairies call it late rising, if they be abed till daybreak! Never mind. There's yet time for the Coyote to get before him on the road! I know that. It must be the same as we followed to the wild horse prairies. He spoke of his hut upon the Alamo. That's the name of the creek where we had our picnic. The hovel cannot be far from there! The Mexican must know the place, or the trail leading to it; which last will be sufficient for his purpose and mine. A fig for the shanty itself! The owner may never reach it. There may be Indians upon the road! There *must* be, before daybreak in the morning!"

As Calhoun concluded this string of strange reflections, he had arrived at the door of another "shanty"—that of the Mexican mustanger. The *jacalé* was the goal of his journey.

Having slipped out of his saddle, and knotted his bridle to a branch, he set foot upon the threshold.

The door was standing wide open. From the inside proceeded a sound, easily identified as the snore of a slumberer.

It was not as of one who sleeps either tranquilly, or continuously. At short intervals it was interrupted—now by silent pauses—anon by hog-like gruntings, interspersed with profane words, not perfectly pronounced, but slurred from a thick tongue, over which, but a short while before, must have passed a stupendous quantity of alcohol.

"*Carrambo! carrai! carajo—chingara! mil diablos!*" mingled with more—perhaps less—reverential exclamations of "*Sangre de Cristo! Jesus! Santissima Virgen! Santa Maria! Dios! Madre de Dios!*" and the like, were uttered inside the *jacalé*, as if the speaker was engaged in an apostrophic conversation with all the principal characters of the Popish Pantheon.

Calhoun paused upon the threshold, and listened.

"*Mal—dit—dit—o!*" muttered the sleeper, concluding the exclamation with a hiccup. "*Buen—buenos nove-dad-es!* Good news, *por sangre Chrees—Chreest—o! Si S'ñor Merican—cano! Nove—dad—es s'perbos! Los Indyos Co—co—manchees* on the war-trail—*el rastro de guerra.* God bless the Co—co—manchees!"

207

"The brute's drunk!" said his visitor, mechanically speaking aloud.

"*H'la S'ñor!*" exclaimed the owner of the *jacalé*, aroused to a state of semi-consciousness by the sound of a human voice. "*Quien llama*! Who has the honour—that is, have I the happiness—I, Miguel Diaz—el Co—coyoté, as the *leperos* call me. Ha, ha! coyo—coyot. Bah! what's in a name? Yours, S'ñor? *Mil demonios*! who are you?"

Partially raising himself from his reed couch, the inebriate remained for a short time in a sitting attitude—glaring, half interrogatively, half unconsciously, at the individual whose voice had intruded itself into his drunken dreams.

The unsteady examination lasted only for a score of seconds. Then the owner of the *jacalé*, with an unintelligible speech, subsided into a recumbent position; when a savage grunt, succeeded by a prolonged snore, proved him to have become oblivious to the fact that his domicile contained a guest.

"Another chance lost!" said the latter, hissing the words through his teeth, as he turned disappointedly from the door.

"A sober fool and a drunken knave—two precious tools wherewith, to accomplish a purpose like mine! Curse the luck! All this night it's been against me! It maybe three long hours before this pig sleeps off the swill that has stupefied him. Three long hours, and then what would be the use of him? 'Twould be too late—too late!"

As he said this, he caught the rein of his bridle, and stood by the head of his horse, as if uncertain what course to pursue.

"No use my staying here! It might be daybreak before the damned liquor gets out of his skull. I may as well go back to the hacienda and wait there; or else—or else—"

The alternative, that at this crisis presented itself, was nor, spoken aloud. Whatever it may have been, it had the effect of terminating the hesitancy that living over him, and stirring him to immediate action.

Roughly tearing his rein from the branch, and passing it over his horse's head, he sprang into the saddle, and rode off from the *jacalé* in a direction the very opposite to that in which he had approached it.

# 36. Three Travellers on the Same Track

No one can deny, that a ride upon a smooth-turfed prairie is one of the most positive pleasures of sublunary existence. No one *will* deny it, who has had the good fortune to experience the delightful sensation. With a spirited horse between your thighs, a well-stocked valise strapped to the cantle of your saddle, a flask of French brandy slung handy over the "horn," and a plethoric cigar-case protruding from under the flap of your pistol holster, you may set forth upon a day's journey, without much fear of feeling weary by the way.

A friend riding by your side—like yourself alive to the beauties of nature, and sensitive to its sublimities—will make the ride, though long, and otherwise arduous, a pleasure to be remembered for many, many years.

If that friend chance to be some fair creature, upon whom you have fixed your affections, then will you experience a delight to remain in your memory for ever.

Ah! if all prairie-travellers were to be favoured with such companionship, the wilderness of Western Texas would soon become crowded with tourists; the great plains would cease to be "pathless,"—the savannas would swarm with snobs.

It is better as it is. As it is, you may launch yourself upon the prairie: and once beyond the precincts of the settlement from which you have started—unless you keep to the customary "road," indicated only by the hoof-prints of half a dozen horsemen who have preceded you—you may ride on for hours, days, weeks, months, perhaps a whole year, without encountering aught that bears the slightest resemblance to yourself, or the image in which you have been made.

Only those who have traversed the great plain of Texas can form a true estimate of its illimitable vastness; impressing the mind with sensations similar to those we feel in the contemplation of infinity.

In some sense may the mariner comprehend my meaning. Just as a ship may cross the Atlantic Ocean—and in tracks most frequented by sailing craft—without sighting a single sail, so upon the prairies of South-western Texas, the traveller may journey on for months, amid a solitude that seems eternal!

Even the ocean itself does not give such an impression of endless space. Moving in its midst you perceive no change—no sign to tell you you are progressing. The broad circular surface of azure blue, with the concave hemisphere of a tint but a few shades lighter, are always around and above you, seeming ever the same. You think they *are* so; and fancy yourself at rest in the centre of a sphere and a circle. You are thus to some extent hindered from having a clear conception of "magnificent distances."

On the prairie it is different. The "landmarks"—there are such, in the shape of "mottes," mounds, trees, ridges, and rocks—constantly changing before your view, admonish you that you are passing through space; and this very knowledge imbues you with the idea of vastness.

It is rare for the prairie traveller to contemplate such scenes alone—rarer still upon the plains of South-western Texas. In twos at least—but oftener in companies of ten or a score—go they, whose need it is to tempt the perils of that wilderness claimed by the Comanches as ancestral soil.

For all this, a solitary traveller may at times be encountered: for on the same night that witnessed the tender and stormy scenes in the garden of Casa del Corvo, no less than three such made the crossing of the plain that stretches south-westward from the banks of the Leona River.

Just at the time that Calhoun was making his discontented departure from the *jacalé* of the Mexican mustanger, the foremost of these nocturnal travellers was clearing the outskirts of the village—going in a direction which, if followed far enough, would conduct him to the Nueces River, or one of its tributary streams.

It is scarcely necessary to say, that he was on horseback. In Texas there are no pedestrians, beyond the precincts of the town or plantation.

The traveller in question bestrode a strong steed; whose tread, at once vigorous and elastic, proclaimed it capable of carrying its rider through a long journey, without danger of breaking down.

Whether such a journey was intended, could not have been told by the bearing of the traveller himself. He was equipped, as any Texan cavalier might have been, for a ten-mile ride—perhaps to his own house. The lateness of the hour forbade the supposition, that he could be going from it. The serapé on his shoulders—somewhat carelessly hanging—might have been only put on to protect them against the dews of the night.

But as there was no dew on that particular night—nor any outlying settlement in the direction he was heading to—the horseman was more like to have been a real traveller—*en route* for some distant point upon the prairies.

For all this he did not appear to be in haste; or uneasy as to the hour at which he might reach his destination.

On the contrary, he seemed absorbed in some thought, that linked itself with the past; sufficiently engrossing to render him unobservant of outward objects, and negligent in the management of his horse.

The latter, with the rein lying loosely upon his neck, was left to take his own way; though instead of stopping, or straying, he kept steadily on, as if over ground oft trodden before.

Thus leaving the animal to its own guidance, and pressing it neither with whip nor spur, the traveller rode tranquilly over the prairie, till lost to view—not by the intervention of any object, but solely through the dimness of the light, where the moon became misty in the far distance.

Almost on the instant of his disappearance—and as if the latter had been taken for a cue—a second horseman spurred out from the suburbs of the village; and proceeded along the same path.

From the fact of his being habited in a fashion to defend him against the chill air of the night, he too might have been taken for a traveller.

A cloak clasped across his breast hung over his shoulders, its ample skirts draping backward to the hips of his horse.

Unlike the horseman who had preceded him, he showed signs of haste—plying both whip and spur as he pressed on.

He appeared intent on overtaking some one. It might be the individual whose form had just faded out of sight?

This was all the more probable from the style of his equitation—at short intervals bending forward in his saddle, and scanning the horizon before him, as if expecting to see some form outlined above the line of the sky.

Continuing to advance in this peculiar fashion, he also disappeared from view—exactly at the same point, where his precursor had ceased to be visible—to any one whose gaze might have been following him from the Fort or village.

An odd contingency—if such it were—that just at that very instant a third horseman rode forth from the outskirts of the little Texan town, and, like the other two, continued advancing in a direct line across the prairie.

He, also, was costumed as if for a journey. A "blanket-coat" of scarlet colour shrouded most of his person from sight—its ample skirts spread over his thighs, half concealing a short jäger rifle, strapped aslant along the flap of his saddle.

Like the foremost of the three, he exhibited no signs of a desire to move rapidly along the road. He was proceeding at a slow pace—even for a traveller. For all that, his manner betokened a state of mind far from tranquil; and in this respect he might be likened to the horseman who had more immediately preceded him.

But there was an essential difference between the actions of the two men. Whereas the cloaked cavalier appeared desirous of overtaking some one in advance, he in the red blanket coat seemed altogether to occupy himself in reconnoitring towards his rear.

At intervals he would slue himself round in the stirrups—sometimes half turn his horse—and scan the track over which he had passed; all the while listening, as though he expected to hear some one who should be coming after him.

Still keeping up this singular surveillance, he likewise in due time reached the point of disappearance, without having overtaken any one, or been himself overtaken.

Though at nearly equal distances apart while making the passage of the prairie, not one of the three horsemen was within sight of either of the others. The second, half-way between the other two, was beyond reach of the vision of either, as they were beyond his.

At the same glance no eye could have taken in all three, or any two of them; unless it had been that of the great Texan owl perched upon the summit of some high eminence, or the "whip-poor-will" soaring still higher in pursuit of the moon-loving moth.

An hour later, and at a point of the prairie ten miles farther from Fort Inge, the relative positions of the three travellers had undergone a considerable change.

The foremost was just entering into a sort of alley or gap in the chapparal forest; which here extended right and left across the plain, far as the eye could trace it. The alley might have been likened to a strait in the sea: its smooth turfed surface contrasting with the darker foliage of the bordering thickets; as water with dry land. It was illumined throughout a part of its length—a half mile or so—the moon showing at its opposite extremity. Beyond this the dark tree line closed it in, where it angled round into sombre shadow.

Before entering the alley the foremost of the trio of travellers, and for the first time, exhibited signs of hesitation. He reined up; and for a second or two sate in his saddle regarding the ground before him. His attention was altogether directed to the opening through the trees in his front. He made no attempt at reconnoitring his rear.

His scrutiny, from whatever cause, was of short continuance.

Seemingly satisfied, he muttered an injunction to his horse, and rode onward into the gap.

Though he saw not him, he was seen by the cavalier in the cloak, following upon the same track, and now scarce half a mile behind.

The latter, on beholding him, gave utterance to a slight exclamation.

It was joyful, nevertheless; as if he was gratified by the prospect of at length overtaking the individual whom he had been for ten miles so earnestly pursuing.

Spurring his horse to a still more rapid pace, he also entered the opening; but only in time to get a glimpse of the other, just passing under the shadow of the trees, at the point where the avenue angled.

Without hesitation, he rode after; soon disappearing at the same place, and in a similar manner.

It was a longer interval before the third and hindmost of the horsemen approached the pass that led through the chapparal.

He did approach it, however; but instead of riding into it, as the others had done, he turned off at an angle towards the edge of the timber; and, after leaving his horse among the trees, crossed a corner of the thicket, and came out into the opening on foot.

Keeping along it—to all appearance still more solicitous about something that might be in his rear than anything that was in front of him—he at length arrived at the shadowy turning; where, like the two others, he abruptly disappeared in the darkness.

An hour elapsed, during which the nocturnal voices of the chapparal—that had been twice temporarily silenced by the hoofstroke of a horse, and once by the footsteps of a man—had kept up their choral cries by a thousand stereotyped repetitions.

Then there came a further interruption; more abrupt in its commencement, and of longer continuance. It was caused by a sound, very different from that made by the passage of either horseman or pedestrian over the prairie turf.

It was the report of a gun, quick, sharp, and clear—the "spang" that denotes the discharge of a rifle.

As to the authoritative wave of the conductor's baton the orchestra yields instant obedience, so did the prairie minstrels simultaneously take their cue from that abrupt detonation, that inspired one and all of them with a peculiar awe.

The tiger cat miaulling in the midst of the chapparal, the coyoté howling along its skirts; even the jaguar who need not fear any forest foe that might approach him, acknowledged his dread of that quick, sharp explosion—to him unexplainable—by instantly discontinuing his cries.

As no other sound succeeded the shot—neither the groan of a wounded man, nor the scream of a stricken animal—the jaguar soon recovered confidence, and once more essayed to frighten the denizens of the thicket with his hoarse growling.

Friends and enemies—birds, beasts, insects, and reptiles— disregarding his voice in the distance, reassumed the thread of their choral strain; until the chapparal was restored to its normal noisy condition, when two individuals standing close together, can only hold converse by speaking in the highest pitch of their voices!

# 37. A Man Missing

The breakfast bell of Casa del Corvo had sounded its second and last summons—preceded by a still earlier signal from a horn, intended to call in the stragglers from remote parts of the plantation.

The "field hands" labouring near had collected around the "quarter;" and in groups, squatted upon the grass, or seated upon stray logs, were discussing their diet—by no means spare—of "hog and hominy" corn-bread and "corn-coffee," with a jocosity that proclaimed a keen relish of these, their ordinary comestibles.

The planter's family assembled in the *sala* were about to begin breakfast, when it was discovered that one of its members was missing.

Henry was the absent one.

At first there was but little notice taken of the circumstance. Only the conjecture: that he would shortly make his appearance.

As several minutes passed without his coming in, the planter quietly observed that it was rather strange of Henry to be behind time, and wonder where he could be.

The breakfast of the South-western American is usually a well appointed meal. It is eaten at a fixed hour, and *table-d'hôte* fashion—all the members of the family meeting at the table.

This habit is exacted by a sort of necessity, arising out of the nature of some of the viands peculiar to the country; many of which, as "Virginia biscuit," "buckwheat cakes," and "waffles," are only relished coming fresh from, the fire: so that the hour when breakfast is being eaten in the dining-room, is that in which the cook is broiling her skin in the kitchen.

As the laggard, or late riser, may have to put up with cold biscuit, and no waffles or buckwheat cakes, there are few such on a Southern plantation.

Considering this custom, it *was* somewhat strange, that Henry Poindexter had not yet put in an appearance.

"Where can the boy be?" asked his father, for the fourth time, in that tone of mild conjecture that scarce calls for reply.

None was made by either of the other two guests at the table. Louise only gave expression to a similar conjecture. For all that, there was a strangeness in her glance—as in the tone of her voice—that might have been observed by one closely scrutinising her features.

It could scarce be caused by the absence of her brother from the breakfast-table? The circumstance was too trifling to call up an emotion; and clearly at that moment was she subject to one.

What was it? No one put the inquiry. Her father did not notice anything odd in her look. Much less Calhoun, who was himself markedly labouring to conceal some disagreeable thought under the guise of an assumed *naïveté*.

Ever since entering the room he had maintained a studied silence; keeping his eyes averted, instead of, according to his usual custom, constantly straying towards his cousin.

He sate nervously in his chair; and once or twice might have been seen to start, as a servant entered the room.

Beyond doubt he was under the influence of some extraordinary agitation.

"Very strange Henry not being here to his breakfast!" remarked the planter, for about the tenth time. "Surely he is not abed till this hour? No—no—he never lies so late. And yet if abroad, he couldn't be at such a distance as not to have heard the horn. He *may* be in his room? It is just possible. Pluto!"

"Ho—ho! d'ye call me, Mass' Woodley? I'se hya." The sable coachee, acting as table waiter, was in the *sala*, hovering around the chairs.

"Go to Henry's sleeping-room. If he's there, tell him we're at breakfast—half through with it."

"He no dar, Mass' Woodley."

"You have been to his room?"

"Ho—ho! Yas. Dat am I'se no been to de room itseff; but I'se been to de 'table, to look atter Massa Henry hoss; an gib um him fodder an corn. Ho—ho! Dat same ole hoss he ain't dar; nor han't a been all ob dis mornin'. I war up by de fuss skreek ob day. No hoss dar, no saddle, no bridle; and ob coass no Massa Henry. Ho—ho! He been an gone out 'fore anb'dy wor 'tirrin' 'bout de place."

"Are you sure?" asked the planter, seriously stirred by the intelligence.

"Satin, shoo, Mass' Woodley. Dar's no hoss doins in dat ere 'table, ceppin de sorrel ob Massa Cahoon. Spotty am in de 'closure outside. Massa Henry hoss ain't nowha."

"It don't follow that Master Henry himself is not in his room. Go instantly, and see!"

"Ho—ho! I'se go on de instum, massr; but f'r all dat dis chile no speck find de young genl'um dar. Ho! ho! wha'ebber de ole hoss am, darr Massr Henry am too."

"There's something strange in all this," pursued the planter, as Pluto shuffled out of the sala. "Henry from home; and at night too. Where can he have gone? I can't think of any one he would be visiting at such unseasonable hours! He must have been out all night, or very early, according to the nigger's account! At the Port, I suppose, with those young fellows. Not at the tavern, I hope?"

"Oh, no! He wouldn't go there," interposed Calhoun, who appeared as much mystified by the absence of Henry as was Poindexter himself. He refrained, however, from suggesting any explanation, or saying aught of the scenes to which he had been witness on the preceding night.

"It is to be hoped *he* knows nothing of it," reflected the young Creole. "If not, it may still remain a secret between brother and myself. I think I can manage Henry. But why is he still absent? I've sate up all night waiting for him. He must have overtaken Maurice, and they have fraternised. I hope so; even though the tavern may have been the scene of their reconciliation. Henry is not much given to dissipation; but after such a burst of passion, followed by his sudden repentance, he may have strayed from his usual habits? Who could blame him if he has? There can be little harm in it: since he has gone astray in good company?"

How far the string of reflections might have extended it is not easy to say: since it did not reach its natural ending.

It was interrupted by the reappearance of Pluto; whose important air, as he re-entered the room, proclaimed him the bearer of eventful tidings.

"Well!" cried his master, without waiting for him to speak, "is he there?"

"No, Mass' Woodley," replied the black, in a voice that betrayed a large measure of emotion, "he are not dar—Massa Henry am not.

But—but," he hesitatingly continued, "dis chile grieb to say dat—dat—*him hoss am dar*."

"His horse there! Not in his sleeping-room, I suppose?"

"No, massa; nor in de 'table neider; but out da, by de big gate."

"His horse at the gate? And why, pray, do you grieve about that?"

"'Ecause, Mass' Woodley, 'ecause de hoss—dat am Massa Henry hoss—'ecause de anymal—"

"Speak out, you stammering nigger! What because? I suppose the horse has his head upon him? Or is it his tail that is missing?"

"Ah, Mass' Woodley, dis nigga fear dat am missin' wuss dan eider him head or him tail. I'se feer'd dat de ole hoss hab loss him rider!"

"What! Henry thrown from his horse? Nonsense, Pluto! My son is too good a rider for that. Impossible that *he* should have been pitched out of the saddle—impossible!"

"Ho! ho! I doan say he war frown out ob de saddle. Gorramity! I fear de trouble wuss dan dat. O! dear ole Massa, I tell you no mo'. Come to de gate ob do hashashanty, and see fo youseff."

By this time the impression conveyed by Pluto's speech—much more by his manner—notwithstanding its ambiguity, had become sufficiently alarming; and not only the planter himself, but his daughter and nephew, hastily forsaking their seats, and preceded by the sable coachman, made their way to the outside gate of the hacienda.

A sight was there awaiting them, calculated to inspire all three with the most terrible apprehensions.

A negro man—one of the field slaves of the plantation—stood holding a horse, that was saddled and bridled. The animal wet with the dews of the night, and having been evidently uncared for in any stable, was snorting and stamping the ground, as if but lately escaped from some scene of excitement, in which he had been compelled to take part.

He was speckled with a colour darker than that of the dewdrops—darker than his own coat of bay-brown. The spots scattered over his shoulders—the streaks that ran parallel with the downward direction of his limbs, the blotches showing conspicuously on the saddle-flaps, were all of the colour of coagulated blood. Blood had caused them—spots, streaks, and blotches!

Whence came that horse?

From the prairies. The negro had caught him, on the outside plain, as, with the bridle trailing among his feet, he was instinctively straying towards the hacienda.

To whom did he belong?

The question was not asked. All present knew him to be the horse of Henry Poindexter.

Nor did any one ask whose blood bedaubed the saddle-flaps. The three individuals most interested could think only of that one, who stood to them in the triple relationship of son, brother, and cousin.

The dark red spots on which they were distractedly gazing had spurted from the veins of Henry Poindexter. They had no other thought.

# 38. The Avengers

Hastily—perhaps too truly—construing the sinister evidence, the half-frantic father leaped into the bloody saddle, and galloped direct for the Fort.

Calhoun, upon his own horse, followed close after.

The hue and cry soon spread abroad. Rapid riders carried it up and down the river, to the remotest plantations of the settlement.

The Indians were out, and near at hand, reaping their harvest of scalps! That of young Poindexter was the firstfruits of their sanguinary gleaning!

Henry Poindexter—the noble generous youth who had not an enemy in all Texas! Who but Indians could have spilled such innocent blood? Only the Comanches could have been so cruel?

Among the horsemen, who came quickly together on the parade ground of Port Inge, no one doubted that the Comanches had done the deed. It was simply a question of how, when, and where.

The blood drops pretty clearly, proclaimed the first. He who had shed them must have been shot, or speared, while sitting in his saddle. They were mostly on the off side; where they presented an appearance, as if something had been slaked over them. This was seen both on the shoulders of the horse, and the flap of the saddle. Of course it was the body of the rider as it slipped lifeless to the earth.

There were some who spoke with equal certainty as to the time—old frontiersmen experienced in such matters.

According to them the blood was scarce "ten hours old:" in other words, must have been shed about ten hours before.

It was now noon. The murder must have been committed at *two* o'clock in the morning.

The third query was, perhaps, the most important—at least now that the deed was done.

*Where* had it been done? Where was the body to be found?

After that, where should the assassins be sought for?

These were the questions discussed by the mixed council of settlers and soldiers, hastily assembled at Port Inge, and presided over by the commandant of the Fort—the afflicted father standing speechless by his side.

The last was of special importance. There are thirty-two points in the compass of the prairies, as well as in that which guides the ocean wanderer; and, therefore, in any expedition going in search of a war-party of Comanches, there would be thirty-two chances to one against its taking the right track.

It mattered not that the home of these nomadic savages was in the west. That was a wide word; and signified anywhere within a semicircle of some hundreds of miles.

Besides, the Indians were now upon the *war-trail*; and, in an isolated settlement such as that of the Leona, as likely to make their appearance from the east. More likely, indeed, since such is a common strategic trick of these astute warriors.

To have ridden forth at random would have been sheer folly; with such odds against going the right way, as thirty-two to one.

A proposal to separate the command into several parties, and proceed in different directions, met with little favour from any one. It was directly negatived by the major himself.

The murderers might be a thousand, the avengers were but the tenth of that number: consisting of some fifty dragoons who chanced to be in garrison, with about as many mounted civilians. The party must be kept together, or run the risk of being attacked, and perhaps cut off, in detail!

The argument was deemed conclusive. Even, the bereaved father—and cousin, who appeared equally the victim of a voiceless grief—consented to shape their course according to the counsels of the more prudent majority, backed by the authority of the major himself.

It was decided that the searchers should proceed in a body.

In what direction? This still remained the subject of discussion.

The thoughtful captain of infantry now became a conspicuous figure, by suggesting that some inquiry should be made, as to what direction had been last taken by the man who was supposed to be murdered. Who last saw Henry Poindexter?

His father and cousin were first appealed to.

The former had last seen his son at the supper table; and supposed him to have gone thence to his bed.

The answer of Calhoun was less direct, and, perhaps, less satisfactory. He had conversed with his cousin at a later hour, and had bidden him good night, under the impression that he was retiring to his room.

Why was Calhoun concealing what had really occurred? Why did he refrain from giving a narration of that garden scene to which he had been witness?

Was it, that he feared humiliation by disclosing the part he had himself played?

Whatever was the reason, the truth was shunned; and an answer given, the sincerity of which was suspected by more than one who listened to it.

The evasiveness might have been more apparent, had there been any reason for suspicion, or had the bystanders been allowed longer time to reflect upon it.

While the inquiry was going on, light came in from a quartet hitherto unthought of. The landlord of the Rough and Ready, who had come uncalled to the council, after forcing his way through the crowd, proclaimed himself willing to communicate some facts worth their hearing—in short, the very facts they were endeavouring to find out: when Henry Poindexter had been last seen, and what the direction he had taken.

Oberdoffer's testimony, delivered in a semi-Teutonic tongue, was to the effect: that Maurice the mustanger—who had been staying at his hotel ever since his fight with Captain Calhoun—had that night ridden out at a late hour, as he had done for several nights before.

He had returned to the hotel at a still later hour; and finding it open—on account of a party of *bons vivants* who had supped there—had done that which he had not done for a long time before—demanded his bill, and to Old Duffer's astonishment—as the latter naïvely confessed—settled every cent of it!

Where he had procured the money "Gott" only knew, or why he left the hotel in such a hurry. Oberdoffer himself only knew that he had left it, and taken all his 'trapsh' along with him—just as he was in the habit of doing, whenever he went off upon one of his horse-catching expeditions.

On one of these the village Boniface supposed him to have gone.

What had all this to do with the question before the council? Much indeed; though it did not appear till the last moment of his examination, when the witness revealed the more pertinent facts:—that about twenty minutes after the mustanger had taken his departure from the hotel, "Heinrich Poindexter" knocked at the door, and inquired after Mr Maurice Gerald;—that on being told the latter was gone, as also the time, and probable direction he had taken, the "young gentle-mans" rode off a a quick pace, as if with the intention of overtaking him.

This was all Mr Oberdoffer knew of the matter; and all he could be expected to tell.

The intelligence, though containing several points but ill under-stood, was nevertheless a guide to the expeditionary party. It furnished a sort of clue to the direction they ought to take. If the missing man had gone off with Maurice the mustanger, or after him, he should be looked for on the road the latter himself would be likely to have taken.

Did any one know where the horse-hunter had his home?

No one could state the exact locality; though there were several who believed it was somewhere among the head-waters of the Nueces, on a creek called the "Alamo."

To the Alamo, then, did they determine upon proceeding in quest of the missing man, or his dead body—perhaps, also, to find that of Maurice the mustanger; and, at the same time, avenge upon the savage assassins two murders instead of one.

# 39. The Pool of Blood

Notwithstanding its number—larger than usual for a party of borderers merely in search of a strayed neighbour—the expedition pursued its way with, considerable caution.

There was reason. The Indians were upon the war-trail. Scouts were sent out in advance; and professed "trackers" employed to pick up, and interpret the "sign."

On the prairie, extending nearly ten miles to the westward of the Leona, no trail was discovered. The turf, hard and dry, only showed the tracks of a horse when going in a gallop. None such were seen along the route.

At ten miles' distance from the Fort the plain is traversed by a tract of chapparal, running north-west and south-east. It is a true Texan jungle, laced by llianas, and almost impenetrable for man and horse.

Through this jungle, directly opposite the Fort, there is an opening, through which passes a path—the shortest that leads to the head waters of the Nueces. It is a sort of natural avenue among the trees that stand closely crowded on each side, but refrain from meeting. It may be artificial: some old "war-trail" of the Comanches, erst trodden by their expeditionary parties on the maraud to Tamaulipas, Coahuila, or New Leon.

The trackers knew that it conducted to the Alamo; and, therefore, guided the expedition into it.

Shortly after entering among the trees, one of the latter, who had gone afoot in the advance, was seen standing by the edge of the thicket, as if waiting to announce some recently discovered fact.

"What is it?" demanded the major, spurring ahead of the others, and riding up to the tracker. "Sign?"

"Ay, that there is, major; and plenty of it. Look there! In that bit of sottish ground you see—"

"The tracks of a horse."

"Of two horses, major," said the man, correcting the officer with an air of deference.

"True. There are two."

"Farther on they become four; though they're all made by the same two horses. They have gone up this openin' a bit, and come back again."

"Well, Spangler, my good fellow; what do you make of it?"

"Not much," replied Spangler, who was one of the paid scouts of the cantonment; "not much of *that*; I hav'n't been far enough up the openin' to make out what it means—only far enough to know that *a man has been murdered*."

"What proof have you of what you say? Is there a dead body?"

"No. Not as much as the little finger; not even a hair of the head, so fur as I can see."

"What then?"

"Blood, a regular pool of it—enough to have cleared out the carcass of a hull buffalo. Come and see for yourself. But," continued the scout in a muttered undertone, "if you wish me to follow up the sign as it ought to be done, you'll order the others to stay back—'specially them as are now nearest you."

This observation appeared to be more particularly pointed at the planter and his nephew; as the tracker, on making it, glanced furtively towards both.

"By all means," replied the major. "Yes, Spangler, you shall have every facility for your work. Gentlemen! may I request you to remain where you are for a few minutes. My tracker, here, has to go through a performance that requires him to have the ground to himself. He can only take me along with him."

Of course the major's request was a command, courteously conveyed, to men who were not exactly his subordinates. It was obeyed, however, just as if they had been; and one and all kept their places, while the officer, following his scout, rode away from the ground.

About fifty yards further on, Spangler came to a stand.

"You see that, major?" said he, pointing to the ground.

"I should be blind if I didn't," replied the officer. "A pool of blood—as you say, big enough to have emptied the veins of a buffalo. If it has come from those of a man, I should say that whoever shed it is no longer in the land of the living."

"Dead!" pronounced the tracker. "Dead before that blood had turned purple—as it is now."

"Whose do you think it is, Spangler?"

225

"That of the man we're in search of—the son of the old gentleman down there. That's why I didn't wish him to come forward."

"He may as well know the worst. He must find it out in time."

"True what you say, major; but we had better first find out how the young fellow has come to be thrown in his tracks. That's what is puzzling me."

"How! by the Indians, of course? The Comanches have done it?"

"Not a bit of it," rejoined the scout, with an air of confidence.

"Hu! why do you say that, Spangler?"

"Because, you see, if the Indyins had a been here, there would be forty horse-tracks instead of four, and them made by only two horses."

"There's truth in that. It isn't likely a single Comanch would have had the daring, even to assassinate—"

"No Comanche, major, no Indyin of any kind committed this murder. There are two horse-tracks along the opening. As you see, both are shod; and they're the same that have come back again. Comanches don't ride shod horses, except when they've stolen them. Both these were ridden by white men. One set of the tracks has been made by a mustang, though it it was a big 'un. The other is the hoof of an American horse. Goin' west the mustang was foremost; you can tell that by the overlap. Comin' back the States horse was in the lead, the other followin' him; though it's hard to say how fur behind. I may be able to tell better, if we keep on to the place whar both must have turned back. It can't be a great ways off."

"Let us proceed thither, then," said the major. "I shall command the people to stay where they are."

Having issued the command, in a voice loud enough to be heard by his following, the major rode away from the bloodstained spot, preceded by the tracker.

For about four hundred yards further on, the two sets of tracks were traceable; but by the eye of the major, only where the turf was softer under the shadow of the trees. So far—the scout said the horses had passed and returned in the order already declared by him:—that is, the mustang in the lead while proceeding westward, and in the rear while going in the opposite direction.

At this point the trail ended—both horses, as was already known, having returned on their own tracks.

Before taking the back track, however, they had halted, and stayed some time in the same place—under the branches of a spreading cottonwood. The turf, much trampled around the trunk of the tree, was evidence of this.

The tracker got off his horse to examine it; and, stooping to the earth, carefully scrutinised the sign.

"They've been here thegither," said he, after several minutes spent in his analysis, "and for some time; though neither's been out of the saddle. They've been on friendly terms, too; which makes it all the more unexplainable. They must have quarrelled afterwards."

"If you are speaking the truth, Spangler, you must be a witch. How on earth can you know all that?"

"By the sign, major; by the sign. It's simple enough. I see the shoes of both horses lapping over each other a score of times; and in such a way that shows they must have been thegither—the animals, it might be, restless and movin' about. As for the time, they've taken long enough to smoke a cigar apiece—close to the teeth too. Here are the stumps; not enough left to fill a fellow's pipe."

The tracker, stooping as he spoke, picked up a brace of cigar stumps, and handed them to the major.

"By the same token," he continued, "I conclude that the two horsemen, whoever they were, while under this tree could not have had any very hostile feelins, the one to the tother. Men don't smoke in company with the design of cutting each other's throats, or blowing out one another's brains, the instant afterwards. The trouble between them must have come on after the cigars were smoked out. That it did come there can be no doubt. As sure, major, as you're sittin' in your saddle, one of them has wiped out the other. I can only guess which has been wiped out, by the errand we're on. Poor Mr Poindexter will niver more see his son alive."

"'Tis very mysterious," remarked the major.

"It is, by jingo!"

"And the body, too; where can *it* be?"

"That's what purplexes me most of all. If 't had been Indyins, I wouldn't a thought much o' its being missin'. They might a carried the man off wi them to make a target of him, if only wounded; and if dead, to eat him, maybe. But there's been no Indyins here—not a redskin. Take my word for it, major, one o' the two men who rid these horses has wiped out the other; and sartinly he *have* wiped him out in the litterlest sense o' the word. What he's done wi' the body beats me; and perhaps only hisself can tell."

"Most strange!" exclaimed the major, pronouncing the words with emphasis—"most mysterious!"

"It's possible we may yet unravel some o' the mystery," pursued Spangler. "We must follow up the tracks of the horses, after they started from this—that is, from where the deed was done. We may make something out of that. There's nothing more to be learnt here. We may as well go back, major. Am I to tell *him*?"

"Mr Poindexter, you mean?"

"Yes. You are convinced that his son is the man who has been murdered?"

"Oh, no; not so much as that comes to. Only convinced that the horse the old gentleman is now riding is one of the two that's been over this ground last night—the States horse I feel sure. I have compared the tracks; and if young Poindexter was the man who was on *his* back, I fear there's not much chance for the poor fellow. It looks ugly that the other *rid after* him."

"Spangler! have you any suspicion as to who the other may be?"

"Not a spark, major. If't hadn't been for the tale of Old Duffer I'd never have thought of Maurice the mustanger. True, it's the track o' a shod mustang; but I don't know it to be hisn. Surely it can't be? The young Irishman aint the man to stand nonsense from nobody; but as little air he the one to do a deed like this—that is, if it's been cold-blooded killin'."

"I think as you about that."

"And you may think so, major. If young Poindexter's been killed, and by Maurice Gerald, there's been a fair stand-up fight atween them, and the planter's son has gone under. That's how I shed reckon it up. As to the disappearance o' the dead body—for them two quarts o' blood could only have come out o' a body that's now dead—that *trees me*. We must follow the trail, howsoever; and maybe it'll fetch us to some sensible concloosion. Am I to tell the old gentleman what I think o't?"

"Perhaps better not. He knows enough already. It will at least fall lighter upon him if he find things out by piecemeal. Say nothing of what we've seen. If you can take up the trail of the two horses after going off from the place where the blood is, I shall manage to bring the command after you without any one suspecting what we've seen."

"All right, major," said the scout, "I think I can guess where the off trail goes. Give me ten minutes upon it, and then come on to my signal."

So saying the tracker rode back to the "place of blood;" and after what appeared a very cursory examination, turned off into a lateral opening in the chapparal.

Within the promised time his shrill whistle announced that he was nearly a mile distant, and in a direction altogether different from the spot that had been profaned by some sanguinary scene.

On hearing the signal, the commander of the expedition—who had in the meantime returned to his party—gave orders to advance; while he himself, with Poindexter and the other principal men, moved ahead, without his revealing to any one of his retinue the chapter of strange disclosures for which he was indebted to the "instincts" of his tracker.

---

# 40. The Marked Bullet

Before coming up with the scout, an incident occurred to vary the monotony of the march. Instead of keeping along the avenue, the major had conducted his command in a diagonal direction through the chapparal. He had done this to avoid giving unnecessary pain to the afflicted father; who would otherwise have looked upon the life-blood of his son, or at least what the major believed to be so. The gory spot was shunned, and as the discovery was not yet known to any other save the major himself, and the tracker who had made it, the party moved on in ignorance of the existence of such a dread sign.

The path they were now pursuing was a mere cattle-track, scarce broad enough for two to ride abreast. Here and there were glades where it widened out for a few yards, again running into the thorny chapparal.

On entering one of these glades, an animal sprang out of the bushes, and bounded off over the sward. A beautiful creature it was, with its fulvous coat ocellated with rows of shining rosettes; its strong lithe limbs supporting a smooth cylindrical body, continued into a long tapering tail; the very type of agility; a creature rare even in these remote solitudes—the jaguar.

Its very rarity rendered it the more desirable as an object to test the skill of the marksman; and, notwithstanding the serious nature of the expedition, two of the party were tempted to discharge their rifles at the retreating animal.

They were Cassius Calhoun, and a young planter who was riding by his side.

The jaguar dropped dead in its tracks: a bullet having entered its body, and traversed the spine in a longitudinal direction.

Which of the two was entitled to the credit of the successful shot? Calhoun claimed it, and so did the young planter.

The shots had been fired simultaneously, and only one of them had hit.

"I shall show you," confidently asserted the ex-officer, dismounting beside the dead jaguar, and unsheathing his knife. "You see, gentlemen, the ball is still in the animal's body? If it's mine, you'll find my initials on it—C.C.—with a crescent. I mould my bullets so that I can always tell when I've killed my game."

The swaggering air with which he held up the leaden missile after extracting it told that he had spoken the truth. A few of the more curious drew near and examined the bullet. Sure enough it was moulded as Calhoun had declared, and the dispute ended in the discomfiture of the young planter.

The party soon after came up with the tracker, waiting to conduct them along a fresh trail.

It was no longer a track made by two horses, with shod hooves. The turf showed only the hoof-marks of one; and so indistinctly, that at times they were undiscernible to all eyes save those of the tracker himself.

The trace carried them through the thicket, from glade to glade—after a circuitous march—bringing them back into the lane-like opening, at a point still further to the west.

Spangler—though far from being the most accomplished of his calling—took it; up as fast as the people could ride after him. In his own mind he had determined the character of the animal whose footmarks he was following. He knew it to be a mustang—the same that had stood under the cottonwood whilst its rider was smoking a cigar—the same whose hoof-mark he had seen deeply indented in a sod saturated with human blood.

The track of the States horse he had also followed for a short distance—in the interval, when he was left alone. He saw that it would conduct him back to the prairie through which they had passed; and thence, in all likelihood, to the settlements on the Leona.

He had forsaken it to trace the footsteps of the shod mustang; more likely to lead him to an explanation of that red mystery of murder—perhaps to the den of the assassin.

Hitherto perplexed by the hoof-prints of two horses alternately overlapping each other, he was not less puzzled now, while scrutinising the tracks of but one.

They went not direct, as those of an animal urged onwards upon a journey; but here and there zigzagging; occasionally turning upon themselves in short curves; then forward for a stretch; and then circling again, as if the mustang was either not mounted, or its rider was asleep in the saddle!

Could these be the hoof-prints of a horse with a man upon his back—an assassin skulking away from the scene of assassination, his conscience freshly excited by the crime?

Spangler did not think so. He knew not what to think. He was mystified more than ever. So confessed he to the major, when being questioned as to the character of the trail.

A spectacle that soon afterwards came under his eyes—simultaneously seen by every individual of the party—so far from solving the mystery, had the effect of rendering it yet more inexplicable.

More than this. What had hitherto been but an ambiguous affair—a subject for guess and speculation—was suddenly transformed into a horror; of that intense kind that can only spring from thoughts of the supernatural.

No one could say that this feeling of horror had arisen without reason.

When a man is seen mounted on a horse's back, seated firmly in the saddle, with limbs astride in the stirrups, body erect, and hand holding the rein—in short, everything in air and attitude required of a rider; when, on closer scrutiny, it is observed: that there is something wanting to complete the idea of a perfect equestrian; and, on still closer scrutiny, that this something is the *head*, it would be strange if the spectacle did not startle the beholder, terrifying him to the very core of his heart.

And this very sight came before their eyes; causing them simultaneously to rein up, and with as much suddenness, as if each had rashly ridden within less than his horse's length of the brink of an abyss!

The sun was low down, almost on a level with the sward. Facing westward, his disc was directly before them. His rays, glaring redly in their eyes, hindered them from having a very accurate view, towards the quarter of the west. Still could they see that strange shape above described—a horseman without a head!

Had only one of the party declared himself to have seen it, he would have been laughed at by his companions as a lunatic. Even two might have been stigmatised in a similar manner.

But what everybody saw at the same time, could not be questioned; and only he would have been thought crazed, who should have expressed incredulity about the presence of the abnormal phenomenon.

No one did. The eyes of all were turned in the same direction, their gaze intently fixed on what was either a horseman without the head, or the best counterfeit that could have been contrived.

Was it this? If not, what was it?

These interrogatories passed simultaneously through the minds of all. As no one could answer them, even to himself, no answer was vouchsafed. Soldiers and civilians sate silent in their saddles—each expecting an explanation, which the other was unable to supply.

There could be heard only mutterings, expressive of surprise and terror. No one even offered a conjecture.

The headless horseman, whether phantom or real, when first seen, was about entering the avenue—near the debouchure of which the searchers had arrived. Had he continued his course, he must have met them in the teeth—supposing their courage to have been equal to the encounter.

As it was, he had halted at the same instant as themselves; and stood regarding them with a mistrust that may have been mutual.

There was an interval of silence on both sides, during which a cigar stump might have been heard falling upon the sward. It was then the strange apparition was most closely scrutinised by those who had the courage: for the majority of the men sate shivering in their stirrups—through sheer terror, incapable even of thought!

The few who dared face the mystery, with any thought of accounting for it, were baffled in their investigation by the glare of the setting sun. They could only see that there was a horse of large size and noble shape, with a man upon his back. The figure of the man was less easily determined, on account of the limbs being inserted into overalls, while his shoulders were enveloped in an ample cloak-like covering.

What signified his shape, so long as it wanted that portion most essential to existence? A man without a head—on horseback, sitting erect in the saddle, in an attitude of ease and grace—with spurs sparkling upon his heels—the bridle-rein held in one hand—the other where it should be, resting lightly upon his thigh!

Great God! what could it mean?

Was it a phantom? Surely it could not be human?

They who viewed it were not the men to have faith either in phantoms, or phantasmagoria. Many of them had met Nature in her remotest solitudes, and wrestled with her in her roughest moods. They were not given to a belief in ghosts.

But the confidence of the most incredulous was shaken by a sight so strange—so absolutely unnatural—and to such an extent, that the stoutest hearted of the party was forced mentally to repeat the words:—

*"Is it a phantom? Surely it cannot be human?"*

Its size favoured the idea of the supernatural. It appeared double that of an ordinary man upon an ordinary horse. It was more like a giant on a gigantic steed; though this might have been owing to the illusory light under which it was seen—the refraction of the sun's rays passing horizontally through the tremulous atmosphere of the parched plain.

There was but little time to philosophise—not enough to complete a careful scrutiny of the unearthly apparition, which every one present, with hand spread over his eyes to shade them from the dazzling glare, was endeavouring to make.

Nothing of colour could be noted—neither the garments of the man, nor the hairy coat of the horse. Only the shape could be traced, outlined in sable silhouette against the golden background of the sky; and this in every change of attitude, whether fronting the spectators, or turned stern towards them, was still the same—still that inexplicable phenomenon: *a horseman without a head*!

Was it a phantom? Surely it could not be human?

"'Tis old Nick upon horseback!" cried a fearless frontiersman, who would scarce have quailed to encounter his Satanic majesty even in that guise. "By the 'tarnal Almighty, it's the devil himself."

The boisterous laugh which succeeded the profane utterance of the reckless speaker, while it only added to the awe of his less courageous comrades, appeared to produce an effect on the headless horseman. Wheeling suddenly round—his horse at the same time sending forth a scream that caused either the earth or the atmosphere to tremble—he commenced galloping away.

He went direct towards the sun; and continued this course, until only by his motion could he be distinguished from one of those spots that have puzzled the philosopher—at length altogether disappearing, as though he had ridden into the dazzling disc!

# 41. Cuatro Cavalleros

The party of searchers, under the command of the major, was not the only one that went forth from Fort Inge on that eventful morning.

Nor was it the earliest to take saddle. Long before—in fact close following the dawn of day—a much smaller party, consisting of only four horsemen, was seen setting out from the suburbs of the village, and heading their horses in the direction of the Nueces.

These could not be going in search of the dead body of Henry Poindexter. At that hour no one suspected that the young man was dead, or even that he was missing. The riderless horse had not yet come in to tell the tale of woe. The settlement was still slumbering, unconscious that innocent blood had been spilt.

Though setting out from nearly the same point, and proceeding in a like direction, there was not the slightest similarity between the two parties of mounted men. Those earliest a-start were all of pure Iberian blood; or this commingled with Aztecan. In other words they were Mexicans.

It required neither skill nor close scrutiny to discover this. A glance at themselves and their horses, their style of equitation, the slight muscular development of their thighs and hips—more strikingly observable in their deep-tree saddles—the gaily coloured serapés shrouding their shoulders, the wide velveteen calzoneros on their legs, the big spurs on their boots, and broad-brimmed sombreros on their heads, declared them either Mexicans, or men who had adopted the Mexican costume.

That they were the former there was not a question. The sallow hue; the pointed Vandyke beard, covering the chin, sparsely—though not from any thinning by the shears—the black, close-cropped *chevelure*; the regular facial outline, were all indisputable characteristics of the Hispano-Moro-Aztecan race, who now occupy the ancient territory of the Moctezumas.

One of the four was a man of larger frame than any of his companions. He rode a better horse; was more richly apparelled; carried upon his person arms and equipments of a superior finish; and was otherwise distinguished, so as to leave no doubt about his being the leader of the *cuartilla*.

He was a man of between thirty and forty years of age, nearer to the latter than the former; though a smooth, rounded cheek—furnished with a short and carefully trimmed whisker—gave him the appearance of being younger than he was.

But for a cold animal eye, and a heaviness of feature that betrayed a tendency to behave with brutality—if not with positive cruelty—the individual in question might have been described as handsome.

A well formed mouth, with twin rows of white teeth between the lips, even when these were exhibited in a smile, did not remove this unpleasant impression. It but reminded the beholder of the sardonic grin that may have been given by Satan, when, after the temptation had succeeded, he gazed contemptuously back upon the mother of mankind.

It was not his looks that had led to his having become known among his comrades by a peculiar nick-name; that of an animal well known upon the plains of Texas.

His deeds and disposition had earned for him the unenviable soubriquet "El Coyote."

How came he to be crossing the prairie at this early hour of the morning—apparently sober, and acting as the leader of others—when on the same morning, but a few hours before, he was seen drunk in his jacalé—so drunk as to be unconscious of having a visitor, or, at all events, incapable of giving that visitor a civil reception?

The change of situation though sudden—and to some extent strange—is not so difficult of explanation. It will be understood after an account has been given of his movements, from the time of Calhoun's leaving him, till the moment of meeting him in the saddle, in company with his three *conpaisanos*.

On riding away from his hut, Calhoun had left the door, as he had found it, ajar; and in this way did it remain until the morning—El Coyote all the time continuing his sonorous slumber.

At daybreak he was aroused by the raw air that came drifting over him in the shape of a chilly fog. This to some extent sobered him; and, springing up from his skin-covered truck, he commenced staggering over the floor—all the while uttering anathemas against the cold, and the door for letting it in.

It might be expected that he would have shut to the latter on the instant; but he did not. It was the only aperture, excepting some holes arising from dilapidation, by which light was admitted into the interior of the jacalé; and light he wanted, to enable him to carry out the design that had summoned him to his feet.

The grey dawn, just commencing to creep in through the open doorway, scarce sufficed for his purpose; and it was only after a good while spent in groping about, interspersed with a series of stumblings, and accompanied by a string of profane exclamations, that he succeeded in finding that he was searching for: a large two-headed gourd, with a strap around its middle, used as a canteen for carrying water, or more frequently *mezcal*.

The odour escaping from its uncorked end told that it had recently contained this potent spirit; but that it was now empty, was announced by another profane ejaculation that came from the lips of its owner, as he made the discovery.

"*Sangre de Cristo*!" he cried, in an accent of angry disappointment, giving the gourd a shake to assure himself of its emptiness. "Not a drop—not enough to drown a chiga! And my tongue sticking to my teeth. My throat feels as if I had bolted a *brazero* of red-hot charcoal. Por Dios! I can't stand it. What's to be done? Daylight? It is. I must up to the *pueblita*. It's possible that Señor Doffer may have his trap open by this time to catch the early birds. If so, he'll find a customer in the Coyote. Ha, ha, ha!"

Slinging the gourd strap around his neck, and thrusting his head through the slit of his serapé, he set forth for the village.

The tavern was but a few hundred yards from his hut, on the same side of the river, and approachable by a path, that he could have travelled with his eyes under "tapojos." In twenty minutes after, he was staggering past the sign-post of the "Rough and Ready."

He chanced to be in luck. Oberdoffer was in his bar-room, serving some early customers—a party of soldiers who had stolen out of quarters to swallow their morning dram.

"Mein Gott, Mishter Dees!" said the landlord, saluting the newly arrived guest, and without ceremony forsaking six *credit* customers, for one that he knew to be *cash*. "Mein Gott! is it you I sees so early ashtir? I knowsh vat you vant. You vant your pig coord fill mit ze Mexican spirits—ag—ag—vat you call it?"

"*Aguardiente*! You've guessed it, cavallero. That's just what I want."

"A tollar—von tollar ish the price."

"*Carrambo*! I've paid it often enough to know that. Here's the coin, and there's the canteen. Fill, and be quick about it!"

"Ha! you ish in a hurry, mein herr. Fel—I von't keeps you waitin'; I suppose you ish off for the wild horsh prairish. If there's anything goot among the droves, I'm afeart that the Irishmans will pick it up before you. He went off lasht night. He left my housh at a late hour—after midnight it wash—a very late hour, to go a shourney! But he's a queer cushtomer is that mushtanger, Mister Maurish Sherralt. Nobody knows his ways. I shouldn't say anythings againsht him. He hash been a goot cushtomer to me. He has paid his bill like a rich man, and he hash plenty peside. Mein Gott! his pockets wash cramm mit tollars!"

On hearing that the Irishman had gone off to the "horsh prairish," as Oberdoffer termed them, the Mexican by his demeanour betrayed more than an ordinary interest in the announcement.

It was proclaimed, first by a slight start of surprise, and then by an impatience of manner that continued to mark his movements, while listening to the long rigmarole that followed.

It was clear that he did not desire anything of this to be observed. Instead of questioning his informant upon the subject thus started, or voluntarily displaying any interest in it, he rejoined in a careless drawl—

"It don't concern me, cavallero. There are plenty of *musteños* on the plains—enough to give employment to all the horse-catchers in Texas. Look alive, señor, and let's have the aguardiente!"

A little chagrined at being thus rudely checked in his attempt at a gossip, the German Boniface hastily filled the gourd canteen; and, without essaying farther speech, handed it across the counter, took the dollar in exchange, chucked the coin into his till, and then moved back to his military customers, more amiable because drinking *upon the score*.

Diaz, notwithstanding the eagerness he had lately exhibited to obtain the liquor, walked out of the bar-room, and away from the hotel, without taking the stopper from his canteen, or even appearing to think of it!

His excited air was no longer that of a man merely longing for a glass of ardent spirits. There was something stronger stirring within, that for the time rendered him oblivious of the appetite.

Whatever it may have been it did not drive him direct to his home: for not until he had paid a visit to three other hovels somewhat similar to his own—all situated in the suburbs of the *pueblita*, and inhabited by men like himself—not till then, did he return to his jacalé.

It was on getting back, that he noticed for the first time the tracks of a shod horse; and saw where the animal had been tied to a tree that stood near the hut.

"*Carrambo!*" he exclaimed, on perceiving this sign, "*the Capitan Americano* has been here in the night. Por Dios! I remember something—I thought I had dreamt it. I can guess his errand. He has heard of Don Mauricio's departure. Perhaps he'll repeat his visit, when he thinks I'm in a proper state to receive him? Ha! ha! It don't matter now. The thing's all understood; and I sha'n't need any further instructions from him, till I've earned his thousand dollars. *Mil pesos!* What a splendid fortune! Once gained, I shall go back to the Rio Grande, and see what can be done with Isidora."

After delivering the above soliloquy, he remained at his hut only long enough to swallow a few mouthfuls of roasted *tasajo*, washing them down with as many gulps of mezcal. Then having caught and caparisoned his horse, buckled on his huge heavy spurs, strapped his short carbine to the saddle, thrust a pair of pistols into their holsters, and belted the leathern sheathed macheté on his hip, he sprang into the stirrups, and rode rapidly away.

The short interval that elapsed, before making his appearance on the open plain, was spent in the suburbs of the village—waiting for the three horsemen who accompanied him, and who had been forewarned of their being wanted to act as his coadjutors, in some secret exploit that required their assistance.

Whatever it was, his trio of *confrères* appeared to have been made acquainted with the scheme; or at all events that the scene of the exploit was to be on the Alamo. When a short distance out upon the plain, seeing Diaz strike off in a diagonal direction, they called out to warn him, that he was not going the right way.

"I know the Alamo well," said one of them, himself a mustanger. "I've hunted horses there many a time. It's southwest from here. The nearest way to it is through an opening in the chapparal you see out yonder. You are heading too much to the west, Don Miguel!"

"Indeed!" contemptuously retorted the leader of the cuartilla. "You're a *gringo*, Señor Vicente Barajo! You forget the errand we're upon; and that we are riding shod horses? Indians don't go out from Port Inge and then direct to the Alamo to do—no matter what. I suppose you understand me?"

"Oh true!" answered Señor Vicente Barajo, "I beg your pardon, Don Miguel. *Carrambo*! I did not think of that."

And without further protest, the three coadjutors of El Coyote fell into his tracks, and followed him in silence—scarce another word passing between him and them, till they had struck the chapparal, at a point several miles above the opening of which Barajo had made mention.

Once under cover of the thicket, the four men dismounted; and, after tying their horses to the trees, commenced a performance that could only be compared to a scene in the gentlemen's dressing-room of a suburban theatre, preliminary to the representation of some savage and sanguinary drama.

# 42. Vultures on the Wing

He who has travelled across the plains of Southern Texas cannot fail to have witnessed a spectacle of common occurrence—a flock of black vultures upon the wing.

An hundred or more in the flock, swooping in circles, or wide spiral gyrations—now descending almost to touch the prairie award, or the spray of the chapparal—anon soaring upward by a power in which the wing bears no part—their pointed pinions sharply cutting against the clear sky—they constitute a picture of rare interest, one truly characteristic of a tropical clime.

The traveller who sees it for the first time will not fail to rein up his horse, and sit in his saddle, viewing it with feelings of curious interest. Even he who is accustomed to the spectacle will not pass on without indulging in a certain train of thought which it is calculated to call forth.

There is a tale told by the assemblage of base birds. On the ground beneath them, whether seen by the traveller or not, is stretched some stricken creature—quadruped, or it may be *man*—dead, or it may be *dying*.

On the morning that succeeded that sombre night, when the three solitary horsemen made the crossing of the plain, a spectacle similar to that described might have been witnessed above the chapparal into which they had ridden. A flock of black vultures, of both species, was disporting above the tops of the trees, near the point where the avenue angled.

At daybreak not one could have been seen. In less than an hour after, hundreds were hovering above the spot, on widespread wings, their shadows sailing darkly over the green spray of the chapparal.

A Texan traveller entering the avenue, and observing the ominous assemblage, would at once have concluded, that there was death upon his track.

Going farther, he would have found confirmatory evidence, in a pool of blood trampled by the hooves of horses.

Not exactly over this were the vultures engaged in their aerial evolutions. The centre of their swoopings appeared to be a point some distance off among the trees; and there, no doubt, would be discovered the quarry that had called them together.

At that early hour there was no traveller—Texan, or stranger—to test the truth of the conjecture; but, for all that, it was true.

At a point in the chapparal, about a quarter of a mile from the blood-stained path, lay stretched upon the ground the object that was engaging the attention of the vultures.

It was not carrion, nor yet a quadruped; but a human being—a man!

A young man, too, of noble lineaments and graceful shape—so far as could be seen under the cloak that shrouded his recumbent form—with a face fair to look upon, even in death.

Was he dead?

At first sight any one would have said so, and the black birds believed it. His attitude and countenance seemed to proclaim it beyond question.

He was lying upon his back, with face upturned to the sky—no care being taken to shelter it from the sun. His limbs, too, were not in a natural posture; but extended stiffly along the stony surface, as if he had lost the power to control them.

A colossal tree was near, a live oak, but it did not shadow him. He was outside the canopy of its frondage; and the sun's beams, just beginning to penetrate the chapparal, were slanting down upon his pale face—paler by reflection from a white Panama hat that but partially shaded it.

His features did not seem set in death: and as little was it like sleep. It had more the look of death than sleep. The eyes were but half closed; and the pupils could be seen glancing through the lashes, glassy and dilated. Was the man dead?

Beyond doubt, the black birds believed that he was. But the black birds were judging only by appearances. Their wish was parent to the thought. They were mistaken.

Whether it was the glint of the sun striking into his half-screened orbs, or nature becoming restored after a period of repose, the eyes of the prostrate man were seen to open to their full extent, while a movement was perceptible throughout his whole frame.

Soon after he raised himself a little; and, resting upon his elbow, stared confusedly around him.

The vultures soared upward into the air, and for the time maintained a higher flight.

"Am I dead, or living?" muttered he to himself. "Dreaming, or awake? Which is it? Where am I?"

The sunlight was blinding him. He could see nothing, till he had shaded his eyes with his hand; then only indistinctly.

"Trees above—around me! Stones underneath! That I can tell by the aching of my bones. A chapparal forest! How came I into it?

"Now I have it," continued he, after a short spell of reflection. "My head was dashed against a tree. There it is—the very limb that lifted me out of the saddle. My left leg pains me. Ah! I remember; it came in contact with the trunk. By heavens, I believe it is broken!"

As he said this, he made an effort to raise himself into an erect attitude. It proved a failure. His sinister limb would lend him no assistance: it was swollen at the knee-joint—either shattered or dislocated.

"Where is the horse? Gone off, of course. By this time, in the stables of Casa del Corvo. I need not care now. I could not mount him, if he were standing by my side.

"The other?" he added, after a pause. "Good heavens! what a spectacle it was! No wonder it scared the one I was riding!

"What am I to do? My leg may be broken. I can't stir from this spot, without some one to help me. Ten chances to one—a hundred—a thousand—against any one coming this way; at least not till I've become food for those filthy birds. Ugh! the hideous brutes; they stretch out their beaks, as if already sure of making a meal upon me!

"How long have I been lying here? The surf don't seem very high. It was just daybreak, as I climbed into the saddle. I suppose I've been unconscious about an hour. By my faith, I'm in a serious scrape? In all likelihood a broken limb—it feels broken—with no surgeon to set it; a stony couch in the heart of a Texan chapparal—the thicket around me, perhaps for miles—no chance to escape from it of myself—no hope of human creature coming to help me—wolves on the earth, and vultures in the air! Great God! why did I mount, without making sure of the rein? I may have ridden my last ride!"

The countenance of the young man became clouded; and the cloud grew darker, and deeper, as he continued to reflect upon the perilous position in which a simple accident had placed him.

Once more he essayed to rise to his feet, and succeeded; only to find, that he had but one leg on which he could rely! It was no use, standing upon it; and he lay down again.

Two hours were passed without any change in his situation; during which he had caused the chapparal to ring with a loud hallooing. He only desisted from this, under the conviction: that there was no one at all likely to hear him.

The shouting caused thirst; or at all events hastened the advent of this appetite—surely coming on as the concomitant of the injuries he had received.

The sensation was soon experienced to such an extent that everything else—even the pain of his wounds—became of trifling consideration.

"It will kill me, if I stay here?" reflected the sufferer. "I must make an effort to reach water. If I remember aright there's a stream somewhere in this chapparal, and not such a great way off. I must get to it, if I have to crawl upon my hands and knees. Knees! and only one in a condition to support me! There's no help for it but try. The longer I stay here, the worse it will be. The sun grows hotter. It already burns into my brain. I may lose my senses, and then—the wolves—the vultures—"

The horrid apprehension caused silence and shuddering. After a time he continued:

"If I but knew the right way to go. I remember the stream well enough. It runs towards the chalk prairie. It should be south-east, from here. I shall try that way. By good luck the sun guides me. If I find water all may yet be well. God give me strength to reach it!"

With this prayer upon his lips, he commenced making his way through the thicket—creeping over the stony ground, and dragging after him his disabled leg, like some huge Saurian whose vertebrae have been disjointed by a blow!

Lizard-like, he continued his crawl.

The effort was painful in the extreme; but the apprehension from which he suffered was still more painful, and urged him to continue it.

He well knew there was a chance of his falling a victim to thirst—almost a certainty, if he did not succeed in finding water.

Stimulated by this knowledge he crept on.

244

At short intervals he was compelled to pause, and recruit his strength by a little rest. A man does not travel far, on his hands and knees, without feeling fatigued. Much more, when one of the four members cannot be employed in the effort.

His progress was slow and irksome. Besides, it was being made under the most discouraging circumstances. He might not be going in the right direction? Nothing but the dread of death could have induced him to keep on.

He had made about a quarter of a mile from the point of starting, when it occurred to him that a better plan of locomotion might be adopted—one that would, at all events, vary the monotony of his march.

"Perhaps," said he, "I might manage to hobble a bit, if I only had a crutch? Ho! my knife is still here. Thank fortune for that! And there's a sapling of the right size—a bit of blackjack. It will do."

Drawing the knife—a "bowie"—from his belt, he cut down the dwarf-oak; and soon reduced it to a rude kind of crutch; a fork in the tree serving for the head.

Then rising erect, and fitting the fork into his armpit, he proceeded with his exploration.

He knew the necessity of keeping to one course; and, as he had chosen the south-east, he continued in this direction.

It was not so easy. The sun was his only compass; but this had now reached the meridian, and, in the latitude of Southern Texas, at that season of the year, the midday sun is almost in the zenith. Moreover, he had the chapparal to contend with, requiring constant détours to take advantage of its openings. He had a sort of guide in the sloping of the ground: for he knew that downward he was more likely to find the stream.

After proceeding about a mile—not in one continued march, but by short stages, with intervals of rest between—he came upon a track made by the wild animals that frequent the chapparal. It was slight, but running in a direct line—a proof that it led to some point of peculiar consideration—in all likelihood a watering-place—stream, pond, or spring.

Any of these three would serve his purpose; and, without longer looking to the sun, or the slope of the ground, he advanced along the trail—now hobbling upon his crutch, and at times, when tired of this mode, dropping down upon his hands and crawling as before.

The cheerful anticipations he had indulged in, on discovering the trail, soon, came to a termination. It became *blind*. In other words it ran out—ending in a glade surrounded by impervious masses of underwood. He saw, to his dismay, that it led *from* the glade, instead of *towards* it. He had been following it the wrong way!

Unpleasant as was the alternative, there was no other than to return upon his track. To stay in the glade would have been to die there.

He retraced the trodden path—going on beyond the point where he had first struck it.

Nothing but the torture of thirst could have endowed him with strength or spirit to proceed. And this was every moment becoming more unendurable.

The trees through which he was making way were mostly acacias, interspersed with cactus and wild agave. They afforded scarce any shelter from the sun, that now in mid-heaven glared down through their gossamer foliage with the fervour of fire itself.

The perspiration, oozing through every pore of his skin, increased the tendency to thirst—until the appetite became an agony!

Within reach of his hand were the glutinous legumes of the *mezquites*, filled with mellifluous moisture. The agaves and cactus plants, if tapped, would have exuded an abundance of juice. The former was too sweet, the latter too acrid to tempt him.

He was acquainted with the character of both. He knew that, instead of allaying his thirst, they would only have added to its intensity.

He passed the depending pods, without plucking them. He passed the succulent stalks, without tapping thorn.

To augment his anguish, he now discovered that the wounded limb was, every moment, becoming more unmanageable. It had swollen to enormous dimensions. Every step caused him a spasm of pain. Even if going in the direction of the doubtful streamlet, he might never succeed in reaching it? If not, there was no hope for him. He could but lie down in the thicket, and die!

Death would not be immediate. Although suffering acute pain in his head, neither the shock it had received, nor the damage done to his knee, were like to prove speedily fatal. He might dread a more painful way of dying than from wounds. Thirst would be his destroyer—of all shapes of death perhaps the most agonising.

The thought stimulated him to renewed efforts; and despite the slow progress he was able to make—despite the pain experienced in making it—he toiled on.

The black birds hovering above, kept pace with his halting step and laborious crawl. Now more than a mile from the point of their first segregation, they were all of them still there—their numbers even augmented by fresh detachments that had become warned of the expected prey. Though aware that the quarry still lived and moved, they saw that it was stricken. Instinct—perhaps rather experience—told them it must soon succumb.

Their shadows crossed and recrossed the track upon which he advanced—filling him with ominous fears for the end.

There was no noise: for these birds are silent in their flight—even when excited by the prospect of a repast. The hot sun had stilled the voices of the crickets and tree-toads. Even the hideous "horned frog" reclined listless along the earth, sheltering its tuberculated body under the stones.

The only sounds to disturb the solitude of the chapparal were those made by the sufferer himself—the swishing of his garments, as they brushed against the hirsute plants that beset the path; and occasionally his cries, sent forth in the faint hope of their being heard.

By this time, blood was mingling with the sweat upon his skin. The spines of the cactus, and the clawlike thorns of the agave, had been doing their work; and scarce an inch of the epidermis upon his face, hands, and limbs, that was not rent with a laceration.

He was near to the point of despondence—in real truth, he had reached it: for after a spell of shouting he had flung himself prostrate along the earth, despairingly indifferent about proceeding farther.

In all likelihood it was the attitude that saved him. Lying with his ear close to the surface, he heard a sound—so slight, that it would not have been otherwise discernible.

Slight as it was, he could distinguish it, as the very sound for which his senses were sharpened. It was the murmur of moving water!

With an ejaculation of joy, he sprang to his feet, as if nothing were amiss; and made direct towards the point whence proceeded the sound.

He plied his improvised crutch with redoubled energy. Even the disabled leg appeared to sustain him. It was strength and the love of life, struggling against decrepitude and the fear of death.

The former proved victorious; and, in ten minutes after, he lay stretched along the sward, on the banks of a crystal streamlet—wondering why the want of water could have caused him such indescribable agony!

# 43. The Cup and the Jar

Once more the mustanger's hut! Once more his henchman, astride of a stool in the middle of the floor! Once more his hound lying astretch upon the skin-covered hearth, with snout half buried in the cinders!

The relative positions of the man and the dog are essentially the same—as when seen on a former occasion—their attitudes almost identical. Otherwise there is a change in the picture since last painted—a transformation at once striking and significant.

The horse-hide door, standing ajar, still hangs upon its hinges; and the smooth coats of the wild steeds shine lustrously along the walls. The slab table, too, is there, the trestle bedstead, the two stools, and the "shake down" of the servitor.

But the other "chattels" wont to be displayed against the skin tapestry are either out of sight, or displaced. The double gun has been removed from its rack; the silver cup, hunting horn, and dog-call, are no longer suspended from their respective pegs; the saddle, bridles, ropes, and serapés are unslung; and the books, ink, pens, and *papeterie* have entirely disappeared.

At first sight it might be supposed that Indians have paid a visit to the jacalé, and pillaged it of its *penates*.

But no. Had this been the case, Phelim would not be sitting so unconcernedly on the stool, with his carroty scalp still upon his head.

Though the walls are stripped nothing has been carried away. The articles are still there, only with a change of place; and the presence of several corded packages, lying irregularly over the floor—among which is the leathern portmanteau—proclaims the purpose of the transposition.

Though a clearing out has not been made, it is evident that one is intended.

In the midst of the general displacement, one piece of plenishing was still seen in its accustomed corner—the demijohn. It was seen by Phelim, oftener than any other article in the room: for no matter in what direction he might turn his eyes, they were sure to come round again to that wicker-covered vessel that stood so temptingly in the angle.

"Ach! me jewel, it's there yez are!" said he, apostrophising the demijohn for about the twentieth time, "wid more than two quarts av the crayther inside yer bewtifull belly, and not doin' ye a bit av good, nayther. If the tinth part av it was inside av me, it wud be a moighty binnefit to me intistines. Trath wud it that same. Wudn't it, Tara?"

On hearing his name pronounced, the dog raised his head and looked inquiringly around, to see what was wanted of him.

Perceiving that his human companion was but talking to himself, he resumed his attitude of repose.

"Faix! I don't want any answer to that, owld boy. It's meself that knows it, widout tillin'. A hape av good a glass of that same potyeen would do me; and I dar'n't touch a dhrap, afther fwhat the masther sid to me about it. Afther all that packin', too, till me throat is stickin' to me tongue, as if I had been thryin' to swallow a pitch plaster. Sowl! it's a shame av Masther Maurice to make me promise agaynst touchin' the dhrink—espacially when it's not goin' to be wanted. Didn't he say he wudn't stay more than wan night, whin he come back heeur; an shure he won't conshume two quarts in wan night—unless that owld sinner Stump comes along wid him. Bad luck to his greedy gut! he gets more av the Manongahayla than the masther himsilf.

"There's wan consolashun, an thank the Lord for it, we're goin' back to the owld *sad*, an the owld place at Ballyballagh. Won't I have a skinful when I get thare—av the raal stuff too, instid of this Amerikyan rotgut! Hooch—hoop—horoo! The thought av it's enough to sit a man mad wid deloight. Hooch—hoop—horoo!"

Tossing his wide-awake up among the rafters, and catching it as it came down again, the excited Galwegian several times repeated his ludicrous shibboleth. Then becoming tranquil he sate for awhile in silence—his thoughts dwelling with pleasant anticipation on the joys that awaited him at Ballyballagh.

They soon reverted to the objects around him—more especially to the demijohn in the corner. On this once more his eyes became fixed in a gaze, in which increasing covetousness was manifestly visible.

"Arrah, me jewel!" said he, again apostrophising the vessel, "ye're extremely bewtifull to look at—that same ye arr. Shure now, yez wudn't till upon me, if I gave yez a thrifle av a kiss? Ye wudn't be the thraiter to bethray me? Wan smack only. Thare can be no harum in that. Trath, I don't think the masther 'ud mind it—when he thinks av the throuble I've had wid this packin', an the dhry dust gettin' down me throat. Shure he didn't mane me to kape that promise for this time—which differs intirely from all the rest, by razon av our goin' away. A dhry flittin', they say, makes a short sittin'. I'll tell the masther that, whin he comes back; an shure it 'll pacify him. Besoides, there's another ixcuse. He's all av tin hours beyant his time; an I'll say I took a thriflin' dhrap to kape me from thinkin' long for him. Shure he won't say a word about it. Be Sant Pathrick! I'll take a smell at the dimmyjan, an trust to good luck for the rist. Loy down, Tara, I'm not agoin' out."

The staghound had risen, seeing the speaker step towards the door.

But the dumb creature had misinterpreted the purpose—which was simply to take a survey of the path by which the jacalé was approached, and make sure, that, his master was not likely to interrupt him in his intended dealings with the demijohn.

Becoming satisfied that the coast was clear, he glided back across the floor; uncorked the jar; and, raising it to his lips, swallowed something more than a "thriflin' dhrap av its contints."

Then putting it back in its place, he returned to his seat on the stool.

After remaining quiescent for a considerable time, he once more proceeded to soliloquise—now and then changing his speech to the apostrophic form—Tara and the demijohn being the individuals honoured by his discourse.

"In the name av all the angels, an the divils to boot, I wondher what's kapin' the masther! He sid he wud be heeur by eight av the clock in the marnin', and it's now good six in the afthernoon, if thare's any truth in a Tixas sun. Shure thare's somethin' detainin' him? Don't yez think so, Tara?"

This time Tara did vouchsafe the affirmative "sniff"—having poked his nose too far into the ashes.

"Be the powers! then, I hope it's no harum that's befallen him! If there has, owld dog, fwhat 'ud become av you an me? Thare might be no Ballyballagh for miny a month to come; unliss we cowld pay our passage wid these thraps av the masther's. The drinkin' cup—raal silver it is—wud cover the whole expinse av the voyage. Be japers! now that it stroikes me, I niver had a dhrink out av that purty little vessel.

I'm shure the liquor must taste swater that way. Does it, I wondher—trath, now's just the time to thry."

Saying this, he took the cup out of the portmanteau, in which he had packed it; and, once more uncorking the demijohn, poured out a portion of its contents—of about the measure of a wineglassful.

Quaffing it off at a single gulp, he stood smacking his lips—as if to assure himself of the quality of the liquor.

"Sowl! I don't know that it *does* taste betther," said he, still holding the cup in one hand, and the jar in the other. "Afther all, I think, it's swater out av the dimmyjan itself, that is, as far as I cyan remimber. But it isn't givin' the gawblet fair play. It's so long since I had the jar to me mouth, that I a'most forget how it tasted that way. I cowld till betther if I thryed thim thegither. I'll do that, before I decoide."

The demijohn was now raised to his lips; and, after several "glucks" was again taken away.

Then succeeded a second series of smacking, in true connoisseur fashion, with the head held reflectingly steadfast.

"Trath! an I'm wrong agane!" said he, accompanying the remark with another doubtful shake of the head. "Althegither asthray. It's swater from the silver. Or, is it only me imaginayshin that's desavin' me? It's worth while to make shure, an I can only do that by tastin' another thrifle out av the cup. That wud be givin' fair play to both av the vessels; for I've dhrunk twice from the jar, an only wanst from the silver. Fair play's a jewil all the world over; and thare's no raison why this bewtiful little mug showldn't be trated as dacently as that big basket av a jar. Be japers! but it shall tho'!"

The cup was again called into requisition; and once more a portion of the contents of the demijohn were transferred to it—to be poured immediately after down the insatiable throat of the unsatisfied connoisseur.

Whether he eventually decided in favour of the cup, or whether he retained his preference for the jar, is not known. After the fourth potation, which was also the final one, he appeared to think he had tasted sufficiently for the time, and laid both vessels aside.

Instead of returning to his stool, however, a new idea came across his mind; which was to go forth from the hut, and see whether there was any sign to indicate the advent of his master.

"Come, Tara!" cried he, striding towards the door. "Let us stip up to the bluff beyant, and take a look over the big plain. If masther's comin' at all, he shud be in sight by this. Come along, ye owld dog!

Masther Maurice 'll think all the betther av us, for bein' a little unazy about his gettin' back."

Taking the path through the wooded bottom—with the staghound close at his heels—the Galwegian ascended the bluff, by one of its sloping ravines, and stood upon the edge of the upper plateau.

From this point he commanded a view of a somewhat sterile plain; that stretched away eastward, more than a mile, from the spot where he was standing.

The sun was on his back, low down on the horizon, but shining from a cloudless sky. There was nothing to interrupt his view. Here and there, a stray cactus plant, or a solitary stem of the arborescent yucca, raised its hirsute form above the level of the plain. Otherwise the surface was smooth; and a coyoté could not have crossed it without being seen.

Beyond, in the far distance, could be traced the darker outline of trees—where a tract of chapparal, or the wooded selvedge of a stream stretched transversely across the *llano*.

The Galwegian bent his gaze over the ground, in the direction in which he expected his master should appear; and stood silently watching for him.

Ere long his vigil was rewarded. A horseman was seen coming out from among the trees upon the other side, and heading towards the Alamo.

He was still more than a mile distant; but, even at that distance, the faithful servant could identify his master. The striped serapé of brilliant hues—a true Navajo blanket, which Maurice was accustomed to take with him when travelling—was not to be mistaken. It gleamed gaudily under the glare of the setting sun—its bands of red, white, and blue, contrasting with the sombre tints of the sterile plain.

Phelim only wondered, that his master should have it spread over his shoulders on such a sultry evening instead of folded up, and strapped to the cantle of his saddle!

"Trath, Tara! it looks quare, doesn't it? It's hot enough to roast a stake upon these stones; an yit the masther don't seem to think so. I hope he hasn't caught a cowld from stayin' in that close crib at owld Duffer's tavern. It wasn't fit for a pig to dwill in. Our own shanty's a splindid parlour to it."

The speaker was for a time silent, watching the movements of the approaching horseman—by this time about half a mile distant, and still drawing nearer.

When his voice was put forth again it was in a tone altogether changed. It was still that of surprise, with an approach towards merriment. But it was mirth that doubted of the ludicrous; and seemed to struggle under restraint.

"Mother av Moses!" cried he. "What can the masther mane? Not contint with havin' the blankyet upon his showldhers, be japers, he's got it over his head!

"He's playin' us a thrick, Tara. He wants to give you an me a surproise. He wants to have a joke agaynst us!

"Sowl! but it's quare anyhow. It looks as if he *had* no head. In faix does it! Ach! what cyan it mane? Be the Howly Virgin! it's enough to frighten wan, av they didn't know it was the masther!

"*Is* it the masther? Be the powers, it's too short for him! The head? Saint Patrick presarve us, whare is it? It cyan't be smothered up in the blankyet? Thare's no shape thare! Be Jaysus, thare's somethin' wrong! What does it mane, Tara?"

The tone of the speaker had again undergone a change. It was now close bordering upon terror—as was also the expression of his countenance.

The look and attitude of the staghound were not very different. He stood a little in advance—half cowering, half inclined to spring forward—with eyes glaring wildly, while fixed upon the approaching horseman—now scarce two hundred yards from the spot!

As Phelim put the question that terminated his last soliloquy, the hound gave out a lugubrious howl, that seemed intended for an answer.

Then, as if urged by some canine instinct, he bounded off towards the strange object, which puzzled his human companion, and was equally puzzling him.

Rushing straight on, he gave utterance to a series of shrill yelps; far different from the soft sonorous baying, with which he was accustomed to welcome the coming home of the mustanger.

If Phelim was surprised at what he had already seen, he was still further astonished by what now appeared to him.

As the dog drew near, still yelping as he ran, the blood-bay— which the ex-groom had long before identified as his master's horse— turned sharply round, and commenced galloping back across the plain!

While performing the wheel, Phelim saw—or fancied he saw— that, which not only astounded him, but caused the blood to run chill through his veins, and his frame to tremble to the very tips of his toes.

253

It was a head—that of the man on horseback; but, instead of being in its proper place, upon his shoulders, it was held in the rider's hand, just behind the pommel of the saddle!

As the horse turned side towards him, Phelim saw, or fancied he saw, the face—ghastly and covered with gore—half hidden behind the shaggy hair of the holster!

He saw no more. In another instant his back was turned towards the plain; and, in another, he was rushing down the ravine, as fast as his enfeebled limbs would carry him!

# 44. A Quartette of Comanches

With his flame-coloured curls bristling upward—almost raising the hat from his head—the Galwegian continued his retreat—pausing not—scarce looking back, till he had re-entered the jacalé, closed the skin door behind him, and barricaded it with several large packages that lay near.

Even then he did not feel secure. What protection could there be in a shut door, barred and bolted besides, against that which was not earthly?

And surely what he had seen was not of the earth—not of this world! Who on earth had ever witnessed such a spectacle—a man mounted upon horseback, and carrying his head in his hand? Who had ever heard of a phenomenon so unnatural? Certainly not "Phaylim Onale."

His horror still continuing, he rushed to and fro across the floor of the hut; now dropping down upon the stool, anon rising up, and gliding to the door; but without daring either to open it, or look out through the chinks.

At intervals he tore the hair out of his head, striking his clenched hand against his temples, and roughly rubbing his eyes—as if to make sure that he was not asleep, but had really seen the shape that was horrifying him.

One thing alone gave him a moiety of comfort; though it was of the slightest. While retreating down the ravine, before his head had sunk below the level of the plain, he had given a glance backward. He had derived some gratification from that glance; as it showed the headless rider afar off on the prairie, and with back turned toward the Alamo, going on at a gallop.

But for the remembrance of this, the Galwegian might have been still more terrified—if that were possible—while striding back and forth upon the floor of the jacalé.

For a long time he was speechless—not knowing what to say—and only giving utterance to such exclamations as came mechanically to his lips.

As the time passed, and he began to feel, not so much a return of confidence, as of the power of ratiocination, his tongue became restored to him; and a continuous fire of questions and exclamations succeeded. They were all addressed to himself. Tara was no longer there, to take part in the conversation.

They were put, moreover, in a low whispered tone, as if in fear that his voice might be heard outside the jacalé.

"Ochone! Ochone! it cyan't av been him! Sant Pathrick protict me, but fwhat was it thin?

"Thare was iverything av his—the horse—the sthriped blankyet—them spotted wather guards upon his legs—an the head itself—all except the faytures. Thim I saw too, but wasn't shure about eyedintifycashin; for who kud till a face all covered over wid rid blood?

"Ach! it cudn't be Masther Maurice at all, at all!

"It's all a dhrame. I must have been aslape, an dhramin? Or, was it the whisky that did it?

"Shure, I wasn't dhrunk enough for that. Two goes out av the little cup, an two more from the dimmyjan—not over a kupple av naggins in all! That wudn't make me dhrunk. I've taken twice that, widout as much as thrippin in my spache. Trath have I. Besoides, if I had been the worse for the liquor, why am I not so still?

"Thare's not half an hour passed since I saw it; an I'm as sober as a judge upon the binch av magistrates.

"Sowl! a dhrap 'ud do me a power av good just now. If I don't take wan, I'll not get a wink av slape. I'll be shure to kape awake all the night long thinkin' about it. Ochone! ochone! what cyan it be anyhow? An' where cyan the masther be, if it wasn't him? Howly Sant Pathrick! look down an watch over a miserable sinner, that's lift all alone be himself, wid nothin' but ghosts an goblins around him!"

After this appeal to the Catholic saint, the Connemara man addressed himself with still more zealous devotion to the worship of a very different divinity, known among the ancients as Bacchus.

His suit in this quarter proved perfectly successful; for in less than an hour after he had entered upon his genuflexions at the shrine of the pagan god—represented by the demijohn of Monongahela whisky—he was shrived of all his sufferings—if not of his sins—and lay stretched along the floor of the jacalé, not only oblivious of the

256

spectacle that had so late terrified him to the very centre of his soul, but utterly unconscious of his soul's existence.

---

There is no sound within the hut of Maurice the mustanger—not even a clock, to tell, by its continuous ticking, that the hours are passing into eternity, and that another midnight is mantling over the earth.

There are sounds outside; but only as usual. The rippling of the stream close by, the whispering of the leaves stirred by the night wind, the chirrup of cicadas, the occasional cry of some wild creature, are but the natural voices of the nocturnal forest.

Midnight has arrived, with a moon that assimilates it to morning. Her light illumines the earth; here and there penetrating through the shadowy trees, and flinging broad silvery lists between them.

Passing through these alternations of light and shadow— apparently avoiding the former, as much as possible—goes a group of mounted men.

Though few in number—as there are only four of them—they are formidable to look upon. The vermilion glaring redly over their naked skins, the striped and spotted tatooing upon their cheeks, the scarlet feathers standing stiffly upright above their heads, and the gleaming of weapons held in their hands, all bespeak strength of a savage and dangerous kind.

Whence come they?

They are in the war costume of the Comanche. Their paint proclaims it. There is the skin fillet around the temples, with the eagle plumes stuck behind it. The bare breasts and arms; the buckskin breech-clouts—everything in the shape of sign by which these Ishmaelites of Texas may be recognised, when out upon the *maraud*.

They must be Comanches: and, therefore, have come from the west.

Whither go they?

This is a question more easily answered. They are closing in upon the hut, where lies the unconscious inebriate. The jacalé of Maurice Gerald is evidently the *butt* of their expedition.

That their intentions are hostile, is to be inferred from the fact of their wearing the war costume. It is also apparent from their manner of making approach. Still further, by their dismounting at some distance from the hut, securing their horses in the underwood, and continuing their advance on foot.

Their stealthy tread—taking care to plant the foot lightly upon the fallen leaves—the precaution to keep inside the shadow—the frequent pauses, spent in looking ahead and listening—the silent gestures with which these movements are directed by him who appears to be the leader—all proclaim design, to reach the jacalé unperceived by whoever may chance to be inside it.

In this they are successful—so far as may be judged by appearances. They stand by the stockade walls, without any sign being given to show that they have been seen.

The silence inside is complete, as that they are themselves observing. There is nothing heard—not so much as the screech of a hearth-cricket.

And yet the hut is inhabited. But a man may get drunk beyond the power of speech, snoring, or even audibly breathing; and in this condition is the tenant of the jacalé.

The four Comanches steal up to the door; and in skulking attitudes scrutinise it.

It is shut; but there are chinks at the sides. To these the savages set their ears—all at the same time—and stand silently listening.

No snoring, no breathing, no noise of any kind!

"It is possible," says their chief to the follower nearest him—speaking in a whisper, but in good grammatical Castilian, "just possible he has not yet got home; though by the time of his starting he should have reached here long before this. He may have ridden out again? Now I remember: there's a horse-shed at the back. If the man be inside the house, the beast should be found in the shed. Stay here, *camarados*, till I go round and see."

Six seconds suffice to examine the substitute for a stable. No horse in it.

As many more are spent in scrutinising the path that leads to it. No horse has been there—at least not lately.

These points determined, the chief returns to his followers—still standing by the doorway in front.

"*Maldito!*" he exclaims, giving freer scope to his voice, "he's *not* here, nor has he been this day."

"We had better go inside, and make sure?" suggests one of the common warriors, in Spanish fairly pronounced. "There can be no harm in our seeing how the *Irlandes* has housed himself out here?"

"Certainly not!" answers a third, equally well versed in the language of Cervantes. "Let's have a look at his larder too. I'm hungry enough to eat raw tasajo."

"*Por Dios!*" adds the fourth and last of the quartette, in the same sonorous tongue. "I've heard that he keeps a cellar. If so—"

The chief does not wait for his follower to finish the hypothetical speech. The thought of a cellar appears to produce a powerful effect upon him—stimulating to immediate action.

He sets his heel upon the skin door, with the intention of pushing it open.

It resists the effort.

"*Carrambo*! it's barred inside! Done to keep out intruders in his absence! Lions, tigers, bears, buffaloes—perhaps Indians. Ha! ha! ha!"

Another kick is given with greater force. The door still keeps its place.

"Barricaded with something—something heavy too. It won't yield to kicking. No matter. I'll soon see what's inside."

The macheté is drawn from its sheath; and a large hole cut through the stretched skin, that covers the light framework of wood.

Into this the Indian thrusts his arm; and groping about, discovers the nature of the obstruction.

The packages are soon displaced, and the door thrown open.

The savages enter, preceded by a broad moonbeam, that lights them on their way, and enables them to observe the condition of the interior.

A man lying in the middle of the floor!

"*Carajo!*"

"Is he asleep?"

"He must be dead not to have heard us?"

"Neither," says the chief, after stooping to examine him, "only dead drunk—*boracho*—*embriaguado*! He's the servitor of the Irlandes. I've seen this fellow before. From his manner one may safely conclude, that his master is not at home, nor has been lately. I hope the brute hasn't used up the cellar in getting himself into this comfortable condition. Ah! a jar. And smelling like a rose! There's a rattle among these rods. There's stuff inside. Thank the Lady Guadaloupe for this!"

A few seconds suffice for distributing what remains of the contents of the demijohn. There is enough to give each of the four a drink, with two to their chief; who, notwithstanding his high rank, has not the superior politeness to protest against this unequal distribution. In a trice the jar is empty. What next?

The master of the house must come home, some time or other. An interview with him is desired by the men, who have made a call upon him—particularly desired, as may be told by the unseasonable hour of their visit. The chief is especially anxious to see him.

What can four Comanche Indians want with Maurice the mustanger?

Their talk discloses their intentions: for among themselves they make no secret of their object in being there.

*They have come to murder him!*

Their chief is the instigator; the others are only his instruments and assistants.

The business is too important to permit of his trifling. He will gain a thousand dollars by the deed—besides a certain gratification independent of the money motive. His three braves will earn a hundred each—a sum sufficient to tempt the cupidity of a Comanche, and purchase him for any purpose.

The travesty need not be carried any further. By this time the mask must have fallen off. Our Comanches are mere Mexicans; their chief, Miguel Diaz, the mustanger.

"We must lie in wait for him."

This is the counsel of El Coyote.

"He cannot be much longer now, whatever may have detained him. You, Barajo, go up to the bluff, and keep a look-out over the plain. The rest remain here with me. He must come that way from the Leona. We can meet him at the bottom of the gorge under the big cypress tree. 'Tis the best place for our purpose."

"Had we not better silence *him*?" hints the bloodthirsty Barajo, pointing to the Galwegian—fortunately unconscious of what is transpiring around him.

"Dead men tell no tales!" adds another of the conspirators, repeating the proverb in its original language.

"It would tell a worse tale were we to kill him," rejoins Diaz. "Besides, it's of no use. He's silent enough as it is, the droll devil. Let the dog have his day. I've only bargained for the life of his master. Come, Barajo! *Vayate! vayate*! Up to the cliff. We can't tell the moment Don Mauricio may drop in upon us. A miscarriage must not be made. We may never have such a chance again. Take your stand at the top of the gorge. From that point you have a view of the whole plain. He cannot come near without your seeing him, in such a moonlight as this. As soon as you've set eyes on him, hasten down and let us know. Be sure you give us time to get under the cypress."

Barajo is proceeding to yield obedience to this chapter of instructions, but with evident reluctance. He has, the night before, been in ill luck, having lost to El Coyote a large sum at the game of *monté*. He is desirous of having his *revanche*: for he well knows how his *confrères* will spend the time in his absence.

"Quick. Señor Vicente!" commands Diaz, observing his dislike to the duty imposed upon him; "if we fail in this business, you will lose more than you can gain at an *albur* of monté. Go, man!" continues El Coyote, in an encouraging way. "If he come not within the hour, some one will relieve you. Go!"

Barajo obeys, and, stepping out of the jacalé, proceeds to his post upon the top of the cliff.

The others seat themselves inside the hut—having already established a light.

Men of their class and calling generally go provided with the means of killing time, or, at all events, hindering it from hanging on their hands.

The slab table is between them, upon which is soon displayed, not their supper, but a pack of Spanish cards, which every Mexican *vagabondo* carries under his serapé.

*Cavallo* and *soto* (queen and knave) are laid face upward; a monté table is established; the cards are shuffled; and the play proceeds.

Absorbed in calculating the chances of the game, an hour passes without note being taken of the time.

El Coyote is banker, and also croupier.

The cries "*Cavallo en la puerta!*" "*Soto mozo!*" "The queen in the gate!" "The knave winner!"—at intervals announced in set phrase—echo from the skin-covered walls.

The silver dollars are raked along the rough table, their sharp chink contrasting with the soft shuffle of the cards.

All at once a more stentorous sound interrupts the play, causing a cessation of the game.

It is the screech of the inebriate, who, awaking from his trance of intoxication, perceives for the first time the queer company that share with him the shelter of the jacalé.

The players spring to their feet, and draw their machetés. Phelim stands a fair chance of being skewered on three long Toledos.

He is only saved by a contingency—another interruption that has the effect of staying the intent.

Barajo appears in the doorway panting for breath.

It is scarce necessary for him to announce his errand, though he contrives to gasp out—

"He is *coming*—on the bluff already—at the head of the *cañada*—quick, comrades, quick!"

The Galwegian is saved. There is scarce time to kill him—even were it worth while.

But it is not—at least so think the masqueraders; who leave him to resume his disturbed slumber, and rush forth to accomplish the more profitable assassination.

In a score of seconds they are under the cliff, at the bottom of the sloping gorge by which it must be descended.

They take stand under the branches of a spreading cypress; and await the approach of their victim.

They listen for the hoofstrokes that should announce it.

These are soon heard. There is the clinking of a shod hoof—not in regular strokes, but as if a horse was passing over an uneven surface. One is descending the slope!

He is not yet visible to the eyes of the ambuscaders. Even the gorge is in gloom—like the valley below, shadowed by tall trees.

There is but one spot where the moon throws light upon the turf—a narrow space outside the sombre shadow that conceals the assassins. Unfortunately this does not lie in the path of their intended victim. He must pass under the canopy of the cypress!

"Don't kill him!" mutters Miguel Diaz to his men, speaking in an earnest tone. "There's no need for that just yet. I want to have him alive—for the matter of an hour or so. I have my reasons. Lay hold of him and his horse. There can be no danger, as he will be taken by surprise, and unprepared. If there be resistance, we must shoot him down; but let me fire first."

The confederates promise compliance.

They have soon an opportunity of proving the sincerity of their promise. He for whom they are waiting has accomplished the descent of the slope, and is passing under the shadow of the cypress.

"*Abajo las armas! A tierra!*" ("Down with your weapons. To the ground!") cries El Coyote, rushing forward and seizing the bridle, while the other three fling themselves upon the man who is seated in the saddle.

There is no resistance, either by struggle or blow; no blade drawn; no shot discharged: not even a word spoken in protest!

They see a man standing upright in the stirrups; they lay their hands upon limbs that feel solid flesh and bone, and yet seem insensible to the touch!

The horse alone shows resistance. He rears upon his hind legs, makes ground backward, and draws his captors after him.

He carries them into the light, where the moon is shining outside the shadow.

Merciful heaven! what does it mean?

His captors let go their hold, and fall back with a simultaneous shout. It is a scream of wild terror!

Not another instant do they stay under the cypress; but commence retreating at top speed towards the thicket where their own steeds have been left tied.

Mounting in mad haste, they ride rapidly away.

They have seen that which has already stricken terror into hearts more courageous than theirs—*a horseman without a head*!

---

# 45. A Trail Gone Blind

Was it a phantom? Surely it could not be human?

So questioned El Coyote and his terrified companions. So, too, had the scared Galwegian interrogated himself, until his mind, clouded by repeated appeals to the demijohn, became temporarily relieved of the terror.

In a similar strain had run the thoughts of more than a hundred others, to whom the headless horseman had shown himself—the party of searchers who accompanied the major.

It was at an earlier hour, and a point in the prairie five miles farther east, that to these the weird figure had made itself manifest.

Looking westward, with the sun-glare in their eyes, they had seen only its shape, and nothing more—at least nothing to connect it with Maurice the mustanger.

Viewing it from the west, with the sun at his back, the Galwegian had seen enough to make out a resemblance to his master—if not an absolute identification.

Under the light of the moon the four Mexicans, who knew Maurice Gerald by sight, had arrived at a similar conclusion.

If the impression made upon the servant was one of the wildest awe, equally had it stricken the conspirators.

The searchers, though less frightened by the strange phenomenon, were none the less puzzled to explain it.

Up to the instant of its disappearance no explanation had been attempted—save that jocularly conveyed in the bizarre speech of the borderer.

"What *do* you make of it, gentlemen?" said the major, addressing those that had clustered around him: "I confess it mystifies me."

"An Indian trick?" suggested one. "Some decoy to draw us into an ambuscade?"

"A most unlikely lure, then;" remarked another; "certainly the last that would attract me."

"I don't think it's Indian," said the major; "I don't know what to think. What's your opinion of it, Spangler?"

The tracker shook his head, as if equally uncertain.

"Do you think it's an Indian in disguise?" urged the officer, pressing him for an answer.

"I know no more than yourself, major," replied he. "It *should* be somethin' of that kind: for what else *can* it be? It must eyther be a man, or a dummy!"

"That's it—a dummy!" cried several, evidently relieved by his hypothesis.

"Whatsomever it is—man, dummy, or devil," said the frontiersman, who had already pronounced upon it, "thar's no reason why we should be frightened from followin' its trail. Has it left any, I wonder?"

"If it has," replied Spangler, "we'll soon see. Ours goes the same way—so fur as can be judged from here. Shall we move forr'ad, major?"

"By all means. We must not be turned from our purpose by a trifle like that. Forward!"

The horsemen again advanced—some of them not without a show of reluctance. There were among them men, who, if left to themselves, would have taken the back track. Of this number was Calhoun, who, from the first moment of sighting the strange apparition, had shown signs of affright even beyond the rest of his companions. His eyes had suddenly assumed an unnatural glassiness; his lips were white as ashes; while his drooping jaw laid bare two rows of teeth, which he appeared with difficulty to restrain from chattering!

But for the universal confusion, his wild manner might have been observed. So long as the singular form was in sight, there were eyes only for it; and when it had at length disappeared, and the party advanced along the trail, the ex-captain hung back, riding unobserved among the rearmost.

The tracker had guessed aright. The spot upon which the ghostly shape had for the moment stood still, lay direct upon the trail they were already taking up.

But, as if to prove the apparition a spirit, on reaching the place there were no tracks to be seen!

The explanation, however, was altogether natural. Where the horse had wheeled round, and for miles beyond, the plain was thickly

265

strewn with white shingle. It was, in trapper parlance, a "chalk prairie." The stones showed displacement; and here and there an abrasion that appeared to have been made by the hoof of a horse. But these marks were scarce discernible, and only to the eyes of the skilled tracker.

It was the case with the trail they had been taking up—that of the shod mustang; and as the surface had lately been disturbed by a wild herd, the particular hoof-marks could no longer be distinguished.

They might have gone further in the direction taken by the headless rider. The sun would have been their guide, and after that the evening star. But it was the rider of the shod mustang they were desirous to overtake; and the half hour of daylight that followed was spent in fruitless search for his trail—gone blind among the shingle.

Spangler proclaimed himself at fault, as the sun disappeared over the horizon.

They had no alternative but to ride back to the chapparal, and bivouac among the bushes.

The intention was to make a fresh trial for the recovery of the trail, at the earliest hour of the morning.

It was not fulfilled, at least as regarded time. The trial was postponed by an unexpected circumstance.

Scarce had they formed camp, when a courier arrived, bringing a despatch for the major. It was from the commanding officer of the district, whose head-quarters were at San Antonio do Bexar. It had been sent to Fort Inge, and thence forwarded.

The major made known its tenor by ordering "boots and saddles" to be sounded; and before the sweat had become dry upon the horses, the dragoons were once more upon their backs.

The despatch had conveyed the intelligence, that the Comanches were committing outrage, not upon the Leona, but fifty miles farther to the eastward, close to the town of San Antonio itself.

It was no longer a mere rumour. The maraud had commenced by the murder of men, women, and children, with the firing of their houses.

The major was commanded to lose no time, but bring what troops he could spare to the scene of operations. Hence his hurried decampment.

The civilians might have stayed; but friendship—even parental affection—must yield to the necessities of nature. Most of them had set forth without further preparation than the saddling of their horses, and shouldering their guns; and hunger now called them home.

There was no intention to abandon the search. That was to be resumed as soon as they could change horses, and establish a better system of commissariat. Then would it be continued—as one and all declared, to the "bitter end."

A small party was left with Spangler to take up the trail of the American horse, which according to the tracker's forecast would lead back to the Leona. The rest returned along with the dragoons.

Before parting with Poindexter and his friends, the major made known to them—what he had hitherto kept back—the facts relating to the bloody sign, and the tracker's interpretation of it. As he was no longer to take part in the search, he thought it better to communicate to those who should, a circumstance so important.

It pained him to direct suspicion upon the young Irishman, with whom in the way of his calling he had held some pleasant intercourse. But duty was paramount; and, notwithstanding his disbelief in the mustanger's guilt, or rather his belief in its improbability, he could not help acknowledging that appearances were against him.

With the planter and his party it was no longer a suspicion. Now that the question of Indians was disposed of, men boldly proclaimed Maurice Gerald a murderer.

That the deed had been done no one thought of doubting.

Oberdoffer's story had furnished the first chapter of the evidence. Henry's horse returning with the blood-stained saddle the last. The intermediate links were readily supplied—partly by the interpretations of the tracker, and partly by conjecture.

No one paused to investigate the motive—at least with any degree of closeness. The hostility of Gerald was accounted for by his quarrel with Calhoun; on the supposition that it might have extended to the whole family of the Poindexters!

It was very absurd reasoning; but men upon the track of a supposed murderer rarely reason at all. They think only of destroying him.

With this thought did they separate; intending to start afresh on the following morning, throw themselves once more upon the trail of the two men who were missing, and follow it up, till one or both should be found—one or both, living or dead.

The party left with Spangler remained upon the spot which the major had chosen as a camping ground.

They were in all less than a dozen. A larger number was deemed unnecessary. Comanches, in that quarter, were no longer to be looked for; nor was there any other danger that called for a strength of men. Two or three would have been sufficient for the duty required of them.

Nine or ten stayed—some out of curiosity, others for the sake of companionship. They were chiefly young men—sons of planters and the like. Calhoun was among them—the acknowledged chief of the party; though Spangler, acting as guide, was tacitly understood to be the man to whom obedience should be given.

Instead of going to sleep, after the others had ridden away, they gathered around a roaring fire, already kindled within the thicket glade.

Among them was no stint for supper—either of eatables or drinkables. The many who had gone back—knowing they would not need them—had surrendered their haversacks, and the "heel-taps" of their canteens, to the few who remained. There was liquor enough to last through the night—even if spent in continuous carousing.

Despite their knowledge of this—despite the cheerful crackling of the logs, as they took their seats around the fire—they were not in high spirits.

One and all appeared to be under some influence, that, like a spell, prevented them from enjoying a pleasure perhaps not surpassed upon earth.

You may talk of the tranquil joys of the domestic hearth. At times, upon the prairie, I have myself thought of, and longed to return to them. But now, looking back upon both, and calmly comparing them, one with the other, I cannot help exclaiming:

"Give me the circle of the camp-fire, with half-a-dozen of my hunter comrades around it—once again give me that, and be welcome to the wealth I have accumulated, and the trivial honours I have gained—thrice welcome to the care and the toil that must still be exerted in retaining them."

The sombre abstraction of their spirits was easily explained. The weird shape was fresh in their thoughts. They were yet under the influence of an indefinable awe.

Account for the apparition as they best could, and laugh at it—as they at intervals affected to do—they could not clear their minds of this unaccountable incubus, nor feel satisfied with any explanation that had been offered.

The guide Spangler partook of the general sentiment, as did their leader Calhoun.

The latter appeared more affected by it than any of the party! Seated, with moody brow, under the shadow of the trees, at some distance from the fire, he had not spoken a word since the departure of the dragoons. Nor did he seem disposed to join the circle of those who were basking in the blaze; but kept himself apart, as if not caring to come under the scrutiny of his companions.

There was still the same wild look in his eyes—the same scared expression upon his features—that had shown itself before sunset.

"I say, Cash Calhoun!" cried one of the young fellows by the fire, who was beginning to talk "tall," under the influence of the oft-repeated potations—"come up, old fellow, and join us in a drink! We all respect your sorrow; and will do what we can to get satisfaction, for you and yours. But a man mustn't always mope, as you're doing. Come along here, and take a 'smile' of the Monongaheela! It'll do you a power of good, I promise you."

Whether it was that he was pleased at the interpretation put upon his silent attitude—which the speech told him had been observed—or whether he had become suddenly inclined towards a feeling of good fellowship, Calhoun accepted the invitation; and stepping up to the fire, fell into line with the rest of the roysterers. Before seating himself, he took a pull at the proffered flask.

From that moment his air changed, as if by enchantment. Instead of showing sombre, he became eminently hilarious—so much so as to cause surprise to more than one of the party. The behaviour seemed odd for a man, whose cousin was supposed to have been murdered that very morning.

Though commencing in the character of an invited guest, he soon exhibited himself as the host of the occasion. After the others had emptied their respective flasks, he proved himself possessed of a supply that seemed inexhaustible. Canteen after canteen came forth, from his capacious saddle-bags—the legacy left by many departed friends, who had gone back with the major.

Partaking of these at the invitation of their leader—encouraged by his example—the young planter "bloods" who encircled the camp fire, talked, sang, danced, roared, and even rolled around it, until the alcohol could no longer keep them awake. Then, yielding to exhausted nature, they sank back upon the sward, some perhaps to experience the dread slumber of a first intoxication.

The ex-officer of volunteers was the last of the number who laid himself along the grass.

If the last to lie down, he was the first to get up. Scarce had the carousal ceased—scarce had the sonorous breathing of his companions proclaimed them asleep—when he rose into an erect attitude, and with cautious steps stole out from among them. With like stealthy tread he kept on to the confines of the camp—to the spot where his horse stood "hitched" to a tree.

Releasing the rein from its knot, and throwing it over the neck of the animal, he clambered into the saddle, and rode noiselessly away.

In all these actions there was no evidence that he was intoxicated. On the contrary, they proclaimed a clear brain, bent upon some purpose previously determined. What could it be?

Urged by affection, was he going forth to trace the mystery of the murder, by finding the body of the murdered man? Did he wish to show his zeal by going alone?

Some such design might have been interpreted from a series of speeches that fell carelessly from his lips, as he rode through the chapparal.

"Thank God, there's a clear moon, and six good hours before those youngsters will think of getting to their feet! I'll have time to search every corner of the thicket, for a couple of miles around the place; and if the body be there I cannot fail to find it. But what could that thing have meant? If I'd been the only one to see it, I might have believed myself mad. But they all saw it—every one of them. Almighty heavens! what could it have been?"

The closing speech ended in an exclamation of terrified surprise—elicited by a spectacle that at the moment presented itself to the eyes of the ex-officer—causing him to rein up his horse, as if some dread danger was before him.

Coming in by a side path, he had arrived on the edge of the opening already described. He was just turning into it, when he saw, that he was not the only horseman, who at that late hour was traversing the chapparal.

Another, to all appearance as well mounted as himself, was approaching along the avenue—not slowly as he, but in a quick trot.

Long before the strange rider had come near, the moonlight, shining fall upon him, enabled Calhoun to see that he was *headless*!

There could be no mistake about the observation. Though quickly made, it was complete. The white moon beams, silvering his shoulders, were reflected from no face, above or between them! It could be no illusion of the moon's light. Calhoun had seen that same shape under the glare of the sun.

He now saw more—the missing head, ghastly and gory, half shrouded behind the hairy holsters! More still—he recognised the horse—the striped serapé upon the shoulders of the rider—the water-guards upon his legs—the complete caparison—all the belongings of Maurice the mustanger!

He had ample time to take in these details. At a stand in the embouchure of the side path, terror held him transfixed to the spot. His horse appeared to share the feeling. Trembling in its tracks, the animal made no effort to escape; even when the headless rider pulled up in front, and, with a snorting, rearing steed, remained for a moment confronting the frightened party.

It was only after the blood bay had given utterance to a wild "whigher"—responded to by the howl of a hound close following at his heels—and turned into the avenue to continue his interrupted trot—only then that Calhoun became sufficiently released from the spell of horror to find speech.

"God of heaven!" he cried, in a quivering voice, "what can it mean? Is it man, or demon, that mocks me? Has the whole day been a dream? Or am I mad—mad—mad?"

The scarce coherent speech was succeeded by action, instantaneous but determined. Whatever the purpose of his exploration, it was evidently abandoned: for, turning his horse with a wrench upon the rein, he rode back by the way he had come—only at a far faster pace,—pausing not till he had re-entered the encampment.

Then stealing up to the edge of the fire, he lay down among the slumbering inebriates—not to sleep, but to stay trembling in their midst, till daylight disclosed a haggard pallor upon his cheeks, and ghastly glances sent forth from his sunken eyes.

# 46. A Secret Confided

The first dawn of day witnessed an unusual stir in and around the hacienda of Casa del Corvo. The courtyard was crowded with men—armed, though not in the regular fashion. They carried long hunting rifles, having a calibre of sixty to the pound; double-barrelled shot guns; single-barrelled pistols; revolvers; knives with long blades; and even tomahawks!

In their varied attire of red flannel shirts, coats of coloured blanket, and "Kentucky jeans," trowsers of brown "homespun," and blue "cottonade," hats of felt and caps of skin, tall boots of tanned leather, and leggings of buck—these stalwart men furnished a faithful picture of an assemblage, such as may be often seen in the frontier settlements of Texas.

Despite the *bizarrerie* of their appearance, and the fact of their carrying weapons, there was nothing in either to proclaim their object in thus coming together. Had it been for the most pacific purpose, they would have been armed and apparelled just the same.

But their object is known.

A number of the men so met, had been out on the day before, along with the dragoons. Others had now joined the assemblage—settlers who lived farther away, and hunters who had been from home.

The muster on this morning was greater than on the preceding day—even exceeding the strength of the searching party when supplemented by the soldiers.

Though all were civilians, there was one portion of the assembled crowd that could boast of an organisation. Irregular it may be deemed, notwithstanding the name by which its members were distinguished. These were the "*Regulators*."

There was nothing distinctive about them, either in their dress, arms, or equipments. A stranger would not have known a Regulator from any other individual. They knew one another.

Their talk was of murder—of the murder of Henry Poindexter—coupled with the name of Maurice the mustanger.

Another subject was discussed of a somewhat cognate character. Those who had seen it, were telling those who had not—of the strange spectacle that had appeared to them the evening before on the prairie.

Some were at first incredulous, and treated the thing as a joke. But the wholesale testimony—and the serious manner in which it was given—could not long be resisted; and the existence of the *headless horseman* became a universal belief. Of course there was an attempt to account for the odd phenomenon, and many forms of explanation were suggested. The only one, that seemed to give even the semblance of satisfaction, was that already set forward by the frontiersman—that the horse was real enough, but the rider was a counterfeit.

For what purpose such a trick should be contrived, or who should be its contriver, no one pretended to explain.

For the business that had brought them togther, there was but little time wasted in preparation. All were prepared already.

Their horses were outside—some of them held in hand by the servants of the establishment, but most "hitched" to whatever would hold them.

They had come warned of their work, and only waited for Woodley Poindexter—on this occasion their chief—to give the signal for setting forth.

He only waited in the hope of procuring a guide; one who could conduct them to the Alamo—who could take them to the domicile of Maurice the mustanger.

There was no such person present. Planters, merchants, shopkeepers, lawyers, hunters, horse and slave-dealers, were all alike ignorant of the Alamo.

There was but one man belonging to the settlement supposed to be capable of performing the required service—old Zeb Stump. But Zeb could not be found. He was absent on one of his stalking expeditions; and the messengers sent to summon him were returning, one after another, to announce a bootless errand.

There was a *woman*, in the hacienda itself, who could have guided the searchers upon their track—to the very hearthstone of the supposed assassin.

Woodley Poindexter knew it not; and perhaps well for him it was so. Had the proud planter suspected that in the person of his own child, there was a guide who could have conducted kim to the lone hut on the

Alamo, his sorrow for a lost son would have been stifled by anguish for an erring daughter.

The last messenger sent in search of Stump came back to the hacienda without him. The thirst for vengeance could be no longer stayed, and the avengers went forth.

---

They were scarce out of sight of Casa del Corvo, when the two individuals, who could have done them such signal service, became engaged in conversation within the walls of the hacienda itself.

There was nothing clandestine in the meeting, nothing designed. It was a simple contingency, Zeb Stump having just come in from his stalking excursion, bringing to the hacienda a portion of the "plunder"—as he was wont to term it—procured by his unerring rifle.

Of course to Zeb Stump, Louise Poindexter was at home. She was even eager for the interview—so eager, as to have kep almost a continual watch along the river road, all the day before, from the rising to the setting of the sun.

Her vigil, resumed on the departure of the noisy crowd, was soon after rewarded by the sight of the hunter, mounted on his old mare—the latter laden with the spoils of the chase—slowly moving along the road on the opposite side of the river, and manifestly making for the hacienda.

A glad sight to her—that rude, but grand shape of colossal manhood. She recognised in it the form of a true friend—to whose keeping she could safely entrust her most secret confidence. And she had now such a secret to confide to him; that for a night and a day had been painfully pent up within her bosom.

Long before Zeb had set foot upon the flagged pavement of the patio, she had gone out into the verandah to receive him.

The air of smiling nonchalance with which he approached, proclaimed him still ignorant of the event which had cast its melancholy shadow over the house. There was just perceptible the slightest expression of surprise, at finding the outer gate shut, chained, and barred.

It had not been the custom of the hacienda—at least during its present proprietary.

The sombre countenance of the black, encountered within the shadow of the saguan, strengthened Zeb's surprise—sufficiently to call forth an inquiry.

"Why, Pluto, ole fellur! whatsomdiver air the matter wi' ye? Yur lookin' like a 'coon wi' his tail chopped off—clost to the stump at thet! An' why air the big gate shet an barred—in the middle o' break-fist time? I hope thur hain't nuthin' gone astray?"

"Ho! ho! Mass 'Tump, dat's jess what dar hab goed stray—dat's preecise de ting, dis chile sorry t' say—berry much goed stray. Ho! berry, berry much!"

"Heigh!" exclaimed the hunter, startled at the lugubrious tone. "Thur air sommeat amiss? What is't, nigger? Tell me sharp quick. It can't be no wuss than yur face shows it. Nothin' happened to yur young mistress, I hope? Miss Lewaze—"

"Ho—ho! nuffin' happen to de young Missa Looey. Ho—ho! Bad enuf 'thout dat. Ho! de young missa inside de house yar, 'Tep in, Mass' 'Tump. She tell you de drefful news herseff."

"Ain't yur master inside, too? He's at home, ain't he?"

"Golly, no. Dis time no. Massa ain't 'bout de house at all nowhar. He wa' hya a'most a quarrer ob an hour ago. He no hya now. He off to de hoss prairas—wha de hab de big hunt 'bout a momf ago. You know, Mass' Zeb?"

"The hoss purayras! What's tuk him thur? Who's along wi' him?"

"Ho! ho! dar's Mass Cahoon, and gobs o' odder white genlum. Ho! ho! Dar's a mighty big crowd ob dem, dis nigga tell you."

"An' yur young Master Henry—air he gone too?"

"O Mass' 'Tump! Dat's wha am be trubble. Dat's de whole ob it. Mass' Hen' he gone too. He nebber mo' come back. De hoss he been brought home all kibbered over wif blood. Ho! ho! de folks say Massa Henry he gone dead."

"Dead! Yur jokin'? Air ye in airnest, nigger?"

"Oh! I is, Mass' 'Tump. Sorry dis chile am to hab say dat am too troo. Dey all gone to sarch atter de body."

"Hyur! Take these things to the kitchen. Thur's a gobbler, an some purayra chickens. Whar kin I find Miss Lewaze?"

"Here, Mr Stump. Come this way!" replied a sweet voice well known to him, but now speaking in accents so sad he would scarce have recognised it.

"Alas! it is too true what Pluto has been telling you. My brother is missing. He has not been seen since the night before last. His horse came home, with spots of blood upon the saddle. O Zeb! it's fearful to think of it!"

"Sure enuf that *air* ugly news. He rud out somewhar, and the hoss kim back 'ithout him? I don't weesh to gie ye unneedcessary pain, Miss Lewaze; but, as they air still sarchin' I mout be some help at that ere bizness; and maybe ye won't mind tellin' me the particklers?"

These were imparted, as far as known to her. The gardes scene and its antecedents were alone kept back. Oberdoffer was given as authority for the belief, that Henry had gone off after the mustanger.

The narrative was interrupted by bursts of grief, changing to indignation, when she came to tell Zeb of the suspicion entertained by the people—that Maurice was the murderer.

"It air a lie!" cried the hunter, partaking of the same sentiment: "a false, parjured lie! an he air a stinkin' skunk that invented it. The thing's impossible. The mowstanger ain't the man to a dud sech a deed as that. An' why shed he have dud it? If thur hed been an ill-feelin' atween them. But thur wa'n't. I kin answer for the mowstanger—for more'n oncest I've heern him talk o' your brother in the tallest kind o' tarms. In coorse he hated yur cousin Cash—an who doesn't, I shed like to know? Excuse me for sayin' it. As for the other, it air different. Ef thar hed been a quarrel an hot blood atween them—"

"No—no!" cried the young Creole, forgetting herself in the agony of her grief. "It was all over. Henry was reconciled. He said so; and Maurice—"

The astounded look of the listener brought a period to her speech. Covering her face with her hands, she buried her confusion in a flood of tears.

"Hoh—oh!" muttered Zeb; "thur *hev* been somethin'? D'ye say, Miss Lewaze, thur war a—a—quarrel atween yur brother—"

"Dear, dear Zeb!" cried she, removing her hands, and confronting the stalwart hunter with an air of earnest entreaty, "promise me, you will keep my secret? Promise it, as a friend—as a brave true-hearted man! You will—you will?"

The pledge was given by the hunter raising his broad palm, and extending it with a sonorous slap over the region of his heart.

In five minutes more he was in possession of a secret which woman rarely confides to man—except to him who can profoundly appreciate the confidence.

The hunter showed less surprise than might have been expected; merely muttering to himself:—

"I thort it wild come to somethin' o' the sort—specially arter thet ere chase acrost the purayra."

"Wal, Miss Lewaze," he continued, speaking in a tone of kindly approval, "Zeb Stump don't see anythin' to be ashamed o' in all thet. Weemen will be weemen all the world over—on the purayras or off o' them; an ef ye have lost yur young heart to the mowstanger, it wud be the tallest kind o' a mistake to serpose ye hev displaced yur affeckshuns, as they calls it. Though he air Irish, he aint none o' the common sort; thet he aint. As for the rest ye've been tellin' me, it only sarves to substantify what I've been sayin'—that it air parfickly unpossible for the mowstanger to hev dud the dark deed; that is, ef thur's been one dud at all. Let's hope thur's nothin' o' the kind. What proof hez been found? Only the hoss comin' home wi' some rid spots on the seddle?"

"Alas! there is more. The people were all out yesterday. They followed a trail, and saw something, they would not tell me what. Father did not appear as if he wished me to know what they had seen; and I—I feared, for reasons, to ask the others. They've gone off again—only a short while—just as you came in sight on the other side."

"But the mowstanger? What do it say for hisself?"

"Oh, I thought you knew. He has not been found either. *Mon Dieu! mon Dieu!* He, too, may have fallen by the same hand that has struck down my brother!"

"Ye say they war on a trail? His'n I serpose? If he be livin' he oughter be foun' at his shanty on the crik. Why didn't they go thar? Ah! now I think o't, thur's nobody knows the adzack sittavashun o' that ere domycile 'ceptin' myself I reckon: an if it war that greenhorn Spangler as war guidin' o' them he'd niver be able to lift a trail acrost the chalk purayra. Hev they gone that way agin?"

"They have. I heard some of them say so."

"Wal, if they're gone in sarch o' the mowstanger I reck'n I mout as well go too. I'll gie tall odds I find him afore they do."

"It is for that I've been so anxious to see you. There am many rough men along with papa. As they went away I heard them use wild words. There were some of those called 'Regulators.' They talked of lynching and the like. Some of them swore terrible oaths of vengeance. O my God! if they should find *him*, and he cannot make clear his innocence, in the height of their angry passions—cousin Cassius among the number—you understand what I mean—who knows what may be done to him? Dear Zeb, for my sake—for his, whom you call friend—go—go! Reach the Alamo before them, and warn him of the danger! Your horse is slow. Take mine—any one you can find in the stable—"

"Thur's some truth in what ye say," interrupted the hunter, preparing to move off. "Thur mout be a smell o' danger for the young fellur; an I'll do what I kin to avart it. Don't be uneezay, Miss Lewaze. Thur's not sech a partickler hurry. Thet ere shanty ain't agoin' ter be foun' 'ithout a spell o' sarchin'. As to ridin' yur spotty I'll manage better on my ole maar. Beside, the critter air reddy now if Plute hain't tuk off the saddle. Don't be greetin' yur eyes out—thet's a good chile!

Maybe it'll be all right yit 'bout yur brother; and as to the mowstanger, I hain't no more surspishun o' his innersense than a unborn babby."

The interview ended by Zeb making obeisance in backwoodsman style, and striding out of the verandah; while the young Creole glided off to her chamber, to soothe her troubled spirit in supplications for his success.

# 47. An Intercepted Epistle

Urged by the most abject fear, had El Coyote and his three comrades rushed back to their horses, and scrambled confusedly into the saddle.

They had no idea of returning to the jacalé of Maurice Gerald. On the contrary, their only thought was to put space between themselves and that solitary dwelling—whose owner they had encountered riding towards it in such strange guise.

That it was "Don Mauricio" not one of them doubted. All four knew him by sight—Diaz better than any—but all well enough to be sure it was the *Irlandes*. There was his horse, known to them; his *armas de agua* of jaguar-skin; his *Navajo* blanket, in shape differing from the ordinary serapé of Saltillo;—and his *head*!

They had not stayed to scrutinise the features; but the hat was still in its place—the sombrero of black glaze which Maurice was accustomed to wear. It had glanced in their eyes, as it came under the light of the moon.

Besides, they had seen the great dog, which Diaz remembered to be his. The staghound had sprung forward in the midst of the struggle, and with a fierce growl attacked the assailant—though it had not needed this to accelerate their retreat.

Fast as their horses could carry them, they rode through the bottom timber; and, ascending the bluff by one of its ravines—not that where they had meant to commit murder—they reached the level of the upper plateau.

Nor did they halt there for a single second; but, galloping across the plain, re-entered the chapparal, and spurred on to the place where they had so skilfully transformed themselves into Comanches.

The reverse metamorphosis, if not so carefully, was more quickly accomplished. In haste they washed the war-paint from their skins—availing themselves of some water carried in their canteens;—in haste they dragged their civilised habiliments from the hollow tree, in which they had hidden them; and, putting them on in like haste, they once more mounted their horses, and rode towards the Leona.

On their homeward way they conversed only of the headless horseman: but, with their thoughts under the influence of a supernatural terror, they could not satisfactorily account for an appearance so unprecedented; and they were still undecided as they parted company on the outskirts of the village—each going to his own jacalé.

"*Carrai!*" exclaimed the Coyote, as he stepped across the threshold of his, and dropped down upon his cane couch. "Not much chance of sleeping after that. *Santos Dios*! such a sight! It has chilled the blood to the very bottom of my veins. And nothing here to warm me. The canteen empty; the posada shut up; everybody in bed!

"*Madre de Dios*! what can it have been? Ghost it could not be; flesh and bones I grasped myself; so did Vicente on the other side? I felt that, or something very like it, under the tiger-skin. *Santissima*! it could not be a cheat!

"If a contrivance, why and to what end? Who cares to play carnival on the prairies—except myself, and my camarados? *Mil demonios*! what a grim masquerader!

"*Carajo*! am I forestalled? Has some other had the offer, and earned the thousand dollars? Was it the Irlandes himself, dead, decapitated, carrying his head in his hand?

"Bah! it could not be—ridiculous, unlikely, altogether improbable!

"But what then?

"Ha! I have it! A hundred to one I have it! He may have got warning of our visit, or, at least, had suspicions of it. 'Twas a trick got up to try us!—perhaps himself in sight, a witness of our disgraceful flight? *Maldito*!

"But who could have betrayed us? No one. Of course no one could tell of *that* intent. How then should he have prepared such an infernal surprise?

"Ah! I forget. It was broad daylight as we made the crossing of the long prairie. We may have been seen, and our purpose suspected? Just so—just so. And then, while we were making our toilet in the chapparal, the other could have been contrived and effected. That, and that only, can be the explanation!

"Fools! to have been frightened at a scarecrow!

"*Carrambo*! It shan't long delay the event. To-morrow I go back to the Alamo. I'll touch that thousand yet, if I should have to spend twelve months in earning it; and, whether or not, the *deed* shall be done all the same. Enough to have lost Isidora. It may not be true; but the very suspicion of it puts me beside myself. If I but find out that she loves him—that they have met since—since—Mother of God! I shall go mad; and in my madness destroy not only the man I hate, but the woman I love! O Dona Isidora Covarubio de los Llanos! Angel of beauty, and demon of mischief! I could kill you with my caresses—I can kill you with my steel! One or other shall be your fate. It is for you to choose between them!"

His spirit becoming a little tranquillised, partly through being relieved by this conditional threat—and partly from the explanation he had been able to arrive at concerning the other thought that had been troubling it—he soon after fell asleep.

Nor did he awake until daylight looked in at his door, and along with it a visitor.

"José!" he cried out in a tone of surprise in which pleasure was perceptible—"you here?"

"*Si, Señor; yo estoy.*"

"Glad to see you, good José. The Doña Isidora here?—on the Leona, I mean?"

"*Si, Señor.*"

"So soon again! She was here scarce two weeks ago, was she not? I was away from the settlement, but had word of it. I was expecting to hear from you, good José. Why did you not write?"

"Only, Señor Don Miguel, for want of a messenger that could be relied upon. I had something to communicate, that could not with safety be entrusted to a stranger. Something, I am sorry to say, you won't thank me for telling you; but my life is yours, and I promised you should know all."

The "prairie wolf" sprang to his feet, as if pricked with a sharp-pointed thorn.

"Of her, and him? I know it by your looks. Your mistress has met him?"

"No, Señor, she hasn't—not that I know of—not since the first time."

"What, then?" inquired Diaz, evidently a little relieved, "She was here while he was at the posada. Something passed between them?"

"True, Don Miguel—something did pass, as I well know, being myself the bearer of it. Three times I carried him a basket of *dulces*, sent by the Doña Isidora—the last time also a letter."

"A letter! You know the contents? You read it?"

"Thanks to your kindness to the poor *peon* boy, I was able to do that; more still—to make a copy of it."

"You have one?"

"I have. You see, Don Miguel, you did not have me sent to school for nothing. This is what the Doña Isidora wrote to him."

Diaz reached out eagerly, and, taking hold of the piece of paper, proceeded to devour its contents.

It was a copy of the note that had been sent among the sweet-meats.

Instead of further exciting, it seemed rather to tranquillise him.

"*Carrambo*!" he carelessly exclaimed, as he folded up the epistle. "There's not much in this, good José. It only proves that your mistress is grateful to one who has done her a service. If that's all—"

"But it is not all, Señor Don Miguel; and that's why I've come to see you now. I'm on an errand to the *pueblita*. This will explain it."

"Ha! Another letter?"

"*Si, Señor*! This time the original itself, and not a poor copy scribbled by me."

With a shaking hand Diaz took hold of the paper, spread it out, and read:—

Al Señor Don Mauricio Gerald.

*Querido amigo!*

*Otra vez aqui estoy—con tio Silvio quedando! Sin novedades de V. no puedo mas tiempo existir. La incertitud me malaba. Digame que es V. convalescente! Ojala, que estuviera asi! Suspiro en vuestros ojos mirar, estos ojos tan lindos y tan espresivos—a ver, si es restablecido vuestra salud. Sea graciosa darme este favor. Hay—opportunidad. En una cortita media de hora, estuviera quedando en la cima de loma, sobre la cosa del tio. Ven, cavallero, ven!*

Isidora Covarubio de los Llanos.

With a curse El Coyote concluded the reading of the letter. Its sense could scarce be mistaken. Literally translated it read thus:—

"Dear Friend,—I am once more here, staying with uncle Silvio. Without hearing of you I could not longer exist. The uncertainty was killing me. Tell me if you are convalescent. Oh! that it may be so. I long to look into your eyes—those eyes so beautiful, so expressive—to make sure that your health is perfectly restored. Be good enough to grant me this favour. There is an opportunity. In a short half hour from this time, I shall be on the top of the hill, above my uncle's house. Come, sir, come!

"Isidora Covarubio De Los Llanos."

"*Carajo*! an assignation!" half shrieked the indignant Diaz. "That and nothing else! She, too, the proposer. Ha! Her invitation shall be answered; though not by him for whom it is so cunningly intended. Kept to the hour—to the very minute; and by the Divinity of Vengeance—

"Here, José! this note's of no use. The man to whom it is addressed isn't any longer in the pueblita, nor anywhere about here. God knows where he is! There's some mystery about it. No matter. You go on to the posada, and make your inquiries all the same. You must do that to fulfil your errand. Never mind the *papelcito*; leave it with me. You can have it to take to your mistress, as you come back this way. Here's a dollar to get you a drink at the inn. Señor Doffer keeps the best kind of aguardiente. *Hasta luejo*!"

Without staying to question the motive for these directions given to him, José, after accepting the *douceur*, yielded tacit obedience to them, and took his departure from the jacalé.

He was scarce out of sight before Diaz also stepped over its threshold. Hastily setting the saddle upon his horse, he sprang into it, and rode off in the opposite direction.

# 48. Isidora

The sun has just risen clear above the prairie horizon, his round disc still resting upon the sward, like a buckler of burnished gold. His rays are struggling into the chapparal, that here and there diversifies the savanna. The dew-beads yet cling upon the acacias, weighting their feathery fronds, and causing them to droop earthward, as if grieving at the departure of the night, whose cool breeze and moist atmosphere are more congenial to them than the fiery sirocco of day. Though the birds are stirring—for what bird could sleep under the shine of such glorious sunrise?—it is almost too early to expect human being abroad—elsewhere than upon the prairies of Texas. There, however, the hour of the sun's rising is the most enjoyable of the day; and few there are who spend it upon the unconscious couch, or in the solitude of the chamber.

By the banks of the Leona, some three miles below Fort Inge, there is one who has forsaken both, to stray through the chapparal. This early wanderer is not afoot, but astride a strong, spirited horse, that seems impatient at being checked in his paces. By this description, you may suppose the rider to be a man; but, remembering that the scene is in Southern Texas still sparsely inhabited by a Spano-Mexican population—you are equally at liberty to conjecture that the equestrian is a woman. And this, too, despite the round hat upon the head— despite the serapé upon the shoulders, worn as a protection against the chill morning air—despite the style of equitation, so *outré* to European ideas, since the days of La Duchesse de Berri; and still further, despite the crayon-like colouring on the upper lip, displayed in the shape of a pair of silken moustaches. More especially may this last mislead; and you may fancy yourself looking upon some Spanish youth, whose dark but delicate features bespeak the *hijo de algo*, with a descent traceable to the times of the Cid.

If acquainted with the character of the Spano-Mexican physiognomy, this last sign of virility does not decide you as to the sex. It may be that the rider in the Texan chapparal, so distinguished, is, after all, a woman!

On closer scrutiny, this proves to be the case. It is proved by the small hand clasping the bridle-rein; by the little foot, whose tiny toes just touch the "estribo"—looking less in contrast with the huge wooden block that serves as a stirrup; by a certain softness of shape, and pleasing rotundity of outline, perceptible even through the thick serapé of Saltillo; and lastly, by the grand luxuriance of hair coiled up at the back of the head, and standing out in shining clump beyond the rim of the sombrero. After noting these points, you become convinced that you are looking upon a woman, though it may be one distinguished by certain idiosyncrasies. You are looking upon the Doña Isidora Covarubio de los Llanos.

You are struck by the strangeness of her costume—still more by the way she sits her horse. In your eyes, unaccustomed to Mexican modes, both may appear odd—unfeminine—perhaps indecorous.

The Doña Isidora has no thought—not even a suspicion—of there being anything odd in either. Why should she? She is but following the fashion of her country and her kindred. In neither respect is she peculiar.

She is young, but yet a woman. She has seen twenty summers, and perhaps one more. Passed under the sun of a Southern sky, it is needless to say that her girlhood is long since gone by. In her beauty there is no sign of decadence. She is fair to look upon, as in her "buen quince" (beautiful fifteen), Perhaps fairer. Do not suppose that the dark lining on her lip damages the feminine expression of her face. Rather does it add to its attractiveness. Accustomed to the glowing complexion of the Saxon blonde, you may at first sight deem it a deformity. Do not so pronounce, till you have looked again. A second glance, and—my word for it—you will modify your opinion. A third will do away with your indifference; a fourth change it to admiration!

Continue the scrutiny, and it will end in your becoming convinced: that a woman wearing a moustache—young, beautiful, and brunette—is one of the grandest sights which a beneficent Nature offers to the eye of man.

It is presented in the person of Isidora Covarubio de los Llanos. If there is anything unfeminine in her face, it is not this; though it may strengthen a wild, almost fierce, expression, at times discernible, when her white teeth gleam conspicuously under the sable shadow of the "bigotite."

Even then is she beautiful; but, like that of the female jaguar, 'tis a beauty that inspires fear rather than affection.

At all times it is a countenance that bespeaks for its owner the possession of mental attributes not ordinarily bestowed upon her sex. Firmness, determination, courage—carried to the extreme of reckless daring—are all legible in its lines. In those cunningly-carved features, slight, sweet, and delicate, there is no sign of fainting or fear. The crimson that has struggled through the brown skin of her cheeks would scarce forsake them in the teeth of the deadliest danger.

She is riding alone, through the timbered bottom of the Leona. There is a house not far off; but she is leaving it behind her. It is the hacienda of her uncle, Don Silvio Martinez, from the portals of which she has late issued forth.

She sits in her saddle as firmly as the skin that covers it. It is a spirited horse, and has the habit of showing it by his prancing paces. But you have no fear for the rider: you are satisfied of her power to control him.

A light lazo, suited to her strength, is suspended from the saddle-bow. Its careful coiling shows that it is never neglected. This almost assures you, that she understands how to use it. She does—can throw it, with the skill of a mustanger.

The accomplishment is one of her conceits; a part of the idiosyncrasy already acknowledged.

She is riding along a road—not the public one that follows the direction of the river. It is a private way leading from the hacienda of her uncle, running into the former near the summit of a hill—the hill itself being only the bluff that abuts upon the bottom lands of the Leona.

She ascends the sloping path—steep enough to try the breathing of her steed. She reaches the crest of the ridge, along which trends the road belonging to everybody.

She reins up; though not to give her horse an opportunity of resting. She has halted, because of having reached the point where her excursion is to terminate.

There is an opening on one side of the road, of circular shape, and having a superficies of some two or three acres. It is grass-covered and treeless—a prairie in *petto*. It is surrounded by the chapparal forest—very different from the bottom timber out of which she has just emerged. On all sides is the enclosing thicket of spinous plants, broken only by the embouchures of three paths, their triple openings scarce perceptible from the middle of the glade.

Near its centre she has pulled up, patting her horse upon the neck to keep him quiet. It is not much needed. The scaling of the "cuesta" has done that for him. He has no inclination either to go on, or tramp impatiently in his place.

"I am before the hour of appointment," mutters she, drawing a gold watch from under her serapé, "if, indeed, I should expect him at all. He may not come? God grant that he be able!

"I am trembling! Or is it the breathing of the horse? *Valga me Dios*, no! 'Tis my own poor nerves!

"I never felt so before! Is it fear? I suppose it is.

"'Tis strange though—to fear the man I love—the only one I over have loved: for it could not have been love I had for Don Miguel. A girl's fancy. Fortunate for me to have got cured of it! Fortunate my discovering him to be a coward. That disenchanted me—quite dispelled the romantic dream in which he was the foremost figure. Thank my good stars, for the disenchantment; for now I hate him, now that I hear he has grown—*Santissima*! can it be true that he has become—a—a *salteador*?

"And yet I should have no fear of meeting him—not even in this lone spot!

"*Ay de mi*! Fearing the man I love, whom I believe to be of kind, noble nature—and having no dread of him I hate, and know to be cruel and remorseless! 'Tis strange—incomprehensible!

"No—there is nothing strange in it. I tremble not from any thought of danger—only the danger of not being beloved. That is why I now shiver in my saddle—why I have not had one night of tranquil sleep since my deliverance from those drunken savages.

"I have never told *him* of this; nor do I know how he may receive the confession. It must, and shall be made. I can endure the uncertainty no longer. In preference I choose despair—death, if my hopes deceive me!

"Ha! There is a hoof stroke! A horse comes down the road! It is his? Yes. I see glancing through the trees the bright hues of our national costume. He delights to wear it. No wonder; it so becomes him!

"*Santa Virgin*! I'm under a serapé, with a sombrero on my head. He'll mistake me for a man! Off, ye ugly disguises, and let me seem what I am—a woman."

Scarce quicker could be the transformation in a pantomime. The casting off the serapé reveals a form that Hebe might have envied; the

287

removal of the hat, a head that would have inspired the chisel of Canova!

A splendid picture is exhibited in that solitary glade; worthy of being framed, by its bordering of spinous trees, whose hirsute arms seem stretched out to protect it.

A horse of symmetrical shape, half backed upon his haunches, with nostrils spread to the sky, and tail sweeping the ground; on his back one whose aspect and attitude suggest a commingling of grand, though somewhat incongruous ideas, uniting to form a picture, statuesque as beautiful.

The *pose* of the rider is perfect. Half sitting in the saddle, half standing upon the stirrup, every undulation of her form is displayed—the limbs just enough relaxed to show that she is a woman.

Notwithstanding what she has said, on her face there is no fear—at least no sign to betray it. There is no quivering lip—no blanching of the cheeks.

The expression is altogether different. It is a look of love—couched under a proud confidence, such as that with which the she-eagle awaits the wooing of her mate.

You may deem the picture overdrawn—perhaps pronounce it unfeminine.

And yet it is a copy from real life—true as I can remember it; and more than once had I the opportunity to fix it in my memory.

The attitude is altered, and with the suddenness of a *coup d'éclair*; the change being caused by recognition of the horseman who comes galloping into the glade. The shine of the gold-laced vestments had misled her. They are worn not by Maurice Gerald, but by Miguel Diaz!

Bright looks become black. From her firm seat in the saddle she subsides into an attitude of listlessness—despairing rather than indifferent; and the sound that escapes her lips, as for an instant they part over her pearl-like teeth, is less a sigh than an exclamation of chagrin.

There is no sign of fear in the altered attitude—only disappointment, dashed with defiance.

El Coyote speaks first.

"*H'la! S'ñorita*, who'd have expected to find your ladyship in this lonely place—wasting your sweetness on the thorny chapparal?"

"In what way can it concern you, Don Miguel Diaz?"

"Absurd question, S'ñorita! You know it can, and does; and the reason why. You well know how madly I love you. Fool was I to confess it, and acknowledge myself your slave. 'Twas that that cooled you so quickly."

"You are mistaken, Señor. I never told you I loved you. If I did admire your feats of horsemanship, and said so, you had no right to construe it as you've done. I meant no more than that I admired *them*—not you. 'Tis three years ago. I was a girl then, of an age when such things have a fascination for our sex—when we are foolish enough to be caught by personal accomplishments rather than moral attributes. I am now a woman. All that is changed, as—it ought to be."

"*Carrai*! Why did you fill me with false hopes? On the day of the *herradero*, when I conquered the fiercest bull and tamed the wildest horse in your father's herds—a horse not one of his *vaqueros* dared so much as lay hands upon—on that day you smiled—ay, looked love upon me. You need not deny it, Doña Isidora! I had experience, and could read the expression—could tell your thoughts, as they were then. They are changed, and why? Because I was conquered by your charms, or rather because I was the silly fool to acknowledge it; and you, like all women, once you had won and knew it, no longer cared for your conquest. It is true, S'ñorita; it is true."

"It is not, Don Miguel Diaz. I never gave you word or sign to say that I loved, or thought of you otherwise than as an accomplished cavalier. You appeared so then—perhaps were so. What are you now? You know what's said of you, both here and on the Rio Grande!"

"I scorn to reply to calumny—whether it proceeds from false friends or lying enemies. I have come here to seek explanations, not to give them."

"Prom whom?"

"Prom your sweet self, Doña Isidora."

"You are presumptive, Don Miguel Diaz! Think, Señor, to whom you are addressing yourself. Remember, I am the daughter of—"

"One of the proudest *Haciendados* in Tamaulipas, and niece to one of the proudest in Texas. I have thought of all that; and thought too that I was once a haciendado myself and am now only a hunter of horses. *Carrambo*! what of that? You're not the woman to despise a man for the inferiority of his rank. A poor mustanger stands as good a chance in your eyes as the owner of a hundred herds. In that respect, *I have proof of your generous spirit*!"

"What proof?" asked she, in a quick, entreating tone, and for the first time showing signs of uneasiness. "What evidence of the generosity you are so good as to ascribe to me?"

"This pretty epistle I hold in my hand, indited by the Doña Isidora Covarubio de los Llanos, to one who, like myself, is but a dealer in horseflesh. I need not submit it to very close inspection. No doubt you can identify it at some distance?"

She could, and did; as was evinced by her starting in the saddle— by her look of angry surprise directed upon Diaz.

"Señor! how came you in possession of this?" she asked, without any attempt to disguise her indignation.

"It matters not. I am in possession of it, and of what for many a day I have been seeking; a proof, not that you had ceased to care for me—for this I had good reason to know—but that you had begun to care for him. This tells that you love him—words could not speak plainer. You long to look into his beautiful eyes. *Mil demonios*! you shall never see them again!"

"What means this, Don Miguel Diaz?"

The question was put not without a slight quivering of the voice that seemed to betray fear. No wonder it should. There was something in the aspect of El Coyote at that moment well calculated to inspire the sentiment.

Observing it, he responded, "You may well show fear: you have reason. If I have lost you, my lady, no other shall enjoy you. I have made up my mind about that."

"About what?"

"What I have said—that no other shall call you his, and least of all Maurice the mustanger."

"Indeed!"

"Ay, indeed! Give me a promise that you and he shall never meet again, or you depart not from this place!"

"You are jesting, Don Miguel?"

"I am in earnest, Doña Isidora."

The manner of the man too truly betrayed the sincerity of his speech. Coward as he was, there was a cold cruel determination in his looks, whilst his hand was seen straying towards the hilt of his ma- cheté.

Despite her Amazonian courage, the woman could not help a feeling of uneasiness. She saw there was a danger, with but slight chance of averting it. Something of this she had felt from the first moment of the encounter; but she had been sustained by the hope, that the unpleasant interview might be interrupted by one who would soon change its character.

During the early part of the dialogue she had been eagerly listening for the sound of a horse's hoof—casting occasional and furtive glances through the chapparal, in the direction where she hoped to hear it.

This hope was no more. The sight of her own letter told its tale: it had not reached its destination.

Deprived of this hope—hitherto sustaining her—she next thought of retreating from the spot.

But this too presented both difficulties and dangers. It was possible for her to wheel round and gallop off; but it was equally possible for her retreat to be intercepted by a bullet. The butt of El Coyote's pistol was as near to his hand as the hilt of his macheté.

She was fully aware of the danger. Almost any other woman would have given way to it. Not so Isidora Covarubio de los Llanos. She did not even show signs of being affected by it.

"Nonsense!" she exclaimed, answering his protestation with an air of well dissembled incredulity. "You are making sport of me, Señor. You wish to frighten me. Ha! ha! ha! Why should I fear *you*? I can ride as well—fling my lazo as sure and far as you, Look at this I see how skilfully I can handle it!"

While so speaking—smiling as she spoke—she had lifted the lazo from her saddle-bow and was winding it round her head, as if to illustrate her observations.

The act had a very different intent, though it was not perceived by Diaz; who, puzzled by her behaviour, sate speechless in his saddle.

Not till he felt the noose closing around his elbows did he suspect her design; and then too late to hinder its execution. In another instant his arms were pinioned to his sides—both the butt of his pistol and the hilt of his macheté beyond the grasp of his fingers!

He had not even time to attempt releasing himself from the loop. Before he could lay hand upon the rope, it tightened around his body, and with a violent pluck jerked him out of his saddle—throwing him stunned and senseless to the ground.

"Now, Don Miguel Diaz!" cried she who had caused this change of situation, and who was now seen upon her horse, with head turned homeward, the lazo strained taut from the saddle-tree. "Menace me no more! Make no attempt to release yourself. Stir but a finger, and I spur on! Cruel villain! coward as you are, you would have killed me—I saw it in your eye. Ha! the tables are turned, and now—"

Perceiving that there was no rejoinder, she interrupted her speech, still keeping the lazo at a stretch, with her eyes fixed upon the fallen man.

El Coyote lay upon the ground, his arms enlaced in the loop, without stirring, and silent as a stick of wood. The fall from his horse had deprived him of speech, and consciousness at the same time. To all appearance he was dead—his steed alone showing life by its loud neighing, as it reared back among the bushes.

"Holy Virgin! have I killed him?" she exclaimed, reining her horse slightly backward, though still keeping him headed away, and ready to spring to the spur. "Mother of God! I did not intend it— though I should be justified in doing even that: for too surely did he intend to kill *me*! Is he dead, or is it a *ruse* to get me near? By our good Guadaloupe! I shall leave others to decide. There's not much fear of his overtaking me, before I can reach home; and if he's in any danger the people of the hacienda will get back soon enough to release him. Good day, Don Miguel Diaz! *Hasta luego*!"

With these words upon her lips—the levity of which proclaimed her conscience clear of having committed a crime she drew a small sharp-bladed knife from beneath the bodice of her dress; severed the rope short off from her saddle-bow; and, driving the spur deep into the flanks of her horse, galloped off out of the glade—leaving Diaz upon the ground, still encircled by the loop of the lazo!

---

# 49. The Lazo Unloosed

An eagle, scared from its perch on a scathed Cottonwood, with a scream, soars upward into the air.

Startled by the outbreak of angry passions, it has risen to reconnoitre.

A single sweep of its majestic wing brings it above the glade. There, poised on tremulous pinions, with eye turned to earth, it scans both the open space and the chapparal that surrounds it. In the former it beholds that which may, perhaps, be gratifying to its glance—a man thrown from his horse, that runs neighing around him—prostrate—apparently dead. In the latter two singular equestrians: one a woman, with bare head and chevelure spread to the breeze, astride a strong steed, going away from the glade in quick earnest gallop; the other, also a woman, mounted on a spotted horse, in more feminine fashion, riding towards it: attired in hat and habit, advancing at a slower pace, but with equal earnestness in her looks.

Such is the *coup d'oeil* presented to the eye of the eagle.

Of these fair equestrians both are already known. She galloping away is Isidora Covarubio de los Llanos; she who approaches, Louise Poindexter.

It is known why the first has gone out of the glade. It remains to be told for what purpose the second is coming into it.

After her interview with Zeb Stump, the young creole re-entered her chamber, and kneeling before an image of the Madonna, surrendered her spirit to prayer.

It is needless to say that, as a Creole, she was a Catholic, and therefore a firm believer in the efficacy of saintly intercession. Strange and sad was the theme of her supplication—the man who had been marked as the murderer of her brother!

She had not the slightest idea that he was guilty of the horrid crime. It could not be. The very suspicion of it would have lacerated her heart.

Her prayer was not for pardon, but protection. She supplicated the Virgin to save him from his enemies—her own friends!

Tears and choking sobs were mingled with her words, low murmured in the ear of Heaven. She had loved her brother with the fondest sisterly affection. She sorrowed sorely; but her sorrow could not stifle that other affection, stronger than the ties of blood. While mourning her brother's loss she prayed for her lover's safety.

As she rose from her knees, her eye fell upon the bow—that implement so cunningly employed to despatch sweet messages to the man she loved.

"Oh! that I could send one of its arrows to warn him of his danger! I may never use it again!"

The reflection was followed by a thought of cognate character. Might there not remain some trace of that clandestine correspondence in the place where it had been carried on?

She remembered that Maurice swam the stream, instead of recrossing in the skiff, to be drawn back again by her own lazo. He must have been left in the boat!

On the day before, in the confusion of her grief, she had not thought of this. It might become evidence of their midnight meeting; of which, as she supposed, no tongue but theirs—and that for ever silent—could tell the tale.

The sun was now fairly up, and gleaming garishly through the glass. She threw open the casement and stepped out, with the design of proceeding towards the skiff. In the *balcon* her steps were arrested, on hearing voices above.

Two persons were conversing. They were her maid Florinde, and the sable groom, who, in the absence of his master, was taking the air of the *azotea*.

Their words could be heard below, though their young mistress did not intentionally listen to them. It was only on their pronouncing a name, that she permitted their patois to make an impression upon her ear.

"Dey calls de young fella Jerrad. Mors Jerrad am de name. Dey do say he Irish, but if folks 'peak de troof, he an't bit like dem Irish dat works on de Lebee at New Orlean. Ho, ho! He more like bos gen'lum planter. Dat's what he like."

"You don't tink, Pluto, he been gone kill Massa Henry?"

"I doan't tink nuffin ob de kind. Ho, ho! He kill Massa Henry! no more dan dis chile hab done dat same. Goramity—Goramity! 'Peak ob de debbil and he dar—de berry individible we talkin' 'bout. Ho, ho! look Florinde; look yonner!"

"Whar?"

"Dar—out dar, on todder side ob de ribber. You see man on horseback. Dat's Mors Jerrad, de berry man we meet on de brack praira. De same dat gub Missa Loode 'potted hoss; de same dey've all gone to sarch for. Ho, ho! Dey gone dey wrong way. Dey no find him out on dem prairas dis day."

"O, Pluto! an't you glad? I'm sure he innocent—dat brave bewful young gen'lum. He nebba could been de man—"

The listener below stayed to hear no more. Gliding back into her chamber she made her way towards the *azotea*. The beating of her heart was almost as loud as the fall of her footsteps while ascending the *escalera*. It was with difficulty she could conceal her emotion from the two individuals whose conversation had caused it. "What have you seen, that you talk so loudly?" said she, trying to hide her agitation under a pretended air of severity, "Ho, ho! Missa Looey—look ober dar. De young fella!"

"What young fellow?"

"Him as dey be gone sarch for—him dat—"

"I see no one."

"Ho, ho! He jess gone in 'mong de tree. See yonner—yonner! You see de black glaze hat, de shinin' jacket ob velvet, an de glancin' silver buttons—dat's him. I sartin sure dat's de same young fella."

"You may be mistaken for all that, Master Pluto. There are many here who dress in that fashion. The distance is too great for you to distinguish; and now that he's almost out of sight—Never mind, Florinde. Hasten below—get out my hat and habit. I'm going out for a ride. You, Pluto! have the saddle on Luna in the shortest time. I must not let the sun get too high. Haste! haste!"

As the servants disappeared down the stairway, she turned once more towards the parapet, her bosom heaving under the revulsion of thoughts. Unobserved she could now freely scan the prairie and chapparal.

She was too late. The horseman had ridden entirely out of sight.

"It was very like him, and yet it was not. It can scarce be possible. If it be he, why should he be going that way?"

A new pang passed through her bosom. She remembered once before having asked herself the same question.

She no longer stayed upon the *azotea* to watch the road. In ten minutes' time she was across the river, entering the chapparal where the horseman had disappeared.

She rode rapidly on, scanning the causeway far in the advance.

Suddenly she reined up, on nearing the crest of the hill that over-looked the Leona. The act was consequent on the hearing of voices.

She listened. Though still distant, and but faintly heard, the voices could be distinguished as those of a man and woman.

What man? What woman? Another pang passed through her heart at these put questions.

She rode nearer; again halted; again listened.

The conversation was carried on in Spanish. There was no relief to her in this. Maurice Gerald would have talked in that tongue to Isidora Covarubio de los Llanos. The Creole was acquainted with it sufficiently to have understood what was said, had she been near enough to distinguish the words. The tone was animated on both sides, as if both speakers were in a passion. The listener was scarce displeased at this.

She rode nearer; once more pulled up; and once more sate listening.

The man's voice was heard no longer. The woman's sounded dear and firm, as if in menace!

There was an interval of silence, succeeded by a quick trampling of horses—another pause—another speech on the part of the woman, at first loud like a threat, and then subdued as in a soliloquy—then another interval of silence, again broken by the sound of hoofs, as if a single horse was galloping away from the ground.

Only this, and the scream of an eagle, that, startled by the angry tones, had swooped aloft, and was now soaring above the glade.

The listener knew of the opening—to her a hallowed spot. The voices had come out of it. She had made her last halt a little way from its edge. She had been restrained from advancing by a fear—the fear of finding out a bitter truth.

Her indecision ending, she spurred on into the glade.

A horse saddled and bridled rushing to and fro—a man prostrate upon the ground, with a lazo looped around his arms, to all appearance dead—a *sombrero* and *serapé* lying near, evidently not the man's! What could be the interpretation of such a tableau?

The man was dressed in the rich costume of the Mexican *ranchero*—the horse also caparisoned in this elaborate and costly fashion.

At sight of both, the heart of the Louisianian leaped with joy. Whether dead or living, the man was the same she had seen from the *azotea*; and he was *not* Maurice Gerald.

She had doubted before—had hoped that it was not he; and her hopes were now sweetly confirmed.

She drew near and examined the prostrate form. She scanned the face, which was turned up—the man lying upon his back. She fancied she had seen it before, but was not certain.

It was plain that he was a Mexican. Not only his dress but his countenance—every line of it betrayed the Spanish-American physiognomy.

He was far from being ill-featured. On the contrary, he might have been pronounced handsome.

It was not this that induced Louise Poindexter to leap down from her saddle, and stoop over him with a kind pitying look.

The joy caused by his presence—by the discovery that he was not somebody else—found gratification in performing an act of humanity.

"He does not seem dead. Surely he is breathing?"

The cord appeared to hinder his respiration.

It was loosened on the instant—the noose giving way to a Woman's strength.

"Now, he can breathe more freely. Pardieu! what can have caused it? Lazoed in his saddle and dragged to the earth? That is most probable. But who could have done it? It was a woman's voice. Surely it was? I could not be mistaken about that.

"And yet there is a man's hat, and a *serapé*, not this man's! Was there another, who has gone away with the woman? Only one horse went off.

"Ah! he is coming to himself! thank Heaven for that! He will be able to explain all. You are recovering, sir?"

"S'ñorita! who are you?" asked Don Miguel Diaz, raising his head, and looking apprehensively around.

"Where is she?" he continued.

"Of whom do you speak? I have seen no one but yourself."

"*Carrambo*! that's queer. Haven't you met a woman astride a grey horse?"

"I heard a woman's voice, as I rode up."

"Say rather a she-devil's voice: for that, sure, is Isidora Covarubio de los Llanos."

"Was it she who has done this?"

"Maldito, yes! Where is she now? Tell me that, s'ñorita."

"I cannot. By the sound of the hoofs I fancy she has gone down the hill. She must have done so, as I came the other way myself."

"Ah—gone down the hill—home, then, to —. You've been very kind, s'ñorita, in loosening this lazo—as I make no doubt you've done. Perhaps you will still further assist me by helping me into the saddle? Once in it, I think I can stay there. At all events, I must not stay here. I have enemies, not far off. Come, Carlito!" he cried to his horse, at the same time summoning the animal by a peculiar whistle. "Come near! Don't be frightened at the presence of this fair lady. She's not the same that parted you and me so rudely—*en verdad*, almost for ever! Come on, *cavallo*! come on!"

The horse, on hearing the whistle, came trotting up, and permitted his master—now upon his feet—to lay hold of the bridle-rein.

"A little help from you, kind s'ñorita, and I think I can climb into my saddle. Once there, I shall be safe from their pursuit."

"You expect to be pursued?"

"*Quien sale*? I have enemies, as I told you. Never mind that. I feel very feeble. You will not refuse to help me?"

"Why should I? You are welcome, sir, to any assistance I can give you."

"*Mil gracias, s'ñorita! Mil, mil gracias!*"

The Creole, exerting all her strength, succeeded in helping the disabled horseman into his saddle; where, after some balancing, he appeared to obtain a tolerably firm seat.

Gathering up his reins, he prepared to depart.

"Adios, s'ñorita!" said he, "I know not who you are. I see you are not one of our people. Americano, I take it. Never mind that. You are good as you are fair; and if ever it should chance to be in his power, Miguel Diaz will not be unmindful of the service you have this day done him."

Saying this El Coyote rode off, not rapidly, but in a slow walk, as if he felt some difficulty in preserving his equilibrium.

Notwithstanding the slowness of the pace—he was soon out of sight,—the trees screening him as he passed the glade. He went not by any of the three roads, but by a narrow track, scarce discernible where it entered the underwood.

To the young Creole the whole thing appeared like a dream— strange, rather than disagreeable.

It was changed to a frightful reality, when, after picking up a sheet of paper left by Diaz where he had been lying, she read what was written upon it. The address was "Don Mauricio Gerald;" the signature, "Isidora Covarubio de los Llanos."

To regain her saddle, Louise Poindexter was almost as much in need of a helping hand as the man who had ridden away.

As she forded the Leona, in returning to Casa del Corvo, she halted her horse in the middle of the stream; and for some time sate gazing into the flood that foamed up to her stirrup. There was a wild expression upon her features that betokened deep despair. One degree deeper, and the waters would have covered as fair a form as was ever sacrificed to their Spirit!

# 50. A Conflict with Coyotes

The purple shadows of a Texan twilight were descending upon the earth, when the wounded man, whose toilsome journey through the chapparal has been recorded, arrived upon the banks of the streamlet.

After quenching his thirst to a surfeit, he stretched himself along the grass, his thoughts relieved from the terrible strain so long and continuously acting upon them.

His limb for the time pained him but little; and his spirit was too much worn to be keenly apprehensive as to the future.

He only desired repose; and the cool evening breeze, sighing through the feathery fronds of the acacias, favoured his chances of obtaining it.

The vultures had dispersed to their roosts in the thicket; and, no longer disturbed by their boding presence, he soon after fell asleep.

His slumber was of short continuance. The pain of his wounds, once more returning, awoke him.

It was this—and not the cry of the coyoté—that kept him from sleeping throughout the remainder of the night.

Little did he regard the sneaking wolf of the prairies—a true jackal—that attacks but the dead; the living, only when dying.

He did not believe that he was dying.

It was a long dismal night to the sufferer; it seemed as if day would never dawn.

The light came at length, but revealed nothing to cheer him. Along with it came the birds, and the beasts went not away.

Over him, in the shine of another sun the vultures once more extended their shadowy wings. Around him he heard the howl-bark of the coyoté, in a hundred hideous repetitions.

Crawling down to the stream, he once more quenched his thirst.

He now hungered; and looked round for something to eat.

A pecân tree stood, near. There were nuts upon its branches, within six feet of the ground.

He was able to reach the pecân upon his hands and knees; though the effort caused agony.

With his crutch he succeeded in detaching some of the nuts; and on these broke his fast.

What was the next step to be taken?

To stir away from the spot was simply impossible. The slightest movement gave him pain; at the same time assuring him of his utter inability to go anywhere.

He was still uncertain as to the nature of the injuries he had sustained—more especially that in his leg, which was so swollen that he could not well examine it. He supposed it to be either a fracture of the knee-cap, or a dislocation of the joint. In either case, it might be days before he could use the limb; and what, meanwhile, was he to do?

He had but little expectation of any one coming that way. He had shouted himself hoarse; and though, at intervals, he still continued to send forth a feeble cry, it was but the intermittent effort of hope struggling against despair.

There was no alternative but stay where he was; and, satisfied of this, he stretched himself along the sward, with the resolve to be as patient as possible.

It required all the stoicism of his nature to bear up against the acute agony he was enduring. Nor did he endure it altogether in silence. At intervals it elicited a groan.

Engrossed by his sufferings, he was for a while unconscious of what was going on around him. Still above him wheeled the black birds; but he had become accustomed to their presence, and no longer regarded it—not even when, at intervals, some of them swooped so near, that he could hear the "wheep" of their wings close to his ears.

Ha! what was that—that sound of different import?

It resembled the pattering of little feet upon the sandy channel of the stream, accompanied by quick breathings, as of animal in a state of excitement.

He looked around for an explanation.

"Only the coyotés!" was his reflection, on seeing a score of these animals flitting to and fro, skulking along both banks of the stream, and "squatting" upon the grass.

Hitherto he had felt no fear—only contempt—for these cowardly creatures.

301

But his sentiments underwent a change, on his noticing their looks and attitudes. The former were fierce; the latter earnest and threatening. Clearly did the coyotés mean mischief.

He now remembered having heard, that these animals—ordinarily innocuous, from sheer cowardice—will attack man when disabled beyond the capability of defending himself. Especially will they do so when stimulated by the smell of blood.

His had flowed freely, and from many veins—punctured by the spines of the cactus. His garments were saturated with it, still but half dry.

On the sultry atmosphere it was sending forth its peculiar odour. The coyotés could not help scenting it.

Was it this that was stirring them to such excited action—apparently making them mad?

Whether or not, he no longer doubted that it was their intention to attack him.

He had no weapon but a bowie knife, which fortunately had kept its place in his belt. His rifle and pistols, attached to the saddle, had been carried off by his horse.

He drew the knife; and, resting upon his right knee, prepared to defend himself.

He did not perform the action a second too soon. Emboldened by having been so long left to make their menaces unmolested—excited to courage by the smell of blood, stronger as they drew nearer—stimulated by their fierce natural appetites—the wolves had by this time reached the turning point of their determination: which was, to spring forward upon the wounded man.

They did so—half a dozen of them simultaneously—fastening their teeth upon his arms, limbs, and body, as they made their impetuous onset.

With a vigorous effort he shook them off, striking out with his knife. One or two were gashed by the shining blade, and went howling away. But a fresh band had by this time entered into the fray, others coming up, till the assailants counted a score. The conflict became desperate, deadly. Several of the animals were slain. But the fate of their fallen comrades did not deter the survivors from continuing the strife. On the contrary, it but maddened them the more.

The struggle became more and more confused—the coyotés crowding over one another to lay hold of their victim. The knife was wielded at random; the arm wielding it every moment becoming weaker, and striking with less fatal effect. The disabled man was soon further disabled. He felt fear for his life. No wonder—death was staring him in the face.

At this crisis a cry escaped his lips. Strange it was not one of terror, but joy! And stranger still that, on hearing it, the coyotés for an instant desisted from their attack!

There was a suspension of the strife—a short interval of silence. It was not the cry of their victim that had caused it, but that which had elicited the exclamation.

There was the sound of a horse's hoofs going at a gallop, followed by the loud baying of a hound.

The wounded man continued to exclaim,—in shouts calling for help. The horse appeared to be close by. A man upon his back could not fail to hear them.

But there was no response. The horse, or horseman, had passed on.

The hoof-strokes became less distinct. Despair once more returned to the antagonist of the coyotés.

At the same time his skulking assailants felt a renewal of their courage, and hastened to renew the conflict.

Once more it commenced, and was soon raging fiercely as before—the wretched man believing himself doomed, and only continuing the strife through sheer desperation.

Once more was it interrupted, this time by an intruder whose presence inspired him with fresh courage and hope.

If the horseman had proved indifferent to his calls for help, not so the hound. A grand creature of the staghound species—of its rarest and finest breed—was seen approaching the spot, uttering a deep sonorous bay, as with impetuous bound it broke through the bushes.

"*A friend! thank Heaven, a friend!*"

The baying ceased, as the hound cleared the selvage of the chapparal, and rushed open-mouthed among the cowed coyotés—already retreating at his approach!

One was instantly seized between the huge jaws; jerked upward from the earth; shaken as if it had been only a rat; and let go again, to writhe over the ground with a shattered spine!

Another was served in a similar manner; but ere a third could be attacked, the terrified survivors dropped their tails to the sward, and went yelping away; one and all retreating whence they had come—into the silent solitudes of the chapparal.

The rescued man saw no more. His strength was completely spent. He had just enough left to stretch forth his arms, and with a smile close them around the neck of his deliverer. Then, murmuring some soft words, he fainted gradually away.

His syncope was soon over, and consciousness once more assumed away.

Supporting himself on his elbow, he looked inquiringly around.

It was a strange, sanguinary spectacle that met his eyes. But for his swoon, he would have seen a still stranger one. During its continuance a horseman had ridden into the glade, and gone out again. He was the same whose hoofstroke had been heard, and who had lent a deaf ear to the cries for help. He had arrived too late, and then without any idea of offering assistance. His design appeared to be the watering of his horse.

The animal plunged straight into the streamlet, drank to its satisfaction, climbed out on the opposite bank, trotted across the open ground, and disappeared in the thicket beyond.

The rider had taken no notice of the prostrate form; the horse only by snorting, as he saw it, and springing from side to side, as he trod amidst the carcases of the coyotés.

The horse was a magnificent animal, not large, but perfect in all his parts. The man was the very reverse—having no head!

There was a head, but not in its proper place. It rested against the holster, seemingly held in the rider's hand!

A fearful apparition.

The dog barked, as it passed through the glade, and followed it to the edge of the underwood. He had been with it for a long time, straying where it strayed, and going where it went.

He now desisted from this fruitless fellowship; and, returning to the sleeper, lay down by his side.

It was then that the latter was restored to consciousness, and remembered what had made him for the moment oblivious.

After caressing the dog he again sank into a prostrate position; and, drawing the skirt of the cloak over his face to shade it from the glare of the sun, he fell asleep.

The staghound lay down at his feet, and also slumbered; but only in short spells. At intervals it raised its head, and uttered an angry growl, as the wings of the vultures came switching too close to its ears.

The young man muttered in his sleep. They were wild words that came from his unconscious lips, and betokened a strange commingling of thoughts: now passionate appeals of love—now disjointed speeches, that pointed to the committal of murder!

# 51. Twice Intoxicated

Our story takes us back to the lone hut on the Alamo, so suddenly forsaken by the gambling guests, who had made themselves welcome in the absence of its owner.

It is near noon of the following day, and he has not yet come home. The *ci-devant* stable-boy of Bally-ballagh is once more sole occupant of the *jacalé*—once more stretched along the floor, in a state of inebriety; though not the same from which we have seen him already aroused. He has been sober since, and the spell now upon him has been produced by a subsequent appeal to the Divinity of drink.

To explain, we must go back to that hour between midnight and morning, when the monté players made their abrupt departure.

The sight of three red savages, seated around the slab table, and industriously engaged in a game of cards, had done more to restore Phelim to a state of sobriety than all the sleep he had obtained.

Despite a certain grotesqueness in the spectacle, he had not seen such a ludicrous sight, as was proved by the terrific screech with which he saluted them. There was nothing laughable in what followed. He had no very clear comprehension of what *did* follow. He only remembered that the trio of painted warriors suddenly gave up their game, flung their cards upon the floor, stood over him for a time with naked blades, threatening his life; and then, along with a fourth who had joined them, turned their backs abruptly, and rushed pellmell out of the place!

All this occupied scarce twenty seconds of time; and when he had recovered from his terrified surprise, he found himself once more alone in the *jacalé*!

Was the sleeping, or awake? Drunk, or dreaming? Was the scene real? Or was it another chapter of incongruous impossibilities, like that still fresh before his mind?

But no. The thing was no fancy. It could not be. He had seen the savages too near to be mistaken as to their reality. He had heard them talking in a tongue unknown to him. What could it be but Indian jargon? Besides, there were the pieces of pasteboard strewn over the floor!

He did not think of picking one up to satisfy himself of *their* reality. He was sober enough, but not sufficiently courageous for that. He could not be sure of their not burning his fingers—those queer cards? They might belong to the devil?

Despite the confusion of his senses, it occurred to him that the hut was no longer a safe place to stay in. The painted players might return to finish their game. They had left behind not only their cards, but everything else the *jacalé* contained; and though some powerful motive seemed to have caused their abrupt departure, they might re-appear with equal abruptness.

The thought prompted the Galwegian to immediate action; and, blowing out the candle, so as to conceal his movements, he stole softly out of the hut.

He did not go by the door. The moon was shining on the grass-plat in front. The savages might still be there.

He found means of exit at the back, by pulling one of the horse hides from its place, and squeezing himself through the stockade wall.

Once outside, he skulked off under the shadow of the trees.

He had not gone far when a clump of dark objects appeared before him. There was a sound, as of horses champing their bitts, and the occasional striking of a hoof. He paused in his steps, screening his body behind the trunk of a cypress.

A short observation convinced him, that what he saw was a group of horses. There appeared to be four of them; no doubt belonging to the four warriors, who had turned the mustanger's hut into a gaming-house. The animals appeared to be tied to a tree, but for all that, their owners might be beside them.

Having made this reflection, he was about to turn back and go the other way; but just at that moment he heard voices in the opposite direction—the voices of several men speaking in tones of menace and command.

Then came short, quick cries of affright, followed by the baying of a hound, and succeeded by silence, at intervals interrupted by a swishing noise, or the snapping of a branch—as if several men were retreating through the underwood in scared confusion!

As he continued to listen, the noises sounded nearer. The men who made them were advancing towards the cypress tree.

The tree was furnished with buttresses all around its base, with shadowy intervals between. Into one of these he stepped hastily; and, crouching close, was completely screened by the shadow.

He had scarce effected his concealment, when four men came rushing up; and, without stopping, hastened on towards the horses.

As they passed by him, they were exchanging speeches which the Irishman could not understand; but their tone betrayed terror. The excited action of the men confirmed it. They were evidently retreating from some enemy that had filled them with fear.

There was a glade where the moon-beams fell upon the grass. It was just outside the shadow of the cypress. To reach the horses they had to cross it; and, as they did so, the vermilion upon their naked skins flashed red under the moonlight.

Phelim identified the four gentlemen who had made so free with the hospitality of the hut.

He kept his place till they had mounted, and rode off—till he could tell by the tramp of their horses that they had ascended the upper plain, and gone off in a gallop—as men who were not likely to come back again.

"Doesn't that bate Banagher?" muttered he, stepping out from his hiding-place, and throwing up his arms in astonishment. "Be japers! it diz. Mother av Moses! fwhat cyan it mane anyhow? What are them divvils afther? An fwhat's afther them? Shure somethin' has given them a scare—that's plain as a pikestaff. I wondher now if it's been that same. Be me sowl it's jist it they've encounthered. I heerd the hound gowlin, an didn't he go afther it. O Lard! what cyan *it* be? May be it'll be comin' this way in purshoot av them?"

The dread of again beholding the unexplained apparition, or being beheld by it, caused him to shrink once more under the shadow of the tree; where he remained for some time longer in a state of trembling suspense.

"Afther all, *it* must be some thrick av Masther Maurice. Maybe to give me a scare; an comin' back he's jist been in time to frighten off these ridskins that intinded to rub an beloike to murther us too. Sowl! I hope it is that. How long since I saw it first? Trath! it must be some considerable time. I remimber having four full naggins, an that's all gone off. I wondher now if them Indyins has come acrass av the dimmyjan? I've heerd that they're as fond of the crayther as if their skins was white. Sowl! if they've smelt the jar there won't be a dhrap in it by this time. I'll jist slip back to the hut an see. If thare's any danger now it won't be from them. By that tarin' gallop, I cyan tell they've gone for good."

Once more emerging from the shadowy stall, he made his way back towards the *jacalé*.

He approached it with caption, stopping at intervals to assure himself that no one was near.

Notwithstanding the plausible hypothesis he had shaped out for himself, he was still in dread of another encounter with the headless horseman—who twice on his way to the hut might now be inside of it.

But for the hope of finding a "dhrap" in the demijohn, he would not have ventured back that night. As it was, the desire to obtain a drink was a trifle stronger than his fears; and yielding to it, he stepped doubtfully into the darkness.

He made no attempt to rekindle the light. Every inch of the floor was familiar to him; and especially that corner where he expected to find the demijohn.

He tried for it. An exclamation uttered in a tone of disappointment told that it was not there.

"Be dad!" muttered he, as he grumblingly groped about; "it looks as if they'd been at it. Av coorse they hav, else fwhy is it not in its place? I lift it thare—shure I lift it thare."

"Ach, me jewel! an it's thare yez are yet," he continued, as his hand came in contact with the wickerwork; "an' bad luck to their imperence—impty as an eggshill! Ach! ye greedy gutted bastes! If I'd a known yez were goin' to do that, I'd av slipped a thrifle av shumach juice into the jar, an made raal firewater av it for ye—jist fwhat yez wants. Divil burn ye for a set av rid-skinned thieves, stalin' a man's liquor when he's aslape! Och-an-anee! fwhat am I to do now? Go to slape agane? I don't belave I cyan, thinkin' av tham an the tother, widout a thrifle av the crayther to comfort me. An' thare isn't a dhrap widin twenty—Fwhat—fwhat! Howly Mary! Mother av Moses! Sant Pathrick and all the others to boot, fwhat am I talkin' about? The pewther flask—the pewther flask! Be japers! it's in the thrunk—full to the very neck! Didn't I fill it for Masther Maurice to take wid him the last time he went to the sittlements? And didn't he forget to take it? Lard have mercy on me! If the Indyins have laid their dhirty claws upon *that* I shall be afther takin' lave at me sinses."

"Hoo—hoop—hoorro!" he cried, after an interval of silence, during which he could be heard fumbling among the contents of the portmanteau. "Hoo—hoop—hoorro! thanks to the Lord for all his mercies. The rid-skins haven't been cunnin' enough to look thare. The flask as full as a tick—not wan av them has had a finger on it. Hoo—hoop—hoorro!"

For some seconds the discoverer of the spirituous treasure, giving way to a joyous excitement, could be heard in the darkness, dancing over the floor of the *jacalé*.

Then there was an interval of silence, succeeded by the screwing of a stopper, and after that a succession of "glucks," that proclaimed the rapid emptying of a narrow-necked vessel.

After a time this sound was suspended, to be replaced by a repeated, smacking of lips, interlarded with grotesque ejaculations.

Again came the gluck-gluck, again the smackings, and so on alternately, till an empty flask was heard falling upon the floor.

After that there were wild shouts—scraps of song intermingled with cheers and laughter—incoherent ravings about red Indians and headless horsemen, repeated over and over again, each time in more subdued tones, till the maudlin gibberish at length ended in loud continuous snoring!

# 52. An Awakener

Phelim's second slumber was destined to endure for a more protracted term than his first. It was nearly noon when he awoke from it; and then only on receiving a bucket of cold water full in his face, that sobered him almost as quickly as the sight of the savages.

It was Zeb Stump who administered the *douche*.

After parting from the precincts of Casa del Corvo, the old hunter had taken the road, or rather *trail*, which he knew to be the most direct one leading to the head waters of the Nueces.

Without staying to notice tracks or other "sign," he rode straight across the prairie, and into the avenue already mentioned.

Prom what Louise Poindexter had told him—from a knowledge of the people who composed the party of searchers—he knew that Maurice Gerald was in danger.

Hence his haste to reach the Alamo before them—coupled with caution to keep out of their way.

He knew that if he came up with the Regulators, equivocation would be a dangerous game; and, *nolens volens*, he should be compelled to guide them to the dwelling of the suspected murderer.

On turning the angle of the avenue, he had the chagrin to see the searchers directly before him, clumped up in a crowd, and apparently engaged in the examination of "sign."

At the same time he had the satisfaction to know that his caution was rewarded, by himself remaining unseen.

"Durn them!" he muttered, with bitter emphasis. "I mout a know'd they'd a bin hyur. I must go back an roun' the tother way. It'll deelay me better'n a hour. Come, ole maar! This air an obstruckshun *you*, won't like. It'll gi'e ye the edition o' six more mile to yur journey. Ee-up, ole gal! Roun' an back we go!"

With a strong pull upon the rein, he brought the mare short round, and rode back towards the embouchure of the avenue.

Once outside, he turned along the edge of the chapparal, again entering it by the path which on the day before had been taken by Diaz and his trio of confederates. From this point he proceeded without pause or adventure until he had descended to the Alamo bottom-land, and arrived within a short distance, though still out of sight of the mustanger's dwelling.

Instead of riding boldly up to it, he dismounted from his mare; and leaving her behind him, approached the *jacalé* with his customary caution.

The horse-hide door was closed; but there was a large aperture in the middle of it, where a portion of the skin had been cut out. What was the meaning of that?

Zeb could not answer the question, even by conjecture.

It increased his caution; and he continued his approach with as much stealth, as if he had been stalking an antelope.

He kept round by the rear—so as to avail himself of the cover afforded by the trees; and at length, having crouched into the horse-shed at the back, he knelt down and listened.

There was an opening before his eyes; where one of the split posts had been pushed out of place, and the skin tapestry torn off. He saw this with some surprise; but, before he could shape any conjecture as to its cause, his ears were saluted with a sonorous breathing, that came out through the aperture. There was also a snore, which he fancied he could recognise, as proceeding from Irish nostrils.

A glance through the opening settled the point. The sleeper was Phelim.

There was an end to the necessity for stealthy manoeuvring. The hunter rose to his feet, and stepping round to the front, entered by the door—which he found unbolted.

He made no attempt to rouse the sleeper, until after he had taken stock of the paraphernalia upon the floor.

"Thur's been packin' up for some purpiss," he observed, after a cursory glance. "Ah! Now I reccollex. The young fellur sayed he war goin' to make a move from hyur some o' these days. Thet ere anymal air not only soun' asleep, but dead drunk. Sartin he air—drunk as Backis. I kin tell that by the smell o' him. I wonder if he hev left any o' the licker? It air dewbious. Not a drop, dog-gone him! Thur's the jar, wi' the stop plug out o' it, lyin' on its side; an thur's the flask, too, in the same preedikamint—both on 'em fall o' empiness. Durn him for a drunken cuss! He kin suck up as much moister as a chalk purayra.

311

"Spanish curds! A hul pack on 'em scattered abeout the place. What kin he ha' been doin' wi' them? S'pose he's been havin' a game o' sollatury along wi' his licker."

"But what's cut the hole in the door, an why's the tother broken out at the back? I reckon he kin tell. I'll roust him, an see. Pheelum! Pheelum!"

Phelim made no reply.

"Pheelum, I say! Pheelum!"

Still no reply. Although the last summons was delivered in a shout loud enough to have been heard half a mile off, there was no sign made by the slumberer to show that he even heard it.

A rude shaking administered by Zeb had no better effect. It only produced a grunt, immediately succeeded by a return to the same stentorous respiration.

"If 'twa'n't for his snorin' I mout b'lieve him to be dead. He *air* dead drunk, an no mistake; intoxerkated to the very eends o' his toenails. Kickin' him 'ud be no use. Dog-goned, ef I don't try *this*."

The old hunter's eye, as he spoke, was resting upon a pail that stood in a corner of the cabin. It was full of water, which Phelim, for some purpose, had fetched from the creek. Unfortunately for himself, he had not wasted it.

With a comical expression in his eye, Zeb took up the pail; and swilled the whole of its contents right down upon the countenance of the sleeper.

It had the effect intended. If not quite sobered, the inebriate was thoroughly awakened; and the string of terrified ejaculations that came from his lips formed a contrasting accompaniment to the loud cachinnations of the hunter.

It was some time before sufficient tranquillity was restored, to admit of the two men entering upon a serious conversation.

Phelim, however, despite his chronic inebriety, was still under the influence of his late fears, and was only too glad to see Zeb Stump, notwithstanding the unceremonious manner in which he had announced himself.

As soon as an understanding was established between them, and without waiting to be questioned, he proceeded to relate in detail, as concisely as an unsteady tongue and disordered brain would permit, the series of strange sights and incidents that had almost deprived him of his senses.

It was the first that Zeb Stump had heard of the *Headless Horseman.*

Although the report concerning this imperfect personage was that morning broadly scattered around Fort Inge, and along the Leona, Zeb, having passed through the settlement at an early hour, and stopped only at Casa del Corvo, had not chanced upon any one who could have communicated such a startling item of intelligence. In fact, he had exchanged speech only with Pluto and Louise Poindexter; neither of whom had at that time heard anything of the strange creature encountered, on the evening before, by the party of searchers. The planter, for some reason or another, had been but little communicative, and his daughter had not held converse with any of the others.

At first Zeb was disposed to ridicule the idea of a man without a head. He called it "a fantassy of Pheelum's brain, owin' to his havin' tuk too much of the corn-juice."

He was puzzled, however, by Phelim's persistence in declaring it to be a fact—more especially when he reflected on the other circumstances known to him.

"Arrah, now, how could I be mistaken?" argued the Irishman. "Didn't I see Masther Maurice, as plain as I see yourself at this minnit? All except the hid, and that I had a peep at as he turned to gallop away. Besides, thare was the Mexican blanket, an the saddle wid the rid cloth, and the wather guards av spotted skin; and who could mistake that purty horse? An' havn't I towld yez that Tara went away afther him, an thin I heerd the dog gowlin', jist afore the Indyins—"

"Injuns!" exclaimed the hunter, with a contemptuous toss of the head. "Injuns playin' wi' Spanish curds! White Injuns, I reck'n."

"Div yez think they waren't Indyins, afther all?"

"Ne'er a matter what I think. Thur's no time to talk o' that now. Go on, an tell me o' all ye seed an heern."

When Phelim had at length unburdened his mind, Zeb ceased to question him; and, striding out of the hut, squatted down, Indian fashion, upon the grass.

His object was, as he said himself, to have "a good think;" which, he had often declared, he could not obtain while "hampered wi' a house abeout him."

It is scarcely necessary to say, that the story told by the Galwegian groom only added to the perplexity he already experienced.

Hitherto there was but the disappearance of Henry Poindexter to be accounted for; now there was the additional circumstance of the non-return of the mustanger to his hut—when it was known that he had started for it, and should, according to a notice given to his servant, have been there at an early hour on the day before.

Far more mystifying was the remarkable story of his being seen riding about the prairie without a head, or with one carried in his hands! This last might be a trick. What else could it be?

Still was it a strange time for tricks—when a man had been murdered, and half the population of the settlement wore out upon the track of the murderer—more especially improbable, that the supposed assassin should be playing them!

Zeb Stump had to deal with, a difficult concatenation—or rather conglomeration of circumstances—events without causes—causes without sequence—crimes committed without any probable motive—mysteries that could only be explained by an appeal to the supernatural.

A midnight meeting between Maurice Gerald and Louise Poindexter—a quarrel with her brother, occasioned by the discovery—Maurice having departed for the prairies—Henry having followed to sue for forgiveness—in all this the sequence was natural and complete.

Beyond began the chapter of confusions and contradictions.

Zeb Stump knew the disposition of Maurice Gerald in regard to Henry Poindexter. More than once he had heard the mustanger speak of the young planter. Instead of having a hostility towards him, he had frequently expressed admiration of his ingenuous and generous character.

That he could have changed from being his friend to become his assassin, was too improbable for belief. Only by the evidence of his eyes could Zeb Stump have been brought to believe it.

After spending a full half hour at his "think," he had made but little progress towards unravelling the network of cognate, yet unconnected, circumstances. Despite an intellect unusually clear, and the possession of strong powers of analysis, he was unable to reach any rational solution of this mysterious drama of many acts.

The only thing clear to him was, that four mounted men—he did not believe them to be Indians—had been making free with the mustanger's hut; and that it was most probable that these had something to do with the murder that had been committed. But the presence of these men at the *jacalé*, coupled with the protracted absence of its owner, conducted his conjectures to a still more melancholy conclusion: that more than one man had fallen a sacrifice to the assassin, and that the thicket might be searched for two bodies, instead of one!

A groan escaped from the bosom of the backwoodsman as this conviction forced itself upon his mind. He entertained for the young Irishman a peculiar affection—strong almost as that felt by a father for his son; and the thought that he had been foully assassinated in some obscure corner of the chapparal, his flesh to be torn by the beak of the buzzard and the teeth of the coyoté, stirred the old hunter to the very core of his heart.

He groaned again, as he reflected upon it; until, without action, he could no longer bear the agonising thought, and, springing to his feet, he strode to and fro over the ground, proclaiming, in loud tones, his purpose of vengeance.

So absorbed was he with his sorrowful indignation, that he saw not the staghound as it came skulking up to the hut.

It was not until he heard Phelim caressing the hound in his grotesque Irish fashion, that he became aware of the creature's presence. And then he remained indifferent to it, until a shout of surprise, coupled with his own name, attracted his attention.

"What is it, Pheelum? What's wrong? Hes a snake bit ye?"

"Oh, Misther Stump, luk at Tara! See! thare's somethin' tied about his neck. It wasn't there when he lift. What do yez think it is?"

The hunter's eyes turned immediately upon the hound. Sure enough there was something around the animal's neck: a piece of buckskin thong. But there was something besides—a tiny packet attached to the thong, and hanging underneath the throat!

Zeb drawing his knife, glided towards the dog. The creature recoiled in fear.

A little coaxing convinced him that there was no hostile intent; and he came up again.

The thong was severed, the packet laid open; it contained a *card*!

There was a name upon the card, and writing—writing in what appeared to be red ink; but it was *blood*!

The rudest backwoodsman knows how to read. Even Zeb Stump was no exception; and he soon deciphered the characters traced upon the bit of pasteboard.

As he finished, a cry rose from his lips, in strange contrast with the groans he had been just uttering. It was a shout of gladness, of joy!

"Thank the Almighty for this!" he added; "and thank my ole Katinuck schoolmaster for puttin' me clar through my Webster's spellin'-book. He lives, Pheelum! he lives! Look at this. Oh, *you* can't read. No matter. He lives! he lives!"

"Who? Masther Maurice? Thin the Lord be thanked—"

"Wagh! thur's no time to thank him now. Get a blanket an some pieces o' horse-hide thong. Ye kin do it while I catch up the ole maar. Quick! Helf an hour lost, an we may be too late!"

# 53. Just in Time

"Half-an-hour lost, and we may be too late!"

They were the last words of the hunter, as he hurried away from the hut.

They were true, except as to the time. Had he said half-a-minute, he would have been nearer the mark. Even at the moment of their utterance, the man, whose red writing had summoned assistance, was once more in dread danger—once more surrounded by the coyotés.

But it was not these he had need to fear. A far more formidable foe was threatening his destruction.

Maurice Gerald—by this time recognised as the man in the cloak and Panama hat—after doing battle with the wolves, as already described, and being rescued by his faithful Tara, had fought repose in sleep.

With full confidence in the ability of his canine companion to protect him against the black birds, or the more dangerous quadrupeds, with which he had been in conflict, he soon found, and for several hours enjoyed it.

He awoke of his own accord. Finding his strength much restored, he once more turned his attention to the perils that surrounded him.

The dog had rescued him from the jackals, and would still protect him against their attacks, should they see fit to renew it. But to what end? The faithful creature could not transport him from the spot; and to stay there would be to die of hunger—perhaps of the wounds he had received?

He rose to his feet, but found that he could not stand upright. Feebleness was now added to his other infirmity; and after struggling a pace or two, he was glad to return to a recumbent position.

At this crisis a happy thought occurred to him. Tara might take a message to the hut!

"If I could but get him to go," said he, as he turned inquiringly towards the dog. "Come hither, old fellow!" he continued, addressing himself to the dumb animal; "I want you to play postman for me—to carry a letter. You understand? Wait till I've got it written. I shall then explain myself more fully."

"By good luck I've got a card," he added, feeling for his case. "No pencil! That don't matter. There's plenty of ink around; and for a pen I can use the thorn of yonder maguey."

He crept up to the plant thus designated; broke off one of the long spines terminating its great leaves; dipped it in the blood of a coyoté that lay near; and drawing forth a card, traced some characters upon it.

With a strip of thong, the card was then attached to the neck of the staghound, after being wrapped up in a piece of oilcloth torn from the lining of the Panama hat.

It only remained to despatch the canine post upon his errand. This proved a somewhat difficult task. The dumb creature, despite a wondrous intelligence, could not comprehend why he should forsake the side of one he had so faithfully befriended; and for a long time resisted the coaxings and chidings, meant to warn him away.

It was only after being scolded in a tone of assumed anger, and beaten by the black-jack crutch—stricken by the man whose life he had so lately saved, that he had consented to leave the spot. Even canine affection could not endure this; and with repeated looks of reproach, cast backwards as he was chased off, he trotted reluctantly into the chapparal.

"Poor fellow!" soliloquised Maurice, as the dog disappeared from his view. "'Tis like boating one's self, or one's dearest friend! Well, I shall make up for it in extra kindness if I have the good fortune to see him again.

"And now, that he is gone, I must provide against the coming back of these villainous coyotés. They will be sure to come, once they discover that I'm alone."

A scheme had been already considered.

A tree stood near—the pecân already alluded to—having two stout branches that extended horizontally and together, at six or seven feet from the ground.

Taking off his cloak, and spreading it out upon the grass, with his knife he cut a row of holes along each edge.

Then unwinding from his waist the sash of china crape, he tore it up the middle, so as to make two strips, each several yards long.

The cloak was now extended between the branches, and fast tied by the strips of crape—thus forming a sort of hammock capable of containing the body of a man laid out at full length.

The maker of it knew that the coyotés are not tree climbers; and, reclining on his suspended couch, he could observe with indifference their efforts to assail him.

He took all this trouble, feeling certain they would return. If he had any doubt, it was soon set at rest, by seeing them, one after the other, come skulking out of the chapparal, lopping a pace or two, at intervals, pausing to reconnoitre, and then advancing towards the scene of their late conflict.

Emboldened by the absence of the enemy most dreaded by them, the pack was soon reassembled, once more exhibiting the truculent ferocity for which these cowardly creatures are celebrated.

It was first displayed in a very unnatural manner—by the devouring of their own dead—which was done in less time than it would have taken the spectator in the tree to have counted a score.

To him their attention was next directed. In swinging his hammock, he had taken no pains to conceal it. He had suspended it high enough to be out of their reach; and that he deemed sufficient for his purpose.

The cloak of dark cloth was conspicuous, as well as the figure outlined within it. The coyotés clustered underneath—their appetites whetted by the taste of blood. It was a sight to see them lick their red lips after their unnatural repast—a fearful sight!

He who saw it scarce regarded them—not even when they were springing up to lay hold of his limbs, or at times attempting to ascend by the trunk of the tree! He supposed there was no danger.

There *was* danger, however, on which he had not reckoned; and not till the coyotés have desisted from their idle attempts, and stretched themselves, panting, under the tree, did he begin to perceive it.

Of all the wild denizens, either of prairie or chapparal, the coyoté is that possessed of the greatest cunning. The trapper will tell you it is the "cunningest varmint in creation." It is a fox in astuteness—a wolf in ferocity. It may be tamed, but it will turn at any time to tear the hand that caresses it. A child can scare it with a stick, but a disabled man may dread its attack. Alone it has the habit of a hare; but in packs—and it hunts only in packs—its poltroonery is less observable; sometimes under the influence of extreme hunger giving place to a savageness of disposition that assumes the semblance of courage.

318

It is the coyotés' cunning that is most to be feared; and it was this that had begun to excite fresh apprehension in the mind of the mustanger.

On discovering that they could not reach him—a discovery they were not long in making—instead of scattering off from the spot, the wolves, one and all, squatted down upon the grass; while others, stragglers from the original troop, were still coming into the glade. He saw that they intended a siege.

This should not have troubled him, seeing that he was secure in his suspended couch.

Nor would it, but for another source of trouble, every moment making itself more manifest—that from which he had so lately had such a narrow escape. He was once more on the eve of being tortured by thirst.

He blamed himself for having been so simple, as not to think of this before climbing up to the tree. He might easily have carried up a supply of water. The stream was there; and for want of a better vessel, the concave blades of the maguey would have served as a cistern.

His self-reproaches came too late. The water was under his eyes, only to tantalise him; and by so doing increase his eagerness to obtain it. He could not return to the stream, without running the gauntlet of the coyotés, and that would be certain death. He had but faint hopes that the hound would return and rescue him a second time—fainter still that his message would reach the man for whom it was intended. A hundred to one against that.

Thirst is quick in coming to a man whose veins are half-emptied of their blood. The torture proclaimed itself apace. How long was it to continue?

This time it was accompanied by a straying of the senses. The wolves, from being a hundred, seemed suddenly to have increased their number tenfold. A thousand appeared to encompass the tree, filling the whole ground of the glade! They came nearer and nearer. Their eyes gave out a lurid light. Their red tongues lapped the hanging cloth; they tore it with their teeth. He could feel their fetid breath, as they sprang up among the branches!

A lucid interval told him that it was all fancy. The wolves were still there; but only a hundred of them—as before, reclining upon the grass, pitiably awaiting a crisis! It came before the period of lucidity had departed; to the spectator unexpected as inexplicable. He saw the coyotés suddenly spring to their feet, and rush off into the thicket, until not one remained within the glade.

Was this, too, a fancy? He doubted the correctness of his vision. He had begun to believe that his brain was distempered.

But it was clear enough now. There were no coyotés. What could have frightened them off?

A cry of joy was sent forth from his lips, as he conjectured a cause. Tara had returned? Perhaps Phelim along with him? There had been time enough for the delivery of the message. For two hours he had been besieged by the coyotés.

He turned upon his knee, and bending over the branch, scanned the circle around him. Neither hound nor henchman was in sight. Nothing but branches and bushes!

He listened. No sound, save an occasional howl, sent back by the coyotés that still seemed to continue their retreat! More than ever was it like an illusion. What could have caused their scampering?

No matter. The coast was clear. The streamlet could now be approached without danger. Its water sparkled under his eyes—its rippling sounded sweet to his ears.

Descending from the tree, he staggered towards its bank, and reached it.

Before stooping to drink, he once more looked around him. Even the agony of thirst could not stifle the surprise, still fresh in his thoughts. To what was he indebted for his strange deliverance?

Despite his hope that it might be the hound, he had an apprehension of danger.

One glance, and he was certain of it. The spotted yellow skin shining among the leaves—the long, lithe form crawling like a snake out of the underwood was not to be mistaken. It was the tiger of the New World—scarce less dreaded than his congener of the Old—the dangerous jaguar.

Its presence accounted for the retreat of the coyotés.

Neither could its intent be mistaken. It, too, had scented blood, and was hastening to the spot where blood had been sprinkled, with that determined air that told it would not be satisfied till after partaking of the banquet.

Its eyes were upon him, who had descended from the tree—its steps were towards him—now in slow, crouching gait; but quicker and quicker, as if preparing for a spring.

To retreat to the tree would have been sheer folly. The jaguar can climb like a cat. The mustanger knew this.

But even had he been ignorant of it, it would have been all the same, as the thing was no longer possible. The animal had already

320

passed that tree, upon which he had found refuge, and there was t'other near that could be reached in time.

He had no thought of climbing to a tree—no thought of any thing, so confused were his senses—partly from present surprise, partly from the bewilderment already within his brain.

It was a simple act of unreasoning impulse that led him to rush on into the stream, until he stood up to his waist in the water.

Had he reasoned, he would have known that this would do nothing to secure his safety. If the jaguar climbs like a cat, it also swims with the ease of an otter; and is as much to be dreaded in the water as upon the land.

Maurice made no such reflection. He suspected that the little pool, towards the centre of which he had waded, would prove but poor protection. He was sure of it when the jaguar, arriving upon the bank above him, set itself in that cowering attitude that told of its intention to spring.

In despair he steadied himself to receive the onset of the fierce animal.

He had nought wherewith to repel it—no knife—no pistol—no weapon of any kind—not even his crutch! A struggle with his bare arms could but end in his destruction.

A wild cry went forth from his lips, as the tawny form was about launching itself for the leap.

There was a simultaneous scream from the jaguar. Something appeared suddenly to impede it; and instead of alighting on the body of its victim, it fell short, with a dead plash upon the water!

Like an echo of his own, a cry came from the chapparal, close following a sound that had preceded it—the sharp "spang" of a rifle.

A huge dog broke through the bushes, and sprang with a plunge into the pool where the jaguar had sunk below the surface. A man of colossal size advanced rapidly towards the bank; another of lesser stature treading close upon his heels, and uttering joyful shouts of triumph.

To the wounded man these sights and sounds were more like a vision than the perception of real phenomena. They were the last thoughts of that day that remained in his memory. His reason, kept too long upon the rack, had given way. He tried to strangle the faithful hound that swam fawningly around him and struggled against the strong arms that, raising him out of the water, bore him in friendly embrace to the bank!

# THE HEADLESS HORSEMAN

His mind had passed from a horrid reality, to a still more horrid dream—the dream of delirium.

# 54. A Prairie Palanquin

The friendly arms, flung around Maurice Gerald, were those of Zeb Stump.

Guided by the instructions written upon the card, the hunter had made all haste towards the rendezvous there given.

He had arrived within sight, and fortunately within rifle-range of the spot, at that critical moment when the jaguar was preparing to spring.

His bullet did not prevent the fierce brute from making the bound—the last of its life—though it had passed right through the animal's heart.

This was a thing thought of afterwards—there was no opportunity then.

On rushing into the water, to make sure that his shot had proved fatal, the hunter was himself attacked; not by the claws of the jaguar, but the hands of the man just rescued from them.

Fortunate for Zeb, that the mustanger's knife had been left upon land. As it was, he came near being throttled; and only after throwing aside his rifle, and employing all his strength, was he able to protect himself against the unlooked-for assault.

A struggle ensued, which ended in Zeb flinging his colossal arms around the young Irishman, and bearing him bodily to the bank.

It was not all over. As soon as the latter was relieved from the embrace, he broke away and made for the pecân tree;—as rapidly as if the injured limb no longer impeded him.

The hunter suspected his intent. Standing over six feet, he saw the bloody knife-blade lying along the cloak. It was for that the mustanger was making!

Zeb bounded after; and once more enfolding the madman in his bear-like embrace, drew him back from the tree.

"Speel up thur, Pheelum!" shouted he. "Git that thing out o' sight. The young fellur hev tuck leeve o' his seven senses. Thur's fever in the feel o' him. He air gone dullerious!"

Phelim instantly obeyed; and, scrambling up the tree-trunk took possession of the knife.

Still the struggle was not over. The delirious man wrestled with his rescuer—not in silence, but with shouts and threatening speeches—his eyes all the time rolling and glaring with a fierce, demoniac light.

For full ten minutes did he continue the mad wrestling match.

At length from sheer exhaustion he sank back upon the grass; and after a few tremulous shiverings, accompanied by sighs heaved from the very bottom of his breast, he lay still, as if the last spark of life had departed from his body!

The Galwegian, believing it so, began uttering a series of lugubrious cries—the "keen" of Connemara.

"Stop yur gowlin, ye durned cuss!" cried Zeb. "It air enuf to scare the breath out o' his karkidge. He's no more dead than you air—only fented. By the way he hev fit me, I reck'n there ain't much the matter wi' him. No," he continued, after stooping down and giving a short examination, "I kin see no wound worth makin' a muss about. Thur's a consid'able swellin' o' the knee; but the leg ain't fructered, else he kudn't a stud up on it. As for them scratches, they ain't much. What kin they be? 'Twarnt the jegwur that gin them. They air more like the claws o' a tom cat. Ho, ho! I sees now. Thur's been a bit o' a skrimmage afore the spotted beest kim up. The young fellur's been attakted by coyoats! Who'd a supposed that the cowardly varmints would a had the owdacity to attakt a human critter? But they *will*, when they gits the chance o' one krippled as he air—durn 'em!"

The hunter had all the talking to himself. Phelim, now overjoyed to know that his master still lived—and furthermore was in no danger of dying—suddenly changed his melancholy whine to a jubilant hullaballoo, and commenced dancing over the ground, all the while snapping his fingers in the most approved Connemara fashion.

His frenzied action provoked the hound to a like pitch of excitement; and the two became engaged in a sort of wild Irish jig.

Zeb took no notice of these grotesque demonstrations; but, once more bending over the prostrate form, proceeded to complete the examination already begun.

Becoming satisfied that there was no serious wound, he rose to his feet, and commenced taking stock of the odd articles around him.

He had already noticed the Panama hat, that still adhered to the head of the mustanger; and a strange thought at seeing it there, had passed through his mind.

Hats of Guayaquil grass—erroneously called Panama—were not uncommon. Scores of Southerners wore them, in Texas as elsewhere. But he knew that the young Irishman was accustomed to carry a Mexican *sombrero*—a very different kind of head-gear. It was possible he might have seen fit to change the fashion.

Still, as Zeb continued to gaze upon it, he fancied he had seen *that* hat before, and on some other head.

It was not from any suspicion of its being honestly in possession of him now wearing it that the hunter stooped down, and took it off with the design to examine it. His object was simply to obtain some explanation of the mystery, or series of mysteries, hitherto baffling his brain.

On looking inside the hat he read two names; first, that of a New Orleans hatter, whose card was pasted in the crown; and then, in writing, another well known to him:—

"HENRY POINDEXTER."

The cloak now came under his notice. It, too, carried marks, by which he was able to identify it as belonging to the same owner.

"Dog-goned kewrious, all this!" muttered the backwoodsman, as he stood with his eyes turned upon the ground, and apparently buried in a profound reflection.

"Hats, heads, an everythin'. Hats on the wrong head; heads i' the wrong place! By the 'tarnal thur's somethin' goed astray! Ef 'twa'nt that I feel a putty consid'able smartin' whar the young fellur gin me a lick over the left eye, I mout be arter believin' my own skull-case wa'nt any longer atween my shoulders!"

"It air no use lookin' to him," he added, glancing towards Maurice, "for an explanation; leastwise till he's slep' off this dullerium thet's on him. When that'll be, ole Nick only knows.

"Wal," he continued after another interval spent in silent reflection, "It won't do no good our stayin' hyur. We must git him to the shanty, an that kin only be did by toatin' him. He sayed on the curd, he cudn't make neer a track. It war only the anger kep' him up a bit. That leg looks wusser and wusser. He's boun to be toated."

The hunter seemed to cogitate on how he was to effect this purpose.

"'Taint no good expektin' *him* to help think it out," he continued looking at the Galwegian, who was busy talking to Tara. "The dumb

325

brute hev more sense than he. Neer a mind. I'd make him take his full share o' the carryin' when it kum to thet. How air it to be done? We must git him on a streetcher. That I reck'n we kin make out o' a kupple o' poles an the cloak; or wi' the blanket Pheelum fetch'd from the shanty. Ye-es! a streetcher. That's the eydentikul eyedee."

The Connemara man was now summoned to lend assistance. Two saplings of at least ten feet in length were cut from the chapparal, and trimmed clear of twigs. Two shorter ones were also selected, and lashed crosswise over the first; and upon these there spread, first the serapé, and afterwards the cloak, to give greater strength.

In this way a rude stretcher was constructed, capable of carrying either an invalid or an inebriate.

In the mode of using it, it more resembled the latter than the former: since he who was to be borne upon it, again deliriously raging, had to be strapped to the trestles!

Unlike the ordinary stretcher, it was not carried between two men; but a man and a mare—the mare at the head, the man bearing behind.

It was he of Connemara who completed the ill-matched team. The old hunter had kept his promise, that Phelim should "take his full share o' the carryin', when it kum to thet."

He was taking it, or rather getting it—Zeb having appointed himself to the easier post of conductor.

The idea was not altogether original. It was a rude copy from the Mexican *litera*, which in Southern Texas Zeb may have seen— differing from the latter only in being without screen, and instead of two mules, having for its *atelage* a mare and a man!

In this improvised palanquin was Maurice Gerald transported to his dwelling.

---

It was night when the grotesque-looking group arrived at the *locale*.

In strong but tender arms the wounded man was transferred from the stretcher to the skin couch, on which he had been accustomed to repose.

He was unconscious of where he was, and knew not the friendly faces bending over him. His thoughts were still astray, though no longer exciting him to violent action. He was experiencing an interval of calm.

He was not silent; though he made no reply to the kind questions addressed to him, or only answered them with an inconsequence that might have provoked mirth. But there were wild words upon his lips that forbade it—suggesting only serious thoughts.

His wounds received such rude dressing as his companions were capable of administering to them; and nothing more could be done but await the return of day.

Phelim went to sleep upon his shake-down; while the other sate up to keep watch by the bedside of the sufferer.

It was not from any unfaithfulness on the part of the foster-brother, that he seemed thus to disregard his duty; but simply because Zeb had requested him to lie down—telling him there was no occasion for both to remain awake.

The old hunter had his reasons. He did not desire that those wild words should be heard even by Phelim. Better he should listen to them alone.

And alone he sate listening to them—throughout the live-long night.

He heard speeches that surprised him, and names that did not. He was not surprised to hear the name "Louise" often repeated, and coupled with fervent protestations of love.

But there was another name also often pronounced—with speeches less pleasant to his ear.

It was the name of Louise's brother.

The speeches were disjointed—incongruous, and almost unintelligible.

Comparing one with the other, however, and assisted by the circumstances already known to him, before the morning light had entered the *jacalé*, Zeb Stump had come to the conclusion: that Henry Poindexter was no longer a living man!

# 55. Un Dia de Novedades

Don Silvio Martinez was one of the few Mexican *ricos*, who had chosen to remain in Texas, after the conquest of that country by the stalwart colonisers from the North.

A man of more than mature age, of peaceful habits, and taking no part in politics, he accepted the new situation without any great regret. He was the more easily reconciled to it, from a knowledge, that his loss of nationality was better than counterbalanced by his gain of security against Comanche incursions; which, previous to the coming of the new colonists, had threatened the complete depopulation of the country.

The savage was not yet entirely subdued; but his maraud was now intermittent, and occurred only at long intervals. Even this was an improvement on the old *régime*.

Don Silvio was a *ganadero*,—a grazier, on a grand scale. So grand that his *ganaderia* was leagues in length and breadth, and contained within its limits many thousands of horses and horned cattle.

He lived in a large rectangular one-storied house—more resembling a jail than a dwelling—surrounded by extensive enclosures—*corrales*.

It was usually a quiet place; except during the time of the *herradero*, or cattle-branding; when for days it became the scene of a festivity almost Homeric.

These occasions were only of annual occurrence.

At all other times the old haciendado—who was a bachelor to boot—led a tranquil and somewhat solitary life; a sister older than himself being his only companion. There were occasional exceptions to this rule: when his charming *sobrina* rode across from the Rio Grande to pay him and his sister a visit. Then the domicile of Don Silvio became a little more lively.

Isidora was welcome whenever she came; welcome to come and go when she pleased; and do as she pleased, while under her uncle's roof. The sprightliness of her character was anything but displeasing to the old haciendado; who was himself far from being of a sombre disposition. Those traits, that might have appeared masculine in many other lands, were not so remarkable in one, where life is held by such precarious tenure; where the country house is oft transformed into a fortress, and the domestic hearth occasionally bedewed with the blood of its inmates!

Is it surprising that in such a land women should be found, endowed with those qualities that have been ascribed to Isidora? If so, it is not the less true that they exist.

As a general thing the Mexican woman is a creature of the most amiable disposition; *douce*—if we may be allowed to borrow from a language that deals more frequently with feminine traits—to such an extent, as to have become a national characteristic. It is to the denizens of the great cities, secure from Indian incursion, that this character more especially applies. On the frontiers, harried for the last half century by the aboriginal freebooter, the case is somewhat different. The amiability still exists; but often combined with a *bravourie* and hardihood masculine in seeming, but in reality heroic.

Since Malinché, more than one fair heroine has figured in the history of Anahuac.

Don Silvio Martinez had himself assisted at many a wild scene and ceremony. His youth had been passed amid perils; and the courage of Isidora—at times degenerating into absolute recklessness—so far from offending, rather gave him gratification.

The old gentleman loved his darling *sobrina*, as if she had been his own child; and had she been so, she would not have been more certain of succeeding to his possessions.

Every one knew, that, when Don Silvio Martinez should take leave of life, Isidora Covarubio de los Llanos would be the owner of—not his broad acres, but—his *leagues* of land, as also his thousands of horses and horned cattle.

With this understanding, it is needless to say, that the señorita carried respect with her wherever she went, or that the vassals of the Hacienda Martinez honoured her as their future mistress.

Independently of this was she regarded. Hers were just the qualities to win the esteem of the dashing *rancheros*; and there was not one upon the estate, but would have drawn his *macheté* at her nod, and used it to the shedding of blood.

Miguel Diaz spoke the truth, when he said he was in danger. Well might he believe it. Had it pleased Isidora to call together her uncle's *vaqueros*, and send them to chastise him, it would have been speedily done—even to hanging him upon the nearest tree!

No wonder he had made such haste to get away from the glade.

As already stated, the real home of Isidora was upon the other side of the Rio Grande—separated by some three-score miles from the Hacienda Martinez. But this did not hinder her from paying frequent visits to her relations upon the Leona.

There was no selfishness in the motive. The prospect of the rich inheritance had nothing to do with it. She was an expectant heiress without that: for her own father was a *rico*. But she liked the company of her uncle and aunt. She also enjoyed the ride from river to river—oft made by her between morning and night, and not unfrequently alone!

Of late these visits had become of much more frequent occurrence.

Had she grown fonder of the society of her Texan relatives—fonder as they grew older? If not, what was her motive?

Imitating her own frankness of character, it may at once be declared.

She came oftener to the Leona, in the hope of meeting with Maurice Gerald.

With like frankness may it be told, that she *loved* him.

Beyond doubt, the young Irishman was in possession of her heart. As already known, he had won it by an act of friendship; though it may have been less the service he had done, than the gallantry displayed in doing it, that had put the love-spell on the daring Isidora.

Perhaps, too, she saw in him other captivating qualities, less easily defined. Whether these had been undesignedly exhibited, or with the intention to effect a conquest, he alone can tell. He has himself said, No; and respect is due to his declaration. But it is difficult to believe, that mortal man could have gazed into the eyes of Isidora de los Llanos without wishing them to look longingly upon him.

Maurice may have spoken the truth; but we could better believe him, had he seen Louise Poindexter before becoming acquainted with Isidora.

The episode of the burnt prairie was several weeks subsequent to the adventure with the intoxicated Indians.

Certainly something appears to have occurred between him and the Mexican maiden, that leads her to believe she has a hope—if not a claim—upon his affections.

It has come to that crisis, that she can no longer rest satisfied. Her impulsive spirit cannot brook ambiguity. She knows that she loves *him*. She has determined to make frank confession of it; and to ask with like frankness whether her passion be reciprocated. Hence her having made an appointment that could not be kept.

For that day Don Miguel Diaz had interfered between her and her purpose.

So thought she, as she galloped out of the glade, and hastened back to the hacienda of her uncle.

Astride her grey steed she goes at a gallop.

Her head is bare; her coiffure disarranged; her rich black tresses streaming back beyond her shoulders, no longer covered by scarf or serapé. The last she has left behind her, and along with it her *vicuña* hat.

Her eyes are flashing with excitement; her cheeks flushed to the colour of carmine.

The cause is known.

And also why she is riding in such hot haste. She has herself declared it.

On nearing the house, she is seen to tighten her rein. The horse is pulled in to a slower pace—a trot; slower still—a walk; and, soon after, he is halted in the middle of the road.

His rider has changed her intention; or stops to reflect whether she should.

She sits reflecting.

"On second thoughts—perhaps—better not have him taken? It would create a terrible scandal, everywhere. So far, no one knows of —. Besides, what can I say myself—the only witness? Ah! were I to tell these gallant Texans the story, my own testimony would be enough to have him punished with a harsh hand. No! let him live. *Ladron* as he is, I do not fear him. After what's happened he will not care to come near me. *Santa Virgen*! to think that I could have felt a fancy for this man—short-lived as it was!

"I must send some one back to release him. One who can keep my secret—who? Benito, the mayor-domo—faithful and brave. *Gracias a Dios*! Yonder's my man—as usual busied in counting his cattle. Benito! Benito!"

"At your orders, s'ñorita?"

331

"Good Benito, I want you to do me a kindness. You consent?"

"At your orders, s'ñorita?" repeats the mayor-domo, bowing low.

"Not *orders*, good Benito. I wish you to do me a *favour*."

"Command me, s'ñorita!"

"You know the spot of open ground at the top of the hill—where the three roads meet?"

"As well as the corral of your uncle's hacienda."

"Good! Go there. You will find a man lying upon the ground, his arms entangled in a lazo. Release, and let him go free. If he be hurt—by a harsh fall he has had—do what you can to restore him; but don't tell him who sent you. You may know the man—I think you do. No matter for that. Ask him no questions, nor answer his, if he should put any. Once you have seen him on his legs, let him make use of them after his own fashion. You understand?"

"*Perfectamente, s'ñorita.* Your orders shall be obeyed to the letter."

"Thanks, good Benito. Uncle Silvio will like you all the better for it; though *you* mustn't tell him of it. Leave that to me. If he shouldn't—if he shouldn't—well! one of these days there may be an estate on the Rio Grande that will stand in need of a brave, faithful steward—such an one as I know you to be."

"Every one knows that the Doña Isidora is gracious as she is fair."

"Thanks—thanks! One more request. The service I ask you to do for me must be known to only three individuals. The third is he whom you are sent to succour. You know the other two?"

"S'ñorita, I comprehend. It shall be as you wish it."

The mayor-domo is moving off on horseback, it need scarce be said. Men of his calling rarely set foot to the earth—never upon a journey of half a league in length.

"Stay! I had forgotten!" calls out the lady, arresting him. "You will find a hat and serapé. They are mine. Bring them, and I shall wait for you here, or meet you somewhere along the way."

Bowing, he again rides away. Again is he summoned to stop.

"On second thoughts, Señor Benito, I've made up my mind to go along with you. *Vamos!*"

The steward of Don Silvio is not surprised at caprice, when exhibited by the niece of his employer. Without questioning, he obeys her command, and once more heads his horse for the hill.

The lady follows. She has told him to ride in the advance. She has her reason for departing from the aristocratic custom.

Benito is astray in his conjecture. It is not to caprice that he is in-debted for the companionship of the señorita. A serious motive takes her back along the road.

She has forgotten something more than her wrapper and hat—that little letter that has caused her so much annoyance.

The "good Benito" has not had *all* her confidence; nor can he be entrusted with this. *It* might prove a scandal, graver than the quarrel with Don Miguel Diaz.

She rides back in hopes of repossessing herself of the epistle. How stupid not to have thought of it before!

How had El Coyote got hold of it? He must have had it from José!

Was her servant a traitor? Or had Diaz met him on the way, and forced the letter from him?

To either of these questions an affirmative answer might be sur-mised.

On the part of Diaz such an act would have been natural enough; and as for José, it is not the first time she has had reason for suspecting his fidelity.

So run her thoughts as she re-ascends the slope, leading up from the river bottom.

The summit is gained, and the opening entered; Isidora now rid-ing side by side with the mayor-domo.

No Miguel Diaz there—no man of any kind; and what gives her far greater chagrin, not a scrap of paper!

There is her hat of vicuña wool—her seraph of Saltillo, and the loop end of her lazo—nothing more.

"You may go home again, Señor Benito! The man thrown from his horse must have recovered his senses—and, I suppose, his saddle too. Blessed be the virgin! But remember, good Benito *Secrecy all the same. Entiende, V?*"

"*Yo entiendo, Doña Isidora.*"

The mayor-domo moves away, and is soon lost to sight behind the crest of the hill.

---

The lady of the lazo is once more alone in the glade. She springs out of her saddle; dons serapé and sombrero; and is again the *beau-ideal* of a youthful hidalgo.

She remounts slowly, mechanically—as if her thoughts do not company the action. Languidly she lifts her limb over the horse. The pretty foot is for a second or two poised in the air.

Her ankle, escaping from the skirt of her *enagua*, displays a tour-nure to have crazed Praxiteles. As it descends on the opposite side of the horse, a cloud seems to overshadow the sun. Simon Stylites could scarce have closed his eyes on the spectacle.

But there is no spectator of this interesting episode; not even the wretched José; who, the moment after, comes skulking into the glade.

He is questioned, without circumlocution, upon the subject of the strayed letter.

"What have you done with it, sirrah?"

"Delivered it, my lady."

"To whom?"

"I left it at—at—the *posada*," he replies, stammering and turning pale. "Don Mauricio had gone out."

"A lie, *lepero*! You gave it to Don Miguel Diaz. No denial, sir! I've seen it since."

"O Señora, pardon! pardon! I am not guilty—indeed I am not."

"Stupid, you should have told your story better. You have com-mitted yourself. How much did Don Miguel pay you for your treason?"

"As I live, lady, it was not treason. He—he—forced it from me—by threats—blows. I—I—was not paid."

"You shall be, then! I discharge you from my service; and for wages take that, and that, and that—"

For at least ten times are the words repeated—the riding whip at each repetition descending upon the shoulders of the dishonest mes-senger.

He essays to escape by running off. In vain. He is brought up again by the dread of being ridden over, and trampled under the hoofs of the excited horse.

Not till the blue wheals appear upon his brown skin, does the chastisement cease.

"Now, sirrah; from my sight! and let me see you no more. *Al monte! al monte!*"

With ludicrous alacrity the command is obeyed. Like a scared cat the discharged servitor rushes out of the glade; only too happy to hide himself, and his shame, under the shadows of the thorny thicket.

But a little while longer does Isidora remain upon the spot—her anger giving place to a profound chagrin. Not only has she been baf-fled from carrying out her design; but her heart's secret is now in the keeping of traitors!

Once more she heads her horse homeward. She arrives in time to be present at a singular spectacle. The people—peons, vaqueros, and employés of every kind—are hurrying to and fro, from field to corral, from corral to courtyard one and all giving tongue to terrified ejaculations. The men are on their feet arming in confused haste; the woman on their knees, praying pitifully to heaven—through the intercession of a score of those saints, profusely furnished by the Mexican hierarchy to suit all times and occasions.

"What is causing the commotion?"

This is the question asked by Isidora.

The mayor-domo—who chances to be the first to present himself—is the individual thus interrogated.

A man has been murdered somewhere out upon the prairie.

The victim is one of the new people who have lately taken possession of Caso del Corvo—the son of the American haciendado himself.

Indians are reported to have done the deed.

Indians! In this word is the key to the excitement among Don Silvio's servitors.

It explains both the praying and the hurried rushing to arms.

The fact that a man has been murdered—a slight circumstance in that land of unbridled emotions—would have produced no such response—more especially when the man was a stranger, an "Americano."

But the report that Indians are abroad, is altogether a different affair. In it there is an idea of danger.

The effect produced on Isidora is different. It is not fear of the savages. The name of the "asesinado" recalls thoughts that have already given her pain. She knows that there is a sister, spoken of as being wonderfully beautiful. She has herself looked upon this beauty, and cannot help believing in it.

A keener pang proceeds from something else she has heard: that this peerless maiden has been seen in the company of Maurice Gerald. There is no fresh jealousy inspired by the news of the brother's death—only the old unpleasantness for the moment revived.

The feeling soon gives place to the ordinary indifference felt for the fate of those with whom we have no acquaintance.

Some hours later, and this indifference becomes changed to a painful interest; in short, an apprehension. There are fresh reports about the murder. It has been committed, not by Comanches; but by a white man—by *Maurice the mustanger*!

335

There are no Indians near.

This later edition of "novedades," while tranquilising Don Silvio's servants, has the contrary effect upon his niece. She cannot rest under the rumour; and half-an-hour afterwards, she is seen reining up her horse in front of the village hotel.

For some weeks, with motive unknown, she has been devoting herself to the study of *La lengua Americana*. Her vocabulary of English words, still scanty, is sufficient for her present purpose; which is to acquire information, not about the murder, but the man accused of committing it.

The landlord, knowing who she is, answers her inquiries with obsequious politeness.

She learns that Maurice Gerald is no longer his guest, with "full particulars of the murder," so far as known.

With a sad heart she rides back to the Hacienda Martinez. On reaching the house, she finds its tranquillity again disturbed. The new cause of excitement might have been deemed ludicrous; though it is not so regarded by the superstitious *peons*. A rare rumour has reached the place. A man without a head—*un hombre descabezado*—has been seen riding about the plains, somewhere near the Rio Nueces!

Despite its apparent absurdity, there can be no doubting the correctness of the report. It is rife throughout the settlement. But there is still surer confirmation of it. A party of Don Silvio's own people—herdsmen out in search of strayed cattle—have seen the *cavallero descabezado*; and, desisting from their search, had ridden away from him, as they would have done from the devil!

The *vaqueros*—there are three of them—are all ready to swear to the account given. But their scared looks furnish a more trustworthy evidence of its truthfulness.

The sun goes down upon a *congeries* of frightful rumours. Neither these nor the protestations of Don Silvio and his sister can prevent their capricious niece from carrying out a resolution she seems suddenly to have formed—which is, to ride back to the Rio Grande. It makes no difference to her, that a murder has been committed on the road she will have to take; much less that near it has been seen the ghastly apparition of a headless horseman! What to any other traveller should cause dismay, seems only to attract Isidora.

She even proposes making the journey *alone*! Don Silvio offers an escort—half a score of his *vaqueros*, armed to the teeth. The offer is rejected. Will she take Benito? No. She prefers journeying alone. In short, she is determined upon it.

Next morning she carries out this determination. By day-break she is in the saddle; and, in less than two hours after, riding, not upon the direct road to the Rio Grande, but along the banks of the Alamo!

Why has she thus deviated from her route? Is she straying?

She looks not like one who has lost her way. There is a sad expression upon her countenance, but not one of inquiry. Besides, her horse steps confidently forward, as if under his rider's direction, and guided by the rein.

Isidora is not straying. She has not lost her way.

Happier for her, if she had.

# 56. A Shot at the Devil

All night long the invalid lay awake; at times tranquil, at times giving way to a paroxysm of unconscious passion.

All night long the hunter sate by his bedside, and listened to his incoherent utterances.

They but confirmed two points of belief already impressed upon Zeb's mind: that Louise Poindexter was beloved; that her brother had been murdered!

The last was a belief that, under any circumstances, would have been painful to the backwoodsman. Coupled with the facts already known, it was agonising.

He thought of the quarrel—the hat—the cloak. He writhed as he contemplated the labyrinth of dark ambiguities that presented itself to his mind. Never in his life had his analytical powers been so completely baffled. He groaned as he felt their impotence.

He kept no watch upon the door. He knew that if *they* came, it would not be in the night.

Once only he went out; but that was near morning, when the light of the moon was beginning to mingle with that of the day.

He had been summoned by a sound. Tara, straying among the trees, had given utterance to a long dismal "gowl," and come running scared-like into the hut.

Extinguishing the light, Zeb stole forth, and stood listening.

There was an interruption to the nocturnal chorus; but that might have been caused by the howling of the hound? What had caused *it*?

The hunter directed his glance first upon the open lawn; then around its edge, and under the shadow of the trees.

There was nothing to be seen there, except what should be.

He raised his eyes to the cliff, that in a dark line trended along the horizon of the sky—broken at both ends by the tops of some tall trees that rose above its crest. There were about fifty paces of clear space, which he knew to be the edge of the upper plain terminating at the brow of the precipice.

The line separating the *chiaro* from the *oscuro* could be traced distinctly as in the day. A brilliant moon was beyond it. A snake could have been seen crawling along the top of the cliff.

There was nothing to be seen there.

But there was something to be heard. As Zeb stood listening there came a sound from the upper plain, that seemed to have been produced not far back from the summit of the cliff. It resembled the clinking of a horse's shoe struck against a loose stone.

So conjectured Zeb, as with open ears he listened to catch its repetition.

It was not repeated; but he soon saw what told him his conjecture was correct—a horse, stepping out from behind the treetops, and advancing along the line of the bluff. There was a man upon his back— both horse and man distinctly seen in dark *silhouette* against the clear sapphire sky.

The figure of the horse was perfect, as in the outlines of a skilfully cast medallion.

That of the man could be traced—only from the saddle to the shoulders. Below, the limbs were lost in the shadow of the animal though the sparkle of spur and stirrup told that they were there. Above, there was nothing—not even the semblance of a head!

Zeb Stump rubbed his eyes and looked; and rubbed them and looked again. It did not change the character of the apparition. If he had rubbed them fourscore times, he would have seen the same—a horseman without a head.

This very sight he saw, beyond the possibility of disbelieving— saw the horse advancing along the level line in a slow but steady pace—without footfall—without sound of any kind—as if gliding rather than walking—like the shifting scene of a cosmorama!

Not for a mere instant had he the opportunity of observing the spectral apparition; but a period long enough to enable him to note every detail—long enough to satisfy him that it could be no illusion of the eye, or in any way a deception of his senses.

Nor did it vanish abruptly from his view; but slowly and gradually: first the head of the horse; then the neck and shoulders; then the shape, half ghastly, half grotesque, of the rider; then the hind-quarters of the animal; the hips; and last of all the long tapering tail!

"Geehosophat!"

It was not surprise at the disappearance of the headless horseman that extorted this exclamation from the lips of Zeb Stump. There was nothing strange about this. The spectacle had simply passed behind the proscenium—represented by the tope of tree tops rising above the bluff.

"Geehosophat!"

Twice did the backwoodsman give utterance to this, his favourite expression of surprise; both times with an emphasis that told of an unlimited astonishment.

His looks betrayed it. Despite his undoubted courage, a shiver passed through his colossal frame; while the pallor upon his lips was perceptible through their brown priming of tobacco juice.

For some time he stood speechless, as if unable to follow up his double ejaculation.

His tongue at length returned to him.

"Dog-gone my cats!" he muttered, but in a very low tone, and with eyes still fixed upon the point where the horse's tail had been last seen. "If that ere don't whip the hul united creashun, my name ain't Zeb'lon Stump! The Irish hev been right arter all. I tho't he hed dreemt o' it in his drink. But no. He hev seed somethin'; and so hev I meself. No wonner the cuss war skeeart. I feel jest a spell shaky in my own narves beout this time. Geehosophat! what kin the durned thing be?"

"What *kin* it be?" he continued, after a period spent in silent reflection. "Dog-goned, ef I kin detarmine one way or the tother. Ef 't hed been only i' the daylight, an I ked a got a good sight on't; or eft hed been a leetle bit cloaster! Ha! Why moutn't I git cloaster to *it*? Dog-goned, ef I don't hev a try! I reck'n it won't eet me—not ef it air ole Nick; an ef it *air* him, I'll jest satersfy meself whether a bullet kin go custrut thro' his infernal karkidge 'ithout throwin' him out o' the seddle. Hyur go for a cloaster akwaintance wi' the varmint, whatsomiver it be."

So saying, the hunter stalked off through the trees—upon the path that led up to the bluff.

He had not needed to go inside for his rifle—having brought that weapon out with him, on hearing the howl of the hound.

If the headless rider was real flesh and blood—earthly and not of the other world—Zeb Stump might confidently count upon seeing him again.

When viewed from the door of the *jacalé*, he was going direct towards the ravine, that permitted passage from the higher level to the bottom lands of the Alamo. As Zeb had started to avail himself of the same path, unless the other should meantime change direction, or his tranquil pace to a trot or gallop, the backwoodsman would be at the head of the pass as soon as he.

Before starting, Zeb had made a calculation of the distance to be done, and the time to do it in.

His estimate proved correct—to a second, and an inch. As his head was brought nearly on a level with the upland plain, he saw the *shoulders* of the horseman rising above it.

Another step upward, and the body was in view. Another, and the horse was outlined against the sky, from hoof to forelock.

He stood at a halt. He was standing, as Zeb first came in sight of him. He was fronting towards the cliff, evidently intending to go down into the gorge. His rider appeared to have pulled him up as a measure of precaution; or he may have heard the hunter scrambling up the ravine; or, what was more likely, scented him.

For whatever reason, he was standing, front face to the spectator.

On seeing him thus, Zeb Stump also came to a stand. Had it been many another man, the same might have been said of his hair; and it is not to be denied, that the old hunter was at that moment, as he acknowledged himself, "a spell shaky 'beout the narves."

He was firm enough, however, to carry out the purpose that had prompted him to seek that singular interview; which was, to discover whether he had to deal with a human being, or the devil!

In an instant his rifle was at his shoulder, his eye glancing along the barrel; the sights, by the help of a brilliant moonlight, bearing upon the heart of the Headless Horseman.

In another, a bullet would have been through it; but for a thought that just then flashed across the brain of the backwoodsman.

Maybe he was about to commit *murder*?

At the thought he lowered the muzzle of his piece, and remained for a time undecided.

"It mout be a man?" muttered he, "though it don't look like it air. Thur ain't room enuf for a head under that ere Mexikin blanket, no how. Ef it be a human critter he hev got a tongue I reck'n, though he ain't much o' a head to hold it in. Hilloo stronger! Ye're out for a putty lateish ride, ain't ye? Hain't yo forgot to fetch yur head wi ye?"

There was no reply. The horse snorted, on hearing the voice. That was all.

"Lookee hyur, strenger! Ole Zeb Stump from the State o' Kintucky, air the individooal who's now speakin' to ye. He ain't one o' thet sort ter be trifled wi'. Don't try to kum none o' yer damfoolery

341

over this hyur coon. I warn ye to declur yur game. If ye're playin pos-sum, ye'd better throw up yur hand; or by the jumpin' Geehosophat, ye may lose both yur stake an yur curds! Speak out now, afore ye gits plugged wi' a piece o' lead!"

Less response than before. This time the horse, becoming accus-tomed to the voice, only tossed up his head.

"Then dog-gone ye!" shouted the hunter, exasperated by what he deemed an insulting silence. "Six seconds more—I'll gie ye six more; an ef ye don't show speech by that time, I'll let drive at yur guts. Ef ye're but a dummy it won't do ye any harm. No more will it, I reckun, ef ye *air* the devil. But ef ye're a man playin' possum, durn me ef ye don't desarve to be shot for bein' sech a damned fool. Sing out!" he continued with increasing anger, "sing out, I tell ye! Ye won't? Then hyur goes! One—two—three—four—five—six!"

Where "seven" should have come in, had the count been contin-ued, was heard the sharp crack of a rifle, followed by the sibillation of a spinning bullet; then the dull "thud" as the deadly missile buried it-self in some solid body.

The only effect produced by the shot, appeared to be the frighten-ing of the horse. The rider still kept his seat in the saddle!

It was not even certain the horse was scared. The clear neigh that responded to the detonation of the rifle, had something in it that sounded derisive!

For all that, the animal went off at a tearing gallop; leaving Zeb Stump a prey to the profoundest surprise he had ever experienced.

After discharging his rifle, he remained upon his knees, for a pe-riod of several seconds.

If his nerves were unsteady before the shot, they had become doubly so now. He was not only surprised at the result, but terrified. He was certain that his bullet had passed through the man's heart—or where it should be—as sure as if his muzzle had been held close to the ribs.

It could not be a man? He did not believe it to be one; and this thought might have reassured him, but for the behaviour of the horse. It was that wild unearthly neigh, that was now chilling his blood, and causing his limbs to shake, as if under an ague.

He would have retreated; but, for a time, he felt absolutely unable to rise to his feet; and he remained kneeling, in a sort of stupefied ter-ror—watching the weird form till it receded out of sight far off over the moonlit plain. Not till then did he recover sufficient courage, to enable him to glide back down the gorge, and on towards the *jacalé*.

And not till he was under its roof, did he feel sufficiently himself, to reflect with any calmness on the odd encounter that had occurred to him.

It was some time before his mind became disabused of the idea that he had been dealing with the devil. Reflection, however, convinced him of the improbability of this; though it gave him no clue as to what the thing really was.

"Shurly," muttered he, his conjectural form of speech showing that he was still undecided, "Shurly arter all it can't be a thing o' the tother world—else I kedn't a heern the *cothug* o' my bullet? Sartin the lead struck agin somethin' solid; an I reck'n thur's nothin' solid in the karkidge o' a ghost?"

"Wagh!" he concluded, apparently resigning the attempt to obtain a solution of the strange physical phenomenon. "Let the durned thing slide! One o' two things it air boun' to be: eyther a bunnel o' rags, or ole Harry from hell?"

As he re-entered the hut, the blue light of morning stole in along with him.

It was time to awaken Phelim, that he might take his turn by the bedside of the invalid.

The Connemara man, now thoroughly restored to sobriety, and under the impression of having been a little derelict in his duty, was ready to undertake the task.

The old hunter, before consigning his charge to the care of his unskilled successor, made a fresh dressing of the scratches—availing himself of the knowledge that a long experience had given him in the pharmacopoeia of the forest.

The *nopal* was near; and its juice inspissated into the fresh wounds would not fail to effect their speedy cure.

Zeb knew that in twenty-four hours after its application, they would be in process of healing; and in three days, entirely cicatrised.

With this confidence—common to every denizen of the cactus-covered land of Mexico—he felt defiant as to doctors; and if a score of them could have been procured upon the instant, he would not have summoned one. He was convinced that Maurice Gerald was in no danger—at least not from his wounds.

There was a danger; but that was of a different kind.

"An' now, Mister Pheelum," said he, on making a finish of his surgical operations; "we hev dud all thet kin be dud for the outard man, an it air full time to look arter the innard. Ye say thur ain't nuthin to eet?"

"Not so much as a purtaty, Misther Stump. An' what's worse thare's nothin' to dhrink—not a dhrap lift in the whole cyabin."

"Durn ye, that's *yur* fault," cried Stump, turning upon the Irishman with a savage scowl that showed equal regret at the announcement. "Eft hadn't a been for you, thur war licker enough to a lasted till the young fellur got roun' agin. What's to be dud now?"

"Sowl, Misther Stump! yez be wrongin' *me* althegither intirely. That same yez are. I hadn't a taste exciptin what came out av the little flask. It wus thim Indyins that imptied the dimmyjan. Trath was it."

"Wagh! ye cudn't a got drunk on what wur contained i' the flask. I know yur durned guts too well for thet. Ye must a had a good pull at the tother, too."

"Be all the saints—"

"Durn yur stinkin' saints! D'you s'pose any man o' sense believes in sech varmint as them?

"Wal; 'tain't no use talkin' any more beout it. Ye've sucked up the corn juice, an thur's an end o't. Thur ain't no more to be hed 'ithin twenty mile, an we must go 'ithout."

"Be Jaysus, but it's bad!"

"Shet up yur head, durn ye, an hear what I've got to say. We'll hev to go 'ithout drinkin'; but thet air no reezun for sturvin' ourselves for want o' somethin' to eet. The young fellur, I don't misdoubt, air by this time half starved hisself. Thur's not much on his stummuk, I reck'n, though thur may be on his mind. As for meself, I'm jest hungry enough to eat coyoat; an I ain't very sure I'd turn away from turkey buzzart; which, as I reck'n, wud be a wusser victual than coyoat. But we ain't obleeged to eet turkey buzzart, whar thur's a chance o' gettin' turkey; an thet ain't so dewbious along the Alamo. You stay hyur, an take care o' the young fellur, whiles I try up the crik, an see if I kin kum acrosst a gobbler."

"I'll do that, Misther Stump, an no mistake. Be me trath—"

"Keep yur palaver to yurself, till I've finished talkin' to ye."

"Sowl! I won't say a word."

"Then don't, but lissen! Thur's somethin 'bout which I don't wait ye to make any mistake. It air this. Ef there shed anybody stray this way dyurin my absince, ye'll let me know. You musn't lose a minnit o' time, but let me know."

"Shure I will—sowl, yis."

"Wal, I'll depend on ye."

"Trath, yez may;—but how Misther Stump? How am I to lit yez know, if you're beyant hearin' av me voice? How thin?"

"Wal, I reck'n, I shan't need to go so fur as thet. Thur ought to be gobblers cloast by—at this time o' the mornin'.

"An yit there moutent," continued Zeb, after reflecting a while. "Ye ain't got sech a thing as a gun in the shanty? A pistol 'ud do."

"Nayther wan nor the tother. The masther tuk both away wid him, when he went last time to the sittlements. He must have lift them thare."

"It air awk'ard. I mout *not* heer yur shout."

Zeb, who had by this time passed through the doorway, again stopped to reflect.

"Heigh!" he exclaimed, after a pause of six seconds. "I've got it. I've treed the eydee. Ye see my ole maar, tethered out thur on the grass?"

"Shure I do, Misther Stump. Av coorse I do."

"Wal, ye see thet ere prickly cacktis plant growin' cloast to the edge o' the openin'?"

"Faith, yis."

"Wal, that's sensible o' ye. Now lissen to what I say. Ye must keep a look out at the door; an ef anybody kums up whiles I'm gone, run straight custrut for the cacktis, cut off one o' its branches—the thorniest ye kin see—an stick it unner the maar's tail."

"Mother av Moses! For what div yez want me to do that?"

"Wal, I reck'n I'd better explain," said Zeb, reflectingly; "otherwise ye'll be makin' a mess o' it."

"Ye see, Pheelum, ef anybody interlopes durin' my absince I hed better be hyur. I ain't a goin' fur off. But howsomediver near, I moutn't hear yur screech; thurfore the maar's 'll do better. You clap the cacktis under her tail, cloast up to the fundament; and ef she don't squeal loud enuf to be heern by me, then ye may konklude that this coon air eyther rubbed out, or hev both his lugs plugged wi picket pins. So, Pheelum; do you adzactly as I've tolt ye."

"I'll do it, be Japers!"

"Be sure now. Yur master's life may depend upon it."

After delivering this last caution, the hunter shouldered his long rifle, and walked away from the hut.

"He's a cute owld chap that same," said Phelim as soon as Zeb was out of hearing. "I wonder what he manes by the master bein' in danger from any wan comin' to the cyabin. He sed, that his life moight depend upon it? Yis—he sed that."

"He towlt me to kape a luk out. I suppose he maned me to begin at wance. I must go to the inthrance thin."

So saying, he stepped outside the door; and proceeded to make an ocular inspection of the paths by which the *jacalé* might be approached.

After completing this, he returned to the threshold; and there took stand, in the attitude of one upon the watch.

# 57. Sounding the Signal

Phelim's vigil was of short duration. Scarce ten minutes had he been keeping it, when he became warned by the sound of a horse's hoof, that some one was coming up the creek in the direction of the hut.

His heart commenced hammering against his ribs.

The trees, standing thickly, hindered him from having a view of the approaching horseman; and he could not tell what sort of guest was about to present himself at the *jacalé*. But the hoofstroke told him there was only *one*; and this it was that excited his apprehension. He would have been less alarmed to hear the trampling of a troop. Though well assured it could no longer be his master, he had no stomach for a second interview with the cavalier who so closely resembled him—in everything except the head.

His first impulse was to rush across the lawn, and carry out the scheme entrusted to him by Zeb. But the indecision springing from his fears kept him to his place—long enough to show him that they were groundless. The strange horseman had a head.

"Shure an that same he hez," said Phelim, as the latter rode out from among the trees, and halted on the edge of the opening; "a raal hid, an a purty face in front av it. An' yit it don't show so plazed nay-ther. He luks as if he'd jist buried his grandmother. Sowl! what a quare young chap he is, wid them toiny mowstacks loike the down upon a two days' goslin'! O Lard! Luk at his little fut! *Be Jaysus, he's a woman!*"

While the Irishman was making these observations—partly in thought, partly in muttered speech—the equestrian advanced a pace or two, and again paused.

On a nearer view of his visitor, Phelim saw that he had correctly guessed the sex; though the moustache, the manner of the mount, the hat, and serapé, might for the moment have misled a keener intellect than his of Connemara.

It *was* a woman. It was Isidora.

It was the first time that Phelim had set eyes on the Mexican maiden—the first that hers had ever rested upon him. They were equally unknown to one another.

He had spoken the truth, when he said that her countenance did not display pleasure. On the contrary, the expression upon it was sad—almost disconsolate.

It had shown distrust, as she was riding under the shadow of the trees. Instead of brightening as she came out into the open ground, the look only changed to one of mingled surprise and disappointment.

Neither could have been caused by her coming within sight of the *jacalé*. She knew of its existence. It was the goal of her journey. It must have been the singular personage standing in the doorway. He was not the man she expected to see there.

In doubt she advanced to address him:

"I may have made a mistake?" said she, speaking in the best "Americana" she could command. "Pardon me, but—I—I thought—that Don Mauricio lived here."

"Dan Marryshow, yez say? Trath, no. Thare's nobody av that name lives heeur. Dan Marryshow? Thare was a man they called Marrish had a dwillin' not far out av Ballyballagh. I remimber the chap will, bekase he chated me wanst in a horse thrade. But his name wasn't Dan. No; it was Pat. Pat Marrish was the name—divil burn him for a desaver!"

"Don Mauricio—Mor-rees—Mor-ees."

"Oh! Maurice! Maybe ye'd be after spakin' av the masther—Misther Gerrald!"

"Si—Si! Señor Zyerral."

"Shure, thin, an if that's fwhat ye're afther, Misther Gerrald diz dwill in this very cyabin—that is, whin he comes to divart hisself, by chasin' the wild horses. He only kapes it for a huntin' box, ye know. Arrah, now; if yez cud only see the great big cyastle he lives in whin he's at home, in owld Ireland; an thy bewtiful crayther that's now cryin' her swate blue eyes out, bekase he won't go back thare. Sowl, if yez saw *her*!"

Despite its *patois*, Phelim's talk was too well understood by her to whom it was addressed. Jealousy is an apt translator. Something like a sigh escaped from Isidora, as he pronounced that little word "her."

"I don't wish to see *her*," was the quick rejoinder; "but him you mention. Is he at home? Is he inside?"

"Is he at home? Thare now, that's comin' to the point—straight as a poike staff. An' supposin' I wuz to say yis, fwhat ud yez be afther wantin' wid him?"

"I wish to see him."

"Div yez? Maybe now ye'll wait till yez be asked. Ye're a purty crayther, notwithstandin' that black strake upon yer lip. But the masther isn't in a condishun jist at this time to see any wan—unless it was the praste or a docthur. Yez cyant see him."

"But I wish very much to see him, señor."

"Trath div yez. Ye've sayed that alriddy. But yez cyant, I till ye. It isn't Phaylim Onale ud deny wan av the fair six—espacially a purty black-eyed colleen loike yerself. But for all that yez cyant see the masther now."

"Why can I not?"

"Why cyant yez not? Will—thare's more than wan rayzon why yez cyant. In the first place, as I've towlt you, he's not in a condishun to resave company—the liss so av its bein' a lady."

"But why, señor? Why?"

"Bekase he's not dacently drissed. He's got nothin' on him but his shirt—exceptin' the rags that Misther Stump's jist tied all roun' him. Be japers! thare's enough av them to make him a whole shoot—coat, waiscoat, and throwsers—trath is thare."

"Señor, I don't understand you."

"Yez don't? Shure an I've spoke plain enough! Don't I till ye that the masther's in bid?"

"In bed! At this hour? I hope there's nothing—"

"The matther wid him, yez wur goin' to say? Alannah, that same is there—a powerful dale the matther wid him—enough to kape him betwane the blankets for weeks to come."

"Oh, señor! Do not tell me that he is ill?"

"Don't I till ye! Arrah now me honey; fwhat ud be the use av consalin' it? It ud do it no good; nayther cyan it do him any harm to spake about it? Yez moight say it afore his face, an he won't conthradict ye."

"He *is* ill, then. O, sir, tell me, what is the nature of his illness—what has caused it?"

"Shure an I cyant answer only wan av thim interrogataries—the first yez hiv phut. His disaze pursades from some ugly tratement he's been resavin—the Lord only knows what, or who administhered it.

He's got a bad lig; an his skin luks as if he'd been tied up in a sack along wid a score av angry cats. Sowl! thare's not the brenth av yer purty little hand widout a scratch upon it. Worse than all, he's besoide hisself."

"Beside himself?"

"Yis, that same. He's ravin' loike wan that had a dhrap too much overnight, an thinks thare's the man wid the poker afther him. Be me trath, I belave the very bist thing for him now ud be a thrifle av potheen—if wan cud only lay hands upon that same. But thare's not the smell av it in the cyabin. Both the dimmy-jan an flask. Arrah, now; *you* wouldn't be afther havin' a little flask upon yer sweet silf? Some av that agwardinty, as yer people call it. Trath, I've tasted worse stuff than it. I'm shure a dhrink av it ud do the masther good. Spake the truth, misthress! Hiv yez any about ye?"

"No, señor. I have nothing of the kind. I am sorry I have not."

"Faugh! The more's the pity for poor Masther Maurice. It ud a done him a dale av good. Well; he must put up widout it."

"But, señor; surely I can see him?"

"Divil a bit. Besides fwhat ud be the use? He wudn't know ye from his great grandmother. I till yez agane, he's been badly thrated, an 's now besoide hisself!"

"All the more reason why I should see him. I may be of service. I owe him a debt—of—of—"

"Oh! yez be owin' him somethin? Yez want to pay it? Faith, that makes it intirely different. But yez needn't see *him* for that. I'm his head man, an thransact all that sort av bizness for him. I cyant write myself, but I'll give ye a resate on the crass wid me mark—which is jist as good, among the lawyers. Yis, misthress; yez may pay the money over to me, an I promise ye the masther 'll niver axe ye for it agane. Trath! it'll come handy jist now, as we're upon the ave av a flittin, an may want it. So if yez have the pewther along wid ye, thare's pins, ink, an paper insoide the cyabin. Say the word, an I'll giv ye the resate!"

"No—no—no! I did not mean money. A debt of—of—gratitude."

"Faugh! only that. Sowl, it's eezy paid, an don't want a resate. But yez needn't return that sort av money now: for the masther woudn't be sinsible av fwhat ye wur sayin. Whin he comes to his sinses, I'll till him yez hiv been heeur, and wiped out the score."

"Surely I can see him?"

"Shurely now yez cyant."

"But I must, señor!"

"Divil a must about it. I've been lift on guard, wid sthrict ordhers to lit no wan go inside."

"They couldn't have been meant for me. I am his friend—the friend of Don Mauricio."

"How is Phaylum Onale to know that? For all yer purty face, yez moight be his didliest innemy. Be Japers! its loike enough, now that I take a second luk at ye."

"I must see him—I must—I will—I shall!"

As Isidora pronounced these words, she flung herself out of the saddle, and advanced in the direction of the door.

Her air of earnest determination combined with the fierce—scarce feminine—expression upon her countenance, convinced the Galwegian, that the contingency had arrived for carrying out the instructions left by Zeb Stump, and that he had been too long neglecting his cue.

Turning hurriedly into the hut, he came out again, armed with a tomahawk; and was about to rush past, when he was brought to a sudden stand, by seeing a pistol in the hands of his lady visitor, pointed straight at his head!

"*Abajo la hacha!*" (Down with the hatchet), cried she. "*Lepero*! lift your arm to strike me, and it will be for the last time!"

"Stroike ye, misthress! Stroike *you*!" blubbered the *ci-devant* stable-boy, as soon as his terror permitted him to speak. "Mother av the Lard! I didn't mane the waypon for you at all, at all! I'll sware it on the crass—or a whole stack av Bibles if yez say so. In trath misthress; I didn't mane the tammyhauk for you!"

"Why have you brought it forth?" inquired the lady, half suspecting that she had made a mistake, and lowering her pistol as she became convinced of it. "Why have you thus armed yourself?"

"As I live, only to ixecute the ordhers, I've resaved—only to cut a branch off av the cyacktus yez see over yander, an phut it undher the tail av the owld mare. Shure yez won't object to my doin' that?"

In her turn, the lady became silent—surprised at the singular proposition.

The odd individual she saw before her, could not mean mischief. His looks, attitude, and gestures were grotesque, rather than threatening; provocative of mirth—not fear, or indignation.

"Silince gives consint. Thank ye," said Phelim, as, no longer in fear of being shot down in his tracks, he ran straight across the lawn, and carried out to the letter, the parting injunctions of Zeb Stump.

The Mexican maiden hitherto held silent by surprise, remained so, on perceiving the absolute idleness of speech.

Further conversation was out of the question. What with the screaming of the mare—continuous from the moment the spinous crupper was inserted under her tail—the loud trampling of her hoofs as she "cavorted" over the turf—the dismal howling of the hound—and the responsive cries of the wild forest denizens—birds, beasts, insects, and reptiles—only the voice of a Stentor could have been heard!

What could be the purpose of the strange proceeding? How was it to terminate?

Isidora looked on in silent astonishment. She could do nothing else. So long as the infernal fracas continued, there was no chance to elicit an explanation from the queer creature who had caused it.

He had returned to the door of the jacalé; and once more taken his stand upon the threshold; where he stood, with the tranquil satisfied air of an actor who has completed the performance of his part in the play, and feels free to range himself among the spectator.

# 58. Recoiling from a Kiss

For full ten minutes was the wild chorus kept up, the mare all the time squealing like a stuck pig; while the dog responded in a series of lugubrious howls, that reverberated along the cliffs on both sides of the creek.

To the distance of a mile might the sounds have been heard; and as Zeb Stump was not likely to be so far from the hut, he would be certain to hear them.

Convinced of this, and that the hunter would soon respond to the signal he had himself arranged, Phelim stood square upon the threshold, in hopes that the lady visitor would stay outside—at least, until he should be relieved of the responsibility of admitting her.

Notwithstanding her earnest protestations of amity, he was still suspicious of some treasonable intention towards his master; else why should Zeb have been so particular about being summoned back?

Of himself, he had abandoned the idea of offering resistance. That shining pistol, still before his eyes, had cured him of all inclination for a quarrel with the strange equestrian; and so far as the Connemara man was concerned, she might have gone unresisted inside.

But there was another from Connemara, who appeared more determined to dispute her passage to the hut—one whom a whole battery of great guns would not have deterred from protecting its owner. This was Tara.

The staghound was not acting as if under the excitement of a mere senseless alarm. Mingling with his prolonged sonorous "gowl" could be heard in repeated interruptions a quick sharp bark, that denoted anger. He had witnessed the attitude of the intruder—its apparent hostility—and drawing his deductions, had taken stand directly in front of Phelim and the door, with the evident determination that neither should be reached except over his own body, and after running the gauntlet of his formidable incisors.

Isidora showed no intention of undertaking the risk. She had none. Astonishment was, for the time, the sole feeling that possessed her.

She remained transfixed to the spot, without attempting to say a word.

She stood expectingly. To such an eccentric prelude there should be a corresponding *finale*. Perplexed, but patiently, she awaited it.

Of her late alarm there was nothing left. What she saw was too ludicrous to allow of apprehension; though it was also too incomprehensible to elicit laughter.

In the mien of the man, who had so oddly comported himself, there was no sign of mirth. If anything, a show of seriousness, oddly contrasting with the comical act he had committed; and which plainly proclaimed that he had not been treating her to a joke.

The expression of helpless perplexity that had become fixed upon her features, continued there; until a tall man, wearing a faded blanket coat, and carrying a six-foot rifle, was seen striding among the tree-trunks, at the rate of ten miles to the hour. He was making direct for the *jacalé*.

At sight of the new-comer her countenance underwent a change. There was now perceptible upon it a shade of apprehension; and the little pistol was clutched with renewed nerve by the delicate hand that still continued to hold it.

The act was partly precautionary, partly mechanical. Nor was it unnatural, in view of the formidable-looking personage who was approaching, and the earnest excited manner with which he was hurrying forward to the hut.

All this became altered, as he advanced into the open ground, and suddenly stopped on its edge; a look of surprise quite as great as that upon the countenance of the lady, supplanting his earnest glances.

Some exclamatory phrases were sent through his teeth, unintelligible in the tumult still continuing, though the gesture that accompanied them seemed to proclaim them of a character anything but gentle.

On giving utterance to them, he turned to one side; strode rapidly towards the screaming mare; and, laying hold of her tail—which no living man save himself would have dared to do—he released her from the torments she had been so long enduring.

Silence was instantly restored; since the mare, abandoned by her fellow choristers, as they became accustomed to her wild neighs, had been, for some time, keeping up the solo by herself.

The lady was not yet enlightened. Her astonishment continued; though a side glance given to the droll individual in the doorway told her, that he had successfully accomplished some scheme with which he had been entrusted.

Phelim's look of satisfaction was of short continuance. It vanished, as Zeb Stump, having effected the deliverance of the tortured quadruped, faced round to the hut—as he did so, showing a cloud upon the corrugations of his countenance, darkly ominous of an angry storm.

Even the presence of beauty did not hinder it from bursting. "Durn, an dog-gone ye, for a Irish eedyit! Air this what ye've brought me back for! An' jest as I wur takin' sight on a turkey, not less 'n thirty poun' weight, I reck'n; skeeart afore he ked touch trigger, wi' the skreek o' thet cussed critter o' a maar. Damned little chance for breakfust now."

"But, Misther Stump, didn't yez till me to do it? Ye sid if any wan showld come to the cyabin—"

"Bah! ye fool! Ye don't serpose I meened weemen, did ye?"

"Trath! I didn't think it wus wan, whin she furst presented hersilf. Yez showld a seen the way she rid up—sittin' astraddle on her horse."

"What matter it, how she wur sittin'! Hain't ye seed thet afore, ye greenhorn? It's thur usooal way 'mong these hyur Mexikin sheemales. Ye're more o' a woman than she air, I guess; an twenty times more o' a fool. Thet I'm sartint o'. I know *her* a leetle by sight, an somethin' more by reeport. What hev fetched the critter hyur ain't so difeequilt to comprehend; tho' it may be to git it out o' her, seein' as she kin only talk thet thur Mexikin lingo; the which this chile can't, nor wudn't ef he kud."

"Sowl, Misther Stump! yez be mistaken. She spakes English too. Don't yez, misthress?"

"Little Inglees," returned the Mexican, who up to this time had remained listening. "Inglees *poco pocito*."

"O—ah!" exclaimed Zeb, slightly abashed at what he had been saying. "I beg your pardin, saynoritta. Ye kin *habla* a bit o' Amerikin, kin ye? *Moocho bono*—so much the betterer. Ye'll be able to tell me what ye mout be a wantin' out hyur. Ye hain't lost yur way, hev ye?"

"No, señor," was the reply, after a pause. "In that case, ye know whar ye air?"

"*Si, señor—si*—yes, of Don Mauricio Zyerral, this the—house?"

355

"Thet air the name, near as a Mexikin mouth kin make it, I reck'n. 'Tain't much o' a house; but it air his'n. Preehaps ye want to see the master o't?"

"O, señor—yees—that is for why I here am—*por esta yo soy aqui*."

"Wal; I reck'n, thur kin be no objecshun to yur seein' him. Yur intenshuns ain't noways hostile to the young fellur, I kalklate. But thur ain't much good in yur talkin' to him now. He won't know yo from a side o' sole-leather."

"He is ill? Has met with some misfortune? *El güero* has said so."

"Yis. I towlt her that," interposed Phelim, whose carroty hair had earned for him the appellation "El güero."

"Sartin," answered Zeb. "He air wounded a bit; an jest now a leetle dulleerious. I reck'n it ain't o' much consekwence. He'll be hisself agin soon's the ravin' fit's gone off o' him."

"O, sir! can I be his nurse till then? *Por amor dios*! Let me enter, and watch over him? I am his friend—*un amigo muy afficionado*."

"Wal; I don't see as thur's any harm in it. Weemen makes the best o' nusses I've heern say; tho', for meself, I hain't hed much chance o' tryin' 'em, sincst I kivered up my ole gurl unner the sods o' Massissipi. Ef ye want to take a spell by the side o' the young fellur, ye're wilkim—seein' ye're his friend. Ye kin look arter him, till we git back, an see thet he don't tummel out o' the bed, or claw off them thur bandidges, I've tied roun him."

"Trust me, good sir, I shall take every care of him. But tell me what has caused it? The Indians? No, they are not near? Has there been a quarrel with any one?"

"In thet, saynoritta; ye're beout as wise as I air meself. Thur's been a quarrel wi' coyeats; but that ain't what's gin him the ugly knee. I foun' him yesterday, clost upon sun-down, in the chapparal beyont. When we kim upon him, he war up to his waist in the water o' a crik as runs through thur, jest beout to be attakted by one o' them spotty critters yur people call tigers. Wal, I relieved him o' that bit o' danger; but what happened afore air a mystery to me. The young fellur had tuk leeve o' his senses, an ked gie no account o' hisself. He hain't rekivered them yet; an', thurfore, we must wait till he do."

"But you are sure, sir, he is not badly injured? His wounds—they are not dangerous?"

"No danger whatsomediver. Nuthin' beyont a bit o' a fever, or maybe a touch o' the agey, when that goes off o' him. As for the wounds, they're only a wheen o' scratches. When the wanderin' hev

356

gone out o' his senses, he'll soon kum roun, I reck'n. In a week's time, ye'll see him as strong as a buck."

"Oh! I shall nurse him tenderly!"

"Wal, that's very kind o' you; but—but—"

Zeb hesitated, as a queer thought came before his mind. It led to a train of reflections kept to himself. They were these:

"This air the same she, as sent them kickshaws to the tavern o' Rough an Ready. Thet she air in love wi' the young fellur is clur as Massissipi mud—in love wi' him to the eends o' her toe nails. So's the tother. But it air equally clur that he's thinkin' o' the tother, an not o' her. Now ef she hears him talk about tother, as he hev been a doin' all o' the night, thur'll be a putty consid'able rumpus riz inside o' her busom. Poor thing! I pity her. She ain't a bad sort. But the Irish—Irish tho' he be—can't belong to both; an I *know* he freezes to the critter from the States. It air durned awkurd—Better ef I ked pursuade her not to go near him—leastwise till he gets over ravin' about Lewaze.

"But, miss," he continued, addressing himself to the Mexican, who during his long string of reflections had stood impatiently silent, "don't ye think ye'd better ride home agin; an kum back to see him arter he gits well. He won't know ye, as I've sayed; an it would be no use yur stayin', since he ain't in any danger o' makin' a die of it."

"No matter, that he may not know me. I should tend him all the same. He may need some things—which I can send, and procure for him."

"Ef ye're boun' to stay then," rejoined Zeb, relentingly, as if some new thought was causing him to consent, "I won't interfere to say, no. But don't you mind what he'll be palaverin' about. Ye may hear some queer talk out o' him, beout a man bein' murdered, an the like. That's natral for any one as is dulleerious. Don't be skeeart at it. Beside, ye may hear him talkin' a deal about a woman, as he's got upon his mind."

"A woman!"

"Jest so. Ye'll hear him make mention o' her name."

"Her name! Señor, what name?"

"Wal, it air the name o' his sister, I reck'n. Fact, I'm sure o' it bein' his sister."

"Oh! Misther Stump. If yez be spakin' av Masther Maurice—"

"Shut up, ye durned fool! What is't to you what I'm speakin' beout? You can't unnerstan sech things. Kum along!" he continued, moving off, and motioning the Connemara man to follow him. "I want ye a leetle way wi' me. I killed a rattle as I wur goin' up the crik, an

357

left it thur. Kum you, an toat it back to the shanty hyur, lest some varmint may make away wi' it; an lest, arter all, I moutn't strike turkey
agin."

"A rattle. Div yez mane a rattle-snake?"

"An' what shed I mean?"

"Shure, Misther Stump, yez wudn't ate a snake. Lard! wudn't it
poison yez?"

"Pisen be durned! Didn't I cut the pisen out, soon 's I killed the
critter, by cuttin' off o' its head?"

"Trath! an for all that, I wudn't ate a morsel av it, if I was
starvin'."

"Sturve, an be durned to ye! Who axes ye to eet it. I only want ye
to toat it home. Kum then, an do as I tell ye; or dog-goned, ef I don't
make ye eet the head o' the reptile,—pisen, fangs an all!"

"Be japers, Misther Stump, I didn't mane to disobey you at all—
at all. Shure it's Phaylim O'Nale that's reddy to do your biddin' anyhow. I'm wid ye for fwhativer yez want; aven to swallowin the snake
whole. Saint Pathrick forgive me!"

"Saint Patrick be durned! Kum along!"

Phelim made no farther remonstrance; but, striking into the tracks
of the backwoodsman, followed him through the wood.

---

Isidora entered the hut; advanced towards the invalid reclining
upon his couch; with fierce fondness kissed his fevered brow, fonder
and fiercer kissed his unconscious lips; and then recoiled from them,
as if she had been stung by a scorpion!

Worse than scorpion's sting was that which had caused her to
spring back.

And yet 'twas but a word—a little word—of only two syllables!

There was nothing strange in this. Oft, on one word—that soft
short syllabic "Yes"—rests the happiness of a life; while oft, too oft,
the harsher negative is the prelude to a world of war!

---

# 59. Another Who Cannot Rest

A dark day for Louise Poindexter—perhaps the darkest in the calendar of her life—was that in which she released Don Miguel Diaz from the lazo.

Sorrow for a brother's loss, with fears for a lover's safety, were yesterday commingled in the cup. To-day it was further embittered by the blackest passion of all—jealousy. Grief—fear—jealousy—what must be the state of the soul in which these emotions are co-existent? A tumult of terrible imaginings.

So was it in the bosom of Louise Poindexter after deciphering the epistle which contained written evidence of her lover's disloyalty.

True, the writing came not from him; nor was the proof conclusive.

But in the first burst of her frenzied rage, the young Creole did not reason thus. In the wording of the letter there was strong presumption, that the relationship between Maurice Gerald and the Mexican was of a more affectionate character than he had represented it to be—that he had, in fact, been practising a deception.

Why should *that* woman write to him in such free strain—giving bold, almost unfeminine, licence to her admiration of his eyes: "*Essos ojos tan lindos y tan espresivos?*"

These were no phrases of friendship; but the expressions of a prurient passion. As such only could the Creole understand them: since they were but a paraphrase of her own feelings.

And then there was the appointment itself—solicited, it is true, in the shape of a request. But this was mere courtesy—the coquetry of an accomplished *maîtresse*. Moreover, the tone of solicitation was abandoned towards the close of the epistle; which terminated in a positive command: "Come, sir! come!"

Something more than jealousy was aroused by the reading of this. A spirit of revenge seemed to dictate the gesture that followed,—and the stray sheet was crushed between the aristocratic fingers into which it had fallen.

"Ah, me!" reflected she, in the acerbity of her soul, "I see it all now. 'Tis not the first time he has answered a similar summons; not the first they have met on that same ground, 'the hill above my uncle's house'—slightly described, but well understood—oft visited before."

Soon the spirit of vengeance gave place to a profound despair. Her heart had its emblem in the piece of paper that lay at her feet upon the floor—like it, crushed and ruined.

For a time she surrendered herself to sad meditation. Wild emotions passed through her mind, suggesting wild resolves. Among others she thought of her beloved Louisiana—of going back there to bury her secret sorrow in the cloisters of the *Sacré Coeur*. Had the Creole convent been near, in that hour of deep despondency, she would, in all probability, have forsaken the paternal home, and sought an asylum within its sacred walls. In very truth was it the darkest day of her existence. After long hours of wretchedness her spirit became calmer, while her thoughts returned to a more rational tone. The letter was re-read; its contents submitted to careful consideration.

There was still a hope—the hope that, after all, Maurice Gerald might *not* be in the Settlement.

It was at best but a faint ray. Surely *she* should know—she who had penned the appointment, and spoken so confidently of his keeping it? Still, as promised, he might have gone away; and upon this supposition hinged that hope, now scintillating like a star through the obscurity of the hour.

It was a delicate matter to make direct inquiries about—to one in the position of Louise Poindexter. But no other course appeared open to her; and as the shadows of twilight shrouded the grass-covered square of the village, she was seen upon her spotted palfrey, riding silently through the streets, and reining up in front of the hotel—on the same spot occupied but a few hours before by the grey steed of Isidora!

As the men of the place were all absent—some on the track of the assassin, others upon the trail of the Comanche, Oberdoffer was the only witness of her indiscretion. But he knew it not as such. It was but natural that the sister of the murdered man should be anxious to obtain news; and so did he construe the motive for the interrogatories addressed to him.

Little did the stolid German suspect the satisfaction which his answers at first gave to his fair questioner; much less the chagrin afterwards caused by that bit of information volunteered by himself, and which abruptly terminated the dialogue between him and his visitor.

On hearing she was not the first of her sex who had that day made inquiries respecting Maurice the mustanger, Louise Poindexter rode back to Casa del Corvo, with a heart writhing under fresh laceration.

A night was spent in the agony of unrest—sleep only obtained in short snatches, and amidst the phantasmagoria of dreamland.

Though the morning restored not her tranquillity, it brought with it a resolve, stern, daring, almost reckless.

It was, at least, daring, for Louise Poindexter to ride to the Alamo alone; and this was her determination.

There was no one to stay her—none to say nay. The searchers out all night had not yet returned. No report had come back to Casa del Corvo. She was sole mistress of the mansion, as of her actions—sole possessor of the motive that was impelling her to this bold step.

But it may be easily guessed. Hers was not a spirit to put up with mere suspicion. Even love, that tames the strongest, had not yet reduced it to that state of helpless submission. Unsatisfied it could no longer exist; and hence her resolve to seek satisfaction.

She might find peace—she might chance upon ruin. Even the last appeared preferable to the agony of uncertainty.

How like to the reasoning of her rival!

It would have been idle to dissuade her, had there been any one to do it. It is doubtful even if parental authority could at that moment have prevented her from carrying out her purpose. Talk to the tigress when frenzied by a similar feeling. With a love unhallowed, the will of the Egyptian queen was not more imperious than is that of the American Creole, when stirred by its holiest passion. It acknowledges no right of contradiction—regards no obstruction save death.

It is a spirit rare upon earth. In its tranquil state, soft as the rays of the Aurora—pure as the prayer of a child; but when stirred by love,—or rather by its too constant concomitant—it becomes proud and perilous as the light of Lucifer!

Of this spirit Louise Poindexter was the truest type. Where love was the lure, to wish was to have, or perish in the attempt to obtain. Jealousy resting upon doubt was neither possible to her nature, or compatible with her existence. She must find proofs to destroy, or confirm it—proofs stronger than those already supplied by the contents of the strayed epistle, which, after all, were only presumptive.

Armed with this, she was in a position to seek them; and they were to be sought upon the Alamo.

---

The first hour of sunrise saw her in the saddle, riding out from the enclosures of Casa del Corvo, and taking a trail across the prairie already known to her.

On passing many a spot, endeared to her—sacred by some of the sweetest souvenirs of her life—her thoughts experienced more than one revulsion.

These were moments when she forgot the motive that originally impelled her to the journey—when she thought only of reaching the man she loved, to rescue him from enemies that might be around him!

Ah! these moments—despite the apprehension for her lover's safety—were happy, when compared with those devoted to the far more painful contemplation of his treachery.

From the point of starting to that of her destination, it was twenty miles. It might seem a journey, to one used to European travelling—that is in the saddle. To the prairie equestrian it is a ride of scarce two hours—quick as a scurry across country, after a stag or fox.

Even with an unwilling steed it is not tedious; but with that lithe-limbed, ocellated creature, Luna, who went willingly towards her prairie home, it was soon over—too soon, perhaps, for the happiness of her rider.

Wretched as Louise Poindexter may have felt before, her misery had scarce reached the point of despair. Through her sadness there still shone a scintillation of hope.

It was extinguished as she set foot upon the threshold of the *jacalé*; and the quick suppressed scream that came from her lips, was like the last utterance of a heart parting in twain.

*There was a woman within the hut*!

From the lips of this woman an exclamation had already escaped, to which her own might have appeared an echo—so closely did the one follow the other—so alike were they in anguish.

Like a second echo, still more intensified, was the cry from Isidora; as turning, she saw in the doorway that woman, whose name had just been pronounced—the "Louise" so fervently praised, so fondly remembered, amidst the vagaries of a distempered brain.

To the young Creole the case was clear—painfully clear. She saw before her the writer of that letter of appointment—which, after all, *had been kept*. In the strife, whose sounds had indistinctly reached her, there may have been a third party—Maurice Gerald? That would account for the condition in which she now saw him; for she was far enough inside the hut to have a view of the invalid upon his couch.

Yes; it was the writer of that bold epistle, who had called Maurice Gerald "querido;"—who had praised his eyes—who had commanded him to come to her side; and who was now by his side, tending him with a solicitude that proclaimed her his! Ah! the thought was too painful to be symbolised in speech.

Equally clear were the conclusions of Isidora—equally agonising. She already knew that she was supplanted. She had been listening too long to the involuntary speeches that told her so, to have any doubt as to their sincerity. On the door-step stood the woman who had succeeded her!

Face to face, with flashing eyes, their bosoms rising and falling as if under one impulse—both distraught with the same dire thought—the two stood eyeing each other.

Alike in love with the same man—alike jealous—they were alongside the object of their burning passion unconscious of the presence of either!

Each believed the other successful: for Louise had not heard the words, that would have given her comfort—those words yet ringing in the ears, and torturing the soul, of Isidora!

It was an attitude of silent hostility—all the more terrible for its silence. Not a word was exchanged between them. Neither deigned to ask explanation of the other; neither needed it. There are occasions when speech is superfluous, and both intuitively felt that this was one. It was a mutual encounter of fell passions; that found expression only in the flashing of eyes, and the scornful curling of lips.

Only for an instant was the attitude kept up. In fact, the whole scene, inside, scarce occupied a score of seconds.

It ended by Louise Poindexter turning round upon the doorstep, and gliding off to regain her saddle. The hut of Maurice Gerald was no place for her!

Isidora too came out, almost treading upon the skirt of the other's dress. The same thought was in her heart—perhaps more emphatically felt. The hut of Maurice Gerald was no place for her!

Both seemed equally intent on departure—alike resolved on forsaking the spot, that had witnessed the desolation of their hearts.

The grey horse stood nearest—the mustang farther out. Isidora was the first to mount—the first to move off; but as she passed, her rival had also got into the saddle, and was holding the ready rein.

Glances were again interchanged—neither triumphant, but neither expressing forgiveness. That of the Creole was a strange mixture of sadness, anger, and surprise; while the last look of Isidora, that accompanied a spiteful *"carajo!"*—a fearful phrase from female lips—was such as the Ephesian goddess may have given to Athenaia, after the award of the apple.

# 60. A Fair Informer

If things physical may be compared with things moral, no greater contrast could have been found, than the bright heavens beaming over the Alamo, and the black thoughts in the bosom of Isidora, as she hastened away from the *jacalé*. Her heart was a focus of fiery passions, revenge predominating over all.

In this there was a sort of demoniac pleasure, that hindered her from giving way to despair; otherwise she might have sunk under the weight of her woe.

With gloomy thoughts she rides under the shadow of the trees. They are not less gloomy, as she gazes up the gorge, and sees the blue sky smiling cheerfully above her. Its cheerfulness seems meant but to mock her!

She pauses before making the ascent. She has reined up under the umbrageous cypress—fit canopy for a sorrowing heart. Its sombre shade appears more desirable than the sunlight above.

It is not this that has caused her to pull up. There is a thought in her soul darker than the shadow of the cypress. It is evinced by her clouded brow; by her black eyebrows contracted over her black flashing eyes; above all, by an expression of fierceness in the contrast of her white teeth gleaming under the moustached lip.

All that is good of woman, except beauty, seems to have forsaken—all that is bad, except ugliness, to have taken possession of her!

She has paused at the prompting of a demon—with an infernal purpose half formed in her mind. Her muttered speeches proclaim it. "I should have killed her upon the spot! Shall I go back, and dare her to deadly strife?"

"If I killed her, what would it avail? It could not win me back *his* heart—lost, lost, without hope! Yes; those words were from the secret depths of his soul; where her image alone has found an abiding place! Oh! there is no hope for me!

"'Tis he who should die; he who has caused my ruin. If I kill him? Ah, then; what would life be to me? Prom that hour an endless anguish!

"Oh! it is anguish now! I cannot endure it. I can think of no solace—if not in revenge. Not only she, he also—both must die!

"But not yet—not till he know, by whose hand it is done. Oh! he shall feel his punishment, and know whence it comes. Mother of God, strengthen me to take vengeance!"

She lances the flank of her horse, and spurs him, up the slope of the ravine.

On reaching the upper plain, she does not stop—even for the animal to breathe itself—but goes on at a reckless gait, and in a direction that appears undetermined. Neither hand nor voice are exerted in the guidance of her steed—only the spur to urge him on.

Left to himself, he returns in the track by which he came. It leads to the Leona. Is it the way he is wanted to go?

His rider seems neither to know nor care. She sits in the saddle, as though she were part of it; with head bent down, in the attitude of one absorbed in a profound reverie, unconscious of outward things—even of the rude pace at which she is riding! She does not observe that black cohort close by; until warned of its proximity by the snorting of her steed, that suddenly comes to a stand.

She sees a *caballada* out upon the open prairie!

Indians? No. White men—less by their colour, than the caparison of their horses, and their style of equitation. Their beards, too, show it; but not their skins, discoloured by the "stoor" of the parched plain.

"*Los Tejanos*!" is the muttered exclamation, as she becomes confirmed in regard to their nationality.

"A troop of their *rangers* scouring the country for Comanches, I suppose? The Indians are not here? If I've heard aright at the Settlement, they should be far on the other side."

Without any strong reason for shunning them, the Mexican maiden has no desire to encounter "Los Tejanos." They are nothing to her, or her purposes; and, at any other time, she would not go out of their way. But in this hour of her wretchedness, she does not wish to run the gauntlet of their questionings, nor become the butt of their curiosity.

It is possible to avoid them. She is yet among the bushes. They do not appear to have observed her. By turning short round, and diving back into the chapparal, she may yet shun being seen.

She is about to do so, when the design is frustrated by the neighing of her horse. A score of theirs respond to him; and he is seen, along with his rider.

It might be still possible for her to escape the encounter, if so inclined. She would be certain of being pursued, but not so sure of being overtaken—especially among the winding ways of the chapparal, well known to her.

At first she *is* so inclined; and completes the turning of her steed. Almost in the same instant, she reins round again; and faces the phalanx of horsemen, already in full gallop towards her.

Her muttered words proclaim a purpose in this sudden change of tactics.

"Rangers—no! Too well dressed for those ragged *vagabundos*? Must be the party of 'searchers,' of which I've heard—led by the father of—Yes—yes it is they. *Ay Dios*! here is a chance of revenge, and without my seeking it; God wills it to be so!"

Instead of turning back among the bushes, she rides out into the open ground; and with an air of bold determination advances towards the horsemen, now near.

She pulls up, and awaits their approach; a black thought in her bosom.

In another minute she is in their midst—the mounted circle close drawn around her.

There are a hundred horsemen, oddly armed, grotesquely attired—uniform only in the coating of clay-coloured dust which adheres to their habiliments, and the stern seriousness observable in the bearing of all; scarce relieved by a slight show of curiosity.

Though it is an *entourage* to cause trembling—especially in a woman—Isidora does not betray it. She is not in the least alarmed. She anticipates no danger from those who have so unceremoniously surrounded her. Some of them she knows by sight; though not the man of more than middle age, who appears to be their leader, and who confronts, to question her.

But she knows him otherwise. Instinct tells her he is the father of the murdered man—of the woman, she may wish to gee slain, but assuredly, shamed. Oh! what an opportunity!

"Can you speak French, mademoiselle?" asks Woodley Poindexter, addressing her in this tongue—in the belief that it may give him a better chance of being understood. "Speak better Inglees—very little, sir."

"Oh! English. So much the better for us. Tell me, miss; have you seen anybody out here—that is—have you met any one, riding about, or camped, or halted anywhere?"

Isidora appears to reflect, or hesitate, before making reply.

The planter pursues the interrogative, with such politeness as the circumstances admit.

"May I ask where you live?"

"On the Rio Grande, señor?"

"Have you come direct from there?"

"No; from the Leona."

"From the Leona!"

"It's the niece of old Martinez," interposes one of the party. "His plantation joins yours, Mister Poindexter."

"Si—yes—true that. *Sobrina*—niece of Don Silvio Martinez. *Yo soy*."

"Then you've come from his place, direct? Pardon me for appearing rude. I assure you, miss, we are not questioning you out of any idle curiosity, or impertinence. We have serious reasons—more than serious: they are solemn."

"From the Hacienda Martinez direct," answers Isidora, without appearing to notice the last remark. "Two hours ago—*un pocito mas*—my uncle's house I leave."

"Then, no doubt, you have heard that there has been a—murder—committed?"

"Si, señor. Yesterday at uncle Silvio's it was told."

"But to-day—when you left—was there any fresh news in the Settlement? We've had word from there; but not so late as you may bring. Have you heard anything, miss?"

"That people were gone after the *asesinado*. Your party, señor?"

"Yes—yes—it meant us, no doubt. You heard nothing more?"

"Oh, yes; something very strange, señores; so strange, you may think I am jesting."

"What is it?" inquire a score of voices in quick simultaneity; while the eyes of all turn with eager interest towards the fair equestrian.

"There is a story of one being seen without a head—on horseback—out here too. *Valga me Dios*! we must now be near the place? It was by the Nueces—not far from the ford—where the road crosses for the Rio Grande. So the vaqueros said."

"Oh; some vaqueros have seen it?"

"Si, señores; three of them will swear to having witnessed the spectacle."

Isidora is a little surprised at the moderate excitement which such a strange story causes among the "Tejanos." There is an exhibition of interest, but no astonishment. A voice explains:

"We've seen it too—that headless horseman—at a distance. Did your vaqueros get close enough to know what it was?"

"*Santissima*! no."

"Can *you* tell us, miss?"

"I? Not I. I only heard of it, as I've said. What it may be, *quien sabe*?"

There is an interval of silence, during which all appear to reflect on what they have heard.

The planter interrupts it, by a recurrence to his original interrogatory.

"Have you met, or seen, any one, miss—out here, I mean?"

"Si—yes—I have."

"You have! What sort of person? Be good enough to describe—"

"A lady."

"Lady!" echo several voices.

"Si, señores."

"What sort of a lady?"

"Una Americana."

"An American lady!—out here? Alone?"

"Si, señores."

"Who?"

"*Quien sabe*?"

"You don't know her? What was she like?"

"Like?—like?"

"Yes; how was she dressed?"

"*Vestido de caballo.*"

"On horseback, then?"

"On horseback."

"Where did you meet the lady you speak of?"

"Not far from this; only on the other side of the chapparal."

"Which way was she going? Is there any house on the other side?"

"A *jacalé*. I only know of that."

Poindexter to one of the party, who understands Spanish: "*A jacalé*?"

"They give that name to their shanties."

"To whom does it belong—this *jacalé*?"

"*Don Mauricio, el musteñero.*"

"Maurice the mustanger!" translates the ready interpreter.

A murmur of mutual congratulation runs through the crowd. After two days of searching—fruitless, as earnest—they have struck a trail,—the trail of the murderer!

Those who have alighted spring back into their saddles. All take up their reins, ready to ride on.

"We don't wish to be rude, Miss Martinez—if that be your name; but you must guide us to this place you speak of."

"It takes me a little out of my way—though not far. Come on, cavalleros! I shall show you, if you are determined on going there."

Isidora re-crosses the belt of chapparal—followed by the hundred horsemen, who ride stragglingly after her.

She halts on its western edge; between which and the Alamo there is a stretch of open prairie.

"Yonder!" says she, pointing over the plain; "you see that black spot on the horizon? It is the top of an *alhuehuete*. Its roots are in the bottom lands of the Alamo. Go there! There is a cañon leading down the cliff. Descend. You will find, a little beyond, the *jacalé* of which I've told you."

The searchers are too much in earnest to stay for further directions. Almost forgetting her who has given them, they spur off across the plain, riding straight for the cypress.

One of the party alone lingers—not the leader, but a man equally interested in all that has transpired. Perhaps more so, in what has been said in relation to the lady seen by Isidora. He is one who knows Isidora's language, as well as his own native tongue.

"Tell me, *niña*," says he, bringing his horse alongside hers, and speaking in a tone of solicitude—almost of entreaty—"Did you take notice of the horse ridden by this lady?"

"*Carrambo*! yes. What a question, cavallero! Who could help noticing it?"

"The colour?" gasps the inquirer.

"*Un musteño pintojo.*"

"A spotted mustang! Holy Heaven!" exclaims Cassius Calhoun, in a half shriek, half groan, as he gallops after the searchers—leaving Isidora in the belief, that, besides her own, there is one other heart burning with that fierce fire which only death can extinguish!

# 61. Angels on Earth

The retreat of her rival—quick and unexpected—held Louise Poindexter, as if spell-bound. She had climbed into the saddle, and was seated, with spur ready to pierce the flanks of the fair Luna. But the stroke was suspended, and she remained in a state of indecision—bewildered by what she saw.

But the moment before she had looked into the *jacalé*—had seen her rival there, apparently at home; mistress both of the mansion and its owner.

What was she to think of that sudden desertion? Why that took of spiteful hatred? Why not the imperious confidence, that should spring from a knowledge of possession?

In place of giving displeasure, Isidora's looks and actions had caused her a secret gratification. Instead of galloping after, or going in any direction, Louise Poindexter once more slipped down from her saddle, and re-entered the hut.

At sight of the pallid cheeks and wild rolling eyes, the young Creole for the moment forgot her wrongs.

"*Mon dieu! Mon dieu!*" she cried, gliding up to the *catré*. "Maurice—wounded—dying! Who has done this?"

There was no reply: only the mutterings of a madman.

"Maurice! Maurice! speak to me! Do you not know me? Louise! Your Louise! You have called me so? Say it—O say it again!"

"Ah! you are very beautiful, you angels here in heaven! Very beautiful. Yes, yes; you look so—to the eyes—to the eyes. But don't say there are none like you upon the Earth; for there are—there are. I know one—ah! more—but one that excels you all, you angels in heaven! I mean in beauty—in goodness, that's another thing. I'm not thinking of goodness—no; no."

"Maurice, dear Maurice! Why do you talk thus? You are not in heaven; you are here with me—with Louise."

"I *am* in heaven; yes, in heaven! I don't wish it, for all they say; that is, unless I can have *her* with me. It may be a pleasant place. Not without her. If she were here, I could be content. Hear it, ye angels, that come hovering around me! Very beautiful, you are, I admit; but none of you like her—her—my angel. Oh! there's a devil, too; a beautiful devil—I don't mean that. I'm thinking only of the angel of the prairies."

"Do you remember her name?"

Perhaps never was question put to a delirious man, where the questioner showed so much interest in the answer.

She bent over him with ears upon the strain—with eyes that marked every movement of his lips.

"Name? name? Did some one say, name? Have you any names here? Oh! I remember—Michael, Gabriel, Azrael—men, all men. Angels, not like my angel—who is a woman. Her name is—"

"Is?"

"Louise—Louise—Louise. Why should I conceal it from you— you up here, who know everything that's down there? Surely you know her—Louise? You should: you could not help loving her—ah! with all your hearts, as I with all mine—all—all!"

Not when these last words were once before spoken—first spoken under the shade of the acacia trees—the speaker in full consciousness of intellect—in the full fervour of his soul—not then were they listened to with such delight. O, happy hour for her who heard them!

Again were soft kisses lavished upon that fevered brow—upon those wan lips; but this time by one who had no need to recoil after the contact.

She only stood up erect—triumphant;—her hand pressing upon her heart, to stay its wild pulsations. It was pleasure too complete, too ecstatic: for there was pain in the thought that it cannot be felt for ever—in the fear of its being too soon interrupted.

The last was but the shadow thrown before, and in such shape it appeared—a shadow that camp darkling through the doorway.

The substance that followed was a man; who, the moment after, was seen standing upon the stoup.

There was nothing terrible in the aspect of the new-comer. On the contrary, his countenance and costume were types of the comical, heightened by contrast with the wild associations of the time and place. Still further, from juxtaposition with the odd objects carried in his hands; in one a tomahawk; in the other a huge snake; with its tail terminating in a string of bead-like rattles, that betrayed its species.

If anything could have added to his air of grotesque drollery, it was the expression of puzzled surprise that came over his countenance; as, stepping upon the threshold, he discovered the change that had taken place in the occupancy of the hut.

"Mother av Moses!" he exclaimed, dropping both snake and tomahawk, and opening his eyes as wide as the lids would allow them; "Shure I must be dhramin? Trath must I! It cyant be yersilf, Miss Pointdixther? Shure now it cyant?"

"But it is, Mr O'Neal. How very ungallant in you to have forgotten me, and so soon!"

"Forgotten yez! Trath, miss, yez needn't accuse me of doin' chat which is intirely impossible. The Oirishman that hiz wance looked in yer swate face will be undher the necissity iver afther to remimber it. Sowl! thare's wan that cyant forgit it, even in his dhrames!"

The speaker glanced significantly towards the couch. A delicious thrill passed through the bosom of the listener.

"But fwhat diz it all mane?" continued Phelim, returning to the unexplained puzzle of the transformation. "Fwhare's the tother—the young chap, or lady, or wuman—whichsomiver she art? Didn't yez see nothin' av a wuman, Miss Pointdixther?"

"Yes—yes."

"Oh! yez did. An fwhere is she now?"

"Gone away, I believe."

"Gone away! Be japers, thin, she hasn't remained long in the wan mind. I lift her heeur in the cyabin not tin minnits ago, takin' aff her bonnit—that was only a man's hat—an sittlin' hersilf down for a stay. Gone, yez say? Sowl! I'm not sorry to hear it. That's a young lady whose room's betther than her company, any day in the twilmonth. She's a dale too handy wid her shootin'-iron. Wud yez belave it, Miss Pointdixther; she prisinted a pistol widin six inches av me nose?"

"*Pardieu*! For what reason?"

"Fwhat rayzun? Only that I thried to hindher her from inthrudin' into the cyabin. She got in for all that; for whin owld Zeb come back, he made no objecshun to it. She sayed she was a frind av the masther, an wanted to nurse him."

"Indeed! Oh! it is strange—very strange!" muttered the Creole, reflectingly.

"Trath, is it. And so is iverything in these times, exciptin' yez own swate silf; that I hope will niver be sthrange in a cyabin frequinted by Phaylim Onale. Shure, now, I'm glad to see yez, miss; an shure so wud the masther, if—"

"Dear Phelim! tell me all that has happened."

"Trath! thin miss, if I'm to till all, ye'll hiv to take off your bonnet, and make up your moind for a long stay—seein' as it 'ut take the big ind av a whole day to relate all the quare things that's happened since the day afore yesthirday."

"Who has been here since then?"

"Who has been heeur?"

"Except the—the—"

"Exceptin' the man-wuman, ye mane?"

"Yes. Has any one else been to this place?"

"Trath has thare—plinty besoides. An av all sorts, an colours too. First an foremost there was wan comin' this way, though he didn't git all the way to the cyabin. But I daren't tell you about him, for it moight frighten ye, miss."

"Tell me. I have no fear."

"Be dad! and I can't make it out meself quite intirely. It was a man upon horseback widout a hid."

"Without a head!"

"Divil a bit av that same on his body."

The statement caused Phelim to be suspected of having lost his.

"An' what's more, miss, he was for all the world like Masther Maurice himself. Wid his horse undher him, an his Mexikin blanket about his showlders, an everything just as the young masther looks, when he's mounted, Sowl! wasn't I scared, whin I sit my eyes on him."

"But where did you see this, Mr O'Neal?"

"Up thare on the top av the bluff. I was out lookin' for the masther to come back from the Sittlement, as he'd promised he wud that mornin', an who showld I see but hisself, as I supposed it to be. An' thin he comes ridin' up, widout his hid, an' stops a bit, an thin goes off at a tarin' gallop, wid Tara gowlin' at his horse's heels, away acrass the big plain, till I saw no more av him. Thin I made back for the cyabin heeur, an shut meself up, and wint to slape; and just in the middle av me dhrames, whin I was dhramin' of—but trath, miss, yez'll be toired standin' on yer feet all this time. Won't yez take aff yer purty little ridin' hat, an sit down on the thrunk thare?—it's asier than the stool. Do plaze take a sate; for if I'm to tell yez all—"

"Never mind me—go on. Please tell me who else has been here besides this strange cavalier; who must have been some one playing a trick upon you, I suppose."

"A thrick, miss! Trath that's just what owld Zeb sayed."

374

"He has been here, then?"

"Yis—yis—but not till long afther the others."

"The others?"

"Yis, miss. Zeb only arroived yestherday marnin'. The others paid their visit the night afore, an at a very unsayzonable hour too, wakin' me out av the middle av my slape."

"But who?—what others?"

"Why the Indyens, to be shure."

"There have been Indians, then?"

"Trath was there—a whole tribe av thim. Well, as I've been tillin' yez, miss, jest as I wus in a soun' slape, I heerd talkin' in the cyabin heern, right over my hid, an the shufflin' av paper, as if somebody was dalin' a pack av cards, an—Mother av Moses! fwhat's that?"

"What?"

"Didn't yez heear somethin'? Wheesht! Thare it is agane! Trath, it's the trampin' av horses! They're jist outside."

Phelim rushed towards the door.

"Be Sant Pathrick! the place is surrounded wid men on horse-back. Thare's a thousand av them! an more comin' behind! Be japers! them's the chaps owld Zeb—Now for a frish spell av squeelin! O Lard! I'll be too late!"

Seizing the cactus-branch—that for convenience he had brought inside the hut—he dashed out through the doorway.

"*Mon Dieu!*" cried the Creole, "'tis they! My father, and I here! How shall I explain it? Holy Virgin, save me from shame!"

Instinctively she sprang towards the door, closing it, as she did so. But a moment's reflection showed her how idle was the act. They who were outside would make light of such obstruction. Already she recognised the voices of the Regulators!

The opening in the skin wall came under her eye. Should she make a retreat through that, undignified as it might be?

It was no longer possible. The sound of hoofs also in the rear! There were horsemen behind the hut!

Besides, her own steed was in front—that ocellated creature not to be mistaken. By this time they must have identified it!

But there was another thought that restrained her from attempting to retreat—one more generous.

*He* was in danger—from which even the unconsciousness of it might not shield him! Who but she could protect him?

"Let my good name go!" thought she. "Father—friends—all—all but him, if God so wills it! Shame, or no shame, to him will I be true!"

# THE HEADLESS HORSEMAN

As these noble thoughts passed through her mind, she took her stand by the bedside of the invalid, like a second Dido, resolved to risk all—even death itself—for the hero of her heart.

# 62. Waiting for the Cue

Never, since its erection, was there such a trampling of hoofs around the hut of the horse-catcher—not even when its corral was filled with fresh-taken mustangs.

Phelim, rushing out from the door, is saluted by a score of voices that summon him to stop.

One is heard louder than the rest, and in tones of command that proclaim the speaker to be chief of the party.

"Pull up, damn you! It's no use—your trying to escape. Another step, and ye'll go tumbling in your tracks. Pull up, I say!"

The command takes effect upon the Connemara man, who has been making direct for Zeb Stump's mare, tethered on the other side of the opening. He stops upon the instant.

"Shure, gintlemen, I don't want to escyape," asseverates he, shivering at the sight of a score of angry faces, and the same number of gun-barrels bearing upon his person; "I had no such intinshuns. I was only goin' to—"

"Run off, if ye'd got the chance. Ye'd made a good beginning. Here, Dick Tracey! half-a-dozen turns of your trail-rope round him. Lend a hand, Shelton! Damned queer-looking curse he is! Surely, gentlemen, this can't be the man we're in search of?"

"No, no! it isn't. Only his man John."

"Ho! hilloa, you round there at the back! Keep your eyes skinned. We havn't got him yet. Don't let as much as a cat creep past you. Now, sirree! who's inside?"

"Who's insoide? The cyabin div yez mane?"

"Damn ye! answer the question that's put to ye!" says Tracey, giving his prisoner a touch of the trail-rope. "Who's inside the shanty?"

"O Lard! Needs must whin the divvel dhrives. Wil, then, thare's the masther for wan—"

"Ho! what's this?" inquires Woodley Poindexter, at this moment, riding up, and seeing the spotted mare. "Why—it—it's Looey's mustang!"

"It is, uncle," answers Cassius Calhoun, who has ridden up along with him.

"I wonder who's brought the beast here?"

"Loo herself, I reckon."

"Nonsense! You're jesting, Cash?"

"No, uncle; I'm in earnest."

"You mean to say my daughter has been here?"

"Has been—still is, I take it."

"Impossible?"

"Look yonder, then!"

The door has just been opened. A female form is seen inside.

"Good God, it is my daughter!"

Poindexter drops from his saddle, and hastens up to the hut—close followed by Calhoun. Both go inside.

"Louises what means this? A wounded man! Is it he—Henry?"

Before an answer can be given, his eye falls upon a cloak and hat—Henry's!

"It is; he's alive! Thank heaven!" He strides towards the couch.

The joy of an instant is in an instant gone. The pale face upon the pillow is not that of his son. The father staggers back with a groan.

Calhoun seems equally affected. But the cry from him is an exclamation of horror; after which he slinks cowed-like out of the cabin.

"Great God!" gasps the planter; "what is it? Can you explain, Louise?"

"I cannot, father. I've been here but a few minutes. I found him as you see. He is delirious."

"And—and—Henry?"

"They have told me nothing. Mr Gerald was alone when I entered. The man outside was absent, and has just returned. I have not had time to question him."

"But—but, how came *you* to be here?"

"I could not stay at home. I could not endure the uncertainty any longer. It was terrible—alone, with no one at the house; and the thought that my poor brother—*Mon dieu! Mon dieu!*"

Poindexter regards his daughter with a perplexed, but still inquiring, look.

"I thought I might find Henry here."

"Here! But how did you know of this place? Who guided you? You are by yourself!"

"Oh, father! I knew the way. You remember the day of the hunt—when the mustang ran away with me. It was beyond this place I was carried. On returning with Mr Gerald, he told me he lived here. I fancied I could find the way back."

Poindexter's look of perplexity does not leave him, though another expression becomes blended with it. His brow contracts; the shadow deepens upon it; though whatever the dark thought, he does not declare it.

"A strange thing for you to have done, my daughter. Imprudent—indeed dangerous. You have acted like a silly girl. Come—come away! This is no place for a lady—for you. Get to your horse, and ride home again. Some one will go with you. There may be a scene here, you should not be present at. Come, come!" The father strides forth from the hut, the daughter following with reluctance scarce concealed; and, with like unwillingness, is conducted to her saddle.

The searchers, now dismounted, are upon the open ground in front.

They are all there. Calhoun has made known the condition of things inside; and there is no need for them to keep up their vigilance.

They stand in groups—some silent, some conversing. A larger crowd is around the Connemara man; who lies upon the grass, last tied in the trail-rope. His tongue is allowed liberty; and they question him, but without giving much credit to his answers.

On the re-appearance of the father and daughter, they face towards them, but stand silent. For all this, they are burning with eagerness to have an explanation of what is passing. Their looks proclaim it.

Most of them know the young lady by sight—all by fame, or name. They feel surprise—almost wonder—at seeing her there. The sister of the murdered man under the roof of his murderer!

More than ever are they convinced that this is the state of the case. Calhoun, coming forth from the hut, has spread fresh intelligence among them—facts that seem to confirm it. He has told them of the hat, the cloak—of the murderer himself, injured in the death-struggle!

But why is Louise Poindexter there—alone—unaccompanied by white or black, by relative or slave? A guest, too: for in this character does she appear! Her cousin does not explain it—perhaps he cannot. Her father—can he? Judging by his embarrassed air, it is doubtful.

Whispers pass from lip to ear—from group to group. There are surmises—many, but none spoken aloud. Even the rude frontiersmen respect the feelings—filial as parental—and patiently await the *éclaircissement*.

"Mount, Louise! Mr Yancey will ride home with you." The young planter thus pledged was never more ready to redeem himself. He is the one who most envies the supposed happiness of Cassius Calhoun. In his soul he thanks Poindexter for the opportunity.

"But, father!" protests the young lady, "why should I no wait for you? You are not going to stay here?" Yancey experiences a shock of apprehension. "It is my wish, daughter, that you do as I tell you. Let that be sufficient."

Yancey's confidence returns. Not quite. He knows enough of that proud spirit to be in doubt whether it may yield obedience—even to the parental command.

It gives way; but with an unwillingness ill disguised, even in the presence of that crowd of attentive spectators.

The two ride off; the young planter taking the lead, his charge slowly following—the former scarce able to conceal his exultation, the latter her chagrin.

Yancey is more distressed than displeased, at the melancholy mood of his companion. How could it be otherwise, with such a sorrow at her heart? Of course he ascribes it to that.

He but half interprets the cause. Were he to look steadfastly into the eye of Louise Poindexter, he might there detect an expression, in which sorrow for the past is less marked, than fear for the future.

They ride on through the trees—but not beyond ear-shot of the people they have left behind them.

Suddenly a change comes over the countenance of the Creole— her features lighting up, as if some thought of joy, or at least of hope, had entered her soul.

She stops reflectingly—her escort constrained to do the same.

"Mr Yancey," says she, after a short pause, "my saddle has got loose. I cannot sit comfortably in it. Have the goodness to look to the girths!"

Yancey leaps to the ground, delighted with the duty thus imposed upon him.

He examines the girths. In his opinion they do not want tightening. He does not say so; but, undoing the buckle, pulls upon the strap with all his strength.

"Stay!" says the fair equestrian, "let me alight. You will get better at it then."

Without waiting for his assistance, she springs from her stirrup, and stands by the side of the mustang.

The young man continues to tug at the straps, pulling with all the power of his arms.

After a prolonged struggle, that turns him red in the face, he succeeds in shortening them by a single hole.

"Now, Miss Poindexter; I think it will do."

"Perhaps it will," rejoins the lady, placing her hand upon the horn of her saddle, and giving it a slight shake. "No doubt it will do now. After all 'tis a pity to start back so soon. I've just arrived here after a fast gallop; and my poor Luna has scarce had time to breathe herself. What if we stop here a while, and let her have a little rest? 'Tis cruel to take her back without it."

"But your father? He seemed desirous you should—"

"That I should go home at once. That's nothing. 'Twas only to get me out of the way of these rough men—that was all. He won't care; so long as I'm out of sight. 'Tis a sweet place, this; so cool, under the shade of these fine trees—just now that the sun is blazing down upon the prairie. Let us stay a while, and give Luna a rest! We can amuse ourselves by watching the gambols of these beautiful silver fish in the stream. Look there, Mr Yancey! What pretty creatures they are!"

The young planter begins to feel flattered. Why should his fair companion wish to linger there with him? Why wish to watch the *iodons*, engaged in their aquatic cotillon—amorous at that time of the year?

He conjectures a reply conformable to his own inclinations.

His compliance is easily obtained.

"Miss Poindexter," says he, "it is for you to command me. I am but too happy to stay here, as long as you wish it."

"Only till Luna be rested. To say the truth, sir, I had scarce got out of the saddle, as the people came up. See! the poor thing is still panting after our long gallop."

Yancey does not take notice whether the spotted mustang is panting or no. He is but too pleased to comply with the wishes of its rider.

They stay by the side of the stream.

He is a little surprised to perceive that his companion gives but slight heed, either to the silver fish, or the spotted mustang. He would have liked this all the better, had her attentions been transferred to himself.

But they are not. He can arrest neither her eye nor her ear. The former seems straying upon vacancy; the latter eagerly bent to catch every sound that comes from the clearing.

Despite his inclinations towards her, he cannot help listening himself. He suspects that a serious scene is there being enacted—a trial before Judge Lynch, with a jury of "Regulators."

Excited talk comes echoing through the tree-trunks. There is an earnestness in its accents that tells of some terrible determination.

Both listen; the lady like some tragic actress, by the side-scene of a theatre, waiting for her cue.

There are speeches in more than one voice; as if made by different men; then one longer than the rest—a harangue.

Louise recognises the voice. It is that of her cousin Cassius. It is urgent—at times angry, at times argumentative: as if persuading his audience to something they are not willing to do.

His speech comes to an end; and immediately after it, there are quick sharp exclamations—cries of assent—one louder than the rest, of fearful import.

While listening, Yancey has forgotten the fair creature by his side.

He is reminded of her presence, by seeing her spring away from the spot, and, with a wild but resolute air, glide towards the *jacalé*!

# 63. A Jury of Regulators

The cry, that had called the young Creole so suddenly from the side of her companion, was the verdict of a jury—in whose rude phrase was also included the pronouncing of the sentence.

The word "hang" was ringing in her ears, as she started away from the spot.

While pretending to take an interest in the play of the silver fish, her thoughts were upon that scene, of less gentle character, transpiring in front of the jacalé.

Though the trees hindered her from having a view of the stage, she knew the actors that were on it; and could tell by their speeches how the play was progressing.

About the time of her dismounting, a tableau had been formed that merits a minute description.

The men, she had left behind, were no longer in scattered groups; but drawn together into a crowd, in shape roughly resembling the circumference of a circle.

Inside it, some half-score figures were conspicuous—among them the tall form of the Regulator Chief, with three or four of his "marshals." Woodley Poindexter was there, and by his side Cassius Calhoun. These no longer appeared to act with authority, but rather as spectators, or witnesses, in the judicial drama about being enacted.

Such in reality was the nature of the scene. It was a trial for Murder—a trial before *Justice Lynch*—this grim dignitary being typified in the person of the Regulator Chief—with a jury composed of all the people upon the ground—all except the prisoners.

Of these there are two—Maurice Gerald and his man Phelim.

They are inside the ring, both prostrate upon the grass; both fast bound in raw-hide ropes, that hinder them from moving hand or foot.

Even their tongues are not free. Phelim has been cursed and scared into silence; while to his master speech is rendered impossible by a piece of stick fastened bitt-like between his teeth. It has been done to prevent interruption by the insane ravings, that would otherwise issue from his lips.

Even the tight-drawn thongs cannot keep him in place. Two men, one at each shoulder, with a third seated upon his knees, hold him to the ground. His eyes alone are free to move; and these rolling in their sockets glare upon his guards with wild unnatural glances, fearful to encounter.

Only one of the prisoners is arraigned on the capital charge; the other is but doubtfully regarded as an accomplice.

The servant alone has been examined—asked to confess all he knows, and what he has to say for himself. It is no use putting questions to his master.

Phelim has told his tale—too strange to be credited; though the strangest part of it—that relating to his having seen a horseman without ahead—is looked upon as the least improbable!

He cannot explain it; and his story but strengthens the suspicion already aroused—that the spectral apparition is a part of the scheme of murder!

"All stuff his tales about tiger-fights and Indians!" say those to whom he has been imparting them. "A pack of lies, contrived to mislead us—nothing else."

The trial has lasted scarce ten minutes; and yet the jury have come to their conclusion.

In the minds of most—already predisposed to it—there is a full conviction that Henry Poindexter is a dead man, and that Maurice Gerald is answerable for his death.

Every circumstance already known has been reconsidered; while to these have been added the new facts discovered at the jacalé—the ugliest of which is the finding of the cloak and hat.

The explanations given by the Galwegian, confused and incongruous, carry no credit. Why should they? They are the inventions of an accomplice.

There are some who will scarce stay to hear them—some who impatiently cry out, "Let the murderer be hanged!"

As if this verdict had been anticipated, a rope lies ready upon the ground, with a noose at its end. It is only a lazo; but for the purpose Calcraft could not produce a more perfect piece of cord.

A sycamore standing near offers a horizontal limb—good enough for a gallows.

The vote is taken *viva voce*.

Eighty out of the hundred jurors express their opinion: that Maurice Gerald must die. His hour appears to have come.

And yet the sentence is not carried into execution. The rope is suffered to lie guileless on the grass. No one seems willing to lay hold of it!

Why that hanging back, as if the thong of horse-hide was a venomous snake, that none dares to touch?

The majority—the *plurality*, to use a true Western word—has pronounced the sentence of death; some strengthening it with rude, even blasphemous, speech. Why is it not carried out?

Why? For want of that unanimity, that stimulates to immediate action—for want of the proofs to produce it.

There is a minority not satisfied—that with less noise, but equally earnest emphasis, have answered "No."

It is this that has caused a suspension of the violent proceedings.

Among this minority is Judge Lynch himself—Sam Manly, the Chief of the Regulators. He has not yet passed sentence; or even signified his acceptance of the acclamatory verdict.

"Fellow citizens!" cries he, as soon as he has an opportunity of making himself heard, "I'm of the opinion, that there's a doubt in this case; and I reckon we ought to give the accused the benefit of it—that is, till he be able to say his own say about it. It's no use questioning him now, as ye all see. We have him tight and fast; and there's not much chance of his getting clear—*if* guilty. Therefore, I move we postpone the trial, till—"

"What's the use of postponing it?" interrupts a voice already loud for the prosecution, and which can be distinguished as that of Cassius Calhoun. "What's the use, Sam Manly? It's all very well for you to talk that way; but if *you* had a friend foully murdered—I won't say cousin, but a son, a brother—you might not be so soft about it. What more do you want to show that the skunk's guilty? Further proofs?"

"That's just what we want, Captain Calhoun."

"Cyan *you* give them, Misther Cashius Calhoun?" inquires a voice from the outside circle, with a strong Irish accent.

"Perhaps I can."

"Let's have them, then!"

"God knows you've had evidence enough. A jury of his own stupid countrymen—"

"Bar that appellashun!" shouts the man, who has demanded the additional evidence. "Just remember, Misther Calhoun, ye're in Texas, and not Mississippi. Bear that in mind; or ye may run your tongue into trouble, sharp as it is."

"I don't mean to offend any one," says Calhoun, backing out of the dilemma into which his Irish antipathies had led him; "even an Englishman, if there's one here."

"Thare ye're welcome—go on!" cries the mollified Milesian.

"Well, then, as I was saying, there's been evidence enough—and more than enough, in my opinion. But if you want more, I can give it."

"Give it—give it!" cry a score of responding voices; that keep up the demand, while Calhoun seems to hesitate.

"Gentlemen!" says he, squaring himself to the crowd, as if for a speech, "what I've got to say now I could have told you long ago. But I didn't think it was needed. You all know what's happened between this man and myself; and I had no wish to be thought revengeful. I'm not; and if it wasn't that I'm sure he has done the deed—sure as the head's on my body—"

Calhoun speaks stammeringly, seeing that the phrase, involuntarily escaping from his lips, has produced a strange effect upon his auditory—as it has upon himself.

"If not sure—I—I should still say nothing of what I've seen, or rather heard: for it was in the night, and I saw nothing."

"What did you hear, Mr Calhoun?" demands the Regulator Chief, resuming his judicial demeanour, for a time forgotten in the confusion of voting the verdict. "Your quarrel with the prisoner, of which I believe everybody has heard, can have nothing to do with your testimony here. Nobody's going to accuse you of false swearing on that account. Please proceed, sir. What did you hear? And where, and when, did you hear it?"

"To begin, then, with the time. It was the night my cousin was missing; though, of course, we didn't miss him till the morning. Last Tuesday night."

"Tuesday night. Well?"

"I'd turned in myself; and thought Henry had done the same. But what with the heat, and the infernal musquitoes, I couldn't get any sleep.

"I started up again; lit a cigar; and, after smoking it awhile in the room, I thought of taking a turn upon the top of the house.

"You know the old hacienda has a flat roof, I suppose? Well, I went up there to get cool; and continued to pull away at the weed.

"It must have been then about midnight, or maybe a little earlier. I can't tell: for I'd been tossing about on my bed, and took no note of the time.

"Just as I had smoked to the end of my cigar, and was about to take a second out of my case, I heard voices. There were two of them.

"They were up the river, as I thought on the other side. They were a good way off, in the direction of the town.

"I mightn't have been able to distinguish them, or tell one from 'tother, if they'd been talking in the ordinary way. But they weren't. There was loud angry talk; and I could tell that two men were quarrelling.

"I supposed it was some drunken rowdies, going home from Oberdoffer's tavern, and I should have thought no more about it. But as I listened, I recognised one of the voices; and then the other. The first was my cousin Henry's—the second that of the man who is there—the man who has murdered him."

"Please proceed, Mr Calhoun! Let us hear the whole of the evidence you have promised to produce. It will be time enough then to state your opinions."

"Well, gentlemen; as you may imagine, I was no little surprised at hearing my cousin's voice—supposing him asleep in his bed. So sure was I of its being him, that I didn't think of going to his room, to see if he was there. I knew it was his voice; and I was quite as sure that the other was that of the horse-catcher.

"I thought it uncommonly queer, in Henry being out at such a late hour: as he was never much given to that sort of thing. But out he was. I couldn't be mistaken about that.

"I listened to catch what the quarrel was about; but though I could distinguish the voices, I couldn't make out anything that was said on either side. What I did hear was Henry calling *him* by some strong names, as if my cousin had been first insulted; and then I heard the Irishman threatening to make him rue it. Each loudly pronounced the other's name; and that convinced me about its being them.

"I should have gone out to see what the trouble was; but I was in my slippers; and before I could draw on a pair of boots, it appeared to be all over.

"I waited for half an hour, for Henry to come home. He didn't come; but, as I supposed he had gone back to Oberdoffer's and fallen in with some of the fellows from the Fort, I concluded he might stay there a spell, and I went back to my bed.

"Now, gentlemen, I've told you all I know. My poor cousin never came back to Casa del Corvo—never more laid his side on a bed,—for that we found by going to his room next morning. His bed that night must have been somewhere upon the prairie, or in the chapparal; and there's the only man who knows where."

With a wave of his hand the speaker triumphantly indicated the accused—whose wild straining eyes told how unconscious he was of the terrible accusation, or of the vengeful looks with which, from all sides, he was now regarded.

Calhoun's story was told with a circumstantiality, that went far to produce conviction of the prisoner's guilt. The concluding speech appeared eloquent of truth, and was followed by a clamourous demand for the execution to proceed.

"Hang! hang!" is the cry from fourscore voices.

The judge himself seems to waver. The minority has been diminished—no longer eighty, out of the hundred, but ninety repeat the cry. The more moderate are overborne by the inundation of vengeful voices.

The crowd sways to and fro—resembling a storm fast increasing to a tempest.

It soon comes to its height. A ruffian rushes towards the rope. Though none seem to have noticed it, he has parted from the side of Calhoun—with whom he has been holding a whispered conversation. One of those "border ruffians" of Southern descent, ever ready by the stake of the philanthropist, or the martyr—such as have been late typified in the *military murderers* of Jamaica, who have disgraced the English name to the limits of all time.

He lays hold of the lazo, and quickly arranges its loop around the neck of the condemned man—alike unconscious of trial and condemnation.

No one steps forward to oppose the act. The ruffian, bristling with bowie-knife and pistols, has it all to himself or, rather, is he assisted by a scoundrel of the same kidney—one of the *ci-devant* guards of the prisoner.

The spectators stand aside, or look tranquilly upon the proceedings. Most express a mute approval—some encouraging the executioners with earnest vociferations of "Up with him! Hang him!"

A few seem stupefied by surprise; a less number show sympathy; but not one dares to give proof of it, by taking part with the prisoner.

The rope is around his neck—the end with the noose upon it. The other is being swung over the sycamore.

"Soon must the soul of Maurice Gerald go back to its God!"

# 64. A Series of Interludes

"Soon the soul of Maurice Gerald must go back to its God!"

It was the thought of every actor in that tragedy among the trees. No one doubted that, in another moment, they would see his body hoisted into the air, and swinging from the branch of the sycamore.

There was an interlude, not provided for in the programme. A farce was being performed simultaneously; and, it might be said, on the same stage. For once the tragedy was more attractive, and the comedy was progressing without spectators.

Not the less earnest were the actors in it. There were only two—a man and a mare. Phelim was once more re-enacting the scenes that had caused surprise to Isidora.

Engrossed by the arguments of Calhoun—by the purposes of vengeance which his story was producing—the Regulators only turned their attention to the chief criminal. No one thought of his companion—whether he was, or was not, an accomplice. His presence was scarce perceived—all eyes being directed with angry intent upon the other.

Still less was it noticed, when the ruffians sprang forward, and commenced adjusting the rope. The Galwegian was then altogether neglected.

There appeared an opportunity of escape, and Phelim was not slow to take advantage of it.

Wriggling himself clear of his fastenings, he crawled off among the legs of the surging crowd.

No one seemed to see, or care about, his movements. Mad with excitement, they were pressing upon each other—the eyes of all turned upward to the gallows tree.

To have seen Phelim skulking off, it might have been supposed, that he was profiting by the chance offered for escape—saving his own life, without thinking of his master.

It is true he could have done nothing, and he knew it. He had exhausted his advocacy; and any further interference on his part would have been an idle effort, or only to aggravate the accusers. It was but slight disloyalty that he should think of saving himself—a mere instinct of self-preservation—to which he seemed yielding, as he stole off among the trees. So one would have conjectured.

But the conjecture would not have done justice to him of Connemara. In his flight the faithful servant had no design to forsake his master—much less leave him to his fate, without making one more effort to effect his delivery from the human bloodhounds who had hold of him. He knew he could do nothing of himself. His hope lay in summoning Zeb Stump, and it was to sound that signal—which had proved so effective before—that he was now stealing off from the scene, alike of trial and execution.

On getting beyond the selvedge of the throng, he had glided in among the trees; and keeping these between him and the angry crowd, he ran on toward the spot where the old mare still grazed upon her tether.

The other horses standing "hitched" to the twigs, formed a tolerably compact tier all round the edge of the timber. This aided in screening his movements from observation, so that he had arrived by the side of the mare, without being seen by any one.

Just then he discovered that he had come without the apparatus necessary to carry out his design. The cactus branch had been dropped where he was first captured, and was still kicking about among the feet of his captors. He could not get hold of it, without exposing himself to a fresh seizure, and this would hinder him from effecting the desired end.

He had no knife—no weapon of any kind—wherewith he might procure another *nopal*.

He paused, in painful uncertainty as to what he should do. Only for an instant. There was no time to be lost. His master's life was in imminent peril, menaced at every moment. No sacrifice would be too great to save him; and with this thought the faithful Phelim rushed towards the cactus-plant; and, seizing one of its spinous branches in his naked hands, wrenched it from the stem.

His fingers were fearfully lacerated in the act; but what mattered that, when weighed against the life of his beloved master? With equal recklessness he ran up to the mare; and, at the risk of being kicked back again, took hold of her tail, and once more applied the instrument of torture!

By this time the noose had been adjusted around the mustanger's neck, carefully adjusted to avoid fluke or failure. The other end, leading over the limb of the tree, was held in hand by the brace of bearded bullies—whose fingers appeared itching to pull upon it. In their eyes and attitudes was an air of deadly determination. They only waited for the word.

Not that any one had the right to pronounce it. And just for this reason was it delayed. No one seemed willing to take the responsibility of giving that signal, which was to send a fellow-creature to his long account. Criminal as they might regard him—murderer as they believed him to be—all shied from doing the sheriff's duty. Even Calhoun instinctively held back.

It was not for the want of will. There was no lack of that on the part of the ex-officer, or among the Regulators. They showed no sign of retreating from the step they had taken. The pause was simply owing to the informality of the proceedings. It was but the lull in the storm that precedes the grand crash.

It was a moment of deep solemnity—every one silent as the tomb. They were in the presence of death, and knew it,—death in its most hideous shape, and darkest guise. Most of them felt that they were abetting it. All believed it to be nigh.

With hushed voice, and hindered gesture, they stood rigid as the tree-trunks around them. Surely the crisis had come?

It had; but not that crisis by everybody expected, by themselves decreed. Instead of seeing Maurice Gerald jerked into the air, far different was the spectacle they were called upon to witness,—one so ludicrous as for a time to interrupt the solemnity of the scene, and cause a suspension of the harsh proceedings.

The old mare—that they knew to be Zeb Stump's—appeared to have gone suddenly mad. She had commenced dancing over the sward, flinging her heels high into the air, and screaming with all her might. She had given the cue to the hundred horses that stood tied to the trees; and all of them had commenced imitating: her wild capers, while loudly responding to her screams!

Enchantment could scarce have produced a quicker transformation than occurred in the tableau formed in front of the jacalé hut. Not only was the execution suspended, but all other proceedings that regarded the condemned captive.

Nor was the change of a comical character. On the contrary, it was accompanied by looks of alarm, and cries of consternation!

The Regulators rushed to their arms—some towards their horses.

"Indians!" was the exclamation upon every lip, though unheard through the din. Nought but the coming of Comanches could have caused such a commotion—threatening to result in a *stampede* of the troop!

For a time men ran shouting over the little lawn, or stood silent with scared countenances.

Most having secured their horses, cowered behind them—using them by way of shield against the chances of an Indian arrow.

There were but few upon the ground accustomed to such prairie escapades; and the fears of the many were exaggerated by their inexperience to the extreme of terror.

It continued, till their steeds, all caught up, had ceased their wild whighering; and only one was heard—the wretched creature that had given them the cue.

Then was discovered the true cause of the alarm; as also that the Connemara man had stolen off.

Fortunate for Phelim he had shown the good sense to betake himself to the bushes. Only by concealment had he saved his skin: for his life was now worth scarce so much as that of his master.

A score of rifles were clutched with angry energy,—their muzzles brought to bear upon the old mare.

But before any of them could be discharged, a man standing near threw his lazo around her neck, and choked her into silence.

Tranquillity is restored, and along with it a resumption of the deadly design. The Regulators are still in the same temper.

The ludicrous incident, whilst perplexing, has not provoked their mirth; but the contrary.

Some feel shame at the sorry figure they have cut, in the face of a false alarm; while others are chafed at the interruption of the solemn ceremonial.

They return to it with increased vindictiveness—as proved by their oaths, and angry exclamations.

Once more the vengeful circle closes around the condemned—the terrible tableau is reconstructed.

Once more the ruffians lay hold of the rope; and for the second time every one is impressed with the solemn thought:

"Soon must the soul of Maurice Gerald go back to its God!"

Thank heaven, there is another interruption to that stern ceremonial of death.

How unlike to death is that bright form flitting under the shadows,—flashing out into the open sunlight.

"A woman! a beautiful woman!"

'Tis only a silent thought; for no one essays to speak. They stand rigid as ever, but with strangely altered looks. Even the rudest of them respect the presence of that fair intruder. There is submission in their attitude, as if from a consciousness of guilt.

Like a meteor she pauses through their midst—glides on without giving a glance on either side—without speech, without halt—till she stoops over the condemned man, still lying gagged the grass.

With a quick clutch she lays hold of the lazo; which the two hangmen, taken by surprise, have let loose.

Grasping it with both her hands, she jerks it from theirs. "Texans! cowards!" she cries, casting a scornful look upon the crowd. "Shame! shame!"

They cower under the stinging reproach. She continues:—

"A trial indeed! A fair trial! The accused without counsel—condemned without being heard! And this you call justice? Texan justice? My scorn upon you—not men, but murderers!"

"What means this?" shouts Poindexter, rushing up, and seizing his daughter by the arm. "You are mad—Loo—mad! How come you to be here? Did I not tell you to go home? Away—this instant away; and do not interfere with what does not concern you!"

"Father, it does concern me!"

"How?—how?—oh true—as a sister! This man is the murderer of your brother."

"I will not—*cannot* believe it. Never—never! There was no motive. O men! if you be men, do not act like savages. Give him a fair trial, and then—then—"

"He's had a fair trial," calls one from the crowd, who seems to speak from instigation; "Ne'er a doubt about his being guilty. It's him that's killed your brother, and nobody else. And it don't look well, Miss Poindexter—excuse me for saying it;—but it don't look just the thing, that *you* should be trying to screen him from his deserving."

"No, that it don't," chime in several voices. "Justice must take its course!" shouts one, in the hackneyed phrase of the law courts.

"It must!—it must!" echoes the chorus. "We are sorry to disoblige you, miss; but we must request you to leave. Mr Poindexter, you'd do well to take your daughter away."

"Come, Loo! 'Tis not the place You must come away. You refuse! Good God! my daughter; do you mean to disobey me? Here, Cash; take hold of her arm, and conduct her from the spot. If you refuse to go willingly, we must use force, Loo. A good girl now. Do as I tell you. Go! Go!"

"No, father, I will not—I shall not—till you have promised—till these men promise—"

"We can't promise you anything, miss—however much we might like it. It ain't a question for women, no how. There's been a crime committed—a murder, as ye yourself know. There must be no cheating of justice. There's no mercy for a murderer!"

"No mercy!" echo a score of angry voices. "Let him be hanged—hanged—hanged!"

The Regulators are no longer restrained by the fair presence. Perhaps it has but hastened the fatal moment. The soul of Cassius Calhoun is not the only one in that crowd stirred by the spirit of envy. The horse hunter is now hated for his supposed good fortune.

In the tumult of revengeful passion, all gallantry is forgotten,—that very virtue for which the Texan is distinguished.

The lady is led aside—dragged rather than led—by her cousin, and at the command of her father. She struggles in the hated arms that hold her—wildly weeping, loudly protesting against the act of inhumanity.

"Monsters! murderers!" are the phrases that fall from her lips.

Her struggles are resisted; her speeches unheeded. She is borne back beyond the confines of the crowd—beyond the hope of giving help to him, for whom she is willing to lay down her life!

Bitter are the speeches Calhoun is constrained to hear—heartbreaking the words now showered upon him. Better for him he had not taken hold of her.

It scarce consoles him—that certainty of revenge. His rival will soon be no more; but what matters it? The fair form writhing in his grasp can never be consentingly embraced. He may kill the hero of her heart, but not conquer for himself its most feeble affection!

# 65. Still Another Interlude

For a third time is the tableau reconstructed—spectators and actors in the dread drama taking their places as before.

The lazo is once more passed over the limb; the same two scoundrels taking hold of its loose end—this time drawing it towards them till it becomes taut.

For the third time arises the reflection:

"Soon must the soul of Maurice Gerald go back to its God!"

Now nearer than ever does the unfortunate man seem to his end. Even love has proved powerless to save him! Wha power on earth can be appealed to after this? None likely to avail.

But there appears no chance of succour—no time for it. There is no mercy in the stern looks of the Regulators—only impatience. The hangmen, too, appear in a hurry—as if they were in dread of another interruption. They manipulate the rope with the ability of experienced executioners. The physiognomy of either would give colour to the assumption, that they had been accustomed to the calling.

In less than sixty seconds they shall have finished the "job."

"Now then, Bill! Are ye ready?" shouts one to the other—by the question proclaiming, that they no longer intend to wait for the word.

"All right!" responds Bill. "Up with the son of a skunk! Up with him!"

There is a pull upon the rope, but not sufficient to raise the body into an erect position. It tightens around the neck; lifts the head a little from the ground, but nothing more!

Only one of the hangmen has given his strength to the pull. "Haul, damn you!" cries Bill, astonished at the inaction of his assistant. "Why the hell don't you haul?"

Bill's back is turned towards an intruder, that, seen by the other, has hindered him from lending a hand. He stands as if suddenly transformed into stone!

"Come!" continues the chief executioner. "Let's go at it again—both together. Yee—up! Up with him!"

"*No ye don't!*" calls out a voice in the tones of a stentor; while a man of colossal frame, carrying a six-foot rifle, is seen rushing out from among the trees, in strides that bring him almost instantly into the thick of the crowd.

"No ye don't!" he repeats, stopping over the prostrate body, and bringing his long rifle to bear upon the ruffians of the rope. "Not yet a bit, as this coon kalkerlates. You, Bill Griffin; pull that piece o' pleeted hoss-hair but the eighth o' an inch tighter, and ye'll git a blue pill in yer stummuk as won't agree wi' ye. Drop the rope, durn ye! Drop it!"

The screaming of Zeb Stump's mare scarce created a more sudden diversion than the appearance of Zeb himself—for it was he who had hurried upon the ground.

He was known to nearly all present; respected by most; and feared by many.

Among the last were Bill Griffin, and his fellow rope-holder. No longer holding it: for at the command to drop it, yielding to a quick perception of danger, both had let go; and the lazo lay loose along the sward.

"What durned tom-foolery's this, boys?" continues the colossus, addressing himself to the crowd, still speechless from surprise. "Ye don't mean hangin', do ye?"

"We do," answers a stern voice. "And why not?" asks another.

"Why not! Ye'd hang a fellur-citizen 'ithout trial, wud ye?"

"Not much of a fellow-citizen—so far as that goes. Besides, he's had a trial—a fair trial."

"I'deed. A human critter to be condemned wi' his brain in a state o' dulleerium! Sent out o' the world 'ithout knowin' that he's in it! Ye call that a fair trial, do ye?"

"What matters it, if we know he's guilty? We're all satisfied about that."

"The hell ye air! Wagh! I aint goin' to waste words wi' sech as you, Jim Stoddars. But for *you*, Sam Manly, an yerself, Mister Peintdexter—shurly ye aint agreed to this hyur proceeding which, in my opeenyun, 'ud be neyther more nor less 'n murder?"

"You haven't heard all, Zeb Stump," interposes the Regulator Chief, with the design to justify his acquiescence in the act. "There are facts—!"

397

"Facts be durned! An' fancies, too! I don't want to hear 'em. It'll be time enuf for thet, when the thing kum to a reg'lar trial; the which shurly nob'dy hyur'll objeck to—seein' as thur aint the ghost o' a chance for *him* to git off. Who air the individooal that objecks?"

"You take too much upon you, Zeb Stump. What is it your business, we'd like to know? The man that's been murdered wasn't *your* son; nor your brother, nor your cousin neither! If he had been, you'd be of a different way of thinking, I take it."

It is Calhoun who has made this interpolation—spoken before with so much success to his scheme.

"I don't see that it concerns you," he continues, "what course we take in this matter."

"But *I do.* It consarns me—fust, because this young fellur's a friend o' mine, though he air Irish, an a strenger; an secondly, because Zeb Stump aint a goin' to stan' by, an see foul play—even tho' it be on the purayras o' Texas."

"Foul play be damned! There's nothing of the sort. And as for standing by, we'll see about that. Boys! you're not going to be scared from your duty by such swagger as this? Let's make a finish of what we've begun. The blood of a murdered man cries out to us. Lay hold of the rope!"

"Do; an by the eturnal! the fust that do 'll drop it a leetle quicker than he grups it. Lay a claw on it—one o' ye—if ye darr. Ye may hang this poor critter as high's ye like; but *not* till ye've laid Zeb'lon Stump streetched dead upon the grass, wi' some o' ye alongside o' him. Now then! Let me see the skunk thet's goin' to tech thet rope!"

Zeb's speech is followed by a profound silence. The people keep their places—partly from the danger of accepting his challenge, and partly from the respect due to his courage and generosity. Also, because there is still some doubt in the minds of the Regulators, both as to the expediency, and fairness, of the course which Calhoun is inciting them to take.

With a quick instinct the old hunter perceives the advantage he has gained, and presses it.

"Gie the young fellur a fair trial," urges he. "Let's take him to the settlement, an hev' him tried thur. Ye've got no clur proof, that he's had any hand in the black bizness; and durn me! if I'd believe it unless I seed it wi' my own eyes. I know how he feeled torst young Peintdexter. Instead o' bein' his enemy, thur aint a man on this ground hed more o' a likin' for him—tho' he did hev a bit o' shindy wi' his precious cousin thur."

398

"You are perhaps not aware, Mr Stump," rejoins the Regulator Chief, in a calm voice, "of what we've just been hearing?"

"What hev ye been hearin'?"

"Evidence to the contrary of what you assert. We have proof, not only that there was bad blood between Gerald and young Poindexter, but that a quarrel took place on the very night—"

"Who sez thet, Sam Manly?"

"I say it," answers Calhoun, stepping a little forward, so as to be seen by Stump.

"O, you it air, Mister Cash Calhoun! You know thur war bad blood atween 'em? You seed the quarrel ye speak o'?"

"I haven't said that I saw it, Zeb Stump. And what's more I'm not going to stand any cross-questioning by you. I have given my evidence, to those who have the right to hear it; and that's enough. I think, gentlemen, you're satisfied as to the verdict. I don't see why this old fool should interrupt—"

"Ole fool!" echoes the hunter, with a screech; "Ole fool! Hell an herrikins! Ye call me an ole fool? By the eturnal God! ye'll live to take back that speech, or my name aint Zeblun Stump, o' Kaintucky. Ne'er a mind now; thur's a time for everythin', an yur time may come, Mister Cash Calhoun, sooner than ye surspecks it."

"As for a quarrel atween Henry Peintdexter an the young fellur hyur," continues Zeb, addressing himself to the Regulator Chief, "I don't believe a word on't; nor won't, so long's thur's no better proof than *his* palaverin'. From what this chile knows, it don't stan' to reezun. Ye say ye've got new facks? So've I too. Facks I reck'n thet'll go a good way torst explicatin o' this mysteerus bizness, twisted up as it air."

"What facts?" demands the Regulator Chief. "Let's hear them, Stump."

"Thur's more than one. Fust place what do ye make o' the young fellur bein' wownded hisself? I don't talk o' them scratches ye see; I believe them's done by coyoats that attackted him, arter they see'd he wur wownded. But look at his knee Somethin' else than coyoats did *that*. What do *you* make o' it, Sam Manly?"

"Well, that—some of the boys here think there's been a struggle between him and—"

"Atween him an who?" sharply interrogates Zeb.

"Why, the man that's missing."

"Yes, that's he who we mean," speaks one of the "boys" referred to. "We all know that Harry Poindexter wouldn't a stood to be shot

399

down like a calf. They've had a tussle, and a fall among the rocks. That's what's given him the swellin' in the knee. Besides, there's the mark of a blow upon his head—looks like it had been the butt of a pistol. As for the scratches, we can't tell what's made them. Thorns may be; or wolves if you like. That foolish fellow of his has a story about a tiger; but it won't do for us."

"What fellur air ye talkin' o'? Ye mean Irish Pheelum? Where air *he*?"

"Stole away to save his carcass. We'll find him, as soon as we've settled this business; and I guess a little hanging will draw the truth out of him."

"If ye mean abeout the tiger, ye'll draw no other truth out o' him than hat ye've got a'ready. I see'd thet varmint myself, an war jest in time to save the young fellur from its claws. But thet aint the peint. Ye've had holt o' the Irish, I 'spose. Did he tell ye o' nothin' else he seed hyur?"

"He had a yarn about Indians. Who believes it?"

"Wal; he tolt me the same story, and that looks like some truth in't. Besides, he declurs they wur playin' curds, an hyur's the things themselves. I found 'em lying scattered about the floor o' the shanty. Spanish curds they air."

Zeb draws the pack out of his pocket, and hands it over to the Regulator Chief.

The cards, on examination, prove to be of Mexican manufacture—such as are used in the universal game of *monté*—the queen upon horseback "cavallo"—the spade represented by a sword "espada"—and the club "baston" symbolised by the huge paviour-like implement, seen in picture-books in the grasp of hairy Orson.

"Who ever heard of Comanches playing cards?" demands he, who has scouted the evidence about the Indians. "Damned ridiculous!"

"Ridiklus ye say!" interposes an old trapper who had been twelve months a prisoner among the Comanches. "Ridiklus it may be; but it's true f'r all that. Many's the game this coon's seed them play, on a dressed burner hide for their table. That same Mexikin *montay* too. I reckon they've larned it from thar Mexikin captives; of the which they've got as good as three thousand in thar different tribes. Yes, sir-ree!" concludes the trapper. "The Keymanchees *do* play cards—sure as shootin'."

Zeb Stump is rejoiced at this bit of evidence, which is more than he could have given himself. It strengthens the case for the accused. The fact, of there having been Indians in the neighbourhood, tends to alter the aspect of the affair in the minds of the Regulators—hitherto under the belief that the Comanches were marauding only on the other side of the settlement.

"Sartin sure," continues Zeb, pressing the point in favour of an adjournment of the trial, "thur's been Injuns hyur, or some thin' durned like—Geesus Geehosofat! Whar's *she* comin' from?"

The clattering of hoofs, borne down from the bluff, salutes the ear of everybody at the same instant of time.

No one needs to inquire, what has caused Stump to give utterance to that abrupt interrogatory. Along the top of the cliff, and close to its edge, a horse is seen, going at a gallop. There is a woman—a lady— upon his back, with hat and hair streaming loosely behind her—the string hindering the hat from being carried altogether away!

So wild is the gallop—so perilous from its proximity to the preci- pice—you might suppose the horse to have run away with his rider.

But no. You may tell that he has not, by the actions of the eques- trian herself. She seems not satisfied with the pace; but with whip, spur, and voice keeps urging him to increase it!

This is plain to the spectators below; though they are puzzled and confused by her riding so close to the cliff.

They stand in silent astonishment. Not that they are ignorant of who it is. It would be strange if they were. That woman equestrian— man-seated in the saddle—once seen was never more to be forgotten.

She is recognised at the first glance. One and all know the reck- less galloper to be the guide—from whom, scarce half-an-hour ago, they had parted upon the prairie.

# 66. Chased by Comanches

It was Isidora who had thus strangely and suddenly shown herself. What was bringing her back? And why was she riding at such a perilous pace?

To explain it, we must return to that dark reverie, from which she was startled by her encounter with the "Tejanos."

While galloping away from the Alamo, she had not thought of looking back, to ascertain whether she was followed. Absorbed in schemes of vengeance, she had gone on—without even giving a glance behind.

It was but slight comfort to her to reflect: that Louise Poindexter had appeared equally determined upon parting from the jacalé. With a woman's intuitive quickness, she suspected the cause; though she knew, too well, it was groundless.

Still, there was some pleasure in the thought: that her rival, ignorant of her happy fortune, was suffering like herself.

There was a hope, too, that the incident might produce estrangement in the heart of this proud Creole lady towards the man so condescendingly beloved; though it was faint, vague, scarce believed in by her who conceived it.

Taking her own heart as a standard, she was not one to lay much stress on the condescension of love: her own history was proof of its levelling power. Still was there the thought that her presence at the jacalé had given pain, and might result in disaster to the happiness of her hated rival.

Isidora had begun to dwell upon this with a sort of subdued pleasure; that continued unchecked, till the time of her rencontre with the Texans.

On turning back with these, her spirits underwent a change. The road to be taken by Louise, should have been the same as that, by which she had herself come. But no lady was upon it.

The Creole must have changed her mind, and stayed by the jacalé—was, perhaps, at that very moment performing the *métier* Isidora had so fondly traced out for herself?

The belief that she was about to bring shame upon the woman who had brought ruin upon her, was the thought that now consoled her.

The questions put by Poindexter, and his companions, sufficiently disclosed the situation. Still clearer was it made by the final interrogations of Calhoun; and, after her interrogators had passed away, she remained by the side of the thicket—half in doubt whether to ride on to the Leona, or go back and be the spectator of a scene, that, by her own contrivance, could scarce fail to be exciting.

She is upon the edge of the chapparal, just inside the shadow of the timber. She is astride her grey steed, that stands with spread nostril and dilated eye, gazing after the *cavallada* that has late parted from the spot—a single horseman in the rear of the rest. Her horse might wonder why he is being thus ridden about; but he is used to sudden changes in the will of his capricious rider.

She is looking in the same direction—towards the *alhuehueté*;—whose dark summit towers above the bluffs of the Alamo.

She sees the searchers descend; and, after them, the man who has so minutely questioned her. As his head sinks below the level of the plain, she fancies herself alone upon it.

In this fancy she is mistaken.

She remains irresolute for a time—ten—fifteen—twenty minutes.

Her thoughts are not to be envied. There is not much sweetness in the revenge, she believes herself instrumental in having accomplished. If she has caused humiliation to the woman she hates, along with it she may have brought ruin upon the man whom she loves? Despite all that has passed, she cannot help loving him!

"*Santissima Virgen!*" she mutters with a fervent earnestness. "What have I done? If these *men—Los Reguladores*—the dreaded judges I've heard of—if they should find him guilty, where may it end? In his death! Mother of God! I do not desire that. Not by their hands—no! no! How wild their looks and gestures—stern—determined! And when I pointed out the way, how quickly they rode off, without further thought of me! Oh, they have made up their minds. Don Mauricio is to die! And he a stranger among them—so have I heard. Not of their country, or kindred; only of the same race. Alone, friendless, with many enemies. *Santissima!* what am I thinking of? Is not he, who has just left me, that cousin of whom I've heard speak! *Ay*

403

*de mi*! Now do I understand the cause of his questioning. His heart, like mine own—like mine own!"

She sits with her gaze bent over the open plain. The grey steed still frets under restraint, though the *cavallada* has long since passed out of sight. He but responds to the spirit of his rider; which he knows to be vacillating—chafing under some irresolution.

'Tis the horse that first discovers a danger, or something that scents of it. He proclaims it by a low tremulous neigh, as if to attract her attention; while his head, tossed back towards the chapparal, shows that the enemy is to be looked for in that direction.

Who, or what is it?

Warned by the behaviour of her steed, Isidora faces to the thicket, and scans the path by which she has lately passed through it. It is the road, or trail, leading to the Leona. 'Tis only open to the eye for a straight stretch of about two hundred yards. Beyond, it becomes screened by the bushes, through which it goes circuitously.

No one is seen upon it—nothing save two or three lean coyotés, that skulk under the shadow of the trees—scenting the shod tracks, in the hope of finding some scrap, that may have fallen from the hurrying horsemen.

It is not these that have caused the grey to show such excitement. He sees them; but what of that? The prairie-wolf is a sight to him neither startling, nor rare. There is something else—something he has either scented, or heard.

Isidora listens: for a time without hearing aught to alarm her. The howl-bark of the jackal does not beget fear at any time; much less in the joy of the daylight. She hears only this. Her thoughts again return to the "Tejanos"—especially to him who has last parted from her side. She is speculating on the purpose of his earnest interrogation; when once more she is interrupted by the action of her horse.

The animal shows impatience at being kept upon the spot; snuffs the air; snorts; and, at length, gives utterance to a neigh, far louder than before!

This time it is answered by several others, from horses that appear to be going along the road—though still hidden behind the trees. Their hoof-strokes are heard at the same time.

But not after. The strange horses have either stopped short, or gone off at a gentle pace, making no noise!

Isidora conjectures the former. She believes the horses to be ridden; and that their riders have checked them up, on hearing the neigh of her own.

She quiets him, and listens.

A humming is heard through the trees. Though indistinct, it can be told to be the sound of men's voices—holding a conversation in a low muttered tone.

Presently it becomes hushed, and the chapparal is again silent. The horsemen, whoever they are, continue halted—perhaps hesitating to advance.

Isidora is scarce astonished at this, and not much alarmed. Some travellers, perhaps, *en route* for the Rio Grande—or, it may be, some stragglers from the Texan troop—who, on hearing a horse neigh, have stopped from an instinct of precaution. It is only natural—at a time, when Indians are known to be on the war-path.

Equally natural, that she should be cautious about encountering the strangers—whoever they may be; and, with this thought, she rides softly to one side—placing herself and her horse under cover of a mezquit tree; where she again sits listening.

Not long, before discovering that the horsemen have commenced advancing towards her—not along the travelled trail, but through the thicket! And not all together, but as if they had separated, and were endeavouring to accomplish a surround!

She can tell this, by hearing the hoof-strokes in different directions: all going gently, but evidently diverging from each other; while the riders are preserving a profound silence, ominous either of cunning or caution—perhaps of evil intent?

They may have discovered her position? The neighing of her steed has betrayed it? They may be riding to get round her—in order to advance from different sides, and make sure of her capture?

How is she to know that their intent is not hostile? She has enemies—one well remembered—Don Miguel Diaz. Besides, there are the Comanches—to be distrusted at all times, and now no longer *en paz*.

She begins to feel alarm. It has been long in arising; but the behaviour of the unseen horsemen is at least suspicious. Ordinary travellers would have continued along the trail. These are sneaking through the chapparal!

She looks around her, scanning her place of concealment. She examines, only to distrust it. The thin, feathery frondage of the mezquit will not screen her from an eye passing near. The hoof-strokes tell, that more than one cavalier is coming that way. She must soon be discovered.

At the thought, she strikes the spur into her horse's side, and rides out from the thicket. Then, turning along the trail, she trots on into the open plain, that extends towards the Alamo.

Her intention is to go two or three hundred yards—beyond range of arrow, or bullet—then halt, until she can discover the character of those who are advancing—whether friends, or to be feared.

If the latter, she will trust to the speed of her gallant grey to carry her on to the protection of the "Tejanos."

She does not make the intended halt. She is hindered by the horsemen, at that moment seen bursting forth from among the bushes, simultaneously with each other, and almost as soon as herself!

They spring out at different points; and, in converging lines, ride rapidly towards her!

A glance shows them to be men of bronze-coloured skins, and half naked bodies—with red paint on their faces, and scarlet feathers sticking up out of their hair.

"*Los Indios!*" mechanically mutters the Mexican, as, driving the rowels against the ribs of her steed, she goes off at full gallop for the *alhuehueté.*

A quick glance behind shows her she is pursued; though she knows it without that. The glance tells her more,—that the pursuit is close and earnest—so earnest that the Indians, contrary to their usual custom, *do not yell!*

Their silence speaks of a determination to capture her; and as if by a plan already preconcerted!

Hitherto she has had but little fear of an encounter with the red rovers of the prairie. For years have they been *en paz*—both with Texans and Mexicans; and the only danger to be dreaded from them was a little rudeness when under the influence of drink—just as a lady, in civilised life, may dislike upon a lonely road, to meet a crowd of "navigators," who have been spending their day at the beer-house.

Isidora has passed through a peril of this kind, and remembers it—with less pain from the thought of the peril itself, than the ruin it has led to.

But her danger is different now. The peace is past. There is war upon the wind. Her pursuers are no longer intoxicated with the fire-water of their foes. They are thirsting for blood; and she flies to escape not only dishonour, but it may be death!

On over that open plain, with all the speed she can take out of her horse,—all that whip, and spur, and voice can accomplish!

She alone speaks. Her pursuers are voiceless—silent as spectres!

Only once does she glance behind. There are still but four of them; but four is too many against one—and that one a woman!

There is no hope, unless she can get within hail of the Texans.

She presses on for the *alhuehueté*.

# 67. Los Indios!

The chased equestrian is within three hundred yards of the bluff, over which the tree towers. She once more glances behind her.

"*Dios me amparé!*" (God preserve me.)

God preserve her! She will be too late!

The foremost of her pursuers has lifted the lazo from his saddle horn: he is winding it over his head!

Before she can reach the head of the pass, the noose will be around her neck, and then—

And then, a sudden thought flashes into her mind—thought that promises escape from the threatened strangulation.

The cliff that overlooks the Alamo is nearer than the gorge, by which the creek bottom must be reached. She remembers that its crest is visible from the jacalé.

With a quick jerk upon the rein, she diverges from her course; and, instead of going on for the *alhuehueté*, she rides directly towards the bluff.

The change puzzles her pursuers—at the same time giving them gratification. They well know the "lay" of the land. They understand the trending of the cliff; and are now confident of a capture.

The leader takes a fresh hold of his lazo, to make more sure of the throw. He is only restrained from launching it, by the certainty she cannot escape.

"*Chingaro!*" mutters he to himself, "if she go much farther, she'll be over the precipice!"

His reflection is false. She goes farther, but not over the precipice. With another quick pull upon the rein she has changed her course, and rides along the edge of it—so close as to attract the attention of the "Tejanos" below, and elicit from Zeb Stump that quaint exclamation— only heard upon extraordinary occasions—

"Geesus Geehosofat!"

As if in answer to the exclamation of the old hunter—or rather to the interrogatory with which he has followed it up—comes the cry of the strange equestrian who has shown herself on the cliff.

"*Los Indios! Los Indios!*"

No one who has spent three days in Southern Texas could mistake the meaning of that phrase—whatever his native tongue. It is the alarm cry which, for three hundred years, has been heard along three thousand miles of frontier, in three different languages—"Les Indiens! Los Indios! the Indians!"

Dull would be the ear, slow the intellect, that did not at once comprehend it, along with the sense of its associated danger.

To those who hear it at the jacalé it needs no translation. They know that she, who has given utterance to it, is pursued by Indians—as certain as if the fact had been announced in their own Saxon vernacular.

They have scarce time to translate it into this—even in thought—when the same voice a second time salutes their ears:—"Tejanos! Cavalleros! save me! save me! Los Indios! I am chased by a troop. They are behind me—close—close—"

Her speech, though continued, is no longer heard distinctly. It is no longer required to explain what is passing upon the plain above.

She has cleared the first clump of tree tops by scarce twenty yards, when the leading savage shoots out from the same cover, and is seen, going in full gallop, against the clear sky.

Like a sling he spins the lazo loop around his head. So eager is he to throw it with sure aim, that he does not appear to take heed of what the fugitive has said—spoken as she went at full speed: for she made no stop, while calling out to the "Tejanos." He may fancy it has been addressed to himself—a final appeal for mercy, uttered in a language he does not understand: for Isidora had spoken in English.

He is only undeceived, as the sharp crack of a rifle comes echoing out of the glen,—or perhaps a little sooner, as a stinging sensation in his wrist causes him to let go his lazo, and look wonderingly for the why!

He perceives a puff of sulphureous smoke rising from below.

A single glance is sufficient to cause a change in his tactics. In that glance he beholds a hundred men, with the gleam of a hundred gun barrels!

His three followers see them at the same time; and as if moved by the same impulse, all four turn in their tracks, and gallop away from the cliff—quite as quickly as they have been approaching it.

409

"'Tur a pity too," says Zeb Stump, proceeding to reload his rifle. "If 't hedn't a been for the savin' o' her, I'd a let 'em come on down the gully. Ef we ked a captered them, we mout a got somethin' out o' 'em consarnin' this queer case o' ourn. Thur aint the smell o' a chance now. It's clur they've goed off; an by the time we git up yander, they'll be hellurd."

---

The sight of the savages has produced another quick change in the tableau formed in front of the mustanger's hut—a change squally sudden in the thoughts of those who compose it.

The majority who deemed Maurice Gerald a murderer has become transformed into a minority; while those who believed him innocent are now the men whose opinions are respected.

Calhoun and his bullies are no longer masters of the situation; and on the motion of their chief the Regulator Jury is adjourned. The new programme is cast in double quick time. A score of words suffice to describe it. The accused is to be carried to the settlement—there to be tried according to the law of the land.

And now for the Indians—whose opportune appearance has caused this sudden change, both of sentiment and design. Are they to be pursued? That of course. But when? Upon the instant? Prudence says, no.

Only four have been seen. But these are not likely to be alone. They may be the rear-guard of four hundred?

"Let us wait till the woman comes down," counsels one of the timid. "They have not followed her any farther. I think I can hear her riding this way through the gulley. Of course she knows it—as it was she who directed us."

The suggestion appears sensible to most upon the ground. They are not cowards. Still there are but few of them, who have encountered the wild Indian in actual strife; and many only know his more debased brethren in the way of trade.

The advice is adopted. They stand waiting for the approach of Isidora.

All are now by their horses; and some have sought shelter among the trees. There are those who have an apprehension: that along with the Mexican, or close after her, may still come a troop of Comanches.

A few are otherwise occupied—Zeb Stump among the number. He takes the gag from between the teeth of the respited prisoner, and unties the thongs hitherto holding him too fast.

There is one who watches him with a strange interest, but takes no part in the proceeding. Her part has been already played—perhaps too prominently. She shuns the risk of appearing farther conspicuous.

Where is the niece of Don Silvio Mortimez? She has not yet come upon the ground! The stroke of her horse's hoof is no longer heard! There has been time—more than time—for her to have reached the jacalé!

Her non-appearance creates surprise—apprehension—alarm. There are men there who admire the Mexican maiden—it is not strange they should—some who have seen her before, and some who never saw her until that day.

Can it be, that she has been overtaken and captured? The interrogatory passes round. No one can answer it; though all are interested in the answer.

The Texans begin to feel something like shame. Their gallantry was appealed to, in that speech sent them from the cliff, "Tejanos! Cavalleros!"

Has she who addressed it succumbed to the pursuer? Is that beauteous form in the embrace of a paint-bedaubed savage?

They listen with ears intent,—many with pulses that beat high, and hearts throbbing with a keen anxiety.

They listen in vain.

There is no sound of hoof—no voice of woman—nothing, except the champing of bitts heard close by their side!

Can it be that she is taken?

Now that the darker design is stifled within their breasts, the hostility against one of their own race is suddenly changed into a more congenial channel.

Their vengeance, rekindled, burns fiercer than ever—since it is directed against the hereditary foe.

The younger and more ardent—among whom are the admirers of the Mexican maiden—can bear the uncertainty no longer. They spring into their saddles, loudly declaring their determination to seek her—to save her, or perish in the attempt.

Who is to gainsay them? Her pursuers—her captors perhaps—may be the very men they have been in search of—the murderers of Henry Poindexter!

No one opposes their intent. They go off in search of Isidora—in pursuit of the prairie pirates.

Those who remain are but few in number; though Zeb Stump is among them.

The old hunter is silent, as to the expediency of pursuing the Indians. He keeps his thoughts to himself: his only seeming care is to look after the invalid prisoner—still unconscious—still guarded by the Regulators.

Zeb is not the only friend who remains true to the mustanger in his hour of distress. There are two others equally faithful. One a fair creature, who watches at a distance, carefully concealing the eager interest that consumes her. The other, a rude, almost ludicrous individual, who, close by his side, addresses the respited man as his "masther." The last is Phelim, who has just descended from his perch among the parasites of an umbrageous oak—where he has for some time stayed—a silent spectator of all that has been transpiring. The change of situation has tempted him back to earth, and the performance of that duty for which he came across the Atlantic.

No longer lies our scene upon the Alamo. In another hour the jacalé is deserted—perhaps never more to extend its protecting roof over Maurice the mustanger.

# 68. The Disappointed Campaigners

The campaign against the Comanches proved one of the shortest—lasting only three or four days. It was discovered that these Ishmaelites of the West did not mean war—at least, on a grand scale. Their descent upon the settlements was only the freak of some young fellows, about to take out their degree as *braves*, desirous of signalising the event by "raising" a few scalps, and capturing some horses and horned cattle.

Forays of this kind are not unfrequent among the Texan Indians. They are made on private account—often without the knowledge of the chief, or elders of the tribe—just as an ambitious young mid, or ensign, may steal off with a score of companions from squadron or camp, to cut out an enemy's craft, or capture his picket guard. These *marauds* are usually made by young Indians out on a hunting party, who wish to return home with something to show besides the spoils of the chase; and the majority of the tribe is often ignorant of them till long after the event. Otherwise, they might be interdicted by the elders; who, as a general thing, are averse to such *filibustering* expeditions—deeming them not only imprudent, but often injurious to the interests of the community. Only when successful are they applauded.

On the present occasion several young Comanches had taken out their war-diploma, by carrying back with them the scalps of a number of white women and boys. The horses and horned cattle were also collected; but these, being less convenient of transport than the light scalp-locks, had been recaptured.

The red-skinned filibusters, overtaken by a detachment of Mounted Rifles, among the hills of the San Saba, were compelled to abandon their four-footed booty, and only saved their own skins by a forced retreat into the fastnesses of the "Llano Estacado."

To follow them beyond the borders of this sterile tract would have required a *commissariat* less hastily established than that with which the troops had sallied forth; and, although the relatives of the scalped settlers clamoured loudly for retaliation, it could only be promised them after due time and preparation.

On discovering that the Comanches had retreated beyond their neutral ground, the soldiers of Uncle Sam had no choice but to return to their ordinary duties—each detachment to its own fort—to await further commands from the head-quarters of the "department."

The troops belonging to Port Inge—entrusted with the guardianship of the country as far as the Rio Nueces—were surprised on getting back to their cantonment to discover that they had been riding in the wrong direction for an encounter with the Indians! Some of them were half mad with disappointment: for there were several—young Hancock among the number—who had not yet run their swords through a red-skin, though keenly desirous of doing so!

No doubt there is inhumanity in the idea. But it must be remembered, that these ruthless savages have given to the white man peculiar provocation, by a thousand repetitions of three diabolical crimes—rape, rapine, and murder.

To talk of their being the aborigines of the country—the real, but dispossessed, owners of the soil—is simple nonsense. This sophism, of the most spurious kind, has too long held dominion over the minds of men. The whole human race has an inherent right to the whole surface of the earth: and if any infinitesimal fraction of the former by chance finds itself idly roaming over an extended portion of the latter, their exclusive claim to it is almost too absurd for argument—even with the narrowest-minded disciple of an aborigines society.

Admit it—give the *hunter* his half-dozen square miles—for he will require that much to maintain him—leave him in undisputed possession to all eternity—and millions of fertile acres must remain untilled, to accommodate this whimsical theory of *national* right. Nay, I will go further, and risk reproach, by asserting:—that not only the savage, so called, but civilised people should be unreservedly dispossessed—whenever they show themselves incapable of turning to a good account the resources which Nature has placed within their limits.

The *exploitation* of Earth's treasures is a question not confined to nations. It concerns the whole family of mankind.

In all this there is not one iota of agrarian doctrine—not a thought of it. He who makes these remarks is the last man to lend countenance to *communism*.

It is true that, at the time spoken of, there were ruffians in Texas who held the life of a red-skin at no higher value than an English gamekeeper does that of a stoat, or any other vermin, that trespasses on his preserves. No doubt these ruffians are there still: for ten years cannot have effected much change in the morality of the Texan frontier.

But, alas! we must now be a little cautious about calling names. Our own story of Jamaica—by heaven! the blackest that has blotted the pages of history—has whitewashed these border *filibusteros* to the seeming purity of snow!

If things are to be judged by comparison, not so fiendish, then, need appear the fact, that the young officers of Fort Inge were some little chagrined at not having an opportunity to slay a score or so of red-skins. On learning that, during their absence, Indians had been seen on the other side, they were inspired by a new hope. They might yet find the opportunity of fleshing their swords, transported without stain—without sharpening, too—from the military school of West Point.

It was a fresh disappointment to them, when a party came in on the same day—civilians who had gone in pursuit of the savages seen on the Alamo—and reported: that no Indians had been there!

They came provided with proofs of their statement, which otherwise would have been received with incredulity—considering what had occurred.

The proofs consisted in a collection of miscellaneous articles—an odd lot, as an auctioneer would describe it—wigs of horse-hair, cocks' feathers stained blue, green, or scarlet, breech-clouts of buckskin, mocassins of the same material, and several packages of paint, all which they had found concealed in the cavity of a cottonwood tree!

There could be no new campaign against Indians; and the aspiring spirits of Fort Inge were, for the time, forced to content themselves with such incidents as the situation afforded.

Notwithstanding its remoteness from any centre of civilised life, these were at the time neither tame nor uninteresting. There were several subjects worth thinking and talking about. There was the arrival, still of recent date, of the most beautiful woman ever seen upon the Alamo; the mysterious disappearance and supposed assassination of her brother; the yet more mysterious appearance of a horseman without a head; the trite story of a party of white men "playing Indian"; and last, though not of least interest, the news that the suspected murderer had been caught, and was now inside the walls of their own guardhouse—mad as a maniac!

There were other tales told to the disappointed campaigners—of sufficient interest to hinder them from thinking: that at Fort Inge they had returned to dull quarters. The name of Isidora Covarubio do los Llanos—with her masculine, but magnificent, beauty—had become a theme of conversation, and something was also said, or surmised, about her connection with the mystery that occupied all minds.

The details of the strange scenes upon the Alamo—the discovery of the mustanger upon his couch—the determination to hang him—the act delayed by the intervention of Louise Poindexter—the respite due to the courage of Zeb Stump—were all points of the most piquant interest—suggestive of the wildest conjectures.

Each became in turn the subject of converse and commentary, but none was discussed with more earnestness than that which related to the innocence, or guilt, of the man accused of murder.

"Murder," said the philosophic Captain Sloman, "is a crime which, in my opinion, Maurice the mustanger is incapable of committing. I think, I know the fellow well enough to be sure about that."

"You'll admit," rejoined Crossman, of the Rifles, "that the circumstances are strong against him? Almost conclusive, I should say."

Crossman had never felt friendly towards the young Irishman. He had an idea, that on one occasion the commissary's niece—the belle of the Fort—had looked too smilingly on the unknown adventurer.

"I consider it anything but conclusive," replied Sloman.

"There's no doubt about young Poindexter being dead, and having been murdered. Every one believes that. Well; who else was likely to have done it? The cousin swears to having overheard a quarrel between him and Gerald."

"That precious cousin would swear to anything that suited his purpose," interposed Hancock, of the Dragoons. "Besides, his own shindy with the same man is suggestive of suspicion—is it not?"

"And if there *was* a quarrel," argued the officer of infantry, "what then? It don't follow there was a murder."

"Then you think the fellow may have killed Poindexter in a fair fight?"

"Something of the sort is possible, and even probable. I will admit that much."

"But what did they have a difficulty about?" asked Hancock. "I heard that young Poindexter was on friendly terms with the horse-hunter—notwithstanding what had happened between him and Calhoun. What could they have quarrelled about?"

"A singular interrogation on *your* part, Lieutenant Hancock!" answered the infantry officer, with a significant emphasis on the pronoun. "As if men ever quarrelled about anything except—"

"Except women," interrupted the dragoon with a laugh.

"But which woman, I wonder? It could not be anything relating to young Poindexter's sister?"

"*Quien sabe?*" answered Sloman, repeating the Spanish phrase with an ambiguous shrug of the shoulders.

"Preposterous!" exclaimed Crossman. "A horse-catcher daring to set his thoughts on Miss Poindexter! Preposterous!"

"What a frightful aristocrat you are, Crossman! Don't you know that love is a natural democrat; and mocks your artificial ideas of distinction. I don't say that in this case there's been anything of the kind. Miss Poindexter's not the only woman that might have caused a quarrel between the two individuals in question. There are other damsels in the settlement worth getting angry about—to say nothing of our own fair following in the Fort; and why not—"

"Captain Sloman," petulantly interrupted the lieutenant of Rifles. "I must say that, for a man of your sense, you talk very inconsiderately. The ladies of the garrison ought to be grateful to you for the insinuation."

"What insinuation, sir?"

"Do you suppose it likely that there's one of them would condescend to speak to the person you've named?"

"Which? I've named two."

"You understand me well enough, Sloman; and I you. Our ladies will, no doubt, feel highly complimented at having their names connected with that of a low adventurer, a horse-thief, and suspected assassin!"

"Maurice the mustanger may be the last—suspected, and that is all. He is neither of the two first; and as for our ladies being above speech with him, in that as in many other things, you may be mistaken, Mr Crossman. I've seen more of this young Irishman than you—enough to satisfy me that, so far as *breeding* goes, he may compare notes with the best of us. Our grand dames needn't be scared at the thought of his acquaintance; and, since you have raised the question, I don't think they would shy from it—some of them at least—if it were

417

offered them. It never has. So far as I have observed, the young fellow has behaved with a modesty that betokens the true gentleman. I have seen him in their presence more than once, and he has conducted himself towards them as if fully sensible of his position. For that matter, I don't think he cares a straw about one or other of them."

"Indeed! How fortunate for those, who might otherwise have been his rivals!"

"Perhaps it is," quietly remarked the captain of infantry.

"Who knows?" asked Hancock, intentionally giving a turn to the ticklish conversation. "Who knows but the cause of quarrel—if there's been one—might not be this splendid señorita so much talked about? I haven't seen her myself; but, by all accounts, she's just the sort to make two fellows as jealous as a pair of tiger-cats."

"It might be—who knows?" drawled Crossman, who found contentment in the thought that the handsome Irishman might have his amorous thoughts turned in any other direction than towards the commissary's quarters.

"They've got him in the guard-house," remarked Hancock, stating a fact that had just been made known to him: for the conversation above detailed occurred shortly after their return from the Comanche campaign. "His droll devil of a serving man is along with him. What's more; the major has just issued an order to double the guard! What does it mean, Captain Sloman—you who know so much of this fellow and his affairs? Surely there's no danger of his making an attempt to steal out of his prison?"

"Not likely," replied the infantry officer, "seeing that he hasn't the slightest idea that he's inside of one. I've just been to the guard-house to have a look at him. He's mad as a March hare; and wouldn't know his own face in a looking-glass."

"Mad! In what way?" asked Hancock and the others, who were yet but half enlightened about the circumstances of the mustanger's capture.

"A brain fever upon him—delirious?"

"Is that why the guards have been doubled? Devilish queer if it is. The major himself must have gone mad!"

"Maybe it's the suggestion—command I should rather say—of the majoress. Ha! ha! ha!"

"But what *does* it mean? Is the old maje really afraid of his getting out of the guard-house?"

"No—not that, I fancy. More likely an apprehension of somebody else getting into it."

"Ah! you mean, that—"

"I mean that for Maurice the Mustanger there's more safety inside than out. Some queer characters are about; and there's been talk of another Lynch trial. The Regulators either repent of having allowed him a respite; or there's somebody hard at work in bringing about this state of public opinion. It's lucky for him that the old hunter has stood his friend; and it's but a continuation of his good luck that we've returned so opportunely. Another day, and we might have found the guardhouse empty—so far as its present occupants are concerned. Now, thank God! the poor fellow shall have a fair trial."

"When is it to take place?"

"Whenever he has recovered his senses, sufficiently to know that he's being tried!"

"It may be weeks before that."

"And it may be only days—hours. He don't appear to be very bad—that is, bodily. It's his mind that's out of order—more, perhaps, from some strange trouble that has come over him, than any serious hurt he has received. A day may make all the difference; and, from what I've just heard, the Regulators will insist on his being tried as soon as he shows a return to consciousness. They say, they won't wait for him to recover from his wounds!"

"Maybe he'll be able to tell a story that'll clear him. I hope so."

This was said by Hancock.

"I doubt it," rejoined Crossman, with an incredulous shake of the head. "*Nous verrons!*"

"I'm sure of it," said Sloman. "*Nos veremos!*" he added, speaking in a tone that seemed founded less upon confidence than a wish that was father to the thought.

# 69. Mystery and Mourning

There is mourning in the mansion of Casa del Corvo, and mystery among the members of Woodley Poindexter's family.

Though now only three in number, their intercourse is less frequent than before, and marked by a degree of reserve that must spring from some deep-seated cause.

They meet only at the hour of meals—then conversing only on such topics as cannot well be shunned.

There is ample explanation of the sorrow, and much of the solemnity.

The death—no longer doubted—of an only son—an only brother—unexpected and still unexplained—should account for the melancholy mien both of father and daughter.

It might also explain the shadow seated constantly on the brow of the cousin.

But there is something beyond this. Each appears to act with an irksome restraint in the presence of the others—even during the rare occasions, on which it becomes necessary to converse on the family misfortune!

Beside the sorrow common to all three, they appear to have separate griefs that do not, and cannot, commingle.

The once proud planter stays within doors—pacing from room to room, or around, the enclosed corridor—bending beneath a weight of woe, that has broken down his pride, and threatens to break his heart. Even strong paternal affection, cruelly bereaved, can scarce account for the groans, oft accompanied by muttered curses, that are heard to issue from his lips!

Calhoun rides abroad as of yore; making his appearance only at the hours of eating and sleeping, and not regularly then.

For a whole day, and part of a night, he has been absent from the place. No one knows where; no one has the right to inquire.

Louise confines herself to her own room, though not continuously. There are times when she may be seen ascending to the azotea—alone and in silent meditation.

There, nearer to Heaven, she seeks solace for the sorrows that have assailed her upon Earth—the loss of a beloved brother—the fear of losing one far more beloved, though in a different sense—perhaps, a little also, the thought of a scandal already attaching to her name.

Of these three sorrows the second is the strongest. The last but little troubles her; and the first, for a while keenly felt, is gradually growing calmer.

But the second—the supreme pain of all—is but strengthened and intensified by time!

She knows that Maurice Gerald is shut up within the walls of a prison—the strong walls of a military guard-house.

It is not their strength that dismays her. On the contrary, she has fears for their weakness!

She has reasons for her apprehension. She has heard of the rumours that are abroad; rumours of sinister significance. She has heard talk of a second trial, under the presidency of Judge Lynch and his rude coadjutors—not the same Judge Lynch who officiated in the Alamo, nor all of the same jury; but a court still less scrupulous than that of the Regulators; composed of the ruffianism, that at any hour can be collected within the bounds of a border settlement—especially when proximate to a military post.

The reports that have thus gone abroad are to some a subject of surprise. Moderate people see no reason why the prisoner should be again brought to trial in that irregular way.

The facts, that have late come to light, do not alter the case—at least, in any way to strengthen the testimony against him.

If the four horsemen seen were not Indians—and this has been clearly shown by the discovery of the disguises—it is not the less likely that they have had to do with the death of young Poindexter. Besides, there is nothing to connect *them* with the mustanger, any more than if they had been real Comanches.

Why, then, this antipathy against the respited prisoner, for the second time surging up?

There is a strangeness about the thing that perplexes a good many people.

There are a few that understand, or suspect, the cause. A very few: perhaps only three individuals.

Two of them are Zeb Stump and Louise Poindexter; the third Captain Cassius Calhoun.

The old hunter, with instinct keenly on the alert, has discovered some underhanded action—the actors being Miguel Diaz and his men, associated with a half-score of like characters of a different race—the "rowdies" of the settlement. Zeb has traced the action to its instigator—the ex-captain of volunteer cavalry.

He has communicated his discovery to the young Creole, who is equal to the understanding of it. It is the too clear comprehension of its truth that now inspires her with a keen solicitude.

Anxiously she awaits every word of news—watches the road leading from the Fort to Casa del Corvo, as if the sentence of her own death, or the security of her life, hung upon the lips of some courier to come that way!

She dares not show herself at the prison. There are soldiers on guard, and spectators around it—a crowd of the idle curious, who, in all countries, seem to feel some sort of sombre enjoyment in the proximity of those who have committed great crimes.

There is an additional piquancy in the circumstances of this one. The criminal is insane; or, at all events, for the time out of his senses.

The guard-house doors are at all hours besieged—to the great discomfort of the sentries—by people eager to listen to the mutterings of the delirious man. A lady could not pass in without having scores of eyes turned inquiringly upon her. Louise Poindexter cannot run the gauntlet of those looks without risk to her reputation.

Left to herself, perhaps she would have attempted it. Watched by a father whose suspicions are already awakened; by a near relation, equally interested in preserving her spotless, before the eyes of the world—she has no opportunity for the act of imprudence.

She can only stay at home; now shut up in her solitary chamber, solaced by the remembrance of those ravings to which she had listened upon the Alamo; now upon the azotea, cheered by the recollection of that sweet time spent among the *mezquite* trees, the spot itself almost discernible, where she had surrendered the proudest passion of her heart; but saddened by the thought that he to whom she surrendered it is now humiliated—disgraced—shut up within the walls of a gaol—perchance to be delivered from it only unto death!

To her it was happy tidings, when, upon the morning of the fourth day, Zeb Stump made his appearance at Casa del Corro, bringing the intelligence; that the "hoss-sogers hed kum back to the Fort."

There was significance in the news thus ungrammatically imparted. There was no longer a danger of the perpetration of that foul act hitherto apprehended: a prisoner taken from his guards, not for rescue, but ruin!

"Ee needn't be uneezy 'beout thet ere ewent," said Zeb, speaking with a confidence he had not shown for some time. "Thur's no longer a danger o' it comin' to pass, Miss Lewaze. I've tuk preecaushins agin it."

"Precautions! How, Zeb?"

"Wal; fust place, I've seed the major clost arter his comin' back, an gied him a bit o' my mind. I tolt him the hul story, as fur's I know it myself. By good luck he ain't agin the young fellur, but the tother way I reck'n. Wal, I tolt him o' the goin's on o' the hul crew—Amerikins, Mexikins, an all o' them—not forgettin' thet ugly Spanyard o' the name o' Dee-ez, thet's been one o' the sarciest o' the lot. The reesult's been thet the major hez doubled the sentries roun' the prison, an's goin' to keep 'em doubled."

"I am so glad! You think there is no longer any fear from that quarter?"

"If you mean the quarter o' Mister Migooel Dee-ez, I kin swar to it. Afore he thinks o' gittin' any b'dy else out o' a prison, he's got to git hisself out."

"What; Diaz in prison! How? When? Where?"

"You've asked three seprit questyuns, Miss Lewaze, all o' a heep. Wal; I reck'n the conveenientest way to answer 'em 'll be to take 'em backurds. An' fust as to the *whar*. As to thet, thur's but one prison in these parts, as 'ud be likely to hold him. Thet is the guard-house at the Fort. He's thur."

"Along with—"

"I know who ye're goin' to name—the young fellur. Jest so. They're in the same buildin', tho' not 'zackly in the same room. Thur's a purtition atween 'em; tho' for thet matter they kin convarse, ef they're so inclined. Thur's three others shet up along wi' the Mexikin—his own cussed cummarades. The three 'll have somethin' to talk 'beout 'mong themselves, I reck'n."

"This is good news, Zeb. You told me yesterday that Diaz was active in—"

"Gittin' hisself into a scrape, which he hev been successful in effectuatin'. He's got hisself into the jug, or someb'y else hev did thet bizness for him."

"But how—when—you've not told me?"

423

"Geehosophat! Miss Lewaze. Gi' me a leetle time. I hain't drew breath yit, since I kim in. Yur second questyun war *when*. It air eezy answered. 'Beout a hour agone thet ere varmint wur trapped an locked up. I war at the shettin' o' the door ahint him, an kum straight custrut hyur arter it war done."

"But you have not yet said why he is arrested."

"I hain't hed a chance. It air a longish story, an 'll take a leetle time in the tellin'. Will ye listen to it now, or arter—?"

"After what, Mr Stump?"

"Wal, Miss Lewaze, I only meened arter—arter—I git the ole mare put up. She air stannin' thur, as if she'd like to chaw a yeer o' corn, an somethin' to wet it down. Both she 'nd me's been on a longish tramp afore we got back to the Fort; which we did scace a hour ago."

"Pardon me, dear Mr Stump, for not thinking of it. Pluto; take Mr Stump's horse to the stable, and see that it is fed. Florinde! Florinde! What will you eat, Mr Stump?"

"Wal, as for thet, Miss Lewaze, thank ye all the same, but I ain't so partikler sharp set. I war only thinkin' o' the maar. For myself, I ked go a kupple o' hours longer 'ithout eetin', but ef thur's sech a thing as a smell o' Monongaheely 'beout the place, it 'ud do this ole karkidge o' mine a power o' good."

"Monongahela? plenty of it. Surely you will allow me to give you something better?"

"Better 'n Monongaheely!"

"Yes. Some sherry—champagne—brandy if you prefer it."

"Let them drink brandy as like it, and kin' git it drinkable. Thur may be some o' it good enuf; an ef thur air, I'm shor it'll be foun' in the house o' a Peintdexter. I only knows o' the sort the sutler keeps up at the Fort. Ef thur ever wur a medicine, thet's one. It 'ud rot the guts out o' a alleygatur. No; darn thur French lickers; an specially thur brandy. Gi' me the pure corn juice; an the best o' all, thet as comes from Pittsburgh on the Monongaheely."

"Florinde! Florinde!"

It was not necessary to tell the waiting-maid for what she was wanted. The presence of Zeb Stump indicated the service for which she had been summoned. Without waiting to receive the order she went off, and the moment after returned, carrying a decanter half-filled with what Zeb called the "pure corn juice," but which was in reality the essence of rye—for from this grain is distilled the celebrated "Monongahela."

Zeb was not slow to refresh himself. A full third of the contents of the decanter were soon put out of sight—the other two-thirds remaining for future potations that might be required in the course of the narration upon which he was about to enter.

# 70. Go, Zeb, and God Speed You!

The old hunter never did things in a hurry. Even his style of drinking was not an exception; and although there was no time wasted, he quaffed the Monongahela in a formal leisurely manner.

The Creole, impatient to hear what he had to relate, did not wait for him to resume speech.

"Tell me, dear Zeb," said she, after directing her maid to withdraw, "why have they arrested this Mexican—Miguel Diaz I mean? I think I know something of the man. I have reasons."

"An' you ain't the only purson may hev reezuns for knowin' him, Miss Lewaze. Yur brother—but never mind 'beout that—leastwise not now. What Zeb Stump *do* know, or strongly surspect, air, thet this same-mentioned Migooel Dee-ez hev had somethin' to do wi'—You know what I'm refarrin' to?"

"Go on, Mr Stump!"

"Wal, the story air this. Arter we kim from the Alamo Crik, the fellurs that went in sarch o' them Injuns, foun' out they wan't Injuns at all. Ye hev heern that yurself. From the fixins that war diskevered in the holler tree, it air clur that what we seed on the Bluff war a party o' whites. I hed a surspishun o't myself—soon as I seed them curds they'd left ahint 'em in the shanty."

"It was the same, then, who visited the jacalé at night—the same Phalim saw?"

"Ne'er a doubt o' it. Them same Mexikins."

"What reason have you to think they were Mexicans?"

"The best o' all reezuns. I foun' 'em out to be; traced the hul kit o' 'em to thur *caché*."

The young Creole made no rejoinder. Zeb's story promised a revelation that might be favourable to her hopes. She stood resignedly waiting for him to continue.

"Ye see, the curds, an also some words, the which the Irish war able to sort o' pernounce, arter a fashun o' his own, tolt me they must a been o' the yeller-belly breed; an sartint 'bout that much, I war able to gie a tol'able guess as to whar they hed kim from. I know'd enuf o' the Mexikins o' these parts to think o' four as answered thar descripshun to a T. As to the Injun duds, thar warn't nuthin' in them to bamboozle me. Arter this, I ked a gone straight to the hul four fellurs, an pinted 'em out for sartin. One o' 'em, for sure sartin. On him I'd made my mark. I war confident o' havin' did thet."

"Your mark! How, Zeb?"

"Ye remimber the shot I fired from the door o' the shanty?"

"Oh, certainly! I did not see the Indians. I was under the trees at the time. I saw you discharge your rifle at something."

"Wal, Miss Lewaze; this hyur coon don't often dischurge thet thur weepun 'ithout drawin' blood. I know'd I hut the skunk; but it war rayther fur for the carry o' the piece, an I reckon'd the ball war a bit spent. F'r all that, I know'd it must a stung him. I seed him squirm to the shot, an I says to myself: Ef ther ain't a hole through his hide somewhar, this coon won't mind changin' skins wi' him. Wal, arter they kim home wi' the story o' whites instead o' red-skins, I hed a tol'able clur idee o' who the sham Injuns wur, an ked a laid my claws on 'em at any minnit. But I didn't."

"And why not, Mr Stump? Surely you haven't allowed them to get away? They might be the very men who are guilty of my poor brother's—"

"That's jest what this coon thort, an it war for that reezun I let 'em slide. There war another reezun besides. I didn't much like goin' fur from the Port, leest somethin' ugly mout turn up in my absince. You unnerstan'? There war another reezun still for not prospectin' arter them jest then. I wanted to make shur o' my game."

"And you have?"

"Shur as shootin'. I guessed thur wan't goin' to be any rain, an thurfor thur war no immeedyit hurry as to what I intended doin'. So I waited till the sogers shed get back, an I ked safely leave him in the guard-house. Soon as they kim in, I tuk the ole maar and rud out to the place whar our fellurs had struck upon the fixing. I eezy foun' it by thur descripshun. Wal; as they'd only got that greenhorn, Spangler, to guide 'em, I war putty sure the sign hedn't been more'n helf read; an that I'd get somethin' out o' it, beside what they'd brought away."

"I wan't disappinted. The durndest fool as ever set fut upon a purayra, mout a follered the back track o' them make-believe Kimanchees. A storekeeper ked a traced it acrost the purayra, though it appears neyther Mister Spangler nor any o' the others did. I foun' it eezy as fallin' off o' a log, not 'ithstandin' thet the sarchers had rud all over it. I tracked every hoss o' the four counterfits to his own stable."

"After that?"

"Arter doin' thet I hed a word wi' the major; an in helf an hour at the most the four beauties wur safe shot up in the guardhouse—the chief o' 'em bein' jugged fust, leest he mout get wind o' what wur goin' forrard, an sneak out o' the way. I wan't fur astray 'beout Mister Migooel Dee-ez bearin' my mark. We foun' the tar o' a bullet through the fleshy part o' his dexter wing; an thet explained why he wur so quick at lettin' go his laryette."

"It was he, then!" mechanically remarked Louise, as she stood reflecting.

"Very strange!" she continued, still muttering the words to herself. "He it was I saw in the chapparal glade! Yes, it must have been! And the woman—this Mexican—Isidora? Ah! There is some deep mystery in all this—some dark design! Who can unravel it?"

"Tell me, dear Zeb," she asked, stepping closer to the old hunter, and speaking with a cartain degree of hesitancy. "That woman—the Mexican lady I mean—who—who was out there. Do you know if she has often visited him?"

"Him! Which him, Miss Lewaze?"

"Mr Gerald, I mean."

"She mout, an she moutn't—'ithout my knowin' eyther one or the tother. I ain't often thur myself. The place air out o' my usooal huntin' ground, an I only go now an then for the sake o' a change. The crik's fust rate for both deer an gobbler. If ye ask my opeenyun, I'd say that thet ere gurl heven't never been thur afore. Leestwise, I hain't heern o' it; an eft hed been so, I reckun Irish Pheelum ud a hed somethin' to say abeout it. Besides, I hev other reezuns for thinkin' so. I've only heern o' one o' the shemale sex bein' on a visit to thet shanty."

"Who?" quickly interrogated the Creole, the instant after regretting that she had asked the question—the colour coming to her cheeks, as she noticed the significant glance with which Zeb had accompanied his concluding remark.

"No matter," she continued, without waiting for the answer.

"So, Zeb," she went on, giving a quick turn to the conversation, "you think that these men have had to do with that which is causing sorrow to all of us,—these Mexicans?"

"To tell ye the truth, Miss Lewaze, I don't know zackly what to think. It air the most musteeriousest consarn as iver kim to pass on these hyur purayras. Sometimes I hev the idea that the Mexikins must a did it; while at others, I'm in the opposite way o' thinkin', an thet some'dy else hev hed a han' in the black bizness. I won't say who."

"Not *him*, Zeb; not *him*!"

"Not the mowstanger. No, neer a bit o' thet. Spite o' all that's sayed agin him, I hain't the leest surspishun o' his innersense."

"Oh! how is he to prove it? It is said, that the testimony is all against him! No one to speak a word in his behalf!"

"Wal, it ain't so sartint as to thet. Keepin' my eye upon the others, an his prison; I hain't hed much chance o' gettin' abeout. Thur's a opportunity now; an I mean to make use o' it. The purayra's a big book, Miss Peintdexter—a wonderful big book—for them as knows how to read the print o't. If not much o' a scholar otherways, Zeb'lon Stump hev larnt to do thet. Thur may be some testymoney that mout help him, scattered over the musquit grass—jest as I've heern a Methody preecher say, thur 'war sarmints in stones, an books in runnin' brutes.' Eft air so, thur oughter be somethin' o' the kind scared up on the Alamo crik."

"You think you might discover some traces?"

"Wal; I'm goin' out to hev a look 'roun' me—speecially at the place whur I foun' the young fellur in the claws o' the spotted painter. I oughter gone afore now, but for the reezun I've tolt ye. Thank the Awlmighty! thur's been no wet—neer y drop; an whatsomiver sign's been made for a week past, kin be understood as well, as if it war did yisterday—that is by them as knows how to read it. I must start straight away, Miss Lewaze. I jest runned down to tell ye what hed been done at the Fort. Thur's no time to be throwed away. They let me in this mornin' to see the young fellur; an I'm sartin his head air gettin' clurrer. Soon as it air all right, the Reg'lators say, they'll insist on the trial takin' place. It may be in less'n three days; an I must git back afore it begins."

"Go, Zeb, and God speed you on your generous errand! Come back with proofs of *his* innocence, and ever after I shall feel indebted to you for—for—more than life!"

# 71. The Sorell Horse

Inspired by this passionate appeal, the hunter hastened towards the stable, where he had stalled his unique specimen of horseflesh.

He found the "critter" sonorously shelling some corn-cobs, which Pluto had placed liberally before her.

Pluto himself was standing by her side.

Contrary to his usual habit, the sable groom was silent: though with an air anything but tranquil. He looked rather *triste* than excited.

It might be easily explained. The loss of his young master—by Pluto much beloved—the sorrow of his young mistress, equally estimated—perhaps some scornful speeches which he had lately been treated to from the lips of Morinda—and still more likely a kick he had received from the boot-toe of Captain Cassius—for several days assuming sole mastery over the mansion—amply accounted for the unquiet expression observable on his countenance.

Zeb was too much occupied with his own thoughts to notice the sorrowful mien of the domestic. He was even in too great a hurry to let the old mare finish her meal of maize, which she stood greatly in need of.

Grasping her by the snout, he stuck the rusty snaffle between her teeth; pulled her long ears through the cracked leathern headstraps; and, turning her in the stall, was about to lead her out.

It was a reluctant movement on the part of the mare—to be dragged away from such provender as she rarely chanced to get between her jaws.

She did not turn without a struggle; and Zeb was obliged to pull vigorously on the bridle-rein before he could detach her muzzle from the manger.

"Ho! ho! Mass' Tump!" interposed Pluto. "Why you be go 'way in dat big hurry? De poor ole ma' she no half got u'm feed. Why you no let her fill her belly wif de corn? Ha! ha! It do her power o' good."

"Han't got time, nigger. Goin' off on a bit o' a jurney. Got abeout a hunderd mile to make in less 'an a kupple o' hours."

"Ho! ho! Dat ere de fassest kind o' trabbelin'. You 'm jokin', Mass' Tump?"

"No, I ain't."

"Gorramity! Wa—dey do make won'full journey on dese hyur prairas. I reck'n dat ere hoss must a trabbled *two* hunner mile de odder night."

"What hoss?"

"De ole sorrel dere—in dat furrest 'tand from de doos—Massa Cahoon hoss."

"What makes ye think he travelled two hunder mile?"

"Kase he turn home all kibbered ober wif de froff. Beside, he wa *so* done up he scace able walk, when dis chile lead um down to de ribba fo' gib um drink. Hee 'tagger like new-drop calf. Ho! ho! he wa broke down—he wa!"

"O' what night air ye palaverin', Plute?"

"Wha night? Le'ss see! Why, ob coas de night Massa Henry wa missed from de plantashun. Dat same night in de mornin', 'bout an hour atter de sun git up into de hebbings. I no see de ole sorrel afore den, kase I no out ob my skeeta-bar till after daylight. Den I kum 'cross to de 'table hya, an den I see dat quadrumpid all kibbered ober wif sweet an froff—lookin' like he'd swimmed through de big ribba, an pantin' 's if he jes finish a fo' mile race on de Metairie course at New Orlean."

"Who had him out thet night?"

"Doan know, Mass' Tump. Only dat nobody 'lowed to ride de sorrel 'cept Massa Cahoon hisself. Ho! ho! Ne'er a body 'lowed lay leg ober dat critter."

"Why, wan't it himself that tuk the anymal out?"

"Doan know, Massa Tump; doan know de why nor de whafor. Dis chile neider see de Cap'n take um out nor fotch um in."

"If yur statement air true 'beout his bein' in sech a sweat, someb'dy must a hed him out, an been ridin' o' him."

"Ha! ha! Someb'dy muss, dat am certing."

"Looke hyur, Plute! Ye ain't a bad sort o' a darkie, though your skin air o' a sut colour. I reck'n you're tellin' the truth; an ye don't know who rud out the sorrel that night. But who do ye *think* it war? I'm only axin' because, as ye know, Mr Peintdexter air a friend o' mine, an I don't want his property to be abused—no more what belongs to Capen Calhoun. Some o' the field niggers, I reck'n, hev stole

431

the anymal out o' the stable, an hev been ridin' it all roun' the country. That's it, ain't it?"

"Well, no, Mass' Tump. Dis chile doan believe dat am it. De fiel' hands not 'lowed inside hyur. *Dey* darn't kum in to de 'table no how. 'Twan't any nigger upon dis plantashun as tooked out de sorrel dat night."

"Durn it, then, who ked a tuk him out? Maybe the overseer? War it him d'ye think?"

"'Twan't him needer."

"Who then ked it be; unless it war the owner o' the hoss hisself? If so, thur's an end o' it. He hed the right to ride his critter wharever he pleased, an gallop it to hell ef thet war agreeable to him. It ain't no bizness o' myen."

"Ho! ho! Nor myen, needer, Mass' Tump. Wish I'd thought dat way dis mornin'."

"Why do ye weesh that? What happened this mornin' to change yur tune?"

"Ho! what happen dis mornin'? Dar happen to dis nigga a great misfortin'. Ho!—ho! berry great misfortin'."

"What war it?"

"Golly, Massa Tump, I'se got kicked—dis berry mornin', jes 'bout an hour arter twelve o'clock in de day."

"Kicked?"

"Dat I did shoo—all round de 'table."

"Oh! by the hosses! Which o' the brutes kicked ye?"

"Ho!—ho! you mistaken! Not any ob de hosses, but de massa ob dem all—'cept little Spotty da, de which he doan't own. I wa kicked by Mass' Cahoon."

"The hell ye wur! For what reezun? Ye must hev *been* misbe-havin' yurself, nigger?"

"Dis nigga wan't mis-b'avin' 't all; not as he knows on. I only ask de cap'n what put de ole sorrel in such a dreful condishin dat ere night, an what make 'im be tired down. He say it not my bizness; an den he kick me; an den he larrup me wif de cow-hide; an den he threaten; an den he tell me, if I ebber 'peak bout dat same ting odder time, he gib me hunder lashes ob de wagon whip. He swa; oh! how he swa! Dis chile nebba see Mass Cahoon so mad—nebba, in all 'im life!"

"But whar's he now? I don't see him nowhar' beout the premises; an I reck'n he ain't rud out, seein' as the sorrel's hyur?"

"Golly, yes, Mass Tump; he jess am rode out at dis time. He ob late go berry much away from de house an tay long time."

432

"A hossback?"

"Jess so. He go on de steel grey. Ha!—ha! he doan' ride de sorrel much now. He hain't mount 'im once since de night de ole hoss wa out—dat night we been 'peakin' 'bout. Maybe he tink he hab enuf hard ridin' den, an need long 'pell ob ress."

"Look'ee hyur, Plute," said Zeb, after standing silent for a second or two, apparently engaged in some abstruse calculation. "Arter all, I reck'n I'd better let the ole maar hev another yeer or two o' the corn. She's got a long spell o' travellin' afore her; an she mout break down on the jurney. The more haste air sometimes the wusser speed; an thurfor, I kalkerlate, I'd better gie the critter her time. While she's munchin' a mouthful, I ked do the same myself. 'Spose, then, you skoot acrosst to the kitchen, an see ef thur ain't some chawin' stuff thur—a bit o' cold meat an a pone o' corn bread 'll do. Yur young mistress wanted me to hev somethin' to eet; but I war skeert abeout delayin', an refused. Now, while I'm waitin' on the maar, I reck'n I ked pick a bone,—jest to pass the time."

"Sartin' ye cud, Mass Tump. I go fotch 'im in de hundreth part ob an instant."

So saying the black-skinned Jehu started off across the *patio*, leaving Zeb Stump sole "master of the stole."

The air of indifference with which he had concluded his dialogue with Pluto disappeared, the moment the latter was outside the door.

It had been altogether assumed: as was proved by the earnest attitude that instantly replaced it.

Striding across the paved causeway, that separated the two rows of stalls, he entered that occupied by the sorrel.

The animal shied off, and stood trembling against the wall—perhaps awed by the look of resolution with which the hunter had approached it.

"Stan' still, ye brute!" chided Zeb. "I don't mean no harm to *you*, tho' by yur looks I reck'n ye're as vicious as yur master. Stan' still, I say, an let's hev a look at yur fut-gear!"

So saying, he stooped forward, and made an attempt to lay hold of one of the fore-legs.

It was unsuccessful. The horse suddenly drew up his hoof; and commenced hammering the flags with it, snorting—as if in fear that some trick was about to be played upon him.

"Durn your ugly karkidge!" cried Zeb, angrily venting the words. "Why don't ye stan' still? Who's goin' to hurt ye? Come, ole critter!" he continued coaxingly, "I only want to see how youv'e been shod."

Again he attempted to lift the hoof, but was prevented by the restive behaviour of the horse.

"Wal, this air a difeequilty I didn't expeck," muttered he, glancing round to see how it might be overcome. "What's to be did? It'll never do to hev the nigger help me—nor yet see what I'm abeout—the which he will ef I don't get quick through wi' it. Dog-gone the hoss! How am I to git his feet up?"

For a short while he stood considering, his countenance showing a peevish impatience.

"Cuss the critter!" he again exclaimed. "I feel like knockin' him over whar he stan's. Ha! now I hev it, if the nigger will only gie time. I hope the wench will keep him waitin'. Durn ye! I'll make ye stan' still, or choke ye dead ef ye don't. Wi' this roun' yur jugewlar, I reck'n ye won't be so skittish."

While speaking he had lifted the trail-rope from his own saddle; and, throwing its noose over the head of the sorrel, he shook it down till it encircled the animal's neck.

Then hauling upon the other end, he drew it taut as a bowstring.

The horse for a time kept starting about the stall, and snorting with rage.

But his snorts were soon changed into a hissing sound, that with difficulty escaped through his nostrils; and his wrath resolved itself into terror. The rope tightly compressing his throat was the cause of the change.

Zeb now approached him without fear; and, after making the slip fast, commenced lifting his feet one after the other—scrutinising each, in great haste, but at the same time with sufficient care. He appeared to take note of the shape, the shoeing, the number and relative position of the nails—in short, everything that might suggest an idiosyncrasy, or assist in a future identification.

On coming to the off hind foot—which he did last of the four—an exclamation escaped him that proclaimed some satisfactory surprise. It was caused by the sight of a broken shoe—nearly a quarter of which was missing from the hoof, the fracture having occurred at the second nail from the canker.

"Ef I'd know'd o' *you*," he muttered in apostrophe to the imperfect shoe, "I mout a' saved myself the trouble o' examinin' the tothers. Thur ain't much chance o' mistakin' the print you'd be likely to leave ahint ye. To make shur, I'll jest take ye along wi me."

In conformity with this resolve, he drew out his huge hunting knife—the blade of which, near the hilt, was a quarter of an inch thick—and, inserting it under the piece of iron, he wrenched it from the hoof.

Taking care to have the nails along, he transferred it to the capacious pocket of his coat.

Then nimbly gliding back to the trail-rope, he undid the knot; and restored the interrupted respiration of the sorrel.

Pluto came in the moment after, bringing a plentiful supply of refreshments—including a tumbler of the Monongahela; and to these Zeb instantly applied himself, without saying a word about the interlude that had occurred during the darkey's absence.

The latter, however, did not fail to perceive that the sorrel was out of sorts: for the animal, on finding itself released, stood shivering in the stall, gazing around in a sort of woe-begone wonder after the rough treatment, to which he had been submitted.

"Gorramity!" exclaimed the black, "what am de matter wif de ole hoss? Ho! ho! he look like he wa afeerd ob you, Mass Tump!"

"Oh, ye-es!" drawled Zeb, with seeming carelessness. "I reck'n he air a bit afeerd. He war makin' to get at my ole maar, so I gied him a larrup or two wi' the eend o' my trail rope. Thet's what has rousted him."

Pluto was perfectly satisfied with the explanation, and the subject was permitted to drop.

"Look hyur, Plute!" said Zeb, starting another. "Who does the shoein' o' yur cattle? Thars some o' the hands air a smith, I reck'n?"

"Ho! ho! Dat dere am. Yella Jake he do shoein'. Fo what you ask, Mass Tump?"

"Wal; I war thinkin' o' havin' a kupple o' shoes put on the hind feet o' the maar. I reck'n Jake ud do it for me."

"Ho! ho! he do it wif a thousan' welkim—dat he will, I'se shoo."

"Questyun is, kin I spare the time to wait. How long do it take him to put on a kupple?"

"Lor, Mass Tamp, berry short while. Jake fust-rate han' lit de bizness. Ebberybody say so."

"He moutn't have the mateerils riddy? It depends on whether he's been shoein' lately. How long's it since he shod any o' yourn?"

"More'n a week I blieb, Mass' Zeb. Ho—ho! Do last war Missa Looey hoss—de beautiful 'potty dar. But dat won't make no differens. I know he hab de fixins all ready. I knows it, kase he go for shoe de sorrel. De ole hoss hab one ob de hind shoe broke. He hab it so de lass ten day; an Mass Cahoon, he gib orders for it be remove. Ho—ho! dis berry mornin' I hear um tell Jake."

435

"Arter all," rejoined Zeb, as if suddenly changing his mind, "I moutn't hev the time to spare. I reck'n I'll let the ole critter do 'ithout till I kum back. The tramp I'm goin' on—most part o' it—lies over grass purayra; an won't hurt her."

"No, I hevn't time," he added, after stepping outside and glancing up towards the sky. "I must be off from hyur in the shakin' o' a goat's tail. Now, ole gal! you've got to stop yur munchin' an take this bit o' iron atwixt yur teeth. Open yur corn trap for it. That's the putty pet!"

And so continuing to talk—now to Pluto, now to the mare—he once more adjusted the headstall; led the animal out; and, clambering into the saddle, rode thoughtfully away.

# 72. Zeb Stump on the Trail

After getting clear of the enclosures of Casa del Corvo, the hunter headed his animal up stream—in the direction of the Port and town.

It was the former he intended to reach—which he did in a ride of less than a quarter of an hour.

Commonly it took him three to accomplish this distance; but on this occasion he was in an unusual state of excitement, and he made speed to correspond. The old mare could go fast enough when required—that is when Zeb required her and he had a mode of quickening her speed—known only to himself, and only employed upon extraordinary occasions. It simply consisted in drawing the bowie knife from his belt, and inserting about in inch of its blade into the mare's hip, close to the termination of the spine.

The effect was like magic; or, if you prefer the figure—electricity. So spurred, Zeb's "critter" could accomplish a mile in three minutes; and more than once had she been called upon to show this capability, when her owner was chased by Comanches.

On the present occasion there was no necessity for such excessive speed; and the Fort was reached after fifteen minutes' sharp trotting.

On reaching it, Zeb slipped out of the saddle, and made his way to the quarters of the commandant; while the mare was left panting upon the parade ground.

The old hunter had no difficulty in obtaining an interview with the military chief of Fort Inge. Looked upon by the officers as a sort of privileged character, he had the entrée at all times, and could go in without countersign, or any of the other formalities usually demanded from a stranger. The sentry passed him, as a matter of course—the officer of the guard only exchanged with him a word of welcome; and the adjutant at once announced his name to the major commanding the cantonment.

From his first words, the latter appeared to have been expecting him.

"Ah! Mr Stump! Glad to see you so soon. Have you made any discovery in this queer affair? From your quick return, I can almost say you have. Something, I hope, in favour of this unfortunate young fellow. Notwithstanding that appearances are strongly against him, I still adhere to my old opinion—that he's innocent. What have you learnt?"

"Wal, Maje," answered Zeb, without making other obeisance than the simple politeness of removing his hat; "what I've larnt aint much, tho' enough to fetch me back to the Fort; where I didn't intend to come, till I'd gone a bit o' a jurney acrosst the purayras. I kim back hyur to hev a word wi' yurself."

"In welcome. What is it you have to say?"

"That ye'll keep back this trial as long's ye kin raisonably do so. I know thur's a pressyur from the outside; but I know, too, that ye've got the power to resist it, an what's more, Maje—yo've got the will."

"I have. You speak quite truly about that, Mr Stump. And as to the power, I have that, too, in a certain sense. But, as you are aware, in our great republic, the military power must always be subservient to the civil—unless under martial-law, which God forbid should ever be required among us—even here in Texas. I can go so far as to hinder any open violation of the law; but I cannot go against the law itself."

"T'ant the law I want ye to go agin. Nothin' o' the sort, Maje. Only them as air like to take it into thur own hands, an twist it abeout to squar it wi' thur own purpisses. Thur's them in this Settlement as 'ud do thet, ef they ain't rustrained. One in espeecial 'ud like to do it; an I knows who thet one air—leestwise I hev a tolable clur guess o' him."

"Who?"

"Yur good to keep a seecret, Maje? I know ye air."

"Mr Stump, what passes here is in confidence. You may speak your mind freely."

"Then my mind air: thet the man who hez dud this murder ain't Maurice the Mowstanger."

"That's my own belief. You know it already. Have you nothing more to communicate?"

"Wal, Maje, preehaps I ked communerkate a leetle more ef you insist upon it. But the time ain't ripe for tellin' ye what I've larnt—the which, arter all, only mounts to surspishuns. I may be wrong; an I'd rayther you'd let me keep 'em to myself till I hev made a short exkurshun acrost to the Nooeces. Arter thet, ye'll be welkum to what I know now, besides what I may be able to gather off o' the parayras."

"So far as I am concerned, I'm quite contented to wait for your return; the more willingly that I know you are acting on the side of justice. But what would you have me do?"

"Keep back the trial, Maje—only that. The rest will be all right."

"How long? You know that it must come on according to the usual process in the Criminal Court. The judge of this circuit will not be ruled by me, though he may yield a little to my advice. But there is a party, who are crying out for vengeance; and he may be ruled by them."

"I know the party ye speak o'. I know their leader; an maybe, afore the trial air over, *he* may be the kriminal afore the bar."

"Ah! you do not believe, then, that these Mexicans are the *men*!"

"Can't tell, Maje, whether they air or ain't. I do b'lieve thet they've hed a hand in the bizness; but I don't b'lieve thet they've been the prime movers in't. It's *him* I want to diskiver. Kin ye promise me three days?"

"Three days! For what?"

"Afore the trial kims on."

"Oh! I think there will be no difficulty about that. He is now a prisoner under military law. Even if the judge of the Supreme Court should require him to be delivered up inside that time, I can make objections that will delay his being taken from the guard-house. I shall undertake to do that."

"Maje! ye'd make a man a'most contented to live under marshul law. No doubt thur air times when it air the best, tho' we independent citizens don't much like it. All I've got to say air, thet ef ye stop this trial for three days, or tharahout, preehaps the prisoner to kim afore the bar may be someb'y else than him who's now in the guard-house— someb'y who jest at this mom't hain't the smallest serspishun o' bein' hisself surspected. Don't ask me who. Only say ye'll streetch a pint, an gi' me three days?"

"I promise it, Mr Stump. Though I may risk my commission as an officer in the American army, I give you an officer's promise, that for three days Maurice the Mustanger shall not go out of my guard-house. Innocent or guilty, for that time he shall be protected."

"Yur the true grit, Maje; an dog-gone me, ef I don't do my beest to show ye some day, thet I'm sensible o't. I've nuthin' more to say now, 'ceptin' to axe thet ye'll not tell out o' doors what I've been tellin' you. Thur's them outside who, ef they only knew what this coon air arter, 'ud move both heving an airth to circumwent his intenshuns."

439

"They'll have no help from me—whoever it is you are speaking of. Mr Stump, you may rely upon my pledged word."

"I know't, Maje, I know't. God bless ye for a good 'un. *Yer* the right sort for Texas!"

With this complimentary leave-taking the hunter strode out of head-quarters, and made his way back to the place where he had left his old mare.

Once more mounting her, he rode rapidly away. Having cleared the parade ground, and afterwards the outskirts of the village, he returned on the same path that had conducted him from Casa Del Corvo.

On reaching the outskirts of Poindexter's plantation, he left the low lands of the Leona bottom, and spurred his old mare 'gainst the steep slope ascending to the upper plain.

He reached it, at a point where the chapparal impinged upon the prairie, and there reined up under the shade of a mezquit tree. He did not alight, nor show any sign of an intention to do so; but sate in the saddle, stooped forward, his eyes turned upon the ground, in that vacant gaze which denotes reflection.

"Dog-gone my cats!" he drawled out in slow soliloquy. "Thet ere sarkimstance are full o' signiferkince. Calhoun's hoss out the same night, an fetched home a' sweetin' all over. What ked that mean? Durn me, ef I don't surspect the foul play hev kum from that quarter. I've thort so all along; only it air so ridiklous to serpose thet he shed a killed his own cousin. He'd do that, or any other villinous thing, ef there war a reezun for it. There ain't—none as I kin think o'. Ef the property hed been a goin' to the young un, then the thing mout a been intellygible enuf. But it want. Ole Peintdexter don't own a acre o' this hyur groun'; nor a nigger thet's upon it. Thet I'm sartin' 'beout. They all belong to that cuss arready; an why shed he want to get shot o' the cousin? Thet's whar this coon gets flummixed in his kalkerlations. Thar want no ill will atween 'em, as ever I heerd o'. Thur's a state o' feelin' twixt him an the gurl, thet *he* don't like, I know. But why shed it temp him to the killin' o' her brother?

"An' then thur's the mowstanger mixed in wi' it, an that shindy 'beout which she tolt me herself; an the sham Injuns, an the Mexikin shemale wi' the har upon her lip; an the hossman 'ithout a head, an hell knows what beside! Geesus Geehosofat! it 'ud puzzle the brain pan o' a Looeyville lawyer!

"Wal—there's no time to stan' speklatin' hyur. Wi' this bit o' iron to assiss me, I may chance upon somethin' thet'll gie a clue to a part o' the bloody bizness, ef not to the hul o' it; an fust, as to the direcshun in which I shed steer?"

He looked round, as if in search of some one to answer the interrogatory.

"It air no use beginnin' neer the Fort or the town. The groun' abeout both on 'em air paddled wi' hoss tracks like a cattle pen. I'd best strike out into the purayra at onst, an take a track crossways o' the Rio Grande route. By doin' thet I may fluke on the futmark I'm in search o'. Yes—ye-es! thet's the most sensiblest idee."

As if fully satisfied on this score, he took up his bridle-rein, muttered some words to his mare, and commenced moving off along the edge of the chapparal.

Having advanced about a mile in the direction of the Nueces river, he abruptly changed his course; but with a coolness that told of a predetermined purpose.

It was now nearly due west, and at right angles to the different trails going towards the Rio Grande.

There was a simultaneous change in his bearing—in the expression of his features—and his attitude in the saddle. No longer looking listlessly around, he sate stooping forward, his eye carefully scanning the sward, over a wide space on both sides of the path he was pursuing.

He had ridden about a mile in the new direction, when something seen upon the ground caused him to start, and simultaneously pull upon the bridle-rein.

Nothing loth, the "critter" came to a stand; Zeb, at the same time, flinging himself out of the saddle.

Leaving the old mare to ruminate upon this eccentric proceeding, he advanced a pace or two, and dropped down upon his knees.

Then drawing the piece of curved iron out of his capacious pocket, he applied it to a hoof-print conspicuously outlined in the turf. It fitted.

"Fits!" he exclaimed, with a triumphant gesticulation, "Doggoned if it don't!"

"Tight as the skin o' a tick!" he continued, after adjusting the broken shoe to the imperfect hoof-print, and taking it up again. "By the eturnal! that ere's *the track o' a creetur—mayhap a murderer!*"

# 73. The Prairie Island

A herd of a hundred horses—or three times the number—pasturing upon a prairie, although a spectacle of the grandest kind furnished by the animal kingdom, is not one that would strike a Texan frontiersman as either strange, or curious. He would think it stranger to see a *single* horse in the same situation.

The former would simply be followed by the reflection: "A drove of mustangs." The latter conducts to a different train of thought, in which there is an ambiguity. The solitary steed might be one of two things: either an exiled stallion, kicked out of his own *cavallada*, or a roadster strayed from some encampment of travellers.

The practised eye of the prairie-man would soon decide which.

If the horse browsed with a bit in his mouth, and a saddle on his shoulders, there would be no ambiguity—only the conjecture, as to how he had escaped from his rider.

If the rider were upon his back, and the horse still browsing, there would be no room for conjecture—only the reflection, that the former must be a lazy thick-headed fellow, not to alight and let his animal graze in a more commodious fashion.

If, however, the rider, instead of being suspected of having a thick head, was seen to have *no head at all*, then would there be cue for a thousand conjectures, not one of which might come within a thousand miles of the truth.

Such a horse; and just such a rider, were seen upon the prairies of South-Western Texas in the year of our Lord 1850 something. I am not certain as to the exact year—the unit of it—though I can with unquestionable certainty record the decade.

I can speak more precisely as to the place; though in this I must be allowed latitude. A circumference of twenty miles will include the different points where the spectral apparition made itself manifest to the eyes of men—both on prairie and in chapparal—in a district of country traversed by several northern tributaries of the Rio de Nueces, and some southern branches of the Rio Leona.

It was seen not only by many people; but at many different times. First, by the searchers for Henry Poindexter and his supposed murderer; second, by the servant of Maurice the mustanger; thirdly, by Cassius Calhoun, on his midnight exploration of the chapparal; fourthly, by the sham Indians on that same night: and, fifthly, by Zeb Stump on the night following.

But there were others who saw it elsewhere and on different occasions—hunters, herdsmen, and travellers—all alike awed, alike perplexed, by the apparition.

It had become the talk not only of the Leona settlement, but of others more distant. Its fame already reached on one side to the Rio Grande, and on the other was rapidly extending to the Sabine. No one doubted that such a thing had been seen. To have done so would have been to ignore the evidence of two hundred pairs of eyes, all belonging to men willing to make affidavit of the fact—for it could not be pronounced a fancy. No one denied that it had been seen. The only question was, how to account for a spectacle so peculiar, as to give the lie to all the known laws of creation.

At least half a score of theories were started—more or less feasible—more or less absurd. Some called it an "Indian dodge;" others believed it a "lay figure;" others that it was not that, but a real rider, only so disguised as to have his head under the serapé that shrouded his shoulders, with perhaps a pair of eye-holes through which he could see to guide his horse; while not a few pertinaciously adhered to the conjecture, started at a very early period, that the Headless Horseman was Lucifer himself!

In addition to the direct attempts at interpreting the abnormal phenomenon, there was a crowd of indirect conjectures relating to it. Some fancied that they could see the head, or the shape of it, down upon the breast, and under the blanket; others affirmed to having actually seen it carried in the rider's hand; while others went still further, and alleged: that upon the head thus seen there was a hat—a black-glaze sombrero of the Mexican sort, with a band of gold bullion above the brim!

There were still further speculations, that related less to the apparition itself than to its connection with the other grand topic of the time—the murder of young Poindexter.

Most people believed there was some connection between the two mysteries; though no one could explain it. He, whom everybody believed, could have thrown some light upon the subject, was still ridden by the night-mare of delirium.

And for a whole week the guessing continued; during which the spectral rider was repeatedly seen; now going at a quick gallop, now moving in slow, tranquil pace, across the treeless prairie: his horse at one time halted and vaguely gazing around him; at another with teeth to the ground, industriously cropping the sweet *gramma* grass, that makes the pasturage of South-Western Texas (in my opinion) the finest in the world.

Rejecting many tales told of the Headless Horseman—most of them too grotesque to be recorded—one truthful episode must needs be given—since it forms an essential chapter of this strange history.

In the midst of the open, prairie there is a "motte"—a coppice, or clump of trees—of perhaps three or four acres in superficial extent. A prairie-man would call it an "island," and with your eyes upon the vast verdant sea that surrounds it, you could not help being struck with the resemblance.

The aboriginal of America might not perceive it. It is a thought of the colonist transmitted to his descendants; who, although they may never have looked upon the great ocean, are nevertheless *au fait* to its phraseology.

By the timber island in question—about two hundred yards from its edge—a horse is quietly pasturing. He is the same that carries the headless rider; and this weird equestrian is still bestriding him, with but little appearance of change, either in apparel or attitude, since first seen by the searchers. The striped blanket still hangs over his shoulders, cloaking the upper half of his person; while the *armas-de-agua*, strapped over his limbs, cover them from thigh to spur, concealing all but their outlines.

His body is bent a little forward, as if to ease the horse in getting his snout to the sward; which the long bridle-rein, surrendered to its full length, enables him to do, though still retained in hand, or resting over the "horn" of the saddle.

Those who asserted that they saw a head, only told the truth. There is a head; and, as also stated, with a hat upon it—a black sombrero, with bullion band as described.

The head rests against the left thigh, the chin being nearly down on a level with the rider's knee. Being on the near side it *can* only be seen, when the spectator is on the same; and not always then, as it is at times concealed by a corner of the serapé.

444

At times too can a glimpse be obtained of the face. Its features are well formed, but wearing a sad expression; the lips of livid colour, slightly parted, showing a double row of white teeth, set in a grim ghastly smile.

Though there is no perceptible change in the *personnel* of the Headless Horseman there is something new to be noted. Hitherto he has been seen going alone. Now he is in company.

It cannot be called agreeable;—consisting as it does of wolves—half a score of them squatting closely upon the plain, and at intervals loping around him.

By the horse they are certainly not liked; as is proved by the snorting and stamping of his hoof, when one of them ventures upon a too close proximity to his heels.

The rider seems more indifferent to a score of birds—large dark birds—that swoop in shadowy circles around his shoulders. Even when one bolder than the rest has the audacity to alight upon him, he has made no attempt to disturb it, raising neither hand nor arm to drive it away!

Three times one of the birds has alighted thus—first upon the right shoulder, then upon the left, and then midway between—upon the spot where the head should be!

The bird does not stay upon its singular perch, or only for an instant. If the rider does not feel the indignity the steed does; and resists it by rearing upward, with a fierce neighing, that frights the vultures off—to return again only after a short interval of shyness.

His steed thus browsing, now in quiet, now disturbed by the too near approach of the wolves—anon by the bold behaviour of the birds—goes the Headless Horseman, step by step, and with long pauses of pasturing, around the prairie island.

# 74. A Solitary Stalker

The singular spectacle described—extraordinary it might be termed—was too grave to appear grotesque. There was some thing about it that savoured of the *outre-monde*. Human eyes could not have beholden it, without the shivering of a human frame, and the chilling of human blood.

Was it seen by human eyes in this fresh phase—with the wolves below, and the vultures above?

It was.

By one pair; and they belonging to the only man in all Texas who had arrived at something like a comprehension of the all-perplexing mystery.

It was not yet altogether clear to him. There were points that still puzzled him. He but know it was neither a dummy, nor the Devil.

His knowledge did not except him from the universal feeling of dread. Despite the understanding of what the thing was, he shuddered as he gazed upon it.

He gazed upon it from the "shore" of the prairie-island; himself unseen under its shadows, and apparently endeavouring to remain so.

And yet, with all his trembling and the desire to keep concealed, he was following it round and round, on the circumference of an inner circle, as if some magnetic power was constraining him to keep on the same radius, of which the point occupied by the Headless Horseman was a prolongation!

More than this. He had seen the latter before entering the island. He had seen him far off, and might easily have shunned him. But instead of doing so, he had immediately commenced making approach towards him!

He had continued it—using the timber as a screen, and acting as one who stalks the timid stag, with the difference of a heart-dread which no deer-stalker could ever know.

He had continued it; until the shelter of the *motte* gave him a momentary respite, not from fear, but the apprehension of a failure.

He had not ridden ten miles across the prairie without a design; and it was this that caused him to go so cautiously—guiding his horse over the softest turf, and through the selvedge of the chapparal—in such a way as neither to expose his person to view, nor cause a rustle among the branches, that might be heard to the distance of ten yards.

No one observing his manoeuvres as he moved amid the timber island, could have mistaken their meaning—at least so far as related to the object for which they were being made.

His eye was upon the Headless Horseman, his whole soul absorbed in watching the movements of the latter—by which he appeared to regulate his own.

At first, fear seemed to be his prevailing thought. After a time, it was succeeded by an impatience that partially emboldened him. The latter plainly sprang from his perceiving, that the Headless Horseman, instead of approaching the timber, still kept at a regular distance of two hundred yards from its edge.

That this chafed him was evident from a string of soliloquies, muttered half aloud. They were not free from blasphemy; but that was characteristic of the man who pronounced them.

"Damn the infernal brute! If he'd only come twenty yards nearer, I could fetch him. My gun won't carry that distance. I'd miss him for sure, and then it'll be all up. I may never get the chance again. Confound him! He's all of twenty yards too far off." As if the last was an ambiguity rather than a conviction, the speaker appeared to measure with his eye the space that separated him from the headless rider—all the while holding in hand a short Yäger rifle, capped and cocked—ready for instant discharge.

"No use," he continued, after a process of silent computation. "I might hit the beast with a spent ball, but only to scare without crippling him. I must have patience, and wait till he gets a little nearer. Damn them wolves! He might come in, if it wasn't for them. So long as they're about him, he'll give the timber a wide berth. It's the nature of these Texas howes—devil skin them!

"I wonder if coaxing would do any good?" he proceeded, after a pause. "Maybe the sound of a man's voice would bring the animal to a stand? Doubtful. He's not likely to 've heard much of that lately. I suppose it would only frighten him! The sight of my horse would be sure to do it, as it did before; though that was in the moonlight. Besides, he was chased by the howling staghound. No wonder his being wild, then, ridden as he is by hell knows what; for it can't be—Bah! After all, there must be some trick in it; some damned infernal trick!"

For a while the speaker checked his horse with a tight rein. And, leaning forward, so as to get a good view through the trees, continued to scan the strange shape that was slowly skirting the timber.

"It's *his* horse—sure as shootin'! His saddle, serapé, and all. How the hell could they have come into the possession of the other?"

Another pause of reflection.

"Trick, or no trick, it's an ugly business. Whoever's planned it, must know all that happened that night; and by God, if that thing lodged there, I've got to get it back. What a fool; to have bragged about it as I did! Curse the crooked luck!

"He *won't* come nearer. He's provokingly shy of the timber. Like all his breed, he knows he's safest in the open ground.

"What's to be done? See if I can call him up. May be he may like to hear a human voice. If it'll only fetch him twenty yards nearer, I'll be satisfied. Hanged if I don't try."

Drawing a little closer to the edge of the thicket, the speaker pronounced that call usually employed by Texans to summon a straying horse.

"Proh—proh—proshow! Come kindly! come, old horse!"

The invitation was extended to no purpose. The Texan steed did not seem to understand it; at all events, as an invitation to friendly companionship. On the contrary, it had the effect of frightening him; for no sooner fell the "proh" upon his ear, than letting go the mouthful of grass already gathered, he tossed his head aloft with a snort that proclaimed far greater fear than that felt for either wolf or vulture!

A mustang, he knew that his greatest enemy was man—a man mounted upon a horse; and by this time his scent had disclosed to him the proximity of such a foe.

He stayed not to see what sort of man, or what kind of horse. His first instinct had told him that both were enemies.

As his rider by this time appeared to have arrived at the same conclusion, there was no tightening of the rein; and he was left free to follow his own course—which carried him straight off over the prairie.

A bitter curse escaped from the lips of the unsuccessful stalker as he spurred out into the open ground.

Still more bitter was his oath, as he beheld the Headless Horseman passing rapidly beyond reach—unscathed by the bullet he had sent to earnestly after him.

# 75. On the Trail

Zeb Stump stayed but a short while on the spot, where he had discovered the hoof-print with the broken shoe.

Six seconds sufficed for its identification; after which he rose to his feet, and continued along the trail of the horse that had made it.

He did not re-mount, but strode forward on foot; the old mare, obedient to a signal he had given her, keeping at a respectful distance behind him.

For more than a mile he moved on in this original fashion—now slowly, as the trail became indistinct—quickening his pace where the print of the imperfect shoe could be seen without difficulty.

Like an archaeologist engaged upon a tablet of hieroglyphic history, long entombed beneath the ruins of a lost metropolis—whose characters appear grotesque to all except himself—so was it with Zeb Stump, as he strode on, translating the "sign" of the prairie.

Absorbed in the act, and the conjectures that accompanied it, he had no eyes for aught else. He glanced neither to the green savannah that stretched inimitably around, nor to the blue sky that spread specklessly above him. Alone to the turf beneath his feet was his eye and attention directed.

A sound—not a sight—startled him from his all-engrossing occupation. It was the report of a rifle; but so distant, as to appear but the detonation of a percussion-cap that had missed fire.

Instinctively he stopped; at the same time raising his eyes, but without unbending his body.

With a quick glance the horizon was swept, along the half dozen points whence the sound should have proceeded.

A spot of bluish smoke—still preserving its balloon shape—was slowly rolling up against the sky. A dark blotch beneath indicated the outlines of an "island" of timber.

So distant was the "motte," the smoke, and the sound, that only the eye of an experienced prairie-man would have seen the first, or his ear heard the last, from the spot where Zeb Stump was standing.

But Zeb saw the one, and heard the other.

"Durned queery!" he muttered, still stooped in the attitude of a gardener dibbing in his young cabbage-plants.

"Dog-goned queery, to say the leest on't. Who in ole Nick's name kin be huntin' out thur—whar theer ain't game enuf to pay for the powder an shet? I've been to thet ere purayra island; an I know there ain't nothin' thur 'ceptin' coyoats. What *they* get to live on, only the Eturnal kin tell!"

"Wagh!" he went on, after a short silence. "Some storekeeper from the town, out on a exkurshun, as he'd call it, who's proud o' poppin' away at them stinkin' varmints, an 'll go hum wi' a story he's been a huntin' *wolves*! Wal. 'Tain't no bizness o' myen. Let yurd-stick hev his belly-ful o' sport. Heigh! thur's somethin' comin' this way. A hoss an somebody on his back—streakin' it as if hell war arter him, wi' a pitchfork o' red-het lightnin'! What! As I live, it air the Headless! It is, by the jumpin' Geehosophat!"

The observation of the old hunter was quite correct. There could be no mistake about the character of the cavalier, who, just clearing himself from the cloud of sulphureous smoke—now falling, dispersed over the prairie—came galloping on towards the spot where Zeb stood. It was the horseman without a head.

Nor could there be any doubt as to the direction he was taking—as straight towards Zeb as if he already saw, and was determined on coming up with him!

A braver man than the backwoodsman could not have been found within the confines of Texas. Cougar, or jaguar—bear, buffalo, or Red Indian—he could have encountered without quailing. Even a troop of Comanches might have come charging on, without causing him half the apprehension felt at sight of that solitary equestrian.

With all his experience of Nature in her most secret haunts—despite the stoicism derived from that experience—Zeb Stump was not altogether free from superstitious fancies. Who is?

With the courage to scorn a human foe—any enemy that might show itself in a natural shape, either of biped or quadruped—still was he not stern enough to defy the *abnormal*; and Bayard himself would have quailed at sight of the cavalier who was advancing to the encounter—apparently determined upon its being deadly!

Zeb Stump not only quailed; but, trembling in his tall boots of alligator leather, sought concealment.

He did so, long before the Headless Horseman had got within hailing distance; or, as he supposed, within *sight* of him.

Some bushes growing close by gave him the chance of a hiding place; of which, with instinctive quickness, he availed himself.

The mare, standing saddled by his side, might still have betrayed him?

But, no. He had not gone to his knees, without thinking of that.

"Hunker down!" he cried, addressing himself to his dumb companion, who, if wanting speech, proved herself perfect in understanding. "Squat, ye ole critter; or by the Eturnal ye'll be switched off into hell!"

As if dreading some such terrible catastrophe, the scraggy quadruped dropped down upon her fore knees; and then, lowering her hind quarters, laid herself along the grass, as though thinking her day's work done—she was free to indulge in a fiesta.

Scarce had Zeb and his roadster composed themselves their new position, when the Headless Horseman came charging up.

He was going at full speed; and Zeb was but too well pleased to perceive that he was likely to continue it.

It was sheer chance that had conducted him that way; and not from having seen either the hunter or his sorry steed.

The former—if not the latter—was satisfied at being treated in that cavalier style; but, long before the Headless Horseman had passed out of sight, Zeb had taken his dimensions, and made himself acquainted with his character.

Though he might be a mystery to all the world beside, he was no longer so to Zebulon Stump.

As the horse shot past in fleet career, the skirt of the serapé, flouted up by the wind, displayed to Stump's optics a form well known to him—in a dress he had seen before. It was a blouse of blue cottonade, box-plaited over the breast; and though its vivid colour was dashed with spots of garish red, the hunter was able to recognise it.

He was not so sure about the face seen low down upon the saddle, and resting against the rider's leg.

There was nothing strange in his inability to recognise it.

The mother, who had oft looked fondly on that once fair countenance, would not have recognised it now.

Zeb Stump only did so by deduction. The horse, the saddle, the holsters, the striped blanket, the sky-blue coat and trousers—even the hat upon the head—were all known to him. So, too, was the figure that stood almost upright in the stirrups. The head and face must belong to the same—notwithstanding their unaccountable displacement.

Zeb saw it by no uncertain glance. He was permitted a full, fair view of the ghastly spectacle.

The steed, though going at a gallop, passed within ten paces of him.

He made no attempt to interrupt the retreating rider—either by word or gesture. Only, as the form became unmasked before his eyes, and its real meaning flashed across his mind, he muttered, in a slow, sad tone:

"Gee-hos-o-phat! It air true, then! *Poor young fellur—dead— dead!*"

# 76. Lost in the Chalk

Still continuing his fleet career, the Headless Horseman galloped on over the prairie—Zeb Stump following only with his eyes; and not until he had passed out of sight, behind some straggling groves of mezquite, did the backwoodsman abandon his kneeling position.

Then only for a second or two did he stand erect—taking council with himself as to what course he should pursue.

The episode—strange as unexpected—had caused some disarrangement in his ideas, and seemed to call for a change in his plans. Should he continue along the trail he was already deciphering; or forsake it for that of the steed that had just swept by?

By keeping to the former, he might find out much; but by changing to the latter he might learn more?

He might capture the Headless Horseman, and ascertain from *him* the why and wherefore of his wild wanderings?

While thus absorbed, in considering what course he had best take, he had forgotten the puff of smoke, and the report heard far off over the prairie.

Only for a moment, however. They were things to be remembered; and he soon remembered them.

Turning his eyes to the quarter where the smoke had appeared, he saw that which caused him to squat down again; and place himself, with more *impressement* than ever, under cover of the mezquites. The old mare, relishing the recumbent attitude, had still kept to it; and there was no necessity for re-disposing of her.

What Zeb now saw was a man on horseback—a real horseman, with a head upon his shoulders.

He was still a long way off; and it was not likely he had seen the tall form of the hunter, standing shored up among the bushes—much less the mare, lying beneath them. He showed no signs of having done so.

On the contrary, he was sitting stooped in the saddle, his breast bent down to the pommel, and his eyes actively engaged in reading the ground, over which he was guiding his horse.

There could be no difficulty in ascertaining his occupation. Zeb Stump guessed it at a glance. He was tracking the headless rider.

"Ho, ho!" muttered Zeb, on making this discovery; "I ain't the only one who's got a reezun for solvin' this hyur myst'ry! Who the hell kin *he* be? I shed jest like to know that."

Zeb had not long to wait for the gratification of his wish. As the trail was fresh, the strange horseman could take it up at a trot—in which pace he was approaching.

He was soon within identifying distance.

"Gee—hosophat!" muttered the backwoodsman; "I mout a know'd it wud be him; an ef I'm not mistook about it, hyurs goin' to be a other chapter out o' the same book—a other link as 'll help me to kumplete the chain o' evydince I'm in sarch for. Lay clost, ye critter! Ef ye make ere a stir—even to the shakin' o' them long lugs o' yourn—I'll cut yur darned throat."

The last speech was an apostrophe to the "maar"—after which Zeb waxed silent, with his head among the spray of the acacias, and his eyes peering through the branches in acute scrutiny of him who was coming along.

This was a man, who, once seen, was not likely to be soon forgotten. Scarce thirty years old, he showed a countenance, scathed, less with care than the play of evil passions.

But there was care upon it now—a care that seemed to speak of apprehension—keen, prolonged, yet looking forward with a hope of being relieved from it.

Withal it was a handsome face: such as a gentleman need not have been ashamed of, but for that sinister expression that told of its belonging to a blackguard.

The dress—but why need we describe it? The blue cloth frock of semi-military cut—the forage cap—the belt sustaining a bowie-knife, with a brace of revolving pistols—all have been mentioned before as enveloping and equipping the person of Captain Cassius Calhoun.

It was he.

It was not the *batterie* of small arms that kept Zeb Stump from showing himself. He had no dread of an encounter with the ex-officer of Volunteers. Though he instinctively felt hostility, he had as yet given no reason to the latter for regarding him as an enemy. He remained in shadow, to have a better view of what was passing under the sunlight.

Still closely scrutinising the trail of the Headless Horseman, Calhoun trotted past.

Still closely keeping among the acacias, Zeb Stump looked after, till the same grove, that had concealed the former, interposed its verdant veil between him and the ex-captain of cavalry.

The backwoodsman's brain having become the recipient of new thoughts, required a fresh exercise of its ingenuity.

If there was reason before for taking the trail of the Headless Horseman, it was redoubled now.

With but short time spent in consideration, so Zeb concluded; and commenced making preparations for a stalk after Cassius Calhoun.

These consisted in taking hold of the bridle, and giving the old mare a kick; that caused her to start instantaneously to her feet.

Zeb stood by her side, intending to climb into the saddle and ride out into the open plain—as soon as Calhoun should be out of sight.

He had no thoughts of keeping the latter in view. He needed no such guidance. The two fresh trails would be sufficient for him; and he felt as sure of finding the direction in which both would lead, as if he had ridden alongside the horseman without a head, or him without a heart.

With this confidence he cleared out from among the acacias, and took the path just trodden by Calhoun.

---

For once in his life, Zeb Stump had made a mistake. On rounding the mezquite grove, behind which both had made disappearance, he discovered he had done so.

Beyond, extended a tract of chalk prairie; over which one of the horsemen appeared to have passed—him without the head.

Zeb guessed so, by seeing the other, at some distance before him, riding to and fro, in transverse stretches, like a pointer quartering the stubble in search of a partridge.

He too had lost the trail, and was endeavouring to recover it.

Crouching under cover of the mezquites, the hunter remained a silent spectator of his movements.

The attempt terminated in a failure. The chalk surface defied interpretation—at least by skill such as that of Cassius Calhoun.

After repeated quarterings he appeared to surrender his design; and, angrily plying the spur, galloped off in the direction of the Leona.

As soon as he was out of sight, Zeb also made an effort to take up the lost trail. But despite his superior attainments in the tracking craft, he was compelled to relinquish it.

A fervid sun was glaring down upon the chalk; and only the eye of a salamander could have withstood the reflection of its rays.

Dazed almost to blindness, the backwoodsman determined upon turning late back; and once more devoting his attention to the trail from which he had been for a time seduced.

He had learnt enough to know that this last promised a rich reward for its exploration.

It took him but a short time to regain it.

Nor did he lose any in following it up. He was too keenly impressed with its value; and with this idea urging him, he strode rapidly on, the mare following as before.

Once only did he make pause; at a point where the tracks of two horses converged with that he was following.

From this point the three coincided—at times parting and running parallel, for a score of yards or so, but again coming together and overlapping one another.

The horses were all shod—like that which carried the broken shoe—and the hunter only stopped to see what he could make out of the hoof marks. One was a "States horse;" the other a mustang—though a stallion of great size, and with a hoof almost as large as that of the American.

Zeb had his conjectures about both.

He did not stay to inquire which had gone first over the ground. That was as clear to him, as if he had been a spectator at their passing. The stallion had been in the lead,—how far Zeb could not exactly tell; but certainly some distance beyond that of companionship. The States horse had followed; and behind him, the roadster with the broken shoe—also an American.

All three had gone over the same ground, at separate times, and each by himself. This Zeb Stump could tell with as much ease and certainty, as one might read the index of a dial, or thermometer.

Whatever may have been in his thoughts, he said nothing, beyond giving utterance to the simple exclamation "Good!" and, with satisfaction stamped upon his features, he moved on, the old mare appearing to mock him by an imitative stride!

"Hyur they've seppurated," he said, once again coming to a stop, and regarding the ground at his feet. "The stellyun an States hoss hev goed thegither—thet air they've tuk the same way. Broken-shoe hev strayed in a diffrent direkshun."

"Wonder now what thet's for?" he continued, after standing awhile to consider. "Durn me ef I iver seed sech perplexin' sign! It ud puzzle ole Dan'l Boone hisself."

"Which on 'em shed I foller fust? Ef I go arter the two I know whar they'll lead. They're boun' to kim up in thet puddle o' blood. Let's track up tother, and see whether he hev rud into the same prock-simmuty! To the right abeout, ole gal, and keep clost ahint me—else ye may get lost in the chapparal, an the coyoats may make thur supper on yur tallow. Ho! ho! ho!"

With this apostrophe to his "critter," ending in a laugh at the conceit of her "tallow," the hunter turned off on the track of the third horse.

It led him along the edge of an extended tract of chapparal; which, following all three, he had approached at a point well known to him, as to the reader,—where it was parted by the open space already described.

The new trail skirted the timber only for a short distance. Two hundred yards from the embouchure of the avenue, it ran into it; and fifty paces further on Zeb came to a spot where the horse had stood tied to a tree.

Zeb saw that the animal had proceeded no further: for there was another set of tracks showing where it had returned to the prairie—though not by the same path.

The rider had gone beyond. The foot-marks of a man could be seen beyond—in the mud of a half-dry *arroyo*—beside which the horse had been "hitched."

Leaving his critter to occupy the "stall" where broken-shoe had for some time fretted himself, the old hunter glided off upon the foot-marks of the dismounted rider.

He soon discovered two sets of them—one going—another coming back.

He followed the former.

He was not surprised at their bringing him out into the avenue—close to the pool of blood—by the coyotés long since licked dry.

He might have traced them right up to it, but for the hundreds of horse tracks that had trodden the ground like a sheep-pen.

But before going so far, he was stayed by the discovery of some fresh "sign"—too interesting to be carelessly examined. In a place where the underwood grew thick, he came upon a spot where a man had remained for some time. There was no turf, and the loose mould was baked hard and smooth, evidently by the sole of a boot or shoe.

There were prints of the same sole leading out towards the place of blood, and similar ones coming back again. But upon the branches of a tree between, Zeb Stump saw something that had escaped the eyes not only of the searchers, but of their guide Spangler—a scrap of paper, blackened and half-burnt—evidently the wadding of a discharged gun!

It was clinging to the twig of a locust-tree, impaled upon one of its spines!

The old hunter took it from the thorn to which, through rain and wind, it had adhered; spread it carefully across the palm of his horny hand; and read upon its smouched surface a name well known to him; which, with its concomitant title, bore the initials, "C.C.C."

458

# 77. Another Link

It was less surprise, than gratification, that showed itself on the countenance of Zeb Stump, as he deciphered the writing on the paper.

"That ere's the backin' o' a letter," muttered he. "Tells a goodish grist o' story; more'n war wrote inside, I reck'n. Been used for the wad' o' a gun! Wal; sarves the cuss right, for rammin' down a rifle ball wi' a patchin' o' scurvy paper, i'stead o' the proper an bessest thing, which air a bit o' greased buckskin."

"The writin' air in a sheemale hand," he continued, looking anew at the piece of paper. "Don't signerfy for thet. It's been sent to *him* all the same; an he's hed it in purzeshun. It air somethin' to be tuk care o'."

So saying, he drew out a small skin wallet, which contained his tinder of "punk," along with his flint and steel; and, after carefully stowing away the scrap of paper, he returned the sack to his pocket.

"Wal!" he went on in soliloquy, as he stood silently considering, "I kalkerlate as how this ole coon 'll be able to unwind a good grist o' this clue o' mystery, tho' thur be a bit o' the thread broken hyur an thur, an a bit o' a puzzle I can't clurly understan'. The man who hev been murdered, whosomdiver *he* may be, war out thur by thet puddle o' blood, an the man as did the deed, whosomdiver *he* be, war a stannin' behint this locust-tree. But for them greenhorns, I mout a got more out o' the sign. Now thur ain't the ghost o' a chance. They've tramped the hul place into a durnationed mess, cuvortin' and caperin' abeout.

"Wal, 'tair no use goin' furrer thet way. The bessest thing now air to take the back track, if it air possable, an diskiver whar the hoss wi' the broke shoe toted his rider arter he went back from this leetle bit o' still-huntin'. Thurfor, ole Zeb'lon Stump, back ye go on the boot tracks!"

With this grotesque apostrophe to himself, he commenced retracing the footmarks that had guided him to the edge of the opening. Only in one or two places were the footprints at all distinct. But Zeb scarce cared for their guidance.

Having already noted that the man who made them had returned to the place where the horse had been left, he knew the back track would lead him there.

There was one place, however, where the two trails did not go over the same ground. There was a forking in the open list, through which the supposed murderer had made his way. It was caused by an obstruction,—a patch of impenetrable thicket. They met again, but not till that on which the hunter was returning straggled off into an open glade of considerable size.

Having become satisfied of this, Zeb looked around into the glade—for a time forsaking the footsteps of the pedestrian.

After a short examination, he observed a trail altogether distinct, and of a different character. It was a well-marked path entering the opening on one side, and going out on the other: in short, a cattle-track.

Zeb saw that several shod horses had passed along it, some days before: and it was this that caused him to come back and examine it.

He could tell to a day—to an hour—*when* the horses had passed; and from the sign itself. But the exercise of his ingenuity was not needed on this occasion. He knew that the hoof-prints were those of the horses ridden by Spangler and his party—after being detached from the main body of searchers who had gone home with the major.

He had heard the whole story of that collateral investigation— how Spangler and his comrades had traced Henry Poindexter's horse to the place where the negro had caught it—on the outskirts of the plantation.

To an ordinary intellect this might have appeared satisfactory. Nothing more could be learnt by any one going over the ground again.

Zeb Stump did not seem to think so. As he stood looking along it, his attitude showed indecision.

"If I ked make shur o' havin' time," he muttered, "I'd foller it fust. Jest as like as not I'll find a *fluke* thur too. But thur's no sartinty 'beout the time, an I'd better purceed to settle wi' the anymal as cast the quarter shoe."

He had turned to go out of the glade, when a thought once more stayed him.

"Arter all, it kin be eezy foun' at any time. I kin guess whar it'll lead, as sartint, as if I'd rud 'longside the skunk thet made it—straight custrut to the stable o' Caser Corver.

460

"It's a durned pity to drop this un,—now whiles I'm hyur upon the spot. It'll gie me the makin' o' another ten-mile jurney, an thur moutn't be time. Dog-goned ef I don't try a leetle way along it. The ole maar kin wait till I kum back."

Bracing himself for a new investigation, he started off upon the cattle-track, trodden by the horses of Spangler and his party.

To the hoof-marks of these he paid but slight attention; at times, none whatever. His eye only sought those of Henry Poindexter's horse. Though the others were of an after time, and often destroyed the traces he was most anxious to examine, he had no difficulty in identifying the latter. As he would have himself said, any greenhorn could do that. The young planter's horse had gone over the ground at a gallop. The trackers had ridden slowly.

As far as Zeb Stump could perceive, the latter had made neither halt nor deviation. The former had.

It was about three-quarters of a mile from the edge of the venue.

It was not a halt the galloping horse had made, but only a slight departure from his direct course; as if something he had seen—wolf, jaguar, cougar, or other beast of prey—had caused him to shy.

Beyond he had continued his career; rapid and reckless as ever.

Beyond the party along with Spangler had proceeded—without staying to inquire why the horse had shied from his track.

Zeb Stump was more inquisitive, and paused upon this spot.

It was a sterile tract, without herbage, and covered with shingle and sand. A huge tree overshadowed it, with limbs extending horizontally. One of these ran transversely to the path over which the horses had passed—so low that a horseman, to shun contact with it, would have to lower his head. At this branch Zeb Stump stood gazing. He observed an abrasion upon the bark; that, though very slight, must have been caused by contact with some substance, as hard, if not sounder, than itself.

"Thet's been done by the skull o' a human critter," reasoned he— "a human critter, that must a been on the back o' a hoss—this side the branch, an off on the t'other. No livin' man ked a stud sech a cullizyun as thet, an kep his seat i' the seddle.

"Hooraw!" he triumphantly exclaimed, after a cursory examination of the ground underneath the tree. "I thort so. Thur's the impreshun o' the throwed rider. An' thur's whar he hez creeped away. Now I've got a explication o' thet big bump as hez been puzzlin' me. I know'd it wan't did by the claws o' any varmint; an it didn't look like

461

the blow eyther o' a stone or a stick. Thet ere's the stick that hez gi'n it."

With an elastic step—his countenance radiant of triumph—the old hunter strode away from the tree, no longer upon the cattle path, but that taken by the man who had been so violently dismounted.

To one unaccustomed to the chapparal, he might have appeared going without a guide, and upon a path never before pressed by human foot.

A portion of it perhaps had not. But Zeb was conducted by signs which, although obscure to the ordinary eye, were to him intelligible as the painted lettering upon a finger-post. The branch contorted to afford passage for a human form—the displaced tendrils of a creeping plant—the scratched surface of the earth—all told that a man had passed that way. The sign signified more—that the man was disabled—had been crawling—a cripple!

Zeb Stump continued on, till he had traced this cripple to the banks of a running stream.

It was not necessary for him to go further. He had made one more splice of the broken thread. Another, and his clue would be complete!

# 78. A Horse-Swop

With an oath, a sullen look, and a brow black as disappointment could make it, Calhoun turned away from the edge of the chalk prairie, where he had lost the traces of the Headless Horseman.

"No use following further! No knowing where he's gone now! No hope of finding him except by a *fluke*! If I go back to the creek I might see him again; but unless I get within range, it'll end as it's done before. The mustang stallion won't let me come near him—as if the brute knows what I'm wanting!

"He's even cunninger than the wild sort—trained to it, I suppose, by the mustanger himself. One fair shot—if I could only get that, I'd settle his courses.

"There appears no chance of stealing upon him; and as to riding him down, it can't be done with a slow mule like this.

"The sorrel's not much better as to speed, though he beats this brute in bottom. I'll try him to-morrow, with the new shoe.

"If I could only get hold of something that's fast enough to overtake the mustang! I'd put down handsomely for a horse that could do it.

"There must be one of the sort in the settlement. I'll see when I get back. If there be, a couple of hundred, ay or three, won't hinder me from having him."

After he had made these mutterings Calhoun rode away from the chalk prairie, his dark countenance strangely contrasting with its snowy sheen. He went at a rapid rate; not sparing his horse, already jaded with a protracted journey—as could be told by his sweating coat, and the clots of half-coagulated blood, where the spur had been freely plied upon his flanks. Fresh drops soon appeared as he cantered somewhat heavily on—his head set for the hacienda of Casa del Corvo.

In less than an hour after, his rider was guiding him among the mezquites that skirted the plantation.

It was a path known to Calhoun. He had ridden over it before, though not upon the same horse. On crossing the bed of an arroyo—dry from a long continuance of drought—he was startled at beholding in the mud the tracks of another horse. One of them showed a broken shoe, an old hoof-print, nearly eight days old. He made no examination to ascertain the time. He knew it to an hour.

He bent over it, with a different thought—a feeling of surprise commingled with a touch of superstition. The track looked recent, as if made on the day before. There had been wind, rain, thunder, and lightning. Not one of these had wasted it. Even the angry elements appeared to have passed over without destroying it—as if to spare it for a testimony against the outraged laws of Nature—their God.

Calhoun dismounted, with the design to obliterate the track of the three-quarter shoe. Better for him to have spared himself the pains. The crease of his boot-heel crushing in the stiff mud was only an additional evidence as to who had ridden the broken-shoed horse. There was one coming close behind capable of collecting it.

Once more in his saddle, the ex-officer rode on—reflecting on his own astuteness.

His reflections had scarce reached the point of reverie, when the hoof-stroke of a horse—not his own—came suddenly within hearing. Not within sight: for the animal making them was still screened by the chapparal.

Plainly was it approaching; and, although at a slow pace, the measured tread told of its being guided, and not straying. It was a horse with a rider upon his back.

In another instant both were in view; and Calhoun saw before him Isidora Covarubio de los Llanos; she at the same instant catching sight of him!

It was a strange circumstance that these two should thus encounter one another—apparently by chance, though perhaps controlled by destiny. Stranger still the thought summoned up in the bosoms of both.

In Calhoun, Isidora saw the man who loved the woman she herself hated. In Isidora, Calhoun saw the woman who loved him he both hated and had determined to destroy.

This mutual knowledge they had derived partly from report, partly from observation, and partly from the suspicious circumstances under which more than once they had met. They were equally convinced of its truth. Each felt certain of the sinister entanglement of the other; while both believed their own to be unsuspected.

The situation was not calculated to create a friendly feeling between them. It is not natural that man, or woman, should like the admirer of a rival. They can only be friends at that point where jealousy prompts to the deadliest vengeance; and then it is but a sinister sympathy.

As yet no such had arisen between Cassius Calhoun and Isidora Covarubio de los Llanos.

If it had been possible, both might have been willing to avoid the encounter. Isidora certainly was.

She had no predilection for the ex-officer of dragoons; and besides the knowledge that he was the lover of her rival, there was another thought that now rendered his presence, if not disagreeable, at least not desirable.

She remembered the chase of the sham Indians, and its ending. She knew that among the Texans there had been much conjecture as to her abrupt disappearance, after appealing to them for protection.

She had her own motive for that, which she did not intend to declare; and the man about meeting her might be inclined to ask questions on the subject.

She would have passed with a simple salutation—she could not give less than that. And perhaps he might have done the same; but for a thought which at that moment came into his mind, entirely unconnected with the reflections already there engendered.

It was not the lady herself who suggested the thought. Despite her splendid beauty, he had no admiration for her. In his breast, ruthless as it might have been, there was no space left for a second passion—not even a sensual one—for her thus encountered in the solitude of the chapparal, with Nature whispering wild, wicked suggestions.

It was no idea of this that caused him to rein up in the middle of the path; remove the cap from his crown; and, by a courtly salutation, invite a dialogue with Isidora.

So challenged, she could not avoid the conversation; that commenced upon the instant—Calhoun taking the initiative.

"Excuse me, señorita," said he, his glance directed more upon her steed than herself; "I know it's very rude thus to interrupt your ride; especially on the part of a stranger, as with sorrow I am compelled to call myself."

"It needs no apology, señor. If I'm not mistaken, we have met before—upon the prairie, out near the Nueces."

"True—true!" stammered Calhoun, not caring to dwell upon the remembrance. "It was not of that encounter I wished to speak; but what I saw afterwards, as you came galloping along the cliff. We all wondered what became of you."

"There was not much cause for wonder, cavallero. The shot which some of your people fired from below, disembarrassed me of my pursuers. I saw that they had turned back, and simply continued my journey."

Calhoun exhibited no chagrin at being thus baffled. The theme upon which he designed to direct his discourse had not yet turned up; and in it he might be more successful.

What it was might have been divined from his glance—half *connoisseur*, half horse-jockey—still directed toward the steed of Isidora.

"I do not say, señorita, that I was one of those who wondered at your sudden disappearance. I presumed you had your own reasons for not coming on to us; and, seeing you ride as you did, I felt no fear for your safety. It was your riding that astonished me, as it did all of my companions. Such a horse you had! He appeared to glide, rather than gallop! If I mistake not, it's the same you are now *astride of.* Am I right, señora? Pardon me for asking such an insignificant question."

"The same? Let me see? I make use of so many. I think I was riding this horse upon that day. Yes, yes; I am sure of it. I remember how the brute betrayed me."

"Betrayed you! How?"

"Twice he did it. Once as you and your people were approaching. The second time, when the Indians—*ay Dios*! not Indians, as I've since heard—were coming through the chapparal."

"But how?"

"By neighing. He should not have done it. He's had training enough to know better than that. No matter. Once I get him back to the Rio Grande he shall stay there. I shan't ride *him* again. He shall return to his Pastures."

"Pardon me, señorita, for speaking to you on such a subject; but I can't help thinking that it's a pity."

"What's a pity?"

"That a steed so splendid as that should be so lightly discarded. I would give much to possess him."

"You are jesting, cavallero. He is nothing beyond the common; perhaps a little pretty, and quick in his paces. My father has five thousand of his sort—many of them prettier, and, no doubt, some faster than he. He's a good roadster; and that's why I'm riding him now. If it weren't that I'm on my way home to the Rio Grande, and the journey is still before me, you'd be welcome to have him, or anybody else who cared for him, as you seem to do. Be still, *musteño mio*! You see there's somebody likes you better than I do."

The last speech was addressed to the mustang, who, like its rider, appeared impatient for the conversation to come to a close.

Calhoun, however, seemed equally desirous of prolonging, or, at all events, bringing it to a different termination.

"Excuse me, señorita," said he, assuming an air of businesslike earnestness, at the same time speaking apologetically; "if that be all the value you set upon the grey mustang, I should be only too glad to make an exchange with you. My horse, if not handsome, is estimated by our Texan dealers as a valuable animal. Though somewhat slow in his paces, I can promise that he will carry you safely to your home, and will serve you well afterwards."

"What, señor!" exclaimed the lady, in evident astonishment, "exchange your grand American *frison* for a Mexican mustang! The offer is too generous to appear other than a jest. You know that on the Rio Grande one of your horses equals in value at least three, sometimes six, of ours?"

Calhoun knew this well enough; but he knew also that the mustang ridden by Isidora would be to him worth a whole stableful of such brutes as that he was bestriding. He had been an eye-witness to its speed, besides having heard of it from others. It was the thing he stood in need of—the very thing. He would have given, not only his "grand *frison*" in exchange, but the full price of the mustang by way of "boot."

Fortunately for him, there was no attempt at extortion. In the composition of the Mexican maiden, however much she might be given to equestrian tastes, there was not much of the "coper." With five thousand horses in the paternal stables, or rather straying over the patrimonial plains, there was but slight motive for sharp practice; and why should she deny such trifling gratification, even though the man seeking it was a stranger—perhaps an enemy?

She did not.

"If you are in earnest, señor," was her response, "you are welcome to what you want."

"I am in earnest, señorita."

"Take him, then!" said she, leaping out of her saddle, and commencing to undo the girths, "We cannot exchange saddles: yours would be a mile too big for me!"

Calhoun was too happy to find words for a rejoinder. He hastened to assist her in removing the saddle; after which he took off his own.

In less than five minutes the horses were exchanged—the saddles and bridles being retained by their respective owners.

To Isidora there was something ludicrous in the transference. She almost laughed while it was being carried on.

Calhoun looked upon it in a different light. There was a purpose present before his mind—one of the utmost importance.

They parted without much further speech—only the usual greetings of adieu—Isidora going off on the *frison*; while the ex-officer, mounted on the grey mustang, continued his course in the direction of Casa del Corvo.

# 79. An Untiring Tracker

Zeb was not long in arriving at the spot where he had "hitched" his mare. The topography of the chapparal was familiar to him; and he crossed it by a less circuitous route than that taken by the cripple.

He once more threw himself upon the trail of the broken shoe, in full belief that it would fetch out not a hundred miles from Casa del Corvo.

It led him along a road running almost direct from one of the crossings of the Rio Grande to Fort Inge. The road was a half-mile in width—a thing not uncommon in Texas, where every traveller selects his own path, alone looking to the general direction.

Along one edge of it had gone the horse with the damaged shoe.

Not all the way to Fort Inge. When within four or five miles of the post, the trail struck off from the road, at an angle of just such degree as followed in a straight line would bring out by Poindexter's plantation. So confident was Zeb of this, that he scarce deigned to keep his eye upon the ground; but rode forwards, as if a finger-post was constantly by his side.

He had long before given up following the trail afoot. Despite his professed contempt for "horse-fixings"—as he called riding—he had no objection to finish his journey in the saddle—fashed as he now was with the fatigue of protracted trailing over prairie and through chapparal. Now and then only did he cast a glance upon the ground—less to assure himself he was on the track of the broken shoe, than to notice whether something else might not be learnt from the sign, besides its mere direction.

There were stretches of the prairie where the turf, hard and dry, had taken no impression. An ordinary traveller might have supposed himself the first to pass over the ground. But Zeb Stump was not of this class; and although he could not always distinguish the hoof marks, he knew within an inch where they would again become visible—on the more moist and softer patches of the prairie.

If at any place conjecture misled him, it was only for a short distance, and he soon corrected himself by a traverse.

In this half-careless, half-cautious way, he had approached within a mile of Poindexter's plantation. Over the tops of the mezquite trees the crenelled parapet was in sight; when something he saw upon the ground caused a sudden change in his demeanour. A change, too, in his attitude; for instead of remaining on the back of his mare, he flung himself out of the saddle; threw the bridle upon her neck; and, rapidly passing in front of her, commenced taking up the trail afoot.

The mare made no stop, but continued on after him—with an air of resignation, as though she was used to such eccentricities.

To an inexperienced eye there was nothing to account for this sudden dismounting. It occurred at a place where the turf appeared untrodden by man, or beast. Alone might it be inferred from Zeb's speech, as he flung himself out of the saddle:

"His track! goin' to hum!" were the words muttered in a slow, measured tone; after which, at a slower pace, the dismounted hunter kept on along the trail.

In a little time after it conducted him into the chapparal; and in less to a stop—sudden, as if the thorny thicket had been transformed into a *chevaux-de-frise*, impenetrable both to him and his "critter."

It was not this. The path was still open before him—more open than ever. It was its openness that had furnished him with a cause for discontinuing his advance.

The path sloped down into a valley below—a depression in the prairie, along the concavity of which, at times, ran a tiny stream—ran arroyo. It was now dry, or only occupied by stagnant pools, at long distances apart. In the mud-covered channel was a man, with a horse close behind him—the latter led by the bridle.

There was nothing remarkable in the behaviour of the horse; he was simply following the lead of his dismounted rider.

But the man—what was he doing? In his movements there was something peculiar—something that would have puzzled an uninitiated spectator.

It did not puzzle Zeb Stump; or but for a second of time.

Almost the instant his eye fell upon it, he read the meaning of the manoeuvre, and mutteringly pronounced it to himself.

"Oblitturatin' the print o' the broken shoe, or tryin' to do thet same! 'Taint no use, Mister Cash Calhoun—no manner o' use. Ye've made yur fut marks too deep to deceive *me*; an by the Eturnal I'll foller them, though they shed conduck me into the fires o' hell?"

470

As the backwoodsman terminated his blasphemous apostrophe, the man to whom it pointed, having finished his task of obscuration, once more leaped into his saddle, and hurried on.

On foot the tracker followed; though without showing any anxiety about keeping him in sight.

There was no need for that. The sleuth hound on a fresh slot could not be more sure of again viewing his victim, than was Zeb Stump of coming up with his. No chicanery of the chapparal—no twistings or doublings—could save Calhoun now.

The tracker advanced freely; not expecting to make halt again, till he should come within sight of Casa del Corvo.

Little blame to him that his reckoning proved wrong. Who could have foretold such an interruption as that occasioned by the encounter between Cassius Calhoun and Isidora Covarubio de los Llanos?

Though at sight of it, taken by surprise—perhaps something more—Zeb did not allow his feelings to betray his presence near the spot.

On the contrary, it seemed to stimulate him to increased caution.

Turning noiselessly round, he whispered some cabalistic words into the care of his "critter;" and then stole silently forward under cover of the acacias.

Without remonstrance, or remark, the mare followed. He soon came to a fall stop—his animal doing the same, in imitation so exact as to appear its counterpart.

A thick growth of mezquite trees separated him from the two individuals, by this time engaged in a lively interchange of speech.

He could not see them, without exposing himself to the danger of being detected in his eaves-dropping; but he heard what they said all the same.

He kept his place—listening till the *horse trade* was concluded, and for some time after.

Only when they had separated, and both taken departure did he venture to come forth from his cover.

Standing upon the spot lately occupied by the "swoppers," and looking "both ways at once," he exclaimed—

"Geehosophat! thur's a compack atween a *he* an' *she*-devil; an' durn'd ef I kin tell, which hez got the bessest o' the bargin!"

# 80. A Doorway Well Watched

It was some time before Zeb Stump sallied forth from the covert where he had been witness to the "horse swop." Not till both the bargainers had ridden entirely out of sight. Then he went not after either; but stayed upon the spot, as if undecided which he should follow.

It was not exactly this that kept him to the place; but the necessity of taking what he was in the habit of calling a "good think."

His thoughts were about the exchange of the horses: for he had heard the whole dialogue relating thereto, and the proposal coming from Calhoun. It was this that puzzled, or rather gave him reason for reflection. What could be the motive?

Zeb knew to be true what the Mexican had said: that the States horse was, in market value, worth far more than the mustang. He knew, moreover, that Cassius Calhoun was the last man to be "coped" in a horse trade. Why, then, had he done the "deal?"

The old hunter pulled off his felt hat; gave his hand a twist or two through his unkempt hair; transferred the caress to the grizzled beard upon his chin—all the while gazing upon the ground, as if the answer to his mental interrogatory was to spring out of the grass.

"Thur air but one explication o't," he at length muttered: "the grey's the faster critter o' the two—ne'er a doubt 'beout thet; an Mister Cash wants him for his fastness: else why the durnation shed he a gin a hoss thet 'ud sell for four o' his sort in any part o' Texas, an twicet thet number in Mexiko? I reck'n he's bargained for the heels. Why? Durn me, ef I don't suspect why. He wants—he—heigh—I hev it—somethin' as kin kum up wi' the Headless!

"Thet's the very thing he's arter—sure as my name's Zeb'lon Stump. He's tried the States hoss an foun' him slow. Thet much I knowd myself. Now he thinks, wi' the mowstang, he may hev a chance to overhaul the tother, ef he kin only find him agin; an for sartin he'll go in sarch o' him.

"He's rad on now to Casser Corver—maybe to git a pick o' some-thin' to eat. He won't stay thur long. 'Fore many hours hev passed, somebody 'll see him out hyur on the purayra; an thet somebody air boun' to be Zeb'lon Stump.

"Come, ye critter!" he continued, turning to the mare, "ye thort ye wur a goin' hum, did ye? Yur mistaken 'beout that. Ye've got to squat hyur for another hour or two—if not the hul o' the night. Never mind, ole gurl! The grass don't look so had; an ye shell hev a chance to git yur snout to it. Thur now—eet your durned gut-full!"

While pronouncing this apostrophe, he drew the head-stall over the ears of his mare; and, chucking the bridle across the projecting tree of the saddle, permitted her to graze at will.

Having secured her in the chapparal where he had halted, he walked on—along the track taken by Calhoun.

Two hundred yards farther on, and the jungle terminated. Beyond stretched an open plain; and on its opposite side could be seen the ha-cienda of Casa del Corvo.

The figure of a horseman could be distinguished against its whitewashed façade—in another moment lost within the dark outline of the entrance.

Zeb knew who went in.

"From this place," he muttered, "I kin see him kum out; an durn me, ef I don't watch till he do kum out—ef it shed be till this time o' the morrow. So hyur goes for a spell o' patience."

He first lowered himself to his knees. Then, "squirming" round till his back came in contact with the trunk of a honey-locust, he ar-ranged himself into a sitting posture. This done, he drew from his capacious pocket a wallet, containing a "pone" of corn-bread, a large "hunk" of fried "hog-meat," and a flask of liquor, whose perfume pro-claimed it "Monongahela."

Having eaten about half the bread, and a like quantity of the meat, he returned the remaining moieties to the wallet; which he suspended over head upon a branch. Then taking a satisfactory swig from the whiskey-flask, and igniting his pipe, he leant back against the locust—with arms folded over his breast, and eyes bent upon the gateway of Casa del Corvo.

In this way he kept watch for a period of full two hours; never changing the direction of his glance; or not long enough for any one to pass out unseen by him.

Forms came out, and went in—several of them—men and women. But even in the distance their scant light-coloured garments, and dusky complexions, told them to be only the domestics of the mansion. Besides, they were all on foot; and he, for whom Zeb was watching, should come on horseback—if at all.

His vigil was only interrupted by the going down of the sun; and then only to cause a change in his post of observation. When twilight began to fling its purple shadows over the plain, he rose to his feet; and, leisurely unfolding his tall figure, stood upright by the stem of the tree—as if this attitude was more favourable for "considering."

"Thur's jest a posserbillity the skunk mout sneak out i' the night?" was his reflection. "Leastways afore the light o' the mornin'; an I must make sure which way he takes purayra.

"'Taint no use my toatin' the maar after me," he continued, glancing in the direction where the animal had been left. "She'd only bother me. Beside, thur's goin' to be a clurrish sort o' moonlight; an she mout be seen from the nigger quarter. She'll be better hyur—both for grass and kiver."

He went back to the mare; took off the saddle; fastened the trail-rope round her neck, tying the other end to a tree; and then, unstrapping his old blanket from the cantle, he threw it across his left arm, and walked off in the direction of Casa del Corvo.

He did not proceed *pari passu*; but now quicker, and now more hesitatingly—timing himself, by the twilight—so that his approach might not be observed from the hacienda.

He had need of this caution: for the ground which he had to pass was like a level lawn, without copse or cover of any kind. Here and there stood a solitary tree—dwarf-oak or *algarobia*, but not close enough to shelter him from being seen through the windows—much less from the azotea.

Now and then he stopped altogether—to wait for the deepening of the twilight.

Working his way in this stealthy manner, he arrived within less than two hundred yards of the walls—just as the last trace of sunlight disappeared from the sky.

He had reached the goal of his journey—for that day—and the spot on which he was likely to pass the night.

A low stemless bush grew near; and, laying himself down behind it, he resumed the espionage, that could scarce be said to have been interrupted.

---

Throughout the live-long night Zeb Stump never closed both eyes at the same time. One was always on the watch; and the unflagging earnestness, with which he maintained it, proclaimed him to be acting under the influence of some motive beyond the common.

During the earlier hours he was not without sounds to cheer, or at least relieve, the monotony of his lonely vigil. There was the hum of voices from the slave cabins; with now and then a peal of laughter. But this was more suppressed than customary; nor was it accompanied by the clear strain of the violin, or the lively tink-a-tink of the banjo— sounds almost characteristic of the "negro-quarter," at night.

The sombre silence that hung over the "big house" extended to the hearths of its sable retainers.

Before midnight the voices became hushed, and stillness reigned everywhere; broken only at intervals by the howl of a straying hound—uttered in response to the howl-bark of a coyoté taking care to keep far out upon the plain.

The watcher had spent a wearisome day, and could have slept— but for his thoughts. Once when these threatened to forsake him, and he was in danger of dozing, he started suddenly to his feet; took a turn or two over the sward; and, then lying down again, re-lit his pipe; stuck his head into the heart of the bush; and smoked away till the bowl was burnt empty.

During all this time, he kept his eyes upon the great gateway of the mansion; whose massive door—he could tell by the moonlight shining upon it—remained shut.

Again did he change his post of observation; the sun's rising—as its setting had done—seeming to give him the cue.

As the first tint of dawn displayed itself on the horizon, he rose gently to his feet; clutched the blanket so as to bring its edges in contact across his breast; and, turning his back upon Casa del Corvo, walked slowly away—taking the same track by which he had approached it on the preceding night.

And again with unequal steps: at short intervals stopping and looking back—under his arm, or over his shoulder.

Nowhere did he make a prolonged pause; until reaching the locust-tree, under whose shade he had made his evening meal; and there, in the same identical attitude, he proceeded to break his fast.

The second half of the "pone" and the remaining moiety of the pork, soon disappeared between his teeth; after which followed the liquor that had been left in his flask.

He had refilled his pipe, and was about relighting it, when an object came before his eyes, that caused him hastily to return his flint and steel to the pouch from which he had taken them.

475

Through the blue mist of the morning the entrance of Casa del Corvo showed a darker disc. The door had been drawn open.

Almost at the same instant a horseman was seen to sally forth, mounted upon a small grey horse; and the door was at once closed behind him.

Zeb Stump made no note of this. He only looked to see what direction the early traveller would take.

Less than a score of seconds sufficed to satisfy him. The horse's head and the face of the rider were turned towards himself.

He lost no time in trying to identify either. He did not doubt of its being the same man and horse, that had passed that spot on the evening before; and he was equally confident they were going to pass it again.

What he did was to shamble up to his mare; in some haste get her saddled and bridled; and then, having taken up his trail rope, lead her off into a cover—from which he could command a view of the chapparal path, without danger of being himself seen.

This done, he awaited the arrival of the traveller on the grey steed—whom he knew to be Captain Cassius Calhoun.

He waited still longer—until the latter had trotted past; until he had gone quite through the belt of chapparal, and in the hazy light of the morning gradually disappeared on the prairie beyond.

Not till then did Zeb Stump clamber into his saddle; and, "prodding" his solitary spur against the ribs of his roadster, cause the latter to move on.

He went after Cassius Calhoun; but without showing the slightest concern about keeping the latter in sight!

He needed not this to guide him. The dew upon the grass was to him a spotless page—the tracks of the grey mustang a type, as legible as the lines of a printed book.

He could read them at a trot; ay, going at a gallop!

---

# 81. Heads Down—Heels Up!

Without suspicion that he had been seen leaving the house—except by Pluto, who had saddled the grey mustang—Calhoun rode on across the prairie.

Equally unsuspicious was he, in passing the point where Zeb Stump stood crouching in concealment.

In the dim light of the morning he supposed himself unseen by human eye; and he recked not of any other.

After parting from the timbered border, he struck off towards the Nueces; riding at a brisk trot—now and then increasing to a canter.

Por the first six or eight miles he took but little note of aught that was around. An occasional glance along the horizon seemed to satisfy him; and this extended only to that portion of the vast circle before his face. He looked neither to the right nor the left; and only once behind—after getting some distance from the skirt of the chapparal.

Before him was the object—still unseen—upon which his thoughts were straying.

What that object was he and only one other knew—that other Zeb Stump—though little did Calhoun imagine that mortal man could have a suspicion of the nature of his early errand.

The old hunter had only conjectured it; but it was a conjecture of the truth of which he was as certain, as if the ex-captain had made him his confidant. He knew that the latter had gone off in search of the Headless Horseman—in hopes of renewing the chase of yesterday, with a better chance of effecting a capture.

Though bestriding a steed fleet as a Texan stag, Calhoun was by no means sanguine of success. There were many chances against his getting sight of the game he intended to take: at least two to one; and this it was that formed the theme of his reflections as he rode onward.

The uncertainty troubled him; but he was solaced by a hope founded upon some late experiences.

There was a particular place where he had twice encountered the thing he was in search of. It might be there again?

This was an embayment of green sward, where the savannah was bordered by the chapparal, and close to the embouchure of that opening—where it was supposed the murder had been committed!

"Odd he should always make back there?" reflected Calhoun, as he pondered upon the circumstance. "Damned ugly odd it is! Looks as if he knew—. Bah! It's only because the grass is better, and that pond by the side of it. Well! I hope he's been thinking that way this morning. If so, there'll be a chance of finding him. If not, I must go on through the chapparal; and hang me if I like it—though it be in the daylight. Ugh!

"Pish! what's there to fear—now that he's safe in limbo? Nothing but the *bit of lead*; and *it* I must have, if I should ride this thing till it drops dead in its tracks. Holy Heaven! what's that out yonder?"

These last six words were spoken aloud. All the rest had been a soliloquy in thought.

The speaker, on pronouncing them, pulled up, almost dragging the mustang on its haunches; and with eyes that seemed ready to start from their sockets, sate gazing across the plain.

There was something more than surprise in that stedfast glance—there was horror.

And no wonder: for the spectacle upon which it rested was one to terrify the stoutest heart.

The sun had stolen up above the horizon of the prairie, and was behind the rider's back, in the direct line of the course he had been pursuing. Before him, along the heaven's edge, extended a belt of bluish mist—the exhalation arising out of the chapparal—now not far distant. The trees themselves were unseen—concealed under the film floating over them, that like a veil of purple gauze, rose to a considerable height above their tops—gradually merging into the deeper azure of the sky.

On this veil, or moving behind it—as in the transparencies of a stage scene—appeared a form strange enough to have left the spectator incredulous, had he not beheld it before. It was that of the Headless Horseman.

But not as seen before—either by Calhoun himself, or any of the others. No. It was now altogether different. In shape the same; but in size it was increased to tenfold its original dimensions!

No longer a man, but a Colossus—a giant. No longer a horse, but an animal of equine shape, with the towering height and huge massive bulk of a mastodon!

Nor was this all of the new to be noted about the Headless Horseman. A still greater change was presented in his appearance; one yet more inexplicable, if that could possibly be. He was no longer walking upon the ground, but against the sky; both horse and rider moving in an inverted position! The hoofs of the former were distinctly perceptible upon the upper edge of the film; while the shoulders—I had almost said *head*—of the latter were close down to the line of the horizon! The serapé shrouding them hung in the right direction—not as regarded the laws of gravity, but the attitude of the wearer. So, too, the bridle reins, the mane, and sweeping tail of the horse. All draped *upwards*!

When first seen, the spectral form—now more spectre-like than ever—was going at a slow, leisurely walk. In this pace it for some time continued—Calhoun gazing upon it with a heart brimful of horror.

All of a sudden it assumed a change. Its regular outlines became confused by a quick transformation; the horse having turned, and gone off at a trot in the opposite direction, though still with his heels against the sky!

The spectre had become alarmed, and was retreating!

Calhoun, half palsied with fear, would have kept his ground, and permitted it to depart, but for his own horse; that, just then shying suddenly round, placed him face to face with the explanation.

As he turned, the tap of a shod hoof upon the prairie turf admonished him that a real horseman was near—if that could be called real, which had thrown such a frightful shadow.

"It's the *mirage*!" he exclaimed, with the addition of an oath to give vent to his chagrin. "What a fool I've been to let it humbug me! There's the damned thing that did it: the very thing I'm in search of. And so close too! If I'd known, I might have got hold of him before he saw me. Now for a chase; and, by God, I'll *grup* him, if I have to gallop to the other end of Texas!"

Voice, spur, and whip were simultaneously exerted to prove the speaker's earnestness; and in five minutes after, two horsemen were going at full stretch across the prairie—their horses both to the prairie born—one closely pursuing the other—the pursued without a head; the pursuer with a heart that throbbed under a desperate determination.

The chase was not a long one—at least, so far as it led over the open prairie; and Calhoun had begun to congratulate himself on the prospect of a capture.

His horse appeared the swifter; but this may have arisen from his being more earnestly urged; or that the other was not sufficiently scared to care for escaping. Certainly the grey steed gained ground—at length getting so close, that Calhoun made ready his rifle.

His intention was to shoot the horse down, and so put an end to the pursuit.

He would have fired on the instant, but for the fear of a miss. But having made more than one already, he restrained himself from pulling trigger, till he could ride close enough to secure killing shot.

While thus hesitating, the chase veered suddenly from off the treeless plain, and dashed into the opening of the timber.

This movement, unexpected by the pursuer, caused him to lose ground; and in the endeavour to regain it, more than a half mile of distance was left behind him.

He was approaching a spot well, too well, known to him—the place where blood had been spilt.

On any other occasion he would have shunned it; but there was in his heart a thought that hindered him from dwelling upon memories of the past—steeling it against all reflection, except a cold fear for the future. The capture of the strange equestrian could alone allay this fear—by removing the danger he dreaded.

Once more he had gained ground in the chase. The spread nostrils of his steed were almost on a line with the sweeping tail of that pursued. His rifle lay ready in his left hand, its trigger guard covered by the fingers of his right. He was searching for a spot to take aim at.

In another second the shot would have been fired, and a bullet sent between the ribs of the retreating horse, when the latter, as if becoming aware of the danger, made a quick curvet to the off side; and then, aiming a kick at the snout of his pursuer, bounded on in a different direction!

The suddenness of the demonstration, with the sharp, spiteful "squeal" that accompanied it—appearing almost to speak of an unearthly intelligence—for the moment disconcerted Calhoun; as it did the horse he was riding.

The latter came to a stop; and refused to go farther; till the spur, plunged deep between his ribs, once more forced him to the gallop.

And now more earnestly than ever did his rider urge him on; for the pursued, no longer keeping to the path, was heading direct for the thicket. The chase might there terminate, without the chased animal being either killed or captured.

Hitherto Calhoun had only been thinking of a trial of speed. He had not anticipated such an ending, as was now both possible and probable; and with a more reckless resolve, he once more raised his rifle for the shot.

By this time both were close in to the bushes—the Headless Horseman already half-screened by the leafy branches that swept swishing along his sides. Only the hips of his horse could be aimed at; and upon these was the gun levelled.

The sulphureous smoke spurted forth from its muzzle; the crack was heard simultaneously; and, as if caused by the discharge, a dark object came whirling through the cloud, and fell with a dull "thud" upon the turf.

With a bound and a roll—that brought it among the feet of Calhoun's horse—it became stationary.

Stationary, but not still. It continued to oscillate from side to side, like a top before ceasing to spin.

The grey steed snorted, and reared back. His rider uttered a cry of intensified alarm.

And no wonder. If read in Shakespearean lore, he might have appropriately repeated the words "Shake not those gory locks": for, on the ground beneath, was the head of a man—still sticking in its hat—whose stiff orbicular brim hindered it from staying still.

The face was toward Calhoun—upturned at just such an angle as to bring it full before him. The features were bloodstained, wan, and shrivelled; the eyes open, but cold and dim, like balls of blown glass; the teeth gleaming white between livid lips, yet seemingly set in an expression of careless contentment.

All this saw Cassius Calhoun.

He saw it with fear and trembling. Not for the supernatural or unknown, but for the real and truly comprehended.

Short was his interview with that silent, but speaking head. Ere it had ceased to oscillate on the smooth sward, he wrenched his horse around; struck the rowels deep; and galloped away from the ground!

No farther went he in pursuit of the Headless Horseman—still heard breaking through the bushes—but back—back to the prairie; and on, on, to Casa del Corvo!

# 82. A Queer Parcel

The backwoodsman, after emerging from the thicket, proceeded as leisurely along the trail, as if he had the whole day before him, and no particular motive for making haste.

And yet, one closely scrutinising his features, might there have observed an expression of intense eagerness; that accorded with his nervous twitching in the saddle, and the sharp glances from time to time cast before him.

He scarce deigned to look upon the "sign" left by Calhoun. It he could read out of the corner of his eye. As to following it, the old mare could have done that without him!

It was not this knowledge that caused him to hang back; for he would have preferred keeping Calhoun in sight. But by doing this, the latter might see *him*; and so frustrate the end he desired to attain.

This end was of more importance than any acts that might occur between; and, to make himself acquainted with the latter, Zeb Stump trusted to the craft of his intellect, rather than the skill of his senses.

Advancing slowly and with caution—but with that constancy that ensures good speed—he arrived at length on the spot where the *mirage* had made itself manifest to Calhoun.

Zeb saw nothing of this. It was gone; and the sky stretched down to the prairie—the blue meeting the green in a straight unbroken line.

He saw, however, what excited him almost as much as the spectre would have done: two sets of horse-tracks going together—those that went after being the hoof-marks of Calhoun's new horse—of which Zeb had already taken the measure.

About the tracks *underneath* he had no conjecture—at least as regarded their identification. These he knew, as well as if his own mare had made them.

"The skunk's hed a find!" were the words that escaped him, as he sate gazing upon the double trail. "It don't foller from thet," he continued, in the same careless drawl, "thet he hez made a catch. An' yit, who knows? Durn me, ef he moutn't! Thur's lots o' chances for his doin' it. The mowstang may a let him come clost up—seein' as he's ridin' one o' its own sort; an ef it dud—ay, ef it dud—

"What the durnation am I stannin' hyur for? Thur ain't no time to be wasted in shiller-shallerin'. Ef he shed grup thet critter, an git what he wants from it, then I mout whissel for what I want, 'ithout the ghost o' a chance for gettin' it.

"I must make a better rate o' speed. Gee-up, ole gurl; an see ef ye can't overtake that ere grey hoss, as scuttled past half-a-hour agone. Now for a spell o' yur swiftness, the which you kin show along wi' any o' them, I reckon—thet air when ye're pressed. Gee-up!"

Instead of using the cruel means employed by him when wanting his mare to make her best speed, he only drove the old spur against her ribs, and started her into a trot. He had no desire to travel more rapidly than was consistent with caution; and while trotting he kept his eyes sharply ranging along the skyline in front of him.

"From the way his track runs," was his reflection, "I kin tell pretty nigh whar it's goin' to fetch out. Everything seems to go that way; an so did he, poor young fellur—never more to come back. Ah, wal! ef t'aint possible to ree-vive him agin, may be it air to squar the yards wi' the skunk as destroyed him. The Scripter sez, 'a eye for a eye, an a tooth for a tooth,' an I reckin I'll shet up somebody's day-lights, an spoil the use o' thur ivories afore I hev done wi' him. Somebody as don't suspeeshun it neyther, an that same—. Heigh! Yonner he goes! An' yonner too the Headless, by Geehosophat! Full gallup both; an durn me, if the grey aint a overtakin' him!

"They aint comin' this way, so 'tain't no use in our squattin', ole gurl. Stan' steady for all that. He *mout* see us movin'.

"No fear. He's too full o' his frolic to look anywhar else, than straight custrut afore him. Ha! jest as I expected—into the openin'! Right down it, fast as heels kin carry 'em!

"Now, my maar, on we go agin!"

Another stage of trotting—with his eyes kept steadfastly fixed upon the chapparal gap—brought Zeb to the timber.

Although the chase had long since turned the angle of the avenue, and was now out of sight, he did not go along the open ground; but among the bushes that bordered it.

He went so as to command a view of the clear track for some distance ahead; at the same time taking care that neither himself, nor his mare, might be seen by any one advancing from the opposite direction.

He did not anticipate meeting any one—much less the man who soon after came in sight.

He was not greatly surprised at hearing a shot: for he had been listening for it, ever since he had set eyes on the chase. He was rather in surprise at not hearing it sooner; and when the crack did come, he recognised the report of a yäger rifle, and knew whose gun had been discharged.

He was more astonished to see its owner returning along the lane—in less than five minutes after the shot had been fired— returning, too, with a rapidity that told of retreat!

"Comin' back agin—an so soon!" he muttered, on perceiving Calhoun. "Dog-goned queery thet air! Thur's somethin' amiss, more'n a miss, I reck'n. Ho, ho, ho! Goin', too, as if hell war arter him! Maybe it's the Headless hisself, and thur's been a changin' about in the chase—tit for tat! Darn me, ef it don't look like it! I'd gie a silver dollar to see thet sort o' a thing. He, he, he, ho, ho, hoo!"

Long before this, the hunter had slipped out of his saddle, and taken the precaution to screen both himself and his animal from the chance of being seen by the retreating rider—who promise soon to pass the spot.

And soon did he pass it, going at such a gait, and with such a wild abstracted air, that Zeb would scarce have been perceived had he been standing uncovered in the avenue!

"Geehosophat!" mentally ejaculated the backwoodsman, as the passion-scathed countenance came near enough to be scrutinised. "If hell ain't *arter*, it's *inside* o' him! Durn me, ef thet face ain't the ugli-est picter this coon ever clapped eyes on. I shed pity the wife as gets him. Poor Miss Peintdexter! I hope she'll be able to steer clur o' havin' sech a cut-throat as him to be her lord an master.

"What's up anyhow? Thar don't 'pear to be anythin' arter him? An' he still keeps on! Whar's he boun' for now? I must foller an see.

"To hum agin!" exclaimed the hunter, after going on to the edge of the chapparal, and observed Calhoun still going at a gallop, with head turned homeward. "Hum agin, for sartin!

"Now, ole gurl!" he continued, having remained silent till the grey horse was nearly out of sight, "You an me goes t'other way. We must find out what thet shot wur fired for."

---

In ten minutes after, Zeb had alighted from his mare, and lifted up from the ground an object, the stoutest heart might have felt horror in taking hold of—disgust, even, in touching!

Not so the old hunter. In that object he beheld the lineaments of a face well known to him—despite the shrivelling of the skin, and the blood streaks that so fearfully falsified its expression—still dear to him, despite death and a merciless mutilation.

He had loved that face, when it belonged to a boy; he now cherished it, belonging not to anybody!

Clasping the rim of the hat that fitted tightly to the temples—Zeb endeavoured to take it off. He did not succeed. The head was swollen so as almost to burst the bullion band twisted around it!

Holding it in its natural position, Zeb stood for a time gazing tenderly on the face.

"Lord, O Lordy!" he drawlingly exclaimed, "what a present to take back to *his* father, to say nothin' o' the sister! I don't think I'll take it. It air better to bury the thing out hyur, an say no more abeout it.

"No; durn me ef I do! What am I thinkin' o'? Tho' I don't exackly see how it may help to sarcumstantiate the chain o' evvydince, it may do somethin' torst it. Durned queery witness *it* 'll be to purduce in a coort o' justis!"

Saying this, he unstrapped his old blanket; and, using it as a wrapper, carefully packed within it head, hat, and all.

Then, hanging the strange bundle over the horn of his saddle, he remounted his mare, and rode reflectingly away.

# 83. Limbs of the Law

On the third day after Maurice Gerald became an inmate of the military prison the fever had forsaken him, and he no longer talked incoherently. On the fourth he was almost restored to his health and strength. The fifth was appointed for his trial!

This haste—that elsewhere would have been considered indecent—was thought nothing of in Texas; where a man may commit a capital offence, be tried, and hanged within the short space of four-and-twenty hours!

His enemies, who were numerous, for some reason of their own, insisted upon despatch: while his friends, who were few, could urge no good reason against it.

Among the populace there was the usual clamouring for prompt and speedy justice; fortified by that exciting phrase, old as the creation itself: "that the blood of the murdered man was calling from the ground for vengeance."

The advocates of an early trial were favoured by a fortuitous circumstance. The judge of the Supreme Court chanced just then to be going his circuit; and the days devoted to clearing the calendar at Fort Inge, had been appointed for that very week.

There was, therefore, a sort of necessity, that the case of Maurice Gerald, as of the other suspected murderers, should be tried within a limited time.

As no one objected, there was no one to ask for a postponement; and it stood upon the docket for the day in question—the fifteenth of the month.

The accused might require the services of a legal adviser. There was no regular practitioner in the place: as in these frontier districts the gentlemen of the long robe usually travel in company with the Court; and the Court had not yet arrived. For all that, a lawyer had appeared: a "counsellor" of distinction; who had come all the way from San Antonio, to conduct the case. As a volunteer he had presented himself!

It may have been generosity on the part of this gentleman, or an eye to Congress, though it was said that gold, presented by fair fingers, had induced him to make the journey.

When it rains, it rains. The adage is true in Texas as regards the elements; and on this occasion it was true of the lawyers.

The day before that appointed for the trial of the mustanger, a second presented himself at Fort Inge, who put forward his claim to be upon the side of the prisoner.

This gentleman had made a still longer journey than he of San Antonio; a voyage, in fact: since he had crossed the great Atlantic, starting from the metropolis of the Emerald Isle. He had come for no other purpose than to hold communication with the man accused of having committed a murder!

It is true, the errand that had brought him did not anticipate this; and the Dublin solicitor was no little astonished when, after depositing his travelling traps under the roof of Mr Oberdoffer's hostelry, and making inquiry about Maurice Gerald, he was told that the young Irishman was shut up in the guard-house.

Still greater the attorney's astonishment on learning the cause of his incarceration.

"Fwhat! the son of a Munsther Gerald accused of murdher! The heir of Castle Ballagh, wid its bewtiful park and demesne. Fwy, I've got the papers in my portmantyee here. Faugh-a-ballagh! Show me the way to him!"

Though the "Texan" Boniface was inclined to consider his re-cently arrived guest entitled to a suspicion of lunacy, he assented to his request; and furnished him with a guide to the guard-house.

If the Irish attorney was mad, there appeared to be method in his madness. Instead of being denied admittance to the accused criminal, he was made welcome to go in and out of the military prison—as often as it seemed good to him.

Some document he had laid before the eyes of the major-commandant, had procured him this privilege; at the same time placing him *en rapport*, in a friendly way, with the Texan "counsellor."

The advent of the Irish attorney at such a crisis gave rise to much speculation at the Port, the village, and throughout the settlement. The bar-room of the "Rough and Ready" was rife with conjecturers—*quidnuncs* they could scarcely be called: since in Texas the genus does not exist.

A certain grotesqueness about the man added to the national instinct for guessing—which had been rendered excruciatingly keen through some revelations, contributed by "Old Duffer."

For all that, the transatlantic limb of the law proved himself tolerably true to the traditions of his craft. With the exception of the trifling imprudences already detailed—drawn from him in the first moments of surprise—he never afterwards committed himself; but kept his lips close as an oyster at ebb tide.

There was not much time for him to use his tongue. On the day after his arrival the trial was to take place; and during most of the interval he was either in the guard-house along with the prisoner, or closeted with the San Antonio counsel.

The rumour became rife that Maurice Gerald had told them a tale—a strange weird story—but of its details the world outside remained in itching ignorance.

There was one who knew it—one able to confirm it—Zeb Stump the hunter.

There may have been another; but this other was not in the confidence either of the accused or his counsel.

Zeb himself did not appear in their company. Only once had he been seen conferring with them. After that he was gone—both from the guard-house and the settlement, as everybody supposed, about his ordinary business—in search of deer, "baar," or "gobbler."

Everybody was in error. Zeb for the time had forsaken his usual pursuits, or, at all events, the game he was accustomed to chase, capture, and kill.

It is true he was out upon a stalking expedition; but instead of birds or beasts, he was after an animal of neither sort; one that could not be classed with creatures either of the earth or the air—a horseman without a head!

# 84. An Affectionate Nephew

"Tried to-morrow—to-morrow, thank God! Not likely that any-body 'll catch that cursed thing before then—to be hoped, never.

"*It* is all I've got to fear. I defy them to tell what's happened without that. Hang me if I know myself! Enough only to—.

"Queer, the coming of this Irish pettifogger!

"Queer, too, the fellow from San Antonio! Wonder who and what's brought him? Somebody's promised him his costs?

"Damn 'em! I don't care, not the value of a red cent. They can make nothing out of it, but that Gerald did the deed. Everything points that way; and everybody thinks so. They're bound to convict him.

"Zeb Stump don't think it, the suspicious old snake! He's no-where to be found. Wonder where he has gone? On a hunt, they say. 'Tain't likely, such time as this. What if he be hunting it? What if he should catch it?

"I'd try again myself, if there was time. There ain't. Before to-morrow night it'll be all over; and afterwards if there should turn up—. Damn afterwards! The thing is to make sure now. Let the future look to itself. With one man hung for the murder, 'tain't likely they'd care to accuse another. Even if something suspicious *did* turn up! they'd be shy to take hold of it. It would be like condemning themselves!

"I reckon, I've got all right with the Regulators. Sam Manley himself appears pretty well convinced. I knocked his doubts upon the head, when I told him what I'd heard that night. A little more than I did hear; though that was enough to make a man stark, staring mad. Damn!

"It's no use crying over spilt milk. She's met the man, and there's an end of it. She'll never meet him again, and that's another end of it—except she meet him in heaven. Well; that will depend upon her-self.

"I don't think *anything has happened between them.* She's not the sort for that, with all her wildness; and it may be what that yellow wench tells me—only *gratitude*. No, no, no! It can't be. Gratitude don't get out of its bed in the middle of the night—to keep appointments at the bottom of a garden? She loves him—she loves him! Let her love and be damned! She shall never have him. She shall never see him again, unless she prove obstinate; and then it will be but to condemn him. A word from her, and he's a hanged man.

"She shall speak it, if she don't say that other word, I've twice asked her for. The third time will be the last. One more refusal, and I show my hand. Not only shall this Irish adventurer meet his doom; but she shall be his condemner; and the plantation, house, niggers, everything—. Ah! uncle Woodley; I wanted to see you."

The soliloquy above reported took place in a chamber, tenanted only by Cassius Calhoun.

It was Woodley Poindexter who interrupted it. Sad, silent, straying through the corridors of Casa del Corvo, he had entered the apartment usually occupied by his nephew—more by chance than from any premeditated purpose.

"Want me! For what, nephew?"

There was a tone of humility, almost obeisance, in the speech of the broken man. The once proud Poindexter—before whom two hundred slaves had trembled every day, every hour of their lives, now stood in the presence of his master!

True, it was his own nephew, who had the power to humiliate him—his sister's son.

But there was not much in that, considering the character of the man.

"I want to talk to you about Loo," was the rejoinder of Calhoun.

It was the very subject Woodley Poindexter would have shunned. It was something he dreaded to think about, much less make the topic of discourse; and less still with him who now challenged it.

Nevertheless, he did not betray surprise. He scarce felt it. Something said or done on the day before had led him to anticipate this request for a conversation—as also the nature of the subject.

The manner in which Calhoun introduced it, did not diminish his uneasiness. It sounded more like a demand than a request.

"About Loo? What of her?" he inquired, with assumed calmness.

"Well," said Calhoun, apparently in reluctant utterance, as if shy about entering upon the subject, or pretending to be so, "I—I—wanted—"

"I'd rather," put in the planter, taking advantage of the other's hesitancy, "I'd rather not speak of *her* now."

This was said almost supplicatingly.

"And why not now, uncle?" asked Calhoun, emboldened by the show of opposition.

"You know my reasons, nephew?"

"Well, I know the time is not pleasant. Poor Henry missing—supposed to be—After all, he may turn up yet, and everything be right again."

"Never! we shall never see him again—living or dead. I have no longer a son?"

"You have a daughter; and she—"

"Has disgraced me!"

"I don't believe it, uncle—no."

"What means those things I've heard—myself seen? What could have taken her there—twenty miles across the country—alone—in the hut of a common horse-trader—standing by his bedside? O God! And why should she have interposed to save him—him, the murderer of my son—her own brother? O God!"

"Her own story explains the first—satisfactorily, as I think."

Calhoun did *not* think so.

"The second is simple enough. Any woman would have done the same—a woman like Loo."

"There is *none* like her. I, her father, say so. Oh! that I could think it is, as you say! My poor daughter! who should now be dearer to me than ever—now that I have no son!"

"It is for her to find you a son—one already related to you; and who can promise to play the part—with perhaps not so much affection as him you have lost, but with all he has the power to give. I won't talk to you in riddles, Uncle Woodley. You know what I mean; and how my mind's made up about this matter. *I want Loo!*"

The planter showed no surprise at the laconic declaration. He expected it. For all that, the shadow became darker on his brow. It was evident he did not relish the proposed alliance.

This may seem strange. Up to a late period, he had been its advocate—in his own mind—and more than once, delicately, in the ear of his daughter.

Previous to the migration into Texas, he had known comparatively little of his nephew.

Since coming to manhood, Calhoun had been a citizen of the state of Mississippi—more frequently a dweller in the dissipated city of New Orleans. An occasional visit to the Louisiana plantation was all his uncle had seen of him; until the developing beauty of his cousin

491

Louise gave him the inducement to make these visits at shorter intervals—each time protracting them to a longer stay.

There was then twelve months of campaigning in Mexico; where he rose to the rank of captain; and, after his conquests in war, he had returned home with the full determination to make a conquest in love—the heart of his Creole cousin.

From that time his residence under his uncle's roof had been more permanent. If not altogether liked by the young lady, he had made himself welcome to her father, by means seldom known to fail.

The planter, once rich, was now poor. Extravagance had reduced his estate to a hopeless indebtedness. With his nephew, the order was reversed: once poor, he was now rich. Chance had made him so. Under the circumstances, it was not surprising, that money had passed between them.

In his native place, and among his old neighbours, Woodley Poindexter still commanded sufficient homage to shield him from the suspicion of being *under* his nephew; as also to restrain the latter from exhibiting the customary arrogance of the creditor.

It was only after the move into Texas, that their relations began to assume that peculiar character observable between mortgagor and mortgagee.

It grew more patent, after several attempts at love-making on the part of Calhoun, with corresponding repulses on the part of Louise.

The planter had now a better opportunity of becoming acquainted with the true character of his nephew; and almost every day; since their arrival at Casa del Corvo, had this been developing itself to his discredit.

Calhoun's quarrel with the mustanger, and its ending, had not strengthened his uncle's respect for him; though, as a kinsman, he was under the necessity of taking sides with him.

There had occurred other circumstances to cause a change in his feelings—to make him, notwithstanding its many advantages, *dislike* the connection.

Alas! there was much also to render it, if not agreeable, at least not to be slightingly set aside.

Indecision—perhaps more than the sorrow for his son's loss dictated the character of his reply.

"If I understand you aright, nephew, you mean *marriage*! Surely it is not the time to talk of it now—while death is in our house! To think of such a thing would cause a scandal throughout the settlement."

"You mistake me, uncle. I do not mean marriage—that is, not *now*. Only something that will secure it—when the proper time arrives."

"I do not understand you, Cash."

"You'll do that, if you only listen to me a minute."

"Go on."

"Well; what I want to say is this. I've made up my mind to get married. I'm now close upon thirty—as you know; and at that time a man begins to get tired of running about the world. I'm damnably tired of it; and don't intend to keep single any longer. *I'm willing to have Loo for my wife.* There need be no hurry about it. All I want now is her promise; signed and sealed, that there may be no *fluke*, or uncertainty. I want the thing settled. When these *bothers* blow past, it will be time enough to talk of the wedding business, and that sort of thing."

The word "bothers," with the speech of which it formed part, grated harshly on the ear of a father, mourning for his murdered son!

The spirit of Woodley Poindexter was aroused—almost to the resumption of its old pride, and the indignation that had oft accompanied it.

It soon cowered again. On one side he saw land, slaves, wealth, position; on the other, penury that seemed perdition.

He did not yield altogether; as may be guessed by the character of his reply.

"Well, nephew; you have certainly spoken plain enough. But I know not my daughter's disposition towards you. You say you are willing to have her for your wife. Is she willing to have you? I suppose there is a question about that?"

"I think, uncle, it will depend a good deal upon yourself. You are her father. Surely you can *convince* her?"

"I'm not so sure of that. She's not of the kind to be convinced— against her will. You, Cash, know that as well as I."

"Well, I only know that I intend getting 'spliced,' as the sailors say; and I'd like Loo for the *mistress of Casa del Corvo*, better than any other woman in the Settlement—in all Texas, for that matter."

Woodley Poindexter recoiled at the ungracious speech. It was the first time he had been told, that he was not the *master* of Casa del Corvo! Indirectly as the information had been conveyed, he understood it.

Once more rose before his mind the reality of lands, slaves, wealth, and social status—alongside, the apparition of poverty and social abasement.

The last looked hideous; though not more so than the man who stood before him—his own nephew—soliciting to become his son!

For purposes impossible to comprehend, God often suffers himself to be defeated by the Devil. In this instance was it so. The good in Poindexter's heart succumbed to the evil. He promised to assist his nephew, in destroying the happiness of his daughter.

"Loo!"

"Father!"

"I come to ask a favour from you."

"What is it, father?"

"You know that your cousin Cash loves you. He is ready to die for—more and better still, to marry you."

"But I am not ready to marry *him*. No, father; *I* shall die first. The presumptuous wretch! I know what it means. And he has sent *you* to make this proposal! Tell him in return, that, sooner than consent to become his wife, I'd go upon the prairies—and seek my living by lassoing wild horses! Tell him that!"

"Reflect, daughter! You are, perhaps, not aware that—"

"That my cousin is your creditor. I know all that, dear father. But I know also that you are Woodley Poindexter, and I your daughter."

Delicately as the hint was given, it produced the desired effect. The spirit of the planter surged up to its ancient pride, His reply was:—

"Dearest Louise! image of your mother! I had doubted you. Forgive me, my noble girl! Let the past be forgotten. I shall leave it to yourself. You are free to refuse him!"

---

# 85. A Kind Cousin

Louise Poindexter made fall use of the liberty allowed by her father. In less than an hour after, Calhoun was flatly refused.

It was his third time of asking. Twice before had the same suit been preferred; informally, and rather by a figure of speech than in the shape of a direct declaration.

It was the third time; and the answer told it would be the last. It was a simple "No," emphatically followed by the equally simple "Never!"

There was no prevarication about the speech—no apology for having made it.

Calhoun listened to his rejection, without much show of surprise. Possibly—in all probability—he expected it.

But instead of the blank look of despair usually observable under the circumstances, his features remained firm, and his cheeks free from blanching.

As he stood confronting his fair cousin, a spectator might have been reminded of the jaguar, as it pauses before springing on its prey.

There was that in his eye which seemed to say:—

"In less than sixty seconds, you'll change your tune."

What he did say was:—

"You're not in earnest, Loo?"

"I am, sir. Have I spoken like one who jests?"

"You've spoken like one, who hasn't taken pains to reflect."

"Upon what?"

"Many things."

"Name them!"

"Well, for one—the way I love you."

She made no rejoinder.

"A love," he continued, in a tone half explanatory, half pleading; "a love, Loo, that no man can feel for a woman, and survive it. It can end only with my life. It could not end with *yours*."

There was a pause, but still no reply.

"'Tis no use my telling you its history. It began on the same day—ay, the same hour—I first saw you.

"I won't say it grew stronger as time passed. It could not. On my first visit to your father's house—now six years ago—you may remember that, after alighting from my horse, you asked me to take a walk with you round the garden—while dinner was being got ready.

"You were but a stripling of a girl; but oh, Loo, you were a woman in beauty—as beautiful as you are at this moment.

"No doubt you little thought, as you took me by the hand, and led me along the gravelled walk, under the shade of the China trees, that the touch of your fingers was sending a thrill into my soul; your pretty prattle making an impression upon my heart, that neither time, nor distance, nor yet *dissipation*, has been able to efface."

The Creole continued to listen, though not without showing sign. Words so eloquent, so earnest, so full of sweet flattery, could scarce fail to have effect upon a woman. By such speech had Lucifer succeeded in the accomplishment of his purpose. There was pity, if not approval, in her look!

Still did she keep silence.

Calhoun continued:—

"Yes, Loo; it's true as I tell you. I've tried all three. Six years may fairly be called time. From Mississippi to Mexico was the distance: for I went there with no other purpose than to forget you. It proved of no avail; and, returning, I entered upon a course of dissipation. New Orleans knows that.

"I won't say, that my passion grew stronger by these attempts to stifle it. I've already told you, it could not. From the hour you first caught hold of my hand, and called me cousin—ah! you called me *handsome* cousin, Loo—from that hour I can remember no change, no degrees, in the fervour of my affection; except when jealousy has made me hate—ay, so much, that I could have *killed* you!"

"Good gracious, Captain Calhoun! This is wild talk of yours. It is even silly!"

"'Tis serious, nevertheless. I've been so jealous with you at times, that it was a task to control myself. My temper I could not—as you have reason to know."

"Alas, cousin, I cannot help what has happened. I never gave you cause, to think—"

"I know what you are going to say; and you may leave it unspoken. I'll say it for you: 'to think that you ever loved me.' Those were the words upon your lips.

"I don't say you did," he continued, with deepening despair: "I don't accuse you of tempting me. Something did. God, who gave you such beauty; or the Devil, who led me to look upon it."

"What you say only causes me pain. I do not suppose you are trying to flatter me. You talk too earnestly for that. But oh, cousin Cassius, 'tis a fancy from which you will easily recover. There are others, far fairer than I; and many, who would feel complimented by such speeches. Why not address yourself to them?"

"Why not?" he echoed, with bitter emphasis. "What an idle question!"

"I repeat it. It is not idle. Far more so is your affection for me: for I must be candid with you, Cassius. I do not—I *cannot*, love you."

"You will not marry me then?"

"That, at least, is an idle question. I've said I do not love you. Surely that is sufficient."

"And I've said I love *you*. I gave it as one reason why I wish you for my wife: but there are *others*. Are you desirous of hearing them?"

As Calhoun asked this question the suppliant air forsook him. The spirit of the jaguar was once more in his eye.

"You said there were other reasons. State them! Do not be backward. I'm not afraid to listen."

"Indeed!" he rejoined, sneeringly. "You're not afraid, ain't you?"

"Not that I know of. What have I to fear?"

"I won't say what *you* have; but what your father has."

"Let me hear it? What concerns him, equally affects me. I am his daughter; and now, alas, his only—. Go on, cousin Calhoun! What is this shadow hanging over him?"

"No shadow, Loo; but something serious, and substantial. A trouble he's no longer able to contend with. You force me to speak of things you shouldn't know anything about."

"Oh! don't I? You're mistaken, cousin Cash. I know them already. I'm aware that my father's in debt; and that you are his creditor. How could I have remained in ignorance of it? Your arrogance about the house—your presumption, shown every hour, and in presence of the domestics—has been evidence sufficient to satisfy even them, that there is something amiss. You are master of Casa del Corvo. I know it. You are not master of *me*!"

497

Calhoun quailed before the defiant speech. The card, upon which he had been counting, was not likely to gain the trick. He declined playing it.

He held a still stronger *in* his hand; which was exhibited without farther delay.

"Indeed!" he retorted, sneeringly. "Well; if I'm not master of your heart, I am of your happiness—or shall be. I know the worthless wretch that's driven you to this denial—"

"Who?"

"How innocent you are!"

"Of that at least I am; unless by worthless wretch you mean yourself. In that sense I can understand you, sir. The description is too true to be mistaken."

"Be it so!" he replied, turning livid with rage, though still keeping himself under a certain restraint. "Well; since you think me so worthless, it won't, I suppose, better your opinion of me, when I tell you what I'm going to do with you?"

"Do with me! You are presumptuous, cousin Cash! You talk as if I were your *protégée*, or slave! I'm neither one, nor the other!"

Calhoun, cowering under the outburst of her indignation, remained silent.

"*Pardieu!*" she continued, "what is this threat? Tell me what you are *going to do with me*! I should like to know that."

"You shall."

"Let me hear it! Am I to be turned adrift upon the prairie, or shut up in a convent? Perhaps it may be a prison?"

"You would like the last, no doubt—provided your incarceration was to be in the company of—"

"Go on, sir! What is to be my destiny? I'm impatient to have it declared."

"Don't be in a hurry. The first act shall be rehearsed tomorrow."

"So soon? And where, may I ask?"

"In a court of justice."

"How, sir?"

"By your standing before a judge, and in presence of a jury."

"You are pleased to be facetious, Captain Calhoun. Let me tell you that I don't like such pleasantries—"

"Pleasantries indeed! I'm stating plain facts. To-morrow is the day of trial. Mr Maurice Gerald, or McSweeney, or O'Hogerty, or whatever's his name, will stand before the bar—accused of murdering your brother."

"'Tis false! Maurice Gerald never—"

"Did the deed, you are going to say? Well, that remains to be proved. It *will* be; and from your own lips will come the words that'll prove it—to the satisfaction of every man upon the jury."

The great gazelle-eyes of the Creole were opened to their fullest extent. They gazed upon the speaker with a look such as is oft given by the gazelle itself—a commingling of fear, wonder, and inquiry.

It was some seconds before she essayed to speak. Thoughts, conjectures, fears, fancies, and suspicions, all had to do in keeping her silent.

"I know not what you mean," she at length rejoined. "You talk of my being called into court. For what purpose? Though I am the sister of him, who—I know nothing—can tell no more than is in the mouth of everybody."

"Yes can you; a great deal more. It's not in the mouth of everybody: that on the night of the murder, you gave Gerald a meeting at the bottom of the garden. No more does all the world know what occurred at that stolen interview. How Henry intruded upon it; how, maddened, as he might well be, by the thought of such a disgrace—not only to his sister, but his family—he threatened to kill the man who had caused it; and was only hindered from carrying out that threat, by the intercession of the woman so damnably deluded!

"All the world don't know what followed: how Henry, like a fool, went after the low hound, and with what intent. Besides themselves, there were but two others who chanced to be spectators of that parting."

"Two—who were they?"

The question was asked mechanically—almost with a tranquil coolness.

It was answered with equal *sang froid*.

"One was Cassius Calhoun—the other Louise Poindexter." She did not start. She did not even show sign of being surprised. What was spoken already had prepared her for the revelation. Her rejoinder was a single word, pronounced in a tone of defiance. "Well!"

"Well!" echoed Calhoun, chagrined at the slight effect his speeches had produced; "I suppose you understand me?"

"Not any more than ever."

"You wish me to speak further?"

"As you please, sir."

"I shall then. I say to you, Loo, there's but one way to save your father from ruin—yourself from shame. You know what I mean?"

"Yes; I know that much."

"You will not refuse me now?"

"*Now* more than *ever!*"

"Be it so! Before this time to-morrow—and, by Heaven! I mean it—before this time *to-morrow*, you shall stand in the witness-box?"

"Vile spy! Anywhere but in your presence! Out of my sight! This instant, or I call my father!"

"You needn't put yourself to the trouble. I'm not going to embarrass you any longer with my company—so disagreeable to you. I leave you to reflect. Perhaps before the trial comes on, you'll see fit to change your mind. If so, I hope you'll give notice of it—in time to stay the summons. Good night, Loo! I'll sleep thinking of you."

With these words of mockery upon his lips—almost as bitter to himself as to her who heard them—Calhoun strode out of the apartment, with an air less of triumph than of guilt.

Louise listened, until his footsteps died away in the distant corridor.

Then, as if the proud angry thoughts hitherto sustaining her had become suddenly relaxed, she sank into a chair; and, with both hands pressing upon her bosom, tried to still the dread throbbings that now, more than ever, distracted it.

# 86. A Texan Court

It is the dawn of another day. The Aurora, rising rose-coloured from the waves of a West Indian sea, flings its sweetest smile athwart the savannas of Texas.

Almost on the same instant that the rosy light kisses the white sand-dunes of the Mexican Gulf, does it salute the flag on Fort Inge, nearly a hundred leagues distant: since there is just this much of an upward inclination between the coast at Matagorda and the spurs of the Guadalupe mountains, near which stand this frontier post.

The Aurora has just lighted up the flag, that at the same time flouting out from its staff spreads its broad field of red, white, and blue to the gentle zephyrs of the morning.

Perhaps never since that staff went up, has the star-spangled banner waved over a scene of more intense interest than is expected to occur on this very day.

Even at the early hour of dawn, the spectacle may be said to have commenced. Along with the first rays of the Aurora, horsemen may be seen approaching the military post from all quarters of the compass. They ride up in squads of two, three, or half a dozen; dismount as they arrive; fasten their horses to the stockade fences, or picket them upon the open prairie.

This done, they gather into groups on the parade-ground; stand conversing or stray down to the village; all, at one time or another, taking a turn into the tavern, and paying their respects to Boniface behind the bar.

The men thus assembling are of many distinct types and nationalities. Almost every country in Europe has furnished its quota; though the majority are of that stalwart race whose ancestors expelled the Indians from the "Bloody Ground;" built log cabins on the sites of their wigwams; and spent the remainder of their lives in felling the forests of the Mississippi. Some of them have been brought up to the cultivation of corn; others understand better the culture of cotton; while a large number, from homes further south, have migrated into Texas to speculate in the growth and manufacture of sugar and tobacco.

Most are planters by calling and inclination; though there are graziers and cattle-dealers, hunters and horse-dealers, storekeepers, and traders of other kinds—not a few of them traffickers in human flesh!

There are lawyers, land-surveyors, and land-speculators, and other speculators of no proclaimed calling—adventurers ready to take a hand in whatever may turn up—whether it be the branding of cattle, a scout against Comanches, or a spell of filibustering across the Rio Grande.

Their costumes are as varied as their callings. They have been already described: for the men now gathering around Fort Inge are the same we have seen before assembled in the courtyard of Casa del Corvo—the same with an augmentation of numbers.

The present assemblage differs in another respect from that composing the expedition of searchers. It is graced by the presence of women—the wives, sisters, and daughters of the men. Some are on horseback; and remain in the saddle—their curtained cotton-bonnets shading their fair faces from the glare of the sun; others are still more commodiously placed for the spectacle—seated under white waggon-tilts, or beneath the more elegant coverings of "carrioles" and "Jerseys."

There is a spectacle—at least there is one looked for. It is a trial long talked of in the Settlement.

Superfluous to say that it is the trial of Maurice Gerald—known as *Maurice the mustanger*.

Equally idle to add, that it is for the murder of Henry Poindexter.

It is not the high nature of the offence that has attracted such a crowd, nor yet the characters of either the accused or his victim—neither much known in the neighbourhood.

The same Court—it is the Supreme Court of the district, Uvalde—has been in session there before—has tried all sorts of cases, and all kinds of men—thieves, swindlers, homicides, and even murderers—with scarce fourscore people caring to be spectators of the trial, or staying to hear the sentence!

It is not this which has brought so many settlers together; but a series of strange circumstances, mysterious and melodramatic; which seem in some way to be connected with the crime, and have been for days the sole talk of the Settlement.

It is not necessary to name these circumstances: they are already known.

All present at Fort Inge have come there anticipating: that the trial about to take place will throw light on the strange problem that has hitherto defied solution.

Of course there are some who, independent of this, have a feeling of interest in the fate of the prisoner. There are others inspired with a still sadder interest—friends and relatives of the man *supposed to have been* murdered: for it must be remembered, that there is yet no evidence of the actuality of the crime.

But there is little doubt entertained of it. Several circumstances—independent of each other—have united to confirm it; and all believe that the foul deed has been done—as firmly as if they had been eye-witnesses of the act.

They only wait to be told the details; to learn the how, and the when, and the wherefore.

---

Ten o'clock, and the Court is in session.

There is not much change in the composition of the crowd; only that a sprinkling of military uniforms has become mixed with the more sober dresses of the citizens. The soldiers of the garrison have been dismissed from morning parade; and, free to take their recreation for the day, have sought it among the ranks of the civilian spectators. There stand they side by side—soldiers and citizens—dragoons, riflemen, infantry, and artillery, interspersed among planters, hunters, horse-dealers, and desperate adventurers, having just heard the "Oyez!" of the Court crier—grotesquely pronounced "O yes!"—determined to stand there till they hear the last solemn formulary from the lips of the judge: "May God have mercy on your soul!"

There is scarce one present who does not expect ere night to listen to this terrible final phrase, spoken from under the shadow of that sable cap, that denotes the death doom of a fellow creature.

There may be only a few who wish it. But there are many who feel certain, that the trial will end in a conviction; and that ere the sun has set, the soul of Maurice Gerald will go back to its God!

---

The Court is in session.

You have before your mind's eye a large hall, with a raised daïs at one side; a space enclosed between panelled partitions; a table inside it; and on its edge a box-like structure, resembling the rostrum of a lecture-room, or the reading-desk in a church.

503

You see judges in ermine robes; barristers in wigs of grey, and gowns of black, with solicitors attending on them; clerks, ushers, and reporters; blue policemen with bright buttons standing here and there; and at the back a sea of heads and faces, not always kempt or clean.

You observe, moreover, a certain subdued look on the countenances of the spectators—not so much an air of decorum, as a fear of infringing the regulations of the Court.

You must get all this out of your mind, if you wish to form an idea of a Court of justice on the frontiers of Texas—as unlike its homonym in England as a bond of guerillas to a brigade of Guardsmen.

There is no court-house, although there is a sort of public room used for this and other purposes. But the day promises to be hot, and the Court has decided to *sit under a tree*!

And under a tree has it established itself—a gigantic live-oak, festooned with Spanish moss—standing by the edge of the parade-ground, and extending its shadow afar over the verdant prairie.

A large deal table is placed underneath, with half a score of skin-bottomed chairs set around it, and on its top a few scattered sheets of foolscap paper, an inkstand with goose-quill pens, a well-thumbed law-book or two, a blown-glass decanter containing peach-brandy, a couple of common tumblers, a box of Havannah cigars, and another of lucifer-matches.

Behind these *paraphernalia* sits the judge, not only un-robed in ermine, but actually un-coated—the temperature of the day having decided him to try the case in his *shirt-sleeves*!

Instead of a wig, he wears his Panama hat, set slouchingly over one cheek, to balance the half-smoked, half-chewed Havannah projecting from the other.

The remaining chairs are occupied by men whose costume gives no indication of their calling.

There are lawyers among them—attorneys, and *counsellors*, there called—with no difference either in social or legal status; the sheriff and his "deputy"; the military commandant of the fort; the chaplain; the doctor; several officers; with one or two men of undeclared occupations.

A little apart are twelve individuals grouped together; about half of them seated on a rough slab bench, the other half "squatted" or reclining along the grass.

It is the *jury*—an "institution" as germane to Texas as to England; and in Texas ten times more true to its trust; scorning to submit to the dictation of the judge—in England but too freely admitted.

Around the Texan judge and jury—close pressing upon the precincts of the Court—is a crowd that may well be called nondescript. Buckskin hunting-shirts; blanket-coats—even under the oppressive heat; frocks of "copperas stripe" and Kentucky jeans; blouses of white linen, or sky-blue *cottonade*; shirts of red flannel or unbleached "domestic"; dragoon, rifle, infantry, and artillery uniforms, blend and mingle in that motley assemblage.

Here and there is seen a more regular costume—one more native to the country—the *jaqueta* and *calzoneros* of the Mexican, with the broad *sombrero* shading his swarthy face of *picaresque* expression.

Time was—and that not very long ago—when men assembled in this same spot would all have been so attired.

But then there was no jury of twelve, and the judge—*Juez de Letras*—was a far more important personage, with death in his nod, and pardon easily obtained by those who could put *onzas* in his pocket.

With all its rude irregularity—despite the absence of effete forms—of white ermine, and black silk—of uniformed *alguazils*, or bright-buttoned policemen—despite the presence of men that, to the civilised eye, may appear uncouth—even savage I hesitate not to say, that among these red flannel-shirts and coats of Kentucky jean, the innocent man is as safe—ay far safer—to obtain justice, and the guilty to get punished, than amidst the formalities and hair-splitting chicaneries of our so-called civilisation.

Do not mistake those men assembled under the Texan tree—however rough their exterior may seem to your hypercritical eye—do not mistake them for a mob of your own "masses," brutalised from their very birth by the curse of over-taxation. Do not mistake them, either, for things like yourselves—filled to the throat with a spirit of flunkeyism—would that it choked you!—scorning all that is grand and progressive—revering only the effete, the superficial, and the selfish.

I am talking to you, my middle-class friend, who fancy yourself a *citizen* of this our English country. A citizen, forsooth; without even the first and scantiest right of citizenship—that of choosing your parliamentary representative.

You fancy you *have* this right. I have scarce patience to tell you, you are mistaken.

Ay, grandly mistaken, when you imagine yourself standing on the same political platform with those quasi-rude frontiersmen of Texas.

Nothing of the kind. *They* are "sovereign citizens"—the peers of your superiors, or of those who assume so to call themselves, and whose assumption you are base enough to permit without struggle—almost without protest!

In most assemblies the inner circle is the more select. The gem is to be found in the centre at Port Inge.

In that now mustered the order is reversed. Outside is the elegance. The fair feminine forms, bedecked in their best dresses, stand up in spring waggons, or sit in more elegant equipages, sufficiently elevated to see over the heads of the male spectators.

It is not upon the judge that their eyes are bent, or only at intervals. The glances are given to a group of three men, placed near the jury, and not very far from the stem of the tree. One is seated, and two standing. The former is the prisoner at the bar; the latter the sheriff's officers in charge of him.

It was originally intended to try several other men for the murder; Miguel Diaz and his associates, as also Phelim O'Neal.

But in the course of a preliminary investigation the Mexican mustanger succeeded in proving an *alibi*, as did also his trio of companions. All four have been consequently discharged.

They acknowledged having disguised themselves as Indians: for the fact being proved home to them, they could not do less.

But they pretended it to have been a joke—a *travestie*; and as there was proof of the others being at home—and Diaz dead drunk—on the night of Henry Poindexter's disappearance, their statement satisfied those who had been entrusted with the inquiry.

As to the Connemara man, it was not thought necessary to put him upon trial. If an accomplice, he could only have acted at the instigation of his master; and he might prove more serviceable in the witness-box than in the dock.

Before the bar, then—if we may be permitted the figure of speech—there stands but one prisoner, Maurice Gerald—known to those gazing upon him as *Maurice the mustanger*.

# 87. A False Witness

There are but few present who have any personal acquaintance with the accused; though there are also but a few who have never before heard his name. Perhaps not any.

It is only of late that this has become generally known: for previous to the six-shot duel with Calhoun, he had no other reputation than that of an accomplished horse-catcher.

All admitted him to be a fine young fellow—handsome, dashing, devoted to a fine horse, and deeming it no sin to look fondly on a fair woman—free of heart, as most Irishmen are, and also of speech, as will be more readily believed.

But neither his good, nor evil, qualities were carried to excess. His daring rarely exhibited itself in reckless rashness; while as rarely did his speech degenerate into "small talk."

In his actions there was observable a certain *juste milieu*. His words were alike well-balanced; displaying, even over his cups, a reticence somewhat rare among his countrymen.

No one seemed to know whence he came; for what reason he had settled in Texas; or why he had taken to such a queer "trade," as that of catching wild horses—a calling not deemed the most reputable.

It seemed all the more strange to those who knew: that he was not only educated, but evidently a "born gentleman"—a phrase, however, of but slight significance upon the frontiers of Texas.

There, too, was the thing itself regarded with no great wonder; where "born noblemen," both of France and the "Faderland," may oft be encountered seeking an honest livelihood by the sweat of their brow.

A fig for all patents of nobility—save those stamped by the true die of Nature!

Such is the sentiment of this far free land.

And this sort of impress the young Irishman carries about him—blazoned like the broad arrow. There is no one likely to mistake him for either fool or villain.

And yet he stands in the presence of an assembly, called upon to regard him as an assassin—one who in the dead hour of night has spilled innocent blood, and taken away the life of a fellow-creature!

Can the charge be true? If so, may God have mercy on his soul!

Some such reflection passes through the minds of the spectators, as they stand with eyes fixed upon him, waiting for his trial to begin.

Some regard him with glances of simple curiosity; others with interrogation; but most with a look that speaks of anger and revenge.

There is one pair of eyes dwelling upon him with an expression altogether unlike the rest—a gaze soft, but steadfast—in which fear and fondness seem strangely commingled.

There are many who notice that look of the lady spectator, whose pale face, half hid behind the curtains of a *calèche*, is too fair to escape observation.

There are few who can interpret it.

But among these, is the prisoner himself; who, observing both the lady and the look, feels a proud thrill passing through his soul, that almost compensates for the humiliation he is called upon to undergo. It is enough to make him, for the time, forget the fearful position in which he is placed.

For the moment, it is one of pleasure. He has been told of much that transpired during those dark oblivious hours. He now knows that what he had fancied to be only a sweet, heavenly vision, was a far sweeter reality of earth.

That woman's face, shining dream-like over his couch, was the same now seen through the curtains of the *calèche*; and the expression upon it tells him: that among the frowning spectators he has one friend who will be true to the end—even though it be death!

The trial begins.

There is not much ceremony in its inception. The judge takes off his hat strikes a lucifer-match; and freshly ignites his cigar.

After half a dozen draws, he takes the "weed" from between his teeth, lays it still smoking along the table, and says—

"Gentlemen of the jury! We are here assembled to try a case, the particulars of which are, I believe, known to all of you. A man has been murdered,—the son of one of our most respected citizens; and the prisoner at the bar is accused of having committed the crime. It is my duty to direct you as to the legal formalities of the trial. It is yours to decide—after hearing the evidence to be laid before you—whether or not the accusation be sustained."

The prisoner is asked, according to the usual formality,—"*Guilty, or not guilty?*"

"Not guilty," is the reply; delivered in a firm, but modest tone.

Cassius Calhoun, and some "rowdies" around him, affect an incredulous sneer.

The judge resumes his cigar, and remains silent.

The counsel for the State, after some introductory remarks, proceeds to introduce the witnesses for the prosecution.

First called is Franz Oberdoffer.

After a few unimportant interrogatories about his calling, and the like, he is requested to state what he knows of the affair. This is the common routine of a Texan trial.

Oberdoffer's evidence coincides with the tale already told by him: how on the night that young Poindexter was missed, Maurice Gerald had left his house at a late hour—after midnight. He had settled his account before leaving; and appeared to have plenty of money. It was not often Oberdoffer had known him so well supplied with cash. He had started for his home on the Nueces; or wherever it was. He had not said where he was going. He was not on the most friendly terms with witness. Witness only supposed he was going there, because his man had gone the day before, taking all his traps upon a pack-mule—everything, except what the mustanger himself carried off on his horse.

What had he carried off?

Witness could not remember much in particular. He was not certain of his having a gun. He rather believed that he had one—strapped, Mexican fashion, along the side of his saddle.

He could speak with certainty of having seen pistols in the holsters, with a bowie-knife in the mustanger's belt. Gerald was dressed as he always went—in Mexican costume, and with a striped Mexican blanket. He had the last over his shoulders as he rode off. The witness thought it strange, his leaving at that late hour of the night. Still stranger, that he had told witness of his intention to start the next morning.

He had been out all the early part of the night, but without his horse—which he kept in the tavern stable. He had started off immediately after returning. He stayed only long enough to settle his account. He appeared excited, and in a hurry. It was not with drink. He filled his flask with *Kirschenwasser*; but did not drink of it before leaving the hotel. Witness could swear to his being sober. He knew that he was excited by his manner. While he was saddling his horse—which he did for himself—he was all the time talking, as if angry. Witness didn't think it was at the animal. He believed he had been crossed by somebody, and was angry at something that had happened to him, before coming back to the hotel. Had no idea where Gerald had been to; but heard afterwards that he had been seen going out of the village, and down the river, in the direction of Mr Poindexter's plantation. He had been seen going that way often for the last three or four days of his sojourn at the hotel—both by day and night—on foot as well as horseback—several times both ways.

Such are the main points of Oberdoffer's evidence relating to the movements of the prisoner.

He is questioned about Henry Poindexter.

Knew the young gentleman but slightly, as he came very seldom to the hotel. He was there on the night when last seen. Witness was surprised to see him there—partly because he was not in the habit of coming, and partly on account of the lateness of the hour.

Young Poindexter did not enter the house. Only looked inside the saloon; and called witness to the door.

He asked after Mr Gerald. He too appeared sober, but excited; and, upon being told that the mustanger was gone away, became very much more excited. Said he wished very much to see Gerald that very night; and asked which way he had gone. Witness directed him along the Rio Grande trace—thinking the mustanger had taken it. Said he knew the road, and went off, as if intending to overtake the mustanger.

A few desultory questions, and Oberdoffer's evidence is exhausted.

On the whole it is unfavourable to the accused; especially the circumstance of Gerald's having changed his intention as to his time of starting. His manner, described as excited and angry,—perhaps somewhat exaggerated by the man who naïvely confesses to a grudge against him. That is especially unfavourable. A murmur through the court tells that it has made this impression.

But why should Henry Poindexter have been excited too? Why should he have been following after Gerald in such hot haste, and at such an unusual hour—unusual for the young planter, both as regarded his haunts and habits?

Had the order been reversed, and Gerald inquiring about and going after him, the case would have been clearer. But even then there would have been an absence of motive. Who can show this, to satisfy the jury?

Several witnesses are called; but their testimony rather favours the reverse view. Some of them testify to the friendly feeling that existed between the prisoner and the man he stands charged with having murdered.

One is at length called up who gives evidence of the opposite. It is Captain Cassius Calhoun.

His story produces a complete change in the character of the trial. It not only discloses a motive for the murder, but darkens the deed tenfold.

After a craftily worded preface, in which he declares his reluctance to make the exposure, he ends by telling all: the scene in the garden; the quarrel; the departure of Gerald, which he describes as having been accompanied by a threat; his being followed by Henry; everything but the true motive for this following, and his own course of action throughout. These two facts he keeps carefully to himself.

The scandalous revelation causes a universal surprise—alike shared by judge, jury, and spectators. It exhibits itself in an unmistakable manner—here in ominous whisperings, there in ejaculations of anger.

These are not directed towards the man who has testified; but against him who stands before them, now presumptively charged with a double crime: the assassination of a son—the defilement of a daughter!

A groan had been heard as the terrible testimony proceeded. It came from a man of more than middle age—of sad subdued aspect—whom all knew to be the father of both these unfortunates.

But the eyes of the spectators dwell not on him. They look beyond, to a curtained *calèche*, in which is seen seated a lady: so fair, as long before to have fixed their attention.

Strange are the glances turned upon her; strange, though not inexplicable: for it is Louise Poindexter who occupies the carriage.

Is she there of her own accord—by her own free will?

So runs the inquiry around, and the whispered reflections that follow it.

There is not much time allowed them for speculation. They have their answer in the crier's voice, heard pronouncing the name—

"Louise Poindexter!"

Calhoun has kept his word.

# 88. An Unwilling Witness

Before the monotonous summons has been three times repeated, the lady is seen descending the steps of her carriage.

Conducted by an officer of the Court, she takes her stand on the spot set apart for the witnesses.

Without flinching—apparently without fear—she faces towards the Court.

All eyes are upon her: some interrogatively; a few, perhaps, in scorn: but many in admiration—that secret approval which female loveliness exacts, even when allied with guilt!

One regards her with an expression different from the rest: a look of tenderest passion, dashed with an almost imperceptible distrust.

It is the prisoner himself. From him her eyes are averted as from everybody else.

Only one man she appears to think worthy of her attention—he who has just forsaken the stand she occupies. She looks at Calhoun, her own cousin—as though with her eyes she would kill him.

Cowering under the glance, he slinks back, until the crowd conceals him from her sight.

"Where were you, Miss Poindexter, on the night when your brother was last seen?"

The question is put by the State counsellor.

"At home,—in my father's house."

"May I ask, if on that night you went into the garden?"

"I did."

"Perhaps you will be good enough to inform the Court at what hour?"

"At the hour of midnight—if I rightly remember."

"Were you alone?"

"Not all the time."

"Part of it there was some one with you?"

"There was."

"Judging by your frankness, Miss Poindexter, you will not refuse to inform the Court who that person was?"

"Certainly not."

"May I ask the name of the individual?"

"There was more than one. My brother was there."

"But before your brother came upon the ground, was there not some one else in your company?"

"There was."

"It is *his* name we wish you to give. I hope you will not withhold it."

"Why should I? You are welcome to know that the gentleman, who was with me, was Mr Maurice Gerald."

The answer causes surprise, and something more. There is a show of scorn, not unmixed with indignation.

There is one on whom it produces a very different effect—the prisoner at the bar—who looks more triumphant than any of his accusers!

"May I ask if this meeting was accidental, or by appointment?"

"By appointment."

"It is a delicate question, Miss Poindexter; you will pardon me for putting it—in the execution of my duty:—What was the nature—the object I should rather term it—of this appointment?"

The witness hesitates to make answer.

Only for an instant. Braising herself from the stooping attitude she has hitherto held, and casting a careless glance upon the faces around her, she replies—

"Motive, or object, it is all the same. I have no intention to conceal it. I went into the garden to meet the man I loved—whom I still love, though he stands before you an accused criminal! Now, sir, I hope you are satisfied?"

"Not quite," continues the prosecuting counsel, unmoved by the murmurs heard around him; "I must ask you another question, Miss Poindexter. The course I am about to take, though a little irregular, will save the time of the Court; and I think no one will object to it. You have heard what has been said by the witness who preceded you. Is it true that your brother parted in anger with the prisoner at the bar?"

"Quite true."

The answer sends a thrill through the crowd—a thrill of indignation. It confirms the story of Calhoun. It establishes the *motive* of the murder!

513

The bystanders do not wait for the explanation the witness designs to give. There is a cry of "Hang—hang him!" and, along with it, a demonstration for this to be done without staying for the verdict of the jury, "Order in the Court!" cries the judge, taking the cigar from between his teeth, and looking authoritatively around him.

"My brother did not *follow him in anger*," pursues the witness, without being further questioned. "He had forgiven Mr Gerald; and went after to apologise."

"*I* have something to say about that," interposes Calhoun, disregarding the irregularity of the act; "they quarrelled *afterwards*. I heard them, from where I was standing on the top of the house."

"Mr Calhoun!" cries the judge rebukingly; "if the counsel for the prosecution desire it, you can be put in the box again. Meanwhile, sir, you will please not interrupt the proceedings."

After a few more questions, eliciting answers explanatory of what she has last alleged, the lady is relieved from her embarrassing situation.

She goes back to her carriage with a cold heaviness at her heart: for she has become conscious that, by telling the truth, she has damaged the cause of him she intended to serve. Her own too: for in passing through the crowd she does not fail to perceive eyes turned upon her, that regard her with an expression too closely resembling contempt!

The "chivalry" is offended by her condescension; the morality shocked by her free confession of that midnight meeting; to say nought of the envy felt for the *bonne fortune* of him who has been so daringly endorsed.

Calhoun is once more called to the stand; and by some additional perjury, strengthens the antipathy already felt for the accused. Every word is a lie; but his statements appear too plausible to be fabrications.

Again breaks forth the clamour of the crowd. Again is heard the cry, "Hang!"—this time more vociferous, more earnest, than ever.

This time, too, the action is more violent. Men strip off their coats, and fling their hats into the air. The women in the waggons—and even those of gentle strain in the carriages—seem, to share the frenzied spite against the prisoner—all save that one, who sits screened behind the curtain.

She too shows indignation; but from a different cause. If she trembles at the commotion, it is not through fear; but from the bitter consciousness that she has herself assisted in stirring it up. In this dark hour she remembers the significant speech of Calhoun: that from her own lips were to come the words that would prove Maurice Gerald a murderer!

The clamour continues, increasing in earnestness. There are things said aloud—insinuations against the accused—designed to inflame the passions of the assembly; and each moment the outcry grows fiercer and more virulent.

Judge Roberts—the name of him who presides—is in peril of being deposed; to be succeeded by the lawless Lynch!

And then what must follow? For Maurice Gerald no more trial; no condemnation: for that has been done already. No shrift neither; but a quick execution, occupying only the time it will take half a score of expert rope-men to throw a noose around his neck, and jerk him up to the limb of the live-oak stretching horizontally over his head!

This is the thought of almost everybody on the ground, as they stand waiting for some one to say the word—some bad, bold borderer daring enough to take the initiative.

Thanks be to God, the spectators are not *all* of this mind. A few have determined on bringing the affair to a different finale.

There is a group of men in uniform, seen in excited consultation. They are the officers of the Fort, with the commandant in their midst.

Only for a score of seconds does their council continue. It ends with the braying of a bugle. It is a signal sounded by command of the major.

Almost at the same instant a troop of two-score dragoons, with a like number of mounted riflemen, is seen filing out from the stockade enclosure that extends rearward from the Fort.

Having cleared the gateway, they advance over the open ground in the direction of the live-oak.

Silently, and as though acting under an instinct, they deploy into an alignment—forming three sides of a square, that partially encloses the Court!

The crowd has ceased its clamouring; and stands gazing at a spectacle, which might be taken for a *coup de théâtre*.

It produces not only silence, but submission: for plainly do they perceive its design, and that the movement is a precautionary measure due to the skill of the commanding officer of the post.

Equally plain is it, that the presidency of Justice Lynch is no longer possible; and that the law of the land is once more in the ascendant.

Without further opposition Judge Roberts is permitted to resume his functions, so rudely interrupted.

"Fellow citizens!" he cries, with a glance towards his auditory, now more reproachful than appealing, "the law is bound to take its course—just the same in Texas as in the States. I need not tell you that, since most of you, I reckon, have seen corn growing on the other side of the Mississippi. Well, taking this for granted, you wouldn't hang a man without first hearing what he's got to say for himself? That would neither be law, nor justice, but downright murder!"

"And hasn't he done murder?" asks one of the rowdies standing near Calhoun. "It's only sarvin' him, as he sarved young Poindexter."

"There is no certainty about that. You've not yet heard all the testimony. Wait till we've examined the witnesses on the other side. Crier!" continues he, turning to the official; "call the witnesses for the defence."

The crier obeys; and Phelim O'Neal is conducted to the stand.

The story of the *ci-devant* stable-boy, confusedly told, full of incongruities—and in many parts altogether improbable—rather injures the chances of his master being thought innocent.

The San Antonio counsel is but too anxious for his testimony to be cut short—having a firmer reliance on the tale to be told by another.

That other is next announced.

"Zebulon Stump!"

Before the voice of the summoning officer has ceased to reverberate among the branches of the live-oak, a tall stalwart specimen of humanity is seen making his way through the throng—whom all recognise as Zeb Stump, the most noted hunter of the Settlement.

Taking three or four strides forward, the backwoodsman comes to a stand upon the spot set apart for the witnesses.

The sacred volume is presented to him in due form; which, after repeating the well-known words of the "affidavit," Zeb is directed to kiss.

He performs this operation with a smack sufficiently sonorous to be heard to the extreme outside circle of the assemblage.

Despite the solemnity of the scene, there is an audible tittering, instantly checked by the judge; a little, perhaps, by Zeb himself, whose glance, cast inquiringly around, seems to search for some one, that may be seen with a sneer upon his face.

The character of the man is too well known, for any one to suppose he might make merry at his expense; and before his searching glance the crowd resumes, or affects to resume, its composure.

After a few preliminary questions, Zeb is invited to give his version of the strange circumstances, which, have been keeping the Settlement in a state of unwonted agitation.

The spectators prick up their ears, and stand in expectant silence. There is a general impression that Zeb holds the key to the whole mystery.

"Wal, Mister Judge!" says he, looking straight in the face of that cigar-smoking functionary; "I've no objection to tell what I know 'beout the bizness; but ef it be all the same to yurself, an the Jewry hyur, I'd preefar that the young fellur shed gie his varsion fust. I kud then foller wi' mine, the which mout sartify and confirm him."

"Of what young fellow do you speak?" inquires the judge.

"The mowstanger thur, in coorse. Him as stan's 'cused o' killin' young Peintdexter."

"It would be somewhat irregular," rejoins the judge—"After all, our object is to get at the truth. For my part, I haven't much faith in old-fashioned forms; and if the jury don't object, let it be as you say."

The "twelve," speaking through their foreman, profess themselves of the same way of thinking. Frontiersmen are not noted for strict adherence to ceremonious forms; and Zeb's request is conceded *nemine dissentiente*.

517

# 89. The Confession of the Accused

Acting under the advice of his counsel, the accused prepares to avail himself of the advantage thus conceded.

Directed by the judge, he stands forward; the sheriff's officers in charge falling a step or two into the rear.

It is superfluous to say that there is universal silence. Even the tree crickets, hitherto "chirping" among the leaves of the live-oak, desist from their shrill stridulation—as if awed by the stillness underneath. Every eye is fixed upon the prisoner; every ear bent to catch the first words of, what may be termed, his *confession*.

"Judge, and gentlemen of the jury!" says he, commencing his speech in true Texan style; "you are good enough to let me speak for myself; and in availing myself of the privilege, I shall not long detain you.

"First, have I to say: that, notwithstanding the many circumstances mentioned during the course of this trial—which to you appear not only odd, but inexplicable—my story is simple enough; and will explain some of them.

"Not all of the statements you have heard are true. Some of them are false as the lips from which they have fallen."

The speaker's glance, directed upon Cassius Calhoun, causes the latter to quail, as if standing before the muzzle of a six-shooter.

"It is true that I met Miss Poindexter, as stated. That noble lady, by her own generous confession, has saved me from the sin of perjuring myself—which otherwise I might have done. In all else I entreat you to believe me.

"It is also true that our interview was a stolen one; and that it was interrupted by him who is not here to speak to what occurred after.

"It is true that angry words passed between us, or rather from him to me: for they were all on his side.

"But it is *not* true that the quarrel was afterwards renewed; and the man who has so sworn dared not say it, were I free to contradict him as he deserves."

Again are the eyes of the accused turned towards Calhoun, still cowering behind the crowd.

"On the contrary," continues he, "the next meeting between Henry Poindexter and myself, was one of apology on his part, and friendship—I might say affection—on mine.

"Who could have helped liking him? As to forgiving him for the few words he had rashly spoken, I need hardly tell you how grateful I felt for that reconciliation."

"There was a reconciliation, then?" asks the judge, taking advantage of a pause in the narration. "Where did it take place?"

"About four hundred yards from the spot *where the murder was committed.*"

The judge starts to his feet. The jury do the same. The spectators, already standing, show signs of a like exciting surprise.

It is the first time any one has spoken positively of the spot where the murder was committed; or even that a murder has been committed at all!

"You mean the place where some blood was found?" doubtingly interrogates the judge.

"I mean the place where *Henry Poindexter was assassinated.*"

There is a fresh exhibition of astonishment in the Court—expressed in muttered speeches and low exclamations. One louder than the rest is a groan. It is given by Woodley Poindexter; now for the first time made certain he has no longer a son! In the heart of the father has still lingered a hope that his son may be alive: that he might be only missing—kept out of the way by accident, illness, Indians, or some other circumstance. As yet there has been no positive proof of his death—only a thread of circumstantial evidence, and it of the slightest.

This hope, by the testimony of the accused himself, is no longer tenable.

"You are sure he is dead, then?" is the question put to the prisoner by the prosecuting counsel.

"Quite sure," responds the accused. "Had you seen him as I did, you would think the interrogatory a very idle one."

"You saw the body?"

"I must take exception to this course of examination," interposes the counsel for the accused. "It is quite irregular."

"Faith! in an Owld Country court it wouldn't be allowed," adds the Cis-Atlantic attorney. "The counsel for the prosecution wouldn't be permitted to spake, till it came to the cross-examination."

"That's the law here, too," says the judge, with a severe gesture towards him who has erred. "Prisoner at the bar! you can continue your story. Your own counsel may ask you what question he pleases; but nobody else, till you have done. Go on! Let us hear all you have to say."

"I have spoken of a reconciliation," resumes the accused, "and have told you where it took place. I must explain how it came to be there.

"It has been made known to you how we parted—Miss Poindexter, her brother, and myself.

"On leaving them I swam across the river; partly because I was too excited to care how I went off, and partly that I did not wish *him* to know how I had got into the garden. I had my reasons for that. I walked on up stream, towards the village. It was a very warm night—as may be remembered by many of you—and my clothes had got nearly dry by the time I reached the hotel.

"The house was still open, and the landlord behind his bar; but as up to that day I had no reason to thank him for any extra hospitality, and as there was nothing to detain me any longer under his roof, I took it into my head to set out at once for the Alamo, and make the journey during the cool hours of the night.

"I had sent my servant before, and intended to follow in the morning; but what happened at Casa del Corvo made me desirous of getting away as soon as possible; and I started off, after settling my account with Mr Oberdoffer."

"And the money with which you paid him?" asks the State prosecutor, "where did you get—?"

"I protest against this!" interrupts the counsel for the accused.

"Bedarrah!" exclaims the Milesian lawyer, looking daggers, or rather *duelling pistols*, at the State counsellor; "if yez were to go on at that rate in a Galway assize, ye'd stand a nate chance of gettin' conthradicted in a different style altogether!"

"Silence, gentlemen!" commands the judge, in an authoritative tone. "Let the accused continue his statement."

"I travelled slowly. There was no reason for being in a hurry. I was in no mood for going to sleep that night; and it mattered little to me where I should spend it—on the prairie, or under the roof of my *jacalé*. I knew I could reach the Alamo before daybreak; and that would be as soon as I desired.

"I never thought of looking behind me. I had no suspicion that any one was coming after; until I had got about half a mile into the chapparal—where the Rio Grande trace runs through it.

"Then I heard the stroke of a horse's hoof, that appeared hurrying up behind.

"I had got round the corner—where the trace makes a sharp turn—and was hindered from seeing the horseman. But I could tell that he was coming on at a trot.

"It might be somebody I wouldn't care to encounter?

"That was the reflection I made; though I wasn't much caring who. It was more from habit—by living in the neighbourhood of the Indians—that I drew in among the trees, and waited until the stranger should show himself.

"He did so shortly after.

"You may judge of my surprise when, instead of a stranger, I saw the man from whom I had so lately parted in anger. When I say anger, I don't speak of myself—only him.

"Was he still in the same temper? Had he been only restrained by the presence of his sister from attacking me? Relieved of this, had he come after me to demand satisfaction for the injury he supposed her to have sustained?

"Gentlemen of the jury! I shall not deny, that this was the impression on my mind when I saw who it was.

"I was determined there should be no concealment—no cowardly shrinking on my part. I was not conscious of having committed crime. True I had met his sister clandestinely; but that was the fault of others—not mine—not hers. I loved her with a pure honest passion, and with my whole heart. I am not afraid to confess it. In the same way I love her still!"

Louise Poindexter, seated in her carriage behind the outer circle of spectators, is not so distant from the speaker, nor are the curtains so closely drawn, but that she can hear every word passing from his lips.

Despite the sadness of her heart, a gleam of joy irradiates her countenance, as she listens to the daring declaration.

It is but the echo of her own; and the glow that comes quickly to her cheeks is not shame, but the expression of a proud triumph.

She makes no attempt to conceal it. Rather does she appear ready to spring up from her seat, rush towards the man who is being tried for the murder of her brother, and with the *abandon* that love alone can impart, bid defiance to the boldest of his accusers!

If the signs of sorrow soon reappear, they are no longer to be traced to jealousy. Those sweet ravings are well remembered, and can now be trusted as truth. They are confirmed by the confession of restored reason—by the avowal of a man who may be standing on the stoup of death, and can have no earthly motive for a deception such as that!

# 90. A Court Quickly Cleared

If the last speech has given satisfaction to Louise Poindexter, there are few who share it with her. Upon most of the spectators it has produced an impression of a totally different character.

It is one of the saddest traits of our ignoble nature; to feel pain in contemplating a love we cannot share—more especially when exhibited in the shape of a grand absorbing passion.

The thing is not so difficult of explanation. *We* know that he, or she, thus sweetly possessed, can feel no interest in ourselves.

It is but the old story of self-esteem, stung by the thought of indifference.

Even some of the spectators unaffected by the charms of the beautiful Creole, cannot restrain themselves from a certain feeling of envy; while others more deeply interested feel chagrined to the heart's core, by what they are pleased to designate an impudent avowal!

If the story of the accused contains no better proofs of his innocence it were better untold. So far, it has but helped his accusers by exciting the antipathy of those who would have been otherwise neutral.

Once more there is a murmuring among the men, and a movement among the rowdies who stand near Calhoun.

Again seems Maurice Gerald in danger of being seized by a lawless mob, and hanged without farther hearing!

The danger exists only in seeming. Once more the major glances significantly towards his well-trained troop; the judge in an authoritative voice commands "Silence in the Court!" the clamouring is subdued; and the prisoner is permitted to proceed.

He continues his recital:—

"On seeing who it was, I rode out from among the trees, and reined up before him.

"There was light enough for him to see who I was; and he at once recognised me.

"Instead of the angry scene I expected—perhaps had reason to expect—I was joyfully surprised by his reception of me. His first words were to ask if I would forgive him for what he had said to me—at the same time holding out his hand in the most frank and friendly manner.

"Need I tell you that I took that hand? Or how heartily I pressed it? I knew it to be a true one; more than that, I had a hope it might one day be the hand of a brother.

"It was the last time, but one, I ever grasped it alive. The last was shortly after—when we bade each other good night, and parted upon the path. I had no thought it was to be for ever.

"Gentlemen of the jury! you do not wish me to take up your time with the conversation that occurred between us? It was upon matters that have nothing to do with this trial.

"We rode together for a short distance; and then drew up under the shadow of a tree.

"Cigars were exchanged, and smoked; and there was another exchange—the more closely to cement the good understanding established between us. It consisted of our hats and cloaks.

"It was a whim of the moment suggested by myself—from a fashion I had been accustomed to among the Comanches. I gave Henry Poindexter my Mexican sombrero and striped blanket—taking his cloth cloak and Panama hat.

"We then parted—he riding away, myself remaining.

"I can give no reason why I stayed upon the spot; unless that I liked it, from being the scene of our reconciliation—by me so little looked for and so much desired.

"I no longer cared for going on to the Alamo that night. I was happy enough to stay under the tree; and, dismounting, I staked out my horse; wrapped myself up in the cloak; and with the hat upon my head, lay down upon the grass.

"In three seconds I was asleep.

"It was rare for sleep to come on me so readily. Half an hour before, and the thing would have been impossible. I can only account for the change by the feeling of contentment that was upon me—after the unpleasant excitement through which I had passed.

"My slumbers could not have been very sound; nor were they long undisturbed.

"I could not have been unconscious for more than two minutes, when a sound awoke me. It was the report of a gun.

"I was not quite sure of its being this. I only fancied that it was.

"My horse seemed to know better than I. As I looked up, he was standing with ears erect, snorting, as if he had been fired at!

"I sprang to my feet, and stood listening.

"But as I could hear nothing more, and the mustang soon quieted down, I came to the conclusion that we had both been mistaken. The horse had heard the footsteps of some straying animal; and that which struck upon my ear might have been the snapping of a branch broken by its passage through the thicket; or perhaps one of the many mysterious sounds—mysterious, because unexplained—often heard in the recesses of the chapparal.

"Dismissing the thing from my mind, I again lay down along the grass; and once more fell asleep.

"This time I was not awakened until the raw air of the morning began to chill me through the cloak.

"It was not pleasant to stay longer under the tree; and, recovering my horse, I was about to continue my journey.

"But the shot seemed still ringing in my ears—even louder than I had heard it while half asleep!

"It appeared, too, to be in the direction in which Henry Poindexter had gone.

"Fancy or no fancy, I could not help connecting it with him; nor yet resist the temptation to go back that way and seek for an explanation of it.

"I did not go far till I found it. Oh, Heavens! What a sight!

"I saw—"

"*The Headless Horseman!*" exclaims a voice from the outer circle of the spectators, causing one and all to turn suddenly in that direction.

"*The Headless Horseman!*" respond fifty others, in a simultaneous shout.

Is it mockery, this seeming contempt of court?

There is no one who takes it in this sense; for by this time every individual in the assemblage has become acquainted with the cause of the interruption. It is the Headless Horseman himself seen out upon the open plain, in all his fearful shape!

"Yonder he goes—yonder! yonder!"

"No, he's coming this way! See! He's making straight for the Fort!"

The latest assertion seems the truer; but only for an instant. As if to contradict it, the strange equestrian makes a sudden pause upon the prairie, and stands eyeing the crowd gathered around the tree.

Then, apparently not liking the looks of what is before him, the horse gives utterance to his dislike with a loud snort, followed by a still louder neighing.

The intense interest excited by the confession of the accused is for the time eclipsed.

There is a universal impression that, in the spectral form thus opportunely presenting itself, will be found the explanation of all that has occurred.

Three-fourths of the spectators forsake the spot, and rush towards their horses. Even the jurymen are not exempt from taking part in the general *débandade*, and at least six out of the twelve go scattering off to join in the chase of the Headless Horseman.

The latter has paused only for an instant—just long enough to scan the crowd of men and horses now moving towards him. Then repeating his wild "whigher," he wheels round, and goes off at full speed—followed by a thick clump of shouting pursuers!

# 91. A Chase through a Thicket

The chase leads straight across the prairie—towards the tract of chapparal, ten miles distant.

Before reaching it, the ruck of riders becomes thinned to a straggling line—one after another falling off,—as their horses become blown by the long sweltering gallop.

But few get within sight of the thicket; and only two enter it, in anything like close proximity to the escaping horseman; who, without making halt, plunges into the timber.

The pursuer nearest him is mounted upon a grey mustang; which is being urged to its utmost speed by whip, spur, and voice.

The one coming after—but with a long interval between—is a tall man in a slouched hat and blanket coat, bestriding a rawboned roadster, that no one would suspect to be capable of such speed.

It is procured not by whip, spur, and voice; but by the more cruel prompting of a knife-blade held in the rider's hand, and at intervals silently applied to the animal's spine, just behind the croup.

The two men, thus leading the chase, are Cassius Calhoun and Zeb Stump.

The swiftness of the grey mustang has given Calhoun the advantage; aided by a determination to be in at the death—as if some desperate necessity required it.

The old hunter appears equally determined. Instead of being contented to proceed at his usual gait, and trusting to his skill as a tracker, he seems aiming to keep the other in sight—as if a like stern necessity was prompting him to do so.

In a short time both have entered the chapparal, and are lost to the eyes of those riding less resolutely behind.

On through the thicket rush the three horsemen; not in a straight line, but along the lists and cattle tracks—now direct, now in sweeping curves, now sharply zigzagging to avoid the obstructions of the timber.

On go they, regardless of bush or brake—fearlessly, buffeted by the sharp spines of the cactus, and the stinging thorns of the mezquites.

The branches snap and crackle, as they cleave their way between; while the birds, scared by the rude intrusion, fly screaming to some safer roost.

A brace of black vultures, who have risen with a croak from their perch upon a scathed branch, soar up into the air. Instinct tells them, that a pursuit so impetuous can end only in death. On broad shadowy wings they keep pace with it.

It is now a chase in which the pursued has the advantage of the pursuers. He can choose his path; while they have no choice but to follow him.

Less from having increased the distance, than by the interposition of the trees, he is soon out of sight of both; as each is of the other.

No one of the three can see either of the other two; though all are under the eyes of the vultures.

Out of sight of his pursuers, the advantage of the pursued is greater than ever. He is free to keep on at full speed; while they must submit to the delay of riding along a trail. He can still be followed by the sound of his hoofstrokes ahead, and the swishing of the branches as he breaks through between them; but for all that the foremost of his two pursuers begins to despair. At every turning of the track, he appears to have gained distance; until at length his footfall ceases to be heard.

"Curse the damned thing!" cries Calhoun, with a gesture of chagrin. "It's going to escape me again! Not so much matter, if there were nobody after it but myself. But there *is* this time. That old hell-hound's coming on through the thicket. I saw him as I entered it—not three hundred yards behind me.

"Is there no chance of shaking him off? No. He's too good a tracker for that.

"By God! *but there is a chance!*"

At the profane utterance, the speaker reins up; wrenches his horse half round; and scans the path over which he has just passed.

He examines it with the look of one who has conceived a scheme, and is reconnoitring the *terrain*, to see if it will suit.

At the same time, his fingers close nervously around his rifle, which he manipulates with a feverish impatience.

Still is there irresolution in his looks; and he hesitates about throwing himself into a fixed attitude.

On reflection the scheme is abandoned.

"It won't do!" he mutters. "There's too many of them fellows coming after—some that can track, too? They'd find his carcase, sure,—maybe hear the shot?

"No—no. It won't do!"

He stays a while longer, listening. There is no sound heard either before or behind—only that overhead made by the soft waving of the vulturine wings. Strange, the birds should keep above *him*!

"Yes—he must be coming on? Damn the crooked luck, that the others should be so close after him! But for that, it would have been just the time to put an end to his spying on me! And so easy, too!"

Not so easy as you think, Cassius Calhoun; and the birds above—were they gifted with the power of speech—could tell you so.

They see Zeb Stump coming on; but in a fashion to frustrate any scheme for his assassination. It is this that hinders him from being heard.

"I'll be in luck, if he should lose the trail!" reflects Calhoun, once more turning away. "In any case, I must keep on till it's lost to me: else some of those fools may be more fortunate.

"What a fool *I've* been in wasting so much time. If I don't look sharp, the old hound will be up with me; and then it would be no use if I did get the chance of a shot. Hell! that would be worse than all!"

Freshly spurring the grey mustang, he rides forward—fast as the circuitous track will allow him.

Two hundred paces further on, and he again comes to a halt—surprise and pleasure simultaneously lighting up his countenance.

The Headless Horseman is in sight, at less than twenty paces' distance!

He is not advancing either; but standing among some low bushes that rise only to the flaps of the saddle.

His horse's head is down. The animal appears to be browsing upon the bean-pods of the mezquites.

At first sight, so thinks Calhoun.

His rifle is carried quickly to his shoulder, and as quickly brought down again. The horse he intends firing at is no longer at rest, nor is he browsing upon the beans. He has become engaged in a sort of spasmodic struggle—with his head half buried among the bushes!

Calhoun sees that it is *held* there, and by the bridle-rein,—that, dragged over the pommel of the saddle, has become entangled around the stem of a mezquite!

"Caught at last! Thank God—thank God!"

He can scarce restrain himself from shout of triumph, as he spurs forward to the spot. He is only withheld by the fear of being heard from behind.

In another instant, he is by the side of the Headless Horseman— that spectral shape he has so long vainly pursued!

530

# 92. A Reluctant Return

Calhoun clutches at the trailing bridle.

The horse tries to avoid him, but cannot. His head is secured by the tangled rein; and he can only bound about in a circle, of which his nose is the centre.

The rider takes no heed, nor makes any attempt to elude the capture; but sits stiff and mute in the saddle, leaving the horse to continue his "cavortings."

After a brief struggle the animal is secured.

The captor utters an exclamation of joy.

It is suddenly checked, and by a thought. He has not yet fully accomplished his purpose.

What is this purpose?

It is a secret known only to himself; and the stealthy glance cast around tells, that he has no wish to share it with another.

After scanning the selvedge of the thicket, and listening a second or two, he resumes action.

A singular action it might appear, to one ignorant of its object. He draws his knife from its sheath; clutches a corner of the serapé; raises it above the breast of the Headless rider; and then bends towards him, as if intending to plunge the blade into his heart!

The arm is uplifted. The blow is not likely to be warded off.

For all that it is not struck. It is stayed by a shout sent forth from the chapparal—by the edge of which a man has just made his appearance. The man is Zeb Stump.

"Stop that game!" cries the hunter, riding out from the underwood and advancing rapidly through the low bushes; "stop it, durn ye!"

"What game?" rejoins the ex-officer with a dismayed look, at the same time stealthily returning his knife to its sheath. "What the devil are you talking about? This brute's got caught by the bridle. I was afraid he might get away again. I was going to cut his damned throat—so as to make sure of him."

"Ah, thet's what ye're arter. Wal, I reck'n thur's no need to cut the critter's throat. We kin skewer it 'ithout thet sort o' bloody bizness. It air the hoss's throat ye mean, I s'pose?"

"Of course I mean the horse."

"In coorse. As for the man, someb'y's dud thet for him arready—*if it be a man.* What do *you* make o' it, Mister Cash Calhoun?"

"Damned if I know what to make of it. I haven't had time to get a good look at it. I've just this minute come up. By heaven!" he continues, feigning a grand surprise, "I believe it's the body of a man; and dead!"

"Thet last air probibble enuf. 'Tain't likely he'd be alive wi' no head on his shoulders. Thar's none under the blanket, is thar?"

"No; I think not. There cannot be?"

"Lift it a leetle, an see."

"I don't like touching it. It's such a cursed queer-looking thing."

"Durn it, ye wan't so partickler a minnit ago. What's kim over ye now?"

"Ah!" stammers Calhoun, "I was excited with chasing it. I'd got angry at the damned thing, and was determined to put an end to its capers."

"Never mind then," interposes Zeb,—"I'll make a inspecshun o' it. Ye-es," he continues, riding nearer, and keeping his eyes fixed upon the strange shape. "Ye-es, it's the body o' a man, an no mistake! Dead as a buck, an stiff as a hunch o' ven'son in a hard frost!"

"Hullo!" he exclaims, on raising the skirt of the serapé, "it's the body o' the man whose murder's bein' tried—yur own cousin—young Peintdexter! It is, by the Eturnal God!"

"I believe you are right. By heaven it is he!"

"Geehosophat!" proceeds Zeb, after counterfeiting surprise at the discovery, "this air the mysteeriousest thing o' all. Wal; I reck'n thur's no use in our stayin' hyur to spek'late upon it. Bessest thing we kin do 's to take the body back, jest as it's sot in the seddle—which it appears putty firm. I know the hoss too; an I reck'n, when he smell my ole maar a bit, he'll kum along 'ithout much coaxin'. Gee up, ole gurl! an make yurself know'd to him. Thur now! Don't ye see it's a preevious acquaintance o' yourn; though sarting the poor critter appears to hev hed rough usage o' late; an ye mout well be excused for not reconisin' him. 'Tair some time since he's hed a curry to his skin."

While the hunter is speaking, the horse bestridden by the dead body, and the old mare, place their snouts in contact—then withdraw them with a sniff of recognition.

"I thort so," exclaims Zeb, taking hold of the strayed bridle, and detaching it from the mezquite; "the stellyun's boun to lead quietly enuf—so long as he's in kumpny with the maar. 'T all events, 'twon't be needcessary to cut his throat to keep him from runnin' away. Now, Mister Calhoun," he continues, glancing stealthily at the other, to witness the effect produced by his speeches; "don't ye think we'd better start right away? The trial may still be goin' on; an', ef so, we may be wanted to take a part in it. I reck'n thet we've got a witness hyur, as 'll do somethin' torst illoocidatin' the case—either to the hangin' the mowstanger, or, what air more likely, clurrin' him althogither o' the churge. Wal, air ye riddy to take the back track?"

"Oh, certainly. As you say, there's no reason for our remaining here."

Zeb moves off first, leading the captive alongside of him. The latter makes no resistance; but rather seems satisfied at being conducted in company.

Calhoun rides slowly—a close observer might say reluctantly in the rear.

At a point where the path angles abruptly round a clump of trees, he reins up, and appears to consider whether he should go on, or gallop back.

His countenance betrays terrible agitation. Zeb Stump, admonished by the interrupted footfall, becomes aware that his travelling companion has stopped.

He pulls up his mare; and facing round, regards the loiterer with a look of interrogation.

He observes the agitated air, and perfectly comprehends its cause.

Without saying a word, he lowers his long rifle from its rest upon his left shoulder; lays it across the hollow of his arm, ready at an instant's notice to be carried to his cheek. In this attitude he sits eyeing the ex-captain of cavalry. There is no remark made. None is needed. Zeb's gesture is sufficient. It plainly says:—"Go back if ye dare!"

The latter, without appearing to notice it, takes the hint; and moves silently on.

But no longer is he permitted to ride in the rear. Without saying it, the old hunter has grown suspicious, and makes an excuse for keeping behind—with which his *compagnon du voyage* is compelled to put up.

The cavalcade advances slowly through the chapparal.

It approaches the open prairie.

At length the sky line comes in sight.

Something seen upon the distant horizon appears to impress Calhoun with a fresh feeling of fear; and, once more reining up, he sits considering.

Dread is the alternative that occupies his mind. Shall he plunge back into the thicket, and hide himself from the eyes of men? Or go on and brave the dark storm that is fast gathering around him?

He would give all he owns in the world—all that he ever hopes to own—even Louise Poindexter herself—to be relieved of the hated presence of Zeb Stump—to be left for ten minutes alone with the Headless Horseman!

It is not to be. The sleuth-hound, that has followed him thus far, seems more than ever inexorable. Though loth to believe it, instinct tells him: that the old hunter regards *him* as the real captive, and any attempt on his part to steal away, will but end in his receiving a bullet in the back!

After all, what can Zeb Stump say, or do? There is no certainty that the backwoodsman knows anything of the circumstance that is troubling him?

And after all, there may be nothing to be known?

It is evident that Zeb is suspicious. But what of that? Only the friendless need fear suspicion; and the ex-officer is not one of these. Unless that little tell-tale be discovered, he has nothing to fear; and what chance of its being discovered? One against ten. In all likelihood it stayed not where it was sent, but was lost in the secret recesses of the chapparal?

Influenced by this hope, Calhoun regains courage; and with an air of indifference, more assumed than real, he rides out into the open prairie—close followed by Zeb Stump on his critter—the dead body of Henry Poindexter bringing up the rear!

# 93. A Body Beheaded

Forsaken by two-thirds of its spectators—abandoned, by one-half of the jury—the trial taking place under the tree is of necessity interrupted.

There is no adjournment of the Court—only an interregnum, unavoidable, and therefore tacitly agreed to.

The interlude occupies about an hour; during which the judge smokes a couple of cigars; takes about twice that number of drinks from the bottle of peach brandy; chats familiarly with the counsel, the fragment of a jury, and such spectators as, not having horses, or not caring to give them a gallop, have stayed by the tree.

There is no difficulty in finding a subject of conversation. That is furnished by the incident that has just transpired—strange enough to be talked about not only for an hour, but an age.

The spectators converse of it, while with excited feelings they await the return of those who have started on the chase.

They are in hopes that the Headless Horseman will be captured. They believe that his capture will not only supply a clue to the mystery of his being, but will also throw light on that of the murder.

There is one among them who could explain the first—though ignorant of the last. The accused could do this; and will, when called upon to continue his confession.

Under the direction of the judge, and by the advice of his counsel, he is for the time preserving silence.

After a while the pursuers return; not all together, but in straggling squads—as they have despairingly abandoned the pursuit.

All bring back the same story. None of them has been near enough to the Headless rider to add one iota to what is already known of him. His entity remains mythical as ever!

It is soon discovered that two who started in the chase have not reappeared. They are the old hunter and the ex-captain of volunteers.

The latter has been last seen heading the field, the former following not far behind him.

No one saw either of them afterward. Are they still continuing on? Perhaps they may have been successful?

All eyes turn towards the prairie, and scan it with inquiring glances. There is an expectation that the missing men may be seen on their way back—with a hope that the Headless Horseman may be along with them.

An hour elapses, and there is no sign of them—either with or without the wished-for captive.

Is the trial to be further postponed?

The counsel for the prosecution urges its continuance; while he for the accused is equally desirous of its being delayed. The latter moves an adjournment till to-morrow; his plea the absence of an important witness in the person of Zeb Stump, who has not yet been examined.

There are voices that clamour for the case to be completed.

There are paid *claquers* in the crowd composing a Texan Court, as in the pit of a Parisian theatre. The real tragedy has its supporters, as well as the sham!

The clamourers succeed in carrying their point. It is decided to go on with the trial—as much of it as can be got through without the witness who is absent. He may be back before the time comes for calling him. If not, the Court can then talk about adjournment.

So rules the judge; and the jury signify their assent. The spectators do the same.

The prisoner is once more directed to stand up, and continue the confession so unexpectedly interrupted.

---

"You were about to tell us what you saw," proceeds the counsel for the accused, addressing himself to his client. "Go on, and complete your statement. What was it you saw?"

"A man lying at full length upon the grass."

"Asleep?"

"Yes; in the sleep of death."

"Dead?"

"More than dead; if that were possible. On bending over him, I saw that he had been beheaded!"

"What! His head cut off?"

"Just so. I did not know it, till I knelt down beside him. He was upon his face—with the head in its natural position. Even the hat was still on it!

"I was in hopes he might be asleep; though I had a presentiment there was something amiss. The arms were extended too stiffly for a sleeping man. So were the legs. Besides, there was something red upon the grass, that in the dim light I had not at first seen.

"As I stooped low to look at it, I perceived a strange odour—the salt smell that proceeds from human blood.

"I no longer doubted that it was a dead body I was bending over; and I set about examining it.

"I saw there was a gash at the back of the neck, filled with red, half-coagulated blood. I saw that the head was severed from the shoulders!"

A sensation of horror runs through the auditory—accompanied by the exclamatory cries heard on such occasions.

"Did you know the man?"

"Alas! yes."

"Without seeing his face?"

"It did not need that. The dress told who it was—too truly."

"What dress?"

"The striped blanket covering his shoulders and the hat upon his head. They were my own. But for the exchange we had made, I might have fancied it was myself. It was Henry Poindexter."

A groan is again heard—rising above the hum of the excited hearers.

"Proceed, sir!" directs the examining counsel. "State what other circumstances came under your observation."

"On touching the body, I found it cold and stiff. I could see that it had been dead for some length of time. The blood was frozen nearly dry; and had turned black. At least, so it appeared in the grey light: for the sun was not yet up.

"I might have mistaken the cause of death, and supposed it to have been by the *beheading*. But, remembering the shot I had heard in the night, it occurred to me that another wound would be found somewhere—in addition to that made by the knife.

"It proved that I was right. On turning the body breast upward, I perceived a hole in the serapé; that all around the place was saturated with blood.

"On lifting it up, and looking underneath, I saw a livid spot just over the breast-bone. I could tell that a bullet had entered there; and as there was no corresponding wound at the back, I knew it must be still inside the body."

"In your opinion, was the shot sufficient to have caused death, without the mutilation that, you think, must have been done afterwards?"

"Most certainly it was. If not instantaneous, in a few minutes—perhaps seconds."

"The head was cut off, you say. Was it quite severed from the body?"

"Quite; though it was lying close up—as if neither head nor body had moved after the dismemberment."

"Was it a clean out—as if done by a sharp-edged weapon?"

"It was."

"What sort of weapon would you say?"

"It looked like the cut of a broad axe; but it might have been done with a bowie-knife; one heavily weighted at the back of the blade."

"Did you notice whether repeated strokes had been given? Or had the severance been effected by a single cut?"

"There might have been more than one. But there was no appearance of chopping. The first cut was a clean slash; and must have gone nearly, if not quite, through. It was made from the back of the neck; and at right angles to the spine. From that I knew that the poor fellow must have been down on his face when the stroke was delivered."

"Had you any suspicion why, or by whom, the foul deed had been done?"

"Not then, not the slightest. I was so horrified, I could not reflect. I could scarce think it real.

"When I became calmer, and saw for certain that a murder had been committed, I could only account for it by supposing that there had been Comanches upon the ground, and that, meeting young Poindexter, they had killed him out of sheer wantonness.

"But then there was his scalp untouched—even the hat still upon his head!"

"You changed your mind about its being Indians?"

"I did."

"Who did you then think it might be?"

"At the time I did not think of any one. I had never heard of Henry Poindexter having an enemy—either here or elsewhere. I have since had my suspicions. I have them now."

"State them."

"I object to the line of examination," interposes the prosecuting counsel. "We don't want to be made acquainted with, the prisoner's suspicions. Surely it is sufficient if he be allowed to proceed with his *very plausible tale?*"

"Let him proceed, then," directs the judge, igniting a fresh Havannah.

"State how you yourself acted," pursues the examiner. "What did you do, after making the observations you have described?"

"For some time I scarce knew what to do—I was so perplexed by what I saw beside me. I felt convinced that there had been a murder; and equally so that it had been done by the shot—the same I had heard.

"But who could have fired it? Not Indians. Of that I felt sure.

"I thought of some *prairie-pirate*, who might have intended plunder. But this was equally improbable. My Mexican blanket was worth a hundred dollars. That would have been taken. It was not, nor anything else that Poindexter had carried about him. Nothing appeared to have been touched. Even the watch was still in his waistcoat pocket, with the chain around his neck glistening through the gore that had spurted over it!

"I came to the conclusion: that the deed must have been done for the satisfaction of some spite or revenge; and I tried to remember whether I had ever heard of any one having a quarrel with young Poindexter, or a grudge against him.

"I never had.

"Besides, why had the head been cut off?

"It was this that filled me with astonishment—with horror.

"Without attempting to explain it, I bethought me of what was best to be done.

"To stay by the dead body could serve no purpose. To bury it would have been equally idle.

"Then I thought of galloping back to the Fort, and getting assistance to carry it to Casa del Corvo.

"But if I left it in the chapparal, the coyotés might discover it; and both they and the buzzards would be at it before we could get back. Already the vultures were above—taking their early flight. They appeared to have espied it.

"Mutilated as was the young man's form, I could not think of leaving it, to be made still more so. I thought of the tender eyes that must soon behold it—in tears."

# 94. The Mystery Made Clear

The accused pauses in his recital. No one offers any observation—either to interrupt, or hurry him on.

There is a reluctance to disturb the chain of a narrative, all know to be unfinished; and every link of which has been binding them to a closer and more earnest attention.

Judge, jury, and spectators remain breathlessly silent; while their eyes—many with mouths agape—are attentively turned upon the prisoner.

Amidst solemn stillness he is permitted to proceed.

"My next idea was to cover the body with the cloak—as well as the serapé still around the shoulders. By so doing it would be protected from both wolves and buzzards—at least till we could get back to fetch it away.

"I had taken off the cloak for this purpose; when a different plan suggested itself—one that appeared in every way better.

"Instead of returning to the Port alone, I should take the body along with me. I fancied I could do this, by laying it across the croup, and lashing it to the saddle with my lazo.

"I led my horse up to the spot, and was preparing to put the body upon him, when I perceived that there was another horse upon the ground. It was that lately ridden by him who was now no more.

"The animal was near by, browsing upon the grass—as tranquilly as if nothing had happened to disturb it.

"As the bridle trailed upon the ground, I had no difficulty in catching hold of it. There was more in getting the horse to stand still—especially when brought alongside what lay upon the ground.

"Holding the reins between my teeth, I lifted the body up, and endeavoured to place it crosswise in the saddle.

"I succeeded in getting it there, but it would not remain. It was too stiff to bend over, and there was no way to steady it.

"Besides, the *horse* became *greatly excited*, at sight of the strange load he was being called upon to carry.

"After several attempts, I saw I could not succeed.

"I was about to give up the idea, when another occurred to me—one that promised better. It was suggested by a remembrance of something I had read, relating to the Gauchos of South America. When one dies, or is killed by accident, in some remote station of the Pampas, his comrades carry his corpse to their distant home—strapped in the saddle, and seated in the same attitude, as though he were still alive.

"Why should I not do the same with the body of Henry Poindexter?

"I made the attempt—first trying to set him on his own horse.

"But the saddle being a flat one, and the animal still remaining restive, I did not succeed.

"There was but one other chance of our making the home journey together: by exchanging horses.

"I knew that my own would not object. Besides, my Mexican saddle, with its deep tree, would answer admirably for the purpose.

"In a short while I had the body in it, seated erect,—in the natural position. Its stiffness, that had obstructed me before, now served to keep it in its place. The rigid limbs were easily drawn into the proper stride; and with the feet inserted into the stirrups, and the water-guards buckled tightly over the thighs, there was little chance of the body slipping off.

"To make it thoroughly secure, I cut a length from my lazo; and, warping it round the waist, fastened one end to the pommel in front, the other to the cantle behind.

"A separate piece tied to the stirrups, and passing under the belly of the horse, kept the feet from swinging about.

"The head still remained to be dealt with. It too must be taken along.

"On lifting it from the ground, and endeavouring to detach it from the hat, I found that this could not be done. It was swollen to enormous dimensions; and the sombrero adhered to it—close as the skin itself.

"Having no fear that they would fall apart, I tied a piece of string to the buckle of the band; and hung both hat and head over the horn of the saddle.

"This completed my preparations for the journey.

"I mounted the horse of the murdered man; and, calling upon my own to follow me—he was accustomed to do so without leading—I started to ride back to the settlement.

"In less than five minutes after, I was knocked out of my saddle—and my senses at the same time.

"But for that circumstance I should not be standing here,—at all events, not in the unpleasant position I now hold."

"Knocked out of your saddle!" exclaims the judge. "How was that?"

"A simple accident; or rather was it due to my own carelessness. On mounting the strange horse I neglected to take hold of the bridle. Accustomed to guide my own—often with only my voice and knees— I had grown regardless of the reins. I did not anticipate an occurrence of the kind that followed.

"The horse I was on, had only stopped three lengths of itself, from the place where I had bestridden him, when something caused him to shy to one side, and break into a gallop.

"I need not say *something*; for I knew what it was. He had looked round, and seen the other coming on behind, with that strange shape upon his back, that now in the broad light of day was enough to frighten horse or man.

"I clutched at the bridle; but, before I could lay my hand upon it, the horse was at his full speed.

"At first I was but little alarmed; indeed not at all. I supposed I should soon recover the reins, and bring the runaway to a stand.

"But I soon found this could not be so easily done. They had strayed forward, almost to the animal's ears; and I could not reach them, without laying myself flat along the neck.

"While endeavouring to secure the bridle, I took no heed of the direction in which the horse was taking me. It was only when I felt a sharp twitching against my cheeks, that I discovered he had forsaken the open tract, and was carrying me through the chapparal.

"After that I had no time to make observations—no chance even to look after the lost reins. I was enough occupied in dodging the branches of the mezquites, that stretched out their spinous arms as if desiring to drag me from the saddle.

"I managed to steer clear of them, though not without getting scratches.

"But there was one I could not avoid—the limb of a large tree that projected across the path. It was low down—on a level with my breast—and the brute, shying from something that had given him a fresh start, shot right under it.

"Where he went afterwards I do not attempt to say. You all know that—I believe, better than I. I can only tell you, that, after unhorsing, he left me under the limb, with a lump upon my forehead and a painful swelling in the knee; neither of which I knew anything about till two hours afterwards.

"When my senses came back to me, I saw the sun high up in the heavens, and some scores of turkey buzzards wheeling in circles above me. I could tell by the craning of their necks what was the prey they were expecting.

"The sight of them, as well as my thirst—that was beginning to grow painful—prompted me to move away from the place.

"On rising to my feet, I discovered that I could not walk. Worse still, I was scarce able to stand.

"To stay on that spot was to perish—at least I so thought at the time.

"Urged by the thought, I exerted all the strength left me, in an effort to reach water.

"I knew there was a stream near by; and partly by crawling,—partly by the help of a rude crutch procured in the thicket—I succeeded in reaching it.

"Having satisfied my thirst, I felt refreshed; and soon after fell asleep.

"I awoke to find myself surrounded by coyotés.

"There were at least two score of them; and although at first I had no fear—knowing their cowardly nature—I was soon brought to a different way of thinking.

"They saw that I was disabled; and for this reason had determined upon attacking me.

"After a time they did so—clustering around and springing upon me in a simultaneous onslaught.

"I had no weapon but my knife; and it was fortunate I had that. Altogether unarmed, I must have been torn to pieces, and devoured.

"With the knife I was able to keep them off, stabbing as many as I could get a fair stroke at. Half-a-dozen, I should think, were killed in this way.

"For all that it would have ended ill for me. I was becoming enfeebled by the blood fast pouring from my veins, and must soon have succumbed, but for an unexpected chance that turned up in my favour.

"I can scarce call it chance. I am more satisfied, to think it was the hand of God."

On pronouncing this speech the young Irishman turns his eyes towards Heaven, and stands for a time as if reflecting reverentially.

Solemn silence around tells that the attitude is respected. The hearts of all, even the rudest of his listeners, seem touched with the confidence so expressed.

"It showed itself," he continues, "in the shape of an old comrade—one ofttimes more faithful than man himself—my staghound, Tara.

"The dog had been straying—perhaps in search of me—though I've since heard a different explanation of it, with which I need not trouble you. At all events, he found me; and just in time to be my rescuer.

"The coyotés scattered at his approach; and I was saved from a fearful fate—I may say, out of the jaws of death.

"I had another spell of sleep, or unconsciousness—whichever it may have been.

"On awaking I was able to reflect. I knew that the dog must have come from my jacalé; which I also knew to be several miles distant. He had been taken thither, the day before, by my servant, Phelim.

"The man should still be there; and I bethought me of sending him a message—the staghound to be its bearer.

"I wrote some words on a card, which I chanced to have about me.

"I was aware that my servant could not read; but on seeing the card he would recognise it as mine, and seek some one who could decipher what I had written upon it.

"There would be the more likelihood of his doing so, seeing that the characters were traced in blood.

"Wrapping the card in a piece of buckskin, to secure it against being destroyed, I attached it to Tara's neck.

"With some difficulty I succeeded in getting the animal to leave me. But he did so at length; and, as I had hoped, to go home to the hut.

"It appears that my message was duly carried; though it was only yesterday I was made acquainted with the result.

"Shortly after the dog took his departure, I once more fell asleep—again awaking to find myself in the presence of an enemy—one more terrible than I had yet encountered.

"It was a jaguar.

"A conflict came off between us; but how it ended, or after what time, I am unable to tell. I leave that to my brave rescuer, Zeb Stump; who, I hope, will soon return to give an account of it—with much besides that is yet mysterious to me, as to yourselves.

"All I can remember since then is a series of incongruous dreams—painful phantasmagoria—mingled with pleasant visions— ah! some that were celestial—until the day before yesterday, when I awoke to find myself the inmate of a prison—with a charge of murder hanging over my head!

"Gentlemen of the jury! I have done."

---

"*Si non vero e ben trovato*," is the reflection of judge, jury, and spectators, as the prisoner completes his recital.

They may not express it in such well-turned phrase; but they feel it—one and all of them.

And not a few believe in the truth, and reject the thought of contrivance. The tale is too simple—too circumstantial—to have been contrived, and by a man whose brain is but just recovered from the confusion of fevered fancies.

It is altogether improbable he should have concocted such a story. So think the majority of those to whom it has been told.

His confession—irregular as it may have been—has done more for his defence than the most eloquent speech his counsel could have delivered.

Still it is but his own tale; and other testimony will be required to clear him.

Where is the witness upon whom so much is supposed to depend. Where is Zeb Stump?

Five hundred pairs of eyes turn towards the prairie, and scan the horizon with inquiring gaze. Five hundred hearts throb with a mad impatience for the return of the old hunter—with or without Cassius Calhoun—with or without the Headless Horse, man—now no longer either myth or mystery, but a natural phenomenon, explained and comprehended.

It is not necessary to say to that assemblage, that the thing is an improbability—much less to pronounce it impossible. They are Texans of the south-west—denizens of the high upland plateau, bordering upon the "Staked Plain," from which springs the lovely Leona, and where the river of Nuts heads in a hundred crystal streams.

They are dwellers in a land, where death can scarce be said to have its successor in decay; where the stag struck down in its tracks— or the wild steed succumbing to some hapless chance—unless by wild beasts devoured, will, after a time, bid defiance both to the laws of corruption and the teeth of the coyoté; where the corpse of mortal man himself, left uncoffined and uncovered, will, in the short period of

545

eight-and-forty hours, exhibit the signs, and partake of the qualities, of a mummy freshly exhumed from the catacombs of Egypt!

But few upon the ground who are not acquainted with this peculiarity of the Texan climate—that section of it close to the Sierra Madro—and more especially among the spurs of the Llano Estacado.

Should the Headless Horseman be led back under the live oak, there is not one who will be surprised to see the dead body of Henry Poindexter scarce showing the incipient signs of decomposition. If there be any incredulity about the story just told them, it is not on this account; and they stand in impatient expectation, not because they require it to be confirmed.

Their impatience may be traced to a different cause—a suspicion, awakened at an early period of the trial, and which, during its progress, has been gradually growing stronger; until it has at length assumed almost the shape of a belief.

It is to confirm, or dissipate this, that nearly every man upon the ground—every woman as well—chafes at the absence of that witness, whose testimony is expected to restore the accused to his liberty, or consign him to the gallows tree.

Under such an impression, they stand interrogating the level line—where sky and savannah mingle the soft blue of the sapphire with the vivid green of the emerald.

# 95. The Last Witness

The watchful air is kept up for a period of full ten minutes, and along with it the solemn silence.

The latter is at intervals interrupted by a word or exclamation—when some one sees, or fancies, a spot upon the prairie. Then there is a buzz of excitement; and men stand on tiptoe to obtain a better view.

Thrice is the crowd stirred by warnings that have proved false. Its patience is becoming exhausted, when a fourth salutes the ear, spoken in a louder voice and more confident tone.

This time the tale is true. There are shadows upon the skyline—shadows fast assuming shape, substance, and motion.

A wild shout—the old Saxon "huzza," swells up among the branches of the live oak, as the figures of three horsemen emerging from the film of the sun-parched prairie are seen coming in the direction of the tree!

Two of them are easily recognised, as Zeb Stump and Cassius Calhoun. The third still more easily: for far as eye can see, that fantastic form cannot be mistaken.

The first cry of the crowd, which but signalled the return of the two men, is followed by another, yet more significant—when it is seen that they are accompanied by a creature, so long the theme of weird thoughts, and strange conjecturings.

Though its nature is now known, and its cause understood still is it regarded with feelings akin to awe.

The shout is succeeded by an interregnum of silence—unbroken, till the three horsemen have come close up; and then only by a hum of whisperings, as if the thoughts of the spectators are too solemn to be spoken aloud.

Many go forward to meet the approaching cortège; and with wondering gaze accompany it back upon the ground.

The trio of equestrians comes to a halt outside the circle of spectators; which soon changes centre, closing excitedly around them.

Two of them dismount; the third remains seated in the saddle.

Calhoun, leading his horse to one side, becomes commingled with the crowd. In the presence of such a companion, he is no longer thought of. All eyes, as well as thoughts, dwell upon the Headless Horseman.

Zeb Stump, abandoning the old mare, takes hold of his bridle-rein, and conducts him under the tree—into the presence of the Court.

"Now, judge!" says he, speaking as one who has command of the situation, "an' you twelve o' the jury! hyur's a witness as air likely to let a glimp o' daylight into yur dulliberashuns. What say ye to examinin' *him*?"

An exclamation is heard, followed by the words, "O God, it is he!" A tall man staggers forward, and stands by the side of the Headless Horseman. *It is his father*!

A cry proceeds from a more distant point—a scream suddenly suppressed, as if uttered by a woman before swooning. *It is his sister*!

After a time, Woodley Poindexter is led away—unresisting,—apparently unconscious of what is going on around him.

He is conducted to a carriage drawn up at a distance, and placed upon a seat beside its only occupant—his daughter.

But the carriage keeps its place. She who commands the check-string intends to stay there, till the Court has declared its sentence—ay, till the hour of execution, if that is to be the end!

Zeb Stump is officially directed to take his place in the "witness-box."

By order of the judge, the examination proceeds—under direction of the counsel for the accused.

Many formalities are dispensed with. The old hunter, who has been already sworn, is simply called to tell what he knows of the affair; and left to take his own way in the telling it; which he does in curt phrases—as if under the belief that such is required by the technicalities of the law!

After the following fashion does Zeb proceed:—

"Fust heerd o' this ugly bizness on the second day arter young Peint war missin'. Heerd on it as I war reeturnin' from a huntin' spell down the river. Heerd thar wur a suspeeshun 'beout the mowstanger hevin' kermitted the murder. Knowd he wan't the man to do sech; but, to be saterfied, rud out to his shanty to see him. He wan't at home, though his man Pheelum war; so skeeart 'beout one thing an the tother he ked gie no clur account o' anythin'.

"Wal, whiles we war palaverin', in kim the dog, wi' somethin' tied roun' his neck—the which, on bein' 'zamined, proved to be the mowstanger's curd. Thur war words on it; wrote in red ink, which I seed to be blood.

"Them words tolt to whosomedever shed read 'em, whar the young fellur war to be foun'.

"I went thar, takin' the other two—thet air Pheelum an the houn'—along wi' me.

"We got to the groun' jest in time to save the mowstanger from hevin' his guts clawed out by one o' them ere spotted painters—the Mexikins call tigers—tho' I've heern the young fellur hisself gie 'em the name o' Jug-wars.

"I put a bullet through the brute; an thet wur the eend o' it.

"Wal, we tuk the mowstanger to his shanty. We hed to toat him thar on a sort o' streetcher; seein' as he wan't able to make trades o' hisself. Beside, he wur as much out o' his senses as a turkey gobber at treadin' time.

"We got him hum; an thur he stayed, till the sarchers kim to the shanty an foun' him."

The witness makes pause: as if pondering within himself, whether he should relate the series of extraordinary incidents that took place during his stay at the jacalé. Would it be for the benefit of the accused to leave them untold? He resolves to be reticent.

This does not suit the counsel for the prosecution, who proceeds to cross-examine him.

It results in his having to give a full and particular account of everything that occurred—up to the time of the prisoner being taken out of his hands, and incarcerated in the guard-house.

"Now," says he, as soon as the cross-questioning comes to a close, "since ye've made me tell all I know 'beout thet part o' the bizness, thur's somethin' ye haint thought o' askin', an the which this child's boun' to make a clean breast o'."

"Proceed, Mr Stump!" says he of San Antonio, entrusted with the direct examination.

"Wal, what I'm goin' to say now haint so much to do wi' the prisoner at the bar, as wi' a man thet in my opeenyun oughter be stannin' in his place. I won't say who thet man air. I'll tell ye what I know, an hev foun' out, an then you o' the jury may reckon it up for yurselves."

The old hunter makes pause, drawing a long breath—as if to prepare himself for a full spell of confession.

No one attempts either to interrupt or urge him on. There is an impression that he can unravel the mystery of the murder. That of the Headless Horseman no longer needs unravelling.

"Wal, fellur citizens!" continues Zeb, assuming a changed style of apostrophe, "arter what I heerd, an more especially what I seed, I knowd that poor young Peint wur gone under—struck down in his tracks—wiped out o' the world.

"I knowd equally well thet he who did the cowardly deed wan't, an kedn't be, the mowstanger—Maurice Gerald.

"Who war it, then? Thet war the questyun thet bamboozled me, as it's done the rest o' ye—them as haint made up thur minds 'ithout re-flekshun.

"Wal; thinkin' as I did that the Irish wur innocent, I bekim detar-mined to diskiver the truth. I ain't goin' to say thet appearances wan't agin him. They wur dog-gonedly agin him.

"For all thet, I wan't goin' to rely on them; an so I tuk purayra to hev a squint at the sign.

"I knowd thur must be hoss-tracks leadin' to the place, an hoss tracks goin' from it; an damn 'em! thur wur too many o' 'em, goin' everywhur—else the thing mout a been eezy enough.

"But thar wur one partickler set I'd got a *down* upon; an them I determined to foller up to the eend o' creashun.

"They war the footmarks o' an Amerikin hoss, hevin' three shoes to the good, an a fourth wi' a bit broken off the eend o' it. This hyur's the eyedentikul piece o' iron!"

The witness draws his hand from the pocket of his blanket coat, in which it has been some time buried. In the fingers are seen the shoe of a horse, only three quarters complete.

He holds it on high—enough for judge, jury, and spectators to see what it is.

"Now, Mr Judge," he continues, "an' you o' the jury, the hoss that carried this shoe went acrosst the purayra the same night thet the murder war committed. He went arter the man thet air murdered, as well as him thet stans thar accused o' it. He went right upon the track o' both, an stopped short o' the place whur the crime wur committed.

"But the man that rud him didn't stop short. He kep on till he war clost up to the bloody spot; an it war through him it arterwards bekim bloody. It war the third hoss—him wi' the broken shoe—thet carried the murderer!"

"Go on, Mr Stump!" directs the judge. "Explain what you mean by this extraordinary statement."

"What I mean, judge, air jest this. The man I'm speakin' o' tuk stan' in the thicket, from which stan' he fired the shet thet killed poor young Peintdexter."

"What man? Who was it? His name! Give his name!" simultaneously interrogate twenty voices.

"I reckon yu'll find it thar."

"Where?"

"Whar! In thet thur body as sits 'ithout a head, lookin' dumbly down on ye!

"Ye kin all see," continues the witness, pointing to the silent shape, "ye kin all see a red patch on the breast o' the striped blanket. Thur's a hole in the centre o' it. Ahint that hole I reck'n thur'll be another, in the young fellur's karkidge. Thar don't appear any to match it at the back. Thurfor I konklude, thet the bullet as did his bizness air still inside o' him. S'posin' we strip off his duds, an see!"

There is a tacit consent to this proposition of the witness. Two or three of the spectators—Sam Manly one of them—step forward; and with due solemnity proceed to remove the serapé.

As at the inauguration of a statue—whose once living original has won the right of such commemoration—the spectators stand in respectful silence at its uncovering, so stand they under the Texan tree, while the serapé is being raised from the shoulders of the Headless Horseman.

It is a silence solemn, profound, unbroken even by whispers. These are heard only after the unrobing is complete, and the dead body becomes revealed to the gaze of the assemblage.

It is dressed in a blouse of sky-blue *cottonade*—box plaited at the breast, and close buttoned to the throat.

The limbs are encased in a cloth of the like colour, with a lighter stripe along the seams. But only the thighs can be seen—the lower extremities being concealed by the "water-guards" of spotted skin tightly stretched over them.

Around the waist—twice twined around it—is a piece of plaited rope, the strands of horse's hair. Before and behind, it is fastened to the projections of the high-peaked saddle. By it is the body retained in its upright attitude. It is further stayed by a section of the same rope, attached to the stirrups, and traversing—surcingle fashion—under the belly of the horse.

Everything as the accused has stated—all except the head.

Where is this?

551

The spectators do not stay to inquire. Guided by the speech of Zeb Stump, their eyes are directed towards the body, carefully scrutinising it.

Two bullet holes are seen; one over the region of the heart; the other piercing the breast-bone just above the abdomen.

It is upon this last that the gaze becomes concentrated: since around its orifice appears a circle of blood with streams straying downward. These have saturated the soft *cottonade*—now seemingly desiccated.

The other shot-hole shows no similar signs. It is a clear round cut in the cloth—about big enough for a pea to have passed through, and scarce discernible at the distance. There is no blood stain around it.

"*It*," says Zeb Stump, pointing to the smaller, "it signifies nothin'. It's the bullet I fired myself out o' the gully; the same I've ben tellin' ye o'. Ye observe thar's no blood abeout it: which prove thet it wur a dead body when it penetrated. The other air different. It wur the shot as settled him; an ef I ain't dog-gonedly mistaken, ye'll find the bit o' lead still inside o' the corp. Suppose ye make a incizyun, an see!"

The proposal meets with no opposition. On the contrary, the judge directs it to be done as Zeb has suggested.

The stays, both fore and back, are unloosed; the water-guards unbuckled; and the body is lifted out of the saddle.

It feels stark and stiff to those who take part in the unpacking,—the arms and limbs as rigid as if they had become fossilised. The lightness tells of desiccation: for its specific gravity scarce exceeds that of a mummy!

With respectful carefulness it is laid at full length along the grass. The operators stoop silently over it—Sam Manly acting as the chief.

Directed by the judge, he makes an incision around the wound—that with the circle of extravasated blood.

The dissection is carried through the ribs, to the lungs underneath.

In the left lobe is discovered the thing searched for. Something firmer than flesh is touched by the probe—the point of a bowie-knife. It has the feel of a leaden bullet. It is one!

It is extracted; rubbed clean of its crimson coating; and submitted to the examination of the jury.

Despite the abrasion caused by the spirally-grooved bore of the barrel—despite an indentation where it came in contact with a creased rib—there is still discernible the outlines of a stamped crescent, and the letters C.C.

Oh! those tell-tale initials! There are some looking on who remember to have heard of them before. Some who can testify to that
boast about a marked bullet—when the killing of the jaguar was con-
tested!

He who made that boast has now reason to regret it!

"But where is he?"

The question is beginning to be asked.

"What's your explanation, Mr Stump?" is another question put by
the counsel for the accused.

"Don't need much, I reck'n," is the reply. "He'd be a durnationed
greenhorn as can't see, clur as the light o' day, thet young Peint war
plugged by thet ere bullet."

"By whom fired, do you think?"

"Wal; thet appear to be eeqully clur. When a man signs his name
to a message, thar's no chance o' mistakin' who it kums from. Thar's
only the ineeshuls thur; but they're plain enuf, I reck'n, an speak for
theirselves."

"I see nothing in all this," interposes the prosecuting counsel.
"There's a marked bullet, it is true—with a symbol and certain letters,
which may, or may not, belong to a gentleman well known in the Settlement. For the sake of argument, let us suppose them to be his—as
also the ball before us. What of that? It wouldn't be the first time that a
murder has been committed—by one who has first stolen his weapon,
and then used it to accomplish the deed. It is but a piece of ordinary
cunning—a common trick. Who can say that this is not something of
the same sort?"

"Besides," continues the specious pleader, "where is the motive
for a murder such as this would be—supposing it to have been committed by the man you are now called upon to suspect? Without
mentioning names, we all know to whom these initials belong. I don't
suppose the gentleman will deny that they are his. But that signifies
nothing: since there is no other circumstance to connect him in any
way with the committal of the crime."

"Ain't thar though?" asks Stump, who has been impatiently
awaiting the wind up of the lawyer's speech. "What do ye call this?"

Zeb, on delivering himself, takes from his tinder-pouch a piece of
paper—crumpled—scorched along the edges—and blackened as with
gunpowder.

"This I foun'," says he, surrendering it to the jury, "stuck fast on
the thorn o' a muskeet tree, whar it hed been blowed out o' the barrel
o' a gun. It kim out o' the same gun as discharged thet bullet—to

553

which it hed served for waddin'. As this chile takes it, it's bin the backin' o' a letter. Thur's a name on it, which hev a kewrious correspondings wi' the ineeshuls on the bit o' lead. The jury kin read the name for tharselves."

The foreman takes the scrap of paper; and, smoothing out the creases, reads aloud:—

Captain Cassius Calhoun!

# 96. Stole Away!

The announcement of the name produces a vivid impression upon the Court.

It is accompanied by a cry—sent up by the spectators, with a simultaneity that proclaims them animated by a common sentiment.

It is not a cry of surprise; but one of far different augury. It has a double meaning, too: at once proclaiming the innocence of the accused, and the guilt of him who has been the most zealous amongst the accusers.

Against the latter, the testimony of Zeb Stump has done more than direct suspicion. It confirms that already aroused; and which has been growing stronger, as fact after fact has been unfolded: until the belief becomes universal: that Maurice Gerald is not the man who should be on trial for the murder of Henry Poindexter.

Equally is it believed that Calhoun is the man. The scrap of smeared paper has furnished the last link in the chain of evidence; and, though this is but circumstantial, and the motive an inconceivable mystery, there is now scarce any one who has a doubt about the doer of the deed.

After a short time spent in examining the envelope—passed from hand to hand among the jurymen—the witness who has hinted at having something more to tell, is directed to continue his narration.

He proceeds to give an account of his suspicions—those that originally prompted him to seek for "sign" upon the prairie. He tells of the shot fired by Calhoun from the copse; of the chase that succeeded; and the horse trade that came after. Last of all, he describes the scene in the chapparal, where the Headless Horseman has been caught—giving this latest episode in all its details, with his own interpretation of it.

This done, he makes a pause, and stands silent, as if awaiting the Court to question him.

But the eyes of the auditory are no longer fixed upon him. They know that his tale is completed; or, if not so, they need no further testimony to guide their conclusions.

They do not even stay for the deliberations of the Court, now proceeding to sift the evidence. Its action is too slow for men who have seen justice so near being duped—themselves along with it; and—swayed by a bitter reactionary spirit—revenge, proceeding from self-reproach—they call loudly for a change in the programme.

The Court is assailed with the cries:—

"Let the Irishman go—he is innocent! We don't want any farther evidence. We're convinced of it. Let him go free!"

Such is the talk that proceeds from the excited spectators.

It is followed by other speeches equally earnest:—

"Let Cassius Calhoun be arrested, and put upon his trial! It's he that's done the deed! That's why he's shown so bitter against the other! If he's innocent, he'll be able to prove it. He shall have a fair trial; but tried he shall be. Come, judge; we're waiting upon you! Order Mr Calhoun to be brought before the Court. An innocent man's been there long enough. Let the guilty take his place!"

The demand, at first made by some half dozen voices, soon becomes a clamour, universally endorsed by the assemblage.

The judge dares not refuse compliance with a proposal so energetically urged: and, despite the informality, Cassius Calhoun is called upon to come before the Court.

The summons of the crier, thrice loudly pronounced, receives no response; and all eyes go in search of Calhoun.

There is only one pair that looks in the right direction—those of Zeb Stump.

The *ci-devant* witness is seen suddenly to forsake the spot on which he has been giving his testimony, and glide towards his old mare—still alongside the horse late relieved of his ghastly rider.

With an agility that surprises every one, the old hunter springs upon the mare's back, and spurs her from under the tree.

At the same instant the spectators catch sight of a man, moving among the horses that stand picketed over the plain.

Though proceeding stealthily, as if to avoid being observed, he moves at a rapid rate—making for a particular quarter of the *cavallada*.

"'Tis he! 'Tis Calhoun!" cries the voice of one who has recognised him.

"Trying to steal off!" proclaims another.

"Follow him!" shouts the judge, in a tone of stern command. "Follow, and bring him back!"

There is no need for the order to be repeated. Ere the words are well out, it is in the act of being obeyed—by scores of men who rush simultaneously towards their horses.

Before reaching them, Calhoun has reached his—a grey mustang, standing on the outskirts of the *cavallada*.

It is the same he has lately ridden in chase of the Headless Horseman. The saddle is still upon its back, and the bitt between its teeth.

From the commotion observable under the tree, and the shouting that accompanies it, he has become cognisant of that terrible signal— the "hue and cry."

Concealment is no longer possible; and, changing from the stealthy pace to a quick earnest run, he bounds upon the animal's back.

Giving a wild glance backward, he heads it towards the prairie— going off at a gallop.

Fifty horses are soon laid along his track—their riders roused to the wildest excitement by some words pronounced at their parting.

"Bring him back—dead or alive!" was the solemn phrase,— supposed to have been spoken by the major.

No matter by whom. It needs not the stamp of official warrant to stimulate the pursuers. Their horror of the foul deed is sufficient for this—coupled with the high respect in which the victim of it had been held.

Each man spurs onward, as if riding to avenge the death of a relative—a brother; as if each was himself eager to become an instrument in the execution of justice!

Never before has the ex-captain of cavalry been in such danger of his life; not while charging over the red battle-field of Buena Vista; not while stretched upon the sanded floor of Oberdoffer's bar-room, with the muzzle of the mustanger's pistol pointed at his head!

He knows as much; and, knowing it, spurs on at a fearful pace— at intervals casting behind a glance, quick, furtive, and fierce.

It is not a look of despair. It has not yet come to this; though at sight of such a following—within hearing of their harsh vengeful cries—one might wonder he could entertain the shadow of a hope.

He has.

He knows that he is mounted on a fleet horse, and that there is a tract of timber before him.

True, it is nearly ten miles distant. But what signify ten miles? He is riding at the rate of twenty to the hour; and in half an hour he may find shelter in the chapparal?

Is this the thought that sustains him?

It can scarce be. Concealment in the thicket—with half a score of skilled trackers in pursuit—Zeb Stump at their head!

No: it cannot be this. There is no hiding-place for him; and he knows it.

What, then, hinders him from sinking under despair, and at once resigning himself to what must be his ultimate destiny?

Is it the mere instinct of the animal, giving way to a blind unreasoning effort at impossible escape?

Nothing of the kind. The murderer of Henry Poindexter is not mad. In his attempt to elude the justice he now dreads, he is not trusting to such slender chances as either a quick gallop across the prairie, or a possible concealment in the timber beyond.

There is a still farther beyond—a *border*. Upon this his thoughts are dwelling, and his hopes have become fixed.

There are, indeed, two *borders*. One that separates two nations termed civilised. There is a law of extradition between them. For all this the red-handed assassin may cheat justice—often does—by an adroit migration from one to the other—a mere change of residence and nationality.

But it is not this course Calhoun intends to take. However ill observed the statute between Texas and Mexico, he has no intention to take advantage of its loose observance. He dreads to risk such a danger. With the consciousness of his great crime, he has reason.

Though riding toward the Rio Grande, it is not with the design of crossing it. He has bethought him of the *other border*—that beyond which roams the savage Comanche—the Ishmaelite of the prairies—whose hand is against every man with a white skin; but will be lifted lightly against him, who has spilled the white man's blood!

In his tent, the murderer may not only find a home, but hope for hospitality—perhaps promotion, in the red career of his adoption!

It is from an understanding of these circumstances, that Calhoun sees a chance of escape, that support him against despair; and, though he has started in a direct line for the Rio Grande, he intends, under cover of the chapparal, to flee towards the *Llano Estacado*.

He does not dread the dangers of this frightful desert; nor any others that may lie before him. They can be but light compared with those threatening behind.

He might feel regret at the terrible expatriation forced upon him—the loss of wealth, friends, social status, and civilisation—more than all, the severance from one too wildly, wickedly loved—perhaps never to be seen again!

---

But he has no time to think even of *her*. To his ignoble nature life is dearer than love. He fancies that life is still before him; but it is no fancy that tells him, death is behind—fast travelling upon his tracks!

The murderer makes haste—all the haste that can be taken out of a Mexican mustang—swift as the steeds of Arabia, from which it can claim descent.

Ere this the creature should be tired. Since the morning it has made more than a score miles—most of them going at a gallop.

But it shows no signs of fatigue. Like all its race—tough as terriers—it will go fifty—if need be a hundred—without staggering in its tracks.

What a stroke of good fortune—that exchange of horses with the Mexican maiden! So reflects its rider. But for it he might now be standing under the sombre shadow of the live oak, in the stern presence of a judge and jury, abetted and urged on to convict him, by the less scrupulous Lynch and his cohort of Regulators.

He is no longer in dread of such a destiny. He begins to fancy himself clear of all danger. He glances back over the plain, and sees his pursuers still far behind him.

He looks forward, and, in the dark line looming above the bright green of the savannah, descries the chapparal. He has no doubt of being able to reach it, and then his chance of escape will be almost certain.

Even if he should not succeed in concealing himself within the thicket, who is there to overtake him? He believes himself to be mounted on the fastest horse that is making the passage of the prairie.

Who, then, can come up with him?

He congratulates himself on the *chance* that has given him such a steed. He may ascribe it to the devil. He cannot attribute it to God!

And will God permit this red-handed ruffian to escape? Will He not stretch forth His almighty arm, and stay the assassin in his flight?

---

# 97. The Chase of the Assassin

Will God permit the red-handed ruffian to escape? Will He not stretch forth His almighty arm, and stay the assassin in his flight?

These interrogatories are put by those who have remained under the tree.

They are answered by an instinct of justice—the first negatively, the second in the affirmative. He will not, and He will.

The answers are but conjectural; doubtfully so, as Calhoun goes galloping off; a little less doubtful as Zeb Stump is descried starting after him; and still less, when a hundred horsemen—soldiers and civilians—spring forward in the pursuit.

The doubt diminishes as the last of the pursuers is seen leaving the ground. All seem to believe that the last at starting will be first in the chase: for they perceive that it is Maurice the mustanger mounted on a horse whose fleetness is now far famed.

The exclamations late ringing through the court have proclaimed not only a fresh postponement of his trial, but its indefinite adjournment. By the consent of the assemblage, vociferously expressed, or tacitly admitted, he feels that he is free.

The first use he makes of his liberty is to rush towards the horse late ridden by the headless rider—as all know—his own.

At his approach the animal recognises its master; proclaims it by trotting towards him, and giving utterance to a glad "whigher!"

Despite the long severance, there is scarce time to exchange congratulations. A single word passes the lips of the mustanger, in response to the neigh of recognition; and in the next instant he is on the back of the blood-bay, with the bridle in his grasp.

He looks round for a lazo; asks for it appealingly, in speech directed to the bystanders.

After a little delay one is thrown to him, and he is off.

The spectators stand gazing after. There is no longer a doubt as to the result. The wish, almost universal, has become a universal belief.

God has decreed that the assassin shall not escape; but that he will be overtaken, captured, and brought back before that same tribunal, where he so late stood a too willing witness!

And the man, so near suffering death through his perjured testimony, is the instrument chosen to carry out the Divine decree!

Even the rude Regulators—with their practical habitudes of life, but little regarding the idea of Divine interference—cannot help having the impression of this poetical justice.

One and all give way to it, as the red stallion springs off over the prairie, carrying Maurice Gerald upon his back.

---

After his departure, an episode occurs under the shadow of the live oak. It is not this that hinders it from being observed; but because every one has turned face towards the plain, and watches the chase, fast receding from view.

There is one scanning it with a look unlike the others. A lady strains her eyes through the curtains of a *calèche*—her glance telling of a thought within dissimilar to that felt by the common spectators.

It is no mere curiosity that causes her twin breasts to sink and swell in quick spasmodic breathing. In her eye, still showing sadness, there is a gleam of triumph as it follows the pursuer—tempered with mercy, as it falls upon the pursued; while from her lips, slightly parted, escapes the prayer: "*God have mercy on the guilty man!*"

---

Delayed a little at mounting—and more in procuring the lazo— Maurice Gerald is the very latest to leave the ground. On clearing the skirt of the crowd, now dispersed over the parade, he sees the others far ahead—a distance of several hundred yards separating him from the rearmost.

He thinks nothing of this. Confident in the qualities of his steed, he knows he will not long ride in the rear.

And the blood-bay answers his expectations. As if joyed at being relieved from his inert load—to him an incubus inexplicable—and inspired by the pressure of his master's knees, the noble horse springs off over the prairie turf—in long sinewy strides, showing that his body still retains its strength, and his limbs their elasticity.

He soon closes upon the hindmost; overtakes one; then another, and another, till he has surged far ahead of the "field."

Still on, over the rolling ridges—across the stream-beds between—on, over soft turf, and sharp shingle, till at length his competitors lose sight of him—as they have already done of the grey mustang and its rider.

There is but one of the pursuing party who continues to keep him in view—a tall man, mounted upon what might be taken for the sorriest of steeds—an old mustang mare.

Her speed tells a different tale; produced though it be by the strangest of spurs—the keen blade of a bowie-knife.

It is Zeb Stump who makes use of this quaint, but cruel, means of persuasion.

Still the old mare cannot keep pace with the magnificent stallion of the mustanger. Nor does Zeb expect it. He but aims at holding the latter in sight; and in this he is so far successful.

There is yet another who beholds the blood-bay making his vigorous bounds. He beholds him with "beard upon the shoulder." It is he who is pursued.

Just as he has begun to feel hopeful of escape, Calhoun, looking back, catches sight of the red stallion; no longer with that strange shape upon his back, but one as well recognised, and to him even more terrible. He perceives it to be Maurice, the mustanger—the man he would have devoted—was so near devoting—to the most disgraceful of deaths!

He sees this man coming after—his own conscience tells him—as an avenger!

Is it the hand of God that directs this enemy on his track? He trembles as he asks himself the question. From any other pursuer there might have been a chance of escaping. There is none from Maurice Gerald!

A cold shiver runs through the frame of the fugitive. He feels as if he were fighting against Fate; and that it is idle to continue the contest!

He sits despairingly in his saddle; scarce caring to ply the spur; no longer believing that speed can avail him!

His flight is now merely mechanical—his mind taking no part in the performance.

His soul is absorbed with the horror of a dread death—not less dread, from his knowing that he deserves it.

The sight of the chapparal, close at hand, inspires him with a fresh hope; and, forcing the fatigued horse into a last feeble effort, he struggles on towards it.

An opening presents itself. He enters it; and continues his gallop for a half mile further.

He arrives at a point, where the path turns sharply round some heavy timber. Beyond that, he might enter the underwood, and get out of sight of his pursuer.

He knows the place, but too well. It has been fatal to him before. Is it to prove so again?

It is. He feels that it is, and rides irresolutely. He hears the hoof-stroke of the red horse close upon the heels of his own; and along with it the voice of the avenging rider, summoning him to stop!

He is too late for turning the corner,—too late to seek conceal-ment in the thicket,—and with a cry he reins up.

It is a cry partly of despair, partly of fierce defiance—like the scream of a chased jaguar under bay of the bloodhounds.

It is accompanied by a gesture; quick followed by a flash, a puff of white smoke, and a sharp detonation, that tell of the discharge of a revolver.

But the bullet whistles harmlessly through the air; while in the opposite direction is heard a hishing sound—as from the winding of a sling—and a long serpent seems to uncoil itself in the air!

Calhoun sees it through the thinning smoke. It is darting straight towards him!

He has no time to draw trigger for a second shot—no time even to avoid the lazo's loop. Before he can do either, he feels it settling over his shoulders; he hears the dread summons, *"Surrender, you assassin!"* he sees the red stallion turn tail towards him; and, in the next instant, experiences the sensation of one who has been kicked from a scaffold!

Beyond this he feels, hears, and sees nothing more.

He has been jerked out of his saddle; and the shock received in his collision with the hard turf has knocked the breath out of his body, as well as the sense out of his soul!

# 98. Not Dead Yet

The assassin lies stretched along the earth—his arms embraced by the raw-hide rope—to all appearance dead.

But his captor does not trust to this. He believes it to be only a faint—it may be a feint—and to make sure it is not the latter, he remains in his saddle, keeping his lazo upon the strain.

The blood-bay, obedient to his will, stands firm as the trunk of a tree—ready to rear back, or bound forward, on receiving the slightest sign.

It is a terrible tableau; though far from being strange in that region of red-handed strife, that lies along the far-stretching frontier of Tamaulipas and Texas.

Oft—too oft—has the soaring vulture looked down upon such a scene—with joy beholding it, as promising a banquet for its filthy beak!

Even now half a score of these ravenous birds, attracted by the report of the pistol, are hovering in the air—their naked necks elongated in eager anticipation of a feast!

One touch of the spur, on the part of him seated in the saddle, would give them what they want.

"It would serve the scoundrel right," mutters the mustanger to himself. "Great God, to think of the crime he has committed! Killed his own cousin, and then cut off his head! There can be no doubt that he has done both; though from what motive, God only can tell,—or himself, if he be still alive.

"I have my own thoughts about it. I know that he loves *her*; and it may be that the brother stood in his way.

"But how, and why? That is the question that requires an answer. Perhaps it can only be answered by God and himself?"

"Yur mistaken beout thet, young fellur," interposes a voice breaking in on the soliloquy. "Thur's one who kin tell the how and the why, jest as well as eyther o' them ye've made mention o'; and thet individooal air ole Zeb Stump, at your sarvice. But 'taint the time to talk o' sech things now; not hyur ain't the place neythur. We must take *him* back unner the live oak, whar he'll git treated accordin' to his desarvins. Durn his ugly picter! It would sarve him right to make it uglier by draggin' him a spell at the eend o' yur trail-rope.

"Never mind beout that. We needn't volunteer to be Henry Peintdexter's 'vengers. From what they know now, I reck'n that kin be trusted to the Regulators."

"How are we to get him back? His horse has galloped away!"

"No difeequilty beout that, Mister Gerald. He's only fainted a bit; or maybe, playin' possum. In eyther case, I'll soon roust him. If he ain't able to make tracks on the hoof he kin go a hossback, and hyur's the critter as 'll carry him. I'm sick o' the seddle myself, an I reck'n the ole gal's a leetle bit sick o' me—leestwise o' the spur I've been a prickin' into her. I've made up my mind to go back on Shanks's maar, an as for Mister Cash Calhoun, he's welkim to hev my seat for the reeturn jerney. Ef he don't stop shammin an sit upright, we kin pack him acrost the crupper, like a side o' dead buck-meat. Yo-ho! he begins to show sign! He'll soon rekiver his senses—all seven o' 'em, I reck'n—an then he kin mount the maar o' hisself.

"Yee-up, ole hoss!" continues Zeb, grasping Calhoun by the collar of his coat, and giving him a vigorous shake. "Yee-up, I say; an kum along wi' us! Ye're wanted. Thar's somebody desirin' to have a talk wi' you!"

"Who? where?" inquires the captive, slowly recovering consciousness, and staring unsteadily around him. "Who wants me?"

"Wal; I do for one; an—"

"Ah! you it is, Zeb Stump! and—and—?"

"An' that air's Mister Maurice Gerald the mowstanger. You've seed him afore, I reck'n? He wants ye for two. Beside, thar's a good grist o' others as ud like to see ye agin—back thar by the Port. So ye'd best get upon yur legs, an' go along wi' us."

The wretched man rises to his feet. In so doing, he discovers that his arms are encircled by a lazo.

"My horse?" he exclaims, looking inquiringly around. "Where is my horse?"

"Ole Nick only knows whar *he* air by this time. Like enuf gone back to the Grand, whar he kim from. Arter the gallupin ye've gi'n him, I reck'n he air sick o' the swop; an's goed off to take a spell o' rest on his native pasters."

Calhoun gazes on the old hunter with something more than aston-ishment. The swop! Even this, too, is known to him!

"Now, then," pursues Zeb, with a gesture of impatience. "'Twon't do to keep the Court a-waitin'. Are ye riddy?"

"Ready for what?"

"Fust an foremost, to go back along wi' me an Mister Gerald. Second an second-most, to stan' yur trial."

"Trial! I stand trial!"

"You, Mister Cash Calhoun."

"On what charge?"

"The churge o' killin' Henry Peintdexter—yur own cousin."

"It's a lie! A damned slanderous lie; and whoever says it—!"

"Shet up yur head!" cries Zeb, with an authoritative gesture. "Ye're only wastin' breath. Ef this chile ain't mistook about it, ye'll need all ye've got afore long. Kum, now! make riddy to reeturn wi' us! The judge air awaitin'; the jury air awaitin'; an *justice* air waitin', too—in the shape o' three score Reg'lators."

"I'm not going back," doggedly responds Calhoun. "By what au-thority do you command me? You have no warrant?"

"Hain't I, though?" interrupts Zeb. "What d'ye call this?" he adds, pointing to his rifle. "Thur's my warrant, by the grace o' God; an by thet same, this chile air a goin' to execute it. So no more o' yur durned palaver: for I ain't the sort to stan' it. Take yur choice, Mister Cash Calhoun. Mount thet old maar o' mine, an kum along quickly; or try the toother dodge, an git toated like a packidge o' merchandice: for back yur boun' to go—I swar it by the Eturnal!"

Calhoun makes no reply. He glances at Stump—at Gerald—despairingly around him; then stealthily towards a six-shooter, pro-truding from the breast-pocket of his coat—the counterpart of that shaken out of his hand, as the rope settled around him.

He makes an effort to reach the pistol—feeble, because only half resolved.

He is restrained by the lazo; perhaps more by a movement on the part of Zeb; who, with a significant gesture, brings his long gun to the level.

"Quick!" exclaims the hunter. "Mount, Mister Calhoun! Thur's the maar awaitin' for ye. Inter the seddle, I say!"

Like a puppet worked by the wires of the showman, the ex-captain of cavalry yields compliance with the commands of the back-woodsman. He does so, from a consciousness that there is death—certain death—in disobeying them.

Mechanically he mounts the mare; and, without resistance, suffers her to be led away from the spot.

Zeb, afoot, strides on in advance.

The mare, at bridle-length, follows upon his tracks.

The mustanger rides reflectingly behind; thinking less of him held at the end of his lazo, than of her, who by a generous self-sacrifice, has that day riveted around his heart a golden chain—only by death to be undone!

# 99. Attempted Murder and Suicide

After its second involuntary recess—less prolonged than the first—the Court has once more resumed its functions under the great evergreen oak.

It is now evening; and the sunbeams, falling aslant, intrude upon the space canopied by the tree.

From the golden brightness, displayed by them at noon, they have changed to a lurid red—as if there was anger in the sky!

It is but an accident of the atmosphere—the portent of an approaching storm.

For all this, it is remarked as singular, that a storm should be coming at the time: since it symbolises the sentiment of the spectators, who look on with sullenness in their hearts, and gloom in their glances.

It would seem as if Heaven's wrath was acting in concert with the passions of Earth!

Maurice Gerald is no longer the cynosure of those scowling eyes. He has been clamorously acquitted, and is henceforth only one of the witnesses.

In the place late occupied by him another stands. Cassius Calhoun is now the prisoner at the bar!

This is the only change observable.

The judge is the same, the jury the same, and the spectators as before; though with very different feelings in regard to the criminality of the accused.

His guilt is no longer the question that is being considered.

It has been established beyond the shadow of a doubt. The evidence is already before them; and though entirely circumstantial—as in most cases of murder—the circumstances form a chain irresistibly conclusive and complete.

There is but one missing link—if link it may be called—the *motive*.

The motive both for the murder and the mutilation: for the testimony of Gerald has been confirmed by a subsequent examination of the dead body. The surgeon of the cantonment has pronounced the two distinct, and that Henry Poindexter's death must have ensued, almost instantaneously after his receiving the shot.

Why should Cassius Calhoun have killed his own cousin? *Why* cut off his head?

No one can answer these questions, save the murderer himself. No one expects him to do so—save to his Maker.

Before Him he must soon stand: for a knowledge of the motive is not deemed essential to his condemnation, and he has been condemned.

The trial has come to a close; the verdict *Guilty* has been given; and the judge, laying aside his Panama hat, is about to put on the black cap—that dread emblem of death—preparatory to pronouncing the sentence.

In the usual solemn manner the condemned man is invited to make his final speech; to avail himself, as it were, of the last forlorn hope for sentence.

He starts at the invitation—falling, as it does, like a death-knell upon his ear.

He looks wildly around. Despairingly: when on the faces that encircle him he sees not one wearing an expression of sympathy.

There is not even pity. All appear to frown upon him.

His confederates—those payed ruffians who have hitherto supported him—are of no use now, and their sympathy of no consequence. They have shrunk out of sight—before the majesty of the law, and the damning evidence of his guilt.

Despite his social standing—and the wealth to sustain it—he sees himself alone; without friend or sympathiser: for so stands the assassin in Texas!

His demeanour is completely changed. In place of that high haughty air—oft exhibited in bold brutal bullyism—he looks cowed and craven.

And not strange that he should.

He feels that there is no chance of escape; that he is standing by the side of his coffin—on the edge of an Eternity too terrible to contemplate.

To a conscience like his, it cannot be otherwise than appalling.

All at once a light is seen to flask into his eyes—sunken as they are in the midst of two livid circles. He has the air of one on the eve of making confession.

Is it to be an acknowledgment of guilt? Is he about to unburden his conscience of the weight that must be on it?

The spectators, guessing his intention, stand breathlessly observing him.

There is silence even among the cicadas.

It is broken by the formalised interrogatory of the judge?

"*Have you anything to say why sentence of death should not be pronounced upon you?*"

"No!" he replies, "I have not. The jury has given a just verdict. I acknowledge that I have forfeited my life, and deserve to lose it."

Not during all the day—despite its many strange incidents and startling surprises—have the spectators been so astonished. They are confounded beyond the power of speech; and in silence permit the condemned man to proceed, with what they now perceive to be his confession.

"It is quite true," continues he, "that I killed Henry Poindexter— shot him dead in the chapparal."

The declaration is answered by a cry from the crowd. It is altogether involuntary, and expresses horror rather than indignation.

Alike involuntary is the groan that goes with it—proceeding from a single individual, whom all know to be the father of the murdered man—once more in their midst.

Beyond these sounds, soon ceasing, there is nothing to hinder the confession from being continued.

"I know that I've got to die," proceeds the prisoner, with an air of seeming recklessness. "You have decreed it; and I can tell by your looks you have no intention to change your minds.

"After what I've confessed, it would be folly in me to expect pardon; and I don't. I've been a bad fellow; and no doubt have done enough to deserve my fate. But, bad as I may have been, I'm not vile enough to be sent out of the world, and leave behind me the horrid imputation of having *murdered* my own cousin. I did take his life, as I've told you. You are all asking why, and conjecturing about the motive. There was none."

A new "sensation" makes itself manifest among the spectators. It partakes of surprise, curiosity, and incredulity.

No one speaks, or in any way attempts interruption.

"You wonder at that. It's easily explained. *I killed him by mistake!*"

The surprise culminates in a shout; suppressed as the speaker proceeds.

"Yes, by mistake; and God knows I was sorry enough, on discovering that I had made it. I didn't know myself till long after."

The condemned man looks up, as if in hopes that he has touched a chord of mercy. There is no sign of it, on the faces that surround him—still solemnly austere.

"I don't deny," continues he; "I needn't—that I intended to kill some one. I did. Nor am I going to deny who it was. It was the cur I *see* standing before me."

In a glance of concentrated hatred, the speaker rests his eye upon Gerald; who only answers with a look, so calm as almost to betray indifference.

"Yes. I intended to kill *him*. I had my reasons. I'm not going to say what they were. It's no use now.

"I thought I *had* killed him; but, as hell's luck would have it, the Irish hound had changed cloaks with my cousin.

"You know the rest. By mistake I fired the shot—meant for an enemy, and fatal to a friend. It was sure enough; and poor Henry dropped from his horse. But to make more sure, I drew out my knife; and the cursed serapé still deceiving me, I hacked off his head."

The "sensation" again expresses itself in shuddering and shouts—the latter prolonged into cries of retribution—mingled with that murmuring which proclaims a story told.

There is no more mystery, either about the murder or its motive; and the prisoner is spared further description of that fiendish deed, that left the dead body of Henry Poindexter without a head.

"Now!" cries he, as the shouting subsides, and the spectators stand glaring upon him, "you know all that's passed; but not what's to come. There's another scene yet. You see me standing on my grave; but I don't go into it, till I've sent *him* to *his*. I don't, by God!"

There is no need to guess at the meaning of this profane speech—the last of Calhoun's life. Its meaning is made clear by the act that accompanies it.

While speaking he has kept his right hand under the left breast of his coat. Along with the oath it comes forth, holding a revolver.

The spectators have just time to see the pistol—as it glints under the slanting sunbeams—when two shots are heard in quick succession.

# THE HEADLESS HORSEMAN

With a like interval between, two men fall forward upon their faces; and lie with their heads closely contiguous!

One is Maurice Gerald, the mustanger,—the other Cassius Calhoun, ex-captain of volunteer cavalry.

The crowd closes around, believing both to be dead; while through the stillness that succeeds is heard a female voice, in those wild plaintive tones that tell of a heart nigh parting in twain!

# 100. Joy

Joy!

There was this under the evergreen oak, when it was discovered that only the suicide was a success, and the attempt at assassination a failure. There was this in the heart of Louise Poindexter, on learning that her lover still lived.

Though saddened by the series of tragedies so quickly transpiring, she was but human; and, being woman, who can blame her for giving way to the subdued happiness that succeeded? Not I. Not you, if you speak truly.

The passion that controlled her may not be popular under a strictly Puritan standard. Still is it according to the dictates of Nature—universal and irresistible—telling us that father, mother, sister, and brother, are all to be forsaken for that love illimitable; on Earth only exceeded—sometimes scarce equalled—by the love of self.

Do not reproach the young Creole, because this passion was paramount in her soul. Do not blame her for feeling pleasure amidst moments that should otherwise have been devoted to sadness. Nor, that her happiness was heightened, on learning from the astonished spectators, how her lover's life had been preserved—as it might seem miraculously.

The aim of the assassin had been true enough. He must have felt sure of it, before turning the muzzle towards his own temples, and firing the bullet that had lodged in his brain. Right over the heart he had hit his intended victim, and through the heart would the leaden missile have made its way, but that a *gage d'amour*—the gift of her who alone could have secured it such a place—turned aside the shot, causing it to *ricochet*!

Not harmlessly, however: since it struck one of the spectators standing too close to the spot.

Not quite harmless, either, was it to him for whom it had been intended.

The stunning shock—with the mental and corporeal excitement—long sustained—did not fail to produce its effect; and the mind of Maurice Gerald once more returned to its delirious dreaming.

But no longer lay his body in danger—in the chapparal, surrounded by wolves, and shadowed by soaring vultures,—in a hut, where he was but ill attended—in a jail, where he was scarce cared for at all.

When again restored to consciousness, it was to discover that the fair vision of his dreams was no vision at all, but a lovely woman—the loveliest on the Leona, or in all Texas if you like—by name Louise Poindexter.

There was now no one to object to her nursing him; not even her own father. The spirit of the aristocratic planter—steeped in sorrow, and humiliated by misfortune—had become purged of its false pride; though it needed not this to make him willingly acquiesce in an alliance, which, instead of a "nobody," gave him a nobleman for his son. Such, in reality, was Sir Maurice Gerald—erst known as Maurice the mustanger!

In Texas the title would have counted for little; nor did its owner care to carry it. But, by a bit of good fortune—not always attendant on an Irish baronetcy—it carried along with it an endowment—ample enough to clear Casa del Corvo of the mortgage held by the late Cassius Calhoun, and claimed by his nearest of kin.

This was not Woodley Poindexter: for after Calhoun's death, it was discovered that the ex-captain had once been a Benedict; and there was a young scion of his stock—living in New Orleans—who had the legal right to say he was his son!

It mattered not to Maurice Gerald; who, now clear of every entanglement, became the husband of the fair Creole.

After a visit to his native land—including the European tour—which was also that of his honeymoon—Sir Maurice, swayed by his inclinations, once more returned to Texas, and made Casa del Corvo his permanent home.

The "blue-eyed colleen" of Castle Ballagh must have been a myth—having existence only in the erratic fancy of Phelim. Or it may have been the bud of a young love, blighted ere it reached blooming—by absence, oft fatal to such tender plants of passion?

Whether or no, Louise Poindexter—Lady Gerald she must now be called—during her sojourn in the Emerald Isle saw nothing to excite her to jealousy.

Only once again did this fell passion take possession of her spirit; and then only in the shape of a shadow soon to pass away.

It was one day when her husband came home to the hacienda—bearing in his arms the body of a beautiful woman!

Not yet dead; though the blood streaming from a wound in her bared bosom showed she had not long to live.

To the question, "Who has done this?" she was only able to answer, "Diaz—Diaz!"

It was the last utterance of Isidora Covarubio de los Llanos!

As the spirit of the unhappy *señorita* passed into eternity, along with it went all rancour from that of her more fortunate rival. There can be no jealousy of the dead. That of Lady Gerald was at rest, and for ever.

It was succeeded by a strong sympathy for the ill-fated Isidora; whose story she now better comprehended. She even assisted her lord in the saddling of his red-bay steed, and encouraged him in the pursuit of the assassin.

She joyed to see the latter led back at the end of a lazo—held in the hand of her husband; and refused to interfere, when a band of Regulators, called hastily together, dealt out summary chastisement—by hanging him to a tree!

It was not cruelty—only a crude kind of justice:—"an eye for an eye, and a tooth for a tooth."

And what a poor compensation it seemed, to those who had taken part in exacting it!

As they stood gazing upon the remains of the villain, and his victim—the swarth ruffian dangling from the branch above, and the fair form lying underneath—the hearts of the Texans were touched—as perhaps they had never been before.

There was a strange thought passing through their minds; a sadness independent of that caused by the spectacle of a murder. It was regret at having so hastily despatched the assassin!

Beautiful, even in death, was Isidora. Such features as she possessed, owe not everything to the light of life. That voluptuous shape—the true form divine—may be admired in the cold statue.

Men stood gazing upon her dead body—long gazing—loth to go away—at length going with thoughts not altogether sacred!

---

In the physical world Time is accounted the destroyer; though in the moral, it is oft the restorer. Nowhere has it effected greater changes than in Texas—during the last decade—and especially in the settlements of the Nueces and Leona.

Plantations have sprung up, where late the *chapparal* thickly covered the earth; and cities stand, where the wild steed once roamed over a pathless prairie.

There are new names for men, places, and things.

For all this, there are those who could conduct you to an ancient hacienda—still known as Casa del Corvo.

Once there, you would become the recipient of a hospitality, unequalled in European lands.

You would have for your host one of the handsomest men in Texas; for your hostess one of its most beautiful women—both still this side of middle life.

Residing under their roof you would find an old gentleman, of aristocratic air and venerable aspect—withal chatty and cheerful—who would conduct you around the *corrales*, show you the stock, and never tire of talking about the hundreds—ay thousands—of horses and horned cattle, seen roaming over the pastures of the plantation.

You would find this old gentleman very proud upon many points: but more especially of his beautiful daughter—the mistress of the mansion—and the half-dozen pretty prattlers who cling to his skirts, and call him their "dear grandpa."

Leaving him for a time, you would come in contact with two other individuals attached to the establishment.

One is the *groom* of the "stole,"—by name Phelim O'Neal—who has full charge of the horses. The other a coachman of sable skin, yclept Pluto Poindexter; who would scorn to look at a horse except when perched upon the "box," and after having the "ribbons" deftly delivered into his hands.

Since we last saw him, the gay Pluto has become tamed down to a staid and sober Benedict—black though he be.

Florinda—now the better half of his life—has effected the transformation.

There is one other name known at Casa del Corvo, with which you cannot fail to become acquainted. You will hear it mentioned, almost every time you sit down to dinner: for you will be told that the turkey at the head of the table, or the venison at its opposite end, is the produce of a rifle that rarely misses its aim.

During the course of the meal—but much more over the wine—you will hear talk of "Zeb Stump the hunter."

You may not often see him. He will be gone from the hacienda, before you are out of your bed; and back only after you have retired. But the huge gobbler seen in the "smoke-house," and the haunch of venison hanging by its side, are evidence he has been there.

While sojourning at Casa del Corvo, you may get hints of a strange story connected with the place—now almost reduced to a legend.

The domestics will tell it you, but only in whispers: since they know that it is a theme *tabooed* by the master and mistress of the mansion, in whom it excites sad souvenirs.

It is the story of the Headless Horseman.

*Also from Benediction Books ...*
**Wandering Between Two Worlds: Essays on Faith and Art**
**Anita Mathias**
Benediction Books, 2007
152 pages
ISBN: 0955373700

Available from www.amazon.com, www.amazon.co.uk

In these wide-ranging lyrical essays, Anita Mathias writes, in lush, lovely prose, of her naughty Catholic childhood in Jamshedpur, India; her large, eccentric family in Mangalore, a sea-coast town converted by the Portuguese in the sixteenth century; her rebellion and atheism as a teenager in her Himalayan boarding school, run by German missionary nuns, St. Mary's Convent, Nainital; and her abrupt religious conversion after which she entered Mother Teresa's convent in Calcutta as a novice. Later rich, elegant essays explore the dualities of her life as a writer, mother, and Christian in the United States-- Domesticity and Art, Writing and Prayer, and the experience of being "an alien and stranger" as an immigrant in America, sensing the need for roots.

**About the Author**

Anita Mathias is the author of *Wandering Between Two Worlds: Essays on Faith and Art.* She has a B.A. and M.A. in English from Somerville College, Oxford University, and an M.A. in Creative Writing from the Ohio State University, USA. Anita won a National Endowment of the Arts fellowship in Creative Nonfiction in 1997. She lives in Oxford, England with her husband, Roy, and her daughters, Zoe and Irene.

Visit Anita's website
  http://www.anitamathias.com,
and Anita's blog
  http://dreamingbeneaththespires.blogspot.com, (Dreaming Beneath the Spires).

**The Church That Had Too Much**
**Anita Mathias**
Benediction Books, 2010
52 pages
ISBN: 9781849026567

Available from www.amazon.com, www.amazon.co.uk

The Church That Had Too Much was very well-intentioned. She
wanted to love God, she wanted to love people, but she was both
hampered by her muchness and the abundance of her possessions, and beset by ambition, power struggles and snobbery.
Read about the surprising way The Church That Had Too Much
began to resolve her problems in this deceptively simple and en-
chanting fable.

## About the Author

Anita Mathias is the author of *Wandering Between Two Worlds:
Essays on Faith and Art.* She has a B.A. and M.A. in English
from Somerville College, Oxford University, and an M.A. in
Creative Writing from the Ohio State University, USA. Anita
won a National Endowment of the Arts fellowship in Creative
Nonfiction in 1997. She lives in Oxford, England with her husband, Roy, and her daughters, Zoe and Irene.

Visit Anita's website
    http://www.anitamathias.com,
and Anita's blog
    http://dreamingbeneaththespires.blogspot.com (Dreaming Beneath the Spires).

www.ingramcontent.com/pod-product-compliance
Lightning Source LLC
Chambersburg PA
CBHW010252030726
47497CB00010BA/5183